The Passage Advocate

The Shimmering Series
Book 1

Eric T. Schönfeld

KWE Publishing

I'd like to thank my parents for encouraging my flights of fancy, those closest to me who stuck by me to light my fires, and the Lord of All who made it possible.

Schönfeld, Eric T. *The Passage Advocate*
Copyright © 2025 by Eric T. Schönfeld, all rights reserved.
ISBNs: 978-1-963850-00-0 (paperback), 978-1-963850-01-7 (ebook), 978-1-963850-02-4 (hardcover)
Library of Congress Catalog Number: 2024918965

Cover illustration by Benlin Alexander.

Published by KWE Publishing, kwepub.com.

Contents

Prologue

T he wind blew wisps of snow in irregular patterns around the sighing pines. Clouds raced along the grey sky, kissing the peaks topped with a frosty wreath of white. The dying sun glistened off the blankets of snow, bidding farewell to a lost season of forgotten warmth. A far-off bird called mournfully in the twilight, echoing softly off the mountains surrounding the valley.

Nicholas heard nor saw any of the beauty around him as he ran hard, the peace from the entire scene completely lost on him. The young lad wept as he raced to reach the upper ridgelines for safety. His lungs burned from the effort as he shuffled his feet through the thin layers of snow, crunching his way up the valley. Rabbit-fur boots and mittens kept him warm, yet his bear fur slowed his progress, making the ascent difficult. He gulped for air, and his breath puffed steadily with each laborious stride.

His dark eyes surveyed the canyon as he ran, desperately searching for where he could discern the trail that would lead him away from town and into the high country. Normally, he used this trail for hunting; today, he needed an escape route.

Below him in the valley, the screams from the dying and the shouts from the Mongol raiders mingled along with the smoke and flames, wafting into the evening air. The brutal intruders torched his quaint Ural Mountain village from horseback, leaving no one alive. Left alone to fend for himself, Nicholas fled from the mayhem up the valley, dutifully following the directions his father had given to him.

Daring only a brief glimpse back, the flickering firelight glistened on his tear-stained face, providing no warmth and illuminating the horror of his village in flames below.

Visions of his older brother, a ruddier, handsomer version of what he always had hoped his future self might become, floated past his mind's eye. His mother's smiling warm embrace. His father's wise confidence and protection for the family, the teacher of his survival skills. All the comforts of home lost in the flames and the screams wafting skyward before him.

He sobbed as he turned again and ran, weeping aloud for his lost family. His voice became muffled as he ran, barely discernible as the sighing wind carried the sounds of the continuing mayhem from the valley below to his ears, overwhelming his cries. Crossing a frozen creek bed, he struggled to climb higher into the narrowing canyon leading up into the high country. *I must put it out of my mind for now; that's what Father would have me do!*

There would be time for mourning later. As Nicholas pressed on, he knew the lands above town better than anyone, but he would need to push on quickly to gain more distance between himself and the marauders.

"Nyet!" he sniffed as the screams followed after him, wafting up the valley walls around him. Their torturous wails propelled him ever faster, even as the snow drifts deepened, slowing his arduous climb as his sobbing cries mingled with those carried on the winds.

If he could just gain the boulders and crags, he would be more difficult to track. Once in the wilds...

"Pssssst!! Hey, Rabbit Boy! Mind sharing some of your furs?" A familiar voice stopped him from behind a nearby tree. The tall form of the town tailor stepped into the light from the forest's edge. Dressed in a fine white shirt with intricate golden stitching, the bald man with bushy eyebrows shivered in the winter cold. In the chaos of the attack on the town, he had clearly missed taking his coat and gloves.

"You...made it out?" Nicholas could do little more than stare at the man in disbelief.

"Not many of us did," the shivering man replied as he held out a shaking hand, pleading yet coaxing. "Come, child, don't be afraid; you remember me! I traded with your mum and your brother in the market. Share with me some of your furs!"

Nicholas nodded, striding toward the lanky man, yet he stopped suddenly when he was within a few feet of him. The man's intimidating frame towered over him despite being hunched over, struggling to keep warm. Yet just behind the tailor, hidden in the shadows of the trees, two Mongol fighters waited with daggers drawn, watching his approach with wicked intent. The tailor followed Nicholas's line of sight until he realized his entourage had been spotted.

"I told you to stay back until I had him!" the tailor shouted as his feigned shivering ceased. He stood tall, continuing to curse his chastisements at the hidden warriors, his own furs hung just out of sight on the tree behind him.

"You're with them? Why?!" Nicholas gasped, stumbling back in retreat, shocked at the clear betrayal. "You were part of our home! You were part of our town! We welcomed you!"

"They pay better," the tall man sneered. The tailor's vicious smile curled through his lips, his teeth clenched impatiently with the cold. "Now give me your furs, and you can go back to town and warm yourself among the ashes of your dead!"

"Nyet!!!" Nicholas screamed as he turned and ran.

"Come back here, Rabbit Boy!" the tailor yelled after him, drawing a long-serrated blade, hidden from behind him before turning back to his entourage. "Don't just stand there; if he gets away and tells others, your surprise raids on these towns are over!"

Nicholas sprinted as if his life depended on it and soon placed some distance between himself and his pursuers. His lungs burned with the effort even as the sounds of the pursuit underway echoed off the surrounding cliffs. It seemed hours, yet only minutes had gone by when he rounded the base of a cliff where the valley narrowed. There before him, a misshapen dead oak tree loomed. Its single barren branch seemed to point forlornly up the valley, as if warning him not to stop.

He glanced back and could still hear the fading sounds of mayhem from his village. The marauders pursuing him remained momentarily out of sight but not out of earshot, the sound of their pursuit intensifying with each passing second. Wide-eyed and shaking in fear, Nicholas clambered around the base of the oak when he gasped.

There, extended from the foot of the tree's two large roots, an inky black shadow roiling within the space between them. Resembling a pool of oil, it pulsed once with a crimson light, rippling without wind once before it stilled, as if suddenly sensing his approach. When he moved to step around it, the sludge slid toward him, and he backed away.

Nicholas rubbed his eyes in disbelief, and the sludge rippled in anticipation before flattening back into place, an opaque and placid enigma with a flat surface. *How easily it blended into the shadows; how easy to miss the presence of...what is that, anyway?!*

Deciding not to trust the strange shadow, Nicholas searched frantically for another hiding place. Spotting a large boulder above the trail, he swiftly took refuge there, careful to utilize stones, logs and brush to limit tracks in the snow.

Just as he ducked into hiding, the tailor followed by the other two Mongols arrived, one now carrying a lit torch. Nicholas could clearly see the bloodstained savagery on their furs cast by the light of the flickering torch.

Speaking in their guttural tongue, they began circling the oak, using the torch to illuminate the branches. The inky shadow at the base of the tree remained still despite the direct light from the torch, glistening as if frozen.

The tailor noticed it too and motioned to his companions. They stared at it dumbly as the torchbearer held the light closer; then, it moved. Akin to molasses, it pooled into the corner where the roots met before sliding up the crevices of the tree in a morose reverse drip. Like an oily patch of night, it clung stubbornly to its space, refusing to give further ground to the men and only retreating from light directly threatening to pierce it.

"Whatever it is doesn't like the light," the tailor muttered in fascination as he reached toward the shadow to probe it with his blade. That's when the shadow struck: whipping upright, past his blade and up his arm, wrapping itself around him up to his shoulder, curling around his appendage like a snake.

The tall man gasped as the shadow stretched itself into a fluidic arch, wrapping itself first around the tailor's arm and then gushing forth over his head and neck. He dropped his knife, gagging and tearing at his face, screaming aloud as it seemed to affix itself around his neck and ears.

"Get it off! Get it off! Get it..." The tailor's shouts rang out initially as his Mongol accomplices stared wide-eyed and uncertain.

The shadow enveloped the man's head, gushing around his mouth and muffling his screams as he gagged before seeming to suddenly flow into his ears, nose and mouth.

The Mongol soldiers stepped back, perplexed and dumbfounded at their companion, splayed out on the ground and twitching in the snow, belching sounds that shouldn't come from a human body. Nicholas recoiled in horror but remained quiet as the tailor's convulsions subsided into vibrating tremors as all fell silent around them.

One of the men prodded his fallen comrade when suddenly, the downed man's eyes snapped open, pulsing a hellish red glow. With inhuman speed, the tailor grabbed his companion by the head and snapped his neck, throwing him aside. The other Mongol jumped back, dropping his torch as the crazed tailor leapt to his feet and lunged at the other man's throat.

The crimson-eyed tailor pinned the other Mongol warrior down, knocking him to the ground. As the struggle ensued, the fighter managed to grab the tailor's knife out of his belt and stab him once in the thigh. The tailor made no sound or even grimace at the knife wound as he mercilessly squeezed his companion's throat. The red glow from his eyes pulsed as he strangled the Mongol thrashing beneath him. The warrior's gasps turned to death throes as he gurgled, final convulsions taking his body before expiring along with the torch lying beside them.

Nicholas wanted to scream but forced himself to stay still, cowering behind the boulder. As the tailor stood, his glowing red eyes scanned around the narrow gulley, a predator searching for prey. For terrible long moments, the crazed man searched for the lad, withdrawing the knife from his leg without so much as a wince, sliding it free almost as an afterthought. The wound dribbled briefly before black tar oozed alongside the blood to seal it.

The tailor's crimson eyes fixed on the rock where Nicholas hid, and he hissed with satisfied glee. Although unseen and out of sight, Nicholas knew he had been found, bolting from his hiding place and sprinting straight up the canyon without looking once behind him.

Possessed with predatory purpose, the tailor gurgled once and limped after him, arm outstretched as if to grasp him from afar. As he pursued Nicholas, the plastered smile left his face, and a new fiery, hateful look possessed him. A loud metallic moan bellowed forth, chilling the lad far more than the frozen landscape around him.

Nicholas tore through the deepening snow drifts as he climbed higher up the canyon, not bothering to turn to see whether the possessed tailor followed, knowing he did. With his last remaining strength, he scrambled higher, the grade steepening as he went. His lungs stung from the effort as he pressed onto the only safety he knew— the wilds of the highlands.

Tears of agony flowed anew as terror ran through him; how he wished his father or brother were here with him! Tiring quickly, he knew he would not be able to continue much further and had to find another place to hide. Fleeing the barbarian attack was one thing, but whatever was pursuing him now was clearly much more than simply a man.

The effort seemed to have paid off; when Nicholas looked back, he had temporarily lost sight of the pursuing tailor. Ahead of him and at the head of the valley, a frozen waterfall offered yet another possible hiding place.

Glancing worriedly over his shoulder to ensure he hadn't been spotted, Nicholas pressed himself between the giant icicles and slippery rocks, attempting to gain the inner recesses of the alcove behind them. Sliding precipitously on an icy rock, he went down hard, bashing his head on a stone.

Nicholas cried out as water and ice spilled over him, mixing with his blood as the frozen creek soaked him to the bone. Dizziness overwhelmed him as he regained his footing. Struggling upright to his feet, he limped onward, pushing behind the ice to a darkened alcove. Soaking wet and bleeding, he looked around, bewildered at how quickly his options dwindled with each passing moment.

A quick survey behind the curtain of ice revealed a cluster of branches, half frozen in the creek and jammed between rocks. He grunted as he pulled forth a long branch resembling a staff. His teeth chattered as hypothermia set in and the world began to spin.

Nicholas's head throbbed as he pushed into a gap, towing his makeshift staff with him. From behind a pair of frozen roots and between the ice stalactites of the waterfall, he could peek through to the canyon he had just climbed. He took a moment to catch his breath, shivering from the cold. *Perhaps this isn't such a good idea after all, but there's nowhere else to go!*

The thought pushed Nicholas further back into the alcove, nestled between the roots. He almost cried aloud when the roots parted, and he nearly fell through. Squinting behind him to see, it was impossible to tell in the darkness just how deep this cave went. Whispers of warning from his father to stay away from unknown caves surfaced, so he sufficed himself with his current station, behind the cover of the frozen waterfall to spy on his pursuer.

With nothing to do but wait, tormenting memories of what he had lost flooded him through the cold and darkness. His brother, Peter, and his father had gone to see the very merchant now pursuing him to trade furs only just this morning. His mother had been at home, cooking the rabbits he had trapped yesterday. His quaint home and the surrounding farms were all lost now to the invading horsemen; the tailor had apparently been helping all along.

Nicholas had heard the screams after the horsemen had galloped into town later that day. He was still dressed for the cold from his earlier hunting trip to obtain more rabbits. His bloodied father had stumbled home amongst the chaos and told him to run for the high country.

He never questioned his father, not ever. Only now in the darkened alcove did he begin to question that decision. Bitter tears flowed as he gripped his staff in anguish; he was sure some of the screams he had heard were theirs.

The sound of footsteps crunching through the snow outside caught Nicholas's attention, stealing the last vestiges of his thoughts as the landscape settled into a disquieting hush. Holding his breath, he stared out between the icy roots at the empty ravine. In the sudden silence, all he could hear was the pursuer's footsteps and the quickening of his own heartbeat, even as the methodical footsteps slowed.

In the fading evening light, the hunched tailor emerged into sight at the far end of the canyon, sniffing the air like a wild animal as he strode forth. As the red-eyed man wandered closer, Nicholas could see that cold seemed to have no effect on him. The tall man's blazing gaze scanned the ravine patiently, searching for his prey as steam rose from his skin and torn shirt.

Then, their eyes met.

The same knowing smile crept over the tailor's face, but in a metallic voice not his own, he cooed to Nicholas, slowly creeping to close the distance between them. He called to the lad with a gentle voice despite brandishing his short hunting blade.

"Come here, little boy, I've got something for you!" a deep voice rumbled, coming from the tailor, yet his lips never moved. As he reached for the lad the towering man began to tremble with a barely containable excitement, a spittle of black drool forming along his lips. "Don't hide from me! I have someone who wants to meet you! Just...a bit closer now; come here! There's no need to fear; you are special! We need you! We want you! We must have you!"

"Nyet!!!" Nicholas sobbed as his knees began to buckle. He gripped his staff before him, trembling in fear and cold, striking out frantically as instinct took over. "Leave me alone! Get away from me!!"

The tailor began to grab at the icicles from the waterfall, ripping them free with his bare hands, tearing at the cave's entrance with frenzied glee. Nicholas began screaming, jabbing futilely at his attacker between the gnarled roots and icicles.

This seemed to only encourage his attacker more as he broke a large section of ice free, tossing it aside before pushing his pale face into the hole he made. The man's eyes blazed beneath his bristly eyebrows as he called to Nicholas in that deceptively gentle voice that wasn't his own.

"I won't hurt you!" The voice from nowhere and yet everywhere assaulted him. His lips parted, and his teeth gnashed in frustration as he grasped for the lad, a dark spittle dripping down his chin. The tailor's breath assailed his senses, smelling sickly sweet as if with the scent of rotting meat. "Just...come...here..."

Nicholas struck with everything left in him, shoving the staff straight into the tailor's nose, cracking it and spurting blood in all directions. The man staggered back, screaming and clutching his face, the red glow briefly fading from his eyes.

"Wait! Don't leave me!" the man whimpered as if suddenly scared, looking about as if he had lost something before turning his attention back to Nicholas. "What have you done?! I...can't...feel my...oh, wait... there you are!"

The crimson light suddenly returned to the man's eyes, blazing with fury as the tailor went berserk, moaning aloud with a metallic roar and tearing at the remaining icicles and even at the roots to get to Nicholas. The explosion of ice and wood from his frenzy sent Nicholas tumbling backward into the cave, dropping his makeshift staff as he fell.

The man lunged again, leaping into Nicholas's enclosure. The crimson glow from the tailor's eyes illuminated their faces inside the cave as the man pressed himself atop him.

"I have you now," the strange voice whispered even as the tailor grinned without moving his lips. The towering man pushed his face closer, his blood mingling with that same black ichor and dripping from his lips. Nicholas could smell his breath, that same rancid odor, and he turned to retch from the overwhelming stench.

Pinned down, Nicholas could do little as he screamed as suddenly, rocks and mud began to fall from the cave ceiling, dislodged with their struggle. As the avalanche of debris continued, the floor seemed to collapse as well, yawning open beneath them.

With a sudden crash, he fell away from his attacker. Down into a dark abyss they plunged, falling together. He could still make out his attacker's luminous eyes, falling after him but quickly vanishing as they separated, falling in different directions. *How large is this cave? Where are we falling to?*

The air grew strangely warm, accompanied by the smell of rich, deep earth...a strange white light flashed, seeming to come from every-where at once...a vortex spinning him in a whirlpool...he screamed again, but his voice seemed to reflect back to him, folding on itself.

All the while, another watchful pair of eyes observed his fall, the image of it spiraling away, as if down a drain...

Chapter 1

Johanna

Johanna Langley found herself staring into a whirlpool of water spiraling down a drain, taking the visions of Nicholas from untold eons ago with it. Gasping for air, she clutched the sides of the bathroom sink to steady herself as the images receded with the waterline. The sounds from her vision faded along with the echoes of her pounding heart in her ears.

Taking a deep breath, she splashed the remainder of the water from the basin on her face, letting the droplets cascade down her cheeks. The tips of her shoulder-length, wavy chestnut hair caught some of the water as she stared back at herself. A single lavender candle burning in the tiny office restroom provided just enough light to illuminate her face and help pull herself together, but not enough to reveal just how bloodshot her normally soft brown eyes must have been. Not bothering to turn on the lights, she tried to collect herself as she washed the stress away. *At least in candlelight, the wrinkle lines of aging on my brow are hidden.*

She didn't use to have such nightmares, particularly while she was awake. They started occurring just prior to her husband's car accident and his passing. Beginning as simple dreams during the night, they eventually evolved into distracting daydreams and visions. When they had escalated further into daytime blackouts, that's when she knew it was time to seek help.

It felt like her life was spinning out of control until she discovered the offices of Maude Anice Brown. Referred to her by the hospital where she worked as part of her mental health program, Dr. Brown had already established a good reputation with other nurses at the hospital.

"Johanna Langley. Johanna Langley," a muffled voice from the waiting room called. She quickly splashed another round of warm water on her face before patting it gently with a towel and returning to the waiting room lobby.

Although warm and inviting, the lobby of the waiting room was still brighter than the restroom she had been in. As she strode past the faux bookcases lining the windowless room, she blinked. The low-level lighting gave guests of the psychologist a sense they were visiting a Victorian library rather than a counselor. Paintings of British lords on a fox hunt alternated with framed awards and credentials of Dr. Brown's hallway. The only sounds permeating the room came from the ticking of an antique clock on the waiting room table and the nondescript receptionist tapping her pen on a clipboard.

"Yes, I'm here," Johanna sighed, walking briskly to the receptionist standing in the waiting room, still propping the hallway door open.

Johanna glanced about the empty waiting room, picked up her jacket, headed down the hall and soon found herself in Dr. Brown's office, which looked very much like the waiting room she was just in. Sitting stiffly on a long leather sofa, she stared up at the ceiling.

She always appreciated that Dr. Brown let her speak her mind first during the appointments before offering the always-insightful advice. Although first impressions of the woman's cold blue eyes and jet-black hair tied back in a bun had left Johanna worried, she had quickly opened up when Dr. Brown's warm yet firm insistence for conversation gained her trust.

Today's appointment seemed to flow much as each of the previous ones had. A nervous start exchanging pleasantries before diving into a careful construct initiated by the therapist. Johanna would initially resist the transition but quickly find her confidence and within moments begin anew in her efforts to uncover some previously undefined stress in her life that she could only hope might be the source of her life's troubles.

"So, let me get this straight," Dr. Brown stated calmly, about halfway through their appointment. "After your husband died last year, you have dated infrequently because your son, Daniel, takes up most of your time. You bury yourself in your work at the hospital taking care of patients because as a medical practitioner—"

"Nurse," Johanna interjected in slight annoyance. "Nurse practitioner, actually. It's a common mistake, but we can substitute for a doctor in many cases."

"Yes, please forgive me, nurse practitioner," Dr. Brown continued, glancing at her notes as she adjusted her reading glasses. "My point is that you haven't had time for dating."

"That's correct," Johanna agreed, a bit defensively as she brushed a brunette lock of hair out of her soft brown eyes. "Being a single mother and holding down a household and a full-time job is demanding on my schedule!"

"I understand that, but what about your late husband's friend, the one you had been spending time with?" Dr. Brown persisted, leaning toward Johanna and annoyingly tapping her pen on the side of her clipboard. This hadn't been the first time she had pushed Johanna about him as she ruffled through her previous notes and looked through the papers in search of the point Johanna had hoped to avoid. "Yes, here's his name: Nate! You spend a lot of time with him, and he seems very taken with you and your son. He's the only individual you've mentioned to me in our sessions other than your late husband."

"I really didn't want to talk about him today." Johanna exhaled to release the tension she felt regarding him, relaxing back into the leather sofa. She looked around the room, trying to regain some level of trust in order to somehow further her progress with the counselor. *This office looks just like the waiting room, and I still feel like I'm waiting! Am I making any progress with these sessions at all?*

"Johanna," Dr. Brown pushed when her patient seemed unwilling to answer. "You've indicated before that you spend time with Nate and admit to even being intimate with him, yet you seem to avoid talking about him in favor of your job, your son and your finances. Why is that?"

"Guilt, I suppose," Johanna whispered, shaking her head before finally blurting the rest out. "He's perfect on paper, but it still doesn't feel right! To begin with, he was my husband's friend. I appreciate everything he's done for Danny and me, yet I cannot help but feel that his attraction to me happened even before Bill and I were married; it feels like it was always there and was wrong before, and maybe it is still wrong now. They knew each other during their military days, and I don't like the feeling that I'm just being handed off!"

"Handed off? You said he treats Daniel very well, he does things for you around the house even though he doesn't live there and he's treated you with nothing but respect." Dr. Brown raised an eyebrow as she continued thoughtfully, "What do you see as the problem here? You weren't intimate with him before the tragedy that took your husband, were you?"

"Certainly not! Never while I was married! He's always been a friend of the family, and I suppose I'm comfortable with that, but nothing further!" Johanna scoffed before reddening. "It happened only one time, and we probably shouldn't have, but I was in a vulnerable position at the time..."

"Once?" The therapist raised an eyebrow, looking down her nose atop the rims of her glasses. "I was under the impression you both had become quite close. Now it seems you've thrown yourself into work by choice. Why are you avoiding him, or are you?"

"It's not that!" Johanna protested, blushing momentarily. "He wanted to start talking children again, and for heaven's sake, we're not even married! I just don't want to go down that road right now!"

"With him," Dr Brown finished for her, watching her reaction. "Is that right?"

"I...don't know!" Johanna threw her hands up in frustration. "It just freaked me out when he asked me about that during sex, and I really wasn't ready to hear that!"

"As long as he respects your boundaries and understands what you've gone through," Dr. Brown pointed out gently. "Have you considered anyone else in the picture? Maybe widening the field a bit, dating others?"

"No, not really," Johanna muttered coolly, reflecting on the implications. "Danny is just so taken with him; I think he reminds Danny of his father, and I don't want to take that away from him. He really could use a father figure, and Nate does a good job at that; a little too good sometimes. I fear as he gets older, he even leans more on Nate than he does me!"

"I wouldn't worry too much about that, Johanna; boys always love their mothers, and no one can take that away," Dr Brown pressed with a thin, reassuring smile. "This is about you though, Johanna. Your son has his own issues to face as he grows into adulthood, and he isn't going to be under your roof forever. Aren't you leaving town with Nate today on an outing? You mentioned it was the reason why you moved your appointment up, is it not?"

"It is!" Johanna clasped her hands together sheepishly, trying to stay constructive yet almost ashamed of what she was about to say next. "I have love for him; I'm just not 'IN love' WITH him. He's just so... blue-collar!"

"That's a bit unfair then, don't you think?" Dr. Brown pointed out. An uncomfortable moment of silence passed, and only the ticking of the clock could be heard. Dr. Brown put her pen down for a moment and adjusted her glasses, looking down her nose at Johanna. "What's wrong with 'blue-collar'?"

"Well, I don't want Danny to grow up with all that." Johanna rolled her eyes.

"Why not?" Dr. Brown shook her head and paused briefly to check her notes. "He's former military, he's been an electrician for eight solid years now, and he's even a partner in his own business. He's more like Bill than most men. He's got a good head on his shoulders and is frankly a good role model for Danny, given the loss of his father. I don't see the issue other than I noticed you quit talking about him after your intimacy."

"Maybe that's the problem." Johanna drifted off again, unsure of what more to say about it as she looked away. "He's too much like my former husband. Our intimate encounter just drove that home; we became too close. I realized then I don't think we are on the same page; he wants more than I can give, and I hope I'm not being unfair to him by letting this go on."

"I'm not sure I know what that means," Dr. Brown sighed. "Do you blame Nate for Bill's passing?"

"N-n-n-no!" Johanna reacted, involuntarily stammering. "Why would I do that?"

"I'm just asking," Dr Brown replied. Sensing Johanna's agitation at the insinuation, she placed a reassuring hand on her arm before sitting back and summarizing the bullet points from the notes she had taken. "Look at it this way. You have a man in your life who has been there for you from the beginning. He consistently pursued you after Bill's passing. He's not 'unattractive,' according to you. You won't date or see anyone else. Do you think your late husband wouldn't approve?"

"Yes, he probably would," Johanna stated quietly before looking away. "I guess it's on me, and I just haven't made up my mind yet."

"Don't misunderstand me, I'm not pushing you to Nate or against him," Dr. Brown clarified. Although the counselor said the words softly, they stabbed like a cold knife in Johanna's heart, yet she knew them to be true. "However, you really need to start asking yourself the tough questions. None of you are getting any younger, and the time for decision-making will one day run its course. Bill isn't coming back, and if all this time you're spending with Nate isn't getting you anywhere, you need to ask yourself, what ARE you doing with him?"

"Bill's car accident was over a year ago, but it still seems like yesterday," Johanna whispered. "I guess I just miss my husband, and Nate is the closest thing to him."

"I know, dear; I also know that you and he may not be on the same page, and all I'm saying is it's something to consider. This doesn't need to be resolved now, but you should keep that in mind whether you continue with Nate or even someone else in the future," Dr. Brown suggested gently before sitting back in her chair, her smile fading as she changed the subject. "Tell me more about the nightmares. Do you think Bill's death has something to do with those? If we can separate—"

"No, that's just it," Johanna interrupted, sitting up abruptly in her chair. "I used to think it was trauma from losing Bill, but these dreams started only months ago. They're not really dreams, though—they're more like premonitions, occurring even while I'm awake. I had several before Bill's passing, and they terrified me. When I was informed of the accident and his death, it's like I already knew, and the incident came as no surprise. I just felt a sad, hollow acceptance of a tremendous loss."

"You feel as if...you predicted it?" the counselor asked skeptically, staring back at Johanna over the rim of her glasses. "If you spend your life worrying about calamity, many times your worry can disguise itself as self-fulfilling prophecies. You just can't live that way expecting the worst of everything. It may have happened this time, but to apply it to everything in life would be unproductive at best, debilitating at worst."

"Perhaps; do you think I'm crazy?" Johanna paused, then chuckled at the irony, her voice trailing off as Dr. Brown began scribbling more notes on her pad. "It's not all the time or anything, but during my down moments. They don't always involve my family either. I had one in your waiting room when I came in today, this time about that boy I told you about from hundreds of years ago. It makes no sense! It's not just a daydream; they're far too intense for that!"

"Well, at least you're consistent." Dr. Brown managed another thin smile as she thumbed through her notes briefly, adjusting her spectacles to read aloud. "Your 'premonitions,' as you call them, involve a young boy called Nicholas. There are mountains, and there's snow. The town is destroyed by raiders, and he is pursued by a tailor into the wilderness where they fall down a hole in a cave."

"You make it sound so silly," Johanna exhaled, shaking her head in dismay. "I'm honestly not sure that it isn't. Maybe I'm making too much of it all."

"I won't say that it's silly because you feel them so intensely. I must admit though, I'm not much for dream interpretation. I think they may represent something for you that could be repressed." Dr Brown grimaced as she stated the admission with unhesitant clarity. "Let's look at this logically, shall we? All I'm saying is perhaps you've blended Bill's, um, mishap with your protective desire to take care of Daniel. The town's destruction could be representative of your previous life. The barbarians could represent your trials in the past year..."

"I thought you were going to say they represented Nate," Johanna joked but immediately felt guilty for saying it.

"I don't think you really view Nate through that lens." The counselor smiled politely. "You may resent his closeness during a time when you were healing on your own and became uncomfortable with him when you allowed an intimate moment with him. Your son Daniel, on the other hand, has found new kinship with him, complicating the matter, and that may bother you. The intensity of these feelings may be leading to these 'visions' you're having."

"Having visions of a car crash and Bill dying made sense to me; it was unpleasant, but it made sense," Johanna countered methodically, suddenly focused as all nervous attempts at jest left her. "The only thing different from that vision to the reality was where it occurred. I SAW Bill roll his car into a frozen lake in the mountains and die. The fact that he rolled his car near Fort Collins and rolled into a frozen ditch is beside the point. All of his injuries were the same as I saw in the vision."

"What does that have to do with your latest vision?" Dr. Brown tipped her reading glasses skeptically. "I don't see where this boy and the village fit in."

"Neither do I, and that's my point; that all happened before his crash—way before! This vision that I've been having is from an ancient time and makes no sense to me!" Johanna shuddered. "It's no one I've ever met, in a place I've never been and either well before I've been born or in a very wild setting; I don't even know if such a place exists! And then there's that terrible shadow..."

"Johanna, let me be frank: I don't deal with the supernatural," Dr. Brown sighed. "Don't get me wrong, I'm not belittling your dreams or the emotional strain they may cause. Whether or not I believe in them is irrelevant—they are real to you. I can only help you focus on what's real, tangible and in front of us. I can help you deal with you, your family and your relationships here in this world. Let's get back to Nate and how that could help you and Daniel."

Johanna nodded reluctantly. *I have to table my visions for now. Either Dr. Brown doesn't believe in them, or she simply doesn't view them as applicable here. In either case, she's right and cannot help me with them.*

"Nate certainly does do Danny some good," Johanna admitted. "I worry about my son since his father's passing. He doesn't have many friends anymore. He and his father were close, and when Bill passed, Danny just seemed to lose interest in having anyone else around. He really became a loner."

"Johanna, as true as that may be, you won't be doing him, Nate or yourself any favors if you don't come to terms with this," the counselor advised. "Daniel does need guidance—I can even see him if he agrees to it. We can work out some of those issues, but those are his to deal with; you cannot fix that for him. Neither can Nate."

"It's just that for Danny, it was just such bad timing," Johanna sighed. "He's in his mid-teens now, and I think he really needs a father figure. He and Nate do very well together—I'm just not so sure Nate and I do so well."

They spoke continuously for the rest of the full hour. Time with Dr. Brown always passed so quickly. Finally, when the hour was over, the therapist gently reminded Johanna of the time and that she would see her next week.

Johanna grimaced as she gathered her belongings before briefly hugging Dr. Brown goodbye, administering a courteous yet brisk pat on the back before abruptly departing. What had started in a friendly exchange seemed to end with obligatory distaste, having not achieved any real resolution, likely resulting in revisiting the same issue later.

As she left the tall office building and stepped out into the bright sunlit day, she heard a familiar honk in the parking lot and turned to see Nate's brown Jeep Grand Cherokee sitting not more than a few parking spots from her. The winch set on the front bumper and the extra lift for height gave it away. As the tinted window rolled down, a grinning, unshaven Nate smiled back at her. Ruddy and handsome as ever, with his square-set jaw, he looked like the Brawny paper towel guy with his mussed sandy hair. He got out of the running vehicle, wearing blue jeans and a plaid button-up shirt.

If only he would work on that gut a little more—"the battle of the bulge" he always called it. She couldn't criticize him there, though, since it wasn't really that bad for a man his age. Besides, it was also a battle she faced, even if she hid it well.

"Nate Livingston, what are you doing here?" She shook her head yet couldn't resist returning his eager smile.

"We thought we'd surprise you!" Nate smirked as he ushered her to his car, his hazel eyes twinkling. "That way you wouldn't have to take the bus again today. Besides, you said you were all ready to go for our trip up into the mountains; I just finished the packing, and now here we are."

"Well, I am ready as long as you are, but did you even shower today?" She poked semi-jokingly. He smelled of sun and hard work as she hugged him.

"Of course I did!" Nate scoffed. "I couldn't smell bad for you, could I?"

"Wouldn't be the first time," she snickered, feigning to pinch her nose as he opened the passenger door to let her in. He gave her a peck on the cheek as she got in the vehicle. "Besides, who's 'we'?"

"Hey, Mom," an unmistakably adolescent male voice from the back seat greeted her. Johanna peeked back into the vehicle, and there sat Daniel, her son. His lanky form was already seat-belted in as he sat grinning back at her. His brown eyes sparkled in anticipation beneath his nondescript mop of sandy brown hair.

"Danny?! What are you doing here?" Johanna exclaimed. "You're supposed to be in school!"

"Don't embarrass me, Mom; I'm practically eighteen, and it's no big deal." Daniel rolled his eyes as he leaned forward to hug his mother. "Nate got me out early, and I made sure that I'm all caught up on my assignments for the week!"

"Oh, Danny, that's not the point! Well anyway, I'm glad you could join us," she exclaimed, beaming with pride and gratitude at his presence.

Tall for his age and a little awkward, Danny's face remained sadly beautiful, especially to her. When he smiled, that's when she saw his father—a mixed blessing, to be sure. Seeing Bill in her son's smile caused her pain and relief simultaneously, but she kept that to herself. She knew she clung to him a bit too much in his teenage years, especially after Bill's passing. Far too often, though, he wore his serious face, losing the similarity with her former husband. Johanna only saw a mirror image of herself looking back at her.

"What about all our things?" Johanna asked, turning to Nate as he settled back behind the steering wheel. "Are we sure we have everything?"

"All packed up—you packed them last night, remember?" Nate said smugly. "All I had to do was load it up!"

"Yes, but did you presume I just had everything I needed? Why did you assume that?" While Johanna smiled, a flash of anger flared inside of her—she hated surprises. She knew the anger was unreasonable, so she silently tamped it down. *Why am I getting upset?*

"Mom, relax—it was my idea to leave early." Daniel flashed her long-lost husband's smile back at her again. "Nate was going to wait until after we got home, but we were already packed. I figured we should beat the traffic."

"Yes, I suppose you're right," Johanna exhaled, sitting back in her seat. Feeling the need to add something further, she intentionally aimed her next comment at Nate.

"Thank you," Nate sighed in relief as he began to drive and shift his attention to the road ahead of them. Another sigh of discontentment along with some shuffling came from the back of the vehicle behind Daniel.

"That's alright, Sammy, we're going now," Daniel said, reaching back to pat the scruffy head of the Australian shepherd dog. Scratching the white spot on her forehead, she poked her cold, wet nose on his neck. He laughed before relenting and giving her a dog biscuit from a bag on the seat. "Who wants to go to the mountains? Who wants to go to the mountains?"

"I see you brought your dog too," Johanna noted with a smirk as she turned to her son. "Keep talking to her like that, Danny, and maybe someday she'll talk back to you!"

"Don't get jealous, sweetie; other than you, she's my girl!" Nate laughed before taking a second glance at Johanna. "You don't mind, do you? Daniel's looking after her as he always does; it's a good lesson for responsibility for him growing up, and I see no reason to interrupt that even as we go on a vacation!"

"Of course not, but she's practically becoming Daniel's dog in the process!" Johanna laughed. She winced as she caught sight of a large old wooden box crammed in with the dog and the suitcases. "But your ammo box? Really? Do we have to take that?"

"You don't remember?" Nate laughed. "I told you I was taking you both shooting. Bill and I had a rifle and handgun collection, and he and I both agreed that you and Daniel should learn how to use them. Before you go on again about how you hate guns, I want to remind you about how important it was for both Bill and me that we do this."

"Nah, I'm fine with Sammy," Johanna exhaled, her anxiety apparent as she sat back in her seat. "I just didn't know we were doing that on THIS trip. The dog is one thing, the guns are another."

"What better time than the present?" Nate insisted. "We're going up to the cabin for three full days, away from the city and away from people. We've got plenty of time and plenty of space to do it right and safely—it's high time you both learned."

"I want to try the handgun first," Daniel chimed in from the back seat before donning a headset to listen to music.

"Yeah, great." Johanna rolled her eyes, glancing back to ensure Daniel wouldn't hear her as she reduced her voice to a harsh whisper. "It's high time! My son has enough issues as it is, and you want to get him to tote a gun now?!"

Nate ignored Johanna's sarcasm, whistling a tune through his charming smile as they drove until they were out of the Denver city limits, climbing steadily on I-70 until they reached the town of Evergreen. The exit off the freeway took them atop Bergen Park, the turnoff to climb Highway 103 and the unique vista of the Rocky Mountain foothills.

Johanna decided at the beginning to let the dispute go; this was an old familiar argument with no resolution. She had the same disagreement over guns many times in the past with her deceased husband, and it was no different with Nate in the present. While she didn't mind road trips, her mind was still focused on her therapy session. Her visions nagged at her, refusing to leave her mind's eye, yet she couldn't allow them to consume the reality she faced each day.

Nate glanced over at his companion, seeming to sense her easing apprehension as they meandered deeper into the mountain scenery, patches of snow peppering the meadow to their left as the narrow highway took them into the forest. He patted her on the knee in reassurance. He could see her continue to visibly relax as they left the town of Evergreen behind and immersed themselves in the forest, climbing steadily up the winding mountain highway through aspen and pines, curving more yet revealing a broader landscape the higher they went.

Since Bill had passed, he had taken to looking after Johanna and Daniel. He could sense the wall she had placed between them, so he dared not mention the love he had already developed for her. He had successfully tamped down his desire for her when Bill had originally introduced them, but since his best friend's passing, his yearning for her only intensified. It was all he could do to prevent himself from responding to her vulnerability by rushing in to fill the void that Bill had left.

Her initial hesitation to embrace his affections had stung, yet he could not find it within himself to resent her for it. Each time he saw her or Daniel, Bill's face would resurface in his mind, speaking to him, privately insisting, "If anything should ever happen to me, look after them!"

Weeks had turned to months, and his persistent efforts to assist them never felt unappreciated; and even if they had, he had long ago resolved to help—if not for himself, then for Bill. *I have to tread carefully with this one!*

Looking briefly in the mirror, he caught sight of Daniel, gently petting Sammy and offering her a treat. His dog briefly chewed down one morsel, inhaling it faster than she could enjoy it.

Nate chuckled to himself and Daniel smiled back before returning his gaze out the passenger window at the scenery spilling by. He wondered how it would have felt to lose his own father before becoming an adult. Lately, Nate could see Daniel burying himself in video games, books and movies instead of joining team sports and the parties that the other kids his age occupied themselves with. It wasn't healthy and certainly not what Bill would have wanted.

Johanna had tried to force the issue with her son, but Nate knew Daniel wouldn't respond to that coercion. This trip was a chance at finding out more about the boy; a chance to really get to know him and find that bit of Bill that was inside him.

"So, you really prepared for everything," Johanna commented, drawing his attention to her as she helped herself to a Thermos of hot cider. The smell of cinnamon and apple permeated the vehicle as they drove, giving a pleasant aroma while they meandered through the mountains on the scenic roadway. "Would you like some?"

"I'll take a cup!" Nate grinned, turning his attention back to the wintry scenery ahead. As Johanna poured a steaming cup into his driver's mug, he noticed the fresh mantles of snow, sloughing off the trees the higher they climbed higher in elevation. He accepted the mug with thanks and took a deep draught. "Looks like a fresh snowfall recently. Roads are still decent though."

"I thought the cabin was near Idaho Springs?" Johanna pointed out. "Why did we turn early at Evergreen?"

"Well, yeah," Nate breathed, slightly annoyed. "It's a prettier drive this way, and I thought you would enjoy the view."

"Well, the road's a bit winding, isn't it?" Johanna commented, turning back to ask Daniel his opinion. "I noticed a couple of icy patches on the road; aren't you worried?"

As pleasant as the drive was, Johanna couldn't help but notice that the ascent switch-backed several times through the forest peppered only occasionally with a mountain cabin and very few other cars. They had even passed a small ski area on the right-hand side but continued the two-lane highway up the mountainside.

Daniel had already dozed off, asleep with his headphones on. Sammy stirred only occasionally behind him amongst their bags.

"We're fine," Nate stated as he pointed. "There—look."

Johanna gazed out the window in wonder. The road they had been winding incessantly for nearly fifteen miles opened ahead of them, giving a view of the snow-capped Rockies off to their right. *No matter how many times I see them, they truly are breathtaking.*

"You're right, Nate; it is beautiful," Johanna agreed with a long sigh, settling back in her seat. "I don't think I thank you enough, and you really do deserve it."

"I really hope you don't mind about the guns," he began with a confident smile, noting an air of contentment beginning to settle over her face. "I know you're not a fan, but Bill wanted you both to learn to shoot. He and I both agreed that when Daniel was older, we'd show the both of you."

"He told you that, did he?" Johanna asked in more of a statement than a question, carefully trying to keep the malice from her voice. The mention of Bill's name always threw a damper on her mood.

"Well, yeah—he did," Nate said, glancing over at her. "You know I care about you and Daniel deeply, but I also lost my best friend," he reiterated the point.

"Yes, well—he was my husband and Daniel's father," Johanna quipped, turning to look out the window again.

"What's that supposed to mean?" Nate let the moment pass only briefly before a shot of annoyance washed over him. "Johanna, come on! It's been a year now, and all I'm saying is that it's an important skill we BOTH wanted to share with you and Daniel."

"No, you're right," Johanna lamented, shaking her head, trying to recapture the peace that had been so quickly disturbed. Johanna returned the comment with a forced smile, nodding in agreement. "It's fine. His ghost just seems to come up a lot lately."

Nate recognized the forced nature in the smile but said nothing, so they continued in silence on the snowy road that had begun to descend. With a line of tall peaks ahead, the vista opened up again, and he knew the view of several mountain peaks would make a good distraction from their last topic.

Towering pines around them maintained their snowy winter mantle, yet icy chunks could be seen dropping off as the air warmed. To her relief, the road ceased climbing and began to descend. A wide valley opened up before them and at the center of it, a broad frozen lake shone in the sun, glistening like a great diamond nestled among the snow-covered trees.

"Looks like a cabin there," Johanna commented, pointing to a large wooden structure they were passing on the left, near the shore of the lake.

"It's a visitor center and gift shop in the summer," Nate explained. "It's closed and boarded up for the season, but I always thought it would make a nice year-round B&B."

"It's beautiful, Nate," Johanna murmured, although a crease of concern lined her face as she sat up attentively. "Yet also strangely familiar..."

"That's why I love coming this way," Nate proclaimed with a broad grin. The vista opened further, and the sight took their breath away, even as the glare made them squint to take it in. The bright sun reflected off the wind-driven snow. Nate's smile faded when he saw Johanna's face pale. "What is it?"

"My God," she gasped. "It's the lake I saw Bill die in; only he's already gone. I don't understand; why am I seeing it here and now? Why have I seen this before?"

Chapter 2

Road Trip

Kevin Micker welcomed the opportunity to get out of the car and stretch his legs at the Georgetown stop in Colorado. Nestled in a narrow valley deep in the Rocky Mountains, the small, picturesque town, looked like a Norman Rockwell painting from I-70, giving the group of four college students the excuse for a long overdue break in their drive. He and his companions had been in the car for over six hours, and even though they were almost to Denver, he took any opportunity possible to put some space between himself and his fellow travelers.

Kevin stole a glance back at the oversized blue Lincoln that Javier Billings had been driving the whole way from Farmington, New Mexico. It had been Javier's bright idea to take the long way through Grand Junction to see western Colorado on their way to visit friends in Boulder at Colorado University. Javier, the tall, muscular jock, seemed to suck all the air out of the room whenever he walked in; he was the bane of Kevin's existence...

Shaking his head with disgust, Kevin watched as Javier got out of the driver's seat to pump gas. Javier stood tall as he always did, flexing his muscular arms as he brushed back his wavy black hair, his blue eyes shining in the sunlight. *He's so full of himself.*

This trip was originally supposed to be just Kevin and his friend, Becky Branson. The cute, short blonde girl on campus had taken a special liking to Kevin early on. Oh, sure, she had a boyfriend—Tim Blaylock, another blonde "Ken doll" with a short goatee beard, but he never minded Kevin and Becky studying together. In fact, she had approached Kevin originally to ask him about going somewhere together for spring break. Kevin could remember it clearly.

"I was just going to go back to Albuquerque and, well, do nothing," Kevin had told her as he laughed. "Why do you ask? What about Tim; isn't he going with you?"

"Nah," she had stated with such certainty. "He and Javier Billings are going to Moab on a guys-only trip, and I don't want to go alone. Do you know Javier?"

Javier Billings—the name turned his stomach even then. The know-it-all jock who always seemed to steal the spotlight in a crowd and only pointed it at you if it was to make fun of you.

"Yeah, I know Javier but don't know why Tim would want to hang out with him," Kevin stated carefully before sidestepping the topic. *I don't want to say anything that might get back to him.* "Either way, you sure Tim doesn't have a problem with us going together?"

"Kevin, please," she admonished, rolling her blue-grey eyes and giving him a big hug. "Tim knows you and I are just friends; he doesn't mind!"

He had smiled in relief then. But that was then; this was now. Plans changed, and not only did Tim decide to come along, but Javier also invited himself along. Before they knew it, Javier was the one driving and throwing jabs at Kevin every few minutes about "who invited the prude" or "why is the boring guy here?"

Kevin's memory of how the plans had shifted so drastically still stung him, even surrounded by the beauty of Georgetown, nestled deep in the Rocky Mountains. The encompassing splendor did little to comfort him and only made him wish he was further away.

"Tim Blaylock! That's my private shit!" Becky shouted playfully from the back seat in the Lincoln, slapping her boyfriend as her long blonde hair tussled with the effort. He rifled through her purse before triumphantly producing a tampon and hitting her over the head with it. "Give that back to me!"

"Guys, I'm going in to use the bathroom and get some snacks," Kevin announced. When no one seemed to hear or respond, he shook his head and exited the vehicle, ambling toward the convenience store.

As Javier pumped the gas, he turned to see another group of spring-skiing girls walking toward Kevin at the convenience store's entrance. They flirted with Javier as they strode past, giggling nervously as he returned their inviting glances. Suddenly serious again, he pushed back his jet-black hair and smiled at them, talking in low tones as he ravished them with his piercing blue eyes.

Kevin scoffed, sick of watching everyone having fun but him, and he turned to enter the convenience store. Catching sight of his own reflection in the window, he wondered, *Why am I the only one not having fun here?*

If the last few hundred miles were any indication of how things were going, Kevin was beginning to regret coming on this trip, wishing he had just gone home to Albuquerque instead. He didn't view himself as unattractive by comparison, to his peers. He just felt more reserved and plain. He had light brown hair and brown eyes and was not nearly as tall as Javier, with more of a lanky swimmer's build. *I suppose I'm just more modest…I'm nothing like these people!*

Once inside, Kevin turned briefly to see Javier still flirting with the girls. The girls giggled as Javier took off his black leather jacket, no doubt to show off his pecs under that skintight shirt of his. Kevin shook his head, *What an ass!*

≈≈≈≈

Outside at the car, Becky had finally stopped playing keep-away with Tim to launch into a short make-out session with her boyfriend.

They kissed in the back seat as Javier finished filling the car with gasoline, turning his full attention to the girls still standing at the front of the car.

"Well at least Javier's having a good time," Becky murmured in Tim's ear.

"Yes, he is," Tim laughed between kisses on Becky's neck. "I'm glad we invited him along."

"You know, this was supposed to be Kevin's trip too," Becky whispered as she stopped him with a finger on his lips, smiling sweetly but locking his gaze seriously eye to eye. "You guys were going to Moab, and I had no one to go with me to Boulder to see Karen and Mike. You guys changed your mind at the last minute, and..."

"What are you saying?" Tim scoffed with a smirk, forcing a kiss onto her neck. "We're ruining Kevin's vacation?"

"Tim!" Becky stopped him after a moment, laughing but still trying to make her point. "The least you guys could do is include him."

"Hey, I include him all the time," Tim complained. "I can't force Javier to like him, and Kevin seems to like being alone. If that's what he enjoys, why should we stop him?"

"No, he doesn't," Becky insisted. "Anyway, maybe you could at least talk to Javier and get him to..."

"Where's the douchebag?" Javier interjected, knocking on the window.

"See what I'm talking about?" she whispered, gesturing at Javier to emphasize her point. The two skier girls had gone into the store and Javier had put on his black jacket again with no one left to impress and rubbing his hands together to regain his body heat lost with his brief display.

"Be nice!" Becky pointed at him sternly, shouting at him through the glass before turning in exasperation back to her boyfriend. "Tim, make him be nice!"

"I AM nice!" Javier shot back with a smirk.

"He went into the store," Tim said in annoyance. "Alright, fine; I'll go get him if it's that important to you."

"No, I'll get him," Javier growled. "This is going to take time I don't feel like wasting!"

"Well, don't be an asshole!" Tim shouted, before turning and raising his eyebrows at his girlfriend, seeking her approval. "See? How was that?"

"Well, that at least was something," Becky sighed, rolling her eyes. "You both need to do better; he's my friend!"

"What else can I do?" Tim exclaimed before resuming their make-out session.

≈≈≈≈

Kevin emerged from the bathroom, drying his hands on his pants as he strolled slowly past the snack aisle. Turning the corner of shelves in the convenience store, he had to squeeze past the two skier girls Javier had been talking to outside.

"Excuse me," he muttered politely.

"No problem," the brunette replied with a wink and a smile. He tossed her long straight hair, smelling faintly of cherries as she giggled. "Sheri, let the guy pass!"

"Sure thing," her dirty-blonde-haired friend said with a sassy smile as she snatched a bag of chips. "Hey, are you with that group outside?"

"Yeah," Kevin said, regretfully non-committed.

"Oh, cool!" the brunette exclaimed. "My name's Kelly, and we should totally hang out! Your friend Javier out there told us you all were going to Boulder. That's where we go to school! We're headed back that way and there's a big party tomorrow night on campus!"

"Yeah, Kelly and I would love to see you guys there," the blonde girl added. "I'm Sheri by the way!"

"Nice to meet you both, I'm Kevin," he managed, smiling back after grabbing a couple of bags of chips. "It would be nice to see some friendly faces; I'm sure my friends are up for it."

"Hey, Micker!" Javier's voice grated on him like sandpaper from across the convenience store. Standing in the doorway as annoyed as ever, he threw his hands up in the air impatiently. They made eye contact, and Kevin immediately noticed Javier's eyes drifting from him to the girls. After a mischievous grin, he added, "You're making us late as usual! Quit bullshitting and get your ass out here!"

"I was getting some chips for everyone—" Kevin started.

"Nobody wants that shit, come on!" Javier snapped his fingers and motioned as the girls giggled and Javier winked at them before turning his attention back to Kevin. "Get your ass out here!"

"To hell with him," Kevin muttered, throwing the chips back on the shelf and leaving the store, not even looking at Javier as he walked out past him.

≈≈≈≈

It was quiet in the car for the next twenty minutes other than the rock music playing in the background. Kevin stared out the window at the tops of the mountains. He could see the outlines of branches, their pinecones, even birds flying above them and wished he was just sitting up there among them.

"Hey, didn't you say you and Becky have been out this way before?" Javier asked, breaking the silence as he drummed his thumbs impatiently on the steering wheel before turning finally to Tim. "Before we rush to campus, we should check out some of the sights!"

"Yeah, we came last year," Tim replied. "Had a really good time— it's a cool group there on campus."

"Remember that lake we stopped at?" Becky asked suddenly.

"Oh, yeah." Tim nodded. "Right outside of town. What was it... Chasm Lake?"

"Echo Lake," Kevin stated.

"You weren't there, how would you know?" Javier turned on him with a sour look.

"I told him about it," Becky interjected heatedly. She sat back, glaring at Javier in the mirror, who shrugged and kept driving. "Yes, Kevin, that's it—Echo Lake. It was beautiful!"

"We should go there again," Tim murmured as he nuzzled Becky's neck. "For old time's sake. We're not far from the turnoff now; what do you think, Javier? You wanna take us there?"

"Sure, why not," Javier stated aloud without hesitation even though he continued to drum his fingers impatiently on the steering wheel. *What do I think?! I won't tell you what I really think!*

He had been irritable since they left Farmington, looking forward to a long-awaited mountain biking in Moab with his best friend Tim. He wanted to put school, studying obligations and Patrice behind him. Ah, yes, Patrice—*that bitch.*

He had a year of dating her, seriously invested in her, before she told him she had had enough. A beautiful girl, soft-spoken but hardly soft, she was athletic and very self-driven. He had worked hard to keep her interested throughout their time together. It had been two weeks ago when she approached him, saying she was leaving for greener pastures.

"Seattle?!" he had exclaimed. "I can't move to Seattle. We're not even done with graduation yet!"

"I know, Javier," she had gently but firmly told him, her deep blue eyes as sincere as they possibly could be. "I'm moving back there to start a new life. I need to do some things for myself, and I'm sorry, it just doesn't include you."

"Not include me?" Javier had smirked even as a sense of dread had opened in his stomach. "What's wrong with me?"

She had taken a deep breath before arriving at the point that stabbed him deeper than even he had known possible.

"Javier, I'm sick of your bullshit," she began, her voice suddenly pinched with annoyance. "I'm sick of your self-centeredness and lack of civility. I need someone in my life who gives a shit about people other than themselves, and let's face facts—that's not you!"

"You don't think I can find someone else?" Javier had exploded. "You think I NEED you?!"

"Javier, I just don't care," Patrice had flatly stated, shaking her head.

"I know I am going to find someone else, and you can go do whatever you want!"

She had started to leave when he grabbed her arm—big mistake. He had underestimated just how frustrated she was with him. The slap she had landed on his cheek still echoed in his head.

"What the fuck is wrong with you?!" he had exclaimed, the breath suddenly seized from his chest. "What is your problem?!"

"Javier, YOU are my problem," she had replied. "I swear to you, one of these days, you will give a shit about someone beyond just how they make you feel! Your good looks will only take you so far, and then they will go away, and you'll be just another lonely middle-aged guy, living alone and drunk, wishing for his glory days! I'm done!"

"Don't worry, I don't need you either!" he had yelled after her.

With that, she had stormed away, leaving him with nothing else left to say. *Small consolation—that bitch. I'll show her.*

The trip to Moab was supposed to be a getaway for him and Tim to help purge Patrice from his mind. Now, plans had been rearranged around Beck and Boulder—and this Kevin guy; *fine, whatever. Tim didn't like Beck going with another guy to Boulder without him, but why does this dweeb have to ruin it all for us?!*

Javier was bound and determined to show his friend and his friend's girlfriend that their sickening romance could be matched. He'd find one too. Pretty girls were no match for him, he'd get one...maybe more than one. He still had Patrice's number and would make sure there was photographic evidence of the good times he'd have without her.

"Javier?" Becky prodded his seat with her foot.

"What?" Javier turned. "Did you say something?"

"Do you mind if we take a detour to that lake?" Tim asked. "We're coming up to that exit!"

"Yeah, sure—whatever you want," Javier muttered.

"You okay, buddy?" Tim patted him on the shoulder and pointed. "You need to slow down if we're going to take that detour; it's right there!"

"Oh, yeah, for sure, just in the zone!" Javier muttered. "I thought this mountain was called Mount Evans."

"Right up there," Kevin stated heatedly, pointing ahead of them. "The sign right there says turnoff for Echo Lake and Mount Blue Sky."

"I saw it, I don't need you to point it out, Captain Obvious!" Javier scoffed as they approached the small town of Idaho Springs. He could now clearly see the exit on the right with the sign Kevin had indicated but decided to joke about it. "Echo Lake and Mount Everest, right ahead!"

"Evans, not Everest," Kevin muttered under his breath, rolling his eyes. "Everest is in the Himalayas; they changed this mountain's name to Mount Blue Sky a while ago."

For once, Javier decided to say nothing, but that was another thing irritating him. This Kevin Micker was really pissing him off. He just wasn't part of their group—why did Tim have to invite him along?

Tim had insisted that Kevin was his girlfriend's friend, but the guy was a real drag. They had him sitting up front with him, sulking in the corner. Kevin clearly had nothing in common with them, and the guy just seemed like he wanted to be somewhere else. The few times they had spoken, it sounded like he was looking down his nose at Javier.

What's your problem? What's wrong with you? It's as if Patrice sent you along just to irritate me!

Javier shook his head. *Technically, Tim and I have invaded Kevin and Becky's trip; but who cares! No one is going to get in my way of having fun, certainly not a nobody like Kevin!*

It made matters worse when those two girls he had been flirting with at the gas station had asked him about Kevin, "the cute, shy, thin guy." Meanwhile, Kevin seemed to have no interest in them, even when he'd been caught speaking to the girls at the convenience store. *If Kevin gets in the way again, I'll just embarrass him more when we get to the party. I'll make sure he knows his place!*

The road ascended to higher elevations and emerged from a wooded valley with steep slopes on either side. Fresh snow lined the roadway to either side as they climbed up out of the valley. The road began to switch-back as they climbed higher, past leafless aspens and above cliff edges, giving them a sweeping view of the mountains around them. The named mountain peak loomed over the valley beside them as they winded up the snow-covered grade.

"Wow, that's beautiful," Kevin whispered.

"Isn't it?!" Becky clapped. "Aren't you glad you came!?"

"So, Kevin," Javier interjected, still stewing over their last quip. He could feel Becky kick him from the back seat, but he pressed on. "What sports do you play?"

"Well, I like to ski and hike and—" Kevin started.

"Those aren't sports," Javier interrupted. "What REAL sports are you in?"

"I used to run cross country and track," Kevin finished.

"Oh, yeah," Tim interjected at Becky's prompts. "I remember running track myself back in high school. Skiing is also a sport, by the way."

"No, that's an activity," Javier corrected. "I'd like to know what actual sports you play!"

"Skiing is most definitely a sport if you're competing," Becky stated.

"Okay, fine, I'll give you that," Javier admitted before turning to Kevin. "Did you compete in skiing?"

"Sure," Kevin lied. "Many times!"

"Hey, remember that ski trip we all took up to Vail?" Tim exclaimed before Javier could say anything further.

"Oh, yeah, when was that anyway? That bus with the whole lot of us?" Javier remembered, reluctantly letting go of the annoyance he harbored toward Kevin still glaring at him from the front passenger seat. "What about it?"

"Wasn't Patrice on that trip too?" Kevin asked, happy to give a dig where he saw the opportunity. "I seem to remember she had a really good time on that trip!"

Javier had a flash of anger but kept it to himself. *So, he DOES know about her, that son of a bitch!*

"Yeah, she was there, but I don't think she had as good of a time as she claims to have had." Javier forced a grin while, in his mind, he was punching Kevin in the face. "Next time, it will be one of those two from the gas station!"

"Javier, why are you speeding up? Slow down!" Becky pointed over Javier's shoulder even as his lead foot led them screeching around the corners he drove. Drifts of snow had accumulated in shaded sections of the road. Where the sun touched the drifts, sheets of ice glistened, reflecting the light. "There's black ice on the road! There, in the shade!"

"Looks like they've had some wind up here," Tim agreed as they continued their winding drive up the mountain road. "Come on, Javier, slow down!"

"Yeah, I see it," Javier muttered, reluctantly complying. "I'm the driver here!"

"Shouldn't you slow down more?" Kevin muttered as he looked away, gripping the dashboard in nervous misery. "You're gonna get us all killed!"

"You want to drive, Puss in Boots?" Javier seethed, even as he relented, noticeably slowing the vehicle a bit more. "If it weren't for me, we'd still be back in—"

"Both of you, just relax; we don't have too much further to go," Tim interrupted nervously while still trying to impress on the scenery. "Just look at the view!"

The towering fourteen-thousand-plus foot peak loomed ahead, snow-capped and glistening in the sun as the car continued its winding course up the mountain road. Large tuffs of snow hung from the boughs of the trees to either side. The higher they went, the thicker it seemed, especially in shaded sections.

"We're almost there." Becky clenched Tim's knee excitedly. "Do you think the lake is still frozen? It would be fun to walk out on it."

"Yeah, I don't know," Tim admitted, leaning forward and pointing. He excitedly unbuckled his seatbelt to lean closer to Javier and point out exactly where he wanted his friend to park the car. "There, right over there. Javier, we're going to miss the parking lot on the right! Watch the ice!"

The road veered to the left, and on the right side, the shoulder of the road opened up with a picnic area visible between the trees and places to park. Between the tree-lined picnic area, the shoreline of the lake buttressed right up against the roadside. The frozen lake glistened in the sun, although dark splotches of water spotting the ice gave the telltale signs of spring melt.

Javier stepped on the brakes and started to turn, but the car began to fishtail. Too late, all four of them saw the slick surface atop the roadway, a solid sheet of ice from an early melt and freeze.

"Black ice! Black ice!" Kevin shouted, scrambling to brace himself.

"Javier!" Becky exclaimed. "We want to visit the lake, not swim in it!"

"Yeah, I see it!" Javier gritted his teeth as he clenched the steering wheel.

Suddenly, the back end of the car swung around to face the lake, sending the car into a tailspin. The group quickly found themselves sliding off the road, still spinning toward the shoreline.

"Javier!" Becky screamed.

"Whoa, buddy!!!" Tim grunted as he grasped helplessly onto the frame of the car with both hands, grimacing as he tensed. "Shit! We're going in!"

Javier downshifted and tried to give it more gas, but it was too late. The back end of the Lincoln swung out over the ledge and dropped immediately over the rocks onto the rocky shoreline with a violent, jarring clang. The clockwise spin of the car carried the tire into a large boulder, stopping the back end abruptly and forcing the vehicle to flip.

Kevin gasped, and it all seemed to go in slow motion as he tried to jam himself deeper into the recesses of the passenger side. Glass shattered around him with each impact as metal and leather caved on to each side, taking up any free space.

Javier threw his hands up to cover his face, no longer in control of the vehicle as the world revolved and then flipped upside down around him.

Becky closed her eyes, screaming as she slammed forcefully into Tim's chest.

Tim bounced upward and then sideways as the car began to roll, shattering the passenger window. He suddenly found himself thrust halfway outside the car as it rolled. He stared, mouth agape and eyes wide, as the full weight of the car rolled over him, pressing his face onto the lake ice, his upper body remaining half out the rear window.

As the tumbling vehicle rolled twice, it came to a halt upside down. A loud crack resounded across the lake as the ice around the car shattered into multiple sections. Freezing water flooded into the car along with jagged sections of ice as the front end began to sink.

"Oh God! Oh God!" Becky screamed as dark water flooded into the vehicle. Upside down and sinking, the freezing lake pressed in around them, liquid pain seeping through their clothing like hypodermic needles.

Kevin tried to scream too, but with an ear-piercing shriek, jagged pieces of ice stabbed their way into the vehicle, and all he could do was clutch his head and curl up. Only when the freezing water hit him did he manage an agonizing cry. He glanced briefly over toward Javier, slumped over the steering wheel and head bleeding, as water and ice flooded in, mingling with broken glass and bent metal all around them.

Chapter 3

The Meeting

Nate did his best to keep Johanna calm as the road became intermittently icy. Drifts of snow blew ahead of them before melting and refreezing, giving treacherous sections a glossy sheet of black ice. He hoped Johanna wouldn't notice and add to her sudden and unexpected recollection of a supposed premonition for disaster at the lake as they came around the bend.

"What do you mean this is the same lake, Johanna?" Nate clenched his teeth as he kept his focus on driving when he felt the Jeep's wheels slip slightly. Luckily, she seemed so fixated on her apprehension that she hadn't noticed his slight course correction to keep the vehicle in their lane.

"This is the place! I saw this place, right before Bill died!" Johanna sputtered. "I know it sounds off, but this is where I saw him crash!"

"Bill died in that crash in Fort Collins more than a year ago, miles away; not here," Nate stated quietly to calm her. "Johanna, not everything you see is a premonition or has a special meaning."

"Maybe we're the ones who are supposed to crash here!" Daniel grinned, eavesdropping from the back seat.

"Not funny," Nate growled as he snapped his fingers at him, glaring at the lad through the rear-view mirror. As they continued around the bend, the full view of the lake splayed out before them. "Don't make your mother any more worried than…"

"Oh my God, Nate! Look!" Johanna gasped, pointing ahead on the road. A crumpled inverted blue Lincoln stuck halfway out of shattered lake ice in front of them on the far northwest corner of the lake. Steam and smoke poured from the back as the car slowly sank into the hole it had created in the ice. "I know it's not Bill, but that car, upside down and where this is, looks exactly like what I saw!"

"Oh, great," Nate muttered as he slowed the Jeep. Bewilderment coursed through him as he ran his hands through his sandy hair, surveying the scene, at a loss for words. His heart pounded as he did his best not to glance in shock at Johanna. *Coincidence?!*

"Whoa! What happened there?" Daniel exhaled in shock as he pulled off his headphones and Johanna fumbled for her cell phone. "Mom, you saw that before?!"

"Calm down, both of you! Looks like they hit that patch of ice there on the road," Nate muttered as he shook his head, bringing the Jeep to a halt at the edge of the road near the scene of the accident. He and Johanna stepped out of the vehicle, slipping and sliding on the road top black ice. "Careful! It's slick as snot here!"

"I can't get a signal!" Johanna exclaimed in frustration, futilely moving her phone around above her as she stepped out on the road. The fresh cold mountain breezes rustled her hair as the scent of pine permeated the scene around her. "Should we drive down into town and get help?"

"No, it looks like it just happened; and they are sinking! We need to help," Nate stated, grasping her shoulders to get her attention and locking her eyes with his. "You are going to have to stay here while I try to winch them out. If we start to slide too, then I'm going to need you to back us out. Just don't gun the engine when you pull the Jeep back!"

Johanna nodded and slid into the driver's seat as Nate shut the door behind her. Turning back to the slowly sinking car, he rubbed his hands together as he considered the matters at hand. Despite the warming spring day, the air still had a winter bite to it.

He could see that the taillights of the Lincoln were still lit and the rear bumper was exposed, rising higher into the air as the front slid deeper. Grabbing the tow hook from the front winch, he crunched through the snow onto the lake ice, pulling the cable as he went. The Lincoln's hood was completely submerged, and Nate noted the blood-stained ice near the smashed back end.

"Hello?" Nate called as he approached. "Is everyone okay in there?"

"Yes! I'm here," a girl's voice screamed back at him from the car. "There's three other guys here with me, but I think they're hurt really bad!"

"I see you," Nate shouted as he attached the tow hook beneath the back bumper of the Lincoln. He could barely make out the blonde hair of the girl staring wide-eyed at him from behind the broken rear window. "Are you able to crawl out?"

"I'm pinned and I can't move!" The girl winced in panic, struggling to move but unable to. "I'm jammed behind this seat and all this stuff!"

"Okay, just hang on! I'm working on it!" he yelled before turning back and running for the Jeep to start the winch.

"Hurry, please, I think we're sinking!" the girl shouted again. "It's so cold, and the guys in the front are almost under!"

Nate climbed back up the embankment and flipped the switch for the winch. He watched carefully as the cable tightened and the machinery spooled in the slack on the cable, making a low hum as it pulled.

As the cable began to tighten, the hook around the Lincoln's bumper looked like it might begin to slip free.

"Damn!" Nate muttered. He quickly slid down the embankment, careful to avoid the broken ice, and tightened the tow cable again around the car's bumper just as the cable went taunt. "Just in time!"

Nodding with satisfaction, he noted the whir of the machinery beginning to strain against the weight of the car. This time, the tie-off held as the car began to inch back out of the ice, water pouring from the smashed windows and caved-in roof. Nate shivered, glancing about nervously; he could only imagine how cold it must be inside that car.

Just then, a loud cracking sound reverberated suddenly like thunder around the valley. *What was that? Gunshots? Thunder?*

Nate felt a sudden sense of dread run through him when with realization, he looked down at his feet, vibrating from the ice he stood on, spider-webbing with cracks. He turned to run and briefly caught a glimpse of Johanna, her eyes wide as she gripped the Jeep's steering wheel in terror. Their eyes met and time stood still for an instant. Just long enough to allow Nate's brain to tell his feet to move...but not long enough to take more than a step.

With a resounding crash, the ice on the lake shattered and the Lincoln plummeted down into the water. Massive sections of ice upended around the sinking car, sending Nate flailing into the icy water. He could only gasp as the slushy mix crushed in brutally around him, the cold blasting in around him from all sides, encapsulating and soaking him to the bone, threatening to freeze solid around him. *Like being trapped in a swirling snow cone.*

The car's submerged front end slammed into an underwater boulder, shattering the driver's side headlamp. With a burst of light underwater, the lake momentarily lit up like a mile-wide flash bulb. As the car sank, a loud pop resounded and half the bumper from the Lincoln's back end wrenched free.

The bumper's jagged metal edge pierced Nate's upper thigh, and he screamed as it sliced through flesh, snagging his jeans and pulling him beneath the surface as the car plummeted.

Nate struggled as he quickly succumbed to the cold, the furious stabbing of knives dulling quickly into numbness to the point he could barely move to keep himself afloat. He could scarcely feel much in the cold, but as he gripped his bleeding leg, another shifting section of ice slid over his head submerging him completely. Sinking below the icy surface, he gurgled in muffled agony as he sank.

At the Jeep, the tow cable became immediately taut as the car and Nate vanished beneath the surface. With a sudden lurch, the SUV started to slide towards the edge of the lake.

"Oh God, we're still attached!" Johanna gasped. She tried to put the Jeep in reverse but quickly noticed something was wrong; the engine suddenly stalled as warning lights flashed across the dashboard. The vehicle began sliding faster toward the lake, pulled by the sinking car. Turning the key over and over resulted in nothing but loud clicks as she struggled to restart the Jeep, even as it slid. "Come on! Come on! No! No! No! No!"

"Mom, what's going on?" Daniel grunted, fussing with Sammy's leash and collar, having missed what had transpired. "What are you—"

"Danny! Get out!" she screamed. "Oh God, Danny, get out! Get out! Get out!" *Too late...*

The Jeep plunged headlong over the embankment and bounced violently twice over the side and into the lake. With a loud splash, water and slush began pouring in from all sides.

"Mom!!!" Daniel exclaimed as he and Sammy rolled together over each other in the back seat, shockingly frigid waters flooding in around them. With a violent jolt, the tow line went taunt, yanking them down beneath the surface. "What the hell?!?! Oh my God! Nate; help!!! Nate!!!"

Sammy yelped in terror as water suddenly began to flood in around the occupants. Johanna and Daniel screamed helplessly as the temperature plunged within the sinking vehicle, their breath puffing like smoke as the vehicle plummeted into the icy depths. Every movement became a sudden slog as their clothing froze to their skin. Gasping for air and clutching at the windows did nothing to stop their sinking. They pried at the door handles, but chunks of ice pressed in around them, pinning the doors shut. The windows began to crack as freezing water sprayed in around the dimly lit interior, and soon, all subsided into darkness and bubbles.

"It shouldn't be this deep!" Johanna gasped as water closed in over her head. She cried aloud, grasping for her son's hand as they began choking and spluttering, recoiling from the icy clench of agony closing in around them in a vise grip.

A sudden rushing sound met their ears, and the water even seemed to reverse, draining around them as a faint light swirled in a vortex around the Jeep. They screamed as a sudden sense of free-falling overtook them.

≈≈≈≈

The sun shimmered high in the afternoon sky, warming the crests and ridges of an idyllic forested vale, a narrow green and winding valley. A mix of pine and fir trees overlooked a lush grassy meadow, peppered with flowers and dry reeds. A fast but deep flowing river flowed quietly past a cliff on the north side. The smooth rock-face slab protruded from the river's edge, forcing the river to bend around it. Only the occasional bird chirping and chattering chipmunk interrupted the warm and peaceful scene.

A peculiar milling sound emerged above the din, and the air around seemed to go silent, except for the errant insect flying by to buzz from flower to flower. At first barely perceivable, the grinding sound grew in intensity, turning into a rumble that vibrated the entire hillside.

Suddenly, a geyser of water erupted from the cliff face, shooting several feet into the air before plummeting into the river below. The disturbance startled the local wildlife, and even the fish scattered as water sprayed out of the rock face. Deer, rabbits, chipmunks—everything ran from the unexpected spout.

More sharp cracking sounds resounded, echoing throughout the valley as chunks of ice and debris blew from the ever-enlarging hole. With a loud boom, a flock of birds took flight in the meadow as the cliff face blew open and a flood of water and ice vomited forth, turning the spout into a flowing river, spilling down into the creek below.

A very crumpled Lincoln Town Car plunged forth and tumbled

onto the sandy bank right side up, miring itself in the mud. A much smaller splash in the water behind it followed as an unconscious man fell into the river, becoming entwined in the looping metal cable. The man floated face down in the deep pool that had formed, bumped into the car and started to drift past it until the cable held him fast.

Another great splash followed as a second vehicle followed. The waterlogged Jeep became stuck in the mouth of the spout briefly before plunging over the precipice. With windows shattered and the body dented, the Jeep was still in much better shape than the car, landing upright and bobbing briefly in the pool before settling in the mud. The two vehicles and the half-submerged man lay in the river as water continued to pour out from the hillside.

Eventually, the waterspout from the cliff subsided from a torrent to a gentler, more constant flow. Then from a flow, it ebbed to a trickle, and the quiet returned to the meadow. Only a gaping black hole in the cliff face and the two vehicles lying on the embankment betrayed any sign of a disturbance ever occurring. Within minutes, the trickle vanished and only a dripping cavern remained.

That's when the door behind the driver's seat of the Jeep opened and water spilled out. A very weary-looking woman half fell out of the damaged SUV, coughing and hacking, trailed by her bewildered son, followed by a wet black dog.

≈≈≈≈

Shivering despite the sun, Johanna stumbled over to where Nate lay face down in the water. Grabbing him by his shoulders, she hoisted his blue face out of the water and pulled him to shore. The cable he had tangled in loosened enough to simply pull him free, but his right leg bled freely where the jagged bumper had caught his thigh.

"Is he alright, Mom? Is Nate going to be okay?" Daniel coughed as they dragged Nate's limp body onto the grass. His mother never answered him as she began mouth-to-mouth resuscitation, sending him into a frenzied panic, his voice cracking. "Mom! Is he going to make it?!"

"Danny...not now!" Johanna gasped between chest compressions. "I'll take care of Nate; go check on the other vehicle! They may need our help...and we may need theirs!"

"Fine! I'll check!" Daniel staggered over to the Lincoln. Bending down to peek inside, he shouted at the despondent passengers slumped inside. "Hey, is anyone in there?"

A groan answered him from somewhere in the back of the vehicle.

"Hang on, I'll get you out!" Daniel shouted as Sammy pranced around him, shaking the water from her fur and barking. "Sammy! Get out of the way!"

Daniel pried at the Lincoln's driver's side door, but it budged only a little and with great effort. Only able to partially open the door, he glanced back at his mother when he heard Nate begin to cough.

"Oh, thank God," Johanna sighed as she sat Nate up. He began to exhume volumes of water as she held him close to her shivering form. She turned to shout to her son. "Danny, get the jack out of the back of the Jeep! Get the first aid kit also while you're at it!"

"The jack to open the door...I'll be right back!" he called to the inhabitants of the car as he ran back to the SUV.

Daniel rifled through the jumble in the cargo area before producing the jack and first aid kit. Dropping the kit with his mother, he returned to the car and fumbled numbly with the jack to force it into the car's partially opened doorway. Pumping furiously at the tool, he began to pry the door open as it screamed in protest.

"What happened?" Nate whispered. His pale face strained with pain as he clutched at his leg, holding the nasty gash in his jeans closed. Johanna held him close, still searching his body for other wounds. "Where are we?"

"I don't know yet, but you're lucky this wasn't worse; hold that cut tight!" Johanna commented as Nate regained consciousness. She provided him with a large bandage and applied it to his leg while tears streamed down her face. "You could have lost more than just your leg, but so far it seems that's the worst you got in this debacle. Take it easy; I'm not finding any broken bones yet, but I need to really check you over. You may have internal injuries I'm not aware of yet!"

The Lincoln's door squealing in protest caught her attention as Daniel finally forced it open with the jack. His efforts allowed enough room for him to unbuckle the driver's seatbelt and pull the tall, dark-haired driver from the vehicle.

Daniel surmised that none of the vehicle's occupants were much older than he was as he pulled the muscular driver forth and spread his unconscious form spread-eagle out on the sand.

"Be careful of the glass and metal!" Johanna shouted over to him as she glanced over her shoulder worriedly at her son. "Is the driver breathing!? The passengers, are they okay?!"

"Yes! I think so; yes! The driver is breathing; I'll check on the others!" her son shouted back before holding his hand in front of the young man's mouth and nose. "How's Nate doing?!"

"He's fine!" his mother shouted back. "Stay on track with them!"

Another young man, curled up in a ball on the passenger side, pushed feebly at chunks of ice and debris before crawling past the steering wheel. Groaning as he emerged, he stretched his tall and lanky form as he stood, shaking from the effort. Cut, bruised and still bleeding, he shivered as he began coughing, falling to the ground next to his still unconscious companion.

"Stay there," Daniel stated to the guy who looked to him not unlike an older version of himself, albeit with lighter hair. "I'll get you guys some blankets, but I've got to get whoever is in the back seat."

Looking back, he could already see a blonde girl's matted hair poking from between the seats as she tried to push herself forward to the driver's seat. Daniel reached in to grasp her hand and help her out, but she mumbled in protest.

"Tim, get Tim—he's on the other side," she groaned, gesturing weakly toward the other side of the car. Daniel relented and walked around to the battered vehicle—and immediately wished he hadn't.

Tim's mangled form lay half in and half out of the car, split nearly in two, bleeding out into the mud.

"Mom!" Daniel shouted as he grew weak in the knees and grasped at the crumpled Lincoln's frame for support. Looking back, he nearly ran into the short blonde girl limping around the car to where he stood.

"Tim!" Becky coughed as she rounded the corner. "Are you okay?!"

"No, don't go over there!" Daniel warned. Still struggling to hold down his nausea, he could barely speak as he grasped at her arm. She shook him loose...and caught sight of Tim as she collapsed to the ground, screaming and holding the sides of her head. Her voice echoed through the valley as Daniel held her close, falling with her to the ground as she wailed aloud.

"Stay here and hold that compress down; at least I don't think the cut hit an artery or a vein! I'll be right back!" Johanna stated to Nate as she stood. Stumbling to the car, she reached Daniel's side and caught his attention. "All right, what's happening here?"

"Two guys, one out cold at the front of the car, the other seems alright," Daniel replied, pointing ahead of him to the side of the car. He held onto his mother as they cautiously approached the other side of the Lincoln.

Even with all of Johanna's medical training, her breath caught in her throat when she saw the mangled body of a young man hanging half out of the vehicle.

"This girl here, and the other one sitting next to her...was not so lucky," Daniel said.

"We can't do anything for him," Johanna stated after taking a quick pulse from his wrist and neck, looking about and nodding soberly. "Danny, get the flares from the back of the Jeep and then see if we can get a fire going—we're going to need some warmth or we're all going to freeze."

"Got it," Daniel grunted as he stood and returned to the SUV. As he began rummaging around through the back, he continued to cast worried glances at Nate, still seated and shivering by the shoreline.

"You, my dear, what's your name?" Johanna asked as she turned back to the girl, helping her to her feet and guiding her back toward where Nate lay.

"I'm Becky, Becky Mastiff," the blonde girl stammered, hugging her folded arms to her chest, shivering. Shock washed through her, and she stood, pale, shivering and hugging herself. A glazed look came over her, and she answered robotically even as her teeth chattered. "The guy on the other side of the car is Tim Blaylock, my boyfriend. The one who's awake is Kevin Micker, and the driver is Javier Billings."

"Nice to meet you, Becky. Go sit next to Nate there, and my son Danny will help you with your wounds. We'll get a fire going and sort this all out." Johanna nodded as her healthcare professional demeanor took over. She turned to Kevin, still shivering on the ground near the other unconscious driver and feeling around him, and asked, "Are you okay? Is anything broken?"

"I-I-I don't think so," Kevin murmured, barely able to open his right eye, swollen nearly shut.

"Okay, join Becky and go sit with Nate, over there." She pointed to the shoreline on the grass. "We'll get a fire going shortly. I'll take care of your friend."

As Kevin stumbled to his feet and limped over to the others, Johanna turned to Javier who had just begun to stir.

"Where are we?" Javier rasped, his blue eyes fluttering open, blood-shot and unseeing.

"I'm not sure," Johanna replied softly. "But we'll find out soon and get some help. Until then, your friends are here, and we're going to get a fire going, but I need to check you first before you move any further. What's your name?"

"I'm Javier," he groaned aloud as he blinked his eyes. Looking around in bewilderment, he exploded into a coughing fit.

"Take it easy," Johanna stated as she finished examining him. "My name is Johanna. You guys were very lucky, but your friend, Tim, though, I'm sorry to say, is no longer with us. I'm afraid you have a broken collarbone and possibly a broken arm, too, but the rest of you are okay from what I can see for now."

Johanna comforted him the best she could, but all he could do was cough as he struggled to stand. She helped him to his feet and glanced around to gauge their surroundings.

The water level in the river had dropped significantly, and the hole they had washed through in the rock face only dribbled now. Both the Jeep and the wrecked car were mired in mud, but the river water continued to flow behind them steadily, no longer fed by the torrent that had brought them here.

It took the remainder of the day to gather supplies and start a fire, but finally, the group gathered around the blaze as the sun began to set. The forested peaks to either side glowed in the orange light of the departing day as the warmth fled with the dying light.

Golden rays of sunset glinted off the mix of yellow and green aspen leaves on the edge of the meadow. As the least injured member of their group, Daniel scoured the meadow for sticks, pinecones and other fuel for their fire.

Johanna rummaged through the first aid kit for a bandage and some aspirin. As Javier groaned in pain, Johanna affixed the dressing with two large sticks and tied it off. Helping him to his feet with his new splint, he cried out with the movement.

"It's getting dark," Kevin moaned, pointing out the obvious as he painfully rubbed his arms to stimulate circulation and warmth back into them. "What do we do now?"

"Well, it looks like we may have washed down the canyon from Echo Lake," Nate pointed out. "I don't see any snow around here, and it looks like we are at a much lower elevation; it's much warmer here. I don't recall ever hearing about a dam or any other drain at the lake, though...I really don't know how we survived that."

"You mean THAT'S a drain?" Becky gestured at the massive hole in the rock.

"It sure doesn't look like one, I'll give you that." Nate shrugged. "Most of the damage to your car came from the crash, it seems. It's like we were flushed down a toilet."

"Yeah." Javier drifted off, looking sadly at his car. His car was a mess, but he was thinking about his friend, lying just on the other side. "Some of us, anyway."

"I'm really sorry about your friend," Nate offered, wincing in pain as he dared to check his leg. Only a small amount of blood resumed to dribble forth, so he reapplied the compress. "What happened anyway?"

"It was actually his idea to come up here—Tim's and Becky's," Javier stated as he glanced sideward at her. "We were supposed to go to Moab, but plans changed for Boulder, and they wanted to see Echo Lake..."

"What about your other friend?" Nate asked.

"Kevin? Him?" Javier scoffed bitterly. "Eh, he's Becky's friend. I suppose without him, I'd be in Moab with Tim right now."

"You all weren't drinking and driving, were you?" Nate asked pointedly.

"No." Javier shot him an irritated glance, spitting onto the ground as if to emphasize his point. "We hit black ice!"

The tension subsided as everyone stood, shivering with even the slightest breeze blowing down the canyon. As the sun set, the temperatures began to fall. Becky and Daniel stoked up enough layered sticks in the center of the pile of rocks to get the campfire roaring higher, providing a bubble of warmth around their meager campsite.

Night soon arrived, and outside the firelight, only the moon provided any light to see by. The shapes of the vehicles barely stood out amidst rocks in the immediate vicinity. The trees at the edge of the meadow descended into nothing more than a shadow wall.

As they stoked the fire higher, they warmed themselves, their clothes steaming as they dried. Only Javier and Nate continued to shiver, their pale forms huddled close to the fireside, still in shock from their injuries.

"Do you suppose anyone will know to look for us here?" Becky finally asked.

"Doubtful," Nate spat as he shook his head. "Has anyone's phone survived or dried out enough to make a call?"

The absence of any answer to that question seemed equally bleak as they stared into the fiery coals of the fire in silence.

"I once had mine survive being dropped in a mud puddle, but it did take a couple of days before I could use it again," Kevin finally offered.

"This wasn't a trip through a mud puddle, dumbass," Javier growled.

"Well, at least we know that's not an option now," Nate interrupted, poking at the fire, eager to dispel yet another fiery interchange among the dark-haired youth. "Tonight, we'll just make the best of it. Tomorrow, I'll try to winch the Jeep out, and by then, maybe search and rescue will come for us."

"What are we going to do with Tim?" Becky asked softly.

"Search and rescue can bring him down, but they have to find us first," Nate stated solemnly. "I'm not surprised though that no one has come looking yet. Unless someone passes by Echo Lake and reports vehicles having gone into the ice at the lake..."

"We were expected at a party," Javier stated, thinking of the girls he had met earlier at the gas station. "Maybe they'll say something..."

"Oh, get real!" Kevin seized the opportunity to retaliate for Javier's earlier dig at him. "They don't even remember you, much less give a shit about any of us!"

"Guys! Put a sock in it!" Becky snapped before composing herself and turning quietly to Johanna. "I don't know what we would have done if you had not come by. Thank you for all your help and for patching us up."

"I'm not sure how much good we've done," Johanna sighed. "After what we've been through, we all need a doctor's office with equipment to really tell."

"I mean here and now." Becky smiled gratefully. "The crash was terrible enough, but we'd be dead by if you weren't here."

"I'm only glad to help." Johanna patted her on the leg before changing the subject. "Is there anything in the car that we can use?"

"Not really," Becky sighed. "The trunk has our suitcases, but we can get those in the morning. There is a flashlight in the glove box—a big black industrial one—it might have survived the water."

"We definitely can use that." Johanna paused, then stood. "I'll get it." *No need for this poor girl to see her boyfriend all mangled.*

Johanna walked reluctantly over to the car and around the front end to the passenger side. The mud had hardened, and the river continued to recede, leaving both vehicles stranded on the sand and out of the water.

Tim's grisly form greeted her, crushed and unmoving. Touching her hand gently to his ruined face, she confirmed that what little warmth was left in the body was gone, growing cold. *Thank God, it must have been quick.*

Johanna turned her attention to the smashed window and the glove box. Bending down, she purposefully began searching through the shattered glove box and chunks of ice until she grasped the long metallic cylinder and pulled it free from the wreckage.

A single click verified that the flashlight still functioned. When she pointed, a stream of white light penetrated the darkness around her. She clicked it off and walked back to the fire, smiling at Becky in acknowledgment as she sat back down beside her.

Their smiles faded as the sky and the woods went dark and the trees seemed to press in even from hundreds of feet away. Something else seemed changed—the woods had gone silent as well. The breeze stilled, and neither leaf nor twig stirred.

"What is that?" Nate muttered, breaking the silence again. *The entire valley seems to be holding its breath...for what?*

"What is what?" Javier grunted.

"The silence; didn't you hear how everything just stopped?" Nate began. "It's like—"

"No, what's THAT?" Daniel interrupted, pointing up at the moon.

"I don't see anything," Kevin began to mutter, but then, he saw it too.

Something immensely large and dark winged its way silently through the moonlight, passing in front of the moon and casting a shadow as it went. Massive yet graceful, it glided effortlessly past the valley. It was there for a moment, and then it was gone.

"A bat?" Javier offered dismissively.

"Maybe," Nate muttered, doubtful as he squinted at the moon, but nothing was there anymore. Whatever it was had moved on. "From here, it looked to be much larger, but as dark as it is and at this distance, it's impossible to tell. You all saw it too?"

Only dumbfounded nods answered him as the breeze picked up again. The hoot of a distant owl echoed gently in the valley and even the crickets chirping returned.

Chapter 4

Campground

Becky slept fitfully throughout the night, shivering with the cold and plagued with images staining her consciousness of what had befallen them. Between the throbbing pain in her neck and the constant reminder of Tim's death, she woke with every crackle of the fire or snapping twig in the forest. Each time she sat upright, a flood of memories would overcome her.

"Tim, oh, Tim," she whispered to herself each time, sobbing softly throughout the night.

Hearing Javier and Kevin moan in their own private agonies was of no help either. She'd open her eyes as the moon traced slowly through the starlit sky, shining a cold and lonely light upon them through the heavens.

Johanna kept the fire stoked for warmth, and only Daniel and Nate seemed to slumber deeply through it all. At one point, she had looked over to Kevin. Although his eyes were closed, his swollen face and shivering betrayed the pain he felt. It was at that moment she heard a low growl and sat up to see Sammy's nose pointing to the woods. The hound's black hair bristled on end as her intense eyes stared into the gloom.

"Come over here, girl," she whispered to the hound, wistfully patting her side. The dog trotted over to her but still kept her snout up anxiously, fixated on an unseen source of concern in the darkness. Petting Sammy only seemed to help momentarily, because within seconds, the hound became even more agitated and began to bark, leaping back and forth, gnashing her teeth.

"What's going on?" Kevin awoke with a disoriented start.

"She smells something," Nate muttered warily, watching Sammy pace nervously in front of them, eyes fixed into the blackness of the not-too-distant forest. "We are in the forest; it's likely an animal passing by."

"It's alright, girl," Daniel coaxed, brushing back her bristling hair. "It's probably a deer or something."

"If it's all the same to you, I think I'll feed the fire again," Johanna stated, shivering with anticipation beyond simply being chilled. The fire sparked briefly as she added a larger log to the top.

"I don't know, Dan, she's kind of freaking me out," Becky complained, her heart pounding in her chest. Although the campfire flared to life, the light it cast seemed to only encompass the immediate vicinity, occupied with dilapidated vehicles and their former occupants, leaving little to see as pitch-blackness permeated the tree line. "What if it was whatever we saw flying by earlier?"

"No, this time is a little different," Nate cautioned as he sat up fully, stoking the fire as he kept a wary eye on the sky. "There are wild animals out here—deer, moose, elk, bear, coyotes, mountain lion, who knows. We'll be fine if we just stay together near the fire."

That seemed to satisfy everyone except Becky, who curled up as close to the flames as possible. Johanna kept the trembling hound under her arm, and everyone lay back down to drift off again.

Sammy's growling finally subsided, although she still stayed silent, staring unnervingly at the tree line. The hound continued to tremble and shake, yet she seemed intent to just stare, the firelight reflecting ominously in her dark eyes.

≈≈≈≈

Morning came with a faint magenta glow in the east, the stars winking out one by one. The fire smoldered to a faint wisp, yet the new light revealed the meadow covered in a thick layer of frost.

"Oh my God—it's freezing!" Becky moaned as she stood, her breath a puff of steam as she shivered. "Let's get this fire going again!"

"Yes, it is freezing, and we need the fire if I'm going to cook something," Johanna agreed, standing to throw some smaller kindling onto the last flickering coals as Sammy stood and shook herself off. They watched as she trotted around the broken Lincoln to relieve herself. The hound, clearly still agitated, sniffed the ground around the car as if searching for something specific.

"Danny, see if you can get that fire going again," Johanna directed to her son before she turned. "Nate, let me check your leg again."

"You're my super nurse," Nate murmured appreciatively as he limped over to her. "You've been tending to it since yesterday, and it actually feels much better today."

"That's what worries me, it's far too soon for it to be feeling better," Johanna sighed as she sat Nate down and began to carefully examine the site of the wound on his leg. Johanna appeared startled, and her soft brown eyes widened in surprise. The bloodied tear in the jeans was much worse than the cut, still raw but very much sealed. "You had a very deep cut! If you've lost feeling, then I wouldn't be surprised if it was infected or...it's just gone, barely a scar! I don't get it!"

"What is it?" Nate asked as she gently picked through the tear in his jeans.

"I guess you heal better than I realized," Johanna muttered, perplexed as she shook her head. "You're even luckier than I thought; I could have sworn the cut was deeper last night! You lost blood, but the cut is completely sealed, without stitches, no less. All I did was use tape!"

"I told you; I've got a super nurse!" Nate winked as he turned to the others. "That's more than I can say for you guys. Kevin, your face is still pretty swollen. How is Javier doing?"

"Not too good, by the looks of it," Kevin groaned. Javier lay on the ground, shivering, pale and sweating. He moaned in agony despite the first rays of the sun warming the glade coursing over them.

"I'll check him in a moment," Johanna stated, gingerly moving over to Kevin, taking his face in her hands and inspecting it. "You may have broken some bones too. Let's start by warming you up though."

She gently held his face in her hands as the glow from the sunrise bathed the valley, lighting up his face as she examined it. He squinted his swollen eyes against the glare as Johanna held him close for inspection. As he warmed, the swelling seemed to visually recede, and he groaned in relief.

"Wow, I feel much better," Kevin stated. "I don't know what you did, but thanks."

"All I did was warm you up, young man," Johanna chided gently. "Be careful, though; no sudden movements or exertion today. I don't like the way that looked before, and you're going to need an X-ray when we get back." *That doesn't make sense—could he just be cold? He should be in much worse pain...*

"Actually, I'd like to check out that drain we came through," Kevin insisted as he stood, brushing himself off.

"I'll come with you," Becky offered, stretching and anxious to distract herself from their ordeal.

"Fine," Johanna acquiesced. "But neither of you should be exerting yourselves. You've both been in a major accident, and for the sake of your recovery, the less you do right now, the better!"

As she moved over to attend to Javier's swollen eye socket, Becky assisted Kevin carefully across the stream. The water level had fallen off during the night, and both vehicles were well clear of the creek yet still mired in the mud. Creek bottom rocks had been exposed during the night, and stepping across by utilizing the exposed stones to access the other side proved easy.

Nate and Daniel opened the hood of the Jeep and began inspecting the engine. A quick glance underneath the vehicle also revealed that while the body had been dented and scraped significantly, the wheels and drive shaft appeared to have escaped damage. There was little more for them to do until the mud dried, so they wound up the tow cable and joined Johanna by the fire as Javier dozed.

At one point, Nate took a break to wake Javier, instructing him to tighten up loose connections with a small wrench under the hood while he sauntered over to Johanna to check on her. She stood attentively over the camping cook stove, heating water and stirring in condiments for soup, looking none too happy.

"I told them no exertions," Johanna muttered in annoyance, glancing worriedly to where Kevin and Becky climbed the rock face into the gaping hole they had come through just yesterday. "They really should be sitting here with us."

"Well, we're all adults here," Nate sighed. "It's their decision."

≈≈≈≈

"Come on, don't look back," Kevin encouraged Becky as they reached the cave. As he helped her up to the entrance, he averted his eyes from the Lincoln's side, where Sammy was sniffing around. "I wish they'd keep their dog away from that spot!"

Heading into the cavern, he ushered Becky in with him, their footsteps echoing off the dripping walls. The air inside became cold and musty as they pushed further in. Becky clicked on the flashlight she carried to illuminate their path. While rounded and wide, the cavern wall proved worn smooth by the ice and stone that had pushed aside earth through sheer force, held together by roots from the hillside trees and shrubs.

"Definitely not manmade," Becky observed, beginning to shiver again. "See? No seams or concrete. It's all natural."

"It ends there; it must have collapsed behind us. There's no going back that way; that's for sure!" Kevin stated, his voice echoing in the chamber-like tube as he pointed. Just ahead, a solid wall of boulders and rocks conglomerated together to form a plug. "Damn, it's freezing in here!"

They stared in awe at the jumbled mass before them, a mix of rock, ice and varying debris. Turning back in defeat, they walked out of the cave and emerged into the blinding light of day.

"It's all caved in," Becky shouted, waving back to the others. "It's..."

Becky's voice caught in her throat. Sammy continued to sniff around the crumpled Lincoln, but what was missing caught her attention. "Oh God, TIM!!!"

"What is it!?" Johanna yelled back.

"Tim's gone!" Becky screamed again, scrambling down the embankment to where her boyfriend's body had lain. Only Tim's shoes and a large bloodstain remained in the clear imprint where he had been on the ground. Paw prints of large animals clustered around the spot, and Sammy took great interest in these tracks, sniffing intently in circles, huffing nervously with each pant. "Something took him!"

As the group convened around the broken car, Becky sobbed helplessly as Kevin tried to console her. Javier pulled himself out from under the Jeep, brushing himself off before joining the group gathered around the car.

"So that's what Sammy was barking at last night," Nate muttered. "Looks like a pack of coyotes came by last night; I'm surprised we didn't hear them."

"Are you sure!?" Daniel asked fearfully. "These pawprints are huge!"

"THOSE were coyotes?" Javier pointed out incredulously. "They actually dragged Tim away!"

"Well, the mud makes them look bigger," Nate advised as he shrugged, pointing to his own dog. "See, look at Sammy's prints; see how they swell in the mud."

"They do swell some," Kevin admitted, pointing out Sammy's pawprints. Sure enough, the dog's prints seemed to expand wherever she pranced around in the mud, but they still did not look as large as whatever had come through the camp last night.

"You guys are missing the point!" Becky shrieked, tears streaming down her face. "Tim's gone! He didn't deserve this, and now we can't even bury him properly!"

"Oh, you poor dear!" Johanna sighed as she tried to comfort Becky through her hysterics, gently hugging her closely and consoling her, but nothing seemed to help. Javier limped around the corner, staring dumbly at where his friend had lain.

"What are YOU going to do about this?" Becky laid the withering accusation at him with a shaking finger. "YOU got us into this!"

"You know I didn't, Becky," Javier choked as he shook his head. His face reddened, and his hands shook at the accusation, but he said nothing further. Tears started to form, and he turned away from everyone. "This whole thing sucks! If Micker hadn't—"

"Don't blame it on him!" Becky cried. "This has nothing to do with him!"

Whether from the pain of his injuries or annoyance with the argument, Nate decided a distraction was best for the group. He quickly pulled Javier and Kevin together and pulled them aside.

"Let's move from pointing blame to doing a quick search around here, agreed?" Nate began. "They couldn't have taken your friend far—I suggest just us going. Dan and the girls can stay with the camp in case a rescue party comes for us. Are you guys up for it?"

"I'm coming with you!" Daniel stood, brushing himself off. Even though Javier and Kevin winced in pain, they agreed.

"No, Daniel," Nate barked, his order firm yet direct. "Stay with your mother and the others! I need you here!"

"But..." Daniel protested but never got the rest out when Nate snapped his fingers to silence him.

"Don't go far," Johanna reminded them, placing a protective arm around her reluctantly accepting son. "Between potential broken bones and cuts, we don't need this situation getting worse. In the meantime, I'll dig through the ice chest and see if I can make us all something to eat."

"Bring him back, Kevin," Becky sobbed. She caught Kevin's arm as they turned to leave, whispering coarsely. "I get it—he's dead. But bring him back anyway!"

"I will," he promised, hugging her closely before setting off after Javier and Nate.

≈≈≈≈

The trio followed the animal tracks directly south across the meadow and into the forest. They fanned out from there, having lost the trail in the foliage and pine needles. Nate could see the other two were nervous at the suggestion of splitting up, but he promised them that the danger was minimal and that coyotes would not attack a fully grown and uninjured man. In broad daylight, they would be safe and wouldn't be far from each other.

With the pep talk concluded, Nate started hiking parallel to the creek upstream, directing Javier to follow the creek downstream and Kevin to climb south directly up the hill until he obtained the ridgeline, concealed in the fragrant pine forest a few hundred yards above.

For Kevin, the terrain quickly became rocky. Although beautifully interspaced with pine trees and great boulders, his joints ached, and he still felt raw from the wreck; progress quickly became painfully slow. He stopped frequently and cursed to himself before finally deciding that there was no way even a pack of coyotes could drag a human body up the hill without some evidence of struggle through the brush and rocks. He eventually came to the ridgeline but could see little over into the next valley, the neighboring valley dense with forest and little else from what he could see from that vantage point.

Instead of heading straight back to camp, he decided to cut diagonally downhill toward where he guessed Javier had gone. Between the pains of his wounds and the heat of midday, he sweated freely. Kevin shook his head despite himself. *Ironic, I'm trying to find Javier, the one guy in my life I can't stand.*

In the meantime, Jaiver had already lost patience with the search. He picked his way around the side of the meadow, weaving in and out of trees, looking for any signs of their quarry. Sweating freely and cursing to himself, the gloomy mood of realization settled over him. *What a sucky spring break! My best friend is dead, and I can't blame it on drugs or alcohol. Literally, my own stupidity and carelessness got us into this!*

Finally, alone and in the privacy of his own thoughts, he double-checked his surroundings to ensure he was alone, then broke out into tears. The pains of his wounds wracked his body while his inner demons whispered accusingly the way Becky had levied the same accusation. *The same way my ex, Patrice, accused me...*

"Self-centered asshole!" he muttered to himself. "You've killed your best friend, destroyed your car and you nearly killed yourself!"

As Javier made his way through the meadow, the grass became higher, and he had to push his way through, continuing his internal rant. After nearly a mile, there remained no indications of any coyotes or a body being dragged.

"This is pointless!" he screamed aloud to no one, sniffing and wiping the tears from his face. He was about to scream again when he noticed a path meandering along the base of the hillside in front of him. Not far off, but at least it was the first sign of human impact in the wilderness. "Finally, a fuckin' road!"

Two clearly cut parallel lines through the grass at the base of the hillside, along the banks of the creek, were unmistakable. It was a far cry from a freeway, but perhaps it was an old Jeep trail or forest service road. *Coyotes wouldn't drag anyone to civilization...*

With that assumption in mind, he turned back toward camp. The relief of finally seeing some signs of humanity put a new spring into his step, and he returned in silence.

It didn't take long before he ran into Kevin, and the two of them stopped, assessing each other in uncomfortable silence.

"I didn't see any sign of coyotes or Tim," Kevin stated, shrugging as he took the opportunity to speak first. "Did you find anything?"

"There's a road or a path about a quarter mile from here, so I doubt they dragged him off that way," Javier grunted as he pointed back over his shoulder, the way he had come. "Maybe Nate had more luck than we did."

"Sure," Kevin agreed as the two of them trudged back toward the meadow where they had started. "Maybe by now, someone from search and rescue has come to help."

"Yeah, maybe," Javier muttered as he looked away, not wanting to converse further or let Kevin see the remnants of the tears in his eyes. They turned and trudged on together in an uncomfortable silence, listening only to the swishing of their feet through the wet grass.

"What do you think that thing was last night?" Kevin finally broke the silence. "That thing flying past the moon; what was that?"

"I told you last night, a bat," Javier spat, quickening his pace to avoid any more conversation than necessary.

"A bat?!" Kevin retorted in dismay, breathing heavily to keep up. "The whole valley went quiet when it flew by. We didn't hear a sound from its wings. We—"

"What do you want it to be, Micker?" Javier stopped suddenly and turned on him in exasperation. "Does it matter? I say it was a bat; everyone was half asleep! Nobody cares! Tim's dead, and we're stranded out here until help comes! You and I are not friends, and I don't care to discuss it with you further, so why don't we focus on what's important?"

"Fine, whatever!" Kevin snapped, stuffing his hands into his pockets and taking the lead, pushing on up the meadow. He didn't look over his shoulder to see if Javier followed. Normally, he would have been bothered by the outburst, but he was too tired and gruff himself to add anything further. *Besides, it's Javier; what more would you expect? Why couldn't he have died and Tim lived?*

It didn't take much longer before they found Nate waiting for them, sitting quietly on a log in the shade. As they strode up, he looked up at them somberly.

"Any luck?" Javier huffed as they approached.

"I'm afraid so," Nate answered quietly. From behind his back, he produced a wad of familiar shredded clothing covered in blood. "I found bones, too, but not much else; I'm sorry, boys. They really got to him."

"What the fuck?!?!" Javier yelled, throwing his hands up in disgust. Wincing in pain, he began to pace, fuming as he did. "Where's the search and rescue? Where's the help? Why does this keep getting worse?!"

"Shhhhhh!" Nate cautioned, pointing back up the hillside behind him. "I don't want to upset the girls, but yeah, it looks like the pack actually consumed him...back there."

"You said coyotes don't do that!" Kevin hissed incredulously. "Coyotes don't consume people!"

"Not typically." Nate scratched his head. "Maybe a mountain lion or bear competing with them; I don't know, but we are in the wild."

"It's the last thing Becky needs to see, and now I can't un-see it!" Javier exhaled, throwing his hands up again in exasperation. Shaking his head in disgust, he choked back his regret. "Let's just bury that for now; it's the last piece of my best friend left, and it's the last thing the others need to see!"

"What are we going to tell his parents?" Kevin asked, mortified beyond further words.

"I don't know, Micker!" Javier shouted, holding his head. "This whole thing..."

A stick snapped, and something stirred in the bushes nearby as the three men turned in silent unison. At first, they saw nothing. Javier was about to say something more, but Nate silenced him with an abrupt wave of his hand.

"Look there," Nate whispered sharply, pulling Javier and Kevin closer to the ground and pointing to a clump of bushes laden with berries...not far from where they stood. "Stay close to each other, boys; don't show fear!"

An enormous black muzzle poked through the branches, pointing back at them, sniffing softly. In the shade behind the snout, two golden eyes watched with curiosity as the three men stared back, their hearts frozen in their throats.

Nate picked up a stick and tossed it at the bushes. With a rush of grey fur, the enormous animal, nearly the size of a full-grown man, crashed through the bramble in a flurry of leaves before they could react. As the three moved, the beast made a sharp turn and fled into the forest, bounding out of sight.

"THAT was a coyote?!" Kevin exclaimed. "It was so big that I thought it was a bear for a second!"

"It looked like a freakin' wolf!" Javier exclaimed. "Much too big to be a coyote!"

"It was rather large, even for a wolf," Nate breathlessly admitted. "But there aren't wolves this far south!"

"If it's all the same to you, I'd just as soon not find out!" Javier bellowed. "Let's get back to the girls; maybe help has come since we left. I found a road or something back my way, so I'm sure it has got to lead somewhere. If search and rescue hasn't come, I vote we leave on our own at this point in case that thing decides to come back and bring some of its friends with it!"

"Our vehicles are stuck until the mud dries, and none of us are in any shape to go anywhere," Nate sighed as he dropped the meager remains of Tim's clothing behind a boulder. "Do you want to say a few words before we leave?"

"May God watch over our friend," Javier began, offering a quick prayer through his pain. "He didn't deserve this, and I hope he didn't suffer!"

"May his family be comforted," Kevin managed to say before shaking his head. "May all our families, for that matter."

They left the silent glade for the quick trek back to camp. When they arrived, Sammy greeted them warmly. Becky, on the other hand, stared up at the sky, catatonic as scattered clouds passed overhead, dissipating and reforming as they billowed by.

"Hey, guys!" Daniel called to them from the cave, waving in excitement at their return. "Did you find anything?"

"We found a road, but not much else," Nate stated wistfully, glancing over at the other two, who simply looked away in disgust. His stomach grumbled as the scent of something cooking permeated the campsite.

"I figured we all would need something to eat," Johanna offered, holding up a steaming plate of diced chicken and vegetables, having cooked a late lunch. "Unfortunately, there hasn't been any rescue or anyone looking for us. I sure hope somebody comes soon!"

"That looks delicious, thanks." Nate hobbled over to Johanna. He sat next to her atop a boulder near the cook fire, reducing his voice to a whisper. "I had hoped you would have seen search and rescue by now."

"Not a soul, Nate. Not a soul," Johanna muttered. "My water-logged phone still isn't working. Danny got his to work, but there's no signal in this valley. How's your leg doing?"

"It's actually much better, surprisingly," Nate admitted, scratching the back of his brawny neck as he sat and stretched out, rubbing his wounded leg. "Unbelievable; we may actually have to take ourselves out of here after all."

"We have enough supplies for a few days, plus water." She gestured at the creek. "I just can't believe that nobody would know about this. Surely, they'd see the wreck site at the lake and come look for us!"

"They may yet still, but timing is not in our favor anymore; we have other problems," Nate murmured as he took a bite of his food. "Javier found the road, but we can't go anywhere just yet. Even if I get the Jeep started, that mud needs to dry a bit more or at least freeze. We may be dealing with some of the local wildlife that dragged their friend's body off, and they may still be hanging around."

"Nothing we can't handle, is it?" Johanna eyed him skeptically. "Should I be worried?"

"Let's just say you and Dan should stay close to the Jeep for now," Nate muttered. "We may also want to break out the guns tonight."

"Are you serious?" Johanna's eyes widened. "What aren't you telling me?"

"I don't want to worry you or the others," Nate stated slowly, carefully choosing his words. "But I'll be taking watch tonight with Sammy.

I think we can handle it, but nobody should wander far from camp, especially at night."

≈≈≈≈

Over by the wrecked Lincoln, Javier glanced uneasily at Kevin as he sat next to Becky. Daniel had clambered down from the cave and joined them; he was snacking on the chips and trail mix Johanna had set out for them.

"This looks great, Johanna," Kevin called out appreciatively, noting an intense discussion between her and Nate. He turned back to his friend and coaxed, "Come on, Becky, have some more!"

"I'm not hungry," Becky moaned as she sat in the grass next to the car, her half-eaten bowl sitting at her feet. "I just wanna go home! You guys didn't find Tim, and now he's out there just laying somewhere!"

"I told you, he was pretty messed up, so we buried him. Now come on, eat something," Kevin persuaded as gently as he could. "You have to eat, even if you don't want to."

"Let her be," Javier snapped. "Becky and I both lost Tim here, and she doesn't need you ordering her around! Go eat something yourself."

"No, Kevin, you're right." Becky turned on Javier, brushing herself off, throwing him a brief glare. "I think I WILL have some. Tell me, did you guys find anything else?"

"Javier found a road, but other than that, not much else," Kevin muttered as he cringed. "If it's all the same to you, I think we should stick close to camp tonight."

"Why?" Daniel chimed in as he sauntered up beside them. "The cave has nothing in it, so I was just about to go further downstream myself and see what was down there."

"No, Dan, Nate said we should stay close in case search and rescue comes," Kevin chided, trying to be helpful. Javier's dig at him still burned, but Becky had chosen his side, so he decided to simply ignore his rival's remark, the image of the enormous canine animal still fresh in his mind. He glanced quickly over at Javier to see him stretch out over a boulder with his eyes closed.

"Come eat some more; I don't want any of this to go to waste," Johanna called to the others as Nate finished off his serving of the lunch she had made. She turned back to Nate and whispered, "So we are just supposed to hang out here and hope help arrives?"

"We don't have much choice for the moment," Nate quipped, keeping his eyes fixed on Johanna's as he sat to eat a handful of nuts. He glanced briefly over at Becky as a hint. "I'll work on getting the Jeep started again, but we should keep what happened to ourselves for now."

"I almost wished you hadn't told me," Johanna sighed. "That has me worried now for all of us! I can't believe they took that poor boy's body!"

"Yeah, well, hopefully that's the last we see of it. Either search and rescue arrives, or I get the Jeep ready to roll," Nate vowed as he shoveled down the food as quickly as he could. Finishing the bowl, he thanked Johanna before standing to go tackle the task at hand. "In either case, I don't intend for us to stay here much longer!"

≈≈≈≈

They rested in silence, waiting out the remainder of the day, Johanna tending to their wounds, muttering at how surprised she was at the speed they all healed. The sun traced overhead, warming the meadow and stirring the occasional insect to buzz by. The vale remained silent other than the rustle in the boughs from the occasional puff of a breeze through the trees or the constant trickle from the creek once the wind subsided. Javier rose from his snooze at one point and slowly walked over to the Jeep, which Nate continued to work on.

"Anything I can do to help?" the younger man offered.

"Not for the moment, but I did want to say I was sorry about your car," Nate muttered from beneath the hood of the Jeep as Javier stood by, assisting in repairs where he could. "If we can get the Jeep going again, maybe we can increase our chances of getting out of here. That mud is going to have to dry or freeze before I get it unstuck."

"You have that winch," Javier reminded him. "Why don't we just tie it off to something?"

"I do, but I need something to tie it to within a hundred feet," Nate countered. "That doesn't mean we can't get ready for that though. These boulders by our campsite might work, but they aren't ideal."

They worked through the afternoon, re-affixing a hose here, a cord there. At one point, Nate was tightening the battery terminals when sparks flew, blowing him and Javier back from the vehicle with a bright flash and an audible *pop*.

"Whoa, dude!" Javier laughed for the first time he could remember in a while. "Be careful!"

"You're not kidding," Nate chuckled. "Damn—that's a live wire!"

"Hey, you guys," Johanna called out. "What's going on over there?"

"Looks like some things were a little loose, but we've got it all tightened down," Javier shouted back. "We may actually be able to drive out of here if we can get it to start."

"Possibly, but let's not get everyone's hopes up yet," Nate cautioned. "The mud does seem to be drying, and we may be able to get the Jeep out by tomorrow. In the meantime, siphon the rest of the gas from the Lincoln. We'll need all the gas we can get. If we don't get any search and rescue help by tomorrow, we can go for that trail you found in the morning."

"So, you don't think they're coming?" Javier asked quietly. "Search and rescue—where are they?"

"I'm frankly surprised they haven't come yet," Nate admitted, changing positions to check under the Jeep again for further damage. "Luckily, the underbody armor seems to still be in place, just a few dents; maybe some leaks."

"What about that wolf?" Javier whispered.

"What about it?" Nate grunted as he strained, tightening a bolt from beneath the drive shaft.

"Do you think what we saw back there was a wolf?" Javier pressed. "I've never seen anything like it before."

"Doubtful; as I said before, there are no wolves in this part of Colorado," Nate muttered as he re-emerged from under the Jeep, refusing to address the matter further. "Now we just need to see if it will start and if we can get it in gear."

"Hey, Micker!" Javier shouted, turning suddenly to Kevin, still comforting Becky. "Get over here and help us!"

"Why do you ride him like that?" Nate seethed, speaking quietly so only Javier could hear him. "Is that really necessary?"

"I didn't think it was a big deal," Javier scoffed, mildly surprised at the rebuke. "He's just some nerd who came along for our ride; he's not really even my friend."

"Well, maybe you should think about that again, considering what you've all just gone through!" Nate growled in annoyance. "If you really don't like him, consider keeping it to yourself and not being such an asshole about it; show some respect!"

Kevin kissed Becky on her forehead as she picked at her remaining food. After making sure she began eating, he slowly walked over to the Jeep, glancing over his shoulder with concern as he came.

"What's up?" Kevin offered as he strode up. Javier said nothing, looking away red-faced and focusing on something else.

"Just get behind the wheel, and when I say, start it up," Nate instructed. He returned to the open hood, gave a thumbs-up signal and gave the order. "Now!"

"Damnit," Nate muttered when Kevin turned the engine over and only a few resounding clicks could be heard. He adjusted a few of the cords attached to the battery. "Battery may have been damaged and gotten water in it. Try again!"

A few more clicks resounded with no results.

"All right!" Nate shouted, using a wrench to crank down hard on the terminals, muttering under his breath in frustration, sweating from the effort. "One more time!"

With another resounding pop, another flurry of sparks flew from where Nate's hands grasped the wrench. Loud crackling ensued as Javier jumped back, yet this time, the clicking seemed to wake the sleeping engine; it groaned in protest before sputtering to life. The engine roared briefly, as if clearing its throat, smoke pouring from the tailpipe.

"What is that?!" Javier blinked in surprise. "Something wrong with your battery?"

"I don't know, but whatever it was worked," Nate proclaimed with a smile, shaking his hands off. "Damn if it didn't electrocute me too!"

"You alright?" Johanna called as she walked over to them.

"Yeah, I just got shocked," Nate said, walking over to the driver's side and shaking his hand to drive feeling back into the fingers. "Leave it on for a while, Kevin. We need to let it run for a bit and clear the lines."

"Shouldn't we drive out of here now?" Kevin asked.

"Not at night without a road to follow, and it's going to be dark soon. I want to see the condition of the Lincoln's battery; maybe get both charged, just in case," Nate reminded them with a grimace. "In the meantime, we should go ahead and consolidate our supplies. I don't want to spend any longer out here than any of you, but if we have to drive out on our own, let's do it right and with plenty of daylight."

The Lincoln's battery ended up being salvageable, and after letting the Jeep's battery charge, they hooked it up to ensure they'd have the backup Nate alluded to. Setting the Jeep's battery in the grass in front of the vehicle, they let the Lincoln's battery charge for a few hours before finally turning the Jeep off. Dusk began to set in as the sun sank again behind the mountain peaks at the head of the valley, leaving the group again for another night in the wilderness.

After briefly testing both batteries, Nate determined that either would be sufficient to start the vehicle in the morning. As everyone turned in for the night, Nate closed up the Jeep, and they settled in for the evening, gathering the last few pieces of firewood closer to the fire.

Satisfied no one was watching him, Nate casually returned to the Jeep's hatchback and began digging through the green box among their bags, pulling out a single handgun. He ensured it was loaded before closing the box and pushing it back into the vehicle. Wadding it carefully into a bundle of clothes he was using for a pillow, he joined the rest of his group near the campfire with everyone else to sleep. *I'll have this handy, just in case.*

As the last rays of the setting sun faded behind the mountains, a curtain of silent dread enveloped Nate as he kept a wary eye on the forest around them. His assurances of safety by the fire felt hollow, even after he had expressed them to the others.

Only Johanna seemed to realize the conceit and insisted Daniel stay by her side near the fire. By the time night fully settled in around them, darkness fell over the lands, and a disquieting hush settled over the valley. All the while, they listened in vain for the sound of a helicopter or vehicle. Only silence answered, and they eventually drifted off to sleep near the crackling of the fire. Sammy's ever-watchful eyes stayed open as the dog stared expectantly at the forest's edge.

Chapter 5

Time to Leave

"Kevin...Kevin...Kevin! Wake up!" Becky's voice whispered to him through his murky sleep. She reached over to nudge him gently. "Come on! Get up!"

"What...what is it?" Kevin slurred sleepily, struggling to open his eyes. "It's still dark!"

"I know; I've got to pee!" Becky urgently pleaded. "Where's the flashlight?"

As Kevin sat up and rubbed his eyes, the crisp night air bit at his face. He didn't want to budge from his sleeping bag, but Becky had already emerged from hers, shivering and standing pigeon-toed above him expectantly.

"Right now?!" he protested. Their breath puffed into the night air as they spoke, and the fire flickered softly in front of them, dying into a pile of glowing coals. Except for the shimmering blanket of stars above, only pitch-blackness surrounded the silent meadow. "It's freezing! Can't this wait for morning?"

"No, now!" Becky insisted, snapping her fingers. "Just give me the flashlight!"

"Okay, okay," he sighed, fumbling in his sleeping bag until he found the cold metal cylinder. Clicking the switch on, he handed it to her, and she promptly clicked it off.

"I don't want to wake anyone," she stated. "I'll be quick; I promise!"

"Nate's asleep?" Kevin asked as he sat up and rubbed his eyes in concern. "I thought he had watch?"

"No, it's fine; don't bother him!" Becky persisted. "I won't go far, and I can see alright; I'm just going over to the trees."

"No! Don't go over there," he warned, suddenly remembering their walk from earlier in the day. "Just stay close by! Go behind the Jeep!"

"I don't want you to see me!" Becky protested. "I'll go behind the car!"

"No, Becky, there's wild animals here!" he tried, intentionally remaining vague while he sat up and pointed. "Just go behind the Jeep!"

"Fine!" Becky scoffed as she waddled over to the other side of the vehicle. Kevin forced himself out of the sleeping bag to stoke the fire, trying not to appear as if he was keeping an eye on her yet scanning the silent clearing for signs of movement; he saw none.

The meadow remained deathly silent as Becky slunk behind the Jeep, surprised at how well she could see in the dark. She started to squat on the other side of the Jeep, but sudden light flared from the campfire as Kevin stoked it higher.

"Kevin! Not so bright! I don't want you guys to see me!" she hissed, but he couldn't hear her. The light being thrown off by the growing fire made Becky uncomfortable and self-conscious, too close to camp to do her business. "Ugh, Kevin!"

She stood and shuffled further from the Jeep and past the wrecked Lincoln. Even though Tim wasn't there anymore, she averted her eyes to the spot where he had lain. The smoky scent from the campfire receded the further out she went, replaced by the pine and earthy smells of the meadow. As she approached a clump of bushes, she thought she heard them rustle. *That's far enough.*

She started squatting, watching the bushes the entire time, alert for any further signs of movement. During the eternity it took to finish emptying her bladder, to her relief, the bushes stayed silent and still.

After she finished, she stood, collected herself and turned to leave, catching her breath. Standing between her and camp stood the silhouettes of three enormous canines, the long shadows they cast illuminated by the flickering campfire. They stared back intensely at her, their ears lay flat and their tails down, eyes glimmering faintly like jewels in the dark. *Are they real? They're huge! Like almost bear-sized! Maybe they're just boulders and a trick of the eyes in the dark?*

Hoping the shadows were her imagination, she clicked on the flashlight. They didn't move at all as her light passed over them, but their eyes glistened, reflecting and intensely fixated on her.

A low growl reverberated from the mongrel trio, revealing rows of fangs along with the fact that indeed, they were quite real. Their fur bristled as their golden eyes shone through the dark, glowering as they watched her.

"Shoo!" she hissed at them, waving her arms above her head as her heart began to pound. "Go on, GET!"

Her pulse raced as she picked up a cluster of stones to throw. They still didn't budge but began to bare their teeth in a loud snarl, sending a shiver up her spine.

"Um, Kevin! Guys!" she shouted nervously as her heart caught in her throat. "HELP!!!"

"What is it?" Kevin called back to her.

"I think they're wolves!!" she shouted as they began to inch toward her in a low crouch. She screamed, throwing her handful of rocks at the nearest one. "BACK!"

Just then, something huge and dark burst from the bushes behind her. In a flurry of leaves, the massive predator slammed into her, knocking the wind out of her, pinning her to the ground and flinging the flashlight away.

≈≈≈≈

Becky's piercing screams shattered the night's peace, waking Javier and the others. They were clearly no longer alone at their campsite.

"Where is she?" Nate shouted as he jolted upright. Kevin had already pulled a burning stick from the fire and rushed past the Jeep toward the cacophony permeating the night just beyond the immobile vehicles.

"She had to go to the bathroom!" Kevin cried out over his shoulder, his mouth suddenly dry and his heart pounding as he charged off into the night with his makeshift torch. "I told her not to go so far!"

"Wait for me, Micker!" Javier called, throwing off his blanket and grabbing a burning stick of his own before racing after him. "BECKY; we're coming!!!"

"What's going on?" Daniel gasped, sitting upright in terror, his eyes immediately wide and alert. He started to clamber for the fire, but his mother held him back. "Mom! Let go!"

"No! Your mother's right; stay here!" Nate hollered as he produced the handgun from the wad of clothes he had used for a pillow and charged after the duo, struggling to keep up as they rushed into the dark.

≈≈≈≈

Kevin quickly found himself sprinting into the middle of the fray with his flaming stick to where Becky struggled beneath a pack of nearly five large wolves, their fangs flashing in the dark as their barking and whining filled the glade. Continuing to scream, she fought back with everything she had as they nipped and bit at her, drawing blood with each bite.

Kevin swung his torch like a madman, throwing sparks and singeing the fur of the immediate attackers, turning to snap at him but yelping in surprise. Becky tried to stand when a couple of the larger ones suddenly lunged and grabbed her by the shirt, knocking her down again and dragging her away from Kevin and camp as she flailed. The rest of the pack turned on her would-be rescuer, closing in on him from all sides.

"Get away from her!" Kevin shouted as Javier joined him, both swinging flaming torches like scythes. They cut their way into the pack, trying to get to Becky, who was rolling on the ground and covering her face and neck.

Nate began shooting into the air to frighten the marauders, but they only ducked in bewilderment as each shot rang out. The pack paused their attack only briefly before turning on the men, snarling and snapping at them while other wolves flooded into the meadow from the forest edge. More than thirty massive canines now filled the meadow, yipping and howling in excitement.

"There's too many of them!" Nate shouted breathlessly as he began targeting individuals, picking one off at a time, dropping them with each thunderous shot. They yelped in response, but the pack kept coming. "Something is wrong; they aren't afraid of us!"

"These are NOT coyotes!" Javier gasped, wide-eyed and trembling as he kept swinging desperately at two of the massive predators snapping at his legs. "They're fucking huge!"

"Hurry! They're taking her again!" Kevin screamed as he chased after the pack. The cluster of chaos had grabbed Becky again by the shirt and hair, dragging her more than halfway to the forest's edge at the far end of the meadow to the south. Her screams persisted yet faded each time they rang out as her attackers muscled her across the uneven ground.

Becky swung desperately at the pack dragging her through the grass as they bit at her legs and clothing. Between snapping jaws, being dragged over stones and cut by the whipping grass, the assault became disorienting. She thrashed, trying to loosen their grip on her, but she seemed unable to break free from the wave of predators carrying her.

Suddenly, she slammed her head against a rock, sending her ears ringing and a rolling wave of dizziness through her. For a moment, all she could do was hang limp as the pack ran with her the rest of the way to the hillside.

Another series of gunshots rang out through the night, followed by a series of yelps, and the pack suddenly dispersed, leaving her in a bloodied heap between two pine trees. The forest loomed menacingly nearby, a dark and impenetrable wall as she stood, wavering in a swooning haze.

"Guys, I'm over here!" Becky called out weakly, gasping for breath. She struggled to stand, holding onto one of the pines for support, sobbing and holding her bleeding head. "Hurry, please, I'm hurt! I think...they may be coming back...for me!"

"We're coming! Stay put!" She heard Nate's voice.

More gunshots rang out, closer this time. She could hear the pack snarling and barking, but they seemed to be focused on the men for now. A few yelps confirmed Nate's bullets had found their mark, and the sudden wounded among the pack seemed to have the predators confused.

"We're almost there!" Javier shouted. "I see you by the tree! Stay there!"

Breathing heavily, she rested against the side of the tree, sap sticking to her arm as she sobbed shakily, blood seeping from her face and arms. It was at that point she heard a discernible heavy breathing coming from the other side of the tree. She froze and listened as twigs snapped and soft footfalls from the forest pierced through the chaos of the meadow.

Squinting in the blackness, she could see something standing tall and upright in front of her, coalescing first as a shadow before lumbering closer. Large and opaque, it approached out of the dark, unmistakably upright, taking swift and heavy strides to reach her.

"Kevin? Nate? Javier? Is that you?" she whispered toward the shape as it towered above her, reaching for her.

≈≈≈≈

"I've got to help them!" Daniel shouted at his mother as she held him back. It was hard enough holding Sammy's leash as she pulled, barking incessantly at the commotion, yet her son seemed intent on joining the fray. "They need me!"

"I told you no, Danny! Nate said to stay here!!" Johanna insisted. "We need you to control Sammy and keep the fire going! We need a larger fire!"

"Fine!" Daniel screamed in exasperation, wrenching free from his mother to grab their remaining firewood.

They stood together in front of the fire, stoking it higher, when Becky's blood-curdling scream resonated loud and clear—before suddenly being cut short. All fell silent around the valley as her cries echoed from peak to peak. Even Sammy stood whimpering and shaking, looking intently out into the darkness.

"Mom, what was that?" Daniel whispered as the color drained from Johanna's face.

"Nate! What's happening?!" Johanna called, dread rapidly filling the hole that had opened in her stomach. Only silence seemed to answer her. That's when she saw movement coming back toward camp.

"Oh my God, Danny—get in the Jeep!" Johanna's eyes widened, and she pushed her son.

"But Mom, I—" Daniel resisted.

"DON'T ARGUE WITH ME, DANNY! GET IN THE DAMN JEEP, NOW!!!" Johanna shouted.

Suddenly, Daniel saw it too. The massive pack of nearly thirty wolves came bounding out of the darkness straight at them. Golden eyes and slobbering jaws reflected the firelight, flashing in sharp contrast to their shadowy forms as they bounded into the campsite. He leapt into the Jeep, screaming for his mother to follow.

Johanna grabbed sticks straight out of the fire. She turned and grabbed a panicked Sammy, heaving the hound into the Jeep, before slamming the SUV's door shut behind them.

The frenzied pack hit the Jeep like an avalanche, rocking it back and forth, jumping, biting and scraping at the metal as if trying to bring down a large prey. Barking and snarling, the pack surrounded the vehicle in a sea of chaos.

Johanna and Daniel gasped at the onslaught, jabbing at the beasts through broken windows, sparks flying from their makeshift torches. Sammy frothed at the mouth, snapping at the invaders as they tried to gain entry.

In desperation, Johanna leaned on the horn, blaring the deafening honk into the chaos of their darkened surroundings.

≈≈≈≈

The commotion back at the Jeep caught Nate's attention, but Javier and Kevin were still frozen in horror at the meadow's edge. Indecision seemed to grip the young men after the pack they were fighting had moved back onto the camp after Becky's scream, leaving them standing virtually unopposed.

"Guys, I gotta go back and help Johanna!" Nate gasped for breath, hearing the horn. Without waiting for a response, he charged back toward the camp where he could make out the pack swarming the Jeep.

"What about Becky?" Kevin shouted after him.

"Fuck him, Kevin—let's go!" Javier pulled at his shirt. "We've got this!"

"You're right," Kevin muttered through clenched teeth. Adrenaline surged through him as he sprinted after Javier. "BECKY, WE'RE COMING!!"

Javier made it to the first tree at the edge of the meadow and froze as Kevin caught up to him. They stood side by side between the two pines, searching with their makeshift torches.

"Becky!!!" Kevin choked, bursting into tears before letting out a mortal cry of his own.

"Oh God, no," Javier breathed as he stopped at the nearest tree, nearly collapsing as he leaned against the trunk for support.

Becky's severed head lay in the grass just feet from where they stood. Her blue-grey eyes stared unseeingly at the stars above even as her face exuded a puzzled expression, never quite knowing what exactly had happened. Her tattered, bloodstained clothes lay shredded, scattered over the grass.

There on the ground lay bits of blonde hair mixed with shredded clothing in a growing pool of blood. Bits of bone fragments littered the ground between larger, snarling pack members, fighting over scraps.

"You BASTARDS!!!" Javier exploded, a wave of revulsion and rage shooting out from him in a metallic ring in his voice.

The pack turned almost in unison, ducking low as if something massive had hit them. They stared back at him in the darkness with their glowing eyes. The predators turned to face the new threat, baring their bloodied teeth.

"Oh, shit," Javier whispered. "Micker, light the grass."

"What?" Kevin sobbed. "What about her..."

"Light the fucking grass!" Javier shouted, already torching the grass in front of him. Unfortunately, the mostly wet grass lit only slowly, but between him and Kevin, they created a small arch of fire between themselves in the pack.

"This isn't going to work!" Kevin cried.

"I know!" Javier shouted. "Do it anyway and run!!"

The two of them turned in unison, racing back to camp. Howls erupted behind them in the night as the pack leapt through the flames spreading in the grass behind them.

Kevin sobbed as he ran; he could still hear Becky's final scream like shattering glass echoing through his mind. He glanced briefly at Javier, a primal fear he'd never seen before etched into his face.

"Don't stop!" Javier gasped. "We're almost there!"

Gunshots rang out ahead of them, and in the firelight, they could make out Nate, closing in on the Jeep, firing into the other pack members as he reentered the light from the campfire. He dropped several of the wolves, and they yelped in surprise, now giving him a cautious, wide berth.

"They aren't backing off!" Kevin exclaimed as they reached Nate's side, gasping for air. "Why aren't they afraid of us!?"

"Are they rabid?" Javier exclaimed in bewilderment.

Nate couldn't answer as he continued firing his handgun but soon heard the telltale click of an empty magazine.

"Guys, I'm out," he gasped, his eyes wide. "Cover me while I go to the back of the Jeep for more ammo! I'll bring the shotguns too!"

The news hung in the air like doom as Javier and Kevin stood with their backs to each other, swinging their torches in an arc in front of them. They moved with Nate in unison back to the Jeep. All the while, Daniel and Johanna argued from within the vehicle, their voices drowned out by Sammy's incessant barking.

Several larger wolves lunged forth, flanking them and blocking their path, testing the perimeter. Javier and Kevin swung wildly with their burning sticks, but it was hardly a barrier to the largest of the invaders.

"Johanna!" Nate shouted over the din. "Let go of Sammy!"

"What?!" Johanna exclaimed. "She can't fight them, they're—"

"NOW!" Nate ordered. "You heard me! Let her go, now!"

"No!" Daniel shouted, but it was too late. Sammy came tearing out of the Jeep's window, barking and snapping at the wolf nearest to Javier. Poor Sammy was only half the size of the wild beast, but it was enough to draw its attention.

It turned at the onrush of the smaller dog, jaws agape. Sammy leapt to the side but continued to press her attack. Two other massive canines rushed the hound from behind, forcing her under the Jeep, snapping her jaws in a defensive yelping retreat. However, the short distraction worked.

Nate gained access to the back of the Jeep and already had another magazine snapped into place. He turned and fired, pressing back into the fray. Shots continued to ring out, sending the pack scattering. Several dropped, yelping, limping back into the dark and dragging bloodied limbs behind them.

"Take that, you motherfuckers!" Nate shouted like a madman. "Guys! There's more in the box! Grab the shotguns and—"

"Nate!! More are coming!!!" Johanna screamed, pointing in slow motion as confusion consumed the clash. The entire pack joined the fray, swarming into camp from out of the dark, converging on the SUV from all sides.

One particularly large wolf knocked Nate off his feet; the impact from the predator sent the gun flying out of his hands. Another went for his throat, pinning him onto the ground in front of the Jeep, beneath Johanna's line of sight and right on top of the car battery they had been charging earlier that day.

An explosive surge of electricity blew out in front of the Jeep in a blinding flash. Like a bomb going off, the thunderclap that followed threw at least four of the attackers clear of the vehicle. One landed in the campfire pit, flames erupting from its fur. It thrashed in agony and panic before taking off in a dead run, disappearing into the night, flames trailing it as it fled.

"Nate!" Kevin shouted, still gripping his useless torch but moving in to shield him from further attack. "Are you okay?!"

"Kevin, wait!" Javier shouted. "We need to get the—" Another massive wolf leapt through the air, hurtling toward his face, and all he could do was shout the word "GUNS" at the top of his lungs in surprise as the gnashing jaws and fur filled his entire field of vision.

Javier's words echoed in a metallic-sounding ripple as he yelled, blasting into the attacker as he caught the frenzied animal midair before ducking and throwing it atop the SUV. There, it writhed in agony before sliding off and twitching to the ground.

A long, low howl, sounding more like a roar, broke through the glade from beyond the meadow, ending the battle just as suddenly as it had begun. The haunting resonance reverberated, repeating through the darkness of night, echoing throughout the valley.

The remaining pack took a final look back at their failed quarry before receding silently back into the night. As the yelps and barks faded, many of the larger wolves grabbed their downed comrades on the way out, dragging the corpses and wounded behind them.

Silence enveloped the disheveled campsite as the pack melted back into the darkness, leaving the campers in a state of bewilderment.

"N-N-Nate?!" Johanna trembled as she finally opened the door, shaking as she turned the corner to find Nate still lying on the ground in front of the Jeep. "Are you okay?"

"W-w-what happened?" Nate stood, brushing at the acidic remains of the car battery tangled in his disheveled hair. He spat grass and dirt out as Kevin helped him to his feet. "What was that horrible sound?"

"I don't know," Kevin whispered, retrieving Nate's gun from the grass. "Something called them back after that explosion. That howl... didn't sound like a howl...I don't know what that was!"

"I'm just glad they're gone, at least for the moment!" Johanna gestured at the smoking remains of the battery, lying next to where Nate had been pushed into the grass. "What made the battery do that?"

"I don't know." Nate coughed, staring warily back into the dark. "An act of God, but whatever it was, saved us."

"For now," Johanna breathed, wiping tears from her face. A small bark caught their attention, and Sammy crawled out from under the Jeep, trembling. "Nate, regardless of what happened, we need to wash the battery acid off you!"

"Oh, thank God," Daniel exclaimed as he gathered up the hound. She had a few scrapes and bites but had escaped any mortal wound from the attackers. "Sammy made it!"

"What about you?" Kevin asked Javier, who was standing quietly by, contemplating the dead canine lying on the ground beside the Jeep. "Did any of them get you?"

"I had a close call, man, that's it," Javier muttered, seething to himself as he stared off into the direction the pack had gone. He choked the rest of what he had to say out, unable to finish. "I can't believe they took her head. We need to at least bury her..."

"I'm very sorry, boys, but if that's the case, then there's nothing we can do for her right now," Nate interjected sadly. Clenching his teeth, he seethed at the helplessness he felt. "We need to stay close to the fire tonight, and we'll have to deal with that in the morning when we don't run the risk of being ambushed in the dark. Get the guns and follow me down to the creek. I need to get this battery acid off me."

They followed him down with two loaded shotguns, warily on the lookout for any moving shadows, yet nothing revealed itself. They listened intently for any sounds of the pack, but only the crackling fire made any noise. With the sudden silence that had enveloped the valley, they could hear their hearts pounding in their ears.

By the time Nate finished scrubbing himself off in the creek, he stood shivering from the cold. They clustered together around the fire in vain attempts to stay warm as the hellish nightmare of the night wore inexorably on.

Every snap or crackle that came from the dark sent Sammy into a barking frenzy and everyone else's nerves frayed. Into the wee hours of the night, sleep became impossible, and exhaustion was the only companion to the tragedy of their loss.

A long-awaited faint pink glow in the east gave the first hallmark of relief as the sun began to rise. As the first rays of dawn flooded the meadow, Javier and Kevin trudged wordlessly over to where they had last seen Becky at the meadow's edge. Daniel started after them, but Johanna held him back.

"Give them a moment, Danny," she quietly told him. He silently relented, so she turned her attention back to Nate. "Let's get the fire stoked up; would you mind?"

"I should have done more!" Nate whispered. "I wish I could have done more! The boys said the pack took her head; that's just not natural behavior!"

"You did all you could. Come, let me have another look at you. Looks like you were lucky yet again," she murmured as he sat in contemplative silence. "No bites or chunks taken out of you or the other two."

"No, we're done here," Nate groaned as she finished inspecting him. "I don't feel lucky at all. We're getting the hell out of here. I don't want to stay here a minute longer. We leave today."

"We're not waiting for search and rescue?" she pressed, handing him a canteen. "I've never seen you this shaken before - I thought that was the plan!"

"We can't keep waiting here, not after last night," Nate stated decisively, gulping down a swallow of water. "I don't think they'll find us here before those animals come back; they're not acting normal – not at all!"

Nate stopped speaking. Javier and Kevin were already returning, glum and dragging their feet as they silently walked, empty-handed.

"What happened to Becky?" Johanna whispered as they stopped in front of her. Kevin shook his head silently, at a loss of words. "Where is she?"

"She's gone; they took her too, just like Tim," Javier whispered. "What was left of her, anyway..."

"I thought wild animals don't do that!" Kevin cried out. "This wasn't supposed to happen!"

"No, it wasn't," Nate muttered through clenched teeth. "That is why I've decided we can't wait any longer. Let's get the hell out of here while we still can!"

Without any argument or delay, they immediately loaded their gear and finished packing what meager supplies they had left in the Lincoln into the Jeep. Holding their breaths as Nate started the Jeep, the vehicle not only started but idled normally without dying; they exhaled in relief.

They pushed the remainder of the firewood under the tires to give the vehicle the traction it needed to break free. It took some negotiating back and forth to finally dislodge the Jeep from the mud, but with the group pushing and heaving, the SUV bounced clear of the mire, and Nate motioned everyone aboard by late morning.

Nate began the bumpy drive with everyone loaded up to the far end of the meadow. Missing two from their group now left them all in a silent sadness. They paused briefly at the base of the bloody tree at the far end of the meadow. Only the bloodstained grass remained. No one said anything further although the pain mirrored in each of their eyes said it all. There would be no burial for their friends.

The cramped seating arrangements were less than desirable, as Daniel squeezed in the center between Javier and Kevin. From the back seat, Javier pointed over Nate's shoulder to the southeast, the direction he had seen the trail the other day.

Nate silently acknowledged the direction, and soon, they were making their way across and out of the meadow. The vehicle jolted violently as it gained the primitive road's dirt surface. However, once squarely on the path, the ride settled. With unspoken agreement, Nate navigated the vehicle downhill, following the trail as it paralleled the valley and the creek down from the high country.

From within the trees behind them, a sea of hungry eyes watched from the shadows of the forest as the Jeep departed and the sound from the engine faded.

Chapter 6

Saving Ourselves

At the dawning of a new day, the uncomfortably cramped passengers in the Jeep tossed about, trying to hold themselves in place as the vehicle jostled its way slowly down the narrow canyon.

"Looks like we're following a trail of some kind all right, hardly a road though," Nate muttered after a time. He stopped the vehicle briefly and took a deep breath. "This is not going to get much smoother from what I can see."

"Yes, but note there are two tracks, so someone drove up here at some point," Johanna grunted, grasping at the dashboard. "It's gotta lead somewhere, either to civilization or at least to another road."

"Looks more like a wagon trail," Kevin struggled to state.

"A wagon trail?!" Javier bitterly laughed at the incredulous suggestion. "Don't you get it, Micker? There are four-wheel drive trails all over the place. I found us one! Pull your head out of your—"

"Whatever!" Kevin exclaimed, looking away in disgust. "You found it; I'll give you a gold star later! It would be worth more if it wasn't so full of obstacles!"

"Guys!" Nate shouted impatiently. "Now's not the time for this!

We found it, and now we're taking it! Let's just hope it leads down to somewhere with more people! Besides, why don't you call Kevin by his first name for once, Javier? I'm sick of you riding him like that!"

"Fuck off!" an indignant Javier raged. "I don't need shitheads like you telling me how to deal with dumbass statements from someone like Micker, or even you, for that matter!!"

"You're in my vehicle; you play by my rules, or you can walk!" Nate bellowed. "I don't care how dumb something is that anyone says!"

Javier's face contorted in rage as he started to say something but stopped himself, resorting to fuming in silence and staring out the window instead.

Nate resumed their drive in silence for a time. The two-tracked trail loosely followed the riverbed through a narrow canyon and down the mountainside. It strayed from the creek when the drop became too steep yet always allowed them to keep the riverbed in sight. Signs of the flood peppered their route with clumps of mud, sections of washed-out embankments and errant logs and boulders, but the path seemed to stay above it all.

The Jeep struggled along through the afternoon, the engine coughing and spluttering with the strain. They stopped several times throughout the day, discovering an oil leak, a radiator leak and even a fuel leak. Water in the fuel line seemed to hamper the engine's cadence, gurgling and variating as it gave an unpredictable and often less than harmonious headway to their descent. Nerves frayed, but they contained their tempers as they continued onward.

With each stop, they listened intently for signs of rescue while nervously watching the forest around them for pursuit by the canine predators from the previous night. The day wore on as the sun trudged through the sky, reflecting a similar trek to their slow, agonizing process.

Finally, the canyon widened to where the meadow stretched into an elongated "S" shape, with the descending elevation of the ridgelines to either side into gentler hillsides. The water from the creek became calm and more like a river that flowed at an even pace, deeper and slower, as other water sources from the hillsides merged into it. The air also warmed with the drop in elevation and deciduous trees mixed in with conifers.

The ride continued while they bounced along throughout the day between trees and boulders. With each jarring bump, Javier winced with pain from his injured shoulder but remained silent, consumed by his own misery.

As they neared the center of the valley, Nate suddenly stopped the Jeep and stood up, pushing his upper torso through the window, gawking in amazement at the scenery around them.

"What is going on here?" Nate breathed.

"What do you mean?" Johanna squinted.

"It's the trees," Kevin whispered. "Look at the trees."

Everyone gawked in awed silence. Before them, the creek widened, meandering through the valley, surrounded on both sides by frosted forested peaks. It wasn't the unfamiliarity of their surroundings that took their breath away.

It was the golden cottonwoods and elms mixed with the reds of maples interspaced between the pines. A brief breeze caressed the grove, showering the meadow's edge in a crimson and golden display of glorious color.

"It's not just there," Nate stated aloud in realization, pointing to the mountainsides above. "Look at all that aspen and the other trees even on the surrounding hillsides!"

"Isn't it supposed to be spring?" Daniel spoke, stating the obvious as he wondered aloud. "This looks like fall!"

"It doesn't look like fall; this IS fall," Kevin muttered, watching as a breeze dislodged countless crimson leaves from the surrounding trees, sending them in a flurry around them. "Look at the bushes and the grass too."

"It's all cured and dry, not like spring at all," Johanna added in wonder. "Everything is turning as if a full summer has already gone by!"

"I don't know or care what's going on here, but let's just get down to civilization," Javier interjected, wincing in pain. "I don't want to spend another night out here!"

"I don't either," Nate muttered more to himself than the others. Nate pushed on, revving the vehicle's engine to keep it alive as it sputtered, following the trail through high grass and mud.

Kevin stared out the passenger window, just wishing it would all be over as the vehicle bounced on. He watched the tops of the trees pass slowly by, the sun glinting through the multi-colored leaves. He wondered the same question that was on everyone's mind: *how and why are there fall colors on the trees?*

He lulled himself into a trance, watching the countryside pass by. A barely perceptible humming sound began to permeate the air, intensifying by the moment. As the sound intensified, the colors around the trees he had fixated on became brighter and seemed to magnify, as if looking through a lens.

"Do you hear that? Are those crickets?" Javier turned to ask the others. "No, wait; it's getting louder...that sound; it's like cicadas."

"Sounds like electric wires," Nate said, stopping the vehicle and craning his neck outside to see. "I suppose it could be cicadas, but I've not seen any yet."

Kevin heard it too and spun to look around, but the sound ceased the moment he turned.

"It's gone," Johanna said, straining to hear it again herself. "I heard it too, but now it's gone."

"I don't see any power lines," Nate said as he craned his head around, searching the treetops. "If it's all the same, I'd feel better finding some other sign of civilization. I had hoped they were power lines, but I don't see any."

Nate pushed the vehicle onward as they continued down the pathway meandering through the valley. As the day wore on into late afternoon, he gambled with the Jeep's condition, driving the vehicle faster, coaxing it to make up distance despite its damaged state. He began to swallow nervously as he drove, sweat forming on his brow as he silently contemplated the late hour of the day against their progress.

A cloud of doubt began to spread from him, settling over them all as no further sign of anyone else in the wilderness transpired. The nagging fact remained that they had seen no one; not a single person, nor even the sign of another vehicle presented itself. All the while, they maintained watch through the shattered rear window, dreading that they might be followed. The uncertainty built into unspoken despair for the Jeep's occupants as the sky in the east turned orange, reflecting off the rock faces in a brilliant alpenglow from the higher peaks.

Johanna continued to ponder the landscape, tiny lines of worry etching her exhausted features. She tried not to show her concern, but the deepening hue of the sky made their reality inescapable: another night in the wilds was becoming increasingly likely.

Nate smiled and patted her leg in reassurance, but when she met his gaze, she could see she wasn't the only one worried. That and the inexplicable and irrefutable signs that fall, not spring, were all around them. Dried grass, multi-colored leaves and a crisp bite to the air left little doubt as to what season they were in yet offered no explanation as to why.

As twilight continued to descend, Nate pushed the Jeep to the top of a knoll and looked out over an expanse that made his heart sink. The river had become a rushing torrent again, dropping into a much larger valley below. The trail they followed switchbacked precariously down the hillside. Although not heavily wooded, the drop was steep and strewn with large rocks and shrubs.

"What is it?" Johanna whispered, scanning his scruff-peppered face with concern.

"How are you all doing back there? You guys alright?" Nate called out over his shoulder, clearly to Johanna an attempt to avoid the topic at hand. Daniel patted him on the shoulder, and the other two gave a thumbs-up.

"Stop trying to change the subject!" Johanna hissed. "Answer my question—what's wrong!?"

"Even with the Jeep in the best of conditions, the way ahead is going to be difficult even in broad daylight," he exhaled before shaking his head. "In the dark, with this descent and in the condition we're in, this is going to be impossible."

Nate struggled to formulate words. With twilight settling across the broader valley ahead of them, the difficult off-road only became worse.

What made matters worse was the unfamiliarity of it all. In the failing light, he could still see a massive snow-capped mountain looming over the north end of the valley, bisecting their path ahead. The lonely mountain loomed uncharacteristically large over every other peak, covered with a mix of steep cliffs and glacial ice near its conical summit.

One reality became clear to everyone; the scene remained absent and devoid of any human life or activity. At the bottom of the great mountain, the forest grew thick, and the river they followed joined an even larger river, flowing through where the foot of the peak headed the valley.

"Say something!" Johanna hissed. "Are you telling me we have to spend another night out here?"

"At another time, this place would even be beautiful," Nate finally stated, pointing to the massive mountain to their left. "I just don't recognize any of this. That peak looks like it has actual glacial ice near the top and is easily over 14,000 feet; I've never seen anything like it before, at least not in Colorado! Mount Evans, Mount Bierstadt, Pikes Peak, Longs Peak—they're all known within the Rocky Mountains. I don't recognize this mountain or any of the others we've passed."

"What do you mean?" Johanna blinked back tears as she choked back the panic in her voice. "This is the way home, isn't it?"

"That's what I'm trying to say; I've never seen that before," he sighed as he gestured again at the enormous mountain at the north end of the valley. "I'm afraid you're correct: we ARE going to have to spend another night up here!"

"No fucking way!" Javier muttered from the back, slamming his fist into the seat back.

"Are you sure? Look at me!" Johanna's voice cracked as she tried to contain her hysteria. Only then did Nate reluctantly turn to her, the helplessness he had tried to hide from her reflecting in his eyes. "We have injured with us, not to mention two that we tried to rescue have already died!"

She glanced back quickly at Javier and Kevin as tears spilled down her face. The two younger men said nothing, contained in their own miseries for the moment, either pretending not to hear or simply blocking the conversation out of their thoughts.

"Johanna," Nate coaxed softly, placing a reassuring hand on her knee as he regained some of his commanding composure again. "If we try to descend in the dark on this steep grade, we risk a wreck that could overturn the vehicle, not to mention injure or kill us all. I can only guarantee one thing—we wouldn't stop rolling until we hit the bottom. There's nothing to stop us on this hillside if we tumble; I don't think we should risk it."

"Shit," she whispered after a long pause, smacking the dashboard with an open hand. She took one final look over the hood to the valley below, yet the glimpse only confirmed in her mind what he already told her. Taking in a deep, shaky breath, she steadied herself. "All right, I guess that means we're making camp again. I'll cook up some vegetables and chicken tonight, and we'll just figure this all out tomorrow."

"That's the spirit! Just no cooking meat though," Nate whispered, meeting her gaze, then glancing back the way they had come. "Keep the fire low. I don't want to attract attention, not until I'm sure I see signs of human civilization."

"Oh," was all she could muster in agreement, looking behind them on the empty trail they had already descended. The trail behind filled with the darkness of the coming night, swirling, with dried leaves blowing across the path. The dread of what had happened to them previously remained fresh on her mind.

Without a second thought on the matter, they unloaded the SUV and prepared camp. Johanna decided to busy herself, content with cooking.

After dinner, the air became cooler again but remained comfortable as the sun completed its journey into the west behind the high peaks.

The crickets chirped softly as the group used what fading light remained to prepare for the evening. It was only then that the faint sounds of a far-off whistle could be heard, a low-pitched noise resembling the melody of an unknown song.

"What is that?" Johanna muttered to herself as she shivered, turning to the enormous mountain to their north as mournful echoes drifted through the night air. Barely audible, the melodies of some unrecognizable sad song seemed to drift yet fade away before she could recognize any aspect of them. "Is that a train?"

"Hard to say," Nate replied. "It's far off whatever it is. It could just as easily be the wind blowing past those cliffs."

They shrugged off the strange echo as Nate washed dishes, and Daniel helped him to clean the scraps from their dinner into the creek. Kevin originally protested the environmental implications, but Nate's warning about the scent of food attracting wildlife quickly silenced any argument.

The rest of the group gathered enough wood for a large fire but agreed to keep the fire this night small. They would only pile on the additional fuel if they needed the added light and fire to fend off potential attackers again.

As the evening activity subsided, Nate decided to take the time to try to calm Johanna's nerves. He could see her struggle earlier to contain her terror and decided to assist in calming her nerves before bedding down for the evening. He walked up behind her as she was stowing the remaining cooking items back in the Jeep and placed a gentle hand around her waist.

"I keep thinking I hear those wolves," she muttered, flinching slightly at his touch. "Then I think I'm hearing someone singing; I must be losing my mind!"

"Like I said, I think it's just the wind blowing through the high peaks and glaciers up there," he assured her, nodding toward the outline of the great mountain to the north. "We'd know if it was something else."

"Think so, huh?" Johanna scoffed, shaking her head. "I'm sorry, I don't doubt you, but it gives me the creeps!"

"The air is warmer down here," he reassured her as he quietly nuzzled her neck. "We've made good progress today, and I think the change in elevation is bringing us to warmer zones. I'm sorry we didn't make it to a town today, but I think we have a good shot at it tomorrow."

"Yeah," she mumbled none too enthusiastically. "If it's all the same to you, while I agree with the decision to stop for the night, I'm still not liking it."

"The drive is pretty taxing, and I'm exhausted," he continued. When Johanna didn't respond, he turned and touched her arm to press for attention. "I may need your help with some of the driving tomorrow."

"Nate, I don't know what to tell you!" she snapped in irritation, pulling away as she bustled about the dishes. Blaming Nate for their situation may not have been rational, but she still reeled at the notion of having to spend another night in the wilderness. "You're the only one who can drive us out of here! We're in the middle of nowhere, and this is your vehicle! This is all off-road driving, and I've never driven your Jeep off-road before. This is hardly the time or place for me to practice; you got us into this, so get us out!"

"That's not true and you know it!" Nate protested, shaking his head. He didn't want to fight with her about it here and now, no matter how unreasonable it seemed. "I'm just asking for some help here!"

"Nate, I don't know where we are, and I can see that you don't either," she snapped again, squaring off with him. "That scares the hell out of me, and I can guarantee you that me driving is not going to change that! Now, my contribution to this effort is the cooking and cleaning for everyone, and I hope you deem it as enough!"

"Fine, let's table this for tonight then," he scoffed, pinching the bridge of his nose to relieve the sudden surge of stress. "We can reassess this once we reach the flatlands. I'll take the first watch for tonight."

Johanna forced herself to not answer, noting his gruffness. As he turned away from her, he hoisted himself atop the Jeep. Slinging both shotguns and his handgun, he stared back at the trail they had come down in brooding silence.

She turned back to the dishes, trying to recall the words from her counselor. *Breathe in the night air, try to relax and don't blame Nate for the situation we are in.*

Javier and Kevin propped themselves up near the front driver's-side tire, while Daniel put the seats down in the back to sleep in what little protection the damaged vehicle offered.

As the group turned in for the night, falling asleep proved to be a challenge. Every rustling leaf and snapping twig sent them on edge again, especially when Sammy spun off into a barking fit. However, throughout the night, they remained otherwise unmolested.

Kevin stared off into the dark, alone in his misery. He lay on the ground with his hands folded behind his head, thinking of Becky. He missed her now more than ever. *She always had a way of bringing people together, and now she's gone.*

Becky had always been more of an adventurer. It had been her idea to go to Boulder in the first place. It had been her idea to go up to Echo Lake. She was always a crowd-pleaser, bringing people together even when they weren't the most compatible.

He had been surprised that she skipped the Moab plans with Tim and Javier to go with him to Boulder; she was always so adventurous and unafraid, just like Tim.

Kevin had seen Tim take a fall and hit a tree once while skiing. He had been cut and bruised but never noticed it until they got home. The guy was truly indestructible, and Becky was always so proud of that about him.

Now, they both were gone. He missed them both, but he missed her most of all. Becky was his rock, and he felt her loss terribly as he drifted off to sleep. As his eyes closed, images began to form themselves in his mind.

Becky sat across from Kevin, smiling, seemingly hovering a few inches above the ground. Daylight spilled over the both of them, and

Kevin glanced around, surprised. Everyone else still slept, but Becky sat patiently, facing Kevin as if nothing had happened.

"Becky?!" Kevin asked as he sat up with a start. "What happened?! How did you find us?! Are you okay?!"

"I'm fine now; Tim and I are both fine now, but we can't move on yet," Becky's voice stated despite her lips never moving from the pleasant smile she wore as she floated above him. "I thought it was you, coming to save me back in the meadow, but it wasn't. Beware of the wolf, Kevin; you and Javier both. Beware of the wolf."

"The wolf? Becky, what's that mean? What..."

"WAKE! WAKE! WAKE! WAKE!" she yelped. The whole scene blurred and...

Kevin jerked upright, waking suddenly and gasping for air. It was still dark, and propped up against the Jeep, he could see that Javier still slumbered next to the front tire beside him. When he turned to the left, he met Sammy's wet tongue right into his mouth. Spluttering, he gently pushed Sammy's face out of his. The hound slurped the side of his face with warm kisses as he wiped the slobber from his cheeks.

"Ack! Sammy, cut it out!" he spat. "What's going on?!"

"Biiiig biiiird," the dog growled, pointing back above the bushes and into the sky. Sammy whined again and pointed her nose at the nearly full moon above. "Biiig biiiird!"

"What?!" Kevin gasped, staring at the talking dog incredulously.

Suddenly, the shadow of something large but far away crossed in front of the moon again, just as it had two nights previously. This time, he could scarcely hear a deep flap as something massive winged its way across the sky. He quickly rubbed his eyes in disbelief, squinting again at the moon, trying to discern what he had suddenly woken up to.

It was there for a moment...and then it was gone again. He thought to wake Javier, but whatever it was vanished quickly behind a cloud, and silence enveloped the land again.

"Biiiig biiiird," the hound growled as sleep overtook him again.

≈≈≈≈

Kevin woke again at first light, standing to stretch his cramped body. A fresh layer of frost glistened on the grassy Ridgeline, and the creek babbled quietly nearby. Although sleep still permeated his mind, he knew he would not be returning to it as dawn broke over the more gently rolling hillsides in front of them. *At least the signs of them coming out of the mountains are all around us, especially ahead of us.*

Nature called, and the need to relieve himself emerged, but he didn't want to stray far from camp. The crisp air bit at him, sending shivers down his spine as he rubbed his hands together for warmth, glancing over the mists clinging to the glazed banks of the icy creek.

"Sammy!" he whispered. He tried again, this time whistling gently and tapping his leg. *The dog will know if anything is amiss.* "Sammy!"

A sudden crashing in the bushes near the creek woke everyone as an explosion of black fur came bounding to him through the brush. A flashback of wolves startled everyone awake, but to their relief, only a very happy Sammy emerged.

The hound trotted up to Kevin, tail wagging and dripping with muck as she clenched an errant stick stubbornly in her jaws. She glistened in the morning sun, wet and covered with mud, burrs and debris.

"No, Sammy! No!" Kevin squealed as he extended his arms to stop the inevitable as the Australian Shepherd began to shake, her short black fur throwing mud and water everywhere. The fresh smell of meadow mud followed the hound wherever she proudly trotted as everyone tried to keep the dog at arm's length. "Oh, you stink!"

Despite the groans of annoyance at being awakened, the rest of the group couldn't help but laugh. Even Javier cracked the first smile that Kevin had seen the entire trip. In the dim twilight of morning, the moment of mirth was unmistakable.

Kevin apologized nevertheless for waking everyone and limped off with the happy hound beside him. He found a secluded spot away from camp to unzip and answer his call to nature. As he urinated, he scanned the valley around him, noticing a tall ponderosa pine at the top of the hill on the far side. Its abnormal height stood out to him among the other trees, branches clearly defined in the faint morning light. He focused on the swaying branches as he finished his business.

The same strange sound, like power lines or cicadas during a hot summer day, permeated the air again.

"There's that sound again," Javier exclaimed, startling him from behind, and immediately the sound ceased. As he reached Kevin's side, he stopped and looked around again, shaking his head in dismay. "Just like last time, the second I hear it, it stops!"

"Oh, man, you scared me," Kevin breathed. "You know, for a second, I heard it too."

"It seemed louder this time," Javier noted as he unzipped his pants and relieved himself as well. "We're going to have to pay closer attention to figure out what that is; catch it before it vanishes. That's weird, though; I don't hear it now."

"Yeah, maybe it's something that flies off," Kevin wondered aloud. "Speaking of which, I think I saw something fly past the moon again last night; thought I heard it too."

"Were you able to get a better look at it?" Javier asked, notably more curious and less antagonizing. "None of that electrical sound though, huh?"

"No, it's definitely different, although I can't say whether they're related or not," Kevin offered tentatively. "I guess I should have woken you or someone else up, but it happened so fast."

"Meh, don't worry about it; Johanna is making breakfast and then we'll all be out of here," Javier exhaled in a long sigh as he zipped his pants again. "To think we came here for spring break and would lose our best friends over this. We're going to have a shit time explaining what happened to Tim and Becky's family. We don't even have their bodies with us to bury!"

The two looked away from each other as Javier said the last bit, his voice catching.

"I wouldn't even know where to start," Kevin whispered.

"Yeah," Javier agreed, composing himself. "So, what exactly are we going to say?"

"The truth; what else can we say?" Kevin squinted at him. "We hit ice, flipped the car and now we're here. We weren't drinking, we weren't irresponsible and this wasn't your fault. Don't worry, Javier, I'm not going to blame you, if that's what you're worried about. We may not be friends, but I'm not like that."

"Thanks, Kevin, I appreciate that, but that's not what I meant," his former nemesis sighed. Something else was clearly on his mind, and Kevin arched an eyebrow.

"Then what is it?" Kevin pressed, noting Javier used his first name instead of calling him the usual dismissive "Micker."

"Hey, bro, I just wanted to apologize to you and say that I'm sorry for being such a dickhead," Javier muttered, looking away uncomfortably. "Becky and Tim were both after me about it before. Seeing how things have gone, the least I can do for them at this point is make it good with you, if you're cool with that."

Kevin stopped and looked Javier in the face. It was clearly an uncomfortable moment for them both, but Javier was the one making the effort.

"No worries," Kevin replied, flashing a brief smile before looking away. He turned back to him and clasped his hand firmly. "If anything good comes out of this disaster, I hope that you and I can at least be acquaintances. If not, I'll understand, and we just part ways on good terms when this is over. I'll leave it up to you, but we've been through a lot together at this point, and I think it's what our friends would have wanted."

"No, I think we can definitely hang more, we can definitely do that!" Javier turned back to him in a whisper. "For Tim and Becky. We owe that to them. Truthfully, I don't mind; I actually want to."

"Yeah, for Tim and Becky," Kevin echoed as they turned and walked back to camp together. He had his doubts about how long this newfound friendship would last, but the apology from Javier was a great way to start the day. "So, how did you sleep?"

"Like shit!" Javier scoffed as he composed himself. "I kept having these weird dreams and waking up. Oh, I also dreamt their dog Sammy could talk."

"So did I!" Kevin turned and looked at him in surprise, the comment stopping them both just short of camp. "The same dream! I wonder what that means?"

"Ask Johanna," Javier huffed. "Dream interpretation and premonitions seem to be her thing. Supposedly she dreamt all this before we got here, at least that's what Daniel told me earlier."

"There's one other thing; I wasn't going to bring it up but since we're talking," Kevin hesitated before choking off a whisper. "I dreamt of Becky; she said, 'Beware of the wolf.'"

"No, Micker," Javier replied, resuming the use of his last name, albeit gently. "I don't want to talk about her; not just yet and not now. We failed her and I can't..."

Kevin nodded solemnly as they returned to camp, noting Johanna had taken the risk to cook bacon and eggs despite Nate's warning about cooking meat. Nate conceded to simply tackle heating some badly needed coffee for himself. She said very little, working feverishly to provide sustenance, only occasionally brushing back her disheveled chestnut hair away from the creases in her normally smooth ivory face.

Daniel struggled with a comb to try and remove the burs from Sammy's fur, focused on the matter at hand rather than the silent cold between his mother and Nate. He looked over their raggedy bunch as the morning rays lit the land around them. The signs of wear were clear from the days spent in the wild. Even Javier and Kevin showed signs of scruff, beginning to look more like Nate, although their youthful exuberance provided more energy as they strode into camp.

"Yeeeeelp!" Sammy squealed. "Awwwrrr, awwwwr, awwwwr!"

"Come on, Sammy, I just gotta take out a few more," Daniel groaned. "You should have stayed out of those bushes by the creek—what if something happened to you?"

"Ouch!" Sammy yelped again.

"Ouch?!" Nate exclaimed. Javier and Kevin shared a glance but said nothing. "That almost sounded like a person!"

After breakfast, Nate inspected the Jeep again, muttering about only having a quarter tank of gasoline left and that the other fluids were low as well. Although they were able to siphon creek water into the radiator, Nate continued to fret about having low power steering fluid and less oil than before, clearly the sign of yet another leak.

As the sun warmed the hillside, the frost lifted, and they loaded back into the Jeep and continued their journey down the mountain. The going was rough and slow, and at times, the SUV clanged as it bounced off a rock and descended unceremoniously down the trail, nauseating the carsick occupants further.

Where the night had been cold and damp, the sun-exposed trail baked in the sunlight, hot and dusty. Opting to forgo lunch, they sufficed with granola bars and sipped canteens of water, but the rough ride frayed their nerves. By mid-afternoon, they finally reached the bottom of the canyon.

It came as a great relief when they finally forded the shallow river at the bottom of the canyon. Once across, Nate threw the Jeep into park and turned to Johanna, fixating her with a glare of intention in his eyes.

"Finally, a dirt road," Johanna commented, avoiding his gaze and pointing not far from where they parked. Paralleling the river to the north and south, a well-traveled dirt road cut through the grasses, meandering gently down the canyon. "We know there's not much but more wilderness to the north, so I'm guessing we should probably go south?"

"Agreed, but we've arrived at a point where it's time to revisit our previous discussion," Nate said, pressing on the point. "As I said last night, I've been driving the past two days, and I'd like you to assist me."

"You're right, Nate, we DID talk about this last night!" Johanna roiled in fury, taken aback by his direct approach to something she had previously refused. "This is your vehicle! I already told you I'm not comfortable driving your vehicle off-road!"

"Johanna, I need you to step up—this is hardly off-road!" he argued, his face reddening as he bellowed louder. "I've gotten us this far, and I need you to..."

"Step up?!" Johanna interrupted. "I'm cooking and cleaning for all of us here! I'm telling you that I'm not comfortable driving YOUR vehicle!"

"Guys, would you mind?" Nate turned in frustration to the backseat passengers. "Would any of you like to try driving for a bit?"

"Don't ask them!" Johanna snapped, jutting a finger into his face. "Javier has a broken arm, and he has no business driving! I don't know the extent of Kevin's injuries just yet, but he took a major blow to the head!"

"I don't mind," Kevin interjected, trying to be helpful. "I could drive if you want."

"I can drive," Daniel offered, increasingly uncomfortable with the bickering. "You haven't asked me yet, and I have my license!"

"Certainly not!" Johanna stated resolutely. "Nate, I'm sorry you're tired, but the outdoor driving is YOUR thing, and you need to see us through this! That is all there is to it!"

"That's ridiculous!" Nate snapped back. "I'm just asking for a bit of help here! I'll drive for another few minutes, but you're up after we pass this next bend, you hear me?"

As the argument continued, Kevin turned to look out the window, wishing he were somewhere else as the Jeep continued to rumble along. The morning had started off so wonderfully, but the trip down had been so miserable; it felt like all the personal gains were being lost. He found himself focused on the ripples of the water in the paralleling river, their tiny V-shaped white caps catching his attention.

Sighing as the bickering escalated, he focused on the ripples in the river, leaning out the window of the Jeep for fresh air. Immediately, the buzzing noise started again, but this time, he didn't care; he just let it continue to build as the sound intensified. The ripples began to glow with a blinding white light, suddenly seeming to build as he focused in on their image...he could see bubbles...

Sammy started to whine, staring intently at Kevin, and the hound's ears perked.

"Hey, guys, there's those power lines again!" Javier tried to interject over the shouting. "Keep your eyes peeled for—"

"Kevin!" Daniel exclaimed as a shimmer, like summer heat, emanated from Kevin, warping wind around him.

In a blast of air, Kevin found the river water rushing up to meet him. In the blink of an eye, he suddenly found himself floating in the river, struggling and bobbing, swept away by the current and tumbling downstream as ice-cold water washed over him. Coughing and spluttering in the frigid water, he tumbled in shock over rocks and branches downstream away from the Jeep. His clothes quickly soaked in the freezing water, weighing him down as he tried to stand, slipping on the rocky river bottom.

"Nate!" Johanna screamed, pointing. "Kevin's in the river!"

"How did he get there?" Nate exclaimed, slamming on the brakes, throwing the vehicle into park and opening the door to run after Kevin. "Did he just jump in?"

"I don't know; I didn't see," Javier stammered. "He was just right here, and then he wasn't."

"Why would he do that!?" Johanna shook her head as Nate jumped out of the vehicle, slogging into the river to help Kevin to his feet. "Why would he just jump out?!"

"He didn't!" Daniel cried out. "He was sucked out!"

"Sucked out?" Johanna turned to her son, squinting at him doubtfully.

"What the hell were you doing?" Nate admonished as he helped Kevin back to the shoreline.

"I-I-I don't know," Kevin stammered as he shivered, wet and dripping. Johanna found a towel buried in their luggage and handed it to him. "I just fell in!"

"No, I saw you get sucked out!" Daniel insisted. "Something pulled you out the window! You were here, and it's like a whirlpool sucked you out into the river!"

"A whirlpool?!" Johanna waved her son off. "Danny, that's enough. Now is not the time for—"

"I'm not making it up!" Daniel snapped. "I saw it, Mom! He was sucked out!"

Nate glanced back at Johanna, but her look told him everything he needed to know; despite the distraction of Kevin's untimely exit from the vehicle, she was not going to do any driving until they reached a paved road.

"Well, let's all buckle up; there's no need for that to happen again," Nate stated, settling back into the driver's seat to continue their drive down the valley. "It's a bumpy road, and we don't need anyone else getting thrown out!"

"That's NOT what happened!" Daniel seethed. "I saw it!"

Johanna and Kevin resettled in the Jeep, and Nate put the vehicle back into drive. They resumed their taxing trek down the valley, but as they rounded the next bend, he began preparing himself to argue with Johanna again about the driving situation.

"There! People!" Javier suddenly exclaimed, pointing at a small cottage ahead of them on the road. "Finally, PEOPLE!"

An elderly man and woman tended a small farm, a crop of corn in their front yard behind a rickety-looking wooden fence. The cottage had a thatched roof, and although small, it retained a clean-looking and well-maintained exterior. A pair of horses tied at the front porch whinnied nervously as the Jeep approached. The smell of meat and herbs cooking filled the glade, and a thin wisp of smoke floated faintly from the stone chimney above the thatched roof.

"Yeah, finally!" Nate grinned. "Let's see if we can use their phone, and maybe they can get us some help."

The elderly couple looked up in bewilderment at their approach and waved nervously. The man wore loose brown coveralls and carried a wooden rake while his wife donned a simple green woolen dress. Their clothing had a very homemade look to it, and as the Jeep closed in on their yard, it became apparent there were no modern amenities in their dwelling or even nearby.

"Man, this is rustic living," Kevin commented quietly, still shivering and wet, clutching his towel as they approached. "I don't see any power lines."

"Maybe they just choose to live simply," Johanna stated to put an end to the conversation. "We need their help nevertheless."

"Hi there!" Nate called out as he parked the SUV. "We're a bit lost here and have been out here for days. May we use your phone?"

The man and woman glanced at each other, the woman wiping her hands nervously on her dress before she nodded to the man, signaling him to approach their vehicle. Her grey eyes surveyed the group suspiciously even as she brushed a lock of silvery hair back beneath her white-laced bonnet.

"Phone?" the man asked dumbly, squinting at Nate in disbelief. "Did you come down from Mondlichtberg?"

"I don't know what a Mondlichtberg is, but we need to call for help," Nate affirmed, scratching at his scruff. "We've been out here for days and frankly have had a rough time out here; we're lost and have injured and need assistance!"

"There's just us here, my wife and I," the man stated in a heavy Germanic accent, pointing further down the roadway. "Levens isn't far off though—you'll get there before dark, depending on how fast this contraption can go. They'll have everything you need."

"Levens?" Johanna asked. "Are we at least close to Evergreen or Bailey?"

"Don't know of those places, but Levens is the closest town to us," the agitated woman spoke up, peering from behind her husband's stocky frame, finally gaining the confidence to approach herself. "Just keep following this road until you exit the valley! Best not dally though; it'll be dark soon!"

"Say, what sort of wagon is this?" the man added, running a trembling hand along the hood. "Heard you coming down the canyon and thought it might be a wild beast or something worse!"

"Jeep Grand Cherokee—got the off-road package and the V-8 engine with well over 400 horses under that hood," Nate said proudly despite being anxious to be on their way or use the phone. "May not look like it now, with the accident we had and all, but…"

"You have 400 horses in that box—are you sure you aren't from Mondlichtberg?" the farmer balked, perplexed and uncomprehending. A sudden dread seemed to seize him, and he stopped and scanned the sky worriedly above. "It's awfully shiny, though, and it may attract unwanted attention!"

"Yes indeed, the beast that hunts from the sky may see this!" the woman agreed suspiciously as she moved beside her husband to pull him back. "If you aren't from Mondlichtberg, then you best be on your way!"

"We came from Denver," Nate answered her. "We're trying to get back."

"We don't know of a Denver," the woman scoffed, eyeing the group distrustfully, also glancing skyward in fear. "We don't have anything for you here. They'll have what you need in Levens! You best clear out before you bring ruin to us all!"

"What we really need is a phone." Nate's smile thinned as he was quickly losing patience. "If you don't have a phone we can use, that's fine, but we need to know where we can find one; our cell phones do not seem to access towers here."

"No, we do not have a phone here," the old man agreed. "Just keep heading to Levens; they'll help you there!"

"Thanks for nothing," Nate muttered before putting the Jeep back into drive and continuing down the darkening road, leaving the odd couple behind in the dust.

"Friendly people," Javier said sarcastically. "You'd think they'd be a bit more welcoming for people who just went through what we did!"

"I'd be pissed, but if this Levens town is only five miles away, we might as well just finish saving ourselves," Nate growled as he shook his head in annoyance.

Chapter 7

Levens

Nate drove onward as the sun began to set behind them. Following the dirt roadway parallel to the river, their journey finally broke out of the valley and onto a vast plain along the base of the mountains. From here, the river widened as it continued in a shallower and gentler flow to the south. Nate began to wonder about the river's destination when the thought became suddenly lost on him.

The road ahead forked, with the more clearly traveled section veering away from the river and to the east. Now a single clearly defined dirt road, the trail led toward a broad dome-shaped knoll in front of a distant set of rolling hills. The less worn two-track road continued into the forest, peppering the way ahead in a foreboding darkness enveloping the land as the sun set behind the mountains.

"What is it?" Johanna asked as Nate brought the vehicle to a halt, shaking his head in confusion.

"I said this before, but this really doesn't look like anywhere I've ever been," Nate groaned, concern creasing the lines in his face just under the scruff. "It looks sort of like the San Luis Valley, but this is greener, and none of the hills further to the east look familiar; at this point, this should all be the Great Plains! There's no traffic, roads, or other landmarks, either. Denver, Colorado Springs, Castle Rock or something else should be there! I'm serious, Johanna, this area just does not look familiar to me at all!"

"How can that be?! You've been up and down the front range for years!" Johanna echoed as she settled back in her seat, confounded and suddenly at a loss for words. She turned to the backseat passengers, but all they could convey was dismayed confusion as they stared dumbfounded out the windows, searching the rolling grasslands in vain for any signs of civilization. Settling back in her seat, all she could do was stare straight ahead in dismay. "What would be your best guess then? At this point, I'm willing to commit to that!"

"I think we should follow the clearer road; that other one just goes back into the forest and...wait a sec," Nate said as he exhaled. An anomaly on the rounded hillside ahead caught his eye as he grabbed a pair of binoculars from the glove box. Standing tall through the broken driver's side window, he scanned the roadway ahead. "I see something at the top of that hill ahead of us, a wall and some torches! There's a gate too! Yes, and more people!"

"I see it now too; it looks like a small town," Johanna stated, squinting, as the others peered over her shoulder. "Levens, do you suppose?"

The group in the Jeep could see the lights of a town crowning the broad hilltop. Nate passed the binoculars around so each person could see for themselves.

Like a crown atop the back of a great turtle, a granite stone wall surrounded the quaint town taking up most of the hill. They could make out lights coming from wooden torches embedded into the sides of the wall as attendants strolled alongside, lighting them for the evening. From this distance, the details of the town remained veiled behind the fortification, but the thatched roofs and stonemasonry poked above, becoming more visible towards the hilltop. The whole scene resembled something like a postcard from central medieval Europe.

Within the walls, a larger octagonal fortress sat atop the hillside amid the village, a squat monstrosity of a structure formed more for utility than beauty it seemed a modest crown atop the hill. Only a neighboring tower stood taller on the south end of the castle, lone and stoic, and almost seemingly as an afterthought. The narrow rock structure stood notably like a watchtower above it all, grey and faded, dwarfed by its squat neighbor in every way but height.

Pedestrians moved in and out of the town through a menacing-looking iron gate, currently retracted to allow commerce through. Chain-mailed guardsmen patrolled the wall tops as below, mule-drawn carts and foot traffic mingled. Attendants wearing faded blue cloaks strode alongside the walls, igniting torches for illumination as they went for the evening's trade and commerce, continuing unabated by the coming nightfall.

"Levens," Javier repeated, breaking into soft cynical laughter as he lay back in his seat, grasping his head between his hands. "We're so screwed!"

"Now let's not jump to conclusions here," Nate murmured, his voice portraying a hope he neglected to feel at his core. "This is the first sign of people we've come across unless we want to go back to the farmer's hut we passed back in the mountains."

Distant peals of thunder rumbled moments later across the valley giving an ominous promise of more to come. As they looked back towards the mountain peaks, strange pulses of white light flashed just over the horizon, reflecting off a low set of angry clouds, clustered over an isolated section of the high country they had just come from.

"We don't want to go back there, do we?" Kevin muttered. "Seems like a storm's coming, and I'd rather be indoors for it rather than trying to weather it with all of us crammed in the Jeep."

"Agreed," Johanna confirmed as more flashes of light ensued. The blinding flashes from the taller mountain peaks behind them faded only to be followed by a series of thunderous echoes. "We've come all this way; let's just start there and get this figured out. It may be two steps forward and one back, but we're getting closer."

"Closer to what though?" Daniel interjected.

"Closer to a hot bath and a phone, and maybe a gas station? Doesn't sound so bad!" Kevin sighed as Nate put the Jeep back into drive. "At this point, I'll take it!"

As if in response, more distant rumbling reverberated throughout the western sky as the Jeep took to the road, bursts of light emanating from behind the peaks as it moved toward the unknown town in its path.

≈≈≈≈

High atop the tower, beneath the gently flapping sigil of the moon and three stars, an ancient man sat alone. He gently puffed on a tobacco pipe, watching thoughtfully as the distant flashes of light illuminated the gathering clouds on the horizon above the mountain peaks. As he rocked back and forth gently beneath the thatched roof of his abode, he took in the vista as wrinkles of concern, both present and past, lined his pale face beneath his flowing white beard.

"Grand Master Nicholas," the voice of a young male page followed a series of knocks, reverberating on the thick oaken door of his chambers. "Are you there, sir?"

Grand Master Nicholas never tired of his perch, the highest point in Levens. Pulling his white flowing robes about him to ward off the coming chill, he listened anxiously to the sounds of thunder over the flowing breeze, ignoring the incessant pleas at his doorstep.

"No scent of rain though, no scent of rain," he wheezed to himself, standing as the sun began to set over the mountains and behind the angry clouds. "Why did they move without me? The fools! What do they hope to accomplish? Searching for...

"Wait a moment," the grand master muttered and suddenly stopped, squinting as he scanned the roadway to town. The strange hum from a beastless carriage wafted back to him on the evening breezes as it had approached Levens. The grand master's eyes widened with realization as he stood tall. "No...it cannot be! They're here?!"

Squinting to make out the details, he stood as it approached the town, making its way through the cattails at the base of the hill. When the carriage entered the city gates, another frantic knock on his door prompted the man to stand and brush the ashes off his snowy beard and robes.

"Yes! Come in!" he shouted in a rough voice, sounding like tree bark in a stiff breeze. "I'm on the porch!"

"Grand Master Nicholas!" the young boy called, swinging the heavy door open and poking his head inside, eyes wide with excitement. "You asked that I notify you if someone strange came to town. Our lookout has spied something strange approaching!"

"Indeed, I did," the old man laughed, grabbing his gnarled wooden staff and grunting as he stood. "It appears they have arrived at the front gate, proceeding my expectations! Good thing I had your keen eyes on this! I half expected them not to come here at all!"

"They have, Grand Master!" The squire was clearly agitated as he glanced over the grand master's shoulder and caught sight of the dust trail leading to the front gate. "They aren't dangerous, are they?"

"Extremely," the ancient man scoffed as he hobbled inside and over to the squire. "However, not to us, and most likely only to themselves. I must come greet our newcomers. They have no idea what awaits them, and frankly, neither do the people of Levens!"

As the old man hobbled to the door, candles fluttered from the cross breeze, and parchments blew about the room.

≈≈≈≈

Nate breathed a sigh of relief after passing over a short wooden drawbridge, spanning the width of a reed-choked spring. Although the bridge was heavily bracketed in iron holdings, it creaked and clanked loudly as they passed over its length.

From there, the roadway narrowed into a cobblestone entry, where pedestrians turned to stare at the newcomers. Nate drove the rest of the way on the road right up to the main gate, as the group stared in amazement at what appeared to be a medieval village before them.

Transfixed by their approach, peasants struggled to keep panicking beasts of burden calm as the crowds gathered beneath the archway entrance where a quaint wooden sign hung, reading, "Welcome to Levens." In tandem with the sign, a banner of golden wheat overlay in a sky-blue field flapped in the evening breeze from above the gate.

The same wheat sigils hung from both sides of the gate and from the parapets high above. The wall stood a good twenty feet high and surrounded the town with a guard box at the entrance. Most of the buildings inside had thatched roofs and the streets were paved in worn cobblestone.

The strangers' approach had certainly caused a stir, and villagers scrambled to get behind the walls as several of the guards moved to block the entrance, spears in hand.

"What is this, Shakespeare land?" Javier called out sarcastically. Everyone was too stunned to answer as Nate brought the Jeep to a stop at the guard box.

"I've heard of a Renaissance festival near Larkspur," Kevin started.

"We are clearly NOT in Larkspur, Micker," Javier exclaimed, breaking out into bitter, sardonic laughter. "This takes the definition of 'being lost' to a whole new level!"

"I just don't know what this place is," Johanna gasped, shaking her head in disbelief. "I've never seen anything like it!"

"Neither do I, but maybe they can help," Nate muttered, pointing to a cluster of guards donning light blue tunics over their chain mail and grey trousers. "Looks like their leader is coming to talk to us now."

A muscular young-looking guard with bright ginger hair stepped forth from the guard's hut near the gate. His rusty goatee accentuated his chiseled face and his green eyes flashed with youthful exuberance and curiosity. As he approached the driver's window, his face betrayed a later age, etched with lines and years of experience, previously hidden with greater distance.

"Strangers from a distant land, I presume," he offered in greeting with a slight Germanic accent. He placed a friendly hand atop the window frame and leaned in to inspect the vehicle, yet his eyes darted suspiciously to the passengers. He offered a disarming smile, yet he clearly noted details quickly as he scanned over the newcomers with a thorough and practiced review. "Welcome to Levens! You sure know how to make an entrance!"

"Thank you, sir, but I'm unsure as to how distant," Nate confessed. "Let's just start with that we're lost for the moment."

"Lost, eh?" The guard scoffed as he rubbed his neatly trimmed rusty beard. "So, you're not from Mondlichtberg? All sorts of surprises have been known to come from there. I must admit though, I've never seen anything like this before!"

"That's the second time I've heard of this Mondlichtberg, but I can assure you that we are not from there," Nate stated. "We're from Denver and are trying to get back there."

"Never heard of a 'Denver' before," the guard laughed before taking on a more serious tone, gripping the window to emphasize his next point. "Regardless of where you're from, I'd prefer you and your strange wagon clear this gate and come with me to answer a few questions. You're causing quite a disruption to our normal flow here."

"We can do that," Nate replied softly as he took notice of a small tattoo on the man's outer palm: a simple image clearly depicting a grain of wheat matching the banners flying high above. The guard smelled of the outdoors, not unclean, yet naturally raw as someone who had labored in the sun all day. "I appreciate your patience since we are new around here, but if you don't mind, I have a few questions of my own."

"Very well, enter, but let's move this discussion behind the guard house," the crimson-haired guard insisted as he pointed inside the fortification, just behind where his other men looked on. The guard's bravado regarding the vehicle seemed to encourage the other onlookers. A murmuring crowd had already emerged out of the gate to gawk at the vehicle. "Best make haste before the locals block your access!"

As Nate maneuvered the vehicle through the entrance and parked, they gained a clearer view up the cobblestone path leading to the top of the hill. The large stone fortress they had seen earlier loomed above the town, crowning the top of the hill. The fortress had a gate and wall of its own, nearly twelve feet high. It was a proud three-story octagonal monstrosity, parapets topped each corner, flying the Levens sigil that they had seen at the front gate. The bold structure stood out in stark contrast to the tight alleys, quaint village marketplace and sparsely placed thatched-roof homes surrounding it.

Only the lone solitary tower stood higher, even above the castle parapets. Notably separate, yet easily accessible to the side of the enormous keep, the narrow tower seemed precariously perched beside its larger squat counterpart. From its top waved a large green banner with a mountain backdrop with three stars and a moon above it.

"Where are my manners?" the guard interrupted their thoughts as his chiseled face broke into a wide grin. He greeted each of them as Nate turned the vehicle off and exited along with his companions. "Clearly you aren't from around here. Let's start over, shall we? I am Brenard, Captain of the Guard for the Royal House of Dade. You must excuse our curiosity, but we've never seen a beastless carriage such as yours. However, it is my duty to ask your business here at this late hour."

"As I said before, we're looking for a phone, a gas station. Maybe some lodging?" Nate explained. "You can see we clearly need it."

"I don't know anything about gas stations or phones, but I must admit to desiring to know your kingdom of origin," Captain Brenard sighed. "Your arrival at the main gate of Levens and our market plaza at this very late hour is quite unusual, but I'm willing to overlook it since my instincts tell me that you do not intend us ill will. You're still welcome to come in and trade, if commerce is your intention. There are several fine inns around the plaza that aren't too pricey and happily accept a variety of coinage from all kingdoms."

"Coins?" Nate scoffed. "Most of us barely carry cash anymore, but we all have credit cards."

"You may leave your carriage, or whatever this contraption is here, near the stables behind the gate," Brenard stated, staring uncomprehendingly back at him and shaking his head. "I don't know what you want to trade, but I would imagine your carriage would fetch quite a bit! I may make an offer for it myself if you aren't asking for too much!"

"It's not for sale, but we really could use some gasoline; we are nearly out of fuel," Nate stated before turning his attention back to the others. "We won't be able to make it anywhere else tonight before it gets dark. At least here, we can get some food, a bath and maybe a bed."

"You mentioned you had some questions for me," the gate captain mused again. "Is there anything I can answer for you?"

"I think we'll look around first and then come back once we have our bearings," Nate replied, deciding not to volunteer more information. "We'll check out this marketplace of yours and get back to you. If you don't mind, can you and your men watch over the vehicle?"

"We'll make sure no one molests it," the captain assured him. "You're causing quite a commotion, but we do welcome all to our marketplace!"

"Thanks," Nate grunted, expressing his forced gratitude through a clenched-teeth smile. The others nodded in agreement as he muttered under his breath, "Come on, let's see if we can find out where the hell we are!"

"Are any of you armed?" Brenard inquired softly to Nate as he escorted them to the plaza entrance. The captain of the guard arched a rusty eyebrow back at the group warily, careful not to be overheard, yet searching the newcomer's eyes for a reaction.

"Um, no," Nate said, distracted by all the noise but deciding to omit the guns he carried in the back of the Jeep along with their ammo. "Nothing to declare *on our persons*."

"Okay, we shall keep watch over your carriage," Captain Brenard assured him, motioning to the other guards to clear the curious onlookers away from the immediate proximity. "In the meantime, you and your people are welcome to enjoy the market."

"Guys, let's stick together!" Nate shouted to his companions exiting the Jeep over the growing cacophony surrounding them. He didn't need to remind them again. As the group approached the marketplace entry, people mulled about them, giving the group uneasy glances and murmuring about the "outsiders' strange clothing."

Daniel walked nervously between Javier and Kevin, his hands jammed deep into his hoodie pockets for warmth. As they passed beneath the hastily constructed wooden poles draped with canvas, the sights, sounds and smells of the marketplace pressed in around them. Vendors were selling boiling pots of stew, live animals milled about mingling with their human counterparts and thin smoke from the torches permeated the air from surrounding walls.

"It looks like we've stepped onto a movie set," Kevin commented in wonder. "This whole market is fenced in this courtyard of sorts?"

"Looks like it," Javier muttered, turning to address the curious onlookers. "Is there a hotel around here? Where can we find a phone? A police officer station? A doctor's office? Anything? Anyone? Maybe we should go back and look at another area in town."

Daniel snickered at the mob, who seemed unwilling to answer Javier yet fired back with questions of their own. "Where are you from?" "Are you witches?" "Did you come from the dragon?"

"This is exasperating; we don't have time for this!" Johanna breathed quietly to Nate. "Have you heard them all speak? They don't sound like anyone from Colorado! Is there no help to be found from anyone here?!"

"I'm doing the best I can, Johanna!" Nate looked around, nodding in greeting through a forced smile before throwing up his hands. "I'm in the same place and position as you! We just need to find someone else with answers; clearly, there's no one here who can help! This isn't much better than that farm back up the road!"

They had barely gone a few steps into the marketplace when commotion from the vehicle's alarm back at the Jeep caught their attention. Nate noticed that the guards and some merchants were running their hands along the vehicle. Just then, he caught sight of the hatchback opening, the reason for the SUV's blaring horn.

"I don't like this; let's get back to the Jeep," Nate stated, clicking the alarm off and motioning for them to return to the vehicle. The throng parted, and Captain Brenard stood at the back of the Jeep, holding one of the shotguns mid-way on the barrel. The guards were already rummaging through their suitcases and boxes. Nate took off running back to the Jeep, his companions hot on his heels. "Hey! Put those back and put that down!"

"Relax, stranger, we just want to know what it is!" the captain of the guard explained as Nate approached, red-faced and fuming. "What exactly is this?"

"I said, NO! Don't touch that!" Nate yelled, lumbering back toward the vehicle, Javier and Kevin right on his heels.

"What's the problem?" Brenard scoffed as he eyed Nate with renewed suspicion, still holding the shotgun at a precarious angle to his own head. "Are these not for sale also? You said you were here to trade, did you not? Are you up to something else we should know about?"

"Nothing!" Nate lied as he quickly gathered the items the captain had just so generously splayed for all to see in the back of the vehicle. "These are most definitely not for sale!"

"Then again, I must ask you: what are they, stranger?" Brenard growled menacingly, placing his hand on the hilt of his sword. All levity had fled the captain's face, and he fixated on the group with a renewed intensity of a serious glare. "What are you hiding from us?!"

"Thunder sticks!" Kevin broke in, arriving behind Nate. "They are for lighting fires, but we need them for our travels!"

Nate snatched the shotgun from the suspicious guard's hands and gently gathered the stash of guns back into the box, padlocking it shut. Slamming the hatchback into place, he locked it before squaring off with the captain.

"You seem mighty touchy about these 'thunder sticks'—maybe I should have you demonstrate one," Brenard persisted in challenge. "Something tells me you're not being completely forthright with us!"

"You know, we've been on the road for days now," Nate fumed, the dam behind his wall of patience beginning to crack. "Two from our group have been killed, and we have injured. I don't know what games you're playing here, but for the last time, we need a phone, gas, lodging and some assistance!"

Javier pushed painfully through the crowd to stand beside Nate and Kevin, squaring off with Brenard, and the other guards noticed the confrontation. One grabbed a crossbow and the others their spears and began sauntering over toward the Jeep, menacing in their approach.

"Out of my way! Out of my way!" An elderly man's breathless voice could be heard above the din. He yelled in a thick Slavic accent as the crowd parted for the hunched man dressed in white flowing robes, cursing and shuffling as he pushed to the forefront.

All eyes turned to the ancient man as he hobbled up to them, leaning heavily on a gnarled wooden staff. He gripped the pale pine walking stick tightly in his slightly withered hand. His skin resembled cracked leather, and his milky grey eyes scanned each of them, seeming to take in every detail quickly, missing nothing as he muttered to himself, as if only confirming suspicions he already knew the answers to. His white and wavy hair dropped to each side of his creased face, circling neatly around his shoulders and over his stooped form.

"May I present myself as Grand Master Nicholas, chief advisor to the royal family and kingdom of Levens," the elderly man stated grandly as he bowed. "My apologies for my tardiness, but the path to the main gate gets longer every time I walk it!"

"Grand Master," Captain Brenard announced as the captain bowed low in warm greeting, waving off the other guards. "My men and I were just welcoming these new strangers!"

"Captain Brenard," the grand master acknowledged with a twinkle in his eye. "I'll handle the strangers from here. They've come a long way and are in need of assistance, which I'm only too happy to provide. I'm familiar with their situation and will see personally to their needs from here!"

"Are you sure, Grand Master?" Captain Brenard protested. "They are certainly not from around here and may be dangerous..."

"I will advocate for them!" Grand Master Nicholas stated as much to all present as to the captain. "I will take full responsibility for them!"

"What about the Jeep?" Nate asked.

"Captain Brenard and his men will ensure that it will remain unmolested during your stay; they will not attempt to examine it further," the grand master assured him, nodding the directive to the guards. "You must forgive their inquisitiveness; they haven't seen anyone like you before nor the beastless carriage you arrived in!"

"As you wish, Grand Master." Brenard stepped aside and motioned his guards back. This seemed to placate the crowd, and the throng reluctantly began to withdraw. He turned and addressed Nate a final time before withdrawing. "You're in good hands with the Wizard of Levens!"

"Wizard?" Nate's brow wrinkled at the title. "What?"

"Never mind that! Such formalities and titles may be broached later!" the elderly man promised, addressing the newcomers and motioning them to his side. Pointing with a slight tremor to the castle at the top of the hill, he said, "Please, follow me; I will explain everything! You are to be guests of King Phillip and the Dade family of Levens! We want to hear all about your journey here. Come! Come!"

Nate turned back for a moment, took the keys back out of his pocket and for good measure, clicked the lock button. The Jeep beeped in response, causing the remaining crowd around it to gasp and jump, giving it a wider berth.

The newcomers followed Grand Master Nicholas up the cobblestone pathway, leaving the smoke and chaos of the marketplace behind. The crazed ambiance of the main gate soon faded into subtle yet musty scents of the aging stone and moss. The cool breeze wafted in gently around them as they ascended the easy grade towards the massive granite fortress at the top. Anyone they encountered seemed to show the elderly man respect, parting before him as he hobbled his way up the road.

"Your technology and odd appearance astound them," Grand Master Nicholas laughed aloud, his mannerisms seemingly oblivious to passerby stares even as he called attention to it. "I think it's best you minimize your displays though; word will travel swiftly through the land of your arrival. You may draw more attention to yourselves, indeed unwanted attention, even under my protection and advocacy."

"I'm not even sure where 'here' is!" Nate huffed as he strode heavily beside the old man. "I'm honored you would volunteer to guide us, but maybe we should at least start with some introductions!"

Nate began introducing the others as they walked. Even Sammy sniffed his hand and wagged her tail in approval after he patted her on the head. They kept pace with the old man for nearly fifteen minutes up the hill, passing quaint houses with alleyways. Along the way, they passed the vine-covered inner wall, made of rounder and older-appearing stone, more worn with time but nonetheless sturdy. As they pressed on toward the octagonal castle, the crowd from the market dispersed, replaced only by the occasional pedestrian or horse-drawn cart.

"It's a pleasure to meet you all!" Grand Master Nicholas stated, locking eyes with each one of them to ensure he had their attention. "I'm most pleased to advocate for you during your stay with us in Levens. I know that up until now, you have not received sensible information from the locals. There are not many people who can tell you where you are, but I am one who can."

"Great," Javier commented, smacking his lips impatiently. "Then tell us: where are we?"

"You have arrived in the kingdom of Levens, but you are no longer home as you know it. You are in a completely different world," Grand Master Nicholas elaborated quietly, gesturing with his hands as they continued up the cobblestone walkway. "In other words, wherever you and your strange beastless carriage came from, I can assure you that you are not there anymore."

"Now wait a second, a different world?" Johanna scoffed. "You can't be serious! We came through a lake, barely survived the trip down the pipe, and..."

"I'm quite serious, and you came through no pipe," the wizard stated abruptly, shaking his head. "Wherever you are from before, you came through a gateway we call the Shimmering to here. My dear

Johanna, it's not like a different world, it IS a different world; Levens and many other kingdoms like it exist in an entirely different world than the one you originated from!"

He let that sink in for good measure before continuing. Javier let out a snicker, but the look on Grand Master Nicholas's face told him the seriousness of the topic.

"I'm not jesting; it also took me quite a while to accept this when I first arrived. Your story is similar to how I came to be here, long ago," the wizard continued. "There's a tremendous amount of energy expended when such a thing occurs. We call it an off-world Shimmering event. That is how I knew someone had come to this world several days ago; I sensed your arrival."

"How exactly do you sense it?" Johanna pursed her lips, squinting skeptically as fresh lines of impatient doubt creased her face.

"For now, let's just say that I am able to do so," the older man stated gently. He paused briefly in the doorway, lowering his voice to a whisper. "I can sense differences in each of you apart from locals and others in my world. I sensed seven of you initially, days ago; where are the other two? Their presence faded when..."

"One died upon our arrival, and the other was taken by wolves," Johanna acknowledged quietly even as Javier and Kevin winced and looked away. "We were hoping to retrieve their bodies, but it doesn't look like that is a possibility."

"No, you are quite correct, I'm afraid. A painful affair, to be certain. I'm terribly sorry for your loss," the grand master sighed, deciding quickly to change the subject.

He turned back to the castle and motioned for them to follow to a large iron gate, leading into a courtyard at the castle's entrance. Narrow casement windows dotted the grey structure, glinting in the sunlight.

Two guards wearing the same faded blue tunics stood stoically in front of the ornate entrance, a great carved oaken door matching much of the granite trim design depicting farming life from around the region. They glanced up and nodded in acknowledgment but said nothing as the group collected themselves in front of a small stone fountain between them and the entrance.

"Some of you may have noticed that you are exhibiting certain abilities you didn't have before," Grand Master Nicholas stated carefully. "While you are safe in Levens, I would recommend that you refrain from using those abilities openly. Others beyond myself can also sense this, and I don't want to draw unwanted attention to you from the locals or otherwise."

"What are you talking about?" Javier laughed incredulously. "This is ridiculous! Can't you take us to a police station or something?! I've had enough of this game!"

"I'm sorry to say, young sir, but this is no game," the older man assured him, pausing sympathetically for a moment before continuing, nothing but the sound of the gentle trickle from the fountain tinkling in the background as he took a deep breath. "It may also help you to receive a change of clothes to better fit in with the locals. As you saw upon your arrival, they become easily agitated and upset by things they do not understand. Even accidental disruptions only exacerbate their anxiety and draw further unwanted attention to yourselves."

"How do you know all this?" Kevin finally blurted out.

"Because, my young friend, it is my trade to know such things," Grand Master Nicholas announced as he smiled knowingly. "Newcomers are blessed or cursed—depending on how they see it—with abilities that reflect their desires at the time they cross. This is the aspect of you all that I can currently sense; it's pouring around you even as we speak as a bright colorful glow, unseen by others yet clear as day to me. That insight is the gift I received upon my arrival, so many eons ago."

The newcomers glanced at one another skeptically even as he said it. Finally, Johanna cleared her throat before speaking.

"We barely know you!" Johanna scoffed. "How can you just expect us to trust you and take your word for it? Now we are to follow you around while you caretake us; what was the word you used, 'advocate,' for us?"

"You are correct, my dear! Trust is earned, not simply given," the grand master chided her gently. "Therefore, I intend for us to get to know each other better during your stay here as guests of the Dades here in their royal home!"

"I don't suppose we have much say in the matter," Nate stated with a feeble grin.

"I would agree with you in that your other options for the moment are quite limited," the wizard concurred, nodding soberly. "However, I promise that your options will become much clearer in due time! For now, I would simply ask that you only indulge in our hospitality!"

As they followed Nicholas and crossed the threshold into the keep, the guards nodded to the grand master in acknowledgment. The guards opened the great oak door with a loud creak and stepped aside, allowing them in. The elegant interior surprised them, warm and inviting, and almost the antithesis of the exterior of the fortress.

A small crackling fireplace warmed the entryway off to the side while a set of great tapestries lined the tall white plastered walls, lined with great support timbers. A double set of veined grey and pearl marble stairs led to the residences to either side. A great chandelier made from antlers swayed gently overhead, lighting the steeple-shaped entryway with a soft flickering light.

"Nicholas," Johanna interjected quietly, her voice echoing in the hallway's stillness. Still distracted along with her group in awe at the inner decorum of the high castle entry, it took a moment to continue while she grasped his arm. "How and when did you come to be here—and from where, exactly?"

"I won't bore you with all the details now, but I can see you're beginning to accept the truth of your circumstances," the elder wizard sighed. "If you really want to know, I suppose it could be somewhat relevant to your situation,"

"I believe it may be," she murmured. "Please, go on, tell us!"

"Well, I was but a young lad, living in the mountains in a poor farming community," the wizard began thoughtfully. "A man who posed as a merchant and tailor betrayed my village to barbarians. They ransacked my village and killed my family. It was actually he who chased me into a cave under a creek in the dead of winter. That's when I fell through a Shimmering and ended up here; quite tragic, really, now that I think about it."

Johanna shivered, briefly haunted by the mere thought of her premonition. Her eyes widened in recognition of the imagery from her counseling session before they left Denver flashed through her mind.

"I'd like to talk to you about that more a little later if you don't mind," she whispered softly, blushing lightly when the others in her company began to stare.

"I wouldn't mind at all," Grand Master Nicholas stated, somehow recognizing the far-off look in her eyes. Waving his hand in the air as if dismissing an errant thought, he addressed the rest of the group. "In fact, I really do need to talk to each of you about your journey here. Even though I sensed your coming from afar, your exact location or who you were wasn't clear to me until you arrived in town. Now that I have a clearer view of you, I'd love to hear about how things are back in your world now. But first, my friends, you look famished—so we shall dine!"

The grand master tapped his staff on the marble floor with a loud retort, and suddenly, servants in flowing sky-blue robes appeared from beneath the stairs. As the group congregated in the forum, a head servant stepped from the shadows, wearing a grey habit and looking somewhat like a middle-aged nun.

"My name is Charla," she stated, bowing her head stiffly for only a moment. She immediately returned her attention to the wizard and began reviewing the lodging arrangement with him, her keen grey eyes ablaze with purpose as she whispered orders to subordinates and moved about with a stern yet kind and subtle grace. "I will be handling your accommodations while you are guests of the Dades."

She turned and ordered the bustling staff, snapping her fingers to gain their attention yet never speaking unkindly as they hastily prepared two guest rooms for them.

The grand master waited patiently for the servants to disperse before addressing the newcomers awkwardly standing in the hall with their luggage and mouths agape.

"I realize you have a multitude of questions to which answers will be provided in time," he gently intoned. "For now, I request your patience be extended until you are appropriately settled. All will be answered in time. Please, make yourself comfortable, and we can eat. Nate, you and your wife and son may take your hound with you into the room closest to the door; it's much larger and suits your family. Javier and Kevin, you will share the one next to it."

"Um, Nate and I aren't..." Johanna began, shifting uncomfortably even as Nate seized her shoulder.

"Come now, sweetie! No need to bother the busy grand master with all the unimportant details of our relationship!" Nate stated boldly with a forced grin. "He's a very busy man with clearly a lot to deal with on our behalf!"

"Up the stairs now, all of you," Charla stated with a soft yet stern authority. "It's all been settled now, and we mustn't delay! Your current attire will be washed and returned to you. We have baths waiting for you down the hall and fresh apparel for you to change into! Mustn't keep the tailors waiting!"

The grand master appeared not to notice the interchange and Charla promptly ushered them up the stairs, showing them to their nearby rooms. He waited patiently in the lobby, taking a nearby seat upon a richly padded royal red bench beside the entryway fireplace.

Several tailors gathered the newcomers' clothing, exchanging robes until something could be fashioned for the group later in the day. It took well into the evening, but soon, each returned with a hastily assembled basic garb that had been provided for them to wear.

Johanna was the first to emerge from the room, wearing a cascading blue dress down to her ankles, her long dark hair tied neatly into a braided bun. Shutting the door quietly behind her, she stepped gingerly down the stairs and walked over to where Grand Master Nicholas sat.

"I feel silly wearing these, even if they are nice," she stammered as she stood before him.

"They are custom-made, and you wear them well," the elder wizard complimented her as he stood. "More importantly, however, they will help you to blend in. Wear them with pride and honor those who painstakingly made them for you!"

"I will certainly honor that effort!" she said, sitting beside him and clasping her hands together. "Nicholas, if you don't mind, I'd like to ask you a little bit about these abilities we may have while we wait for the others."

"They don't manifest themselves immediately, but they will increase in strength with time," the grand master whispered as he beckoned her closer. "We should be discreet about such conversations. Have you noticed anything in particular?"

"Not for myself," she said. "I'm a healer by trade, and I must confess that my companion's injuries were quite severe when we first arrived. I've been baffled with how quickly they've healed, and you would hardly know of their injuries by now."

"Pay close attention when you're in contact with someone in need of healing," the wizard advised. "We have a few healers in this world who heal through touch. If your power manifests itself in that way, you may feel or see it when it happens."

"There's something else," Johanna said. "Is it possible to have more than one ability?"

"It's extremely rare," the elder wizard spoke the admission in low tones. "Those who do are an exception, really, but also quite powerful. Their abilities tend to surpass others; why do you ask?"

"Because I think I also have premonitions," Johanna stated quickly before taking another deep breath. "It's something I've had since I was a child, although I never fully understood what I've seen. I normally wouldn't talk freely about this, but I feel this strange compulsion to share this with you. Unlike other people, I feel like you'd understand."

"I believe I would," the grand master stated thoughtfully as he nodded with a somber smile. "You may trust me with this, although I do understand your hesitation. I suspect it was this bit of information most of all you wish to speak to me about!"

"I think I was MEANT to meet you," she blurted out. "I saw the lake we came through before we even arrived at it. However, one premonition I had prior to our journey here made me think I was supposed to meet you and that you're who I need to talk to."

With that, Johanna told him everything—starting with her late husband Bill and the dreams she had leading up to the accident that killed him. She then told him about the dreams that followed before their accident at the lake, about the young Nicholas in the village. She spilled out every detail she could recall, telling him about the strange dreams that sometimes came true, even though they didn't always make sense.

When she had finished, Nicholas sat back heavily in thought on the cushioned bench in the hallway beneath the flickering chandelier.

"Well, well!" the wizard stated with finality. "It sounds as if you may have had this ability even prior to your arrival through the Shimmering. You may indeed be the rare exception for having two of these powers!"

"Are they premonitions, or am I just dreaming stuff up?" Johanna pressed, wondering if, like her psychiatrist, Nicholas would tell her that she was making too much of her dreams. "Am I just plain crazy?"

"You are not crazy, Johanna," Grand Master Nicholas stated as he looked her in the eye and smiled sadly. "The description of the dream you had before even arriving here is uncannily accurate and exactly what happened to me as a child. I never told you about the black shadow by the tree, yet you knew about it. It was a dark time in my past, but that shadow followed me to this world in the body of that man, the town tailor who betrayed my people. He followed me through the Shimmering and ultimately led a great war in the east, which I will tell you about another time. Needless to say, the conflict was won but at great cost."

"Doesn't that make it something other than a premonition?" she pressed excitedly, nodding thoughtfully with the realization that what he was telling her not only had been accurate, but it had also actually happened centuries ago. "It wasn't about the future—it was about the past. It was also about you, not myself or anyone I knew."

"Premonitions like these often tie us to others who are important to us in life," the wizard added as he placed a reassuring arm on her shoulder. "Your dream of the past was still a link to a future. Premonitions are seldom clearly laid out or identifiable. They are most like missing pieces to a puzzle that only come together after a time when other pieces fall into place."

"But what about..." she began.

"Patience, Johanna," Grand Master Nicholas reassured her. "The answers to your questions will come. You've all had a very traumatic journey to get here, and although I do sense an abnormal duality and large buildup of innate power coming from you, your friends are approaching. We will need to talk more about it later. Rest assured though, you are in good hands and all will be well!"

"I just have so many questions," she sighed in agreement, looking up to see Nate and Daniel leaving their room and approaching the landing just as Javier and Kevin opened their doors. "Are you sure you can't just..."

"You remind me of my student," the elder wizard laughed. "The king's daughter, who you'll meet later this evening. So many questions, so much tenacity. I'll convey to you what I tell her, though: the timing of our lessons is every bit as important as the content!"

Johanna turned to Nate and her son when they emerged from their room as they approached to stand beside her. She almost giggled as they looked like characters from a King Arthur play. Each had long loose grey or brown pants and leather boots along with an ill-fitting belt and a green or brown tunic. All freshly bathed and shaven, they retained glimmers of their former selves, anew with energy and exuberance.

"Is it me, really?" Nate held an exaggerated gesture, posing in the new clothing.

At this, Johanna could not help but giggle. Her first laughter in days brought a smile to Nate's face. Despite everything they had gone through, at least he could still amuse her. She quickly burst into laughter as another door flung open and Javier came stomping out of the room, a flustered Kevin on his heels.

"It's really not all that bad, Javier!" Kevin coaxed. "Come on, man, don't be so rude!"

"Rude is me having to wear this shit, Micker!" Javier exclaimed. "Get a load of this! You can wear whatever you want; I want my clothes back!"

"Wear your new attire proudly and with dignity!" Grand Master Nicholas quietly insisted, unamused at the comment. "You are guests here in Levens, and if I'm to advocate for you, a little appreciation would well be in order!"

Chapter 8

Dinner

The princess of Levens gazed out the open window of her bedroom across the courtyard and down to the whole of the kingdom splayed out before her. Silky jet-black hair spilled straight down her back, highlighting her porcelain face. Her piercing blue eyes skipped no detail on the horizon, yet her deliberations took in none of the scenery.

The strange thunderheads that had built earlier that afternoon appeared to dissipate and the promise of rain with them. Silence enveloped the evening with only the sighing breeze to cool the air for the coming night.

Deep in thought, the daughter of King Phillip and Queen Amora contemplated her reluctance to don her family's royal regalia hanging from her wardrobe for tonight's dinner. As her embroidery waited patiently for her in the corner of the room, she took in the last rays of the setting sun, descending gloriously over the Grenze Mountains to the west. *How I hate the preparation, all the fancy clothing required, not to mention all the responsibility that comes with it. How I wish to be out there...*

Princess Serina should have been a model for young womanhood and an example for all young ladies in all the northern kingdoms to follow. Yet, here she sat, wishing throughout the final moments of daylight for nothing more than her riding boots, rustic trail breeches and travel cloak. She glanced warily back at her wardrobe, where her formal dinner clothing awaited her, hoping it would vanish along with her royal responsibilities.

Recent whispers of outsiders around the castle grounds had her wondering what sorts of strangers required her participation in formal dinner tonight. Interesting travelers seemed a rare diversion here near the northern wilds unless they were wandering to the wizard's keep of Mondlichtberg.

Only a day's ride from Levens, a venture to the mountain castle of the Wizard's Order of the Moon seemed always beckon to her. Yet royal obligations kept such a venture out of reach, at least until recently.

This year had brought strange tidings from the wilds. The newcomers' emergence was only the most recent of many. Wolf pack attacks on the outlying farms, strange wars in the far-off lands to the east, and numerous storms over Long Lake gave an inexplicable uneasiness to this season's harvest.

It all seemed to add to her parents' worries when it came to her and her brother's upbringing as heirs to the throne of Levens. A grim smile crept across her face as she recalled her mother's initial revelation of her own powers as a young girl.

Once her abilities had surfaced, the queen had wanted to bury the scandal, yet it was her father, the king, who had allowed her to explore this uncovered peculiarity. The royal family sent for a discrete audience with Grand Master Yamaro, the head of the order.

The timing had been convenient for both the Grand Master Council of Three and the royal family of Levens. Since only three grand masters could rule the Order of the Moon's council at a time, a replacement for Grand Master Nicholas was already underway.

The outgoing grand master had been reluctant to fully retire, so he publicly took the role as advisor to the Royal House of Dade in Levens.

Normally a post well below his standing, this role also acted as a front and a subtle assignment as a private mentor to the princess and her newfound magical powers. The unique favor not only solidified the relationship between the Order of the Moon and its friendly neighboring kingdom, but the assignment also provided strength to the waning legitimacy of the ancient order through an upcoming new member, a princess and heir to the kingdom of Levens.

Where she acquired these inherited abilities, no one ever really knew. As a young girl, she expressed them in small ways: glowing rose bubbles floating through the air, moving items in a room with a glance, and occasionally breaking them during tantrums.

It certainly made for uncomfortable conversations, even in private quarters, and set her father and mother with opposing viewpoints against each other on what was best for her future.

The queen frequently expressed her viewpoint of magic as "unbefitting of a royal" many times and without subtlety. Her father, on the other hand, was curious and wanted to learn more about the situation without passing judgment. He overrode the queen's plans for the princess's future, exacerbating the already awkward situation between them.

To aggravate the situation further, Grand Master Nicholas seemed like a stranger to the royal court and bewildered the queen as to why Grand Master Yamaro himself did not represent the order directly.

As time passed and Princess Serina grew into the young woman she was today, her relationship with the retired grand master grew with it. The queen's objections subsided over time as the retired wizard regaled the court with his fantastic tales of how he had come to this world as a boy. His origins of being an orphan himself eventually gained the matriarch's sympathies and put her at ease.

Everything in Princess Serina's life seemed to be placed on hold until a resolution between being a royal or a magician could be found. Her family's expectations of her and herself remained an irresolvable enigma. Although the sting of her private battle within herself faded with time, it remained a persistent and nagging pain of disappointment and unresolved anxiety within her to this very day.

"Innate power does come from outsiders like me, but it also may be inherited through family lineage," Grand Master Nicholas had reminded her once, the soft echo of his wise yet stern voice wafting gently in its Slavic tone through her memory. "Regardless of where it came from, it originates inside yourself and is a part of you. Know yourself, and you will come to know the innate nature of your power."

Her daydreaming and reflections were suddenly interrupted by a peculiar snuffing sound at the door as the last rays of sunset beamed into the room. The princess walked over to her chamber's door, listening as the sound intensified. *What was that?!*

As she opened the door, a shorthaired black hound with a white spot on its head greeted her with a wagging tail.

"Well, hello there!" Princess Serina patted the happy canine on the head with a smile. "What are you doing up here, and who do you belong to?"

"Nate! Nate Livingston!" the hound woofed back to her. "I'm Sammy!!"

"A talking dog?!" Princess Serina laughed in surprise, stumbling back as the hound panted, happily mistaking the princess's shock as an invitation to enter. "Will wonders never cease? My goodness! Where did you come from?"

"We came in Jeep," Sammy whined, pointing her snout down the hallway. "Where is Nate?!"

"Well, I don't know where or what 'Jeep' is, but I suppose that answers my question about whether the dinner guests will be of interest or not, assuming you are with them," the princess laughed again, patting her leg and striding down the hallway. "Come, let's find your people!"

Sammy panted happily as she padded after the princess down the torch-lit hall. The sound of their approach broadened as they came to the throne room, spreading out before them in a grand display. Their footfalls echoed quietly in the vacant chamber as the pair strode beneath the unlit iron chandeliers. Atop a single podium of marble sat the two empty thrones for the king and queen, casting phantom shadows on the wall. Their giant marble forms reflected the moonlight now permeating the room through massive and partially opened stained glass windows.

The hound sniffed at the suits of plate-mail armor that lined the dimly lit stonewalls between which hung faint tapestries, billowing occasionally from the gentle evening breezes wafting through the halls.

"Come on, girl," Princess Serina called to the dog, patting her side. "Stay with me; the guest quarters are downstairs, and your people..."

"Well, hullo, Sammy!" A young man's voice startled Princess Serina from the staircase below. An attractively statured tall young man ascended into the throne room, grinning as he ascended the stone steps. His blue eyes flashed mischievously in the torchlight as he pushed back his short dark hair with a confident swagger. He fixated her with a ravishing stare, a broad smile spreading across his face. "Who is this gorgeous beauty you have found?"

"I believe Sammy may belong to you?" Princess Serina arched an eyebrow as she greeted the lad.

"Oh, yes, we were looking for our dog, and it seems you found her, thanks!" he stated as he approached, his gait certainly not from someone from the region. The handsome stranger asserted himself, extending his hand. "Hi, I'm Javier, Javier Billings."

Taking a step back, Princess Serina balked at the forward approach of this man she'd never met before, particularly in her own home. The awkward moment was brief as she stared at his outstretched hand before her own wit and curiosity took over. *Is this one of the newcomers? Clearly this person with a strange accent is not from around here since he has no clue of proper etiquette and protocol.*

"Hello," she replied, extending her hand in return with a sly grin of her own; *I'll play along and see where it leads.* "My name is Serina. Sammy claims to be with someone you know, perhaps a 'Nate Livingston'?"

"Why yes, she is," he laughed, unwilling to release her hand as he pressed his unrepentant flirt. "We came from far away and are having dinner with the royal family tonight. Apparently, we're the talk of the town! Let me be the first of our group to say, I'm VERY pleased to meet you!"

"The pleasure is all mine," Princess Serina intoned as she smiled, doing her best not to burst into laughter as she wrestled her hand free. "Pleased to meet your acquaintance too, um, Javier!" *Is he flirting?! He keeps playing with his hair!*

"So, what do you do around here for fun?" Javier pressed. "If you don't mind me saying so, you're the prettiest thing I've seen since I got here. If you want to catch up when we're done with dinner, I could meet you back here. The royals here seem a bit stiff if you ask me, but I bet you could show me where the real fun is!"

"Javier, I don't know if anyone's told you or not, but that would hardly be appropriate," the princess scoffed. Unable to contain herself any further, she choked off a giggle as she met his gaze. "Our meeting at night under their roof would not be respectable!"

"Oh, yes, protocol!" he conceded, grinning with a wink. "We can play along, and then…"

"There's no playing along, it's the rules of the house," she gently chastised, locking eyes with him while expressing a squinting frown of disapproval.

"Sorry, I didn't mean to offend you." Javier deflated quickly, a bit disappointed. "Honestly, we've been lost for days and have gone through a lot. I-I-I'm mainly just looking for someone to talk to. We could meet outside the castle if you'd like?"

"Meeting in secret?" the princess laughed aloud, smiling disarmingly again to keep the entertaining flirt alive, feigning a swoon. "No offense taken, Javier. However, I hardly believe that would be appropriate either. I'm sure we'll see each other at dinner tonight, and we can catch up then."

"You'll be there at dinner tonight with the royal family?" Javier brightened as he took hold of Sammy's collar. "Do you know the Dades? Are you a guest of theirs here also?"

"You could say that!" Princess Serina replied. She turned to leave but called over her shoulder with a grin of her own. "I look forward to our next encounter, Javier!"

She laughed as she closed her door. For the first time in many years, she rushed back to change into her royal clothing, eager to engage in further game-playing with the newcomers. *This is going to be fun!*

≈≈≈≈

That night, the royal dining hall bustled with guests around a long oak table at the center as servants tended busily to the throng. A massive iron chandelier hung ominously above as a roaring fire in the stone fireplace blasted heat and light throughout the enormous chamber. The scent of roasted pig and a parade of freshly steamed vegetables permeated the room along with laughter and the murmur of conversation even as a minstrel strummed a guitar, quietly singing a melodious tune in the background. Even Sammy lay contently at Daniel's feet, the invited hound quietly gnawing on a dinner bone.

The king of Levens stood up from his chair at the head of the table, appearing tall and muscular with his blazing golden crown reflecting the firelight, flaring as if the very flames themselves were upon his salt-and-pepper hair. Nevertheless, his charm betrayed nothing of aging, exuding a timeless grace with a hint of mirth.

"Grand Master Nicholas! Guests from near and far!" King Phillip announced, holding forth his goblet to all who had been invited. Nearly fifty local lords and ladies of nearby farms and estates filled the room, all lining the long table for the feast that night. "We welcome those who come through Levens from a far-off land!"

"Hear! Hear!" the voices echoed back from the court, the servants and the royal family all present.

"We Dades have led a free Levens kingdom for hundreds of years," King Phillip spoke proudly as he turned to the newcomer guests. "Grand Master Nicholas has informed me that he is officially your Advocate during your stay with us. We welcome you to our kingdom!

Levens is the crossroads for the people of the north, hunters, farmers and fur traders. We are the breadbasket for the west! It is at this table we are proud to share our bounty with you!"

"Thank you, Your Majesty!" Nate stood briefly, quickly assuming the speaking role for the group as he held his chalice forth. "We greatly appreciate your hospitality, although, I must admit, we are still quite disoriented as to where we are and how we got here."

"Yes, I can imagine," King Phillip acknowledged as he smiled, nodding to the wizard standing beside him at the table, donned in white regal robes of his own. "Grand Master Nicholas has also informed me of your predicament. Let me assure you that while you are under his protection, you are welcomed and in good hands here in Levens as our guests. May you consider it your home for as long as you desire."

"Thank you, Your Majesties!" Nate acknowledged. "Please allow me to introduce my companions."

Nate began, nodding to each person and introducing all who had arrived with him in the Jeep before sitting again. Each stood in turn, nodding politely to all strangers present at the table.

"Please allow me to formally present my family as well," the king intoned in reply as he turned to each of them at the table. The monarch gestured as each stood in turn, nodding from their stations, starting from the head of the table. "Queen Amora Vianna-Dade, our son, Prince Griffon, and our daughter, Princess Serina."

"Holy shit!" Javier mouthed to himself as he blushed. Princess Serina lifted a napkin to her lips to hide her grin. All he could do was turn his crimson face away.

"What's wrong?!" Kevin whispered, kicking Javier under the table.

"Nothing, Micker!" Javier snapped with a hoarse whisper of his own. "I'll tell you later!"

Ignoring the brief kerfuffle that had played across the table with the newcomers, Queen Amora watched her daughter beside her and smiled. Her doll-like features rarely creased beneath the silver crown through which her greying hair gently interlaced. Her features remained smooth, soft and supple, with an uncanny resemblance to her daughter. Her icy blue eyes matched her dress, and her smile had motherly warmth to it. She waited patiently for her husband's introductions to finish before speaking herself.

"Welcome to Levens," the queen greeted in a voice like sweet honey. "Grand Master Nicholas has informed us that you are from his home world, albeit his arrival was long ago. Such occurrences are rare, but they do indeed happen. Please excuse our curiosity as this is an unusual occurrence indeed."

"Thank you again, Your Highnesses," Nate stated as he stood again, briefly acknowledging each one with his goblet. "Your hospitality is most appreciated, and your curiosity is not only understood but also matched by our own."

With the brief toast given, the levity that had punctuated the room before their arrival continued. The fire crackled as laughter and voices echoed joyfully throughout the hall.

Princess Serina could scarcely contain her mirth. Dressed in all her finery, Javier could do little more than offer quick glances from across the table, gawking at her uncomfortably and in embarrassment. She laughed and played it all off as nothing more than a secret shared between the two of them, but he remained mortified, having said nothing since taking his seat in the dining hall.

Only when introductions had concluded and the feast had been served did he summon the courage to speak directly to her as more private conversations ensued around the table.

"Your Highness," Javier began in a mutter, leaning over the table to whisper, his face red and beaded with sweat from the strain and memory of their earlier encounter. "I wanted to apologize for earlier. I clearly had no idea..."

"Think nothing of it," she whispered kindly, winking as she sipped her wine. "Let that be a lesson to you though, about wandering the castle. You never know who or what you may run into! You may also find that lesson useful should you decide to travel outside our lands; the neighboring kingdoms may not be as understanding or forgiving as ours."

The princess toyed with the idea of driving his earlier infraction of protocol further with him this evening, yet his shame seemed to already get the better of him. He seemed unable to respond further, just turning brighter red by the moment and content to sit back in his chair and sip at his goblet.

Queen Amora glanced at her daughter as she noticed the familiarity with which her daughter engaged the newcomer. She eyed their conversation with a mix of disapproval yet measured interest as her daughter seemed to skillfully set him right privately without openly embarrassing their guests.

"Your Majesty," Johanna queried as she gently broke the moment, catching the queen's attention. "I was hoping you may have a doctor or a healer of some kind with some medical supplies for my companions. We've gone through quite a bit recently, and I have only a limited supply of first aid items with me."

"I would be happy to oblige, my dear," the queen replied. "I will send our healer after dinner to your quarters if you would like!"

"I am actually a healer of a kind myself," Johanna stated. "Perhaps your healer has access to local herbs and sterile tools?"

"Sterile?" the queen asked, puzzled at the mention of the word. "Are you unable to bear more children?"

"Oh, I'm fine," Johanna clarified, stifling back a chuckle. "In my own world, we cleanse the tools we use on the body to minimize risk of infection or corruption to the patient's wound site."

The queen seemed very interested in what Johanna had to say about medicine, and their conversation continued as Johanna explained some of the nuances of medical application.

In the meantime, Nate carried on a conversation with King Phillip, who appeared fascinated by the technological advances made in the newcomers' world.

"I noticed you haven't said very much since you arrived," Princess Serina said as she pivoted her attention to Daniel. "Are you shy?"

"I'm not shy!" Daniel sat upright as if struck with the sudden attention. His brown eyes glazed in anticipation as he held half a mouthful of food on his fork. His stunned look elicited laughter from the princess as she gently coaxed him out of his state. "My mouth is just full..."

"You're not being interrogated, my young friend," she laughed. "I only wish to know more of where you come from!"

"Talk about being put on the spot!" Daniel retorted before turning to face the princess, mustering his courage to speak. "The food here is good, and I thank you and your family for taking us in. I must admit, though...I'm just a bit lost in all this. I can't figure out if we went back in time or are just somewhere else completely!"

"From what little I know, it's less of a time travel and more a location change," Princess Serina offered. "Grand Master Nicholas will explain more, but he went through something similar when he was young; he came long ago the same way you did."

"In a car?" Daniel arched an eyebrow, his voice drifting off to a mutter as he took another bite from his dinner plate. "He doesn't seem like the type..."

"I don't know what a car is. Please explain," Princess Serina pressed, her azure eyes sparkling in the firelight with curiosity. "Does everyone where you're from have a beastless carriage such as the one you arrived in?"

"Well, not everybody," Daniel admitted. Seeing the sincerity behind the princess's questions, he sat upright, clearing his throat and speaking with greater confidence. "Where I'm from, there are just more things built with science. You know, like the vehicle we came in, airplanes that can fly and take people hundreds, even thousands of miles across oceans and mountains."

"It sounds amazing," the princess encouraged. "Tell me more, please!"

"Well, we cook with something called a microwave oven—it runs off of electricity... errrr, lightning that we pipe into houses. It lets us cook food without fire," he stated even as the princess blinked with a smile still on her face. Fishing through his pocket, he pulled forth his cell phone. "When we're back in our world, this will work, but it won't here. It has to be able to talk to the others just like it."

"I'm sorry to say, dear Daniel, but it all certainly sounded like magic to me!" Princess Serina soothed. "I truly find this all very fascinating! Maybe one day you'll tell me how it works! Piped lightning; that's amazing!"

"I suppose that is rather amazing, now that I think about it!" Daniel admitted. "Come to think of it, Nate may know more about that than me. There's lots in our world that works when most of us really don't know everything about it all."

With newfound trust and excitement, he went on to explain the circuitry, the networks and the batteries. None of it made any sense to her, but she nodded continuously as he spoke, gaining his trust and admiration with each passing moment. As he opened himself to the conversation with the princess, his speech flowed, becoming a testament to how happy he was to be speaking with her.

Simultaneously, as Daniel spoke, Princess Serina found the boy tapping into a feeling she yearned for herself—a feeling of belonging. For him, his arrival into this world would be like getting a second chance to begin again—a new life and a new chance to prove his worth. *How I envy him!*

Prince Griffon mused over the bunch, looking like a lanky yet athletic version of his father. He grinned broadly when he noticed Javier attempting to regain his sister's recent attention from Daniel. *The frustration this newcomer must be feeling to have a younger lad beating him out for the princess's attention!*

"Are you of royal blood, Javier? I can't have you chasing my sister if you're not!" the prince warned. Kevin laughed as his former rival stammered in feigned confusion, quickly turning to relief as the prince sauntered over to him, laughing as he clapped him on the back. "It's okay, my strange suitor! It seems like she's taken an interest in your younger sibling!"

"We're not related," Javier exhaled. "I am surprised, though. She seems to be going for Danny Boy over me. I have to say, my luck is not with me tonight."

"Fret not over it!" Prince Griffon laughed again. "My sister's not taking on suitors; not now, anyway. I suppose Father will eventually force her to marry a lord from Urocia or one of the united houses of the Southern Kingdoms, but who knows, maybe someone at this table. She may spurn them all and run off with a stranger, for all I know. Worse yet, she may join up with Grand Master Nicholas's wizard's order. Regardless, I am certain to marry before she does."

"A whole wizard's order?" Kevin tilted his head into the conversation. "Do you think they could help us get home?"

"If anyone can, they can; although, frankly, you're in the best hands possible with Grand Master Nicholas. He was once the head grand master there at ol' Mondlichtberg!" Prince Griffon confirmed as he casually pulled up another chair, taking a long draught from his goblet. "Their order is rather secretive, but they're always looking for new recruits. I'm sure since my sister discovered her powers, she would love to join them but for Mother."

"Your sister has powers?" Kevin asked. "Like us? Ever since we became lost here, we seem to have developed some unique abilities, although we can barely control them!"

"Oh, yes, she had that issue too at a young age. Thankfully, that burden seems to have skipped me!" Prince Griffon recalled. "I leave that confusion and controversy to my sister. I've been told it's a rare blessing, coming only to an outsider from our world or inherited through generations, but it seems to have skipped me, making my life much simpler."

Javier started to ask more, but the crimson-haired captain of the guard from earlier at the gate stepped into the room, catching Prince Griffon's eye.

"Captain Brenard, come over here!" the prince called, waving the captain of the guard over to pull up a chair. "Join us!"

"Sorry about giving you newcomers problems earlier," the captain of the guard proclaimed as he complied, seizing a mug of ale from one of the server trays and toasting the others with his tattooed hand. "Hope you don't take it personally—strange folks, strange times...we never can be too careful."

"Ahhhh, never mind that," Prince Griffon laughed, welcoming Brenard into the mix, clapping him on the back. "Let us toast to your diligence!"

"Don't mind if I do," Captain Brenard exhaled as he settled beside them. "More reports of the Northern Guardian torching the settlements up north. It's no wonder the wolves are getting feisty with the fire-breather chasing them out of the wilds!"

"What's a Northern Guardian?" Kevin asked.

"Eh, you'd know it if you saw it," Brenard growled as he squinted. "Big fire-breathing dragon, that one is!"

"A fire-breathing WHAT?!?" Nate exclaimed. The newcomers exchanged several glances between them even as Johanna stood, bursting into laughter.

"I'm sorry!" Johanna exclaimed as she sat, dabbing her eyes with a cloth napkin. "I've barely begun to accept that we're in some sort of time warp or alternate dimension. Now you're telling me there's fire-breathing dragons?!"

"Yeah, I'm with her on this one," Javier muttered as he rolled his eyes. Glancing about the room, he craned his neck in exaggerated movements. "I keep waiting for the TV cameras to come out of the walls and tell us we're on some hidden camera prank show!"

"It's no joke," Grand Master Nicholas intoned as he stood, garnering the attention in the hall, and the entire group fell silent. Only the crackling of the fire could be heard for long moments as a tense seriousness seemed to settle about the room like a cold, wet blanket. "I apologize if this is a shock to you, but the sooner you accept what has happened, the better off you will all be. It's as much for our safety as it is yours. Let's start with the very real and present danger of the Northern Guardian; you were most lucky to avoid it!"

"Do you suppose that's what we saw flying past the moon when we first arrived?" Kevin wondered aloud, speaking up to be heard by all. "I mean, it did seem awfully large and..."

"Micker! It was the middle of the night!" Javier snorted. "How would you know—"

"No, no, no," the captain of the guard interrupted gently. "Don't be too hasty to discount your friend's story. Based on where you emerged from the mountain passes, it's entirely possible!"

Not even sure if they believed him, Kevin and Javier glanced at each other before Prince Griffon launched into a litany of questions, sidelining the topic. It was as if they had stumbled onto a topic no one had wanted to talk about. Reluctantly, they let it go as the more casual conversations resumed.

The prince and captain of the guard seemed more fascinated about their lives prior to their arrival. Under the onslaught of questioning, they could scarcely keep up with the conversation before the next point of curiosity was launched into the fray.

Servants continued to drift in and out of the room as the evening wore on, bringing more fare to the table, and they ate to their hearts' content. The outsiders politely acknowledged the other ladies and lords at the table who occasionally aimed questions at the new strangers. As the hours stretched on, many of the locals began filtering out of the festivities one by one, retiring for the evening.

The ambiance of the evening began to wind down as the wax from the candles diminished and the fire in the hearth simmered. When most of the evening guests had left and only a few remained, King Phillip finally stood to propose a final quiet toast to the newcomers still present.

"Before we close out this evening's festivities, I wanted to ensure you all will be comfortable here in Levens," the king began. "You are my guests for as long as you see fit. I do want to encourage you to stay here with us though, before wandering out into the neighboring countryside."

"Yeah, wouldn't want to run into that Northern Guardian fire-breathing dragon, right?" Kevin pressed.

"There's that, but others," the king stated. You must forgive my people's reluctance to talk about it further; they become superstitious when faced with the unknown. However, there are many pitfalls locally and still many others abroad. Grand Master Nicholas will brief you all on the 'morrow before you decide to venture beyond our borders."

"IF you should decide to leave." Queen Amora raised her glass. "After all, we do have much to offer you here in Levens; frankly, much more than our neighboring realms. You may yet decide to make our kingdom your home!"

"Thank you, Your Majesties! We are most humbled by your gracious hospitality," Johanna said. "I truly admit to difficulty in accepting all this, however, if what has been stated tonight is true, I'm hoping that someone may be able to tell us how we got here in the first place. More importantly, I'm hoping they'll be able to tell us how to return."

"Johanna, my dear," Grand Master Nicholas interjected softly. "The Shimmerings between worlds is a rare occurrence, a fluke, really. I'm not saying this to dash your hopes, but at the same time, I do not wish to foster false ones. Although I am quite content here now, it was not always so. I must say my initial quests to return home were abandoned long ago and forgotten."

"I'm sorry, I had assumed you had chosen to stay..." Johanna nearly stood in alarm—the thought had never occurred to her that they might not be able to get back. Nate grasped her hand in reassurance but seemed to share her concern, even as she blurted out the rest. "I mean, you're a wizard and all; you don't know of a way back?"

"She's right; why can't it occur in reverse?" Javier asked. "Doesn't anyone ever go to another world like ours?"

"The instances of crossovers are so random and uncommon that we never found a way to produce or replicate such Shimmerings; they appear to be natural yet rarely observed phenomena," the wizard stated. "If someone or something from our world went to yours, we would be unaware of the result since they would likely be marooned there as well. From your perspective, the individual may appear mad or as a wanderer."

"Unless it was an animal or creature," Prince Griffon added.

"You mean like the Loch Ness monster, Bigfoot, or the Abominable Snowman," Kevin threw in hopefully. "Or maybe certain ghosts or phantoms."

"Perhaps," Grand Master Nicholas muttered thoughtfully. "I can only offer conjecture in that regard, but what you propose seems highly likely. In any case, our order has studied the phenomenon for centuries yet still knows very little about it."

The grand master's proclamation seemed to unsettle the newcomers, so King Phillip cleared his throat to bring the evening's conversation to a comfortable close as he sought to bring some clarity and comfort to Johanna.

"We hope you and your husband could be happy here with us in Levens," the king began. "If not, we want you to know that you're always welcome here. Above all, you should know you're among friends."

"Oh, Nate and I? We're not married." Johanna didn't know what else to say as she sank back into her chair in shock. "We're close family friends; have been so for many years." *What about my life? My job? What about Daniel? What about dreams for the future? What will happen to my house and mortgage?*

Nate threw her a dirty look but said nothing. He noticed immediately that the marital revelation came as a surprise that cast an awkward silence over the table. The servant staff and the royals exchanged glances, yet Johanna seemed preoccupied with something else.

Without missing a beat, Queen Amora rang a tiny bell near her place at the table. A small servant boy responded immediately, racing up alongside the table to attend to her. She discreetly whispered something into his ear, and he promptly left without another thought.

"I will assist the best I can in this matter, and if I find a way back, you will be the first to know," Grand Master Nicholas intoned after clearing his throat, drawing attention back to himself after the brief distraction. "I will say this, though, that such a venture will not be found readily or easily. Even if I found such a way, I would personally never choose to leave. The Dades of Levens have made a most satisfying home for me here."

"We are not a large kingdom, but we are proud," Queen Amora concluded. "We offer you our home and hearth and hope you consider our offer with utmost care."

"I meant no offense," Johanna stated glumly. "You obviously have accomplished a great deal here. I'm just unaccustomed to not having a choice to go home, I suppose."

"None taken, my dear." Queen Amora nodded pleasantly. "The technology of your world sounds impressive, but I am confident you will find opportunity in our world equally inspiring, if given a chance."

"Are we *allowed* to leave?" Javier shifted in his seat uncomfortably.

"Certainly! You are no prisoner here!" King Phillip proclaimed with a laugh. "What we are saying is that it is highly inadvisable to leave at this time. There's a war between the empire of Urocia and the inhabitants of a cursed land to the east. To our west, the mountains are wild and untamed; a great many beasts wander there and to our north, especially since the Northern Guardian began hunting the skies closer to Levens, driving them forth. To our south, people are very suspicious of outsiders and not entirely welcoming."

"Sounds like we were lucky to arrive in one piece," Johanna muttered, feeling the weight of the situation upon her as fresh lines of worry etched her face. "Makes me wonder what lies ahead for us."

"My point is, you are fortunate in arriving here first, so we may help you to avoid these pitfalls," the king continued to encourage. "Despite his retirement, you can count on the grand master and his order to get to the bottom of this. If there is a way to return you to your home, rest assured every effort will be made."

"Well, if we're going to be here a while, I want to thank Your Royal Highness for the generous and warm hospitality you have shown us." Nate stood and toasted the king and his family again, noting Johanna's shock, still plastered clearly on her face. "I know I speak for myself and my companions when I say I appreciate and am indebted to everything you have done and have offered us."

Princess Serina observed intently through her smiles and pleasantries as Johanna withdrew subtly, the newcomer's countenance fading into a somber silence of self-reflection at their new reality. As the meal continued late into the night, the princess's attention wandered to the others. The new guests held a strange fascination with their mannerisms, the way they spoke, their accents and their unique informality. When the servants cleared the main course, goblets of wine and ale flowed alongside freshly made pie, and the guests seemed particularly elated at the sight, eager to dive into the fare.

As the evening finally ended, the remaining local guests departed, and the king and queen excused themselves to their private quarters. Princess Serina and Prince Griffon remained to entertain their guests alongside Captain Brenard into the wee hours of the night. By this time, the roaring fire in the fireplace had died down to glowing red coals, and even the staff departed, leaving only the head servant to tend to the remaining party.

"Well, it's been a pleasure, but it's getting late!" Grand Master Nicholas finally announced. With that, he grasped his gnarled staff and hobbled off into the darkened hallway. "I'm retiring for the evening, as should you all. We will speak more about your situation in the morning."

Princess Serina was about to say something further when she noticed Charla approaching Johanna and placing a hand on her shoulder to gain her attention. She bit her lip in anticipation. *The royal family's head housekeeper is known for tidiness, not her personality.*

"Ma'am," Charla cleared her throat politely to Johanna, accompanied by a brief curtsey. "I am head housekeeper, Charla. We apologize for the mistake earlier and meant no disrespect to your integrity. Please follow us to more private accommodations."

"Oh, I'm fine..." Johanna's face dropped.

"Nothing doing!" Charla insisted, gently but firmly directing

Johanna down the hall by the arm. "We won't have your honor insulted. I've already taken the liberty of moving your belongings!"

"What? My honor is fine," Johanna insisted. "Nate and I—wait, what about my things?"

"We're not married, remember?" Nate cut her off with a whisper, not wanting to cause an issue with their hosts. "Just go with her."

"At least let me take Sammy," Johanna protested.

"The hound may accompany you to your room," the housekeeper stated with finality. Sammy trotted up beside Johanna, and they vanished down the hallway, Charla's voice still clearly echoing back to them. "As I've already stated, we've moved your items to your private quarters. You'll be well tended to, not to worry, mum!"

Javier and Kevin followed, sauntering in a drunken stupor back to their room, waving a friendly goodnight as they went.

"What was that all about?" Daniel asked.

"I'm so sorry," Princess Serina explained. "I know you are all from another world and have different customs, but Charla does keep a tight ship around here."

"The princess is correct," Brenard reiterated. "I am not aware of your customs, but the royals would never have unmarried guests sharing quarters. It would insult the guest's honor as well as the host's."

"I figured as such," Nate sighed. "I just wish she had understood that before making fools out of us during dinner. You people have been nothing but welcoming, and we don't wish to insult you."

"You're newcomers—it's understandable," the captain of the guard stated as he clasped Nate's arm. "These are minor points that we will all work out in time, lending even more weight to the queen's proposal for you to stay as guests in Levens for a time!"

"Point well taken," Nate sighed. "This is a minor issue, but I'm sure there are other potential ones with more far-reaching consequences."

"Exactly!" Brenard took another swig. "If your courtship with Johanna goes well, you will be married soon, and all of this will be forgotten. I'd be happy to guide you locally as you gain knowledge of our customs. There truly are far worse dangers out there beyond simple misunderstandings and insults of cultural differences that you are unaware of, and we can help you identify those too. Well, if there's nothing else, I suppose I'll be turning in as well."

Brenard began to turn before Nate stopped him.

"We ran into one of those dangers you mentioned when we first arrived. A pack of wolves attacked us and killed one in our group," Nate volunteered cautiously. "I was wondering if there were any diseases we should be concerned about, like rabies or something along those lines. I have to admit, I've never seen such large wolves before."

"They do grow quite large in these parts; I've never heard of anything called 'rabies,' but most wild animals with any disease fall as prey fairly quickly," Brenard stated as a new nervous anxiety reflected in his eyes along with the flickering torchlight. He turned to square off with Nate, his face serious again as he asked his question. "I must know if any of you were bitten during the altercation?"

"No, we managed to drive them back," Nate affirmed; he worried that maybe he inadvertently admitted too much already, given the intensity of the captain's inquiry. "To be clear, none of us were bitten."

"What a relief! How exactly did you drive them off, though?" Brenard pressed as he blinked. His nervousness gone, it was suddenly replaced with an intense scrutiny, searching for truth. "The wolves of the north are not known for their timidity."

"We had a large fire," Nate tried, to which Brenard eyed him with a suspicious grin.

"Nate, you may have many talents, but lying isn't one of them," the captain of the guard offered the friendly warning. "Come, tell me. You're among friends now."

"You'll have to trust someone at some point," Prince Griffon prodded. "Come on; start with us!"

"Fine," Nate breathed as his face reddened. "I retain a small cache of weapons we call guns in the back of the Jeep. I believe Kevin called them 'thunder sticks' earlier."

"I knew it!" Brenard clapped him on the back. "I understand your reluctance, but promise me you'll demonstrate one to me! I swear you may keep them, but I would very much like to see them in operation!"

"If it is allowed and we have time, I will." Nate grinned back. "In the meantime, I trust you'll keep them and the Jeep safe. They won't do harm as long as they aren't disturbed, but without proper training and handling, they could be dangerous, even to the handler."

"It is my pleasure! Your belongings will remain unmolested. When this is over, I'm still hoping you'll sell me your beastless carriage!" Brenard insisted before quickly following up. "You're sure none of you were bitten by any of the wolves?"

"Quite sure; although it was a close call, all present emerged unscathed, all except Becky, who was sadly killed in the altercation," Nate recalled glumly. "The other boys had another person with them— Tim, I think was his name—but he died when we arrived through the Shimmering. Wolves got to him almost immediately. Why do you ask?"

"Well, we have something called Grimmigwulf that roams the wilds," Benard stated, lowering his voice to a whisper. As his voice faded, the entire room seemed to go silent as the flames from the dying fire flickered in his eyes, and only the crackle from the coals could be heard. "They're thought to be a legend, but we believe at least a variant of them may be behind most of the aggressive packs being driven out of the wilds by the dragon. Oh, sure, we have wolves aplenty throughout the realms, but larger packs like the ones you described are headed by these, and it's important you aren't bitten by them."

"How would I know a Grimmigwulf from a regular one?" Nate blinked.

"Oh, don't worry, you would know one if you saw it," Brenard assured him. "They walk upright, and they're a lot bigger than the other members of their pack. The important thing is that none of you were bit, regardless."

"They're just a legend to scare children; no need to scare the newcomers, Brenard, they just got here!" Prince Griffon burst into laughter, turning to Nate. "You have to excuse our dear captain of the guard, he's a wee into the old tales, especially over a pint!"

"Hey, I'm just being careful, for all our sakes," the captain of the guard countered.

"Yeah, and they walk among us as people during the day!" Prince Griffon elbowed him, still laughing. "Careful, or they'll seduce you out into the woods for lovemaking, and then suddenly, you become one of them, or you become their next meal!"

"Ah, shut up, you young pup!" the captain of the guard sneered playfully before taking another swig from his pint. Muttering to himself, he elbowed the laughing prince back. "You should have more respect for your elders!"

"Naw, we didn't see anything like that," Nate chuckled as he stood. He was about to turn and retire for the evening when he stopped. "I meant to ask you something, Brenard. Is there a significance to that tattoo on your palm?"

"Indeed, there is, my friend." Brenard smiled, relieved to change the subject from the wolves. "It's a sign of devotion to our king and land."

"Just as in the sigil, I see," Nate recollected as he turned to leave.

"Well, goodnight to you all! I must admit, I'm really looking forward to a real bed tonight!"

Princess Serina watched the newcomer vanish down the hallway before the captain of the guard caught her attention.

"Well, Your Highnesses, I suppose I better be off as well," Brenard sighed as he bade the royals a goodnight. As he pushed back from the table, his gaze lingered on Princess Serina for a moment before he shook his head and left.

"What was that?" Prince Griffon snickered to his sister as he escorted her from the dining hall.

"What was what?" Princess Serina feigned, her heart pounding. She had seen that look from Brenard before. Not often, but more recently since her attaining womanhood. She had first noticed it last year when his hand grazed hers when preparing her horse, Barley, for a ride.

"I saw that look he gave you!" Prince Griffon pressed. "Is there something you need to tell me?"

"Nate's a fantastic man for an outsider; very interesting." Princess Serina blinked, intentionally diverting the topic. "The others also seemed quite naïve to me but no less intriguing!"

"I'm speaking of Brenard, OUR captain of the guard!" Prince Griffon laughed. When she avoided responding, he seemed to contemplate the diversion only for a moment before relenting with a sigh. "He's a fine man, our captain. Don't worry, little sister; we will find you a suitable match one day. Someone with the many fine yet rare qualities Brenard possesses."

"Of course, dear brother." She blushed. "Matchmaking was always easier for you. Between my peculiarities and awkwardness..."

"Don't be so hard on yourself, little sister," he whispered, giving her a gentle kiss on the forehead. "I only jest. Everything will come in its due time. You need not struggle with tomorrow when we have plenty for us both here today."

She smiled at that as she returned his embrace. *If affection from an outsider from another world weren't taboo enough, endearment from the lead captain of the guard would be quite out of place, regardless of how attractive. No, this is something I need to be more careful about revealing, even in front of my brother.*

Chapter 9

Self-Discovery

Despite her last-minute displacement to a new room, Johanna slept well that night. With stone walls and a single porthole-like window overlooking the town, the small space felt safe and comforting. Nearly identical to the room Javier and Kevin shared, the sparsely furnished room was only a bit smaller and further down the guest hallway than the others in her group. She awoke surprised with how refreshed she felt as sunlight spilled into the abode, dancing off the particulates floating between her bed and the lace curtains.

Only then did she hear the first quiet knocks on her wooden door. Sammy perked up and yawned at her feet when she stirred from her slumber. The hound had been resting peacefully, but when the soft knock on the door resounded in the chambers again, she let out a low growl.

"Whoooo, whooooooo?" she growled, rolling off the bed onto her feet and staring at the door.

"It's okay, faithful hound, I'm here for Johanna," Grand Master Nicholas's soft, elderly voice called to Sammy through the keyhole. "It's Grand Master Nicholas."

"Iiiiit's okay!" Sammy woofed softly, turning to Johanna and staring at her panting. "Ni-chollll-as!"

"I'll never get used to you talking," Johanna muttered with a smile. Throwing on the simple peasant dress lying atop a modest bedside chair, she quickly donned her shoes and a shawl. "I'm coming!"

She emerged from her room, refreshed from her rest, tying her hair back in a bun and fumbling awkwardly with her new garb. The grand master patiently took her arm as Johanna closed the door behind her, ushering Sammy out with her.

"I see your hound continues to develop the ability to speak," the wizard mused. "This is an unexpected result for an animal to gain an ability from passing through the Shimmering; most intriguing!"

"It sure is," Johanna admitted. "I thought I was dreaming. I slept so soundly, but yes—she actually was talking to me! How is this possible?"

"Many things are possible for you here in this world, just as the queen said last night," the wizard pointed out. "It is one of many reasons I abandoned my quest to return home; that, and I had nothing to return to. I have breakfast and Myrenth tea waiting for all of you in the Wizard's Tower, my quarters. We may continue the discussion there."

They stopped by Nate's room to collect him and the others, knocking gently on each door to reveal they were already awake, eagerly awaiting the start of the new day. The grand master led them all back out of the castle and around the towering southside stone walls. Sammy dashed around Daniel, marking territory and yipping excitedly as she went. Javier and Kevin stumbled along sleepily as Nate ushered them enthusiastically along.

A light frost layered both plant and stone overnight throughout town, melting quickly as the morning sun struck. The lone tower built with the same stone as the castle stood atop the hill as the tallest building in Levens, clearly seen from everywhere. Adjacent to the monarchy's fortress castle, the Wizard's Tower projected itself taller than even the royal residence, a narrow watchtower on the world at least ten floors high.

Morning mists rose from the frost on the roof tiles, giving the tower a sort of separation from the rest of the population, a solitary sentinel at the town's center. The dissipating clouds gave the top of the tower an appearance of almost floating on a cushion of billowing cotton above it all.

Early morning revealed Levens already alive, bustling with carts as peasants and farmers gathered their equipment for the fall harvest. All greeted Grand Master Nicholas with a reverent nod as he led the group past. Stray hens and hounds crossed their paths, but all the morning activity seemed headed back to the plaza as they made their way through to the Wizard's Tower.

The entrance to the square tower resided in the center of a side courtyard, with nothing but a gnarled yet full apple tree, a quaint stone well and a stone bench for sparse company. Close by, two guards drawing a bucket of water from the well greeted the group with a friendly wave.

The grand master returned the greeting and produced an iron key from within his robes, his wrinkled hands tremoring slightly with the effort. With a loud clank, he unlocked the heavy wooden door at the tower's base.

The door groaned on its iron brackets as he pushed it open. Leading them all up the narrow winding staircase, they passed slotted windows looking out over first the courtyard, then, as they ascended, to the rest of town.

The elderly wizard hobbled steadily along as he led them ever upward, through the narrow hall spot lit by the occasional slats carved into the cold stone walls. From each slat they ascended past, they could soon gain vistas over the castle and out onto the lands beyond. From the towering mountains to the west, sprawling plains north, forests to the south and distant hills in the east, each window provided a unique, expansive scene far beyond the tiny hilltop kingdom. By the time they reached the top, they were all thoroughly out of breath, yet the grand master seemed barely winded.

Grand Master Nicholas opened another wooden door at the top of the stairs with the same key. The entry swung silently open, and they filed inside the room at the top of the tower.

The room bulged out from the rest of the tower structure in a large wooden bulb with a pointed shingled roof at the top. Intermittent diagonally slatted casement windows interspaced between bookshelves, stacked with leather-bound tomes reaching high into the vaulted ceilings. At one end of the room was a small bed and reading nook. Surprisingly warm and cozy, a miniature stone fireplace built into the wall crackled with fire, above which a boiling kettle of Myrenth tea gave off an aroma that smelled like coffee.

At the center of the room, someone had arranged an assortment of pastries and fruit, neatly prepared with cloth napkins atop a large wooden table. Stacks of maps and parchment had been set aside to make room for their breakfast fare but still occupied more than half the table space.

Across the room from their entry, thick curtains billowed in wafts of cool morning breezes from the open patio doorway, giving views to the grand vista outside could be seen while airing the room with fresh air.

"Welcome to my humble abode!" the wizard announced, gesturing grandly as he ushered them in. "As your Advocate, I think we should start here this morning to discuss the situation."

"What a view!" Nate commented, distracted by the balcony. He strode over and parted the veil for a look over the stone railing. "It's surprisingly warm in here despite the cold outside."

"Yes, I try to maintain the basic comforts," Grand Master Nicholas professed, smiling with pride. "A comfortable year-round temperature up here is important, particularly at my age."

"So, why is the banner on this tower different than the others?" Kevin asked as he squeezed in beside Nate, referring to the full moon set amid three stars on the sigil hanging from the balcony. Its field of black provided a stark contrast to the many Levens's grain of wheat standards they had seen flying around town.

"That is the banner of my order, the last remaining Wizard's Council known throughout all the many kingdoms as the Order of the

Moon," Grand Master Nicholas said. "Please, help yourself to refreshments our servants have provided us this morning."

"It looks delicious, thank you, Nicholas," Johanna acknowledged. "Please, tell us more about your order!"

"We devote our lives to the proper study and use of magic," the grand master began as they gathered around the table he gestured, taking a steaming roll for himself. Javier stepped up eagerly, grabbing an apple before stacking a plate with other bits as the others followed suit. "We believe in the sacred duty of dedication to its purity and proper use—knowledge and sacrifice for the betterment of all."

"How long have you been a wizard?" Nate asked between bites.

"My mentor, Kasok the Great, took me into his tutelage at the wizard's keep of Mondlichtberg, up in the mountains not far from here actually, over 400 years ago," the grand master stated. His eyes twinkled with a private pride as the morning sun washed over him. "As a young boy, I fell through a Shimmering that had manifested itself in a cave near my hometown. When I arrived in this world, Kasok found me half drowned and pulled me from the Rhane River, not far from where you came out of the wilds. He sensed the innate power that had bonded itself within me when I came through the Shimmering."

"Wait a sec," Javier interjected, arching an eyebrow. "Did you just say 400 years ago? I call bullshit!"

"It's true," the wizard sighed with a smile. "It seems the use of magic has a unique side effect in prolonging one's life."

"I wonder if that would apply to us?" Kevin stated aloud.

"In time, it very well could, if even in small ways," the grand master acknowledged, his thoughts briefly drifting elsewhere. "General use of innate power has very little effect; wizards' use of magic is widespread and continuous. This culminates in the longevity spread of one's years. This has been a predictable outcome for all save one individual I know of in Tyrna. A dear friend of mine, a priest from your world, came through, and we still cannot explain his unusually long life."

"A priest?" Nate echoed. "So, others from our world have come through this 'Shimmering'?"

"Many others, likely," the wizard confirmed, returning to the matter at hand. "It's impossible to tell whether they were from our mutual originating world or others, yet nevertheless, they have come throughout our known history. They may not share my friend's longevity of years, but they share the simple fact that upon their arrival, they are blessed with an innate ability as unique and individual as their own spiritual essence may be."

"The Shimmering," Johanna echoed. "That's what you call the portal we came through."

"It is so called," the wizard affirmed. "Just as you all are developing innate abilities from your brush with it, the same happened with me as well. Kasok the Great guided me over the years to develop it and nurture my innate power until I was ready."

"Ready for what?" Javier blinked.

"When I entered manhood, he took me to harvest the staff I now hold from the slopes of Mount Bard, at the foot of the Ice Mountains," he stated, rolling it loosely in his hand, pivoting the base on the floor. "It was the first step to becoming an actual wizard and the pivotal moment in my life when I decided to join the order."

"All because of a staff?" Javier seemed unconvinced.

"This staff exhibits a power of its own," Grand Master Nicholas explained, displaying the length of it in the sunlight streaming through the window. "It lends me strength and support more than just physically; it enhances and magnifies my own powers. It even allows me to utilize other powers beyond my primary innate ability. That is what leads to and even prolongs life. For me, this extension is for over 400 years. It, however, is the only exception to *the* rule."

"What rule?" Daniel asked.

"The primary rule of all magic users," the grand master stated. "We must never, NEVER use non-like magic origins together: innate, elemental, learned, life and spiritual. Combining such powers creates unpredictable and dangerous consequences, particularly in conjunction. My staff is an exception to this rule because it's a tool of *enhancement*. Enhancement talismans complement, neither mixing nor competing with the other magical sources. Other differing magic sources tend to transfigure unpredictably when combined."

"So, you still can't combine other powers, but the staff enhances which one you bring to bear," Kevin restated in understanding. "What exactly is innate power though?"

"Innate powers are a part of the user at birth or upon their arrival to this world through the Shimmering," Grand Master Nicholas explained. "It's the one and only that comes from within. I daresay you are either born with it or it manifests itself within your life force as you enter adulthood."

"How is that any different from the other abilities?" Javier pressed, uncomprehending.

"Other powers originating outside the user are gathered, learned, and utilized," the grand master confirmed. "They may eventually become part of the user over time. This is how the use of magic may imbue or corrupt the user, dependent on proper discipline and knowledge employed. My Order of the Moon believes in proper guidance and practice so that the user may utilize these new abilities without fear and with confidence."

"I understood from last night's dinner that your involvement with the order is drawing down," Johanna stated carefully. "Are you retiring?"

"While that is the truth at face value, the context of that topic is a bit of a controversy outside of the kingdom; therefore, I ask that you keep this in confidence if you are to venture beyond Levens," the wizard stated and then paused with a grimace. "During a great disagreement among the Grand Master Council, I was asked to take up residence in Levens and tutor King Phillip's daughter personally. Since I was already overdue to retire, this move kept me active within the order. It also maintained discretion for Princess Serina's house and family."

"Why would she hide such an ability?" Javier interjected. "I would think such a power would make her quite popular!"

"Infamous would be a more accurate description; most of the kingdoms to the south outright ban the use of magic," the wizard sighed. "For our eastern neighbors in Urocia, it's hardly an issue. In fact, a group called the Order of Etoilenoir has recently emerged and become quite popular among the youth in the limited magic they utilize. Their lack of discipline and their tendency to resort to the practice on a whim is a debate with varying levels of criticism among my order."

"Where are all these places you're referring to?" Nate asked, rifling through the parchments on the table near the food. "I hope you don't mind me looking through these, but I do love maps!"

"Here's Levens, where we are now." Grand Master Nicholas pointed, helping Nate to lock down four corners of one of the largest parchments with stone paperweights. "To the northwest is Mondlicht-berg, high in the wilds of the Grenze Mountains, not far from where you arrived. East of here, you see the plains of Urocia and its capital city of Latana on the shores of the Great Bay. Follow the Rhane River where you came in, south of Levens, and then to the town of North Lake and the great Long Lake."

"What's all in here?" Nate asked, pointing to a vast stretch in the east of unmarked land between Urocia and the Southern Kingdoms.

"Cursed land; frankly, many of the reasons now behind the rules we have in our wizard's order." Grand Master Nicholas cringed. "Once, two great kingdoms warred over that territory, but the terrible powers they wielded destroyed that land, spreading a deadly blight, transforming it into a vast desert wasteland where most dare not venture. Caravans occasionally skirt it at their peril for valuable trade between Urocia and the Southern Kingdoms, but none stay long. It is said they are haunted, and nothing grows there. Their evil was contained in that desert by a strong curse that is maintained to this day."

"This peak here." Johanna pointed, moving back to the north end of the map. "We saw that large mountain there, in the northwest—at the head of a great valley."

"That is Mount Bard, so named from the mournful songs the great mountain sings when the winds blow across the high crags and peaks.

This marks the southern boundary of the northern wilds and the Ice Mountains, where few dare go and where I harvested my staff," the wizard recapped, stroking his long white beard. "The wilderness stretches into the mountains west and south, interrupted by only Mondlichtberg and one other castle to the southwest. Only the occasional trapper or wayward hunters dare venture into the Grenze Mountains; many go in and never return. Some say if you were to go west of the mountains, you'd eventually reach the great Aprinises Ocean, but only the sea-faring merchants from the Southern Kingdoms could verify that claim; and none ever land on those shores since they are quite rocky, swamp-ridden and inhospitable."

"So, the Rhane River flows along the eastern foot of these Grenze mountains, marking the end of known civilization. Once we crossed the river, the going got much easier," Nate recalled. "I suppose we were lucky to have made it out of the wilderness in one piece!"

"Quite lucky, despite your technology and budding abilities," the wizard agreed. "Since the Northern Guardian began hunting that region, many have fallen victim to it or the creatures it displaces, driving them out of the wilds before it."

"Is that Northern Guardian really a fire-breathing dragon?" Daniel asked. "We saw something flying by the moon when we arrived."

"It is indeed, a wild creature that normally stays well to the north," Grand Master Nicholas acknowledged. "The Guardians are mythical beasts of terrible power, originally placed by the wizards of old to guard boundaries into the wild areas of the world. The wards and spells that kept them there have since been forgotten, and the beasts have reverted to their natural states. The other Guardians have vanished off this map, but the Northern Guardian wandered south into the fringes of Levens. Normally, it resides deep in the high mountain passes of the northern wilds. We'd never even seen it until decades ago, and it only became a problem recently."

"Sounds like the wolves weren't the worst thing we could have come across," Johanna sighed. "I'm amazed we emerged from this in as good a condition as we did."

"As am I, frankly, but I think we can get to the bottom of that now," the grand master proclaimed. With an audible huff, he took a seat on a plain wooden chair at the head of the table. "It so happens my original innate power is that of perception; I can use my innate power to see what's in your mind's eye. We can link our minds so that you may also see what I see—if I have your permission, of course."

"I've got to see this in action," Nate stated, deciding almost instantly. "Let's go, Grand Master; show me how this is done!"

"Aha! We already have our first volunteer!" Grand Master Nicholas grinned as Nate eagerly stepped in front of him, sitting on another stool beside the wizard. "Very well, we can start with you then!"

The wizard closed his eyes and gently grasped Nate's head in his hands. Nate could only vaguely feel the wizard's fingers rustling through the scruff of his beard and over his temples when he began seeing images flashing before his eyes. Memories—his memories—began to waft in front of him as he spun through them one at a time.

A large metropolis called Denver with immensely tall glass buildings...a box called a television projecting images on a screen...large birds called airplanes filled with people taking off and landing...people talking to each other over long distances through a device they carried in their pockets...Bill and Nate firing thunder sticks they called guns at a shooting range...

"I had no idea, they've come so far," the wizard muttered, distracted by the images as they faded in and out of Nate's mind. "Your world is indeed the one I came from, yet so much has truly changed!"

"I suppose it has since you last were there," Nate pondered. "Four hundred years; a lot has happened since then."

"I would love to learn more about what has become of my former world, but let us not distract from our pursuits," the wizard muttered as he reconfigured his handhold around Nate's temples. "I suspect each of you may have been imbued with an innate power when you came through the Shimmering; I just need to see when and where it was expressed..."

"Really?" Nate grinned, his eyes still squinted closed. "How would we know?"

"I want you to think specifically about what you were thinking of when you came through," the grand master encouraged. "What passions do you enjoy back in your home? What is it that fascinates you, and did any of those desires pass through your mind as you arrived?"

"I'm not sure," Nate began. He drifted off as images began to flash again. "I love the outdoors, but I'm an electrician by trade. I think..."

I see Johanna tending to the wounded in the meadow, touching the deep cut on my leg.

I used to enjoy working with wires and electricity...sparks flying. Where was that? Oh, yes—the Jeep. AFTER we had arrived in this world. Had the charging battery been overloaded...by me?

After that, the attacking wolf lunging for my throat, pinning me to the ground, gnashing its teeth together, trying to grasp my neck. I threw up my hands in defense and...then what happened? Explosions of electricity like lightning.

"I saw you," the wizard stated, turning to Johanna as he released Nate's head and turned to her. "I saw what you did. You're a healer! In addition to your premonitions, you're a healer! You may indeed retain two distinct abilities!"

"So, it is possible that I may have more than one innate power?" Johanna confirmed.

"Not only possible but also documented," the grand master pridefully announced with a broad grin. "That explains how your care enabled your companions to emerge from the wilds unscathed."

"It makes sense, with my nursing background," Johanna recalled. "I was doing everything I could to help everyone, especially our injured."

"Indeed! We will need more time to explore this, as I would really also like to see some of your premonitions firsthand!" the elderly wizard remarked as he turned back to Nate. "You, my friend, have harnessed lightning!"

"What?!" Nate laughed, almost scoffing at the idea.

"Extend your hands, about shoulder's width in front of you," the wizard instructed. Nate wasn't sure where this was going but did it anyway.

"I saw inside your mind, Nate. All those years in your daily labors, you've worked with harnessed lightning," Grand Master Nicholas affirmed, pointing in front of him as his voice quieted to a whisper. "One commonality I saw with the harnessed lightning was that there was a positive end and a negative end. Make your left hand negative and your right hand positive; release what you have harnessed!"

"How..." Nate began. "Am I supposed to feel something?"

"Just close your eyes and SEE it," Grand Master Nicholas instructed with emphasis. "What does lightning feel like to you? You called it electricity; what does electricity *feel* like?"

Nate did as the wizard directed; he shut his eyes and could see his hands and pictured them like the ends of a battery. A loud CRACK resounded, a bright flash of light pierced the room and the smell of ozone stung his nostrils. He was about to apologize when he noticed everyone laughing.

"Let's try it again, only this time with your eyes open," the wizard said, struggling to contain his mirth. "You can do it!"

Nate did and this time, it came right away. Gently at first, but he could see tiny purple-blue rivulets of electricity coursing between his two hands. They combined into larger ones, so he pulled his hands further apart. The rivulets became small again but continued to build and intensify, loud and crackling as the smell of ozone permeated the room.

"Very good! Now, let's try exerting some control over this," the grand master suggested as he pulled an unlit torch from a wall mount and set it in front of Nate. "Close your eyes and think of the wolf— think of it lunging at your throat—FEEL the danger you were in."

"I think I know what you mean," Nate grunted as he strained. Closing his eyes again, he focused on the event in his mind. "Okay, I have it!"

"Now, open your eyes and see the wolf in the torch." The wizard's whisper hissed in his ear. "Light the torch!"

Nate stretched out his hand over the torch, but the electricity coursing over it faded...and nothing happened.

"NATE—IT'S GOING TO KILL YOU!!! DO SOMETHING!!!" Grand Master Nicholas roared.

Nate jumped as his heart caught in his throat. With a thunderous crack, white-hot lightning exploded from his hand, vaporizing the torch, ricocheting off the wall and lighting the table afire. Everyone ducked for cover as earsplitting thunder resounded through the room, leaving the remaining fruits and pastries dripping from the walls.

"There, you see? You can do it!" Grand Master Nicholas exclaimed, grabbing for a bucket of water tableside to douse the flames. Everyone coughed, regaining their composure amidst the mess he had created in the room. "Once my ears stop ringing, we may continue."

"I am so sorry," Nate muttered as he blushed, tamping his hands nervously on the table to extinguish the flames. "I had no idea."

"Nothing to apologize for!" the wizard laughed, clapping his back with encouragement. "We will continue to hone your skill to control it and in time, you will master this ability!"

Kevin stepped up next, taking Nate's seat. He was encouraged by what had transpired and Grand Master Nicholas repeated the link with him. He saw the images almost immediately when the grand master's fingers touched his temples.

Longing to be somewhere else...my whole life; wishing I was away from people and places I knew. I always saw items in the distance and wanted to bring them closer to myself...just like when I rode in the Jeep after coming here. The water in the river...I was in the river.

"Kevin, this power will come very easy for you. Be careful about that though. For now, until you are able to exercise control over your ability, let's just keep your practice close by the tower," the wizard advised. He led Kevin to the balcony and turned him around, pointing across the room. "There, look back at the door."

"The door?" Kevin questioned.

"Yes, look at it closely," the wizard directed. "Notice the grain of the wood. Focus on the shadow from the door handle. See the iron brackets and the nails."

"I see it." Kevin squinted, concentrating on it.

"Now, bring it to you," the grand master whispered. "In your mind, watch it come to you! Focus on the unique details and see them in detail; examine them closely!"

An all-too-familiar hum, like electricity, filled the room, and Kevin's outline appeared to warp between where he stood and the door itself. With a crash, Kevin briefly seemed to appear in two places at once, his second image smashing into the door as his first vanished. He bounced painfully off the door frame and fell back into the bookshelf, scattering tomes and papers before falling to the floor.

"That's the sound we were hearing back on the trail!" Javier exclaimed. "It was coming from Kevin this whole time?!"

"There, you see how easy that was?" Grand Master Nicholas smiled with satisfaction. "As I said, though, Kevin, stay close by until we can test the limitations of this power. I don't know just how far you can transport yourself and wouldn't want you to get lost!"

"Agreed," Kevin sighed, rubbing his head still smarting from the impact. "I better work on that landing though!"

"Let's see, that leaves the two more," the wizard stated before turning to Javier. "Now, how about you, my boy?"

To everyone's surprise, Javier flinched.

"What's wrong?" Kevin asked. "We're all doing it; is there a problem?"

"Nothing, Micker!" Javier shot him a glare but caught himself. "I'm just not used to having someone in my head."

"It's okay—trust me!" Kevin's smile faded as he encouraged. "He's only trying to see what drives you. You see what he sees the whole time; really, no one here is judging you!"

"Fine! Let's get this over with," Javier muttered as he sat down reluctantly in front of the wizard, staring back at the old man suspiciously. As the grand master reached to him, gently clasping his head with slightly trembling hands, the visions began. "I'm not worried about anyone judging me! I don't need anyone's approval or…"

I see friends…Becky and Tim and others from school, beautiful yet unsatisfied Patrice, my ex-girlfriend. All of them talked AT me; none of them talked WITH me. Did they ever really know me at all; were they ever really listening? I was always the fun one, and it was easy to gain their attention and their approval; but did they ever really hear me when it mattered?

"Stop," Javier heard himself say aloud. "I said STOP!"

The voice had been his, not Nicholas's or anyone else, but it had a deep metallic ring to it. The entire room seemed to reverberate when he said it.

"You okay, Javier?" Johanna asked.

"Yeah, I'm fine," Javier said, glaring back at the grand master. "I don't need anyone fussing over me, but I didn't see anything that cleared this up, did you?"

"Don't be angry, Javier," Grand Master Nicholas chastised softly. "I understand your trepidations with this process. This is frankly similar to and not unlike many young men in any world—not just yours, but most young men, even in my order, for that matter. I won't talk about it unless you desire to, but allow me to tell you this: you overcoming your trepidation and coming to an understanding is the key to unlocking your power."

"Being pissed about people not listening to me is the key to unlocking my power? Sounds like a crock of shit to me!" Javier snapped again as he stood, tossing aside the chair he sat in. Standing tall, his face reddened before he seemed to deflate, muttering aloud a truth to himself and unable to look at the others. "You all don't need to know how big of an asshole I am!"

"Frankly, yes. It *is* a 'crock of shit,' as you say," the grand master gently intoned. "You told me to stop so, I did. Go to the door; tell IT to stop the same way you did me."

"The door?" Javier blinked in quizzical surprise. "What the hell are you…"

"Yes, I'm serious!" The grand master pointed. "Go on, tell it! Don't look at me, tell that door!"

"The door? Tell the door?" Javier shrugged, turning to the door, and stated, "Stop."

"It's not listening," Grand Master Nicholas pressed. "It's still there, ignoring you!"

"Stop! Stop! Stop!" Javier spoke louder, almost shouting.

"IT'S IGNORING YOU, JAVIER!" the wizard shouted. "IT DOESN'T CARE WHAT YOU HAVE TO SAY! IT'S BLOCKING YOU OUT! IT'S NOT GIVING YOU THE RESPECT AND DIGNITY YOU DESERVE!!"

"STOP!!!" Javier shouted in fury as that same strange and unmistakable metallic sound reverberated from his mouth. The energy from it merged into his voice into a visible distortion wave, rippling out from his lips and blowing the door apart, lifting it clear off its hinges. Everyone covered their faces, but when the dust cleared, no door remained. Javier stumbled back giddy, nearly falling back onto the floor. "I did that! I really did that..."

"Yes, you did," Grand Master Nicholas confirmed. He winked as he patted him on the back. "Now I need a new door."

"Oh, I'm sorry," Javier stammered, turning to the grand master with newfound respect. "I finally understand what you were getting at."

"Understanding your power will ultimately lead to understanding yourself," the grand master advised. "There's no shame in any of it! Taking the first step is always the hardest but is also the most important."

"What about your door?" Johanna coughed, waving the dust from in front of her face.

"This is the Wizard's Tower; I will have it replaced." The grand master chuckled as he turned to see Daniel skulking near the table unhappily. "What's wrong, my young friend?"

"Everyone else has shown signs of this over the past couple of days," the unhappy lad sighed. "I've shown nothing. What if I have something stupid or nothing at all?"

"I highly doubt it," the wizard chided him, gesturing at the chair. "Come, Daniel. If you're worried about it, I suggest we find out right away. Come, sit!"

Daniel plopped down reluctantly and closed his eyes.

As Grand Master Nicholas placed his hands around Daniel's temples, he smiled despite himself with deep satisfaction. He could see the adolescent was truly worried about this.

My mom has been so distracted with Nate since my dad's death...my happiness lately is only when I'm alone...my last time being happy was in one of those big airplanes to visit my grandparents. The journey had been just as exciting as the visit. The wings and the engines of the plane...the roar...the air...the clouds...the only time I felt free with the world's problems below...

"Daniel, I know what your innate power is," the wizard announced. A broad grin spread over the grand master's wrinkled face, a slight tremor in his voice. "I think you're going to like this!"

Chapter 10

Morning After

Princess Serina awoke early that same morning, her long black hair draped around a sea of pillows as the morning sun spilled across her face. She only rose from her bed when she heard the muffled voices outside, followed by the sound of Sammy's yipping below her window in the courtyard. Glancing out the window with her icy blue eyes, she watched briefly as Grand Master Nicholas led the entourage of strangers around the side of the castle to his tower.

Last night's dinner had been intriguing for her. Other than Nicholas, she had never personally met people from another world before, even if she had heard of such visitors arriving in past historic events. To be a firsthand witness of it was a rare privilege and bonded her to them in a private way few others understood. These people would likely develop innate magic, much like she had.

As she got out of bed, she walked over to a washbasin and splashed her face with water. Finding a hairpin, she quickly tidied her hair and dressed herself. A soft knock on the door distracted her as a meek young woman's voice called in.

"Are you awake, Your Highness? Anything I can get for you?" her personal lady's maid called through the door.

"Sorry, Sophie, I seemed to beat you to it this morning," Princess Serina sighed as she opened the door. Sophie greeted her with feigned disappointment. Her soft brown eyes scanned the princess up and down, noting the royal had already prepped herself for the day.

Although her servant donned the same matching grey habit the other Levenese royal servants wore, Princess Serina could spot Sophie's unique eyes from a lineup of the whole staff. Her slightly oversized doe eyes gave her the look of a doll and her gentle demeanor only furthered that appearance.

"You didn't allow me to assist you this morning!" Sophie chastised softly. "You know Charla won't be happy with me if she catches you handling all this on your own!"

"I understand, Sophie, but thank you," Princess Serina sighed. "If Charla or anyone asks for me, you tell them I've taken Barley out for my morning ride. I was trying to get out before anyone noticed, and I prefer to be discreet about such things."

"I will, Your Highness, but remember to at least send word to myself or Charla," she sighed, nodding solemnly. "Just be safe out there! All the talk of wolves from the wilds and new strangers about, not to mention sightings of that northern dragon, makes me nervous!"

"Come now, Sophie; I'm not riding that far!" the princess laughed. "Just over to the river. Please be discreet; I'd rather the others not know. I'll be back before anyone knows I've gone!"

"As long as you are," the lady's maid stated as she winked before sauntering on down the hall.

Princess Serina shook her head with a smile before returning to her room to finish her morning preparations. Nothing would ever get past Sophie, her loyal servant since she was a little girl; Sophie knew the princess was an early riser. As Princess Serina had grown older, she had developed a love affair with her horse, Barley. She could never get enough of his billowing, blond mane whisking through the countryside, free of the castle and all of the tedious obligations she had as a royal court member.

After slipping on her leather riding boots and long blue cloak, she quietly opened the door to her quarters the rest of the way. Sophie had returned and waited patiently for her outside her door. With a brief curtsy, she produced a wicker basket.

"Since you are intent on your escapade, I thought you might enjoy this for your morning ride," the maid offered. "Remember your promise, though; be back before anyone knows you're gone!"

"Oh, Sophie, thank you!" Princess Serina smiled, taking the basket and a quick inventory. Packed inside with a wool blanket were hard-boiled eggs, ham slices and a loaf of bread with jam, along with fresh berries and a sealed flask of tea and cream.

"Your family seems quite taken with the strangers," the maid commented.

"As was I," the princess admitted. "I'm frankly surprised they fared as well as they did, coming out of the wilds like that. I'm just glad they made it here without further mishap!"

"You took a liking to the young one?" Sophie prodded with a twinkle in her eye.

"Oh, Sophie, come now," Princess Serina scoffed. "He's cute, but he is surely ten years younger than I am. He reminds me of what a little brother would be, but he's nothing like Prince Griffon."

"The prince is your elder though," Sophie reminded her. "The tall, dark-haired one certainly had his eyes on you."

"He did, didn't he?" Princess Serina mused. "Javier, I believe his name is. Alas, I'm not destined for a stranger. Father will someday likely pair me with a lord from Tyrna or perhaps one of the Long Lake towns. Who knows, one day, perhaps sooner than I'd care for, to be certain."

"No hopes of claiming a lord from Urocia or one of the Southern Kingdoms?" Sophie asked.

"Are you joking?" Princess Serina squinted. "I can't stand the pretentiousness of the Urocians, and with my condition, a pairing with a southern lord would go over as well as horseflies at a picnic. I'll leave the greater cities to my brother—as for me, I only hope to stay in the country with my horse!"

Princess Serina smiled before setting off, and within moments, she exited the castle, quietly striding out a side door in the keep. Like a shade of night fleeing the coming dawn, she crept on cat's feet down several flights of stone steps and past the Wizard's Tower.

Continuing through narrow alleyways, she increased her pace in excited anticipation, her riding boots clicking softly with each step, their taps echoing off the stone walls. As she neared the front gate and the stables, she could smell fresh bread baking from the market ovens wafting to her from the marketplace. A mix of steam and smoke filled the chilly morning air, and she smiled as she clutched her cloak closer around her shoulders. *I do love the mornings!*

Her brother had always made fun of her about becoming a man faster than he had, but she didn't care. He could have all of the late-night parties, the receptions and the matters of state. Princess Serina loved the wilds and the early mornings; this was her time!

As she approached the guardhouse and the stables, she noted the marketplace had barely even stirred at this early hour. The colorful tents and banners flapped gently in the morning breeze, the bazaar quiet and absent of the day's activity sure to come. Brenard stepped from behind the newcomers' beastless carriage, already leading Barley by the reins.

"Out for your morning ride, are you?" the captain of the guard sighed. "Shouldn't you have someone with you?"

"Who did you have in mind?" Princess Serina smirked, blushing slightly and looking away. *His lingering stare from last night is still fresh in my mind.* "Sophie seems to have been very thorough in keeping others well-informed of my movements, even when I seek discretion."

"Well, don't ride too far—your father will have my head if you go out into the mountains again," he warned sternly. "It's not as if you're riding to Mondlichtberg, are you?"

"As much as I would like to make that ride to the wizard's keep, I'm just headed to the river crossroads," she promised abruptly before mounting her steed. "No need to tease me, Brenard. I'll be back before anyone knows the better!"

Astride Barley, Princess Serina galloped through the front gates, glad to be free of the town and its constraints. She found it annoying that everyone was always so worried about her out near the wilds alone. Perhaps they were worried that someday she would just keep going to Mondlichtberg to join the wizard's order. *Maybe one day that temptation will overcome me, but they underestimate my willingness to find satisfaction in my current circumstances! I don't always have to run to something else!*

Perhaps that was why she had taken such a liking to Daniel last night. He seemed to be the only newcomer excited about being in their land, yet he kept so much inside. For him, the whole ordeal appeared as nothing but an opportunity. When she had asked him about obligations for his future, it hadn't seemed to be an issue for him. At one point, he had commented, "Whatever happens will happen, and I'll deal with it then."

"I wish I could be so cavalier about events in my life," she had replied, watching his face and wondering if he had even thought about it. His response told her not only that he had but that he had an approach she had never considered in her own life.

"Well, I don't know if it's the best thing," he had stated. "I first consider what influence I could possibly have on the outcome. If the answer is 'none,' then I refuse to worry about it and leave it up to God to decide."

She admired his openness to their circumstances and reliance on his faith's deity despite having no apparent control over the direction of his life. The wisdom of utilizing such nuanced discipline from someone so young seemed uncanny to her. Perhaps it wasn't wisdom so much to him, but she saw parallels to herself that had given her pause.

Additionally, Daniel had no preconceptions as to who she was or what she *should* be. She was simply someone who would listen to him and be there. And listen she did—Daniel had raved non-stop about his home in a land called Colorado.

Princess Serina continued riding over the rolling hills until she came to the base of the mountains. The pounding of Barley's hooves matched the beating of her heart until they came to a stop. Here at the crossroads, the Rhane River met the road to Levens and the base of the Grenze Mountains all at once.

Flowers still peppered the meadow grass and the occasional honeybee buzzed by in search of any last calls for remaining season pollen. Here, the scent of spring lingered in the air, even as summer fled and fall visibly loomed among the trees and hillsides above.

As she dismounted her steed, she spread out the blanket from her basket under the shade of a lone stunted birch tree and prepared her breakfast. The morning sun spilled warmly around her, and the Rhane River murmured behind her in a dull wash. *This is how I prefer to eat!*

As Princess Serina savored the cheese and berries from her basket, something moving through the air caught her eye. She squinted in the morning light—whatever it was came from the direction of Levens and moved rapidly in her direction. High above, it cast an erratic shadow as it lurched through the sky.

Cutting another slice of bread, she sat staring intently as the sounds of distant barking met her ears along with a familiar voice on the morning breeze.

"Come on, Sammy! Come on!" she recognized Daniel's voice, distant yet clear.

"Daniel! Over here!" Princess Serina shouted, a slow smile creeping over her face. Full recognition came, and she stood and waved, calling out to him. "What are you doing?!"

"Princess Serina!" Daniel shouted back as he closed in on her position. "Look! I can fly!"

Indeed, the boy flew, albeit awkwardly so. Hovering erratically nearly fifty feet in the air, he lurched about, waving his arms frantically to gain control of himself. The grey cape he wore hardly fulfilled its purpose, billowing about him like a flag in a stiff breeze. Sammy had followed him out of the town, barking incessantly in distress as she caught up to him, running below and constantly checking his position. It looked comical, as if the hound flew Daniel as a kite.

"I'm having some trouble controlling this," the newcomer lad admitted as he drew closer, sometimes falling precariously and then catching himself before dropping again.

"Daniel, be careful!" Princess Serina gasped as he nearly collided with a nearby tree, snapping several branches near the top.

"I'm going to aim for the road," he gasped, straining for concentration before suddenly dropping like a stone, his lanky form falling diagonally out of the sky. He screamed as he fell, careening sharply towards the river.

Princess Serina acted instinctively, extending her arms. She cast her own innate power forth, wrapping Daniel in glowing cherry strings of light and drawing him to her from the air. She drew the field around him by moving her hands in a circular motion as transparent rose fields extending from her arms, encircling the lad, stopping his fall and gently depositing him upon the ground in front of her.

Within seconds, the magical field around Daniel dissipated, and he stood, grinning, brushing himself off. Sammy padded up to them, panting in satisfaction that Daniel was no longer in danger. The hound plopped down with a groan from her exertions, resting beside them on the picnic blanket.

"Takeoff and flying fast is easy, it's the landing I still need to work out," Daniel admitted, blushing in embarrassment. "Thanks for the save though! Hey, that's a pretty amazing gift you have yourself!"

"I appreciate that, and you're most welcome," Princess Serina laughed. "How did you manage this, though? How did you find me?"

"Well, Nick was showing us how to use our powers this morning," Daniel began. "I was worried I wouldn't have any, but he read my mind and knew I loved to fly. Next thing I know, I'm running around like a little kid, pretending my arms are like the wings of an airplane and my hands are the engines. Nick said that if I focus on those thoughts and those memories of flying, I could get it to work. He said not to go far, but when I saw you riding off, I figured it would be okay if I followed you."

"Nick!" She laughed despite herself at how casually Daniel spoke her master's name. "You're calling the former Grand Master Council member and current Head Wizard of Levens 'Nick' now?"

"Meh—Nick, Nicholas...what's the difference?" He shrugged, his mirthful smile revealing he neither understood nor comprehended the significance.

"You really are a newcomer to this world!" Princess Serina laughed aloud and sighed. "Please, sit down and join me for some breakfast!"

She gestured to her blanket in the grass while Barley grazed peacefully nearby. As Daniel sat down and began helping himself, he looked over at the princess.

"So, tell me a little more about your ability," he stated inquisitively. "What is that you threw around me, magnetism?"

"I don't know what magnetism is, but I thought it was wind at first," the princess stated as her face turned more serious, although she still beamed with pride. "Grand Master Nicholas showed me it's more of a bubble. I'm still learning, but I can control the size and the shape of the bubble as well as where it goes."

"So, does everyone here have powers like these?" he asked.

"No, actually very few of us," she corrected matter-of-factly. "Some like me are born with it, while others develop an instinct for other abilities over time. The wizard's order searches for such people to help them develop their abilities. Alas, there are so few of us anymore!"

"Well, hopefully soon I'll be able to control my landings better," Daniel muttered hungrily between bites.

"Until then, maybe you should stay lower to the ground," Princess Serina advised. "What are the rest of your friends doing?"

"Mom is staying with Nick—errr, Nicholas, up in the tower. Apparently, she has two powers, and he wants to see inside her head," Daniel managed between bites. "She can heal people, but it's her ability to see things in daydreams that he's really interested in."

"Daydreams? I hardly think Grand Master Nicholas would be interested in simple daydreams; it sounds like something more than that," she commented as she perked up. "If she has two unique and separate abilities, that would be extraordinary."

"She sees things, but she always has," Daniel commented, pondering the point even as he said it. "She saw Nicholas before he came here when he was young. Sometimes, she just sees things and they happen."

"I guess in this case, she saw something that had happened a long time ago," Princess Serina stated quietly. "If the grand master can accompany your mother in her premonitions, he would have direct insights into your world and into her visions. Even if she doesn't understand what she was seeing, he might."

An errant cloud of doubt washed a cold realization over her; these newcomer abilities could be very useful for Levens or the Wizard's Order of the Moon—anyone with a thirst for power. However, it could also attract others' attention. These outsiders could quickly become hot commodities to less-savory parties and anyone who thought to make use of them.

"Daniel, I'm sure Grand Master Nicholas has told you this, but I think you, your mother, and frankly, your whole group had better keep your new abilities to yourselves for the time being," she warned, a wrinkle forming on her brow as she considered the matter further. "Until you have more control, it's best you practice in discretion with the grand master or me—at least ensure no one else is about."

"Yeah, Nicholas told us about that." Daniel nodded, finishing his food. "I don't get why, but if you're saying the same thing, it must be important."

"Daniel, there are others out there who would seek to misguide your talents or even try to claim them for themselves," she stated in earnest, frowning at his nonchalance. "You mustn't leave this to chance or treat this lightly! I won't go into whom and how at this point, but you must heed Grand Master Nicholas on this. He's very wise and knows the pitfalls that are out there."

"Yeah, I already agreed to that with him," he retorted, looking the princess square in the eye as she stood with him. "I'll be careful; I've already promised that to him, but I'll do the same for you if it makes you feel better. I just don't get why everyone must get all dramatic about it!"

"Come, let's take a walk," Princess Serina said suddenly, offering Daniel her arm and noting his defensive counter. Satisfied that he spoke the truth, she decided not to pursue the matter further in such a direct manner. She took a deep breath before finally exhaling, guiding Daniel gently as the two began to stroll near the river's edge. "You really have no idea how this world works yet, do you? I envy you newcomers, I really do."

"Why is that?" Daniel looked at her quizzically as they walked, his curiosity quickly overcoming his ire. "You're a princess! You have everything you could want!"

"That's just it," she whispered. "I do not. I have duties and obligations that extend well beyond my wishes. I have everything I need, but if I followed my heart, I would be more like you: speaking my mind, wandering new lands and discovering my place in this world according to what I want, not what I was obligated to do."

"Wait for me!" Sammy grunted as she rose to join them, padding alongside and sniffing at the water. A school of trout swam lazily in an alcove under the shade of a cluster of trees. The hound leapt into the swirling eddy, barking excitedly at the fish that darted at the dog's approach. "STOP, STOP!"

"What would you do if you could have it all your way?" Daniel quietly asked as they watched Sammy splash in the river. "What if you were like Sammy, just following whatever caught your interest?"

"I'd go to the Mondlichtberg, deep in the wilds west of here, and discover the depths of my power rather than trying to hide it," she sighed. "Alas, that option is not open to me, at least not yet."

"I'm sorry, I guess I never saw things that way," Daniel admitted. "Where I'm from, I guess we're encouraged to find out who we are first before obligating ourselves to responsibilities. I guess I just never thought about it."

"Now, do you see what I mean? You are coming up on that age of decision," the princess gently stated. "I was born with no decisions to make into an honorable house yet saddled with expectations and obligations. This world, like it or not, will come with expectations tied to your being here and your actions. There are consequences behind the decisions you will all make in the coming days. It may be something you'll want to consider."

"Yeah, I guess," he grumbled. "If we're so different, I suppose we would stand out in that way. You would know, being a princess and all. Your royalty makes you stand out too, even if it's in a different way."

"It's important to remember that in how it affects us," the princess reminded him. "But also remember, your decisions affect others too."

"Stick, stick!" Sammy barked. Daniel threw a stick into the river and the hound immediately went after it, yelping excitedly. As they continued to walk, Sammy dove playfully under the water time and time again, chasing the fish that seemed within reach but always twirled just beyond her grasp.

"Your hound seems to be developing the ability to speak," the princess noted, satisfied that Daniel had heeded her warning. She changed the subject, laughing musically as they strode along the banks, keeping a careful watch on Sammy at play. "Do other hounds in your world talk, or do you suppose the brush with the Shimmering affected even her?"

"Yeah, it's pretty cool but definitely not something dogs in my world do!" Daniel snickered. "I've always wanted a talking dog! That could have been from that Shimmering of yours, same as us, I suppose."

"Your father and your friends, how are they adjusting to all this?" the princess gently prodded. "I'm sure this must be a shock for you all!"

"Nate's not my father," Daniel admitted, appearing somewhat downcast. "I sometimes wish that he would be, but my mom's not sure she wants to marry him. My real dad died a year ago—Nate was his best friend."

"Oh, I'm so sorry, Daniel!" she sighed in sympathy. "It seems I have much to learn about you as well before I levy my envy upon you and your companions."

"Thanks, but the worst thing is that my mom saw my dad's death too, before it happened. She tried to warn him, but he didn't listen," Daniel recalled bitterly. "If he had believed in her visions, he'd still be with us. I used to doubt her too, but not anymore! They don't always turn out exactly as she sees them, but they usually do happen regardless."

"That is a terrible burden for you both to bear," Princess Serina agreed as she clasped her hands. They strode along in silence for a bit, listening to the distant melodies of far-off songbirds and the burbling river as she thought of another way to change the topic from a difficult subject. "So, what about your friends?"

"Javier and Kevin? We only met them a few days ago—just before we came here," Daniel stated, looking away. "Kevin seems nice, a bit like me, but Javier doesn't seem to like him very much. I'm surprised the two of them were together when we found them. They came with two others, but Becky's boyfriend, Tim, was killed in the car crash, and Becky...well, the wolves got her."

"You were lucky to get away; the wolves of the wild here do not let their prey go so easily," she pondered aloud before deciding to change the topic, noting Daniel's sensitivity to what had happened. "What about your world? Do you miss any of your friends at home?"

"No, not really. I mostly just go to school and hang out with Nate afterward," he said quietly, looking back at her with a weak smile. "I'm really not that interesting, Your Highness; not like you. Do you have many friends?"

"On the contrary, Daniel, I'm actually quite a bit like you," Princess Serina sighed, caught a little off guard by the shift of attention to her. She pursed her rosy lips as she carefully entertained his query. "My servant Sophie is kind of my friend. We used to play a lot when I was a child, but when I got older my attention became divided between my royal duties and my studies with the grand master. We're still close, but sadly things are different now. There's a definite separation, and I do miss the times when we were younger, closer and things were just so much simpler."

"So, you don't have other friends?" he pressed. "Is that not part of the obligations of a princess?"

"I have certain acquaintances, but honestly, out here on my own is where I love to be," she confirmed, gesturing to the land around them. "One day soon though, I hope to make the ride to Mondlichtberg and study more for my craft and my innate power."

"Isn't that where all the wolves are?" Daniel asked uncomfortably, shuddering at the memory as he scanned the hillsides across the river as if to ensure their safety. "I heard we came in from near there, and you just got done telling me it isn't safe."

"Well, the fortress is located deep in the wilderness," Princess Serina reminded him. "However, yes, while the journey there may be perilous, it's safe once you reach Mondlichtberg. The wizard's keep is a place of solace where you focus on your studies. That's why the Order of the Moon chose that location, far away from civilization. Grand Master Yamaro is the current head of the Order of the Moon now, and he's been a friend of my family for generations."

"Sounds isolated," Daniel mused. "You sure you want to do that? To give up being a princess to go hang out in the wilderness with wolves and wizards?"

"It is isolated, but that's the point." She laughed briefly before allowing her mirth to subside into a quiet contemplation. "I hope to join them one day, Daniel. Maybe it's a fool's hope, but I wish for it nonetheless."

"What does your family think about that?" he asked. "What about your brother?"

"Well, my mother and father are not fond of that notion, but as for my brother; he'll be king someday," the princess sighed. "I love him— but he's very busy with matters of court and being a prince. I would do anything for him, but we rarely relate or speak about such things very often. It's a shame, really; we are blood but scarcely know each other anymore. I wish I could be like him sometimes and just laugh it all away. I wish I did not take everything so seriously, but I do."

"I wish I had a sister like you," Daniel confessed as he impulsively hugged her close. He felt her tense briefly and let go. "Sorry if I surprised you, I meant nothing by it but support."

She was caught off guard by the sudden show of affection but simultaneously relieved by it. She gently hugged him back before separating. *The unbridled show of affection seems so rare; I wish I had more of that in my family.*

"You are wise and sweet beyond your years," she said as she stepped away from him. "Your magic is a talent you happen to possess. It reflects your ability but also who you are. Don't ever forget, though, that you are loved by your mother and others around you. Just be careful with who you allow within that circle of love and trust; not everyone you meet will have your best interests at heart."

≈≈≈≈

Nate, Kevin and Javier practiced together in the courtyard below the Wizard's Tower, waiting for Johanna. Boredom had begun to set in after lunch had been brought to them. They continued to snack on sandwiches between the practices Grand Master Nicholas had given them to do, pressing on and gaining control over their newfound abilities. Broken stones with burn marks and splintered boards littered the once serene courtyard, and it began to resemble a junkyard instead.

"How much longer do you suppose we have to stay here?" Javier mused, clearing his throat. "I could use a drink after all this yelling!"

"Come on, there's the well with water right there; I hoisted the bucket an hour ago!" Nate pointed at the tiny structure, letting loose a tiny bolt to accentuate his point. The bucket swung briefly, creaking with the impact. "You have magical powers! Doesn't that mean something to you?"

"I'm getting worried about Daniel; I haven't seen him since he learned to fly," Kevin wondered aloud. "I'm hoping he didn't wander off too far!"

"Yeah, that kid flying around might catch some unwanted attention, but leave the worrying to his mother!" Javier laughed. "Speaking of getting unwanted attention, you'd think someone would complain with all the noise we are making!"

"Just keep practicing," Nate huffed, scratching his head and sighing. He glanced worriedly at the balcony high above. "I do wonder what they are up to though! Since Daniel leapt off the balcony up there, I haven't seen nor heard him return. His mother will likely have a fit if she hasn't already!"

"It's been hours!" Kevin threw his hands up in the air. "I'm sick of just transporting myself around this courtyard. We should go look for him!"

"Nicholas said that the small courtyard and fewer distractions would help us to focus our powers more," Nate reminded them as he vaporized another errant brick lying at their feet. "We were also told that the locals are also used to strange sights and sounds near the tower and won't question it here."

"We've been at this ALL day!" Kevin stated again in exasperation. "I'm desperate for a change of scenery!"

"Micker has a point there," Javier grunted, eliciting a smile from Kevin. "Surely at least the two of us can go do something else!"

"All right, all right," Nate relented, throwing his hands up. "I'm kind of sick of sitting around here too. I'm going to go up and see what is taking Johanna and Nicholas so long. If you two want to explore a little and see if you can find Daniel, go for it. If you see him, tell him to come back to the tower and that his mother and I are looking for him."

"Sounds good to me," Javier exhaled in relief. He walked up to the stone well, grabbed the wooden bucket hanging by the lowering rope and took a long draught directly from it. Wiping his face, he turned to Kevin and said, "Come on, Micker; let's go check out the town!"

"Remember, guys, no using your powers where others will see," Nate stated, turning to move into the open doorway of the tower and spinning suddenly. "Practice is just supposed to be here in this courtyard! If you guys aren't back in the next two hours, we'll come out looking for you too!"

"Yeah, yeah; I'm sick of yelling at rocks and sticks for today anyway," Javier muttered, gesturing in frustration at the splintered posts around the courtyard. "This courtyard stinks like burnt toast now."

Nate shrugged as he watched the pair leave. *Those guys are going to do whatever they want.*

He slowly climbed the winding stairs until he reached the door to Grand Master Nicholas's chambers. The magic use did seem to have a draining effect on his energy reserves and although he had healed, he still favored the leg that bore the wound from their trip through the Shimmering, and he limped with the effort.

Sweating profusely at the top, he took a deep breath and pushed open the door, seeing Johanna hunched over a cot with one of Captain Brenard's men lying in it. His chain mail and boots lay beside him, and he moaned in pain as Johanna was tending to him.

"Why can't she just heal all of me at once?" the guard complained. "I'm covered in welts, and if she can heal all of me, why not get on with it?!"

"Sit still, sir! Your sacrifice for ridding the baker of that wasp nest is appreciated, but we're trying to do something here!" the grand master barked before turning back to Johanna. "One wound at a time, again; you may proceed when ready!"

Johanna sighed, and with a single finger, focused on each of the painful-looking welts covering the man's arm. A flickering white light emanated from her finger with each press and the welt promptly vanished. Johanna strained, concentrating with each effort, but soon all the man's welts were gone. He stood and brushed himself off as Johanna gasped in relief.

"Good, good," Nicholas encouraged her. "Continue measuring each effort—note how little you need and administer; that amount, no more, no less."

"Thank you, ma'am," the patient muttered, bowing awkwardly in suspicious amazement. He gathered his things, continuing to mutter to himself about having to endure the painstaking one-welt-at-a-time treatment.

"You're welcome," Johanna sighed, collapsing in her chair as she finished. "I won't lie; that was effort!"

"Remember, not a word," Grand Master Nicholas told the man as he escorted him sternly to the door where Nate stood. "Don't forget to drink a single cup of whim thistle tea for your throat—that should help with the swelling."

"Thank you, Grand Master," the soldier promised. "Not a word to anyone, and I'll drink the whim thistle tea as soon as I'm home!"

"Not too much now, or you'll...Nate! Come in!" the grand master bellowed when he caught sight of him standing in the doorway. The soldier nodded in acknowledgment and departed as Nate entered the room. "Come join us, my boy! Where are the others?"

"Yeah, the guys went out to look for Daniel, and I think I'm about ready for a break too," Nate started to say when he caught sight of a single strand of blood trickling from Johanna's nose. "Hey, are you alright?"

"What? Wha..." Johanna stammered as she noted the nosebleed.

"The overuse of innate power can sometimes be taxing and cause nosebleeds," Grand Master Nicholas advised as he turned and snatched a small towel from the table. "They heal right up as long as you don't continue to overuse them—but I think we've all done enough for today."

"Did I hear you correctly?" Johanna asked, dabbing her nose with the cloth as a fresh wave of concern surged through her. "Daniel's not back yet?"

"Not to worry, my dear, he's with the princess," the wizard gently interjected as he dabbed her nose with the towel. "I maintain a mind link with her, and I assure you, they aren't far away."

≈≈≈≈

Javier and Kevin walked silently, glad to be free from the tight confines of the courtyard as they wandered back down the cobblestone street to the marketplace. The alleyways were bustling with activity, and the two young men took it all in, eyes wide in wonder at the multi-faceted aspects of the traders flocking to the bazaar.

Trading activity was in full swing when they arrived at the market and the front gate. The sounds of livestock and merchants making deals were everywhere. As the two young men gently pushed their way through the crowd, several young maidens carrying jugs of milk caught Javier's eye.

Javier flirted briefly, and they giggled before rushing off to an impatiently waving merchant. The portly merchant glared momentarily at them before scolding the girls to drop off the merchandise before tending to their socializing.

"I think I may see what they're up to," Javier laughed mischievously with a smirk. "You want in on that action, Micker?"

"Go ahead, I'll go look for Daniel, like we told Nate we would do," Kevin sighed, waving him off, anxious to be rid of the crowds. He turned back briefly to verify that Javier had not only taken him up on his offer, but he was also already conversing with the girls, pointing at the Jeep parked near the guard box, obviously claiming ownership of it. The girls seemed impressed, and Kevin shook his head. *Same old Javier.*

Turning to leave, he nearly plowed into a large bearded man, brooding in the shadows of a vendor's wooden alcove. The man donned a wolf-skin cloak and had stepped forth, nearly colliding with him.

"Whoah!" the jovial giant boomed in a thunderous voice. He caught Kevin mid-stride with a hairy and muscular arm. Thick salt-and-pepper hair matted his chest, arms and legs. He towered over Kevin's lanky form yet remained friendly as the surprise of their near collision seemed a source of amusement to the stranger. "Didn't mean to bump into you like that!"

"Oh, sorry," Kevin mumbled as he attempted to squeeze by.

"Care to buy furs or pelts from the wild?" the man offered with a friendly grin, his massive frame obstructing Kevin's path. "I've got some in your size too! Very warm for the coming cold months ahead!"

"Oh, no thank you; I'm just passing through," Kevin politely replied. The stranger smelled of sun, dust and the wild; not unpleasant yet somehow also out of place. "I gotta get going; I'm looking for a friend."

"I would say you've found a friend!" the towering bear-sized man laughed, his arms spread wide in welcome. "Come to my wagon, where I have the finest pelts in the land, the heartiest for when the winter snows blow! I've got much more than that too; many other trinkets and oddities may tickle your fancy from the lands abroad!"

"No, really," Kevin protested, blushing and gently smiling in response as he averted his eyes from the stranger's intense stare. "I'm looking for someone specific. We have somewhere we have to be. Besides, I have no money with me."

"Are you sure?" The vendor pressed closer, his oppressive size normally intimidating, though Kevin found him oddly charismatic. "Strangers from another land have a difficult time blending in here, but if you return to the wilds, it will only be harder there."

"Excuse me?" Kevin turned, suddenly off-put by the comment. "How did you know..."

"Let's just say I have a sixth sense about these sorts of things," the wild man rumbled, grinning a toothy smile before gesturing with his thumb over his shoulder to a darkened side street. The way the wild man indicated closed in on all sides with windowless buildings in a tight yet shadowed alcove. "Come! I have another wagon with plenty to choose from back here, in the alley!"

"Eh, maybe another time," Kevin stammered as he beheld the darkened alley. Becky's voice echoed in his mind. *Beware of the wolf...*

"Really! Come with me; it will only take a moment!" the man insisted as he grabbed for Kevin's arm.

Kevin was faster though, and he withdrew his arm quickly, the man's colossal hand missing and closing in around air instead.

"I said not now!" Kevin snapped, unintentionally sharp. Immediately flustered he backed away, blushing as he apologized. "I'm sorry, but I have to find someone, and I don't have time right now. You seem really nice, but I have to go!"

"Awww, don't be shy!" the man grunted in reply as Kevin turned to leave, pressing onward through the marketplace. "C'mon, don't be like that! I meant no harm!"

"No offense, but I have things to do!" Kevin called back with a smile, glancing back over his shoulder to briefly notice the man's uncomfortably heavy gaze on him. The vendor's friendly face was frozen in a smile, yet he seemed to be deciding whether to pursue him or not. "I promise I'll be sure to stop back by later and find you!"

"Well, you know where to find me when you change your mind!" the stranger shouted back with a wave, a practiced smile upon his lips.

"Definitely!" Kevin called back over his shoulder, but when he looked back again, the man had vanished. He paused, briefly entertaining a strange urge to go back and find the man. Shaking his head and dispelling the notion instead, he pressed on.

As Kevin left the bazaar behind, he passed through the main gate in front of the guards. They watched him wordlessly, glancing at him in mild curiosity as the newcomer exited the town along the very road they had arrived on just the other day. As the crowds thinned, the haunting urge to find the strange man faded, leaving him with relief as he greeted the open field before him.

The scene ahead offered a much more serene environment than the heated crush from the marketplace or the doldrums of the Wizard's Tower. He pressed on through another throng of peasants filing through the town's entrance and soon found himself alone.

As the hubbub faded behind him, Kevin soon found himself traversing the iron-clad drawbridge alone and back on the dirt road they had rode in on. Cattails grew on either side of the road, hemming in on the thoroughfare from the small streambed that fronted the city, waving gently in the breeze.

He trudged down the dirt road slowly toward the distant mountains, placing further distance between himself and the town. The peace and serenity wrapped around him, the warming day giving a reprieve from the cacophony he had left behind. Even songbirds could be heard above the whispering breezes caressing the tall grass around him.

I'm not supposed to use my powers out in the open, but who else is out here? I'm far enough...no one will see...

Kevin scanned the horizon, looking intently for any sign of Daniel. He could make out a single horse grazing near a lone birch tree at the foot of the forested mountains, not more than a mile away. Next to the birch tree, he thought he could see the shadow of the tree. As he stared more intently at the spot, a square blanket stood out to him on the hillside as not being the shadow from the tree. He could see some movement nearby. *Maybe Daniel and the princess?*

Something else seemed to approach from the north, coming from the direction of the river and the road. He could clearly see puffs of dust near the tree line, just exiting the foothills.

Turning his attention back to the birch tree and shadow, he brought his power to bear as he focused. Now, here alone, it would be a great opportunity to test himself and his newfound powers. He returned his focus to the blanket itself, noticing the detail of the checkered pattern, trying to draw it closer to himself in his mind...

≈≈≈≈

Princess Serina and Daniel had spent much of the morning by the river and now that afternoon was setting in, they decided to go back and collect Barley, her horse still grazing peacefully but wandering further away with each passing moment.

Sammy trotted alongside them, wet from the river and chasing fish. As they neared the single birch tree and the picnic blanket, Sammy looked back north on the road and froze.

"Whoooooooo's that?" she growled. A low rumble rose in her throat. "Whooooooooooo's that?"

Daniel and the princess looked back up the road as well but saw nothing.

"I don't see anything," Daniel began. "Sammy, you're just hearing things..."

"Wait; the hound is more sensitive than we are," Princess Serina said abruptly. "I hear them also, even if only faintly—horses."

Daniel listened intently again but didn't hear anything, save for the breeze through the trees. Gold and crimson leaves rustled in the wind, and a far-off crow cawed. Just when he was about to speak again, he heard distant hoofbeats. Although they weren't yet close, the air seemed to vibrate with the approaching cadence.

Just then, four black horses drawing an elegant-looking carriage sped into view, approaching from their north upon the road. Dust kicked up as the carriage drew closer to where they stood.

The coach built from dark-stained wood glistened in the sunlight. Clearly a transport for high purpose, it bore the wizard's sigil painted on the doorway. Unlit ornate lanterns stood out of the four corners from the top, bearing flying sigils resembling a single tower and another matching the Order of the Moon.

The driver seemed young, a pasty lad wearing a long grey cloak, flapping in the breeze like the wing of a pigeon in flight. His sandy hair was mussed and dusty from the road travel. He surveyed the roadside gawkers with wide, suspicious hazel eyes and a slightly unpleasant pale face, reddened only by the exposure to the sun.

The coach rumbled closer, and just as it looked like the carriage was going to pass them by, a deep, rich voice called out to the driver to halt. The chauffeur promptly obeyed, and the passenger wagon came to a dusty stop in front of them. The driver's eyes shifted nervously as he observed the princess and her companion.

Daniel gawked at the dark threads mingling within the driver's cloak, continuously shifting and forming shapes of leaves along a vine, much the same as oil moving along the surface of water. The cloak itself shimmered and glinted, reflecting the sun's light as if coated with a lacquer, the varnish concealing the fine intricacies of the threads, silently weaving their mysterious patterns before his eyes. He had a brief flash of memory that reminded him of an Etch A Sketch toy that he had once played with in childhood.

"We're stopping here, Master Aros?" the disgruntled chauffeur called impatiently over his shoulder. "We have a tight schedule in Levens and must be getting along back to Tyrna!"

"The Grand Master Council can afford a few minutes for me to stop along the way!" the deep voice boomed the reply from within. A tall man emerged, opening the narrow carriage door. Strong-looking and ruddy, he stepped from the carriage grasping a long mahogany staff. He wore a long blue robe, and his short beard matched his dark hair, giving him more of the appearance of a lumberjack than the wizard he was. "I have a few moments to say hello to my favorite princess from all the kingdoms!"

"Who is that?" the hound growled quietly. Daniel held Sammy back, whispering to her to keep her calm.

"That is a friend I haven't seen for a long time!" Princess Serina stated, smiling as she strode toward her with open arms. "He is the Wizard of Tyrna, Master Aros!"

The wizard's dark eyes twinkled in recognition as he greeted the princess with a low bow. Only slightly younger than her own father, the wizard's familiarity with the princess was a luxury that few were afforded, and she welcomed him as she would a long-missed uncle.

"Princess Serina," he chastised playfully in a low voice. "What are you doing out here?"

"Oh, you know me," she stated, giving the larger man a hug. "The day was far too beautiful for me to remain indoors. What brings you to Levens though? I thought you were in Tyrna?"

"I was until the Grand Master Council summoned me. I was on my way back from their summons with orders to convey their tidings to Grand Master Nicholas," the wizard sighed unhappily. He gestured at the intricately cloaked driver who waved in return. "Allow me to introduce my chauffeur and new apprentice, Sottis."

"Your Highness," the driver grunted, bowing his head in brief acknowledgment, even as he swiped in annoyance at an errant fly buzzing his head.

"Pleased to make your acquaintance," Princess Serina said, shaking her head at the driver's lack of engagement before quietly turning to her friend. "Don't tell me you're fighting with the council again. You really shouldn't challenge Grand Master Yamaro like you do."

"No, thankfully our purpose was for something else," Master Aros breathed in relief. "Finally, I was called to assist with something that had nothing to do with me!"

"Why would the council summon you all the way from Tyrna?" she laughed, simultaneously puzzled as her levity subsided. "Why not just send you a message through carrier pigeon or other means?"

"Well, I can't really go into that right now," Master Aros stated, glancing back and hinting in annoyance at his grey-cloaked driver, who seemed to only partially veil his attempt to listen in on their conversation. "The council wanted me to brief Grand Master Nicholas personally on my way back to Tyrna. Grand Master Yamaro instructed me to confer the details of my summoning directly and only to him."

"Odd that they didn't just contact him themselves, isn't it?" the princess pressed. "Maybe that's a good sign, them trusting you with the news?"

"I'm always getting into trouble with them," Master Aros complained. "I'm just thankful they allowed my ascension as a master wizard in the first place. To be Wizard of Tyrna carries prestige I never expected, and it's all I can do to uphold that honor. I'm hoping my answering their summons this time around may earn a better opinion of me at Mondlichtberg."

"Still, Nicholas's title is 'grand master wizard.' He is and was that before he came to Levens. You'd think they'd still include him on a summoning, especially being so close to Mondlichtberg!" Princess Serina stated, miffed. "Grand Master Yamaro and he were close for so long! Surely something so important could be discussed among them!?"

"I like that you stick up for these old men!" Master Aros winked, hugging the princess close to his massive chest again as he whispered the rest in her ear. "They seem to quibble nowadays more than they used to. I'd suggest you leave these grand masters to their arguments and let them sort it out for themselves; it's what I do anymore!"

"I can't do that, and you know it." She laughed again, shaking her head. "Grand Master Nicholas has tutored me for years now, and Grand Master Yamaro is like a grandfather to me. I cannot stand to see this ongoing rivalry between them; they're both so important to me and to each other, even if they don't realize it!"

"Suit yourself, but I tell you that it's just unnecessary heartache with these senile old men!" the wizard retorted. In a clear move to change the subject, he pulled back to eye Daniel and Sammy standing silently by, offering a friendly smile. "So, who are your friends?"

Princess Serina introduced them as her friend Daniel and his dog Sammy but omitted anything other than they were passing through, staying in Levens as their guests.

The wizard was beginning to ask another question when he perked up in surprise, seemingly startled by something undetectable to the others on the road. Staring ahead at the town atop a hill, he squinted intently at the distant Levens.

"What is it?" Princess Serina asked.

"I sense something...approaching," Master Aros whispered. "Something...from over by the main gate. Something coming this way..."

Daniel looked around but could see nothing. Only then did he hear the familiar sound of cicadas and electrical wires. The low hum became a crackle in the very air as a distortion formed above the picnic blanket.

With a flash of light, Kevin appeared, stumbling and tripping over the blanket before falling to the ground near their feet. Princess Serina helped him up as he brushed himself off, apologizing profusely.

"Sorry, guys, I didn't mean to crash in on you," Kevin sputtered, wiping his face with his sleeve. "I—oh, crap, I've got a bloody nose!"

"Kevin!" Princess Serina exclaimed, glancing back with a mixture of embarrassed surprise at Master Aros and his driver. "You scared me...you shouldn't have...oh, Kevin!"

"I know, Nicholas said not to practice outside of the courtyard, but..." Kevin fumbled, straightening up when he saw the large man standing in front of the carriage. "Oh, shit; I didn't realize you already had company! I saw someone coming but..."

"This is my friend, Master Aros, Wizard of Tyrna, the neighboring kingdom to our southeast," she sighed, introducing him while shaking her head in disapproval. She was about to introduce the carriage driver, but Sottis already had uncomfortably fixated his attention on the newcomer. "And that's his..."

"Hi, I'm Kevin Micker. I'm from, well...not here," Kevin stammered in surprise, grasping the wizard's hand in a handshake and waving to the chauffeur. "Sorry if I startled you; I was just out for a walk..."

"Kevin, huh?" Master Aros nodded cordially and stared back in wonder before speaking further. "This may be a fortuitous meeting after all!"

"Yeah, I'm not so sure about that," Kevin muttered in embarrassment, looking back towards Levens in guilt. "I wonder if I may have already done something wrong."

"You do need to be more discreet in your entrances, young man. However, this incident is quite helpful to my cause," Master Aros corrected him. "Let's not confer more here in the open. I need to speak with Grand Master Nicholas immediately. However, I believe you are the very reason I was summoned to Mondlichtberg!"

"Master Aros!" the driver called from behind the wizard, eyeing Kevin and Daniel with a wary eye. "Shouldn't we be moving on?!!"

"Yes, yes, of course! After we give our friends a ride back to town!" the wizard fumed, rolling his eyes and ushering the princess and the others inside the carriage. "These new apprentices are riding me as much as the Grand Master Council. Being a master wizard doesn't carry the prestige it once did!"

"New apprentices?" Princess Serina balked. "The order is having apprentices on ferry duty? What happened to your friend, Durant?"

"We aren't staffed the way we used to be; many are taking double duties just to maintain the basic functional requirements of the wizard's keep!" Master Aros grimaced, pointing over his shoulder. "Sottis here was specifically assigned by the Grand Master Council to keep me in line and on schedule!"

"You're joking?!" Princess Serina scoffed, glancing back at the driver, impatiently fondling his whip as he looked away.

"I'm afraid not," Master Aros sighed, keeping his voice low to avoid being overheard and gesturing inside the carriage to Kevin and Daniel. "Come now, we have much to talk about, and we mustn't keep him waiting any longer. I'm on thin ice with the council as it is!"

"I'll lead the way," Princess Serina called out as she remounted Barley and escorted the group back to town.

"I see we are taking in strays," Sottis grumbled aloud. "This may delay us further, unless...are they part of the reason for us stopping here?"

"Never you mind, Sottis!" Aros rebuked the driver. "Prepare to drive on! We'll make up any lost time on the road!"

As Kevin and Daniel entered the carriage, they couldn't help but notice Sottis's intense glance through the pastel curtains at them. The carriage retained a plush interior with patchouli-scented pillows and cushions matching the curtains. Once everyone was seated and the door secured, the driver spurred the horses on.

"What's his problem?" Kevin muttered, noticing the glare the driver shot back over his shoulder at them from time to time.

"What isn't?" Master Aros laughed, having overheard. As the carriage began bumping along the roadway back to Levens, the wizard's demeanor sobered. "I'm afraid you all have found yourselves in the midst of something bigger than yourselves—in fact, something even bigger than Grand Master Nicholas or myself. We will need a plan, and soon."

The wizard drifted off into silence, catching a glimpse of his driver's sideways piercing glare through the curtains.

Chapter 11

Master Aros

Javier watched from the Wizard's Tower balcony as four dark horses drew the ornate carriage from the river and closer to town. Having returned empty-handed from the plaza, Johanna had greeted him less than enthusiastically when he had arrived.

Nate made him promise to keep watch outside, and as soon as he spotted the carriage escorted by Princess Serina, he called to the others inside the tower room.

Dust kicked up from the hooves of the horses as they trotted toward the main gate, pausing only for Brenard to check them in as Princess Serina led the way. The banners from the Order of the Moon and of Tyrna flew clearly from the tops of the carriage in the afternoon sun.

"Who's that?" Nate asked, looking over Javier's shoulder.

"That is Master Aros, my old protégé—much as Princess Serina is now," Grand Master Nicholas proudly announced. "He's one of my greatest accomplishments from my tenure with the order and remains a good friend to this day."

"Daniel and Kevin are with them?" Johanna gazed over their shoulders.

"They are with him at this very moment, as is the princess," the wizard reassured her with a knowing smile. "When I entered your minds, I established a link. It fades with time, although I can still sense each of you in close proximity. Through our many years of mentorship, the link is much stronger with Master Aros and Princess Serina. I can sense them at great distances and even see images of what they experience in my mind's eye."

"That sounds intrusive," Javier grumbled with a frown, running his hand through his dark hair. Maintaining his commanding posture to cover his unease over this revelation sent jitters through his composure.

"It is a bond of mutual trust and respect, and we utilize it only when necessary," the grand master refuted unequivocally. "The permanent bond only exists between the best of friends, not the temporary one that teachers and students employ. We hold such links in rare esteem and with the greatest care for privacy. It is an intimate bond reserved for very few in a lifetime."

"I meant no offense," Javier muttered, looking away. "I just don't know that I'd want someone watching me with my girlfriend or taking a shower."

"Think of it more like your 'telephone,'" the wizard explained with a patient understanding. "I can see best when you answer and I have your consensual reply. Otherwise, you appear as a vague globe of light in my mind's eye that I'm simply familiar with."

"How large is this order of yours?" Nate interjected. "I'm assuming it's quite extensive with some in this Mondlichtberg I keep hearing about, and others scattered as representatives across the other kingdoms."

"It is, or at least, it once was," the wizard somberly agreed. "We still maintain the traditional three grand masters to head the order. I was proud to have been one of the three lead council members before I retired. In the hierarchy, there are fourteen master wizards beneath them who act as counselors and liaisons for the order of the kingdoms. They also recruit and instruct apprentices from their assigned outposts throughout the known world. Master Aros is one of the fourteen advisory council members."

"How many of you are there in total?" Johanna asked in amazement. "It seems like a good model for sustained growth."

"So it was for many a century," Grand Master Nicholas sighed. "Nowadays, there's but a few hundred of us left. Most apprentices and magicians now are stationed at Mondlichtberg. Since our rift with the Order of the Sun long ago, our numbers have been in a sad but steady decline."

"Order of the Sun?" Nate asked. "Another wizard's order?"

"There was a disagreement in the unified order, long before my tenure as grand master and after the great wars, about how best to serve our craft," the wizard recalled aloud. "Humanity had developed a distrust of magic and the practitioners of it. The wizard's order split, and the predominant group abandoned their charter of service, instead embracing service to self and a pursuit of knowledge above wisdom. They called themselves the Order of the Sun and disappeared over the Grenze Mountains, taking with them much of our power and history, along with the spells controlling the Guardians."

"Descension in the ranks, eh?" Nate commented.

"The Order of the Moon stayed behind to pick up the pieces and continue with our original charter," Grand Master Nicholas confirmed. "Despite the kingdoms' growing reluctance to engage with wizards, the Order of the Moon believed in our original charter concerning the realms of men."

"Surely not all is lost?" Johanna sympathized thoughtfully. "Magic is obviously still a big part of this world, even if a few heads of state reject it presently."

"True, but time is not on our side," the wizard reminded her. "My order believes in strict discipline and centuries of learned practice. Now that times have changed, our new leadership seems bent on compromise with this new Order of Etoilenoir in the east. The temptation to unify our ranks and replenish our membership increases with each new generation yet would alter our practice irrevocably."

"Why not compromise?" Javier asked.

"Their ways are easier to follow and less demanding," the grand master admitted, his worry wrinkles etched deep as he reflected on the implications behind such a suggestion. "This is more attractive to a newer generation, particularly in Urocia, one of the few kingdoms that still not only welcomes magic but also embraces it."

"Doesn't sound so bad," Javier remarked.

"It is if you want to prevent misuse of such power, corruption or outright warfare over such differences," the wizard scoffed. "To keep the peace, between their watered-down version of the true practice and the outright hostility by the other kingdoms to magic, I fear we may be forced to either disband or embrace Urocia's vision within my lifetime. Either case is unacceptable to me and fundamentally alters thousands of years of proven tradition."

"Disband?!" Johanna wrinkled her brow. "Sounds to me like it's a more important time than ever to step up!"

"One would hope, but age has taught me over eons that upkeep for the outposts and Mondlichtberg is costly. Such endeavors require the dedication and funding from many who are less likely to provide that than they used to," Grand Master Nicholas sighed as his voice wavered. "We do not take our craft lightly, as the Order of Etoilenoir does. We meticulously examine the character of the wielder to measure how and when they would best handle the responsibility of power entrusted to them. Without proper training, some magic users are overcome by the powers they brandish. This is ultimately at the core of our disagreement with the Order of Etoilenoir and ourselves and remains the source of our divide, not to mention a constant temptation to take, as you would say, 'shortcuts.'"

"Power corrupts; absolute power corrupts absolutely," Nate pondered.

"Wise words, especially when not having the insight of centuries on your side," the wizard agreed. "It was the basis for my final argument with the council before I stepped down from leadership. Grand Master Yamaro argued to give my younger replacement, Grand Master Encara, time to engage with the Order of Etoilenoir and persuade them to align their practices with ours. I felt we should have negotiated from a greater position of strength, demanding they come to us or break relations entirely."

"So that's why you're now here in Levens and not at Mondlichtberg," Javier surmised.

"You're correct," the elder grand master confirmed. "Encara was charismatic and quite persuasive; I have no doubt that's what won him the Urocian station in Latana. He insisted on accommodation, even if it meant compromising our own standards. Against my advice, he took most of the Advisory Council of Master Wizards with him to Latana in order to directly advise on our differences and bridge our commonalities."

"I take it that compromise bothered you," Johanna stated, sensing Grand Master Nicholas's ire.

"You are damned right it did!" The grand master coughed as he seethed in a brief flash of anger. "They gutted our order of its most valuable resource by removing the support structure of the entire Advisory Council of Fourteen! They sent it all with the least experienced grand master to Urocia while intentionally leaving out two of my protégés, knowing full well they would be an obstacle to their appeasement objectives! They're also cheating our youth out of the discipline and wisdom gained by the Master Council's presence, the fundamental core of what it means to be part of the Order of the Moon!!"

"Whoa, Nicholas, let's take it down a notch!" Nate tried to calm the older man. "Maybe that was some of the compromise necessary to break ground?"

"The advisory's function is part of a careful check and balance, yet they disposed of it like a soiled rag!" Grand Master Nicholas sputtered before regrouping his wits about him as the rapid flush left his face. "By that time, I realized I had not only lost my seat on the council, but I had also lost my influence with them. Their reckless pursuit of progress with the Order of Etoilenoir at all costs has already weakened our very foundation. They've also silenced any dissent, creating further division. I tried to tell them this when I promoted Mistress Amina and Master Aros to the council of the fourteen master wizards, but my words fell on deaf ears, and my two choices have been effectively marginalized."

"They didn't listen, did they?" Javier nodded. "I know what that's like!"

"Not only did they not listen, but in hindsight, I fear that my display of favor for them did them more harm than good," the wizard groaned. "Master Aros was ferried off to Tyrna, a good post for him to be sure, but also well out of their way. Sorceress Amina was more headstrong and therefore relegated to nothing more than mentoring others at Mondlichtberg, always under their strict and watchful supervision."

"Sounds like bad management," Johanna scoffed. "I can certainly relate."

"I apologize for the outburst, however, my issues with the other two senior members of the Grand Master Council run deep—far deeper than that of shallow Encara and his harebrained schemes," Grand Master Nicholas sighed sadly. "For centuries, I collaborated with Grand Master Yamaro and Grand Master Oaxro on the betterment of the order. They threw all our dedication and work away in less than a year. I've often been accused of being a 'purist' while Grand Master Encara is often welcomed in kingdoms not normally amicable to our order. The temptation for acceptance became too much for them over time. I wouldn't share my past political challenges with you, except I think it valuable you understand that your being here has implications beyond simply helping misplaced souls from another..."

Just then, the door at the tower's base creaked, then slammed shut. As the footsteps reached the top of the stairs, the door opened. A tall man wearing a blue robe strode into the room, escorting Princess Serina, Daniel and Kevin as a happy Sammy, who trotted in beside them.

"Master Aros, my boy!" Grand Master Nicholas exclaimed, holding his arms wide to embrace his former apprentice. The younger wizard towered over his former master, yet the warmth of their greeting was one shared among peers.

"Grand Master Nicholas!" the other wizard exclaimed through the embrace as he grinned through a full dark beard. "So good to see you!"

Though Master Aros's russet hair revealed him as far younger than Grand Master Nicholas, his demeanor still reflected someone of high status. His bulky size gave him an impressive presence and his billowing blue robes concealed much of what Johanna guessed were likely the muscles of a man accustomed to lifting heavy objects.

"The pleasure is all mine, I can assure you!" the grand master exclaimed. "Please, make yourself at home!"

"You must be getting senile, old man," the taller and younger dark-bearded wizard announced, gesturing at Kevin and Daniel, who filed in behind him. The two wizards embraced as old colleagues reunited after an untold length of time. "I believe I've picked up something you've lost from the road!"

"As their Advocate under my protection, I told them to remain close to the tower," the older mentor laughed. "Clearly, my advice was not heeded!"

"Advocate, huh?" Master Aros turned to the others in a feigned scolding. "Pay attention to this old coot! He's a purist, but he always has your best interests closest to his heart!"

"What's this business about an Advocate?" Johanna queried, squinting at the reference in annoyance. "I keep hearing that title but am unfamiliar with it; are you not telling us something?"

"Not at all, my dear," the grand master assured her before addressing everyone. "I may as well explain it to you: assuming the Advocacy for you is most important since it extends the protection of the Order of the Moon over you, initiates my responsibility for your well-being and guarantees my welcome to any known associates of mine. In return, the expectation is that you follow my directions to avoid pitfalls or hazards of this world that you may not be aware of!"

"That's partially why I'm here," Aros whispered hastily, searching his former master's eyes, looking away as sudden agitation seized him. "I was summoned to Mondlichtberg to assist in locating these newcomers. When we couldn't find them, we had to deal with the threat from the Northern Guardian. We dealt with the dragon, but we still couldn't locate whoever came through the Shimmering. They sent me back to confer with you but also sent a new apprentice whose motivations I cannot make out. He's been my driver and has stuck to me like glue since we left Mondlichtberg and this is the first chance I've had to be rid of him! It's most annoying!"

"I thought Durant was your valet?" Grand Master Nicholas arched his eyebrow. "You both were inseparable!"

"They promoted my beloved Durant right out from under me and sent him off to the Master Advisory Council at Latana under Grand Master Encara's watchful eye," the younger wizard sighed. "I have the ever-brooding Sottis now, thanks to the council's insistence. Supposedly, he's a goodwill exchange with the Order of Etoilenoir in Urocia, but honestly, I sense no goodwill of purpose with him."

"I'm not going to start second-guessing the Grand Master Council's on-duty placements; that's what got us all in trouble last time," the elder wizard gently chastised. "I'm sure this Sottis will come around."

"He's no Durant!" Master Aros stated with regret before dismissing further thought on the topic. "These newcomers are why I was summoned to Mondlichtberg in the first place, and why I am here before you now."

"How interesting," Grand Master Nicholas growled before turning to Princess Serina. "My dear, would you be so kind as to take our guests back to their quarters and prepare for dinner tonight? I have much to catch up on with my old friend. Perhaps include Sottis in the Levenese hospitality we are extending our new friends?"

"Of course," the princess replied, flashing a smile before beckoning to the others to follow her down the tower stairs. The group bade the two wizards farewell and departed, Sammy padding close behind.

"I'd like to hear more about your intended advocacy!" Nate called back up the stairs. "We need to communicate more about this!"

"So we shall," the grand master laughed aloud, grasping the bridge of his nose with his fingers and shaking his head. When the tower door creaked shut, the two wizards were left alone, waiting for the others to descend the stairs out of earshot. "These newcomers are going to be quite a headache!"

"You can count on it!" the younger protégé scoffed. He shuffled around briefly before throwing a quick quizzical glance at his former master. "Do I still have to call you 'Grand Master'? I won't use titles if you don't!"

"No further titles needed, my boy! However, I do suggest dispensing with the pleasantries," Nicholas began. "These newcomers entered our world not far from Mondlichtberg; I can only assume the council sensed this as I did!"

"Indeed, they did, but clearly the Northern Guardian and the wolves sensed it too," Aros stated, nodding soberly. "By the time the council arrived at the *expected* site of entry, the newcomers were gone. The council feared the wolves and the dragon got there first."

"Expected?" Nicholas seemed taken aback. "Shimmerings are natural events and cannot be predicted. How could they anticipate and search for such a thing?"

"I asked them the same question, and they only told me they were able to sense the formation of it prior but had anticipated their arrival nearer to Mondlichtberg!" the younger wizard exclaimed, rolling his eyes. "It's clearly a cover story with an implicit desire for me not to ask or challenge it any further! I tell you, Nicholas, this time, they've gone too far with all their secrecy and subterfuge!!"

"What?! That makes no sense, though!" Nicholas stared wide-eyed at his former pupil, nearly dropping his staff as he started in surprise. "For one, it's a bit odd to summon you all the way from Tyrna, isn't it? Why didn't they ask Mistress Amina, stationed with them AT Mondlichtberg? Even I am half the distance you were, yet they summoned you for this task? I mean no disrespect, my boy you are a quite capable master wizard, but surely more convenient resources were readily available?"

"I'm afraid their suspicious nature and secrecy have only been exacerbated by your absence over the years; it has not improved in the least!" Master Aros's eyes narrowed, his face suddenly serious. "You know how they feel about the sorceress, and I was sworn to total secrecy until I could deliver my message to you personally!"

"I sensed a great expenditure of power last night, but I couldn't believe they'd move on the Guardian without me," Nicholas scoffed in bewilderment. "That thunderstorm over the mountains to the north the other night, that was you?"

"All three of us," Aros confirmed. "We caught the Northern Guardian hunting a wolf pack that had been sniffing around the site of the newcomers' Shimmering entry. The wolves scattered at the Guardian's approach, but the dragon took an interest in something the newcomers left behind. I'm telling you, Nicholas! The newcomers' arrival has drawn a lot of attention lately!"

"We've never been tested against the Guardians before," Grand Master Nicholas breathed. "How did we fare against the northern one?"

"We managed," Master Aros assured his mentor yet remained sober. "I doubt we hurt the beast; you must know that the Guardians are dangerously resilient. However, we were able to drive it off after a bit of intense fighting. Let's just say it won't be returning to the skies over Levens or Mondlichtberg anytime soon!"

"I sense that despite your success in driving off the Northern Guardian, something else weighs on your mind," the elder wizard surmised, cocking a bushy white eyebrow. "What troubles you further, dear Aros?"

"It's probably nothing," Aros exhaled yet appeared unconvinced, his lumberjack-like features knotted in anxious self-dismay. "Just the tenacity of Grand Master Oaxro and Grand Master Encara to dismiss me after our battle with the Northern Guardian. I had thought to investigate what the newcomers had left behind. I had only begun to examine it when they interrupted. They became adamant that 'my work there was finished,' for me to 'be on my way' and to 'leave the remaining investigation to them.'"

"Curious, that they wouldn't involve you further. After all, that is your specialty—to decipher such mysterious objects," Grand Master

Nicholas scoffed at the irony. "Were you able to learn anything from it?"

"Very little," the younger wizard exclaimed in agitation at the memory of being ushered away from the prize he had come so close to claiming. "Only that it seemed to be a carriage of some sort; it had a power source of its own, badly damaged from what I could tell. I could only deem it was technological in nature and not magical. The other grand masters' over-exuberance in caution, given my innate ability to discern such items, seemed contradictory to logic. However, I deferred to their judgment and followed their command to leave it to them."

"Wise, given the circumstances, yet still most surprising and disappointing!" Nicholas sighed. "However, your assumptions on the beast-less carriage are most likely correct; the newcomers arrived in one prior to your arrival. It's parked at the front gate!"

"I saw it, and while I would love some time with it, we are under pressure to act. The council is still looking for them!" Aros warned. "Especially after they found the strange tracks leading this direction!"

"From what you're telling me, it seems that beyond simply investigating the Shimmering appearance, Yamaro and Oaxro know more about the newcomers than they have stated," the elder wizard exhaled. "The council engaged in this search, fought off the Northern Guardian without notifying me, and now they want me to send the newcomers to them?"

"Nicholas, they don't know that you have the newcomers, much less have assumed Advocacy for them!" Aros stated, punctuating the seriousness of the statement with a grimace. "However, word is bound to get out. I'm a little surprised you didn't reach out to the council about them the moment they arrived! You play a dangerous game keeping them here, my friend! The longer they stay here, the more likely this will jeopardize your legacy and standing with the council!"

"What you're saying troubles but does not surprise me given the distance they place their affairs from me," Nicholas stated as he lit a long wooden tobacco pipe and settled into a high-back chair near his bed. A long pause ensued as Nicholas puffed thoughtfully on his cig, a faraway look glazed in his eyes. Finally, he stirred, a sense of frustration building from within as he clenched his teeth, quietly seething. "The council is led by fools!"

"They're still in charge," the younger wizard reminded him. "You agreed to the council's makeup when you stepped down. We handled the Northern Guardian on our own; let it go, Nicholas! For now, you can claim ignorance of the newcomers, but that claim won't be viable for long."

"The council members are still fools, nonetheless. You know it, I know it, and the surrounding kingdoms all know it," Nicholas proclaimed with chagrin. "Their inability to locate the newcomers so close to Mondlichtberg only proves it to me. The concealment of this confrontation with the Northern Guardian smells more of a cover-up, a greater desperation and a lapse of wisdom than I could never have imagined."

"We still have to respect them, do we not?" Aros blinked in confusion at the sudden turn of the conversation. "You taught me that; we still must do all we can to uphold the order."

"Does that include lying?" Nicholas glowered from the shadows as he puffed his pipe, the embers lighting his face ominously as he awaited an answer, carefully observing his protégé's response.

"Lying?!" Aros scoffed. "That's a bit strong, wouldn't you say? To whom? What exactly do you mean by that?"

"You were sent here to notify me of the newcomers, not just of your action against the Northern Guardian," Nicholas stated as he leaned in closer. "Why exactly did you come in person to deliver this message? For that matter, what IS your message to me from the council, and why am I hearing it from you and not them directly through a magic mirror or other means?"

"I was to notify you of the Shimmering event and that anyone coming through that portal should be rescued and delivered to Mondlichtberg immediately," Aros admitted. "Hiding them away in Levens is hardly what was requested."

"There's something else you're not telling me," Nicholas intoned.

"Never mind their flimsy excuses. I don't believe for a moment that they need you to run courier for them any more than you do. I can tell there's something else bothering you beyond their ridiculous assignment well below your station. There's something that you aren't telling me."

"You're right, Grand Master," Aros sighed, settling back in his chair. "I think they utilized me because of my distance from this region and the fact that I've had my hands full lately. They had hoped I would overlook their cover-up, and when I didn't, they sent me away. They're clearly trying to keep something from all of us; I tire of making excuses for them. I've been respectful of their authority, and it has earned me little more than the disdain they show for Sorceress Amina."

"But that's not all, is it?" The older mentor's eyes narrowed. "There's something more, my young friend—what is it?"

"Grand Master, I believe the Wizard's Council may have been compromised," the younger wizard exhaled, letting the statement hang in the air for effect, using his official title to drive home the point before continuing. "We've been far too passive in the face of Encara's demands since you left, and for that matter, less involved with the other kingdoms outside Urocia. In total, we are out of touch with the realities of today!"

"I thank you for your candor, but what do you mean 'compromised'?" Nicholas pressed. "'Compromised' is a far cry from incompetent. We've always known they were going soft, but outright betrayal?"

"Hear me out," Aros whispered as he leaned in. "Encara does nothing to answer my direct inquiries regarding the flagrant demands Urocia places on Tyrna for supplies and men in their war efforts. As liaison to Tyrna, I have a responsibility to account for this support, yet I am shut out of any negotiating in these matters. At first, I thought it was a simple delay, but this has gone on for far too long for it to be that. I believe he's deliberately ignoring my inquiries."

"Other than Mistress Amina, you are the last counselor from the Advisory Council of Fourteen with any proximity to the other two grand master heads of our order," Nicholas pressed. "This is clearly within your jurisdiction and charter to obtain answers. Why don't you say something to them?"

"When I was summoned to Mondlichtberg, I pressed the matter in person," Aros stated somberly. "I was summarily dismissed for 'challenging their authority' in these matters. I only succeeded in acquiring that imbecile Sottis, hovering over everything I do. All I've accomplished is placing myself under the same sequestration as Sorceress Amina. At least they've allowed me to play courier, as you put it, and return to my post, although for how long I'm unsure."

"So now there's absolutely no dissent or debate in any of their decision-making at Mondlichtberg," Nicholas acknowledged bitterly, squinting at the news.

"Come back with me!" Aros stood, unable to contain himself any longer. "Let us return to the council together! With a united front, we can force the issue and make the three grand masters listen! Encara, Oaxro and Yamaro—they will listen to you, especially if you deliver the newcomers to them!"

"This isn't my fight anymore," Nicholas whispered as he inhaled on his pipe. "What of the advisory? Where are their voices in all of this?"

"No one hears from them anymore!" Aros seethed. "It's as if they've all been cut off, instructed not to correspond. I haven't even heard from Durant, whom I had regularly corresponded with until the summer!"

"I can't just go taking matters into my own hands; we have protocols to follow, and I'm retired!" Nicholas waved off the fragrant cloud of smoke filling the air, settling back in his chair. "Yes, I'm bothered by being pushed out of any influence over the catastrophe that is the Order of the Moon now, but ultimately, this is their hour; mine has long since passed!"

"Grand Master, there's something further I must confess," Aros sighed before taking a deep breath. "Forgive me, I know it was unconscionable, but I was desperate for information, and the king of Tyrna is the only other one with knowledge of this affair. I probed King Faund's mind for the answers I was not getting from the Wizard's Council or Urocia."

"Ah, my young protégé; we come to it at last!" Nicholas's eyes widened at Aros's revelation. The elder wizard stood in alarm, flushed from the gravity of the surprise and the weight it carried. "Without his consent?! You know such an action is forbidden! What did you find out?"

"King Faund believes in unconditional support for Urocia; he feels it's his duty as part of our allegiance." Aros met his former teacher's glare head-on. "I found out something more concerning, though; he harbored a great fear. Not for his soldiers, not for his kingdom—he was afraid of *me*!"

"With good reason, apparently!" Nicholas coughed before closing his eyes in disbelief, whispering the transgression aloud, hoping it to be untrue. "You probed his mind, that of a king, your charge, without consent!"

"He was unaware, I assure you," Aros wheezed as his throat constricted at the admission. "I realize that doesn't excuse my transgression, but in my desperation, I discovered this deep mistrust, established well before it was earned."

"Well, then, that does change things," Nicholas muttered. His eyes snapped open, and he began to pace the room, stroking his beard, deep in thought. "The Austriks have always been friends to the Order of the Moon, even their latest in the line, King Faund's father! What is the current ruler thinking? Why is the council supporting this?"

"I tell you, Nicholas, I'm supposed to be in King Faund's inner circle—damnit! I AM his inner circle!" Aros insisted. "I'm also counselor to the three grand masters! I'm being sidelined from all of them, and I don't know why! Someone is poisoning my reputation at a time when my presence is most needed! I need to find a way to earn their trust back!"

"Say nothing about this to anyone; you were wise to come to me with this!" Nicholas snapped as he stopped pacing and turned to Aros. "Although I'm not yet willing to say this is some grand conspiracy, this may be nothing more than a personal vendetta against you. Any one of these circumstances alone would not be enough, but the potential link between all of this is what I find disturbing; someone may be orchestrating this from the shadows!"

"Yes, but who? And why?" Aros seethed. "We must start somewhere! Should we not bring the newcomers before the council?"

"Not just yet," Nicholas stated slowly, shaking his head. "One thing still troubles me. Every recorded Shimmering event, including the one I experienced myself, has typically been brief, natural and randomly occurring. The Shimmering is known to flash open and then close. It usually allows one, maybe two individuals at most to come through," he stated, clapping his hands together in a sharp retort for effect.

"Yes?" Aros pressed.

"With this Shimmering event, we had seven newcomers, including the hound and two of their beastless carriages, not to mention a great volume of water come through," Nicholas affirmed suspiciously. "Additionally, the council *anticipated* the event, at least, that's what they mentioned to you, even if they did so incorrectly. In their bungling, they also called you from far away to deal with them and the Northern Guardian, not Mistress Amina nor myself; do you not find that odd?"

"Are you thinking they opened the Shimmering themselves and that is their cover-up?" Aros contemplated aloud. "I must wonder, is it possible to OPEN a Shimmering intentionally?"

"I'm not sure if it's possible, and to my knowledge, it's never been tried, at least by our order," Nicholas murmured. "Such action was proposed long ago and quashed during my days on the council. I fear my divide with Yamaro may run deeper than I suspected. By sending you here to deliver their message, it only illustrates to me that BOTH of us are sidelined. No, my friend—to find the answer to this riddle, we are going to need to keep our own counsel and play along for the time being."

"How is that going to help?" Aros asked.

"Sometimes, the best place to hide is in plain sight," Nicholas stated. A bitter smile crept over his face as he crafted new ideas. "The first step is for me to come out of retirement. It's time to heal some of these old wounds."

"Won't that attract attention?" Aros asked doubtfully.

"It most certainly will." Nicholas glowered. "However, we need to get ahead of this, not stay behind it. If you're right about a breach of trust in the council, then our actions are long overdue, and we have some catching up to do."

"On that we are in agreement," Aros stated, exhaling a sigh of relief.

"Don't be so quick to rejoice; do you still trust me, my friend— without any hesitancy or doubt?" The retired grand master abruptly placed his hands on his protégé's shoulders and locked his gaze again. "I need to know this before we take the matter any further. I promise you that I have your best interests at heart at all times, as well as that of the order's. We may need to appear at odds in the coming days, but if we see this through, we will get to the bottom of this!"

"I've always been with you, Nicholas; that will never change," Aros whispered. "What are we to do?"

"I'm still working out the details, but it will become more apparent soon, which is why I asked for your unwavering trust here and now," Nicholas contemplated aloud, grabbing his gleaming white staff and heading to the door. "In the meantime, let's get ready for dinner. You are our guest here in Levens; dine with us tonight!"

"Very well," Aros sighed, muttering to himself. "I just wish I knew what you had in mind."

Chapter 12

Demotion

Dinner that night was a much quieter affair compared to that of the previous night's gala. The torches and chandeliers still flickered merrily, but the minstrel and the other ladies and lords were absent that evening. Nearly half the servants from the previous affair quietly served steaming plates of pork roast and greens to the massive yet mostly vacant table.

The newcomers and the Dade family members dined together with Master Aros as the introduced dinner guest, yet it was mainly Grand Master Nicholas who spoke. A hush fell over the great hall, and only the popping and cracking from the hearth's fire could be heard.

"Long ago, before Urocia or Tyrna, there was a great kingdom in the east called Naehfalar," the grand master began his tale as he lifted his chalice. His shadow cast erratically upon the stone wall behind the table as he stood, a ghostly outline projected by the crackling fire in the hearth. "Naehfalar was said to be the center of the known world, an empire the likes of which has never been seen before nor will likely ever be seen again. It was once considered to be a great republic whose people extended influence and goodwill to all. Their capital lay in what is now the cursed mountains of the far east, a once rich and fertile land on the doorsteps of a great plain, separating them from their only rival at the time, the kingdom of Charzera."

"The two vied for control of the lands between them, which yielded fruitful harvests and was a breadbasket for both," Master Aros quietly interjected. "The rivalry between the two kingdoms was a friendly one for hundreds of years before relations soured."

"Yes, and Charzera also relied on Naehfalar for half their water in that region at the time," Grand Master Nicholas reminded him before continuing as all eyes fixed upon him. "Under the leadership of a young and dynamic King Ma'sum, the larger Charzera actively competed with Naehfalar for water, trade and status."

"After several skirmishes and hastily drawn treaties, Naehfalar and Charzera enjoyed an uneasy peace for centuries, eventually even founding the seaside trading posts that became much of what today is known as the Southern Kingdoms," Master Aros pointed out. "Their close proximity to each other and limited resources became a thorn in the side of both their kings. The power base of both were too evenly matched to best the other, so instead, they spread out."

"That stalemate would eventually be broken by Naehfalar," the elder wizard stated. "Most of Naehfalar's citizenry at the time paid very little attention to the rest of the world, keeping very much to themselves, confident in their positions at the top of everything. In the height of their sloth and revelry, an opportunistic foreigner known only as Lord Gathin arrived."

"He was not only highly influential but also a very potent magic user," the younger wizard explained. "The distrust of magic in our world began with him!"

"He was also a skillful politician and a great divider," Grand Master Nicholas emphasized. "He called attention to every plight he could find, turning people against each other and creating strife among them in the name of forced nobility and charity. Most of the citizenry believed in him, handing over to him their freedoms and their faith, and eventually, even their governance, making him king. They did away with their representative republic structure in the name of 'faster results' and 'more effective leadership.' Detractors were dealt with swiftly and were either converted or quickly vanished."

"This is the very reason most republics fail," Queen Amora sighed. "Without a unified people, you have nothing but chaos, and only the most powerful survive."

"A sad truth," Grand Master Nicholas agreed. "After King Gathin completely consolidated power, he arranged to meet King Ma'sum to negotiate a lasting settlement for peace between the two kingdoms. One of the most infamous events in our history called 'The Great Betrayal' arose from that meeting."

"One incident did all that?" Johanna balked.

"It involved a great deal of magic and shifted the very power structure throughout the known world," Grand Master Nicholas explained. "In good faith, King Ma'sum gifted King Gathin a magic cornerstone meant to seal a permanent friendship between the two kingdoms. Intended for the main gate of Rasha, the capital of Naehfalar, it was meant to instill an honored blessing of longevity and permanence to the life and health of the kingdom."

"It was the pivotal moment meant to bring peace and prosperity to all!" Master Aros shook his head in disgust. "Leave it to power-hungry fools to ruin it all!"

"That's exactly what happened," Grand Master Nicholas agreed. "King Gathin gifted the king of Charzera a chest containing a vicious concoction of death and destruction, the darkest of magic. When opened, it unleashed a horrific blight that consumed not just plants but animals and people. It erupted forth in a swarm that moved in a cloud of death, destroying King Ma'sum and his party on sight. From there, it grew, spreading over the entire kingdom of Charzera, swelling in an unmanageable wave that engulfed the empire's capital of Kallah, destroying the last known Moleifera tree and threatening all surrounding lands."

"What stopped it?" Johanna recoiled.

"Only when the elves combined forces with the wizard's orders and the budding Southern Kingdoms were they able to levy a curse to contain it," the elder wizard concluded. "All that exists of Charzera is but a few ruins within the great desert that remained after the blight had passed through the once green and fertile land. The curse swept everything up and sealed the blight away within Naehfalar's borders. Even the great walls of Kallah, known for their height and decorative beauty, are little more than scattered stone remnants, mounds of intermittent stone buried within the timeless sands of the desert."

"That's also why Urocia and Tyrna grew, founded after the great wars," King Phillip added. "From the ashes of the ancient conflict between Naehfalar and Charzera, kingdoms such as Levens then flourished. With the lands in the east having turned sour, many of the people fled to friendlier and more productive lands."

"Although it's been nearly a millennium, the shades of that realm remain," Grand Master Nicholas stated. "The inhabitants within are always seeking to influence those without. Although trapped, the shades that reside there remain malicious and resentful of anyone who may wander within their reach."

"It also explains why magic is so distrusted abroad, especially by kingdoms nearest to the cursed lands," Princess Serina stated quietly. "It's why we continue to caution you newcomers on travel outside of Levens. While the curse contains whatever is left over from the blight and the destruction it wrought, the boundaries are not visible, and the lands nearest to them are fraught with lawlessness and chaos."

"So that's why you want to be our Advocate," Nate broke in, contemplating the matter aloud. "Even with our newfound abilities, we're likely to bump into hazards and situations that could really land us in a heap of trouble!"

"Or even outright danger," Grand Master Nicholas added, nodding soberly. "Not to worry, my new friends; as your Advocate, I will be looking out for you and your better interests!"

"You hear that, Daniel?" Nate leaned forward over the table, careful not to embarrass the lad yet serious even as he stated it. "Keep close to me or your mother at all times; no running off without at least consulting us or Grand Master Nicholas here!"

"Got it!" Daniel hissed, blushing slightly as he eyed others at the table who, to his relief, seemed not to have heard Nate's direction.

Servants quietly bustled about as the oration continued. Javier eyed a large fruit tart being brought in for dessert and elbowed Kevin as they brought it in.

"I could get used to this," Javier whispered over to Nate at one point, gesturing to the last servant girl, who smiled as she retrieved his plate to replace it with a slice of tart.

"Don't you want to go back?" Johanna spoke softly, careful not to insult their hosts. "There's talk of wars, and we're strangers here; this is medieval living at best, Javier. I'm not sure if you know what that means—living without modern medicine, running water and electricity."

"I'd love to return home, but we need to be realistic about this," Kevin interjected, leaning in and whispering. "I'm betting that tunnel we came through no longer connects to Echo Lake and our world! For that matter, I don't even know how we got here in the first place!"

"You are correct, Kevin," Grand Master Nicholas proclaimed aloud, bringing the discussion back into full display for all to hear. "I didn't mean to eavesdrop, but that is an important point you are making, balancing your desire to return home even while you find your footing in a new world. Your plight has not been lost to me, and we shall be exploring both scenarios in the coming days."

"These 'Shimmerings,' as you've called them, have occurred before," Johanna stated. "Why can't we just find another one to send us back?"

"Normally, I'd say they just don't occur that often; these events are extremely rare!" Grand Master Nicholas explained. "They are quick, like a flash of lightning, and allow very little to come through, much akin to a soap bubble bursting. The one you came through has defied all known characteristics that I am aware of. It's been something of an enigma I am pondering as of late."

"So, what do you propose?" Queen Amora raised an eyebrow as the court turned to the elder wizard. "I take it you have something in mind?"

"Your Majesties, my newcomer friends and my friends of old: I've arrived at a decision. On the morrow, I will depart for Tyrna with the newcomers," the grand master announced, eliciting a collective gasp from all present. "The Wizard's Tower in Tyrna is larger and has the more extensive library I need in order to research this issue more thoroughly."

"What of your duties in Levens?" King Phillip quipped. His forehead wrinkled with distaste at the notion of losing their chief advisor. "What of your lessons with Princess Serina?"

"Your Highness, your daughter has been an excellent student, and there's very little I can tutor her further on," the grand master gently reassured the monarch. "I propose to elevate her status from apprentice to magician by submitting her name directly to Grand Master Yamaro at Mondlichtberg for confirmation. The time has come for her to cut the strings and begin a new journey at the wizard's keep!"

"We're speaking of the princess's obligations to the Order of the Moon, but what of her duties here?" Queen Amora scoffed. "We've still not addressed that sore and lingering topic! She is yet a member of this royal family and belongs here in Levens!"

"The temporary nature of her journey to Mondlichtberg still aligns with her royal duties," Grand Master Nicholas insisted. "Upon completion of the trials, within a few weeks' time, also comes her assignment, which was prearranged long ago as assurances to the house of Dade. Magician or royal princess, once she officiates a true magician's level, she may continue to satisfy both here in Levens indefinitely."

"Mondlichtberg is still close to home," Princess Serina said in a measured tone, barely able to conceal her delight at the proposition. "However, what about Levens, Grand Master? Who would advise the kingdom with both of us gone?"

"I am leaving you in good hands with Master Aros in my stead," Grand Master Nicholas stated resolutely. "I must admit, the circumstances are highly irregular and hardly ideal, but he is most capable and quite suited for this assignment."

"Another master wizard assigned to Levens?" Princess Serina asked, arching an eyebrow. "Won't the council have a problem with that?"

"Yes, but we are coming to that, aren't we," the elder wizard sighed, his face souring, and he turned to address the Master Aros directly. "Master Aros, it has come to light that certain infractions occurred between yourself and the Wizard's Council as well as your assignment in Tyrna with King Faund that deem you unfit to hold the title of master. Since only a master-level wizard may serve in Tyrna, I hereby assign you as Wizard of Levens, advisor to the House of Dade. In the meantime, I will assume your current post as Acting Master of Tyrna. I will also communicate this reassignment to the Grand Master Council of Three upon my arrival there."

The public demotion hung in the air as an awkward moment of silence enveloped the table. All eyes turned to Aros, the former Master Wizard of Tyrna, as he stood, shock clearly etched on his face.

"Your Majesty," Aros stammered, turning to King Phillip. "I hope you will accept me into your inner circle. It would be my honor to serve you and your beautiful kingdom, the gem in the west."

"Thank you for your kind words, Wizard Aros." King Phillip eyed Grand Master Nicholas warily before turning back to the newly demoted wizard. "Levens has not the glory nor stature of Tyrna, but we are a proud people with an honored history. I hope you will find peace here, and we are honored to have you!"

"Thank you, Your Majesties," the newly demoted wizard sighed, and his face reddened as he looked away. "Frankly, the city was wearing on me. Now, if you don't mind, may I be excused to get myself settled? I'm sure my driver will have a thing or two to say about this."

"Of course," King Phillip replied, nodding to his captain of the guard. "Captain Brenard, please assign someone to assist Aros with his items."

"You know what, I think I'd like to help him," Kevin stated spontaneously, pushing back his chair and joining Aros as he left the room.

"That's fine, but when you return, I'll need you all to be packed and ready to leave," Nicholas called after him. "We will be departing before first light!"

"Well, I guess we all had better get ready, given that the plans seemed to have changed," Nate sighed. He eyed the rest of the table before standing and dabbing the napkin on his chin. "Anyone care to join me?"

"I think it best," Grand Master Nicholas agreed. "This gives me a chance to brief the king and queen on the changes."

Motioning to Johanna, Daniel and Javier, they retreated to their rooms to pack their items. The shroud of silence descended over the room again, and only the crackling of the fire could be heard.

"Really, Grand Master Nicholas!" Queen Amora shifted uncomfortably in her chair, barely able to contain her dismay. "Was that necessary? In front of everyone?"

"I'm afraid so," Grand Master Nicholas exhaled. "Tyrna is no longer a fit for Aros. Circumstances have arisen there that demand my attention. I must address the order's affairs there until an appropriate replacement may be found. This move also allows me to address the needs of our newcomers with the additional libraries housed in Tyrna's Wizard's Tower."

"Far be it for us to intrude on the affairs of wizards," Prince Griffon intoned slowly, "but why not send them with my sister to Mondlichtberg? Seems to me that their arrival would be something of great interest to the order, even something they could assist with."

"Indeed, it seems that is the reason for my protégé's visit this day. Under normal circumstances, I would do just that!" Grand Master Nicholas agreed. He paused as he waited for the last of the servants to exit before taking a deep breath. "Your Majesties, I must make an unusual request of you; do not mention the newcomers to anyone. It is likely that the council may eventually discover their whereabouts.

However, I'd like to keep their issues separated from those of the kingdom's."

"They've been seen everywhere!" King Phillip exclaimed incredulously. "Our servants, the farmers, the merchants—people know they are here! Word will spread, and I don't want to tarnish the good standing we have with the Order of the Moon!"

"I know," the grand master stated softly. "I'm not asking you to lie, simply omit the timing of their whereabouts for a short time. Trust me when I say it is as much for your protection as it is Grand Master Yamaro's protection and mine."

"What are we to say when we are asked about them?" Queen Amora gestured to the hall the newcomers had just departed through.

"For now, a simple acknowledgment that you knew them as strangers from outside the kingdom, passing through," the grand master replied. "This not only rings true, but the omission also keeps the royal household out of the controversy."

"Controversy? What controversy? What *is* actually happening?" King Phillip exclaimed, throwing his hands up. "This is highly irregular and places Levens in a very difficult position! Grand Master Yamaro may be seeking these people!"

"Honestly, sire, I am not quite sure just yet," the elder wizard proclaimed, scratching his beard as his voice descended to a whisper. "However, currently, as their Advocate, I am certain the council is NOT the best place for the newcomers. I know this: your daughter is about to receive an honor and a promotion that is long-awaited and well-deserved. Your new wizard is receiving an undeserved demotion yet will serve you well. Trust me in this; I have his interests at heart too, and you are in excellent hands while I am away, I promise you that!"

"With everything happening these days, I suppose you're right," King Phillip sighed, leaning back into his chair to drink another sip from his goblet of wine, warily eyeing the grand master in the firelight. "We will follow your instructions on this, for now; you have my word and my trust. You play a complicated and dangerous game, Nicholas. Be sure you do not needlessly disappoint me or my family!"

≈≈≈≈

"Master Aros, wait up!" Kevin called out to the wizard as he caught up with him halfway down the cobblestone road to the courtyard gate.

"I'm not a master anymore, my friend—what is it?" Aros sighed wearily. Hardly pleased with the way the evening had turned out, he had departed the royal banquet hall looking forward to being alone. "Shouldn't you be finishing up with dinner?"

"Nah, we're done. The others have gone to pack, but I just thought I'd come to help you first," Kevin volunteered sympathetically. "I may be a stranger here, but I know bad news when I see it."

"Many thanks, my friend," Aros sighed, grimacing as he waited for Kevin to catch up.

Once Kevin caught his breath, they continued their stroll together down the darkened cobblestone thoroughfare in silence, the great stone wall looming to one side. Sleepy residential cottages to their other side cast faint light upon their pathway from flickering candles within their windows, their occupants preparing to retire preparing for the evening.

"Your new home doesn't seem so bad," Kevin offered. "It's quite peaceful here, actually."

"That is true," Aros replied glumly, not entirely convinced, although his mind seemed occupied with other thoughts. He seemed to consider the matter further before turning to his companion and refocusing on the newcomer with a smile. "Is everyone so kind from your world?"

"No, not really," Kevin admitted even as he grinned. "I guess you can say I'm just a bit more familiar with disappointment and certainly sympathetic to it."

They approached the carriage under the moonlight for a time in silence, greeted by the flickering candles casting a low light from either side of the coach. A lone howl from a distant wolf filtered gently over the night air, and Kevin shuddered. Becky's words from his dream filtered back to him: *beware of the wolf.*

"They're a long way off and won't come here," Aros offered,

seeming to sense his walking companion's apprehension. The main gate of Levens was closed for the evening, and the entry to the market-place stood dark and empty. A lone guard stood watch, standing beside Aros's carriage and the Jeep, parked side by side.

"I see you've returned from your festivities," Sottis' voice called out, less a question and more a statement. As the driver emerged from the shadows, his grey cloak billowed like a rolling thundercloud behind him. The driver strode forth, and the intricate dark threads silently weaved their hypnotic patterns atop the garment under the moonlight. "Are we staying here tonight or moving on to civilization?"

"I am unpacking and staying here for quite a while longer," Aros sighed. "You are now Grand Master Nicholas's ward since he now has seen fit to assume my duties in Tyrna."

"Well, this is unexpected," Sottis declared, blinking as the implications settled, his own thoughts churning at the change of plans. The news clearly surprised him as his eager gaze turned to Kevin and pointed. "What of them? I understood the council was looking for them!"

"We aren't completely sure who the council is looking for," Aros announced in annoyance. "In either case, they are under Grand Master Nicholas's protection and his responsibility. They are hardly my concern now; you may discuss it further with Nicholas on the morrow if you wish."

The wizard hinted at the chauffeur for assistance to no avail until Kevin assumed the driver's responsibility, taking on an armload of luggage from within the wagon. Sottis finally took notice and slung himself atop the carriage to throw down one of the remaining bags with a gleam in his eye.

"So, Grand Master Nicholas rejoins the fold, eh?" the chauffeur surmised, a thin smile spreading across his pasty face. "Your former master leaves you here to tend sheep while he usurps your role in Tyrna, perhaps producing the newcomers to redeem his position along the way?"

"Hardly that dramatic," Aros replied through a yawn. "You'll be driving on with the grand master's guests for Tyrna at first light. I suggest you get some rest as you have a two-day journey ahead of you."

"I'll just speak with Grand Master Nicholas about it directly then if you don't want to discuss it," Sottis snapped. The flash of anger surged through the driver briefly, and then, it vanished as quickly as it had appeared. "I don't know why he insists on retaining that 'grand master' title since he's retired. At any rate, I'm certain that the council will want to be briefed on all this sooner rather than later!"

"I'll leave that to him after he's settled in Tyrna," Aros sighed, clearly miffed, grabbing the largest two bags. "If I may offer you one last bit of advice, apprentice—mind your station. You may be a guest of the order and given certain privileges as a chauffeur, but your attempts at involving yourself in matters of the grand master will bring you trouble!"

"You wizards take yourselves too seriously," the chauffeur snickered before shaking his head and feigning a salute. "Best of luck to you then, Aros. Enjoy your new assignment!"

Kevin gathered the few remaining smaller bags, pausing to gawk again at the driver's mesmerizing cloak. The dark threads seemed to coalesce at a point before dispersing again, even as he watched.

"Like my cloak, do you?" Sottis grinned.

"It's certainly like nothing I've ever seen before," Kevin commented, nodding politely before turning to pursue Aros, already departing up the hill. He waited until they were out of earshot before commenting to the wizard. "Isn't that guy supposed to be your valet? Shouldn't he be handling these bags?"

"You have no idea," Aros laughed. "Being rid of Sottis is the first bit of good news in this whole ordeal! His assistance, albeit owed, is the last thing I desire this evening. I appreciate you helping me with these and giving me a break from him. I for one am glad to release him from that duty!"

"The pleasure is all mine," Kevin assured him as they entered the courtyard of the Wizard's Tower. "Once we get these up the tower stairs..."

"No, that's alright. There's a hoist at the top, and I'll manage," the wizard pointed to the balcony high above, stacking the bags near the water well. "You had better get packed and prepare for a very early ride to Tyrna. It was a pleasure meeting you, Kevin! I wish you and your friends the best of luck in the coming days!"

"I guess you're right," Kevin sighed, shaking his hand and departing. "Good luck to you also, Master Aros!"

Aros smiled to himself and headed up the stairs. Trudging wearily up the long climb, he opened the door when he reached the top of the Wizard's Tower. There, he found Grand Master Nicholas with Princess Serina already waiting for him in front of the roaring fire. He said nothing as he entered the silent chamber; his colleagues' eyes were upon him.

"So, is this the insult I'm meant to endure, Grand Master?" Aros huffed as he rubbed his hands together for warmth beside the hearth. "I don't suppose one of you could lower the hoist for the rest of my items?"

"I told you before, no titles necessary among us," Nicholas stated softly. "However, there's something I would like you to do while I'm gone."

"You want another favor from me after what just transpired at dinner?" Aros arched an eyebrow in surprise. "What further insult must I endure?"

"The newcomers came in a vehicle—a beastless carriage that is in need of repair and fuel." Nicholas ignored the quip and continued, "No one will understand the technology, but with your innate power, you will be able to decipher it."

"So, this is your reason for leaving me here in Levens?" the newly demoted wizard guessed, cooling his demeanor into a mild curiosity.

"One of many, none of which I gave publicly at dinner," Nicholas stated poignantly. "You are going to be encountering something far more advanced than anything the engineers in Tyrna conceived. I am affording you the opportunity you were denied by the others; something you were owed and particularly uniquely suited for someone with your talents."

"Suddenly the demotion doesn't seem so bad; you're repositioning me to regain the council's trust while giving me a chance to investigate the outsiders' technology," Aros surmised with a grin. A new understanding settled over him, and he notably relaxed. "So that's it then, this is the plan you're developing!"

"Some of it," Nicholas confirmed. "I do not yet understand the interests the council holds with the newcomers, and until I do, I'm not prepared to release them into their custody. We're far too close to Mondlichtberg here in Levens, and I need an excuse to keep the council from obtaining them until I have a clearer vision as to what their intentions are. I did declare Advocacy for them, and I intend to keep my word!"

"Wise choice; however, watch my driver, Sottis," Aros warned. "His involvement with all of this may extend beyond his simple unpleasantness. He seemed quite preoccupied with these newcomers and our apparent disagreement. He assumed you were bringing the newcomers back to Mondlichtberg and seemed most disappointed when I informed him that your destination was Tyrna. I told him we hadn't confirmed their number yet or if indeed these people were them, but that will quickly become apparent during your travels."

"No one ever mentioned to Sottis that these people were the newcomers," Princess Serina offered. "He only met Kevin and Daniel earlier today, and for all he knew..."

"That's exactly my point," Aros stated. "Sottis knows more than he lets on. I'm certain he was assigned to watch me, but I'm unsure by whom. The assignment came as I was leaving Mondlichtberg as I departed. Durant was switched out, and Sottis stepped in; it seems his charter may go further than that of a simple valet. Keep a close eye on him, especially if you plan on withholding information from the council."

"I will indeed!" Nicholas nodded as he turned to Princess Serina. "As for you, my dear, I need you to ride for Mondlichtberg in two days.

That should give me enough time to reach Tyrna and contact the Grand Master Council myself. They will hopefully agree to confer the title of magician to you after your trials. That should also give you some time to poke around and find out what is going on there."

"Who do I trust then if not the council?" Princess Serina protested. "Won't I be on my own then?"

"Seek out Sorceress Amina," Nicholas confirmed. "I would place my trust in her. She would have taken my place on the council now had it not been for my falling out with Grand Master Yamaro. Our past disagreements may have clouded his trust in me, but she is still loyal to their original charter."

"Are you asking me to spy on the Grand Master Council?" Princess Serina's eyes widened. "Isn't it enough that we're already lying to them about the newcomers?"

"I want eyes and ears there that will protect the order's interests, the leadership, including Grand Master Yamaro," Nicholas clarified. "I ask only that you refrain from talking about the newcomers as much as possible. I will be talking to the council directly about them myself, thereby assuming full responsibility for them and the situation around them. If asked, just say that they were strangers passing through— nothing more, nothing less. That keeps Levens, you and your family out of the controversy."

"I can do that," she agreed. "I will also keep an eye out for Mistress Amina."

"Timing is of the utmost importance here," Nicholas stated as he stood and moved out onto the balcony. Using a pulley hanging from an overhead beam, he began lowering a hook at the end of a thick rope to the ground below. "The council has made it clear that they want the newcomers. If they learn that I had them prior to my departure for Tyrna, they won't trust me. They have to believe that I came across them on the way to Tyrna and that my reasons are centered on repositioning you, Aros. The truth may come out eventually, but I'm counting on you both to ensure that we fulfill our parts in this plan before it does!"

"Won't the council demand you bring them to Mondlichtberg regardless?" Aros asked. "Even without a direct report from Sottis, they are going to discover their whereabouts eventually."

"They may." Nicholas smiled. "However, if they believe you left Tyrna in shambles and I'm delayed getting to them because you left it in such a state…"

"Now, *that* they might just believe!" Aros laughed bitterly. "My demotion suddenly makes more sense in gaining the council's trust while getting to the bottom of this all. What are you going to do in Tyrna?"

"Find out who's been slandering my favorite protégé and look for a possible way to return the newcomers home," Nicholas sighed. "For them and hopefully the council, the trip appears as nothing more than a tour, prior to finding out exactly who and what they are."

"Perhaps I may be of further service here!" Aros exclaimed as he snapped his fingers. "While you're in the tower library, I suggest beginning your search in elemental magic."

"Why elemental?" Nicholas squinted.

"Something I overheard the Grand Master Council talking about while I was at Mondlichtberg." Aros nodded, recalling the memory. "The Shimmerings are a convergence of great energy, and they suspected it may have to do with seeds from the Moleifera tree."

"There are no such trees anymore." Nicholas blinked. "The last one was destroyed by the blight in the great wars."

"Indeed," sighed Aros. "Nevertheless, that is what they were talking about. Those seeds contained the core powers of elemental magic. Even without the great trees of old, some of the seeds may have survived."

"There may be other ways of tapping into that magic, though; we should keep our eyes out for anything with elemental power of that magnitude," Princess Serina cautioned. "Until we find something tangible, I suppose we have our specific missions."

She bade them both a good night and turned to depart. Nicholas stopped Aros as his protégé turned to leave and follow the princess down the tower stairs.

"A moment, please," Nicholas whispered to the younger wizard. The grand master reached inside the pockets of his robes and produced the keys to the Jeep. "Nate gave me these to give to you before they retired for the evening."

"What are those?" Aros arched an eyebrow.

"The keys for the beastless carriage to work, or so Nate described them," Nicholas pondered as he handed them over to his protégé, who grinned in anticipation. "He did tell me that it is low on fuel, the food that carriage consumes, so do not allow it to run long."

"Thank you for that advice," Aros replied with glee as he accepted the keys, dropping them into a deep pocket on his long blue robe. "I shall heed it!"

"Aros, this whole business with the newcomers aside, I need you to make me a promise," Grand Master Nicholas intoned darkly. "If I find nothing in my investigation of the council, you will not pursue this matter any further. I'm going out on a limb here to investigate, but if they are found blameless, we must adhere to the council's wishes!"

"You believe me, don't you?" Aros balked.

"I know you believe what you're telling me," Nicholas assured his protégé. "However, I've been a part of this order for hundreds of years, and I know that you are ambitious. This can be off-putting for some in positions of power. If I find that this is all simply a misunderstanding or a conflict of personalities, you may have to accept your new assignment as permanent. I am sorry, my friend, but to challenge the council carries a deep price to be paid. If you're correct, though, I fear the price we may all pay will be much deeper!"

"Understood." Aros nodded somberly before turning and walking to the balcony to secure the rigging. When he had finished, he turned to leave when Nicholas stopped him. "If you don't mind, I'll go secure my bags if you don't mind hoisting them up."

"I will assist you with your luggage. However, I need you to understand: this reassignment gives me no pleasure," Nicholas reassured him.

"You may have the lesser assignment in Levens, but I am not looking forward to coming out of retirement, either. At the very least, I'm stuck for a minimum of another ten years in a city when I'd much prefer to fade quietly into the sunset here in Levens!"

"Well, I suppose it just means a longer wait for me to get my mineral assignment," Aros jested. "I had my eye set on Opal."

"Don't tell me you bought into that ridiculous notion of monetizing our ranks!" Nicholas scoffed. "Grand Master Encara embraced that 'golden wizard' nonsense all too readily, flaunting his wealth and fixation on his status; he's no better than the rest of them, whose years of service and experience far outrank his!"

"Well, I hate to tell you, dear friend, but it seems to have stuck," Aros sighed, placing a reassuring arm on his former master's shoulder and cracking a smile. "Grand Master Yamaro has taken to silver, which frankly matches his hair, and Oaxro..."

"Say nothing further!" Nicholas shook his head in disgust. "He retains the copper nickname from his upbringing near copper mines; pathetic!"

"I suppose that would make you a crusty old diamond?" Aros quipped. The look he received in return made him break out into laughter. "Old and unyielding?"

"Don't you dare!" Nicholas whispered, barely containing his mirth at the notion.

Chapter 13

Tyrna

As Kevin slept, he dreamt of floating in a cloud of feathers. His mother and father suddenly appeared with him; they walked with him as they strode together through a golden forest of oaks and cottonwood trees. He couldn't clearly see their faces, but he could hear their voices. They spoke to him about his classes, school and why he didn't have more friends in his life.

The conversation quickly became more heated as Kevin insisted that he had friends, even though he knew it wasn't true. He just couldn't make them understand. Javier, Tim and Becky manifested through a mist in front of them.

"See—those are my friends!" he stated, waving to them. "We're going on a trip together for spring break to Colorado."

"You and I both know those aren't real friends," his mother chided him. "They are just acquaintances. They don't really care about you."

He turned to his mother and father to continue the argument, but they were nowhere to be seen. Tim and Becky's faces turned ashen, and they slumped over, falling to the ground. Javier stared blankly at him as leaves began falling from the trees in a sudden curtain of swirling orange and red.

"Tim!! Becky!!" Kevin shouted, kneeling next to his fallen friends. "Javier!! Do something!!"

Looking about, Javier had also vanished. Only Becky and Tim's deteriorating forms lay stretched out on the ground in front of him.

"Tim, Becky—wake up!!" Kevin cried as he tried to brush the leaves from their faces.

"I told you to beware of the wolf!" Becky's voice floated back to him from everywhere. "It is too late for us; make sure it is not too late for you!"

Dry and brittle Becky and Tim's bodies became, wilting like dying flowers whose petals crumple into a brown and grey lifeless wafer-like crust. Leaves fell around them as barren trees creaked with the sighing breeze, their branches crackling in the wind.

"Don't worry about us now. We will be at peace once we are released from the wolf; the wolf stole our legacy! The wolf is our bane and will be yours too if you are not wary!" Becky's voice rippled again around him. "You and Javier need to look after each other until then. He needs you just as much as you need him."

"Don't doubt yourself or our friendship—it is real," Tim's voice assured him through an echo of his own. "He doesn't realize it yet, but Javier is also your friend now; trust him."

"What do you mean 'he doesn't understand'? I don't understand!" Kevin shouted, looking every which way. "Where are you?!"

Tim and Becky's bodies continued to pale, fading suddenly into piles of leaves. A brisk gust kicked up, scattering the dried leaves everywhere. Kevin tried to hold them together, but they seemed to blow apart. When he opened his hands, all he held were crumbling leaves.

"NO!" he screamed, holding the piles to his chest, sobbing as the leaves blew apart, swirling around him in a whirlwind of sadness. The forest groaned as trees creaked in the wind. The dust and leaves that were his friends dispersed around him and blew away.

"You and Javier must end this for us!" their voices called out in unison before fading with the wind. "We will only fully be at peace once you do!"

"*Javier!*" *Kevin screamed, turning to find he was alone. "Where are you, Javier!? Javier!!*"

"I'm right here, geeesh!" Javier exclaimed in annoyance, waking Kevin the rest of the way as his eyes fluttered open. "You're not having another sex dream about me, are you?"

Kevin rubbed his eyes, slightly embarrassed as Daniel chuckled. Sitting up to regain his bearings, he realized they were all crammed together in Aros's carriage, rocking gently down the road in the twilight of early morning. He sneezed once as the scent of patchouli from the pillows mingled with the dust kicked up from the road. His eyes watered briefly as he pulled a linen curtain aside to see the darkened twilight forest drifting by, only slightly illuminated by the dull, hazy, silvery light from the lamps at the front of the wagon.

"What?!" Javier snapped when Nate kicked at him. "I was just kidding!"

"Sorry, I was just dreaming," Kevin mumbled, looking away out the window while reaching down to pet Sammy, sitting dutifully at their feet. "I just thought..."

"No, I get it," Javier snickered. "You find me hot!"

Kevin returned his attention to the inside of the carriage and, other than Javier smirking at him, Johanna and Nicholas sat across from each other in a linked state. With their hands on each other's temples and both with their eyes closed, they paid no mind to the others in the cramped quarters. Their eyes darted under their closed lids as if in REM sleep.

"No reason for Javier to be an asshole; just keep resting, Kevin, you're fine," Nate growled disapprovingly. "We've got a way to go, crammed in here like this. You may as well rest where and when you can."

Kevin reclined, rubbing his temples. He sighed, taking a long draught from the canteen in the seat beside him as memory flooded through him, the recollection of the wee hours of twilight resurfacing in his mind's eye. They had all packed the night before and had little sleep when Nicholas had awakened them while the darkness of night still permeated the windows of their rooms. He had led them to the main gate, where the coach had already been prepared for departure. It had been a cold, crisp morning, and Sophie had handed them individual wool blankets for the ride.

The seats inside Aros's carriage proved to be comfortable enough, plush and filled with a mix of wool and cotton. The sides were lined with linen tapestry to dampen the road noise and add color and coolness to the interior while keeping most of the road dust at bay. Sottis had already lit the lanterns, the ghostly light reflected in his curious eyes as he had motioned them aboard.

Sottis had said very little to them as he shuffled their bags atop the carriage. The early start had not yet awakened the valet's unpleasant demeanor as he had climbed to the driver's seat without even a mutter, his grey cloak with mysterious, animated black ink fluttering behind him.

The journey had started out quite rocky departing Levens, particularly in the dark with only the lanterns lit, dim globes alongside the carriage. The road felt bumpy, primitive compared to the ride they had prior in the Jeep, tossing the carriage about as the horses trotted along. The carriage they rode in had been bouncing down the road for hours now.

As they continued through the early morning, the rising sun cast the first rays of light through the long navy linen curtains. The road near the base of the mountains meandered south into the forest; the ride smoothed and became more bearable. This gave the indication that the road was more traveled, and indeed, they passed the occasional horseman or cart-toting mule.

Fully awake now, Kevin parted the drapery again to peer out the window; they were deep within the forest with no river or mountains in sight. As the first hint of dawn approached, he could make out pines and firs clustered tightly on both sides of the road, mixed with occasional birches, oaks and cottonwoods.

"How far is Tyrna?" Nate called to the driver.

"We won't reach the city until tomorrow," Sottis stated with a yawn. "I was assured that the drive would be strenuous for you all, so we break the trip in half. Tonight, we make for the town of Millstead, the halfway station between Levens and Tyrna."

"Sounds like this is going to take a while," Nate grumbled, sitting back in the seat. He glanced over at Johanna and Nicholas, still locked in whatever mental state anyone could guess. Turning to Daniel, he patted him briefly on the leg. "You doing alright there, buddy?"

"Yeah, I'd rather fly to wherever we're going, though," Daniel huffed. "I'm barely getting the hang of all this, and now we're being told to keep it under wraps!"

"I hear ya," Nate replied with sympathy, shaking his head. He sufficed himself to merely close his eyes and settle back into the seat to take a nap of his own. "Just relax for now; we need to follow Grand Master Nicholas's advice until we get a better lay of the land! He's our Advocate now, and we need to let him do his job!"

Johanna remained in a dream state of her own. Nicholas accompanied her, sitting across from her and grasping her head within his withered hands in concentration. She couldn't see him, but she could hear his breathing and his heartbeat.

"Think, Johanna," the grand master's voice rumbled through her mind in a thundercloud. "Think back to the boy at the tree."

Flashes of memory flew by her as if on a movie screen; she scrolled through her memories as she used to look through microfiche in a library years ago. She saw Bill playing with a much younger Daniel. She caught glimpses of the church they used to attend as the cross on top of the doorway stood out in her mind several times, intermittently interjecting itself between visions. She saw the hospital she worked at and some of the patients she had tended to. She saw the man whose wasp stings she had healed back in Levens, one at a time with her finger. All these images were from her actual recent past; she searched for something else.

"The dream, Johanna, take me to the dream," Nicholas's voice echoed again.

She could see the young boy again. Mussed brown hair barely moved from under his wool hat, and gloves, along with his oversized bearskin coat, protected him from winter's chill. She could see him make his way through a quaint village with three rabbit furs slung over his shoulder. Surrounded by friendly faces, mainly hunters and trappers, the boy hummed to himself as he crunched his way through the snowy streets. The boy sauntered on to where a strapping lad stood in waiting, looking much like himself with a bit of facial stubble, yet older and nearly a man. He embraced the boy, lifting him up into the air with gusto, laughing with welcome as a proud mother and father looked on.

"My family," Nicholas's voice breathed sadly through Johanna's mind as he paused. "Another life...another time. We mustn't linger here, albeit a beautiful and intriguing reminiscence for me. I miss them even today, hundreds of years later. Can you move forward just a bit? Think of the tree..."

More flashes of light, and then, there—she had it. As if frozen in time, she could see the young Nicholas frozen in terror behind the boulder in the dead of winter. She could see the misshapen tree, twisted in death. In front of the tree, the pool of blackness was extending halfway up the village tailor's arm and inside his nose and mouth, trailing like thick syrup.

As she froze the image in her mind, the blackness was the only movement, and she focused on it; it pulsed rhythmically.

"Yes, that's it!" Nicholas's voice whispered, his voice trailing off in amazement. "Can we move forward from here? It's so shocking even for me to see the clarity of my memory in your mind!"

Everything blurred forward as she watched young Nicholas run up the creek bed in triple time, leaving behind the other men killed so rapidly; she scarcely observed it.

"Slowly now...there! There!" Nicholas boomed excitedly. "Stop here!"

The scene did not stop as Nicholas's voice had asked but played on as if in slow motion. Young Nicholas hid behind the roots in the cave, and the maddened tailor with the glowing red eyes and frothing mouth reached through the roots for him. The boy bashed the man in the face, releasing a torrent of blood from the tailor's nose, and the red glow in the man's eyes flickered.

"His hold was weakened there!" Nicholas's voice noted. "Go on, more...slowly," he instructed, and the scene moved on at normal speed.

Suddenly, the man lunged through the roots and into Nicholas, and the two went tumbling down the dark hole. Branches, ice and rocks tumbled with the pair as they fell, assailing the young Nicholas and his attacker. Young Nicholas flailed wildly, trying to slow his descent, and missed grabbing an outcropping of rock...only to hit his forehead on it.

A cry of pain and fear reverberated throughout the cavern, and Johanna realized the echo came not only from young Nicholas but also from the elder currently sharing the vision with her. The smell of sulfur mingled with the dank wetness of the earth.

Just as it was becoming more difficult to focus on young Nicholas's surroundings, the darkness swirled into lights, and she slowed the imagery down in her mind.

"Yes, very good," Nicholas's thunderous voice boomed. "We are seeing the Shimmering itself!"

In the past, she had always taken the swirling lights as a sign she was waking up from her dream. Now that she was watching this event unfold slowly, she realized she could still see the faint outline of young Nicholas tumbling amidst the lights. She could also see the outline of the tailor tumbling alongside Nicholas only a few feet away. The tailor's body suddenly stretched as if being pulled apart like taffy, spaghetti-fied, and drawn away from Nicholas...but to where?

She managed to briefly pause the image, the dancing lights highlighting the tortured image of the tailor's face contorted face, stretched into an impossible warped feature of rage and...

Why didn't we notice those lights when we came through? Suddenly, the frozen image in Johanna's mind seemed to melt again, morphing back to the Jeep and the Lincoln embedded in the muddy banks next to the river.

Nicholas released Johanna's head from his hands and patted her on the shoulders as she gasped for breath. It took a moment to get her bearings, and she blinked her eyes as a single drop of blood dripped from her nostril.

"I'm sorry," she said, shaking her head in frustration. "I got distracted by the lights—we can try again."

"I think not," Nicholas stated softly. Smiling, he handed her a white lace handkerchief to dab the nosebleed. "We've done enough for today."

"You okay?" Nate asked with a note of concern, having stirred awake as well with the activity in the carriage.

"I'm fine," Johanna huffed in frustration, waving him off. She turned to look out the window and held the hankie close to her face. "It's...it's just a nosebleed."

"Don't be so hard on yourself or him," Nicholas whispered reassuringly. "He's just trying to help, and frankly, you still uncovered details of great value to me in your vision!"

"Really?" Johanna arched an eyebrow. "How so?"

"You don't know how many years I thought that dark shade had succeeded in acquiring me," Nicholas laughed, sitting back in his seat. "After I came to this world, I secretly blamed myself for allowing it to take hold and thought that *it* was the source of my power, lurking somewhere deep inside me. Although I later learned that was not the case, it is still reassuring to witness proof!"

"That's all you got from all this?" Johanna shook her head. "I must tell you, I don't enjoy reliving that event over again! It was bad enough when I was dreaming it, but to learn it was real is making it worse for me. I can only imagine what this is like for you, seeing it all again!"

"I could see that when I hit the tailor on the nose, full possession of his body had not taken place; otherwise, I wouldn't have been able to interrupt its connection," Nicholas sighed. "It seems, however, that their connection was more than a simple involuntary seizure by the shade. That man, the tailor, he welcomed and relished the possession. It makes the cursed one's bond and possession much stronger with a willing host."

"So, what happened to him?" Johanna asked.

"Their connection wasn't broken," Nicholas stated resolutely. "When we passed through the Shimmering into this world, the curse levied against Naehfalar took hold immediately and seized the tailor along with the shade, binding them both to the cursed lands. These nuances from your visions could only be surmised before; as a witness, I have now confirmed them."

"So that shade was from Naehfalar?" Johanna asked. "How did it get out in the first place?"

"Quite a disturbing notion, really. A fluke, I suppose, although it's difficult to say," Nicholas sighed. "The fact that a Shimmering can open anywhere might suggest that the curse meant to contain the evil ones can be—and in this case, was—temporarily circumvented."

That news sent a shudder through Johanna as she contemplated it.

"Not to worry, my dear." Nicholas patted her knee. "We also know that the shades, or wraiths, as we call them, can only infect one person at a time. The key importance was that the moment it came through, it was returned to Naehfalar, where it belonged. You witnessed proof that the curse stands and is still effective to this day."

"What are they capable of, though?" Johanna shifted uncomfortably at the thought. "What could they do if they got out and went through a Shimmering to our world or somebody else's?"

"They are just darkened spirits from another age with only power that is given to them by those who embrace them," the wizard assured her. "Naehfalar's shades are just that—wraiths from a different era and time. Their time has come and gone."

"What of a Grimmigwulf?" Nate asked suddenly.

"Sorry, what?" asked Javier, scoffing after an attempt to pronounce the word.

"'Grimmig,' then 'wulf,'" Nate clarified. "Brenard mentioned them to me the other night. Since we were talking about all these legends, I thought I'd ask."

"Shape-shifters from an afflicted human to wolf that lurk in the deep wilds, very dangerous," Nicholas clarified. "They're a legend among the western and northern wilds, although supposedly, they used to roam all the lands long before the Moleifera trees died out. They stick mainly to the deep wilds now and avoid human civilization; frankly, they are quite rare. The Northern Guardian and the wizard's order at Mondlichtberg in the west generally keep them away, or at least in docile and manageable numbers."

"Brenard seemed worried enough about it to bring it up." Nate shrugged.

"The northern kingdoms have had some issues with aggressive wolf packs over the years," Nicholas acknowledged. "With the increased unpredictability of the Northern Guardian and our waning numbers at the Mondlichtberg, it's always a possibility the Grimmigwulf could resurface again. They haven't been seen in eons though, not since the dark days. Most people don't believe they even ever existed anymore! I believe the good captain is just being cautious."

"Werewolves?" breathed Kevin. "That's how the description sounded to me, but do they exist here? I mean, even if they do, isn't that just when the moon is full?"

"I surmise from your reaction and your term 'werewolves' that this means they are legends in your world. In our world, they are quite real, even if rare," Grand Master Nicholas explained. "Their only tie with the moon is how well you can see them at night."

"Well, that's not much help; do you mean they can change at will?" Javier snorted even as he shrugged. "All the stories from our world have werewolves as mean evil hunting machines, like vampires."

"Vampires, huh?" the grand master laughed. "I believe the shades of Naehfalar are the closest thing we have to the undead in this realm! No, those are locked away, but I assure you, the Grimmigwulf remains free and very real."

"Well, perhaps we should know a little more about them then," Johanna muttered, raising an eyebrow. "Should we be worried about this Grimmigwulf?"

"They're generally very solitary creatures," Nicholas started almost dismissively. "These days, they choose to commune with actual wolves in the wild rather than subject themselves to people or civilization. Legends say they can change at will, even in daylight. Others say it's a curse they cannot escape that manifests itself only at night. The point is that their human relations are so chaotic and rare that they generally avoid each other and humankind."

"I wonder what drives them?" Kevin pondered the thought and shuddered as Becky's warning in his dream to "beware the wolf" whispered as an echo in his mind. "I wonder if any of them were involved with that pack that attacked us when we first arrived. You said we came through in a very isolated region."

"You did, but it's doubtful a Grimmigwulf would be involved; plenty of normal wild wolf packs exist in the frontier," the older wizard assured him. "Long ago, in the dark days, even before Naehfalar, the Grimmigwulf lusted for power and magic they could consume and ingest. The wizards' orders were only just being formed, and elves ruled the lands. The Grimmigwulf of that time hunted not just for food but to expand their own powers, and that was something beings of magic simply could not tolerate. With their voracious appetites unchecked, Grimmigwulf proliferation became so intrusive and terrible, it was said the wizards and elves hunted them nearly to extinction to drive them away and into the wilds."

"So, these beings were content to just be driven away?" Johanna asked, incredulous in her skeptical tone. "It seems rather harsh!"

"Contentment is seldom the way of the Grimmig! I assure you, it was most necessary!" Nicholas countered. "Most were destroyed since they were viewed as a plague in a great culling. They were cunning foes and would spread among the tribes of humans in order to take down someone with power. The elves and wizards of that time period could not tolerate a threat of that magnitude."

"With no elves today and fewer wizards, what's to stop them from coming back?" Kevin thought aloud.

"The Grimmigwulf of old were true hybrids, retaining human

drives and desires," the wizard explained. "Any existing today are likely mostly wolf, if not completely wolf, at this point. It was why the survivors were driven into the wild. Their human cravings and tendencies have been diluted out by this time, replaced with only the wild."

"Never to return again," Johanna sighed. "How would we be able to know one if we saw one?"

"Not as anything you'd differentiate from another common wolf, at least not these days," Nicholas added with a shrug. "It's just the nature of that aberration. Yet another example of a creature from another era whose time has passed. In legend and eons ago, they walked on two feet instead of four with their forepaws as great claws. Quite fearsome to behold!"

Their ride plodded on well through the morning as the sun brightened the land around them. They only stopped briefly by a stream for water and to hand out packed lunches, courtesy of Charla's meticulous planning and stowing of the basket atop the carriage.

Sottis's interest in the group seemed awakened at this juncture, and he surveyed each of them wordlessly as he handed out the rations with a gleam in his eye. Grand Master Nicholas either didn't notice or didn't care, so no one else called attention to the matter.

The remaining part of the afternoon proceeded without incident as the sun trekked steadily through the sky with only the errant crow or forest bird cawing occasionally overhead, a distant reminder of being the only ones on the frontier roads. Only after dusk settled over the land did the carriage finally pull into Millstead.

The town had a rustic yet homey feeling to it, buried in the woods while offering a sanctuary for weary travelers passing through the wilds. Nate pointed out that the town resembled something like a set from a Western movie. Narrow wooden buildings, hastily assembled and even leaning somewhat, lined both sides of the roadway. Wayward livestock wandered into the roadway as local farmers hastily chased after them.

The carriage pulled up to the only two-story structure in town, an inn whose name, "The Wanderer," hung from a splintered sign, swinging lazily from above the doorway. To each side, small misshapen cabins and barns were interspaced with stables and storage yards.

"What's his problem?" Javier mocked, noting Sottis's watchful eye from atop the carriage. He gently elbowed Kevin with a whisper as he disembarked. "That Sottis is clearly obsessed with us! Hey, maybe he's got the hots for you, Micker!"

"Or maybe you, Javier," Kevin retorted with a grin, glancing back to see the driver's gaze boring down on them as he stepped gingerly down from the coach. "You seem to always want to steal the show; maybe this time you finally succeeded!"

"Finally, Micker, a good answer!" Javier winked. Kevin smiled, noting the banter had not descended into a heated argument with his normally annoying companion.

As Nicholas parted the double doors to The Wanderer, a lulling fire in the stone fireplace greeted the travelers. The scent of pine mingled with the lingering aroma of beef stew as a sparse collection of solitary patrons finished the evening meal. The innkeeper nodded in welcome from behind the reception desk, a gnarled elderly man perched behind an ornate-looking wooden table looking almost misplaced in the otherwise plain-looking lobby.

Only a few side tables with scattered and lonely patrons drowning their unknown worries in pints of ale dotted the otherwise empty room. They wore cowls tightly around their faces, glancing at the odd group entering the establishment with mild disinterest.

The innkeeper's smile widened when he recognized Nicholas, his wrinkled features brightening as the firelight and candles gleamed off his bald head and the spectacles on the tip of his nose. He dropped from his highchair and waddled around the side of the desk to greet his new visitors, hunched over and leaning heavily on his cane.

"Grand Master Nicholas! Welcome again, sir!" the innkeeper rasped, his voice sounding like sandpaper as he gripped Nicholas's hands in a more personalized greeting. "It has been some time, hasn't it?!"

"Yes, Wilhelm," Nicholas laughed. "It's good to see you too. It has been far too long—I don't get out much anymore. I offer my best regards to your wife and family. I see the logging business is still as good as ever."

"Well, you know this old forest. Cut something down and it grows back rather fast here." The innkeeper turned and eyed Nicholas's companions suspiciously, pushing his spectacles back up on the bridge of his nose, his oversized eyebrows arching like those of a wise old owl. "Traveling with an entourage this time?"

"Yes, I was en route to Tyrna when we came across them on the road," Nicholas intoned loudly as he stroked his beard. "I suppose I'll need several rooms for them as well."

"Well, that's rather generous of you," Wilhelm replied as he raised an eyebrow. "What's the occasion? Are they of some importance to the order?"

"Never you mind, my nosy friend," the wizard laughed nonchalantly, pulling a bag of silver coins from a fold in his robes and carefully dolling out a handful, counting them individually on the counter. "Let's just say I'm overdue for a good deed."

"Very well, that's more than enough," Wilhelm commented before turning to the others. "Follow me, everyone!"

"I hope we aren't crowding out anyone," Grand Master Nicholas offered. "We are a large group, after all."

"Not at all! Top floor is all yours," Wilhelm explained, motioning for them to follow him to the corner of the room. The narrow hall led up a set of creaking stairs as they climbed to the top floor. "Four rooms to divvy up as you see fit. Breakfast is at sunrise, and if any of you want a bath, we have two of the four tubs in the back with hot water prepared and unused for tonight!"

Wilhelm handed the keys to Nicholas before turning around and heading back down to the lobby. Sottis grabbed his key from out of Nicholas's hand without a word to anyone else, chose the room closest to them, went inside and closed the door behind him.

"Well, I guess he's made his decision," Nate chuckled to himself sarcastically. "Such a friendly guy!"

"Nate and I can share here, along with Daniel," Johanna intoned the statement as more of a question, to which Nicholas affirmed.

"Micker and I can share," Javier said, looking down from the second-story window to the backyard below. The group gathered around him and could see flickering torches lighting a fenced-in area at the back of the inn. "Looks like they have hot tubs out here!"

"A bath!" murmured Johanna, to which the rest of the group sighed happily in agreement. "You guys go first; I won't be far behind you."

Below the window the group stared out of, The Wanderer's property backed up right to the edge of the forest. Large cedar tubs had fire pits dug beneath them, and two of the four still had smoldering fires and hot coals beneath their metal bases. Halfway up each tub, cedar panels had been banded together with metal bracings and sealed in tar. They simmered pleasantly, and the steam released aromas of herbs and spices pleasantly into the evening air, already cooling with the coming night and the scent of pine.

"Whatever they are, I'm in," Javier stated with an eager grin. "Micker, you're with me! Don't get any ideas now!"

Kevin laughed but said nothing, staring at Javier in amazement. *To think I'm about to take a bath and share a room with a guy I really hated; I would never have placed myself in this moment, ever! Can this world get any stranger?*

≈≈≈≈

The next morning, Daniel arose first, clean and refreshed, eager to see what the new day held. He and Sammy padded quietly out the door past the other's doors. While his mother and Nate slept peacefully, he knew the others would be equally difficult to rouse, all except Nicholas. The wizard had chosen the room closest to the stairs and would be on guard for any coming and going to the second floor. He cautiously descended the creaky wooden stairs, careful to avoid rousing their host.

After taking Sammy out back to let her do her business, he decided to preempt his companions in search of breakfast. The hound sniffed around the tubs first, their fires long since grown cold and nothing but ash at their base, the relaxing waters drained away and the tops covered with a thick canvas, covered by frost.

When the dog finished, Daniel sauntered into the lobby, rubbing his hands together as he approached the hearth to warm himself. Sammy curled up next to the fire herself, content to snooze.

"How did you sleep, my lad?" Wilhelm smiled a toothless grin from behind the front desk. He grabbed a plate from behind the counter, offering a plate of various muffins, cheeses, berries, cold cuts and nuts as he brushed back his wispy white hair. "I hope you found the baths to your satisfaction. We pride ourselves in offering that to our guests!"

"Amazing night's sleep!" Daniel thanked him, taking a seat at the bar and settling upon one of the stools at the center. "The beds were comfortable, but I had no idea we would sleep so well, especially after those baths!"

"The secret is the tubs, my young friend," the innkeeper commented. "We heat the water with a mix of sweet grass and Glymous Cave salts. The water we pipe in from a local spring."

"Sweet grass? Glymous Cave salts?" Daniel asked, to which the innkeeper perked in a bit of surprise. "What's that?"

"Sweet grass is gentler than whim thistle," Sottis's voice interrupted his thoughts from a darkened corner beside the fireplace hearth. The valet stood and strode forth with a smile as he continued. "It has some of the medicinal effects without the risk of consequence from overindulging, a pleasant numbing for sore muscles. The Glymous Caves in the dwarf kingdoms have an effective mild salt that they mine for sore muscles; it complements the Whim thistle nicely."

"Oh, that sounds good." Daniel shrugged, cautiously extending his hand to the chauffeur. "We haven't actually met, although you are our driver, right? I'm Daniel!"

"I'm called Sottis, valet and apprentice to the Order of Etoilenoir," their driver corrected, extending his own hand from the inside of his misty, opaque grey cloak, simultaneously shooing the curious innkeeper away as he took a seat of his own next to Daniel. "It's a pleasure to make your acquaintance. I must say though, the benefits of sweet grass are common knowledge even outside Levens. Where exactly did you say you are from?"

"I never said I was from anywhere, but we are from nowhere special," Daniel retorted jovially, his smirk fading as he became mesmerized by the shifting black threads weaving leafy patterns throughout the misty grey backdrop of the driver's cloak. "Seriously, how does your cloak do that?"

"It's just a bit of magic, courtesy of Latana, capital city for the kingdom of Urocia." Sottis grinned pleasantly yet with purpose. "We've produced many more wonders in my home capital of Latana; have you ever been there?"

"Um, no," Daniel feigned a struggle with a full mouth, stuffing his mouth with a muffin and holding up a finger to stall having to answer.

"Never been to Latana?" Sottis exclaimed with an exaggerated feigned surprise. "You must really be from somewhere far away! How is it that you met the acquaintance of the grand master?"

"Oh, Nicholas and us?" Daniel coughed, looking away. *This feels more like an interrogation!* "Sorry, we were on the road in the wilds... and...Nicholas came upon us..."

"They are visitors from a far-off land," Grand Master Nicholas stated from the hallway, striding in with long purposeful gaits to interpose himself between the two. Daniel nodded in relief as Nicholas pulled up a seat next to him. "They are unfamiliar with our kingdom and are considering establishing a homestead."

"Good morning to you, Grand Master," Sottis deferred in half-hearted reverence. "I didn't realize you were so familiar with our travelers. Such a kindness you've shown them, taking them with you on your journey to Tyrna. I would imagine the council would love to recognize such generosity. They may have a thing or two to say about such charity, particularly since I note we are headed away from Mondlichtberg and not to it."

"That's a tremendous leap of judgment, particularly for an apprentice and a valet, wouldn't you say?" Nicholas smiled back through clenched teeth. "Besides, I'm retired, or have you forgotten? No matter, my business and counsel are my own; I suggest you mind your own affairs!"

"I meant no offense, Grand Master!" Sottis protested. Clearly shaken by the rebuke, his face reddened as he looked away. Several pencil-like outlines of leaves falling from the vines and regrowing new ones on his cloak seemed to accentuate his mood. "I merely look out for the order's interest and..."

"Of course," the older wizard cut him off gently, clearly uninterested in the explanation. "Rest assured, my ambitious apprentice, I keep the council well-informed in matters that concern them on a regular basis."

"I've got your favorite morning tea, Nicholas," Wilhelm interrupted mildly, returning with a steaming cup and handing it to the wizard as footsteps resounded from the rooms above. "It sounds like the others have arisen. I'll prepare your fare before you depart."

Sottis stood, brushing himself off and looking away as Nicholas became distracted by the newcomers descending the stairs. Wilhelm turned, motioning the group to a set of tables, and began serving breakfast.

"Join us, Sottis," Daniel offered.

"I'll see you all outside," the driver politely declined with a wave. "I've already eaten and must gather my items; it's time to prepare the carriage."

Wilhelm served up a sumptuous fare for breakfast, offering everyone several identical plates to the one Daniel had already picked halfway through. By mid-morning, they returned to the carriage and the road.

Sottis had already arranged everything, preparing their bags atop the coach and awaiting them outside the front porch as they climbed aboard. Seemingly subdued since the morning's conversation, he said very little to everyone as he took his station.

With a crack from the reigns, the valet drove the carriage into the rising sun, barely beginning to peak over the treetops and breaking the frost-covered leaves into a cool morning dew. From Milstead, the road descended gently from the high-country forests into a broad valley to the east. Shorter yet rocky hills running north to south emerged ahead of them, paralleling the much taller and more forested mountains behind them.

As Sottis drove onward, the journey turned southward at the base of the sparsely vegetated hills, the tree line steadily thinning as they passed a field of boulders. Soon, the forest vanished altogether into widening grassland with only a smattering of squat, sparsely strewn elms and cottonwoods, and they descended in elevation and further from the feet of the Grenze Mountains.

The hills ahead punctuated sharply into a single tall yet narrow mountain peak, forming a horseshoe curve around which the city of Tyrna resided. The mountain itself dwarfed the surrounding rolling hills, sharp and pointed, intermittent snow glistening from the top third of the rocky heights.

Even at the still great distance of nearly twenty miles, they could make out massive red walls of mortar and brick projecting out of the alluvial fan at the mountain's base. Lines of people and livestock peppered the landscape, forming caravans coming and going from the valley as they drew ever nearer.

They rounded the bend well past noon and could finally see the city of Tyrna in all its glory, unhindered by Tyrna's Peak, the ridgeway wings of which surrounded the city to either side. The outer wall encircled the front of the city in a great crimson ring, protecting all approaches to the front while the mountain made any approach to the rear impossible. Behind the wall, the city rose in elevation, right up to the base of the lone mountain.

As the carriage approached, the outer wall grew closer, looming above them to either side. What they saw ahead through the yawning great gate made Levens look tiny in comparison. All visible buildings behind the wall consistently maintained A-framed roofs, looking like spires reaching for the sky. Everything vertically clustered behind the walls; the buildings and the walls all had the same red brick and mortar stone. This gave a slight industrial flair to the otherwise medieval capital. The whole city seemed to glow in welcome beneath the afternoon sun.

Soldiers appeared as small as ants, patrolling the upper walls in pairs, nearly 100 feet above their heads. White pennants and standards flew everywhere, bearing a simple crimson wall with ramparts atop, resembling the very walls they flew from.

In contrast, the newer settlement outside the walls buzzed with activity as wooden cranes lifted stone, mortar and planking to the massive undertaking. New stone buildings, white with fresh plaster and thatched roofs awaited new tenants, dotted the landscape around them, spreading out from the mouth of the main gate.

Sottis guided the carriage into the line of traffic moving into the city, gently mingling with mule-drawn carts and pedestrians on foot. The occupants inside pulled the linen curtains to gawk out the windows at the spectacle moving around them.

A cluster of cats larger than mountain lions strode upright beside them, covered from head to toe in richly ordained, multi-colored clothing. Their eyes gleamed in annoyance at Daniel when he opened his window for a closer look.

"Mrreeeeooooow!" one with luminous emerald-green eyes said. "Haven't you seen anyone from Carthen before?"

"Um, no—sorry," Daniel muttered quietly, embarrassed. The lad just couldn't take his eyes off cat-people dressed in human garb; they even had customized ornate jackets where their tails could poke through.

"Whoooooo's that?" Sammy growled, sniffing the air as Nate stroked her to keep her calm.

"A talking dog!" the cat-man gasped in horror. "How? Where?"

"Never mind us; my friends here are from the north, and this is their first trip this far south!" Nicholas pulled Daniel back and poked his head through apologetically.

"Grand Master Nicholas the Great!" one of the females with snow-white fur and blue eyes purred. "What brings you to Tyrna?! Such a welcomed surprise!"

"I'm taking a holiday," the wizard stated nonchalantly. "I'm showing my new friends the city, and who knows, maybe the lake later."

"Welcome to Tyrna then!" a tall black one with yellow eyes mewed blissfully, and all three bowed low. The cat-people moved fluidly, bobbing their heads as curiosity set in. "The cat-people of Carthen bid you welcome! We hope you have a pleasant visit and a wonderful day! Please excuse our surprise!"

"Not to worry; carry on!" Nicholas laughed musically to set everyone at ease.

The crowd thickened as they moved on, and a group of dwarves emerged from a nearby tavern. The Carthenians continued to gawk, standing tall among the crowd of squat miners and craftsmen as the carriage lumbered on.

Daniel watched in awe through the back window, taking the scene behind them. The valley and a long way off on the horizon, Long Lake stretched further than the eye could see, all along the base of the Grenze Mountains.

Within moments, they passed beneath the great crimson archway that formed the top of the main gates, over 100 feet above their heads. Within the red brick wall, the retracted gate was mostly hidden from the outside until they passed beneath it. Comprised of thick wooden beams and held together by rusted iron grating, the hulking monstrosity loomed menacingly high above. A particularly large pennant bearing the crimson wall flew vertically from above, traipsing nearly half the distance from the top of the archway, covering most of the giant mechanism.

Between the slats of darkened recesses to each side, Nate could make out the giant chains dangling ancient house-sized boulders. Melded to the chains as counterweights, the gargantuan weights held the rusted gate open.

"This must have taken years to build!" Nate breathed as they passed beneath the superstructure, the clopping of their horses' hooves reverberating around them.

"Eons, my friend—whole generations," Nicholas stated with awe. "They were built for a time when the city-states were at war. Those were days of strife, yet days of greatness. Much has changed since then. I don't believe these doors have closed in hundreds of years. If they were, I doubt we could get them to open again."

"Those chains actually function?!" Javier commented. "This place is magnificent!"

"You should have seen it back in the day when it was new," the wizard sighed. "The decline began with the death of wonder; just look at the people coming and going beneath these great gates! This city was made great by people who wanted to be a part of something bigger than themselves. Many come here now to make quick and easy money, drawn to the success rather than the reasons behind the success. These peasants today are lesser sires of greater men. When you stop appreciating what was given to you, then you run the risk of losing it; and I fear that time may come sooner than most expect."

"What is it?" Johanna asked softly, catching the darkened glimpse of his face.

"It's truth, my dear," he sighed. "Despite its magnificence, this city is dying. Sometimes, living in a lie is easier than facing the truth. When I left this post decades ago, the city was already showing signs of degradation. I fear the decay such lethargy fosters also invites predators who take advantage of such conditions."

"Like who?" Nate shifted warily.

"That has yet to be revealed and is also one of the reasons we are here," Nicholas stated soberly. "I have a few suspicions based on petty jealousies in the Wizard's Council and neighboring kingdom royal rivalries, but something tells me there may be something more that."

As the carriage drove on, they couldn't help but notice the throngs of people passing beneath the massive archway. The great rusted chains dwarfed all that passed by yet caught attention from neither beast nor traveler. Great stone carvings cried aloud in silence at the passersby, neglected for eons, displaying missing letters labeling dust-covered memorials of long-forgotten heroes, lining the busy thoroughfare.

All that remained intact were the massive, derelict chains, each link dwarfing even the carriage yet rusting in quiet agony under the assault of suffocating time and neglect.

Chapter 14

King Faund

As the carriage moved further into the city proper, manicured trees and bushes lined the cobblestone road to either side. The thoroughfare ascended gently between older white stone buildings that gradually increased in height.

Although the city's interior remained quieter than the construction activity occurring outside of the great crimson walls, Tyrna had a crowded feel to it, bordering on claustrophobic. Causeways narrowed between slender homes and businesses with carefully manicured miniature parks crammed intermittently between, intended to compliment the architecture and break the sense of congestion.

A small creek shone in the afternoon sun like a pearl. Yet merely a narrow ribbon, the water source for the city meandered through a series of parks. Paralleling the roadway, the babbling brook ran over cobblestone beneath many fruit trees and manicured bushes, complementing the narrow havens of nature with a serene peace amongst the hustle and bustle of the city. At times, the road traversed it in a series of low-arched stone bridges in miniature gardens, interrupted only by the occasional stone bench and torch lamp.

As the grade of the road gradually steepened, the crowds dispersed, and another wall and gate loomed ahead. Older and smaller, the inner wall of Tyrna rose ahead of them, formed from dark grey granite, heavily worn with age, covered with ivy and dotted with moss. Everyone noted that the rusted iron spikes retracted above their heads as they rode beneath. It reminded Johanna of Levens's walls, albeit older and more worn in appearance, choked with a variety of vines and moss.

They passed beneath the archway and rounded a corner where the royal palace gleamed ahead in the sunlight. At the base of the mountain, the palace towered as a vertical overlay in front of the massive peak, mimicking its taller and wider backdrop. Made from the same red brick as the outer walls of the city, it towered above as a tight cluster of spires, with the southernmost Wizard's Tower overshadowing all, being more than double the height of the next tallest.

Sottis parked the carriage beneath the porte-cochere where the street ended in an abrupt cul-de-sac courtyard. The courtyard featured a small, grassy alcove at its center, where a circular cascading fountain lay, gleaming marble white in the sun, matching the ascending staircase into the stronghold.

The fountain bubbled over into a reflection pool where colorful fish leisurely glided about at its bottom, sliding along curtains of translucent draping tails and fins. Two guards stood silently at the base of a rose marble staircase leading up to the main palace. They held nothing more than ornate standards depicting Tyrna's red brick walls atop decorative spears. The banners matched their uniforms, and they stood dressed in crimson finery to match the stone around them.

Nicholas disembarked and helped Johanna and the others onto the cobblestone way when a loud horn blew, heralding their arrival.

"All hail his grace, King Faund, head of the House of Austrik!" one of the sentinels proclaimed aloud. "Welcome to the city of Tyrna, capital of the kingdom of Tyrna! Announcing the arrival of Grand Master Nicholas from the Order of the Moon and distinguished guests!"

Two massive oak doors bearing detailed carvings of crowns set within a frame swung open at the castle's base. A grinning young man sporting a long flowing red robe eagerly descended the white marble stairs, flanked by two royal guards. His tussled brown hair curled above his slightly freckled face as he grinned enthusiastically at his new arrivals.

The king's entourage wore light helmets, obviously more for decoration than for combat. The garishly decorated royal guard wore a large decorative collection of red feathers at the top and an opening at the front, forming a large "T" for their eyes and nose. Crimson capes flowed around their shoulders, matching the king's garb. They flanked the monarch in formation, sun glinting off their helms as they marched forth.

Javier looked on unimpressed as he agilely sprung down from the carriage. The king was likely not much older than Kevin or him. His auburn facial hair was neatly trimmed, yet it could not disguise his inability to grow a full beard.

Kevin and Daniel eagerly disembarked before an aggravated Sottis pulled the steps out properly for the stiff and wary remainder of their troupe.

"Grand Master Nicholas, what an unexpected surprise this is!" King Faund exclaimed in a well-practiced voice of formality as the elder wizard emerged. "I only recently received word of your coming!"

King Faund gripped Nicholas's hands in his and kissed both his cheeks. The whole group knelt, although the newcomers looked clumsy doing it, and the young monarch noticed immediately, smiling in amusement.

"My apologies for not sending word earlier, Your Majesty," Nicholas began. Through his smile and greeting, Nicholas watched the king carefully for a reaction. "I won't bore you with the details, but I will cut to the chase. I've relieved Master Aros of his duties here in Tyrna and exchanged them with my own in Levens. I hope I did not overstep my bounds with you or the Wizard's Council but felt it necessary."

"This is quite unexpected but not unfortunate," King Faund

exclaimed with gratitude. He paused only momentarily as if considering the matter further as he managed to smile. "I cannot speak for the council, but I am not displeased with this outcome. I know you were very fond of your protégé, but ultimately, things were just not well-suited for him here. Your arrival, on the other hand, is most welcomed!"

"It's been a rather long journey, my friend," Nicholas sighed, gesturing to the newcomers. "Perhaps we can discuss our being here over some refreshment?"

"Of course, come! Come!" King Faund exclaimed, pausing as the wizard's companions disembarked. "Who, may I ask, are your companions?"

"These are my guests, whom I am advocating for and are under my protection," Nicholas stated as he introduced each of the newcomers by name. They each bowed awkwardly in turn as King Faund smiled and nodded.

"Welcome to Tyrna—any friend or ward of Nicholas the Great is certainly as welcomed as he is," the monarch stated. "It is obvious to me that you are not from this land or Levens, and I'm most pleased that Nicholas has chosen to show you our proud city in your travels."

"I must inform you; they are more than simply from a land far from here," the wizard stated before lowering his voice to a whisper so that only the king could hear. "In fact, they are from an entirely different world altogether; I suspect the one I originated from. They arrived through a Shimmering event detected only a few days ago."

"A Shimmering?! What a rare occasion of legend to revisit our time! Splendid!" The king could barely contain his excitement under his whisper and wide eyes. "Nicholas, you hero! You have brought them to me first! You shall be well rewarded!"

"Perhaps we can discuss this further in a more private setting," Nicholas intoned with a disquieting grimace. He glanced warily about, his smile fading. "I certainly do not intend to make a spectacle of them in public."

"Of course! My apologies, Grand Master, but it has been quite some time since we've had newcomers to this land!" the monarch exclaimed, beaming with exuberance. "Wherever did you find them?"

"I happened upon them on the road while departing Levens, frankly only becoming acquainted with them on our travels here," Nicholas sighed a little louder for Sottis's ears, noting the driver's barely veiled attempts to overhear from atop the carriage. "If it pleases Your Majesty, I would like to maintain some discretion about their arrival for the time being—at least until they've had a chance to receive a proper orientation. It's the reason I've assumed their advocacy for the time being."

"Of course!" King Faund grinned, turning to one of the guards at his side. "Grand Master Nicholas and I have much to catch up on. Sir Caspin? Sottis? Would you both be so kind as to take our new friends and show them proper hospitality? Perhaps a diversion at the Pratenvike!"

When the lead guard removed his helmet and introduced himself as Sir Caspin of the king's guard, Sottis clambered down from atop the carriage, embracing him with gusto. Sir Caspin was the taller of the two, with thinning sandy hair, twinkling green eyes and a thin moustache; the two seemed very glad to see each other.

"That's the first time I've seen any joy in that lad's face," Nicholas muttered to himself.

"The Pratenvike, Your Majesty?! You aim to shock these strangers into fun?" Sir Caspin's playful demeanor gave Javier the impression they were indeed going to have a good time. "It's a bit early, isn't it? Nevertheless, even mid-afternoon, the activity, food and fare should prove ample!"

"I suppose I could deal with a bit of food and ale before my day ends. If it pleases you, sir?" Sottis grinned before turning warily to Nicholas, who nodded his approval. "Very well then; it's decided!"

"Is this normally where you go when you have time off?" Johanna intoned politely.

"It's a great place to meet people, and I'm most pleased we're meeting you!" Sir Caspin flashed Johanna a flirtatious smile, fixating her with his bright curious eyes. "We so rarely get to be ambassadors of sorts to gracious new guests such as yourself and your entourage!"

The captain of the guard grinned, taking her hand and giving it a long kiss. Nate looked on with annoyance, particularly when she blushed.

"Oh, thank you. If you don't mind, though, I'm rather tired from our journey and would like to get settled," Johanna stated gently as she pulled her hand away to Nate's satisfaction. "Perhaps just the men should go this evening; guy's night on the town?"

"Yes, well, the men then! The king and I have much to catch up on," Nicholas repeated, interrupting the awkward moment. He turned to the others in a low voice of warning and reminder. "Remember our talks about discretion, my new friends!"

"Very well, men only then! Follow me!" Sir Caspin gestured as they followed him back down the road. Talking excitedly among themselves, the newcomers mingled quickly with the guards, peppering them with questions about what might be awaiting them at the Pratenvike. "We're off to a good time this evening! I promise you that!"

"Just stick with Nate and don't stay out too late," Johanna muttered to her son as she took Sammy by the leash. "I'm trusting you now; don't make me worry about you!"

"Mother! I'm not twelve!" Daniel scoffed angrily at his mother before running to catch up to the others, already turning to eagerly walk on foot back down the road, several guards in friendly escort.

The remainder of the garrison stepped forth to unload the carriage as Johanna watched the troupe vanish back through the inner gate. Turning back to King Faund and Grand Master Nicholas, they ascended the marble stairs together as peace and tranquility returned to the courtyard.

"I fear you have chosen the least entertaining option for your first day here," the king said to Johanna as they climbed the stairs. "However, I am proud to welcome you to the royal palace, where you will all stay as my guests! My valets are seeing your personal effects to each of your quarters, even as we speak."

As they passed through the ornately carved wooden doors, another one of the guards stood within the entryway, a short hall entrance to the palace where crimson yet slightly transparent linen curtains billowed inside the double doorway. The king led them inside, and the guard pulled the drapery aside, allowing them to pass through the massive entryway.

Red stone archways and columns supported a steep and high ceiling above, giving Johanna the impression of a cathedral. Massive chandeliers hung from a seemingly impossible height, swaying gently in the draft that moved unseen through the rafters.

Above the entryway, an ornate stained-glass window spilled colorful daylight through it to display the single golden throne, imbued in soft-colored light. The chair oversaw a long, luxuriant wooden table, casting reflected light upon its dark lacquered surface.

"It's magnificent!" Johanna breathed. Even Sammy barked once in approval, her call echoing several times before fading, causing her to perk her ears in curiosity. "I've never seen anything like it! It's as if it was from a storybook!"

"I'm glad you like it," the king replied with a sparkle of pride in his eye. "You should see when the court is in session and the place is full of life. For now, many are celebrating the fall harvest at the Pratenvike and in the marketplaces of New Tyrna below."

"New Tyrna, is that the town just outside the main gate?" Johanna inquired.

"Indeed, yes, it is," the king acknowledged. "You will find many new diversions there, such as the Harvest Festival. New Tyrna is the crossroads where the old and new are exchanged."

"I'd love to explore! Perhaps tomorrow when the others are back and I'm more rested," Johanna decided, pointing to a steep winding staircase at the far end of the hall. "What's up there?"

"That, my dear, is where you will be staying. The guest quarters are on the second level," Nicholas answered. "Beyond that and further up is the tallest point in all Tyrna, the Wizard's Tower. That is where I was once stationed as grand master and will be staying again now."

"I tell you this: Nicholas will not be far from you," King Faund reassured her. "My head maid, Gertrude, and her daughter, Tanny, are in the kitchen now. If you have need of anything, please ask them. They will see to your needs if you should require anything further and tend to our guest quarters. In the meantime, Nicholas and I have business to attend to."

"That sounds lovely; thank you, Your Majesty," Johanna stated as she bowed.

"Oh, one more item that as newcomers you may not be aware of!" the monarch exclaimed, snapping his fingers. "Behind the throne room are my royal quarters. I simply ask that you do not venture there unaccompanied."

"I will certainly pass that on to my friends when they return," Johanna acknowledged. She curtsied to them both before taking her leave and walking briskly off to the kitchen.

"She's remarkably graceful despite being a foreigner," King Faund noted. "I can see why she turned Sir Caspin's head."

"Yes, yes, yes. They shall learn proper protocol and much more about our world, given time. It is why I have chosen to be their Advocate!" Nicholas acknowledged as he followed King Faund up the long winding staircase to the Wizard's Tower. "I also noticed your king's guard seems familiar with my valet."

"They were acquainted some time ago, back in Urocia, if memory serves me," King Faund recalled. "It was good fortune that brought the two together again here in Tyrna. Something about a goodwill exchange between your Order of the Moon and the Order of Etoilenoir that brought his assignment to Aros and now to you."

"Ah, yes, of course," Nicholas acknowledged with a smile, despite harboring dissatisfaction with the answer as they continued up the long winding staircase. "Your Highness, tell me, how are matters of the kingdom these days? I haven't seen you since your father's funeral when my protégé replaced me here in Tyrna."

"My father's passing is still fresh for me," the king replied sadly. "To lose both you and my father was quite a blow to my household."

"I am hardly dead, Your Majesty—and I'm here now," Nicholas scoffed. "I too miss your father's wisdom and guidance, yet you clearly have shown yourself to be most capable in his absence. New Tyrna is getting along fine; the populace will have further room to expand as the city-state continues to prosper."

"Yes, but he was the great King Harmon!" King Faund bemoaned. "I have massive shoes to fill, and I fear my not taking on a queen before his passing was a great disappointment to him."

"Perhaps so; however, you've always been selective in important decisions, Your Majesty." Nicholas stopped him briefly. "Taking on a queen is not something you took lightly, and I can hardly blame you for not doing it. The Southern Kingdoms have little to offer other than instilling resource obligations for our people. Urocia has already siphoned enough from our lands, and to accept a bride from that city-state carries conditions of their own. I understand you waiting for the right one with more of a localized value in mind."

"I'm relieved to hear you say that since I share your concerns," King Faund breathed as they started up the stairs again. "I was beginning to second-guess my position on this matter with the pressure from the Wizard's Council and Emperor Vandroff of Urocia."

"The council said this to you directly?" Nicholas nearly tripped on the next step in surprise as they resumed their climb. "They side with Urocian interests on this matter?"

"Well, not in so many words," King Faund scoffed as he hesitated. "In a way, it makes sense though, with so many of our resources already flowing to Urocia for the war effort."

"It makes sense for Urocia, but does it for Tyrna?" Nicholas's eyes narrowed. "I apologize for my frankness, Your Majesty, but I fail to see the advantage for your kingdom. What did my protégé advise in this matter?"

"Master Aros advised as you do now," the king stated quietly as they approached a plain but thick wooden door at the top of the spire. King Faund seemed downcast momentarily, looking down at the winding stone steps. "In that matter, I wish I had listened more closely to him."

"Why didn't you?" Nicholas whispered, less as an accusation and more as an inquiry, yet nevertheless wondering.

"We had many disagreements, your protégé and I; that may have tainted my trust in him," King Faund sighed as he produced a large key from his robes and handed it to Nicholas. "I believe this is yours now."

With a great clank, Nicholas released the latch. Opening the door to the Wizard's Tower with a loud creak, the grand master beheld his new home for the foreseeable future with an audible sigh.

"Something wrong with the arrangements?" The king arched an eyebrow in curiosity. "It's just the way you left it. Your successor changed very little about it during his tenure. That surprised me, given the differences in your experience and style."

"Nothing wrong with it at all; it's just like I remember!" the grand master intoned with nostalgia as he smiled. Taking a deep breath, he pointedly spoke, allowing the prod to hang in the air for effect. "Your Majesty, please forgive me my blunt inquiry, but I must know—what misgivings did you have with Master Aros? What prevented you from trusting him?"

"We were already in disagreement on other matters," King Faund fumbled, attempting to dismiss the direct approach Nicholas had to the topic. "I hope our misunderstandings have not caused him difficulty with you or the council. It's just that he seemed at odds with them lately as well, and on a multitude of issues. With all the talk of replacing him...let me just say, I'm glad to see they sent you."

"Sent me?!" Nicholas was taken aback. *I brought myself. Someone had been already speaking of replacing Aros? Who would suggest such a thing? And why? So many questions spun out of that assumption.*

"Yes; is that not the case?" The monarch's brow wrinkled in confusion. "I had assumed..."

"Correctly, of course," the wizard corrected himself, smiling disarmingly. "My dear protégé was clearly in over his head, and we've found an assignment more suited to his liking."

"I'm ever so pleased to hear that." King Faund exhaled in relief. "He really is a nice fellow and had some good advice initially. It just became so tiresome for me to choose whose advice to follow."

"Whose advice exactly, Your Majesty?" Nicholas gently probed. "Who else is advising you? I need to know before I can effectively serve you. Who else should I be conferring with in order to achieve your objectives while I'm here?"

"The Wizard's Council, my advisors...they kept me informed of their wishes months prior," King Faund stuttered as he piecemealed the incomplete, vague identities aloud. King Faund became increasingly agitated and began to fidget, his eyes shifting around the doorframe as he shuffled his feet. The king pursed his lips carefully, wrinkling his brow again in contemplation. "Did not Grand Master Yamaro brief you before sending you here to Tyrna? I do not wish to create further trouble among the myriad of individuals who assist me these days."

"Grand Master Yamaro informed me well," Nicholas lied immediately, noting the king had avoided answering his question. "However, I am concerned others may be involved, and in order for anyone to be effective on your behalf, I need to know who they are. The support you have received lately has been, shall we say, inconsistent. I'm not looking to usurp your leadership, merely consolidate it and focus it more closely to your vision."

"What a relief! Never spoken truer! I make it a practice to try not to mix my kingdom's affairs with the affairs of wizards, for one," King Faund nervously laughed. "Secondly, I retain a council of loyal advisors to communicate with the Wizard's Council. I cross-reference their views when my schedule becomes difficult."

"A wise course of action," the wizard agreed and nodded. "Go on."

"I view it as a compromise with the governing styles of the Southern Kingdoms. It served me well until recently," the king stated and then shrugged. "When my disagreements with Master Aros became apparent to my advisors, it became extremely uncomfortable, to say the least."

"I can imagine," Nicholas sighed. "It certainly cannot be an easy compromise to talk about since the Southern Kingdom's ban on the Order of the Moon's involvement in governance."

"Nicholas, I pride myself in Tyrna retaining our own governance, but I have many constituents to keep happy," the monarch confided. "I'm glad you understand the knife edge I must walk."

The grand master glanced about the room in satisfaction; it had a similar feel to the Wizard's Tower in Levens. A bed in the corner, a fireplace in the other corner, walls stacked high with books and a large table in the center of the room, covered with maps. Tapestries of maps also hung from the walls. From there, the similarities ended.

The room was large and circular, with a conical ceiling from which hung a single chandelier. The balcony, however, was a different story entirely. It was a single step up to opened double-shuttered doors. The room smelled of pine yet remained above the riffraff of the city, free from the aromas and muffled sounds from the beasts of burden and activities below. All was reduced to a low rumble from this height.

"I never tire of this view," Nicholas laughed softly as the pair approached and ascended the single step to the balcony. Throwing open the double-slatted doors, they breathed in fresh air while taking in the vista. "You can see half the Grenze Range and the eastern shores of Long Lake from here. On a clear day, I could even see smoke from Levens."

"We have missed you too, my friend." King Faund stood beside him. They stood beside each other in silence, taking it all in as the setting sun lit the entire landscape in a golden hue, revealing the sight much as the grand master had just described it.

Finally, Nicholas turned to the king, fixing him with a gentle stare.

"Tell me, Your Highness," he began slowly, letting his voice drift off before speaking again, "what specifically led you to withdraw from receiving counsel from Master Aros? I assure you; your answer will be kept in the strictest confidence!"

King Faund became quietly subdued and withdrawn before answering as if carefully considering his answer. Even the room fell silent, and the bustle down in the city below seemed to fade.

"It started with our disagreement on New Tyrna," the young monarch whispered the confession, his lip trembling briefly through a grimace. "I believe it only grew from there."

"The budding settlement outside the gate?" Nicholas blinked. "It seems like a bustling, thriving town—it's relieving traffic to the inner city, is it not?"

"It's the issue of where we will obtain the additional resources needed for expansion of New Tyrna," the king said and then took a deep breath, searching the grand master's face for a reaction. "Tyrna henceforth shall be an open society; everyone will be welcomed! Both New Tyrna and Old Tyrna are loved by all, and love will be shown to all. They shall merge as one; we have no need for walls in this new order, and we shall use them for such purpose!"

"You mean to take down the fabled walls of Tyrna?" Nicholas choked back a laugh until he realized the king was serious. He remained emotionless on the outside, while on the inside, he felt a gut-wrenching pit in his stomach open. *Ah, now we arrive to it at last.*

"I do," King Faund whispered. "It's revolutionary, I know. However, it is necessary."

"Sounds rather...economical," Nicholas managed to say, searching for the words as he spoke, struggling to avoid choking on them to reveal his revulsion to the idea. "However, Tyrna's walls have been a source of pride for the kingdom. They are on your very sigil!"

It wasn't so much that the new king was deciding not to place walls around the new city; it was the way he spat out the words regarding the walls in general. Such disregard and disdain had never been applied to the walls of Tyrna, and certainly not by their reigning monarch.

"You don't like the idea; I can see it!" King Faund muttered as he turned away from the wizard to the view again, overlooking the city. A sense of grim determination seemed to settle over him. "Aros didn't like it either."

"Your Highness, it's not that I don't like it," Nicholas stated, catching the king's arm and turning to meet his eyes. "It's that I don't understand it. Tell me—the walls were so important to Tyrna of old;

why detest them now?" *He's so anxious to make a legacy for himself that he doesn't realize that his efforts will be seen as weakness by the council and by even friendly neighbors.*

"I tire of the old Tyrna," the king sighed as he began to pace. His eyes sparkled as he withdrew briefly into his own fancies. "The old city is like a bitter old man, refusing to accept change and surrounded by impenetrable walls of biases and protection from a bygone era. The city grows crowded and congested and is in need of expansion and diversity. We languish in our efforts to maintain this bloated old goat geared for a war that will never come. Meanwhile, Urocia sets the example for the world to follow..."

"Yes? Go on," Nicholas pressed when the king paused.

"Urocia thrives and waxes while we wane and rot away," King Faund spat, searching the wizard's face for a reaction as if testing what he was saying to ascertain whether to say more or not. "When you were in service to my father here, he spoke to you about having a forum located in Tyrna for every voice to be heard from all the kingdoms across the land—there!"

The king pointed to the northwestern corner of the city, splayed out before them. Looking out of the balcony between the billowing curtains, the evening light from the setting sun made it difficult to discern individual homes and structures. One, however, stood out quite easily: a behemoth dome on the northern side of the city. Encircled within the walls, it stood out as mismatched among the other buildings of Tyrna. Ivory-white, it gleamed in the evening sun with many banners rippling off the giant dome in the breeze.

"Isn't that the Pratenvike? I heard much about it during construction from Levens, but we somehow missed seeing it, even when we drove past it upon entry." Nicholas squinted in the evening light. The Pratenvikes' canvas and wooden beams projected well above and around any of the other buildings. The stone-walled base stood as a massive form, clearly crowding out the other structures. Bolstering boldly amid the neatly lined streets of the city, the bulky structure stood out of place and in contrast to the rest of the ancient city, blocking access and ballooning above the surrounding quaint homesteads. "Considering the limited real estate, I'm surprised to see it as large as it is."

"It is indeed, yet even now, I am dissatisfied with its paltry presence; I wanted more," King Faund breathed deeply with pride. "After much cost of time and treasure to our kingdom, it is finally built. Now, *we* have something to be proud of. The Southern Kingdoms have their unity; Urocia has its splendor and style. We have the Pratenvike—a place where everyone wants to be seen and heard and to visit!"

"I see," Nicholas said hesitantly. "Why construct it there and not in the new city where you had access to more unoccupied land?"

"I wanted it at our heart, equal to that of the church," the king proclaimed. "The devotion of the people shouldn't be centered on only one aspect of our history."

"The church has always been a central part of Tyrna's culture and heritage and is unique to the kingdom!" Nicholas stated carefully as he took in the king's words. "Tyrna is the church's capital here in this world, and it has existed alongside the crown without conflict all these eons; why introduce a competing presence?" *This monstrosity is out of character for Tyrna considering the historical significance for the city-state has always been that of labor and strength as its primary resource and commodity.*

"It's not competing!" the king scoffed. "The Pratenvike is a newfound source of pride for the independent nature of our people! The church will always be there, but the people need a diversion, something to bring them status that marks Tyrna for its proper place in the world!"

"Very inspirational, sire," the wizard managed to say, to which the king turned suddenly to him, beaming with pride.

"You think so?" The monarch grinned. "You really think so?!"

"It's certainly a very large structure, occupying a very valuable piece of land within the city," Nicholas sighed. "What happened to the residences and shops that were there before?"

"They were peasants who have found much less expensive and better suited accommodation in New Tyrna," King Faund explained. "I have been encouraging those who don't wish to pay tribute to move into New Tyrna."

"Outside of the protection of the walls?" Nicholas asked softly.

"Protection?!" King Faund laughed. "Old Tyrna and its great walls are relics of the past. The walls served their purpose in the days of old as the fortress bastion for the peoples of the west. Those days are over, my friend. The elves have vanished, and no offense to you, my dear friend, but the wizard's order is a dying dynasty! I mean no personal disrespect to you, but old relics head your order now, afraid of their own shadows and desperate to remain relevant in the new age. I tell you, Nicholas—mark my words! They are not going to pressure me into anything. This will be MY legacy! I came to this on my own with my council of advisors, not by my father, and certainly not by a doting Wizard's Council!"

"So, the council was not as supportive of this grand project of yours?" Nicholas asked, barely containing his distaste at the monarch's insult to his order.

"They said I should have the Urocians build it in exchange for our military and supplies for their war efforts in the east!" King Faund seethed. "They also suggested I incorporate their builders for tribute. I tell you, I'm making this in MY image, not theirs!"

"How did Master Aros feel about it?" Nicholas pressed again, still struggling to contain his disbelief.

"Please don't tell me you and Aros were talking about this before your arrival," King Faund exclaimed, startled momentarily. "I appreciated his rejection of the Wizard's Council's advice, but he too was against constructing even the Pratenvike, particularly when it came to the high cost to the royal treasury. He said it was a 'waste of our resources' and wanted to focus instead upon curtailing the Urocian demands on our military and resources sent to the eastern front."

"He actually never mentioned it to me," Nicholas assured him blandly.

"No, I don't suppose he would have," King Faund reflected, calming a bit. "I told him that I had conceded to the council's demands and that the Urocians were building it. That kept the council out of my business and Master Aros at bay."

Nicholas nodded, thinking to himself. *It finally makes sense. King Faund's own ambition and pride are a third party to this whole mess. The monarch is clearly being pulled in a multitude of directions on these matters. No wonder Aros broke protocol and probed him.*

"What of his requests to follow up on our resources being sent to Urocia?" the wizard asked the king.

"What of it?" King Faund seemed annoyed again with the question. "He was bothered by my sending a third of our forces there to help in the effort. They aren't doing anything here; why shouldn't I send them to help an ally? Can you imagine how he would have reacted if he had learned I'd already sent such a large contingent to the front?"

"A third?!" Nicholas nearly choked. Instead, he reached for his tobacco pipe and lit it with a shaky hand, inhaling long and strong to calm himself. "Did I hear you correctly at a third?"

"You did," King Faund stated, squinting as he studied Nicholas's agitation. "You don't approve?"

"Quite to the contrary," the grand master lied again through a coughing fit. He had to think fast if he was to get more information. He could see trust fast eroding with the king with each reaction. "I can see that you are a man of your own vision. I'm thrilled to see such a young king have such passion and drive for his ideals yet navigate difficulties surrounding him with precision. Your father would have been proud!"

"You think so?" King Faund grinned at the compliment. His shoulders set back, less rigid as he contemplated the matter further. "Maybe he would have been!"

"Oh, yes, such decisive action!" The wizard squared off with the king, searching his eyes for a response. "I am, however, surprised that you would send a third of your military and commodity resources to your neighbor, particularly on the eve of winter. To be sure, you sent only a third and not more?"

"Approximately a third, and not more; what need have we for a standing military anyway? What would it matter?" King Faund smiled. "If our neighbors and friends need help, we help them. In return, they will send us trade supplies we need for winter—we will be fine. We are the western province and have nothing on our doorstep save wilderness. Our friends to the east fight the real war; if they need our strength for that, we shall lend it!"

"I'm assuming Your Majesty has received such assurances and that the supplies they promised are on their way?" Nicholas blinked.

"Not yet, but they will be. I have received the required assurances," King Faund stated confidently. "Until then, we will begin by dismantling our walls."

"What of the historic value?" Nicholas whispered, leaning heavily on his staff in shock. "Surely they retain value there!"

"I will leave the main gate standing as a reminder of our isolation and militaristic past," the king decided. "However, the rest of the walls must come down. We have already received a robust shipment of Urocian crystal to complement the obelisk at the center of the Pratenvike and many other such structures to come."

"Sire," Nicholas began, unable to hold back, "peace is a noble goal, but to pursue it at any and all costs has risks and consequences of its own. Trust must be earned, not merely given. Peace without strength to back it will not result in lasting peace. Have you spoken to the council about this?"

This seemed to give King Faund pause, and he paced the room for a moment, deep in thought. Nicholas risked placing a hand on the king's shoulder; disguised as a gesture of reassurance, he gently probed the king's mind, looking only for where these ideas may have originated. *The very sin I had chastised Aros for!*

"The Wizard's Council is mired in the past..." King Faund began, his voice fading out as the wizard concentrated. As the monarch babbled on about the justification for dismantling Tyrna's walls, a vision flashed before Nicholas's mind: the long wooden table in front of the throne. He saw King Faund at the head and several men whose faces were shrouded in shadow to his left and his right. The only feature he could make out was that each man wore the same intricate grey shimmering cloaks draped over their chairs as gossamer dark threads weaved in leafy patterns. *He IS receiving advice elsewhere... outside the traditional council.*

"Sire," Nicholas stated carefully, gently interrupting the king's monologue. "Perhaps you could arrange for me to speak with some of your advisory panel on this matter. I would love very much to understand more of the planning involved with your noble undertaking and how best I may support it!"

"What?!" The king's exclamation had a shrill ring to it as if cold water had been thrown on him. "You don't think I came up with the idea?!"

"Of course you did, Your Highness!" Nicholas laughed to place the erratic monarch at ease. "The project has simply piqued my interest! I've lived in these lands for over 400 years, and I have never heard of or seen anything like it. I'm not closed to your ideas, sire; I simply want to know more and how best I can support it."

"Really?!" The young king's eyes beamed with hope. The sudden flip of the monarch's emotional state amazed the grand master. *Something is truly off...*

Nicholas nodded with faux enthusiasm as King Faund once again embraced him.

"You won't regret this!" King Faund exclaimed. He withdrew momentarily, his thoughts jumbled with his speech. "I will ask my advisors about meeting with you tomorrow."

"Your Majesty, I don't mean to interrupt; please remember that my loyalty is always to the crown. So, let's have that meeting tomorrow, shall we?" Nicholas stated, inwardly glowering. "I am most looking forward to it!"

"Yes, of course!" King Faund exclaimed, oblivious to the dark mood that had enveloped Nicholas. "I shall arrange it immediately!"

The king embraced the grand master again before striding excitedly down the stairway of the Wizard's Tower. Nicholas watched him go, brooding through a cloud of smoke, fuming from his pipe.

Returning to the balcony, the wizard looked over the city again to the gleaming Pratenvike, coming alive with fluttering torches in the approaching dusk. *What a monstrosity!*

Up here, in the Wizard's Tower of Tyrna, at this height, the wind carried the sounds of the city to his ears. The city itself had a heartbeat —he could hear it. The murmur of the citizenry in the marketplaces, the creaking of the cranes straining to lift the final loads of the day over New Tyrna and the wagons pulled by beasts of burden. *Yes, I can hear them all.*

He missed the quieter quaintness of Levens already, and he closed his eyes briefly as if to try to capture the fleeting moments of peace he had there in the other tower. *Alas, my quiet retirement will have to wait; I'm needed here in this city. I've got my work cut out for me.*

He opened his eyes and searched the hazy city skyline within the walls. There was another building he was searching for as the sun set, sending rays of light like orange curtains through the Wizard's Tower room, high above the palace.

Opposite the Pratenvike, on the southern edge of town, stood a stone cathedral atop a knoll. The building was small in comparison but quite tall. Its steeple housed a great bell that would toll the hours and mark the daily mass. Atop the steeple was a gold cross that reflected the sunlight like a spectacular bright beacon.

Nicholas grimaced in determination as the beginning of a plan formulated. *I must consult with the friar; wisdom may be found there...*

Chapter 15

Pratenvike

Javier grinned from ear to ear as he beheld the Pratenvike. The raucous affair blazed in front of them as music from lutes and drums called out in a disharmonious cacophony to the city's crowds. The aroma of a diverse variety of foods mingled with the crowds of people and livestock as the cluster all seemed to come to a chaotic focal point there.

The grand entrance looked more like a circus pavilion with street entertainers and vendors all vying for attention. Many colorful tents lined the cobblestone streets, leading to the yawning entrance ahead of them. Through the masses of people, they could make out the two great stone pillars of the main entrance to the squat building, lined with an array of blazing torches.

"Let's go in!" Javier shouted excitedly over the din to Sir Caspin. He strode confidently to the forefront as if leading the way himself.

The sandy-haired captain grinned to the others and raised his eyebrows as if daring him with a "you-know-you-want-to" look.

"What's going on?" Kevin balked at the intensity of the noise, reluctant to enter. The place was so crowded that he was certain to lose the others if they went inside. "Is this a festival? Is there someplace a little quieter?"

"It's always a festival here!" the pale Sottis laughed, more at ease than the others had seen him in recent days. "In particular today, they are celebrating the anniversary of the Centerpiece."

"The Centerpiece?" Nate scoffed. "We can't even get through the front door! I'm with Kevin on this one. Can we find a quieter spot?"

"Aw, c'mon! We just gotta push a little," Daniel challenged with a grin, shoving his way into the crowd, only to be stopped by Nate's firm hand.

"Hang on, let's not get separated," Nate cautioned, grabbing the scruff of his shirt to hold him back before turning and stating loud enough for Sir Caspin to hear. "Your mother isn't with us, and I'm sure she'd like to see this place too."

"Yes, we should wait for your companion," Sir Caspin replied, smiling disarmingly after catching Nate's hint. "I'm certain she would enjoy the full tour and wouldn't want to miss any of it. Come, I know a more subdued location at the eastern entrance that will suffice nicely!"

"I know exactly where you're thinking; follow me!" Sottis led the group as they sauntered around the large, oblong building against the flow of the crowd. He snapped authoritatively at any who hindered their path as his shimmering grey cloak billowed behind him, gossamer threads gently weaving throughout. "Move aside, Etoilenoir coming through!"

When the crowd thinned, he beckoned the group around the south end of the main structure, walking single file on the grass. They passed similar yet smaller entrances, interspaced between massive timber-like sections constructed from whole trees supporting the grey stones carefully set between even larger stone columns.

They stopped to peer through one of the less crowded entrances to gain a look inside. From within, the structure appeared like the inside of a massive rib cage. The supports arched upward toward the center, covered by a thick canvas where ventilation could escape through the center hole while letting light in during the daytime. Additional ventilation encircled the sides and between the support beams as puffs of smoke wafted gently into the night from skylights built into the wooden timber roofing.

They continued around the outside, passing occasional archways dividing the outdoor courtyards where a broad array of people, cat-people and stocky dwarves mingled, holding pints of ale and laughing. Each side entrance and courtyard alternated with neatly manicured shrubs, hugging the base of the building and lined with torchlight.

"This place is huge!" Daniel exclaimed.

"Yes, it was quite an undertaking for His Majesty, and the idea originated while he was but a young prince," Sir Caspin agreed. "We opened it last year, but it wasn't completed until recently. You see, Prince Faund wanted to have a central place for the people to gather, and his father only reluctantly entertained the idea."

"Why is that?" Nate asked. "It seems like a noble venture."

"It is, but traditionally, the Austrik's line focused on matters of commerce, industry and productivity," Sir Caspin explained, lovingly running his hand alongside the building. "Many viewed Prince Faund's ideas as an unnecessary expense to the royal treasury and a 'flight of fancy.' Tyrna's prior ruler, King Harmon, initially allowed the young prince a brief dalliance in the matter to satisfy his creative passions, but that proved nowhere substantial enough for what the prince truly wanted. When King Harmon passed, the newly crowned King Faund was able to reprioritize his own vision."

"I take it you were part of the construction effort?" Kevin asked, noting the captain's nostalgia as he spoke about it.

"Oh, I may have helped in some of the less critical details," Sir Caspin admitted with a nonchalant smile. "I'm a guardsman first, with a mild passion and interest for finance. When it comes to these sorts of things, I'm more of an 'ideas' man."

"An 'ideas' man," Sottis scoffed. "Sir Caspin here will talk anyone into anything; it's like an innate talent of his! You'll see, he'll talk his way into a free meal up here!"

They arrived at the east entrance with a more modest crowd gathered. Two large boars rotated on spits between two cloth tents lit like lanterns. Four large, busty women bustled about, serving a cluster of off-duty guards, and as Sir Caspin approached, they snapped to attention.

"At ease," Sir Caspin announced with a grin as he saluted back to the troops. "We're all off duty here."

Everyone relaxed, and after a bit of back-clapping and hand-clasping, returned to their food and drink as the group sauntered up to one of the tents.

"What are we having tonight, boys?" one of the younger maidens behind a long wooden table stacked full of ale pints shouted to them. "I'm assuming your guests are part of your usual tab?"

Her bright eyes twinkled from beneath her sandy hair tossed around both sides of her shoulders. She wiped her hands on a long white apron protecting her light blue dress. The apron was smudged with food and drink yet also noticeably failed to cover her pleasantly voluptuous form.

"For me and my men, we'll have the usual," Sir Caspin ordered, turning to the others with a smile. "As for our new guests, I'm sure they'll be having the same."

"I don't know, what do you have? It all looks so pleasing to me!" Javier affirmed as he winked, flirting through his stare into her soft brown eyes.

"Well, what you see is what you get!" she exclaimed, smiling back at him, batting her eyes and tossing her hair.

"It ALL looks good to me." Daniel tried, a little less subtle, comically leaning over the table in a vain attempt to compete with Javier for attention.

The bar maiden laughed musically, bringing a slight blush to the lad's face. After she composed herself, she pointed to a table set up underneath one of the torches near one of the Pratenvike's side entrances.

"I can take care of all of you all over there," she indicated with a nod of her head before patting Daniel on the arm and whispering to him with playful mercy. "Sorry, my boy, I'm not on the menu!"

Daniel blushed again in silence as she led them to a table to the side of the clearing. Within moments, she brought them steaming plates of boar meat with roasted vegetables and pints of ale.

Kevin sat quietly and listened to Sir Caspin flirt with the servers and chat with the other men. He watched with envy as Javier joined in the mêlée to fit right in. He turned his attention to the less obtuse Sottis, who seemed content to eat.

"I can't help but notice you seem happier now that we're in the city," Kevin tried, gaining the attention of their former carriage driver sitting across from him. "Is it because you're friends with Sir Caspin?"

"Yeah, Sir Caspin and I go way back," Sottis stated as he settled. "I'm sorry I didn't give the best impression of myself back in Levens. These older wizards really have a way of looking down on you. I'm here on a goodwill exchange, but it seems the 'goodwill' only flows in one direction. Their sour attitude brings out the worst in me."

"Really?" Kevin pressed. "Nicholas and Aros seemed awfully nice to us. Maybe if you just gave them a chance—"

"Oh, please," Sottis interrupted. "I don't mean to be rude, but their silk glove treatments of you outsiders are because of what you can bring to their order, not out of any gift from their meager charitable nature. I'm sorry to break it to you that way, Kevin, but it's the truth! Where exactly are you from, anyway?"

"You know I can't talk about that," Kevin quipped, sitting back ready to withdraw from the conversation.

"I'm not trying to offend you," Sottis offered in a whisper. "Let's be honest with each other for just a moment; you don't have to answer me if you don't want to. Let me just state what I already know, and we can take it wherever you want from there. I promise to stay discreet."

"Alright," Kevin agreed reluctantly. "Tell me what you know."

"You're from outside of this world, and you came through the Shimmering," Sottis stated softly. When Kevin simply nodded, Sottis continued. "Each of you is likely showing an ability you didn't have before. It would express itself as an innate magical power."

"I'll just say that we have some skills heightened since our arrival," Kevin deflected, suddenly regretting the conversation, shifting uncomfortably atop the already hard wooden bench. "Go on."

"Retired Grand Master Nicholas got to you first. While I'm sure he means well, he doesn't have to be your only friend around here," Sottis offered. "I understand his wanting to keep you a secret, and I'll play along; all I'm saying is that you should have some say in this matter. Trust me when I say you don't need an Advocate!"

"He's done alright by us so far," Kevin retorted, looking away and wishing he were somewhere else. "I appreciate his stepping up for us when we knew no one else here. Frankly, we'd be lost without him!"

"I know, I know! He helped you all out when you arrived! All I'm saying is that you really should give others a chance to welcome you too," the valet clarified, throwing his hands up in frustration. "Just consider for a moment that your single source of information may be tainted with superstition and hyper-vigilance from a bygone age! He means well, and you apparently share a world of origin, but that doesn't make him right! He's not the only friend you can have! Many of us here embrace a new way of living that you really should get to know; it would do you some good!"

"I'll take that into consideration," Kevin continued with a polite smile. "We're new here, just as you pointed out before. I thank you for your promise to keep our secret, and I'll hold you to it!"

"Your consideration is all I'm asking for," Sottis stated, toasting him quietly with his chalice. "I am completely sympathetic to your situation. In the meantime, have some fun! You're in a different world, my friend! Many new experiences await you! This cloak I wear, for example, you could have one too, in due time! This experience doesn't have to be all doom and gloom; you can learn to live a little!"

"So, I hear you came down from Levens?" Sir Caspin slid over closer on the bench, gently shifting the conversation from the quiet exchange between Kevin and Sottis. "How are things up north? Winter setting in yet?"

"Still fall harvest up there, but I hear the wolves are getting feisty up that way," one of the off-duty guards commented. "Patrol reported a run-in with 'em up that way last week."

"You could say that again." Daniel lifted his ale mug in agreement, slurring his words as he drank, still miffed at his fumbling of flirtation alongside Javier's. "Damned wolves..."

"We had a brief run-in with them also, but we stayed on the main road after that," Nate interjected the explanation. "Locals there recommended we stick to more traveled routes."

"Sound advice," Sir Caspin toasted. "Especially if you're unfamiliar with the territory."

Relieved to have the attention diverted from him and a tipsy Daniel, Kevin took a long draught from his cup, content to resume dining on the food before him and let the locals talk. A buzz had begun to settle in on him, and his mind swam in the oily haze of mild intoxication.

Kevin noticed Sottis beginning to shift his attention back to him as Sir Caspin prattled on, bragging about the latest patrol assignments. The urge to urinate suddenly overcame him just as Sottis leaned in closer to resume what he presumed would be a continuation of the conversation around either his origins, his budding innate power, or Grand Master Nicholas.

"Do you know where I can find a restroom?" Kevin slurred, interjecting the question before Sottis could speak.

"A...what?" Sottis blinked.

"A place where he can take a piss," interjected a grinning Javier, pointing off to the side of the glade near a cluster of trees. "Hey, Micker, I saw a set of pissers over by the bushes. Don't get lost over there!"

"Thanks for your colorful translation, Javier!" Kevin blushed as he stood abruptly and left. "I'll be right back."

Sauntering over to the cluster of trees and bushes, Kevin could make out a set of troughs emptying into a stone grate. The crowds thinned off to the side, nearer to the cobblestone main road, giving him a chance to clear his mind as well as his bladder.

A cool breeze blew through the alleyway, and he shivered as he answered nature's call. Sensing someone standing close by, he glanced sideways to see the shadow of a large man standing in the dark, utilizing the same troughs, down a bit and across from him.

"Well, if it isn't my jittery young friend from a few days ago; fancy meeting you here!" the man's deep voice offered. "If you had bought that wolf pelt from me back in Levens, you wouldn't be cold right now!"

"Sorry, what?" Kevin replied as he finished. He turned to face the mysterious speaker, his lanky form clearly dwarfed by the stranger's imposing form. He could scarcely make out the larger man's outline in the dark, much less recognize him. "Do I know you?"

"Well, we really didn't have much of a chance to talk when we ran into each other back in Levens," the stranger laughed as he completed his business and collected himself. "You rushed off before I could show you my inventory of furs!"

"Levens?" Kevin laughed, suddenly recognizing the man's voice, remembering his salty appearance despite now not being able to make out more than just his looming shadow. "Oh, yeah! I kind of remember that now, from the marketplace! As I said before, though, I don't really have any money so wouldn't be able to buy anything. Funny meeting you here; what a coincidence!"

"Indeed! We could still work out a trade if you want," the stranger rumbled as he stepped around the trough closer to him. Kevin could feel the heat coming from the large man, and a sudden giddiness penetrated his being. Even through his intoxicated haze, he suddenly felt compelled to listen to the trapper. "Perhaps an item from your beastless carriage or something you carry? Or maybe another trinket from your far-off place?"

"Wait a minute," Kevin slurred, shaking his head and trying to clear his thoughts as he took a step back. "Who did you say you were? What are you doing here in Tyrna?"

"Don't worry, my suspicious young friend!" the salt-and-pepper-bearded man said as he stepped forward into clearer light. He chuckled a deep belly laugh beneath a hooded cloak. "I represent a group of fur traders in the wilds, and we travel frequently between Levens, Tyrna and Long Lake. We were already headed south for the coming winter when I recognized you and your friends over by the Pratenvike. It's not too late if you want to shop our inventory; my wagon isn't far from here!"

"Well, I suppose a quick look wouldn't hurt," Kevin commented, tempted by the offer, his heart pounding. He paused only briefly before looking back to the table, surrounded by his companions and the firelight. "I need to go back to the others; they may be interested, too."

"Why don't you come with me and see what I have first," the man pressed in a low, husky tone, stepping closer. "I have some appointments I must keep and don't have time to wait..."

"Hey, Micker!" Javier's voice called to him from outside the glade. "Who you talking to?"

"It's the guy from the Levens market!" Kevin shouted back. "He made it here the same time we did and wants to sell us some..."

"I don't see anyone," Javier commented as he strode up, pulling alongside Kevin to utilize the troughs. "Are you sure you weren't just playing with yourself in the dark here?"

"What?" Kevin turned to find the stranger had vanished. "He was just right here!"

"What did he look like?" Javier asked.

"He was big, burly, and..." Kevin stopped talking, shaking his head. "I actually didn't get a good look at him; it was dark."

"Well, there's no one here now except us, and we're getting ready to head back to the palace," Javier grunted and sighed as he finished relieving himself. "Danny Boy can't hold his liquor, and as much as I'd like to stay, there's always tomorrow!"

"Yeah...tomorrow," Kevin sighed. The strange giddy feeling he had felt when the large man had stood nearby had also fled, leaving him unsure if the incident had ever even occurred.

≈≈≈≈

Many drinks and many hours later, Sir Caspin led the group back to the palace, stumbling along the cobblestone roadway. Nate had Daniel drooped over his shoulders as they helped him up the palace stairs. Their mirthful jibes at each other carried above the peaceful babbling of the fountain, echoing off the walls of the courtyard.

Awakened by the raucous laughter, Johanna met them at the entrance in a fuming rage, her normally smooth face etched with a mother's worry. She stood accompanied by a young maiden who introduced herself as Tanny, one of the housemaids. The housemaid's light blue eyes twinkled from beneath her white maid's hat covering her dark hair as she whispered a soft warning that everyone was asleep but that she would be happy to show them to their quarters.

"Hey, Danny," Javier called to the barely conscious lad as Nate set him down. "Maybe you should meet up with Tanny later? She looks like she's more your age range than the barmaid, and she's cute!"

"What took you all so long?" Johanna demanded, quickly drawing Nate's attention. He abruptly sobered as she stood in red-faced rage in front of him. "Your voices carry all through the halls, and you're announcing yourself like a bunch of back-alley drunkards!"

"Sorry, ma'am, we didn't mean to stay so late, but it was quite a walk, and there's the festival on tonight." Sir Caspin stepped up to Nate's side. "We had hoped you'd join us, and..."

"Yes, but you brought my son back like a drunken casualty of war!" Johanna spat.

"Oh, give it a rest!" Nate shook his head in annoyance. "He's a young man, and we've all been through a lot. He just had a few drinks along with many of the other men that were there, some the same age as he!"

"Bill would never have done that to him!" Johanna seethed. "He's going to sleep with me in my room tonight!"

"Suit yourself!" Nate retorted, waving her off dismissively. "You're overprotecting him as usual, and it's only going to drive him away!"

"My apologies, my lady," Sir Caspin offered, his eyebrows arched at the brief confrontation. "Your husband is correct, though. Your lad will sleep it off, and with a cup of sweet grass tea in the morning and a good hearty breakfast, he'll be fine."

"Thank you, Sir Caspin, but that will be quite enough!" Johanna turned away in a huff. She shot an icy glance back at Nate before adding, "Now, would you gentlemen be so kind as to hoist him upstairs? Nate's not my husband, but Daniel is my son, so it's not an improper request that you put him in my room!"

The deliberate nature of her words stung Nate, but he remained silent as they trudged up the winding stone steps, following Tanny to the guest level in the simmering silence. As the narrow staircase opened to the wide hallway with the guest rooms, Nate hesitated, looking at Johanna questioningly.

"That room is yours!" Johanna hissed as she pointed to another door across the hall as Sir Caspin and Sottis relieved Nate from carrying the boy. They took him inside Johanna's chambers and departed quickly without another word. "You said yourself, we have to respect their customs, so respect them!"

With that, she entered her chambers and closed the door quietly in his face, leaving him to fume alone in the hallways outside. Johanna's room faced west in a circular stone turret, jutting out from the palace's structure. The position afforded a full three-quarter circular view of the courtyard and city below.

Complete with a hutch and washbasin, the room was sparse yet comfortably furnished with handmade wood-carved chairs and an ornate bed. Daniel slumbered peacefully on the sofa near the window, and Johanna finally felt the first vestiges of sleep weigh on her.

She stood silently, listening to the muffled sounds outside her door as a young maid departed, showing Kevin and Javier to their rooms. Johanna noted with relief that Nate had already gone to his quarters. Shaking her head in dismay, she returned to bed, glancing over at her son passed out on the sofa.

"Nate, you bastard, you should have known better," she muttered under her breath.

Chapter 16

The Old and the New

The bright light of morning highlighted the Royal Palace of Tyrna in a harsh morning glare. The wooden build-out to Tyrna's palace jutted into the sunlight from the palace side, just under the first sentry ramparts above and to the left of the main entrance.

The dining nook stood out as a misplaced natural sanctuary, jutting out from cold brick and monotonous mortar. Although blended with exterior paint to match the red brick of the palace walls, it still contrasted as an architectural curiosity. Here, the musty smells of stone and moss from the castle gave way to the earthly scents of wood and flowers.

Made entirely of a blend of timbers, its presence gave the impression of a hunting lodge with large casement windows, allowing sunlight in as well as fresh air, given the ability to open onto a narrow ledge. Windowsill flowerpots highlighted the ledge outside, nestled within a grooved depression and interspaced between smaller stained glass picture windows. The cool breezes wafted in sweet floral scents of the dew-laced flowers from outside, to mingle with the aromas of freshly baked breads inside. Thick wooden beams line the A-framed structure.

Ornate tapestries lined the inside walls, intermixed with occasional taxidermy obtained from the local fauna.

Servants clad in grey liveries busied themselves about the long wooden table in preparation for their new guests gathered around the table for breakfast. The aromas of fresh-baked bread and fruits wafted in each time the servants entered.

Everyone at the table stood when King Faund entered, escorted by a man who was clearly a priest noted by his collar tab. Nicholas introduced the priest as Father Rafael Jaramillo, a ruddy, clean and kept man with salt-and-pepper hair, yet he retained a still youthful appearance with a hint of athletic physique.

"Nicholas mentioned you earlier when we were in Levens," Johanna commented as they dined. "Have others from the church made it here as well? How do you still maintain your connection to Rome?"

"Unfortunately no; I'm the only Christian priest from our world that I'm aware of," the priest replied with a thick Spanish accent. "Sadly, my connection to Rome ceased when I arrived here. I left many of my fellow brothers behind when traveling along the roads of Cibola. My missions brought me along those paths to wherever God's word is needed. Apparently, I was needed here, and thus God sent me long ago to fulfill that call."

"Cibola?" chimed Daniel in amazement as he shoveled down a mix of eggs and sausage, clearly feeling recovered from the previous night's escapades. "How long ago was that?"

"I must confess, I've lost track, but what matter is age within the measurement of what one may accomplish in that time?" Father Jaramillo's pleasant demeanor never flickered as he laughed. "More importantly, what have we for breakfast today?"

"Father Jaramillo is far too modest; he has been with us for half a millennium," King Faund interjected proudly.

At this, the table grew silent, and the newcomers looked to the priest and then to Grand Master Nicholas for an explanation.

"Well, I don't know if it's quite been *that* long!" Father Jaramillo blushed in a vain attempt to downplay the shock. "I originally was sent to New Spain to help educate native peoples in the New World. I became lost in the desert when I happened upon El Morro, a site many travelers passed by to replenish their reserves on the road to Cibola and the supposed Seven Cities of Gold. When I waded into the spring to get water, I slipped and hit my head on a stone and fell into a deep sleep. When I awoke, I was here, or rather, in the Lost Valley south of here. The people known as the Clay Tribe fished me out of their spring, explained to me where I was, and that I would find more of 'my people' here in Tyrna. They escorted me to the city and here is where I made my home ever since."

"Cibola; that was the colonial times!" Johanna shook her head. "How is this possible? That was hundreds of years ago!"

"Indeed, perhaps it was! I interpreted the whole incident as a sign from God and let Him lead me," Father Jaramillo sighed as he took a long sip of his morning tea. "I was grateful to be taken in by the Austriks and welcomed by this community. I turned my work to them and established our Lady of Tyrna's parish in the heart of the city. This became my mission and my reason for living so long, over 400 years ago."

"You're far too modest, Father; you have much to be proud of!" King Faund insisted. "Father Jaramillo single-handedly established our Lady of Tyrna's parish, yes, but he's not telling you of the missions he's built since—seven in total across my kingdom and three others in southeastern Levens. Even the Dades are considering a parish within the township! He's managed to convert nearly half of Tyrna's population as well as a third of the Carthenians, a number of the Clay Tribesmen and even whole sects of the southern dwarf mining colonies!"

"Carthenians," Nate muttered, surmising aloud. "Is that those cat-people we've been seeing around town?"

"They are indeed," Grand Master Nicholas confirmed. "Most of the lands east of Long Lake right up to Tyrna Pass would be wild if not for their lovely collection of kingdoms!"

"That's very admirable, Father!" Johanna stammered, "But how? I mean—you look barely over forty years old!"

"You're far too kind," Father Jaramillo said as he blushed, glancing uncomfortably at Nicholas, who smiled and nodded. The priest simply stated, "The Lord has chosen to bless me with long life, and I use it for Him and His will. I must confess, though, a long life sometimes does not feel like a blessing, and the weight of many years weighs upon me more than my appearance reveals."

"I have always enjoyed Father Jaramillo's uncanny wisdom and advice," Nicholas gently interjected, cheerfully raising his cup to the priest. "As he would put it, his longevity is a miracle that carries a heavy price without the support of his faith and a core focused on truth and service."

"You're far too kind," Father Jaramillo laughed, blushing lightly at the compliment. As his laughter subsided, a long faraway look took his face as his tone sobered. "I find that a long earthly life is frankly wearisome. I long for the day the Lord sees fit to take me home. This path He has laid before me is sometimes fraught with toil and other times lulling with the temptation of a rest I have not yet earned. I am most grateful for your presence and company in this journey, Grand Master. Without our mutual dedication to the service of the Lord's work, albeit in different ways, I fear I would go mad."

"Yet with your uncanny words dedicated to such service comes forth the pearls of your words that are a credit to you and your profession!" the wizard gently reminded the priest, nodding in deference. "He will one day call us all home to account, but until that time, we are most grateful for your wisdom!"

"Hear, hear! As have I," King Faund echoed enthusiastically. "His wisdom is only rivaled by your own, dear Grand Master!"

"The ability to live forever and look young?" Javier scoffed. "Why would anyone want to pass up on that?"

"The grand master and I have seen friends, colleagues and families come and go. They are born, grow, get older, falter, wither and eventually pass on," the priest countered. "The simple pleasures in life no longer satiate, and indeed in time cease to carry the same meaning they once did. Within normal life spans, this is noticed; within ours, it is a most trying and wearisome burden."

"All that remains is our missions," the wizard quietly acknowledged. "Our lives' work, central to serving others, keeps us centered."

"Although we have some differences in our spiritual beliefs, we've honored and respected each other through these long centuries." Father Jaramillo nodded respectfully to the wizard before turning to the group. "I've appreciated Nicholas's friendship, debates and frank conversations."

"As have I, my old friend," the grand master stated as he smiled, raising his own steaming cup of tea to the priest.

They relaxed through the rest of the meal, lingering as the sun continued to pour in through windows, warming the crisp morning air. After breakfast concluded, Father Jaramillo turned to the group and graciously thanked them for their sharing of their morning meal with him.

"I do hope you come by and visit our Lady of Tyrna Parish to celebrate mass," the priest invited. "We'd love to have you, particularly since we haven't had any Christians from my home world to visit in such a long time. I would also love to hear more about what has transpired there since my departure."

"We would be honored to," Johanna commented, turning to the others, who nodded in agreement. "We will definitely make it a point to come by!"

"Splendid! I must go to attend to my flock now!" the priest stated as he stood, bowing to the king before turning back to the others in the room. "We hear confessions this time of day."

With a spin of his black robes, the priest turned and departed. Grand Master Nicholas waited until he was down the hall and out of sight before speaking.

"Father Jaramillo is the only person still alive from our world who has been here for as long as I have; he is a very special man," Grand Master Nicholas admired.

"Here, here!" King Faund broke in, drinking down the last of his tea. "Tales of his establishment of the church have been handed down by my family over generations! Most admirable; I hope to only reproduce such success in many of our endeavors!"

"When Father Jaramillo came through the Shimmering to our world, I asked him about his order since the construct is very similar to our own," Nicholas chuckled at the irony. "He described Jesus Christ as their head and challenged me to come to mass, and so I did. I was amazed that many of our ideals around service were the same, even if our purposes differed."

"Oh, yes," Johanna commented. "The charters would be quite different."

"They are indeed, yet no matter how wise we are and how long we are alive, we can always do better, for ourselves and others," Nicholas reflected. "I couldn't give up the wizard's order, but I continued to attend mass where and when I could, even unto this day to gain a better understanding of the Son of God. In the process, I've come to identify greater worth in myself and others through his teachings. I understand there are some conflicts within each of us throughout our lives, but this does not lessen the love that binds us to God."

"What about your views on his long life?" Nate asked. "Four hundred years is a long time to be alive without some sort of assistance."

"I believe that Father Jaramillo gained an innate power coming through the Shimmering for long life." The grand master smiled knowingly as he took another sip. "He interprets it as a gift from God in order to spread the gospel here in our world. Perhaps it's both. No one really knows the answer to that question. Blessing or curse, it's nevertheless the reality and the source of debate we still argue to this very day!"

"Speaking of debates," King Faund interjected with an impulsive sigh. "I must attend one with the treasury shortly. Another necessary annoyance when I'd rather be here, but please, continue to enjoy yourselves!"

The king excused himself from the room to attend to his daily duties, quickly vanishing down the hall. After a moment of silent eating, Kevin turned to Nicholas and gently prodded his arm.

"I didn't realize you had shared our coming through the Shimmering with Sottis," Kevin gently admitted to the wizard. "I know you told us to be careful when talking to others in this world about where we are from, but are there any others that we should know about that it's okay to talk to?"

"I've mentioned nothing of the sort to Sottis!" Nicholas recoiled in surprise. Squinting, his brow creased in concern. "Are you sure?"

"He was very clear about it," Kevin insisted. "He told me, 'I know you're from outside of this world,' that we 'came through the Shimmering,' and that we could 'skip the pretense' with him."

"It would seem my valet's interest in you all has extended well beyond the ride from Levens," the wizard intoned darkly. "I already spoke with him about minding his station earlier!"

"I hope I'm not getting anyone into trouble here," Kevin conceded, biting his lip as he recalled the conversation from the previous night. "I just want to be sure who we are cleared to share our origins with. I got the impression from him that you had already shared our backgrounds with him."

"It would appear your secret is getting increasingly difficult to keep, despite your naiveté and at no fault of your own," Nicholas muttered. "I may have to move quickly or risk losing you to the council!"

"He's not the only one," Kevin offered. "While we were at the Pratenvike, a fur trader recognized us from Levens. He was wanting to sell me some furs and when I told him we had no money, he offered a trade for something in our beastless carriage."

"Gypsies and fur traders I'm as not concerned with, although it is worrisome that even they are beginning to perceive your truth," Nicholas sighed. "They are common in this area, and it does only further allude to the fact the council is likely to hear of your whereabouts sooner rather than later."

"If you don't mind me asking, does that matter?" Nate asked. "They are *your* council, are they not?"

"They are, or rather, they were," Nicholas exhaled, glowering momentarily before making up his mind. "With Sottis's revelation on your arrival, others may soon know if they don't already. Please continue to refrain from discussing this topic in any great length with anyone outside of our circle. In fact, report to me if anyone else should attempt to broach that subject with you while you're here."

"We can be taught to blend in eventually," Nate pointed out. "However, we left my Jeep right out there in the open back in Levens. Many have seen it by now; maybe we should have covered it?"

"I had someone address that issue when we left," Nicholas stated with a smile. Retrieving a small slip of paper from the cuff in his robes, he cleared his throat for the announcement. "Aros has informed me that your beastless carriage is in good hands. The time will come when we stand before the council, but until then, you must trust me to ensure your safety and well-being under my Advocacy. While we are awaiting him, I will uncover how and why you were brought here to begin with. I also must tend to the duties that Aros held while he was here and assist King Faund out of the latest quagmire involving the Pratenvike and Urocia."

"What are we to do in the meantime?" Johanna pressed.

"Sir Caspin will see to your needs while I am indisposed," Nicholas exhaled as he stood and snatched his staff from the side of the table. "Please, take in the sights and follow his lead, yet remember the discretion I've advised. Lay low, do not attract attention to yourselves. Do not practice your innate abilities in public or even in front of your guardians other than myself. Speaking of which, your guide arrives!"

Almost as if on cue, Sir Caspin strode in from the hall with Sottis in tow. The captain wore full-court attire instead of his military garb, his sandy hair tussled and certainly more casual yet still regal in appearance. They politely acknowledged Nicholas as they strode past him before turning to address the others.

"Well, hello there!" Johanna greeted Sir Caspin as he sauntered inside. Glancing back at Nate nervously, she briefly blushed and looked away, suddenly self-conscious at her greeting.

"Hello yourself! I'm thrilled you'll be able to join our happy troupe today!" The captain smiled flirtatiously again in greeting. Noting Nate's frown, he pulled himself back and cleared his throat. "Today, a new and unique assignment has come to me. I am honored to be your private guide as I orient you around the great city of Tyrna."

"How are you doing this morning? Watch out for our ales; they may be stronger than what you are used to!" Sottis laughed heartily, clapping Daniel on the back, who blushed at the attention. "Come, all of you. Sir Caspin and I will show you around. I assure you, the fog of hangover will soon pass."

"I'm doing just fine," Daniel growled as he stood. "A few beers aren't going to keep me down!"

Nate took the opportunity as they sauntered out of the dining hall to carefully insert himself between Johanna and Sir Caspin. Sottis watched the interaction with scandalous glee and was about to follow the group out when Nicholas cleared his throat from behind.

"Ahem! A word if you don't mind, Apprentice Sottis," Grand Master Nicholas called. "I have need of you for other tasks today."

"As a guest member of your wizard's order, shouldn't I accompany them?" the valet protested, the color draining from his face as he nervously fondled his grey cloak. The dark threads began intertwining rapidly around where his fingers gripped the shimmering cloth. "Surely my continuing with our guests..."

"Not today, my ambitious apprentice," Nicholas stated through a brief grimace. "Please, accompany me to the Wizard's Tower; as my valet, we have an important matter to discuss."

Sottis reluctantly complied as they all left the breakfast nook together. He followed the grand master as they split off from the rest of the group in the throne room.

≈≈≈≈

Sir Caspin led the newcomers to the courtyard and down the marble stairs past the fountain. Across the courtyard, he led them to an ancient moss-covered stone staircase, then to the top of the inner wall, where they climbed atop the battlements, the water feature babbling behind them in a happy ambience.

"The outer wall contains the old city, and the inner wall contains the royal palace grounds," Sir Caspin explained as they strode the parapets. "Both walls originate together at the base of the mountain and encircle Tyrna from there. Where the walls converge is not only the junction for strength in the city's defenses but also a great vantage point to see Tyrna in its entirety. Other than that, the royal palace and the Wizard's Tower afford the best view at the top of the city since the whole city just slopes down from there."

"Yeah, I noticed that inner wall separates the palace from the rest of town," Johanna quipped. "Doesn't that create resentment among the people?"

"Not at all!" Sir Caspin smiled as he ushered them across the battlements. "The palace is far older than the rest of Tyrna. The outer wall was built out later to protect Tyrna's residents that encircled the inner wall during a time of strife in the early days of the city, nearly a thousand years ago."

"There are sure a lot of mouths in this city to feed," Nate stated. "What about water and waste? How do they maintain the needs of a city this size?"

"Tyrna Creek flows right through the center of both walls, the lifeblood of the city, feeding both the palace and the city alike." The captain of the guard gestured at the key points he indicated as they strolled south along the ivy-lined inner wall.

Within moments, they arrived at the spot where the inner and outer walls of Tyrna met. Grey granite mingled with red brick, and the walls of Tyrna were thickest there. From the vantage point atop the convergence, they could see behind the city the narrow switchback road winding its way up the slender canyon and up the mountain. Faint yet well-worn, the path was unmistakable between all the boulders and bushes.

"The reservoir is at the top, near the peak," Sir Caspin stated as he pointed at the sharp, high peak, looming over the city in the east as if pointing to the sun. "There was always a small lake, but with flash floods and inconsistent flow of the creek, the builders dammed it centuries ago in order to maintain water flow year-round for use here in Tyrna. They were even able to provide actual running water to the kitchens of the royal palace, the palace fountains behind us, and some of the original homes around the oldest parts of the city!"

"I'd like to hear more about the construction planning behind it," Nate indicated eagerly, anxious to keep the captain's wandering eyes off Johanna. "As an electrician back home, infrastructure is my specialty. I basically saw the flow of electrical power to homes and businesses, much the same way these aqueducts flow water to the city. To have running water in a place like this is most impressive."

"Power and water! You are describing wonders I can scarcely imagine," admitted Sir Caspin. "I'm afraid much of the aqueduct knowledge you refer to here was lost with the builders. Much of that knowledge has been lost in pursuits of other trades over the centuries."

"Well, I'm sure the aqueduct system here wouldn't be too difficult to figure out," Nate offered. "As far as electricity goes, just think of it like harnessing lightning. Ultimately, the flow concepts at their most basic are the same, although I admit they are much more complex when you get down to the electricity aspects."

"You people truly are amazing!" the captain laughed as he shook his head. "Perhaps visitors like you could renew some of those interests locally? Someone with your background could really make a difference here!"

"Too bad for them we're looking to leave," Johanna whispered to Nate as they continued with their tour. "Once a way home is found, maybe we could just leave them with a few friendly pointers."

"Somehow, I don't think that would be enough," Nate muttered thoughtfully under his breath. "I'm not sure how eager even those who are helping us would be for us to actually leave. Think about it Johanna; with our powers and technology, there's a lot we could do here!"

"You're not suggesting..." she started, taken aback. "You're not wanting to stay here, are you?!"

"No, of course not, and keep your voice down!" Nate shushed her. "I want to go home as much as you do; I'm just saying, they may not want us to leave! We may want to remember that in our dealings with them."

"How far do you think they'd go to keep us?" Johanna whispered, paling at the notion, but she said nothing further as they continued back. The question went unanswered as Nate waved it off, indicating the time wasn't right for that discussion.

Sir Caspin continued the tour, pointing out the masonry aspects that siphoned the creek off through the walls. From there, stone-lined aqueducts and piping provided water to the various fountains and the palace grounds as they strode along the grey stone parapets.

As the captain led them back over the stream flowing under the mossy grate at the base of the inner wall, they paused to take in the view. Unable to see over the mammoth outer wall, the vista still afforded a view of the entire city splayed out before them. Sir Caspin pointed to where the creek flowed through rows of quaint townhomes and greenway parks as it meandered through town. The narrow ribbon glinted in the sunlight before draining through a large grate installed at the base of the outer wall.

"The builders had the foresight to join the wastewater through underground channels, routing eventually to the creek, however within the confines of the outer wall. From the palace, the fountains and the neighborhoods, then to the wall where it all recombines," Sir Caspin explained. "Quite ingenious, really; it all ends up there, where holding ponds cleanse it through steep gravel beds before rejoining its natural flow down to Long Lake. Most of the stench stays clear of the city that way."

"That is quite impressive," Nate marveled as they descended the stone stairs back to the courtyard and the babbling fountain. "They've applied modern principles to maintaining a healthy infrastructure."

"Maybe someday you'll see my home city of Latana," Sir Caspin commented as he ushered them back down the cobblestone road toward the inner gate. "It once was a frontier sister city to Tyrna. Now, though, it is very different."

"Really?" Johanna interjected with curiosity as they passed under the inner wall's moss-covered gate. "How so?"

"Well, the size and population are about the same," Sir Caspin began. "Latana is the capital of Urocia. Long ago, Latana replaced walls of stone with walls of crystal. Tyrna relied on science for its construction, whereas Latana harnessed magical properties found within the bedrock stones and the crystalline structures of the region."

"Sounds interesting," Nate muttered, disappointed in the eagerness with which Johanna joined the conversation.

"I'd love to take you there myself, but my assignments keep me anchored to Tyrna for now," Sir Caspin sighed as they passed through the inner gate. "For now, I wanted you all to see the Pratenvike for all its glory when it's not hosting a festival."

Their host smiled thoughtfully as they rounded the corner where the dome of the Pratenvike loomed before them. The enormous turtle-shell shape of the building soon sprawled before them, the white roof glistening in the sun even as the grey stone wall supports dominated the base.

"You should have seen this place last night," Javier exclaimed excitedly. "It was packed full of people! What a difference a day makes!"

Indeed, the revelers from the previous night had gone, and surprisingly, very little evidence from the previous night's festivities remained. The grass and shrubs were neatly trimmed, and most of the tents had been packed up and stowed. The grounds were meticulously maintained with no trash to be found. It was as if the previous night had never happened.

"This place reminds me of a convention center," Johanna commented, keeping her enthusiasm in check. "I'm amazed at how well the grounds are kept, especially with what you told me about last night."

They followed their guide through the grand entrance, taking in the interior of the great building. The massive stone and wooden arches pointed toward the circular center, where it became narrower and supported white canvas tarps instead of a wooden roof. The place had the feel of a massive cavern but was much better lit and well ventilated. Streams of light poured through skylights, but the largest light came through the center of the high ceiling.

Under the spotlight at the center, a cluster of peasants lingered around a massive violet crystalline obelisk. They sauntered over to the small crowd, eyeing the dark spire at its center.

"What's with all the attention on this rock?" Javier asked.

"It's the Centerpiece: a gift from Urocia," Sir Caspin proclaimed proudly, motioning them closer. The group strode over to the crystalline obelisk, and they gathered around him. "When King Faund declared the construction of the Pratenvike, he wanted a structure to rival those of any other kingdom. Urocia has many of these crystals—as I mentioned earlier, our capital, Latana, incorporates them into every building."

"I take it you miss your home in Urocia?" asked Johanna, sensing a tinge of nostalgia in the captain's voice. The crowd parted for him as he led them to the very base of the spire.

"Born and raised. I came to Tyrna with my father as a boy on the goodwill mission with Lord Morvean to improve relations with the West. When I get homesick, I come here. The sheer perfection of it, the simplicity, the reassurance, the strength, the power..." The captain's breath caught as he reached out with a shaky hand and touched the crystal's mammoth base. A brief yet soft violet pulse emanated to his hand, reflecting in his hazel eyes as he exhaled in a whisper of adulation. "Yes, the comfort it brings me!"

"What's that light do?" Kevin asked, voicing the same surprise at what everyone had just witnessed in silence.

"It's a kiss from the crystal, a blessing of good luck," Sir Caspin reflected. "Would you like to try?"

Not wanting to offend their host, they each took a turn. Indeed, the flash of light touched each of their hands, sending a pleasurable pulse coursing through each of them. What began as an aching warmth at the point of contact quickly flooded through their entire bodies as contentment, followed by a tingling sensation of complete fulfillment.

"Whoa!" Javier exclaimed, followed by a mischievous snicker. "Wanna ask me what that feels like?!"

"Yeah, that could be habit-forming," Kevin observed. "It's a wonder people get anything done around here; I could see many just parking themselves beside this thing!"

"It's nothing so diverting as that! It's just a simple blessing and a kiss." Sir Caspin smiled. "Shall we move along?"

They all mumbled in agreement, still staring at the obelisk as the residual buzz of pleasure slowly faded. As they turned to leave, Nate reached out his hand a second time and touched it.

Instant warmth flooded again into his arm. He felt relaxed, a little sleepy, and his body tingled. As soon as he retracted his hand, he wanted to touch it again. His hand began to shake as he reached out to the obelisk a third time.

"What are you doing?" Johanna whispered. "I'm not sure I would keep doing that! We don't know what it is or what's causing that!"

"When in Rome..." Nate began, but he also noticed that the group was leaving without them. Other peasants had crowded in front of him, blocking his access to the giant crystal.

"Rome didn't have the knowledge we have now, particularly on the topic of addiction!" she whispered in a harsh reminder. "I'm still pissed at you, but until we know what that light actually is, I'd be more careful! Remember, Nicholas advised discretion! What if it's radioactive?"

"Radioactive!" he scoffed initially before giving it a second thought. Muttering to himself, he shrugged off Johanna's rebuff and followed the group back outside. "I highly doubt it's anything so dramatic, but you're right, as usual!"

They headed south this time, crossing the main road behind the still distant gargantuan outer wall's gate. A steady stream of commerce flowed, and they pushed through the crowds, quickly leaving the Pratenvike and commotion of the main thoroughfare behind. Sir

Caspin led them onto a narrow pathway between several quaint street-side shops.

Crossing a footbridge over the creek, the cobblestone pathway climbed slightly, and quaint residences pressed in gently around them. Only the occasional greenway interspaced sections of the creek. These neatly manicured miniature parks retained cobblestone trails, the occasional willow and short grass with benches to provide breaks in the otherwise clustered living.

As they climbed up an alleyway, the neighborhood around them grew much quieter, cleanly maintained, with alternating delicate-looking lampposts and ornately carved benches along the walkway. The narrow stone houses lined the alleyways in tight vertical living, white plastered homes atop red stone foundations and terra-cotta roof shingles.

"We're now passing south through the Christian Quarter," Sir Caspin announced, gesturing ahead through the tight collection of homes and the church ahead of them on the top of the rise. "Despite being an older neighborhood, they tend to keep their homesteads clean and tidy. From here, they overlook the creek and those parkways; nice places!"

"I noticed that most of this city is actually quite hilly," Nate stated, noting that the grounds within Old Tyrna proper had varying degrees of grade. "It climbs the closer you get to the royal palace and the Wizard's Tower closest to the mountain."

"Indeed, it is," Sir Caspin noted. "The original builders utilized Tyrna Peak for its protection. Most of the residential buildings came after the wall, except for the palace and the church that I'm taking you to. They are the oldest structures of the city."

They rounded a corner near the creek, and Sir Caspin pointed to the church surrounded by houses on the hill before them. The basilica stood out around its surroundings. In a traditional Spanish style, the spires reached toward the heavens, and its stained-glass windows gleamed in the sunlight. It had the look of a smaller version of many of the great cathedrals he had seen once in pictures.

"So much detail," Kevin commented in awe. "It's so tall, so huge, yet so beautiful!"

The Lady of Tyrna's high rafters and spires soared high over the medieval homes of the Christian Quarter. Apart from its locale atop the hill, the church stood out differently from any other structure in the city. Forming the steep ceiling sheltering the interior, a single belfry in its northern tower signified the only taller point than the church's roof, a single golden cross glittering atop the height.

"Like the royal palace, the Lady of Tyrna was intended for height. The architecture was meant to inspire all who passed along its base to look up," the captain recalled. "I would say they accomplished their mission in that regard! I would note that this structure and the surrounding grounds occupy nearly the same amount of space as the Pratenvike."

At the front entrance, a garden served to welcome all onto the hallowed grounds. As they approached, Father Jaramillo greeted them, tending to the many flowers and vegetables. He waved a friendly hello and dusted himself off to join their group.

The outsiders gawked at the main entrance, where two massive stone carvings stood at the church's entrance. The pair of great marble angels guarded the doorway on both sides, holding in welcome each one of the two Ten Commandments tablets, each with their arm closest to the doors. The statues' other arms held aloft swords of righteousness, extended high in either welcome or defiance, guarding the entrance.

"Quite the greeters!" Nate pointed to the towering angels to each side of the doorway as they gathered at the entry, the two massive ivory statues looming above. "Welcome or a threat?"

"They're the protection to the sanctuary and all who love God," Father Jaramillo laughed. "Protection from the outside while welcoming those whose hearts seek God inside! So many generations have come and gone through these doors since then; it's just so hard to believe how the time has flown under their watchful gaze, yet I have witnessed it all!"

"Come in or else?" Nate joked as he wiped a bead of sweat from his forehead, catching his breath from their trek up the hill.

"Not at all; come and see, my friends!" Father Jaramillo pulled open the great oaken doors and motioned them inside. "I'm so happy to see you here; allow me to show you the house of our Lord here in Tyrna! It only seems like yesterday when we first built her; I can remember the first day so clearly!"

As they entered, the air around them immediately cooled, and the scent of the old stone permeated the softly lit interior of the great house of worship. The silence echoed in the great chamber as the group shuffled quietly through the entry.

They marveled at the morning sunlight spilling in through the colorful stained glass behind the marble altar and narrow windows at the sides of the church. The ornate glass on the sides illuminated the interior, depicting the Stations of the Cross by illustrating a haunting reminder of the Lord's sacrifice on Calvary. Iron chandeliers remained unlit high above the nearly fifty rows of wooden pews, lining the church with a wide single aisle down the center. Two lesser aisles paralleled the main one to each side, broken only by the occasional stone support pillar and further subdividing the pews and sections of the cathedral.

Votive candles intermittently lined the walls in tiny makeshift sanctuaries, glimmering with ghostly light and highlighting the occasional shadowy figures silently kneeling before them. Silent prayers uttered from the alcoves seemed to be answered by the flickering flames, casting a warm glow that danced in a multicolored display upon the stone walls.

Kevin caught the movement of a dwarf in a monk's robe, quietly stacking books atop built-in shelves near the confessionals along the walls of the church. The monk worked quietly beside a winding metal staircase leading to the choir loft at the back. Somewhere in the recesses of the shadows, musical chants wafted and echoed softly through darkened corners of the high ceilings.

Bells began to toll, pealing from above and dissipating out into the city. Here in the cathedral, the echo rang solemnly inside the church. A tiny robin flew in behind them and wound in circles before settling on the edge of the baptismal fountain, chirping pleasantly near the altar. In the dim light, a Carthenian nun silently crossed the landing high above in the choir loft, dusting off the music stands in the threshold, high above in the choir loft.

"Well, we must be going," Sir Caspin whispered, motioning everyone back to the doors. "You may return later if you'd like, but we have a lot of ground still to cover."

Kevin became so lost in the moment that he didn't notice his entourage leaving. Father Jaramillo watched him with an approving smile before gently tapping his shoulder.

"You may spend all the time here you wish," the priest stated in welcome with his thick, heavy Spanish accent. "Please feel free to come by again anytime you like!"

"It's just so beautiful," Kevin whispered. "It just reminds me of home, though."

"This is one of the oldest structures in Tyrna. We built it with the help of the faithful and the memory of what I retained from the great cathedrals in Europe," Father Jaramillo stated proudly. The priest sighed before pointing to the others quietly exiting back the way they had come. "I would love to show you more when you have time, but it seems your friends are leaving without you! Perhaps another time we may discuss more on what has transpired in your world since I left!"

"I would enjoy that and will return so we may do just that!!" Kevin promised. He thanked Father Jaramillo profusely for his time and promised to return before darting back out into the bright sunlight to catch his entourage. Racing down the hill to catch his friends, he left the stoic marveling statues and the church they guarded behind as they watched, silently glistening blindingly white in the afternoon sun.

As Kevin caught up to the group, they followed Sir Caspin down through a series of alleys toward the base of the great outer wall. Massive and crimson, the outer wall stood like a sheer cliff before them, casting its shadow over the rows of homes nearest to it.

A small, rickety guard's house stood by the entrance to the great wall, looking very much like a tiny burrow, dwarfed by the massive, impenetrable wall it entered. Three guards in chain mail stood idly by, holding ceremonial spears and banners. They greeted Sir Caspin with a salute, snapping to attention as the group approached.

"I'm taking them inside the stairwell onto the walkway," the captain announced as they moved aside.

The lead acknowledged the information with a grunt before noting it in the station log inside the guard shack.

The narrow doorway in the wall looked dark except for the flickering torches lighting the simple yet cramped stone staircase. They climbed up the claustrophobic stairs as their legs throbbed with the effort. When they emerged from a trap door atop the wall's parapets, just south of the main gate, Sir Caspin helped Johanna and Nate onto the landing as the younger lads pressed excitedly by.

The parapet walkway stretched to each side of the main gate atop the wall, interspaced with trebuchets. The wooden latticework structures stood tall, like silent dinosaur skeletons from another time. The rusting machines of war towered over them as tributes to a bygone era of bolstered defense to the impregnable walls.

Yet even they were dwarfed by the stone gate housings at the end of the walkway. A set of steep ladders on each side of the gate allowed guards to climb higher and traverse forty feet above the massive city's entryway. Guards in chain mail leisurely patrolled the parapets with disinterest, almost in ceremony rather than in purpose.

Behind the ladder, they could see a yawning gap slicked with smears of oil. The crevice marked the service access in the gate's mechanism. From within the cavernous chamber, they could make out massive counterweights of stone and brick fastened to giant iron chains. The structure rolled onto itself from within the bricked columns.

"Is this all for the main gate? Looks like a giant garage door, but it rolls up like those gates you see at the mall!" Javier commented, careful to not lean up against the brick enclosure. One could easily fall through the crevice if they stepped behind the ladder, but even if such catastrophe were avoided, the grease and eons of dirt collected around the sides would soil anyone standing too close. "Doesn't look like they use it very often."

"I'm not sure they could move, even if we wanted them to," Sir Caspin mused. "This gate has stayed open for nearly a century now; we've had no reason to close it. They are caked with rust at this point and jammed into place. The mechanisms that moved it are frankly in worse shape than it is, likely rusted into the wall, I suppose."

"What are these for?" Daniel called out, pointing to several depressions with grates interspaced between the trebuchets.

"Drainage, I suppose," Johanna pondered aloud as she caught her breath after their climb.

"Not quite: boiling oil to repel an attack," Sir Caspin corrected with a grin. "In the event of a siege, they pour it down these grates, and momentum carries it down these chutes. It's designed to really spray out into the field below. Once the passages are well-lubricated, the grates can also be removed, and specially designed projectiles are rolled down the slats. With the momentum they gain, they become quite deadly when they exit along the base of the wall."

"Hell of a defense!" Nate admired, scratching his head. "How do you get it all up here?!"

"They employed cranes and pulleys for the heavy lifting," the captain concluded as he pointed to the disassembled machinery, neatly stacked, covered and tightly stored under the base of the trebuchets. "The necessity of all this is long gone yet remains impressive, nonetheless. Come, see the view of the rest of the land from here."

The group's attention drawn, they sauntered over to the ramparts, looking out over the broad expanse below. While the view in the morning had been impressive at the junction of the inner and outer walls, the view from atop the outer wall splayed out before them completely unhindered. They stood atop the battlements of the outer wall, and the entire plain opened out before them.

The Grenze Mountains dominated the distant landscape, with Long Lake splayed out at their feet. Between the lake and the city, grassy fields rippled like waves on the sea in the late afternoon breeze as hints of sunset dotted the intermittent clouds crowning the peaks.

"Only from the Wizard's Tower can you gain this same perspective," Sir Caspin declared. "Takes my breath every time I see it!"

≈≈≈≈

It was nearing evening again when they returned to the royal palace. Sir Caspin turned to the group as they completed their climb up the cobblestone walkway. The captain's eyes glittered in satisfaction, like the twilight upon the waters of the peaceful fountain burbling quietly behind where he stood.

"I hope you've enjoyed your tour, but I must take my leave for now," the captain announced. "I will come back to collect you for dinner. Please feel free to refresh yourselves or wander about until then."

With that, he bade them farewell and departed, flashing a brief wink over to Johanna. She glanced over to Nate, who, to her relief, had missed the flirtation. Nate's attention had been drawn to his dog, Sammy, who had come running up from around the garden, chasing a cat and barking wildly in excitement.

"Sammy! Come back here!" Daniel shouted, racing after the hound.

"Catch me! Catch me!" Sammy yelped.

Johanna rolled her eyes and let him go. She had given up trying to get her son's attention and departed with Nate to their rooms. Javier and Kevin stayed outside on the entrance stairs to watch Daniel play in the garden with the hound.

As Nate and Johanna ascended the stairs back to their rooms, he took their solitude as an opportunity to strike up a conversation with her.

"Nothing like a little privacy finally," he hinted, trying to stir conversation and make amends. "We haven't had any alone time since we got here. Daniel is out at the fountains with Kevin and Javier, so he ought to be fine for now. What do you say you and I...?"

"Not now!" Johanna snapped, pulling back from Nate in irritation, surprising him and even herself. *Am I still that annoyed?*

"Really, Johanna?" Nate balked as a terse wrinkle lined his forehead. "You're still mad at me, and now you're rejecting me?"

"It's not that; I think I need some time to just sleep," Johanna retracted, forcing a smile through her flimsy excuse as she recollected herself. "You don't need to try so hard. I think I just need a nap."

"Are you sure I can't keep you company?" Nate pressed invitingly. "C'mon!"

"That's okay," she blustered as she opened the door. "I'm really just not in the mood; see you at dinner."

She gently shut the door in his face, leaving him dumbfounded. He stood there for a moment, rattled yet unbelieving.

"Maybe you'd prefer that Sir Caspin come knocking!" he yelled after a long moment, punching the door, immediately regretting the decision. Luckily, she seemed to ignore his outburst, and only silence followed.

"Fuck!" he muttered under his breath, turning to go to his own room.

Chapter 17

Mondlichtberg

Princess Serina departed Levens before dawn, dressed in long riding boots and riders' garb. Only to her parents, the king and queen, did she quietly bade a farewell in their chambers. She and her mother had exchanged a few tears, but since she never liked long goodbyes, the exchange had been mercifully brief. She scarcely remembered the walk from the castle to the stables, set in her one-track mind to be on her way.

The town barely noticed her departure in the wee morning hours and was only just beginning to bustle with morning activity as she passed through the arches of the main gate and over the short drawbridge clogged with reeds. Only her long blue cloak flowed behind her and provided some protection from wind and sun as she rode Barley out of Levens's gates.

She rode, galloping past it all swiftly, angling her steed northwest along the roadway Aros had traveled to where she had met up with him only days ago. Her destination: the wilderness beyond.

Most of her early morning rides had been for fun; this time, that was not the case. She had waited two days as Nicholas had requested, but now, the time had arrived for her to be on her way to Mondlichtberg. The journey she had long anticipated had finally come, although attached with conditions she had not anticipated.

Her face set like flint, her thoughts drifted as she trotted past the kingdom's boundaries into unfamiliar territory, the mountains rising all around her. The solitude of the wilds enveloped her, and only sounds came from the rushing torrent of the Rhane River, the occasional breeze through the trees and the clopping of Barley's hooves.

Nicholas's meeting with her and Aros days ago before he had left with the newcomers remained fresh in her mind. Aros was to stay in Levens and quietly obtain supplies for a possible long journey, as well as tend to the beastless carriage the outsiders had come in. Nicholas was to gather trusted associates he still maintained in Tyrna while keeping tabs on the newcomers, all while posing as Aros's replacement in the capital.

That left Princess Serina to set out on her own vital mission, one she wasn't looking forward to. Yes, she had always wanted to visit the wizard's keep, Grand Master Yamaro and the other wizards. Now, she dreaded visiting them under false pretenses with a motive other than to expand her knowledge and ability.

The princess had protested initially, but Nicholas reminded her that Aros was already compromised in the eyes of the Wizard's Council and the monarchy in Tyrna. He also explained Aros would not be staying in Levens and that he had other plans for him. The mission to Mondlichtberg simply *had* to be hers.

The road led past Mondlichtberg Crossroads, a place where wild land trails crossed, leading into either the northern wilds or the western high passes to Mondlichtberg. A small farm stood off to the side, smoke rising sleepily from the cottage nestled in amongst the pines in the clearing.

Crossing the Rhane River, she noted signs of fall well underway; it was warm as ever yet with the warning that it wouldn't last. Bumblebees buzzed around last-minute blooms for last-call pollen as the sun shone brightly overhead.

Telltale patches of changing leaves littered the path ahead in a kaleidoscope of color as she ascended the incline of the ever-narrowing valley. Speckles of red and yellow peppered the roadway leading into the wilds. The scents of fall with decaying leaves and still muddied earth drying slowly in the sun carried on the cool breeze as she rode higher into the alpine environment.

By late afternoon and with a substantial increase in elevation, the fall colors had dropped off in favor of mostly pine forests. She made her way up the tapered valley, coming to a bend in the road near a vast meadow. The telltale tracks from the beastless carriage led off through the grass over to where the creek had joined the road. *So close to Mondlichtberg the newcomers had emerged, yet no one noticed them?*

The grade steepened from here, and the trail led away southwest into another valley. The pleasant scents of grass, flowers and mud followed her from the meadow she left behind as she ascended higher still, passing through thick steeper stands of aspen and pine.

Her trail led over a series of narrow and steep finger valleys, filled with tall pines and firs, intermittently peppered with large boulders that only became sparser towards the tops of the valley rim. Three identical gorges in, her ride turned west again, and broad, grassy dale spread out wider as she entered, the incline tapering off into a gentle rise.

As the afternoon progressed into early evening, she rode more warily as shadows lengthened and darker colors began to permeate the sky. Keeping a constant watch on the sides of the trail, she prepared herself to respond should reports of aggressive wolf packs prove to be true. The grade eased, but the forest thickened into groves of pines and colorful aspen, littering the ground and forests with flecks of crimson and gold. Beautiful to behold yet deceptive in the peace it beckoned with, thoughts of potential clashes with aggressive wildlife bubbled to the surface of her consciousness. Shadows from the trees teased of the coming night, a gloom with potential to hide danger, so she proceeded with caution, nonetheless.

Her father had demanded she take an escort, but headstrong as she was, the princess had left before one could be assembled, promising she would send word of her safe arrival once she had accomplished it. Now, with only the occasional breeze whispering warnings through the trees, she began to second-guess her decision over the hasty departure she had chosen.

A blue jay suddenly darting out from the underbrush flew past her head, startling her into a scream as she flung her arms about her. Heart still pounding, she laughed aloud to calm herself, following the flight path of the errant bird up the valley when she realized, at long last, her goal appeared before her.

At the head of the valley, she caught sight of the large stone fortress straddling a spring at the top. A wide creek spilled from the base of the grand squat fortress, birthed from a miraculous spring on site, cascading out the base and through the broad meadow she now ascended.

The windows glowed with candlelit lamps from within, a warm and friendly greeting to her, given the coming night. As she neared the castle, she sighed in relief, clearing her nerves as she made out the finer details of the keep itself. *Mondlichtberg—finally!*

The grey stone structure retained a squat, plain rectangular width, yet anchored near the center stood timbers at sharp angles to ward off the winter snow, giving the central structure height. The appearance at the middle gave an almost lodge-like quality towards the castle yet retained a fortress quality towards the outside.

The top of the unique "Y" shape of the structure, and the known rear, was built directly into the side of the mountain at the ridgeline, giving occupants of either wing a wide and unobstructed vista of the wilderness to the west. Constructed low at the top of the ridge, the engineers had been careful to not overexpose the structure to the inclement weather of the mountaintop. Both wings stood out as great arms at the back, reaching out to either side, joining to and burring themselves with the stone wall that encircled the tri-winged keep, into the ridgeline.

Conversely, the foremost corner stood quite high, allowing lookouts a complete overview of the valley and anyone approaching from the east. The trail led to the front gate and main entrance, where the wall and base of the "Y" shape stood at its highest. A long, dark pennant hung, the telltale order's full moon set amid three stars in a velvet field of black, waving proudly above the closed entryway.

At the very center of the structure stood the lone Wizard's Tower, tall and imposing. The torchlight coming from the room at the top shone brighter than the light from all the other windows, reminding her of a great scepter her father held for ceremonies when firelight gleamed off the gold at its tip. With only a narrow balcony off the top to observe all four directions, the parapets seemed so close to the main structure that it made her wonder if one could ever stand outside upon them at all.

She dismounted as she neared the front gate and peered through the iron bars to see if anyone was about. While the outside of the keep had a stoic and stern appearance of metal and stone, the grounds inside the walls revealed themselves to be meticulously manicured. *A welcoming sight if I can just get inside!*

Dried yet un-replaced green shrubs and flowers separated cold grey stone from the lawn between the gate and the inner walls of the keep. The wooden doors to the castle remained closed and the only sign of life came from torches, jutting from the walls and freshly lit. The place certainly appeared lively with all the light, yet no sound other than the evening breeze through the trees could be heard.

The howl of a lone wolf, miles away, echoed with the wind. *I certainly cannot stay out here!*

"Princess Serina of Levens!" she shouted to announce herself, swallowing hard as her voice echoed. "Is there anyone within to treat without?"

For a moment, nothing but silence answered her. Another gust of wind whistled around corners in the structure, chilling the evening air and warning of the coming night. She looked around nervously, not relishing the prospect of camping outside.

Suddenly, a loud metallic groan emanated from the gate. A cloud of dust puffed from the guide rails, followed by clanking as counterweights pulled on iron chains, and the grate blocking her entrance slowly rose.

The wooden door to the Keep opened with a creak, and out waddled a modestly stout man carrying a long, gnarled wooden staff. A silvery light shone from the top of the grey staff where a tiny silver lantern cast away the gloom and shadows as he shuffled forth. His white robes and balding head gave him the appearance of a monk, yet he smiled welcomingly as he approached. His features appeared bronze and leathery, yet he displayed few wrinkles, etching his ancient face delicately through the tufts of white hair, highlighting his hairline. He maintained only a thin wisp of a beard, and his eyes were as narrow as his eyebrows.

"My dear, it's been ages since I've heard that lovely voice," he exclaimed in a musical tone as sweet as honey, betraying nothing of the age or the eons of wisdom behind the man who spoke. "What are you doing out here at such a late hour? I had heard you were coming to Mondlichtberg, but now? Without escort?"

"Grand Master Yamaro!" Princess Serina grinned as she led Barley into the courtyard. "I was just beginning to worry; the place has gone from looking understaffed to outright deserted!"

"Sometimes it may feel that way, my child," he soothed, smiling disarmingly. He warmly embraced her first before turning back, beckoning for her to follow. "Please, come in! We are most happy to receive you!"

As they filed over the grassy pathway he offered her his arm, which she gladly took. They proceeded to the petite entrance courtyard where a similarly clad attendant emerged to lead her steed to the stables.

"My name's Ollen, Your Highness! I'll take good care of Barley." The lad with a pinch of red hair and spectacles grinned from underneath the silver cowl and stated eagerly, "We'll ensure he gets a good grooming and something to eat!"

"Also see to it that he's returned to Levens on the morrow," the older wizard sighed before turning to the princess. "Best say your goodbyes now, my dear. The Mondlichtberg is for magic users, and your equestrian companion will be better suited under your father's care."

"I understand; goodbye for now, dear Barley," the princess exhaled. She nuzzled the great beast's nose before turning back to the attendant. "He knows the way home; give him his lead and he'll take you safely to Levens."

"You'll see him again," the younger lad encouraged. "Levens isn't far, and we have carriages making the trip for supplies often! Our quartermaster is leaving on the morrow to meet with the hermit at the Mondlichtberg Crossroads; your kingdom is our only trading partner for leagues!"

"A hermit? At the Mondlichtberg Crossroads?" she laughed. "I know Levens supplies food and clothing in exchange for the ale and wisdom you send across the lands, but what does a hermit have to trade?"

"I must admit, our quartermaster's supply of magical items has never been better!" the grand master exclaimed, shaking his head as he marveled at the irony. "We used to scavenge the hillsides ourselves for stone and wood with unique properties. Seldom in the order's history have we found consistent quality as we have from the hermit's selections!"

"Who exactly is he and where is he from?" the princess queried as she arched an eyebrow with curiosity. "Funny we never heard about him in Levens, not even through Grand Master Nicholas."

"An old Levenese farmer with a passion for herbology and alchemy," the old wizard sighed. "Apparently, he's a distant relation to the couple that lives at the junction near the bottom of the canyon. He prefers his privacy, and we grant him that. During our supply runs, we merely pause at the junction to see if he shows himself. He's quite eccentric and possibly insane, yet his collections are most reliable in their nature!"

"Well, our subjects tend to get a little crazier the further out from town they live!" The princess returned the joke with a wink and continued walking with Grand Master Yamaro through the castle's main entrance. From there, the entry to Mondlichtberg began as a great hallway, yawning open before her as Grand Master Yamaro ushered her inside behind the heavy yet intricately carved oak doors. "I haven't been here in years! I had forgotten how big this place is!"

"Grand Master Nicholas is well, I trust?" mused Grand Master Yamaro, notably looking away from her. "I frankly envy him and miss the company of your family. You are lucky to have such a fine mentor on hand in Levens. However, I must question his judgment of late. I see no escort for you on your journey, and the road through the wilds isn't as safe as it used to be."

"I've heard as such, but nothing Barley and I couldn't handle," Princess Serina assured him, patting his arm gently. "We knew to come quick and not dally!"

"I was warned long ago of your headstrong nature," the silvery wizard gently scolded. "I must have words with your father and Nicholas, nevertheless. To send you on your own, I would never have approved!"

"I simply didn't give them a choice this time," she laughed with a wink. "Really, Grand Master, an escort would only have slowed me!"

As they entered the main hall, the cavernous room buzzed with a quiet simplicity of at least a hundred plainly cloaked occupants dining by candlelight. Dishes clinked and murmurs of low conversation muttered under the din of the crackling fire. The room appeared other-wise empty since the great hall could clearly accommodate a far greater number than the scattered apprentices currently finishing their evening meals.

No one stirred as the princess of Levens strode by, low conversations halting briefly as the diners observed her passing with curiosity. She marveled at the scene nonetheless, gesturing a friendly nod to the half-occupied bench tables lined neatly throughout. A few smiled or waved in return before pulling their dark cloaks around them and returning to their meals after a wary glance at her escort.

Although utilized for dining, the great hall was more of a library. Tomes and books from centuries stacked to the ceiling filled the dusty shelves on both sides of the walls. The great room smelled of old leather, with a hint of fragrant smoke and a promise to her of something delicious to come for the evening meal.

Candles lined the tables but most of the ambient light came from greater sources. Great stone pillars lined the walkway with nothing but torches and massive chandeliers illuminating every corner. The windows were surprisingly tall, yet slender, cranked open to let in the evening breeze. They afforded little light in the daytime but plenty for ventilation after warm days such as this one.

From the central hearth, the heart of Mondlichtberg, the castle divided evenly into the main three wings. The main hall entrance was full of desks and books for studying, serving as both dining hall and study hall, lined with tables and benches three rows wide and many lines deep.

The remaining two wings split evenly into residences on the north-west and southwest ends. The kitchen, stables and washrooms snuggled up against the mountain's rim with the windows almost at ground level.

At the center, a great fireplace opened to all three sections, with iron grating and piping leading the warmer air to each wing, inter-woven with the tower's stone staircase. Massive stone supports for Mondlichtberg's Wizard's Tower stood squarely to each side, supporting the staircase as it wound its way up the rounded central structure. Ascending into the ceiling lined with timbered beams and stonemasonry stood the main office for the Wizard's Council of the Order of the Moon.

Princess Serina followed Grand Master Yamaro to the roaring fire-place at the center of the hall, where a winding stone staircase awaited them. She let him take the lead up the tower stairs. As they continued to exchange pleasantries on the way up, he fretted about her coming alone despite her insistence that her journey had been uneventful. He opened the folds of his robes, shuffling through oversized iron keys.

With a loud clank and a creak, the grand master opened the door and ushered her in. The office felt homey, albeit in a bit of disarray, with books and papers scattered about. Otherwise, the clearly active office space was lined with shelves with a large balcony outside facing east over the valley she had traveled, currently closed off by an ornate stained-glass door. A large mirror stood across from an enormous table at the center, opposite a modest fireplace crackling with warmth.

As Grand Master Yamaro closed the door behind Princess Serina, she took the opportunity to warm herself by the fire. She took a deep breath as she soaked in the warmth, smelling the familiar scents of books and shelves she had been accustomed to in the Wizard's Tower of Levens.

"Accommodations are being prepared for you at this very moment," the grand master began. "I'm so pleased Nicholas has finally come to his senses, handed you over to us, and allowed us to begin your next stage of growth. I must admit, I've been anticipating this for quite some time; it's long overdue!"

"Thank you, dear Grand Master!" she stated, pausing in exuberance. "I must admit, I too have dreamt of this moment for years now!"

"We are most joyous for your arrival," the silvery wizard replied solemnly. "The timing of your arrival couldn't have been better, and we have much planned for you during your stay! New recruits are so rare these days, but one of your stature is most exceptional! You didn't see all the other students staring at you when you came in?"

"You're too kind, Grand Master!" she sighed, changing the topic to her mission's purpose as almost an afterthought. "Master Aros told us to be on the lookout for some newcomers to our world. More than one I'm told, as a result of a rare Shimmering event."

"There has been one indeed," he whispered excitedly. "They are but the first of many to come! Perhaps you may even be involved with them once these first newcomers are located and settled appropriately."

"Wait, more than one event? More to come, you say?" Princess Serina balked but kept her surprised appearance in check at the open admission. "So, the Shimmering opening was no fluke? This was an intentional act of the council?"

"It was indeed!" Grand Master Yamaro confirmed with a broad grin. "I'm quite proud that we were able to accomplish it! My dear, I must confess that this is not yet common knowledge. I must insist on your discretion, and I only share it with you out of respect for the history I share with your family.”

“But why?” she pressed. Princess Serina blinked, still unbelieving at what she was hearing. “This seems so contrary to our order’s charter of non-interference and only practiced and measured use of our craft!”

“As you may have observed, Mondlichtberg was built for many. Indeed, we have room for over a thousand souls here, yet in these recent years, we house barely over a hundred!” The grand master exhaled sadly, shaking his head. “I’m old, my dear. Grand Master Nicholas is older still. Even our ‘Copper Master,’ Grand Master Oaxro, is nearly as old as I am! Our order is aged and becoming obsolete in the eyes of the world, all except Grand Master Encara. Yet he is only one man and his duties at Urocia demand constant attention.”

“To bring in newcomers from another world though,” she exhaled as she shook her head. “That’s a bit extreme, isn’t it? I mean; it is quite a feat, yet so drastic!”

“Time has challenged us all in ways I never thought possible before to find new ways of ensuring our legacy,” he stated softly as he lifted his head to search her eyes. “The old ways do not serve us any longer; it was Grand Master Encara and his fresh perspective that convinced us to change our ways and work with him to force open the Shimmering from this very room!”

Suddenly, Princess Serina realized he was looking for an opinion, not necessarily hers, but perhaps one Nicholas may have shared with her. *I must tread carefully.*

“What a relief!” she exclaimed, plopping down into a chair next to his desk. “Nicholas sensed it, and we weren’t sure what had happened, how they got here or why indeed it had happened at all! It seems we may have indeed met your missing newcomers!”

“So, they did come through after all,” he whispered.

“Yes, Grand Master! They are with Nicholas now, in Tyrna,” she gently informed him without hesitation, luminous blue eyes piercing. “A pity we didn’t realize who they were sooner. What a tremendous amount of power that must have taken! But why, Grand Master? Why them? Is it right to just snatch people out of their own worlds to satisfy our needs?"

"Our intention wasn't to 'snatch' anyone!" Grand Master Yamaro exclaimed, half in apology yet half irritated at the implication as he sat heavily behind his desk. "We only meant to open the Shimmering and see what would come through. It's a very delicate process and involves a great amount of concentration and energy. I cannot say what happened on their end that caused it to open there, but only that it coincided with ours."

"Oh, that's certainly understandable; how would anyone be able to predict what would happen?" Trying not to convey her surprise at the admission of their involvement, she lowered her voice to a whisper. "This is all for the survival of the order?"

"Young lady, our ranks are running critically few and far between these days. In fact, we've recorded fewer recruits from the kingdoms than ever," the elder wizard explained. "We will find a way to return those who truly want to go back, but for now, we've determined that the 'ends justify the means,' and the methods that we employed are sound!"

"Well, it's certainly a novel idea," the princess stated carefully, pursing her lips as she measured out her cautionary opinion around the matter. *I just got here and need to earn trust; I can't let them think I'll be a hindrance!*

"We live in a world that is much different than the one of old," he sighed, gesturing toward the darkening east-facing window. "The kingdoms of men are distracted by customs that don't value the old ways. Many more believe they don't need us anymore. We're desperate to replenish our numbers, and once we do, we will ensure proper compensation to those we inconvenienced."

"I understand your reasons, yet it all seems so contrary to our teachings!" Princess Serina proposed. "Why not share this information with Grand Master Nicholas? I'm certain he would assist the order once he understood the full scope of the predicament!"

"We spoke about it long ago, Nicholas and I," the silvery wizard mused, standing and pulling a large bound book from the wall before settling again across from her at the table. "He had warned us about being too aggressive in our recruitment efforts. Time and circumstances have changed though, and not for the better! Grand Master Encara was more sympathetic to supporting our efforts. It was one of the reasons we waited for Nicholas's retirement and Encara's ascension into our ranks before pursuing this course."

"Still, you all had been so close for so long," the princess countered gently. "It seems like a missed opportunity to make amends!"

"Frankly, we weren't sure we could count on Nicholas's support," Grand Master Yamaro laughed dryly. He turned and she found him studying her face again. "Besides, we wanted to test it first to see if we'd even be successful. We had no intention of pulling anyone through, at least not with this, our first attempt."

"Nicholas is still loyal to Mondlichtberg, the Order of the Moon and all its inhabitants," she stated again without hesitation. "Despite old arguments and academic debates, you must remember that he was with you on the council for over 400 years!"

"That's good to hear, my dear. He used to be so rigid about 'utilizing the resources at hand' and 'maximizing our local resources,'" he emphasized, using Nicholas's own intonations, at which Princess Serina giggled. Grand Master Yamaro laughed with her, setting the mood at ease before continuing the serious aspect of the conversation. "The truth is, we just don't have the luxury of time anymore. I know this was a point of contention with Nicholas, but times have changed. We simply had to act, and we may yet again, and very soon!"

"I know Grand Master Nicholas will understand," Princess Serina assured him. "He's not completely unaware of the situation, nor is he immune to change. He mentioned it to me before I left."

"Did he now?" Grand Master Yamaro seemed surprised as he arched an eyebrow. "In what context?"

"Well, he only mentioned that the Grand Master Council was not in agreement on this topic when he had originally retired," she stated as casually as she could, burying deep inside the resentment she knew that the retired grand master harbored about it. "He only stated, just as you did, that 'times have changed' and that 'you may have been right,' whatever that meant."

"That's very good to hear! Very good indeed." The silvery wizard nodded, retreating into his own thoughts. He paused only momentarily before shrugging it off and producing a room key from within his robes. "Breakfast is at daybreak, and we will complete your trials for your next level in our order! I suggest you get settled and rest up; you're going to need a good night's sleep!"

"Thank you, Grand Master! I'm in desperate need of a bath and dinner as well as..." She was about to leave the room but paused when she noticed Grand Master Yamaro still staring at her expectantly. "Is there something else, Grand Master?"

"What exactly has become of our newcomer friends?" Yamaro interjected, pressing home the point. "You said you met them; why did they not accompany you here?"

"They are Nicholas's wards and guests of King Faund in Tyrna until arrangements can be made otherwise," the princess recalled, giving her best dazzling smile. "They would have come here, but Nicholas didn't realize who they were until well on his way to Tyrna with them! He was in such a rush to get to Tyrna; something about helping Aros out there so Aros could stay in Levens to take his place."

"A most wise move, given his protégé's difficulties in Tyrna," Grand Master Yamaro interpreted aloud before pressing the matter further. "I'm assuming the newcomers are displaying some unique abilities at this point?"

"Well, according to Nicholas's last note, Johanna is a healer, and Javier can project his voice," she stated matter-of-factly. "Seems as though Daniel can fly, and Kevin can project himself over great distances. Nate seems to have a grasp of lightning..."

There is no point in lying about any of this if I can just keep the truth centered on what Nicholas had instructed me.

"You seem to know a great deal about them and are even on a first-name basis," Grand Master Yamaro probed more pointedly, the mirth she had already become accustomed to suddenly fading. He stared at her with a piercing gaze, hard and stern. "Again, I ask, why are you here and they are not?"

This was the question she had been waiting for; the one she dreaded having to answer. However, this question was one she had prepared for.

"Well, as I said before, we didn't know who they were initially; they simply had emerged from the wilds," she carefully began. "He had sensed the Shimmering but also your battle with the dragon and had assumed they were related. When he relieved Aros of his duties in Tyrna and was headed out to assume that post, they expressed an interest in wanting to see the city. My master took a charitable interest in their well-being, so I personally assisted with the extra provisioning for their journey to the capital. By the time he realized who there were, he had already reached King Faund. I received word of this via a message bird, just prior to my departure from Levens this morning."

"I see." Grand Master Yamaro nodded with a sigh, squinting as if he had swallowed a lemon. "That fool Aros didn't convey enough to Nicholas, and as a result, they're all in Tyrna now! Nicholas acted wisely after the fact and in the interests of the order, which is more than I can say for his protégé! I'm sorry, my dear, I don't mean to speak ill of your friend, but Nicholas did the right thing, and his actions are most welcomed and blessed by the council! We're glad to have him back in service!"

"Well, I'm sure Aros tried!" Princess Serina protested, balking at the grand master's assessment. "He wasn't aware of the newcomers' arrival since he was otherwise occupied assisting you with the Northern Guardian. He also had that surprise change of post and needed to ready the Wizard's Tower in Levens for his residency!" *If Grand Master Yamaro knew the truth...*

"Perhaps I should have contacted Nicholas myself; the folly may be my own in this case," the silvery grand master muttered, briefly pinching the bridge of his nose before staring into the flames of his tiny hearth with a far-off look in his eyes. "Nicholas has always been wise, and I regret the words we exchanged during his departure from the order. However, I am glad that he's not afraid to assist our cause when he's needed!"

"Always," the princess stated absolutely and without hesitation. "That has never changed for him!"

"You know that when he retired, we didn't exactly part on the best of terms," Grand Master Yamaro bemoaned. "I state that with sad regret, for my part."

"I'm aware of it," she admitted quietly. "Both of you are like family to me. I can tell you that—at least, for his part—that argument is in the past. He's been retired for over a decade now and I daresay even enjoys the respite. As you've stated, Grand Master, times have changed!"

"They have indeed, my dear!" The grand master smiled, regressing briefly deep back into his own thoughts. "They have indeed!"

"I'm to report back to Nicholas in a week on my progress," she added quietly. "In the meantime, as he has handed over my training to you, he recommended my promotion to a magician level. That is why I am here. I'm ready for the trials!"

"Your father also made me aware of that!" Grand Master Yamaro announced, straightening as he took on a more formal stance with the proclamation. "We shall see to the completion of your training then, although I doubt your mother is as thrilled!"

"I can handle the Queen of Levens in this regard," Princess Serina proclaimed as she lowered her voice again to a whisper. "Regarding Grand Master Nicholas though, the handoff of my training need not be solely a formal matter. I'm sure if you were to reach out to him for other matters, he would be very receptive!"

"I get your meaning and of course I will, once we have this business with your promotion settled," the elder wizard stated as a broad smile spread across his face, a sense of resolution having been achieved. "You have no idea how pleasing I find your being here, along with the news you bring!"

"I can't tell you how thrilled I am to finally be here, free of the mundane obligations of my house, at least for now," she confirmed with a laugh.

"Splendid!" Grand Master Yamaro exclaimed. "Nicholas shall have his replacement for Tyrna in due time. In the meantime, our books, beds and refreshments are at your disposal. I'm in agreement with Nicholas on this; you are ready for the trials. Perhaps his recommendation will help bring us all closer again, my dear! I look forward to validating your promotion to magician!"

"Excellent!" Princess Serina mused, noting the grand master beaming with some hesitation, a hidden excitement he had not yet revealed. "What is it, Grand Master?"

"Just a private satisfaction: it looks as though we've managed to pull old Nicholas out of retirement after all," the great wizard laughed in a sudden coughing fit. "A feat equal to that of opening a Shimmering!"

"Indeed, although I'm uncertain as to how pleased he'll be with that." Princess Serina chuckled at the notion. "You know how stubborn he can be, especially once he realizes the truth of that statement!"

"I'll be gentle in broaching the topic with him, I promise!" Grand Master Yamaro acknowledged as he dismissed her. "Well, go on then, make yourself at home; your trials start tomorrow! You are most welcome here, Your Highness! Go and rest this evening! Mondlichtberg receives you!"

"Dear Grand Master, it's wonderful to finally see you again! Thank you!" the princess added before marching proudly down the stairs. *For now, Grand Master Yamaro seems satisfied with the answers given.*

She was uncomfortable not being fully honest with her father's friend, but if this was the extent of the lie that she was required to spin, then perhaps it was all worth it. With great relief, she would try to communicate with Nicholas tonight, but for now, she couldn't wait for dinner. Perhaps she would run across this Sorceress Amina Nicholas had told her about along the way.

As Princess Serina left, Grand Master Yamaro jotted a few more notes into an open book before blowing a few drying puffs onto the ink. He turned and sauntered over to the long mirror across from the table.

It was a tall and narrow reflective mirror encased in a thin golden frame. Fairly nondescript but nonetheless a special item to him and with hidden value.

Grand Master Yamaro closed his eyes in concentration. *Encara.*

His reflection in the mirror shimmered, no longer his own, but that of Grand Master Encara, staring back at him. The younger grand master's image appeared faint, donning long yellow robes with a high collar. A slender bald man with narrow, dark, arching eyebrows, he implacably stared back at Yamaro, his lips tight and cheekbones set. The light glimmered off the jewel-encrusted robes in a garish glare, giving the newest and younger grand master the informal title of the Golden Wizard.

"What is it, my friend?" Grand Master Encara spoke in a low tone, soothing yet with concern. He maintained a surprisingly high-pitched voice despite his imposing figure, and his calm tone still maintained an edge to it.

"An emissary from former Grand Master Nicholas with news has arrived to Mondlichtberg," the elder grand master replied. "Princess Serina of Levens brought word today regarding the fruits of our labors!"

"Really? Good news, I hope." The Golden Wizard's reflection leaned in closer, a twinkle in his eye as he arched a pencil-thin eyebrow. "Our forces in Urocia grow weary, and our direct intervention may be needed soon!"

"Oh, yes, very encouraging!" intoned the elder, twittering anew with excitement. "Retired Grand Master Nicholas sent the Princess Serina personally to inform us. He appears to be supportive of our new initiatives after all. He happened upon the newcomers on his way to Tyrna, after assuming that post from Master Aros, taking it upon himself to anchor his former pupil in Levens!"

"This is far better than even I'd hoped for," Grand Master Encara intoned as he stroked his chin thoughtfully, contemplating the news. "I hadn't anticipated the old coot would come out of hiding on our side, much less at all. What a stroke of luck that he found the newcomers on his way there; that's two events in our favor!"

"With this change, we may not only be unhindered; we may yet have further assistance if needed," Grand Master Yamaro breathed excitedly. "The princess has assured me that Nicholas is not only aware of our situation, but he may also already be on board and of like mind!"

"Brilliant! Further evidence that the retired Grand Master Nicholas may have finally come to his senses!" the Golden Wizard replied with a smile. "Sad business with Master Aros, but it cannot be helped; he was an unfortunate disappointment, promoted into a situation hardly deemed as appropriate. I always said he was in over his head. Poor Aros; if only I had been there to assist him—alas, my plate is quite full here in Latana!"

"Nicholas will advocate directly for the newcomers there until we send a replacement. In the meantime, they are guests of King Faund," finished Grand Master Yamaro. "Our retired grand master only realized who they were after their arrival in King Faund's court."

"While not ideal, this may still provide an advantage for the order," Grand Master Encara muttered as he contemplated the matter further. "Given the circumstances, I see no need to rush a replacement. Nicholas's change of heart and emergence from retirement may work to our advantage. He has been stationed in Tyrna before and can certainly handle the post for now."

"My thoughts exactly," the silvery Yamaro acknowledged. "How would you like to proceed at this point?"

"I shall return to Mondlichtberg personally within the week," Grand Master Encara offered. "We shall hand-pick Tyrna's replacement together. In the meantime, see to it that the newcomers stay in Tyrna—for their own safety, of course. Once we have a replacement for Tyrna's seat selected, we will send for them in due time. Nicholas can then return to his quiet retirement, and all will be well again."

"Yes," Grand Master Yamaro agreed. "How fare your recruiting efforts in Urocia? Have you obtained any additional interest from the so-called 'Order of Etoilenoir'?"

"I have indeed!" Encara the Golden grinned. "Several leaders from the new order here in Urocia have expressed great interest in taking their newfound powers beyond simple parlor tricks and embracing the visions laid out by our order's traditions."

"Wonderful," the elder Silver Wizard sighed. "However, when can we expect this shift of devotion fully to our side on the level of a tangible commitment?"

"Soon! Very soon!" Grand Master Encara assured him. "I will personally escort the interested leaders as well as their students to your very doorstep to deliver my promise to you! Our enrollment will triple, and then, we three grand masters may turn our attention to opening yet another Shimmering, bringing forth more newcomers to also join our ranks!"

"Your plan. Yes, of course." Grand Master Yamaro nodded, careful to do so without any sarcasm in his tone. His colleague's golden flair was wearing thin with him. He fidgeted slightly with the tip of his robe, anxious to complete the topics at hand. "We handed over an enormous responsibility to you when we sent the Master Advisory Council with you to Latana. You say they are assisting you in Urocia's capital, but when are you returning them to Mondlichtberg here, where they belong?"

"That is still our plan; I just need them for a few more weeks. Their Urocian service here is invaluable!" Grand Master Encara exclaimed, clasping his hands together appreciatively. "We are making great strides in their progress with the other order's leaders. They truly are an exemplary model for the Order of Etoilenoir to follow and they have performed even beyond my expectations! They do miss Sorceress Amina's presence, but her disruptive outbursts would have set us back. Between her station at Mondlichtberg and Aros's new placement at Levens, I suppose those are the best substitutes I can offer for the near term in the advisory's absence."

"Well, it's good to see that at least our plan's validity still holds," Grand Master Yamaro sighed with a grimace. "Continue your work there and let me know when you are coming; I request you reconsider the advisory's assignment and bring them with you upon your return!"

The two men smiled and bowed their heads in acknowledgment

before the mirror's reflection faded again to the elder grand master's tired likeness. He paused briefly before heading down the stairs himself for some dinner, grasping the bridge of his nose in his fingers. *Such decisions these days...the headaches and the decisions...Encara's brashness grates my nerves, but his boldness currently seems necessary to endure. Perhaps he will need to be reined in with due time.*

≈≈≈≈

Princess Serina had business to attend to before cleaning up for dinner and settling into her new accommodations. She made her way through the great hall and into the entrance courtyard.

She happened across the modest stable where Barley grazed silently on hay, nearly oversized for the quaint and leaning structure. She had seen the avian scroll master at dinner along with the quartermaster, consumed in a conversation around late shipments of trade. This allowed her the brief opportunity to communicate with Nicholas unhindered.

Scrawling a quick note, she rolled it and found the carrier pigeons also housed in the stable. The soft coos relaxed her, and she began searching among the many cages labeled with the names of the kingdoms on the outside.

The one marked "Tyrna" was large and right up front. Opening the cage, she grabbed one of the pigeons, slid the rolled message into the carrier on its foot and sealed it. Leaving the barn, bird in hand, she tossed the pigeon into the night air and watched as it fluttered away.

≈≈≈≈

Back in Levens, Aros laid low for two days until Princess Serina's departure. He spent his time reviewing Nicholas's notes and getting settled in Levens's Wizard's Tower. The day Princess Serina left for Mondlichtberg was the day he decided to act.

Aros smiled to himself in anticipation as he headed to the barn he knew would house the Jeep, just across from the main gate's entrance. Levens was the perfect place for Nicholas to hide him for the very same reason Nicholas had originally taken his retirement in the tiny kingdom.

With Princess Serina out on assignment and Nicholas himself out, Aros would be viewed as simply occupying Nicholas's office while he was away. No one would question what he was up to. No one would miss his coming absence for days, possibly weeks.

As a precaution, he would keep a rucksack always prepared for a sudden departure. At ready, he'd keep his stash in a small closet at the base of the stone stairs of the Wizard's Tower.

The only question remaining to him was when he would be summoned to Tyrna. Not knowing seemed a bother, but in the meantime, he would utilize his time to familiarize himself with the newcomers' beastless carriage.

This morning, Aros walked briefly with the same royal squire that had serviced Nicholas in the tower. On the way to Levens's front gate, the wizard handed him the iron key ring to Nicholas's office as they sauntered along the cobblestone walkway.

"I would like you to light a candle in the balcony window of the Wizard's Tower each night," Aros explained. "I may or may not be present in the office when you are there, but regardless, please be sure to lock up when leaving."

The young lad nodded—he would no doubt inform the queen, who would confer with Aros's orders and approve them without a second thought.

Aros soon arrived at the barn where the newcomers' beastless carriage was held, and he threw open the double doors. The cowshed was empty other than a few horses idly swishing their tails as several errant pigeons fluttered past. The Jeep stood alone in the center of the barn as he approached its muddy, shattered and scraped form. The smell of hay permeated the air as he sauntered over to the vehicle to examine it more closely.

He ran his hands down the side to the driver's side door and stopped. He closed his eyes and used his focus to make out the locking mechanism in his mind's eye. Using his mind and his innate power, Aros patiently explored the vehicle inside and out. He probed its inner workings, patiently and methodically ran through each mechanism and system, learning not only of its construction but also the subtleties of its composition.

Just as his Grand Master Nicholas had taught him all those years ago, he emptied his mind of everything until all he could see was a dark, blank canvas. His power reached out and coursed through the workings of the unfamiliar object. In the darkness of his mind, he could see colorful lines appearing, spreading out like spider webs, forming grids and circuits. They formed an image that made no sense to him, but like pieces of a puzzle, they came together.

He could see the metal's intricate workings, the circuitry and how it connected to the lock. With a click, the door unlocked, and he opened the door for closer inspection. Over the next few hours, he took his time, methodically examining the vehicle. He popped open the hood, coming around to the front to scrutinize the engine. *This is going to take some time.*

Time ticked on beyond perception; throughout the day and into the evening, he explored different sections of the Jeep, slowly repairing systems he knew nothing about but could see how they were intended to come together. Where something was bent or disconnected, he willed it to return to its original shape and status, and it did.

It was nearing nightfall when the galloping of hooves outside and footsteps revealed two men approaching reached his ears. The footsteps stopped, and Aros could sense the men watching from the doorway.

"Well, out with it, lads!" the wizard called, his eyes aglow in concentration. He didn't even bother to turn even as the men arriving entered the barn behind him. "Announce yourselves!"

"My name is Dex," a wiry, sandy voice grated. "This here is Crand; Grand Master Nicholas sent us to accompany you for a summons to Tyrna!"

"Indeed, did he now?" Aros smiled, still focused on probing the Jeep's inner workings. His eyes, still white and aglow, remained unseeing in concentration. "Let's start with this, shall we? Help me find a very large and sturdy wagon that can house this contraption and an oxen team that can pull it!"

"We have one; the retired grand master has not lost his touch for anticipating needs," Dex replied impatiently. "Let's be quick about it, though. We were warned others may take an interest in what you were doing in here."

"Can't be too careful," Aros acknowledged as the glow from his eyes faded. The wizard wiped his hands and introduced himself, grinning as he shook the hands of the two who had entered. "I agree, let's make haste."

Chapter 18

A Good Steward

As Sottis ascended the stairway behind Nicholas in the Wizard's Tower, he continued to fidget nervously with his grey cloak as if trying to find a hidden strength somewhere within the folds where the dark gossamer threads seemed to shiver in anticipation. The entire morning had been spent silently alongside the grand master, attending to his finance meetings with King Faund and other matters of state in the throne room. The awkward silence between them only became more tense when the elder wizard finally indicated the time had arrived for a private conference up in the tower of his abode.

The two climbed the cold tower stairs in silence, with only the sound of their breathing and shuffling feet resounding in the steep, narrow corridor. When they reached the top, the grand master ushered him into the room, closing the door behind them. He took a deep breath before turning to confront the valet.

"I'm not actually sure where to begin," Grand Master Nicholas finally laughed, more to himself than to anyone. "This has been weighing on me since Levens, though, and I feel it's high time you and I had a conversation."

"I'm not sure what you mean by that or why I'm here," Sottis replied and squinted back nervously, a bit flustered at the grand master's authoritative tone.

"Well, let's start there, shall we?" The elder wizard pointed, suddenly focused. "Why exactly *are* you here?"

"You brought me here," Sottis started. "I was going to accompany Sir Caspin and the others—"

"I'm not referring to the tower," the grand master snapped. "I'm talking about why you are here in Tyrna! Why you spied on Master Aros and who you report to since it clearly was not Master Aros!"

"I'm no spy!" Sottis spat, his face reddening. "I'm a guest of the Order of the Moon at the behest of the Grand Master Council. I'll have you know I'm also a senior member of the Order of Etoilenoir and..."

"Yessssss, a 'guest,'" Grand Master Nicholas repeated sarcastically. "As a 'guest,' who informed you about the newcomers we transported from Levens yesterday?"

"Kevin did! He told me all about it when we were at The Wanderer Inn in Millstead," Sottis advised. "I told him to be careful about who he told these things to—"

"That's a lie," the wizard interrupted. "I've searched Kevin's thoughts on this matter, and *you* came to *him* with that information, not the other way around."

"I don't appreciate your innuendo," Sottis hissed as his face darkened. "Aros told me before we left Levens—there, now you have it! Are we done here?"

"No, he did not either; I know that for a fact," Grand Master Nicholas stated softly. The gentle mirth entirely faded from the wizard's face as he leaned in, locking eyes with the valet. "I'm surprised your superiors didn't warn you about my ability to see the thoughts of others. I don't suppose they accounted for your encounter with me, though."

"*Former* Grand Master, what you or I say here is of no consequence," Sottis stated, his own tone shifting defiantly as he pointedly stated the wizard's title. The valet's cloak seemed to shimmer briefly with a rosy hue as he barely concealed his rage. "The *current* Grand Master Council is looking for these people, and you seem to have decided to advocate for them without the council's approval! You say you are in contact with them, yet your actions seem to defy my understanding of what the council's latest directives on this matter are! What right have you to declare yourself Advocate for them?"

"Who gave you this information?!" The wizard suddenly stood tall, looming over the valet and shouting. "Why are you involved with this at all?! What is your interest in the newcomers?! Who told you to spy on my protégé?!"

"Spy? Just listen to yourself, you paranoid old man! You are an outdated relic and barely functional!" Sottis breathed in frustration as his voice escalated to match the wizard's intensity. "Your protégé Aros is a disgrace! You're a disgrace! Your own Grand Master Council welcomed me in and stationed me here to keep Aros in line! When they hear of your interference with the newcomers they brought here..."

"The *council* brought them?" Grand Master Nicholas balked, his eyes widening as he silenced the valet with a wave of his hand. "Thank you, Sottis; now, I know who brought them. There's no way I'm going to give them back to the council until I know *how* and *why* they did this!"

"That's not your call, *former* Grand Master!" Sottis raged. "YOU have no right to declare yourself Advocate!"

"It is my call, and as the officially stationed wizard in Tyrna, I have ranking authority for them, and for that matter, you," Grand Master Nicholas stated, pausing to let the last word hang in the air. "Sottis Bisset of the Order of Etoilenoir, your services here in Tyrna are no longer required. Whether current grand master or former grand master, Tyrna now has a grand master in its service. A second posting alongside is not only no longer required but also no longer appropriate; your services here are now fulfilled and completed. You may return to Urocia or wherever it is you came from, effective immediately!"

"You're terminating my position here!?" Sottis seethed. "What am I to do? I can't just go home!"

"If returning to Urocia doesn't suit you, return to Mondlichtberg first if you must. You may lodge your complaint with them as you see fit," Nicholas stated, laying the case out flatly. "However, if you choose that path, then you can explain to Grand Master Yamaro that I will speak only to him about these newcomers and..."

Nicholas stopped talking when a wicked smile spread across Sottis's face.

"Grand Master Yamaro?!" Sottis sneered. "That old fool knows about as much as you do! He's as incapable and clueless as..." He stopped himself, flustered and shaking with rage.

"Go on," Nicholas coaxed with a cool sarcasm. "Since it's now clear to me that you do not report to Grand Master Yamaro, who exactly do you report to? I'm beginning to suspect I know exactly where this is coming from..."

"I report to the council in its entirety!" Sottis screamed in a twisted and sudden rage. With a resounding swish and a flick of the wrist, he flung his grey cloak aside, producing a wicked-looking emerald-green dagger. With blinding speed, he lunged at the elder, eyes wide with vengeance, slicing through the air at the wizard's throat.

The grand master ducked in reflex as the assassin's dagger clipped his shoulder, tearing at his robes and biting down into his skin, drawing first blood.

"*D'eAK,LeA!!*" the wizard boomed, casting a spell of restraint at his attacker as he fell back, clutching at his wound. Sparks of blinding white light enveloped Sottis, and he dropped the dagger with a shrill scream. Coils of searing white light bound his hands, legs and mouth, drawing taut as they dimmed, mild burn marks swelling on his skin.

The valet struggled briefly before falling to the floor, gasping for breath and choking on a long, dry laugh. The cloak shimmered briefly before the dark threads seemed to sink into the folds and vanish, leaving only the grey opaque cloth reflecting the light from the bonds in a garish glint.

Grand Master Nicholas stood, fuming over his attacker. He examined the cut on his shoulder and quickly determined it as inconsequential before turning his attention back to the valet. The quivering driver lay upon the surface of the stone floor in the plain grey cloak, looking suddenly small and helpless, nowhere near the menace he had just been.

"I don't need to probe you to know you are foul!" Nicholas fumed as he picked up the discarded weapon, trembling with a newfound rage of his own. "I will get to the bottom of this, and you will not see the light of day until I have a full account of your treachery! I swear it!"

Sottis seemed to relax, soft laughter fluttering from his thin lips as the dagger disintegrated into dust within Nicholas's grasp. The former grand master shook his hands free of the crumbling weapon in disgust. He lunged forward, gripping the would-be assassin's head in his hands.

"I swore I would never do this," the elder wizard muttered in vexed fury as he conjured forth the white light from his hands, his eyes rolling back into his head in concentration. "You leave me no choice!"

Projecting himself into Sottis's mind, he searched forcibly, penetrating the apprentice's thoughts. The valet squirmed in his grasp, gasping for air as Nicholas probed. He searched and searched...yet found nothing. *Sottis's image appeared doubled and blurred, floating in a pool of black nothingness.*

"And you thought I didn't know about your innate power!" Sottis gurgled with glee as the white-robed wizard released the valet's head in frustration. "Probe all you want, old fool! You'll find *nothing!*"

"No matter, GUARDS!" the grand master shouted, throwing the valet to the cold stone floor. Footsteps echoed in the stairwell, and soon, the door swung open. Nicholas turned to greet the pair of guards that entered.

"Not a word to anyone!" the wizard told them, breathless as he struggled to regain his composure. "Take this man and lock him in the dungeon until I figure out what to do with him! Make sure he's fed and watered, but not a word to anyone!"

"I know all about the newcomers! You can't keep them!" Sottis howled in triumph as the guards seized him by the arms to drag him away. "We're coming for them! We all are coming, and soon, you and your precious followers will be answering to us!"

≈≈≈≈

The rest of the afternoon, Grand Master Nicholas sat in King Faund's office with several meek advisors, still fuming and sore from Sottis's earlier attack. He had a brief change of clothes into yet another plain white robe. The bleeding had stopped, yet anxiety over the implications of the confrontation ran far deeper than any physical injury. *Had the Wizard's Council truly approved of Sottis? If so, the decision to keep the newcomers in Tyrna was the right one.*

The apprentice clearly had friends here in Tyrna, so keeping him prisoner indefinitely was not an option. Nicholas would have to figure something else out since interrogating him had revealed the valet had been able to employ a surprisingly effective block against any forced extraction of information.

In the meantime, he had to tend to the other matters at hand and couldn't afford to be distracted by the morning's failures. The matter of Tyrna's monarchy proved to be yet another challenge, and it quickly became apparent why Master Aros had difficulty with the post.

The meeting with King Faund continued all afternoon in an erratic fashion as Nicholas struggled to rein the young monarch's temper in. The cramped quarters of the closed-door meeting room made matters worse as occupants were forced to breathe the stale air without respite as the day wore on. Unlike the fresh air in the cavernous throne room, the tiny meeting space near the king's quarters had once only likely been a bedroom in the royal palace, with only a single tiny window for air through the thick stone wall. Dimly lit through a series of low-hanging iron chandeliers, the candles provided more heat and smoke to the room than light.

The advisory board and the king seemed at odds with how best to explain the situation to a grand master who clearly did not like what he was hearing. The Pratenvike mason, the royal master of coin, the market master—all appeared individually like competent advisors with vital information. They all donned a uniform and the official-looking shimmering grey cloak he had seen in his vision when he had probed King Faund, looking elegant and full of expertise. Each cloak swam with its own set of gossamer midnight-black threads, weaving patterns of leaves and vines in an unsettling, hypnotic effect.

When the advisors spoke, however, what they conveyed seemed to defy common sense. As they took turns parading their ideas to the king, their speech flowed like silk, matching the tenor of the intricate cloaks they wore. The grand master struggled to hold his composure as he watched the advisors reveal the status of the kingdom to the monarch with little or no reaction from the ruler.

At one point, the grand master shifted from the cloaked advisors to re-read the tally to King Faund aloud. The records scribed clearly confirmed Tyrna had actually sent nearly half the active guard squadrons to Urocia after all, not a third! No matter how official his advisors carried themselves, the facts remained: King Faund had also committed over half of the entire royal treasury to building projects such as New Tyrna and the Pratenvike.

With little to say, all the grand master could do was shake his head in disbelief. As the day wore on, the meeting became more disorderly. While the fanciful ideas coming from the king's advisory worried Nicholas, King Faund's counterproposals seemed downright baffling.

"Your Majesty, pardon my insertion here, but this is rather important," a thin, raspy voice spoke from between two larger men who had been seated next to each other across the table. A short, stout advisor pressed between them, licking his thin lips behind a forced smile before he spoke again. "May I draw your attention back to the relocation of additional residents to the Christian Quarter; can they afford to relinquish some space to make room for Pratenvike expansion since New Tyrna isn't quite completed?"

"Oh, bother! It's large enough already, wouldn't you say?" the king retorted. "We should focus on expanding our efforts to finish New

Tyrna instead! Besides, if we're to relocate anyone further, we need to have a place to put them!"

"Eh, that wasn't my point, Your Highness," the plump advisor sighed, shrugging helplessly as he glanced back to the others in the room, who seemed equally perplexed on how to get their points across. His grey cloak shimmered briefly in a soft red hue in the chamber's light as the dark gossamer threads swam upon the opaque grey surface. "A royal decree is needed in either case since we've already surpassed the original budget..."

"More talk of budgets? I have assurances from the royal treasury that we have more than enough to cover current relocation efforts, don't we?" the monarch queried aloud as he drifted off in thought. Just then, he caught sight of yet another advisor who had been pacing nervously in the background. "Percy, that is your name, isn't it?"

"Yes, Your Majesty," the shorter man's voice squeaked. His face openly winced, and his eyes widened at being named. He hugged his cloud-grey cloak about him as he quivered. "I'm not here about the budget, though, sire. I'm here to speak to you about Lady Adriana and Lady Charlotta's delegation."

"Tell the Urocian delegation that I have not forgotten their marriage proposals and that I will address them in due time." King Faund seemed to take brief pleasure at catching Percy off guard, but his smile faded quickly. "What is it, six potential brides now?"

"Eh, eight, Your Majesty," the narrow man sighed. "Customarily, you would approach them, but you already invited them here months ago."

"I invited their fathers to discuss matters of trade, but I can never keep count of it all," the king sighed before snapping his fingers in the air. "Oh, yes, who was I talking to about the stonemasons? Let's get back to the important matters at hand."

"Stonemasons?" several unseen voices murmured in protest across the room.

"It was I, sire!" a voice called from the hidden recesses at the back of the room. By this time, several other advisors had crowded out the portly man who had spoken about the finances. He jumped up, waving his hand behind the throng, trying to regain the monarch's attention.

With Nicholas's practiced smile becoming more strained by the hour, he resorted to stroking his snowy beard and muttering aloud. The grand master still played the part of the observer, keeping his comments positive and at a minimum. The guise became increasingly difficult by the minute as the chaotic advisors scurried around the king like rats in a cage, lurching awkwardly from topic to topic while accomplishing nothing.

To make matters worse, interruptions from the builders, masons and planners came with unpredictable intermittence. The monarch seemed hugely burdened about how to prioritize the issues at hand and refused recommendations from anyone present. Instead, he seemed to glean pleasure at simply having the attention centered on him.

With all the competing agendas, the struggle for resulting progress was minimal at best. The grand master couldn't discern nefarious intentions from simply progress-oriented ones because, through the chaos, no one was getting anything they wanted.

At one point, Nicholas politely stepped forward and suggested a brief respite but was swiftly rebuked by the Pratenvike mason while the king took little notice. The wizard quietly retreated to continue watching as the royal charade resumed.

As evening neared, Sir Caspin poked his head through the doorway. Before an exhausted Nicholas could say a word, King Faund greeted his captain of the guard with a relief that the grand master had not seen from the monarch all day. He noted the release seemed to flood the advisors as well as murmurs of gratitude at the captain of the guard's appearance.

"How are our guests enjoying the city?" the king asked inquisitively, again welcoming yet another interruption.

"They absolutely loved it, Your Majesty!" Sir Caspin smiled glowingly. "They have taken their leave to revive themselves before dinner, but I thought I would catch up with you on financial matters for the kingdom. I hope I am not interrupting; is now still a good time?"

"Not a moment too soon; please, sit!" The king gestured to a chair near the side of the dusky table. "Oh, and I've invited Grand Master Nicholas to join us today!"

"Indeed!" Sir Caspin seemed surprised. "Will Sottis be joining us as well?"

"I've dispatched Sottis back to Mondlichtberg on an urgent matter," Nicholas lied with a dismissive gesture. Turning back to the matter at hand, he arched an eyebrow in curiosity. "In the meantime, I'm anxious to learn about this project you...are also...apparently involved with."

The comment seemed to silence the room as the advisors present suddenly had nothing to say.

"Grand Master Nicholas has had quite a morning learning of our ventures, haven't you, Grand Master?" King Faund interjected, anticipating further approval.

The wizard turned to Sir Caspin, whose eyes had widened at the king's pronouncement. Nicholas also noted that all the other advisors in the room sat back to drink and gather their notes, making notable efforts to avoid eye contact with him.

"Most definitely, Your Majesty," Nicholas stated dryly. "I'm quite fond of all of them, but I'm especially interested in how exactly we are paying for all this. I noticed how little attention the finance minister received in these proceedings. Perhaps this is something the captain of the guard may shed some insight on? Forgive me, this is most unusual!"

"I hadn't realized your duties were to extend beyond our new guests, Grand Master." Sir Caspin stalled for a moment before reluctantly entering the room.

"Indeed, I had the very same impression of your duties," Nicholas remarked pointedly. "I'm very interested in what you have to say here, particularly since your talents seem to extend further than captain of the guard and into arenas where the advisors present are, shall we say, challenged."

"I'm not sure I know what that means," Sir Caspin replied in confusion, turning doubtfully to the king. "Should I be worried?"

"Not at all!" the grand master assured the captain, spitting the words out as best he could without sounding sarcastic. "I'm only concerned with the king's success in all these matters and how best I may be able to support them. My protégé was not able to brief me on the magnificence of these undertakings and I'm having some challenges getting caught up on it all!"

"Oh! Well, if that's the case, I have some notes for you both to review," Sir Caspin stated amicably, nodding warily to Nicholas as he strode to the king. "I just happen to share a passion with King Faund in this matter. I'm more of an ideas man with a few talents for this sort of thing!"

Nicholas's eyes widened. *A captain of the guard advising the king on financial matters? This seems highly irregular. Sir Caspin is clearly trusted with matters of the king's security, but finances are a different matter entirely...*

"Well then, here we are!" Sir Caspin stated as he produced a rolled parchment and stepped up to the table, spreading it out before them both and began reading, "The treasury stands at twenty percent of last year's balance, Your Highness. However, with the new taxes we've raised on the population, we should be able to bolster that up to near thirty percent by next harvest."

"Wait a moment!" Nicholas exclaimed, feeling his throat constrict in surprise as he coughed aloud. "Thirty percent?!"

"Why, yes, sir," Sir Caspin replied. "The Pratenvike expansion demanded thirty-eight percent of our gold and silver stores. New Tyrna is running about twenty-four percent of that as well. We've donated another fifteen percent towards the war effort in the east to Latana and another three percent for the first annual grand ball and tournament to be held once Pratenvike's completion is achieved."

"You're telling me there's *more* expansion still required at the Pratenvike?" Nicholas balked. "This goes even beyond what the stonemason advisor stated earlier today?"

"Quite a bit more; is something the matter?" Sir Caspin's eyes narrowed, glancing nervously to the king and back to Nicholas. "I double-checked the numbers myself with the master of coin!"

"What of our armory, our armies?" Nicholas exclaimed. "What of repairs to the walls—inner or outer? What of our commerce on Long Lake? What of the king's usual expenses with travel, court and staff?"

"Grand Master! We already discussed the walls; they are of no consequence!" King Faund exclaimed, suddenly enraged by Nicholas's inquiry for accountability. "I thought you were on board here! Greatness requires sacrifice for the good of the people! The new taxes cover it all; tell him, Sir Caspin!"

"Oh, um, yes." Sir Caspin blushed slightly, stalling as he produced supporting documents and began shuffling through the pages. "Most wages are now being paid by the moon cycle rather than daily, so we are able to balance the deficit with the new taxes levied on merchants and estates residing within the walls of Tyrna, considering the nature of these estates now to be a luxury."

"Deficit?!" Nicholas gasped, turning to King Faund, whose face was turning equally bright red. "Your predecessors kept the city strong, both on the walls and in its vaults! When did Tyrna ever incur a peacetime debt?"

"I can see the day is getting to you," the young monarch seethed in embarrassment and anger at the grand master for the unexpected opposition. "Perhaps you should retire, and we can talk about this in the morning, when you are more...refreshed."

"I must protest, Your Majesty! Where is your master of coin on this?" Grand Master Nicholas grasped, searching around the room for a friendly face, yet finding none, his voice drifted off. A bitter laugh escaped his lips before he asked the next question. "Why is the captain of the guard suddenly heading this effort?"

The room had fallen silent, and King Faund, Sir Caspin, the advisory board and the guards lining the wall in the office stood glowering at Nicholas. Anxiety and apprehension about what would happen next seeped in around him as tension built palpably around the table.

"Yes, Grand Master, you were saying?" King Faund growled. "Perhaps your vision is closer to the one Master Aros had advised after all? He too did not appreciate that we all have a part to play in this endeavor!"

"Uh, not at all, Your Majesty," the wizard stammered. "I'm just surprised is all!" *How am I going gracefully exit the scene I just created?*

"Would you recommend raising taxes higher?" Sir Caspin offered, his eyes narrowing, clearly displeased.

"Uh, no—not at this point. You appear to have it under control," Nicholas muttered. "I had been under the impression that our contributions to the war efforts in the east came strictly from our manpower, not the treasury or our winter stores."

"Well, yes! Initially, that was the case, but more was required by our allies in the east!" Sir Caspin retorted, still flustered. "We believed with the council that Tyrna could rise to the occasion and meet these demands as they surfaced. This is hardly a peacetime debt; we *are* at war, even if the war is not here. Urocia fights on our behalf..."

"I'm confused as to why the captain of the guard is advising the king on this matter and not—" Nicholas whispered to keep the conversation between the three of them.

"Yes, Grand Master, you are correct: you are confused!" the king snapped, shooting Nicholas a withering glance before drawing Sir Caspin's attention back to the matters at hand. "Grand Master Nicholas may need a recess!"

From that point on, Nicholas watched in silence as Sir Caspin took over the meeting, reviewing the balance sheet before them. The wizard could do little more than sit back and let it happen.

While the grand master listened, he reflected on what had transpired and what he continued to hear as the meeting dragged on. While Nicholas listened, he thought about what he was hearing. *To be envied and accepted by other kingdoms is one thing, but to spend yourself into oblivion in order to achieve stature seems ludicrous! People in this kingdom work hard but keep the fruits of their labors! This is so uncharacteristic of this kingdom!*

Sir Caspin and King Faund seemed to take great glee in the social engineering it took to turn farmers into Pratenvike vendors, metal-smiths into sculpture artists, guards into gardeners. It all seemed ludicrous to Nicholas but appeared to make perfect sense to everyone else in the room as the rest of the advisors took turns backing the captain of the guard to simply agree with whatever idea involved them.

King Faund never looked back at Nicholas until he and Sir Caspin had finished reviewing the scroll. The previous hours of futility seemed to be single-handedly resolved by the captain of the guard and yet the balance sheets clearly depicted a kingdom nearing financial collapse; yet the monarch never looked more pleased.

"I believe we have solved all of our problems, for now; thank you, Sir Caspin!" King Faund sighed. He turned to the grand master and quietly offered, "Are you hungry, my friend?"

"Yes, Your Majesty, famished," Nicholas managed without stammering.

"Good, let's meet with our guests and feast, shall we?" King Faund insisted. As the advisors and everyone else filtered out of the room, the king caught Grand Master Nicholas's arm and whispered, "A moment, Grand Master, if you don't mind."

Nicholas leaned on his staff, patiently waiting for the room to empty. Once they were alone, the king continued, his demeanor souring and his voice descending into a low cold tone.

"Don't you ever question me about my finances again; are we clear on this?" the young monarch seethed. "Particularly not in front of my most trusted men! That was most unacceptable and will not be tolerated again!"

"Yes, Your Majesty—I beg a thousand pardons," Nicholas sighed.

"I am taking my kingdom in a new direction, with or without our silly walls!" the king continued, unconvinced and determined to make his point. "I will be loved by all, and Tyrna will know greatness that it's never known! We *will* be the shining new example for all to follow, do you hear me?"

"Yes, sire," Nicholas rasped. "Completely understand!"

"I swear to you, so help me!" King Faund exhaled. The monarch paused and turned to fix the wizard in an icy glare. He let his next statement hang after he spoke it for effect. "I will establish greatness for my kingdom unknown even by my predecessors...or yours!"

"Of course, Your Highness; it won't happen again," the elder wizard recited, eyes downcast. "Perhaps we should see to our dinner now, and perhaps invite our new guests as well?"

"Yes, about these newcomers," King Faund growled, not ready to let the admonishment lay. "Are you sure they aren't a distraction for you? Perhaps their advocacy would be better suited for your Wizard's Council?"

"It's under consideration," Nicholas muttered as a chill ran through him. "In the meantime, allow me to assure you that their well-being will not interfere with my duties to the crown!"

"Very good! I too only want what's best for them, be it with the Wizard's Council or settled here; safe and settled, but not in our way," the king exclaimed before clapping a single retort that reverberated through the chamber. He summarily dismissed the grand master with a wave of his hand and a promise to join them all shortly. "Then we are done here, as long as I have made myself clear in these matters!"

"Crystal!" Nicholas exclaimed before the monarch motioned for him to leave, signifying the end of the conversation. The wizard shuffled out of the room in defeat. "All is as you would wish it, sire!"

"Very good!" King Faund quipped as he watched the wizard leave, breathing a sigh of relief once the door closed.

Finally alone, he turned in silence to the window looking out the north side of the palace. Expecting to see the ridgeline of the mountain, the king instead caught a glimpse of his own reflection.

Locking eyes with himself, he searched his reflection for reassurance and support.

Am I doing the right thing? This all seemed so clear before, but the grand master seems more disturbed than his predecessor regarding the Pratenvike-centered vision for the future. Only Sir Caspin seems to still grasp the purpose. Is that so wrong?

After what seemed like an eternity, King Faund dismissively shook his head to regain his focus and clarity. This pandering to his thoughts and self-reflection would have to wait. His dinner guests would be waiting for him.

≈≈≈≈

The festivities of the evening seemed to drive the terse meeting from earlier into a distant memory. A roasted boar with an apple in its mouth took up most of the table at the center of the dining hall. Lords and ladies with great goblets of wine sat around the table alongside elaborate grey-cloaked guests from Urocia. Others from more distant lands came, including dignitaries from the dwarf mines, cat lords of Carthen, the Southern Kingdoms and Levens.

They all came to toast the king and his accomplishments and occasionally jibe at him about taking on a wife. Between the clinking of silverware, the bustling servants and the conversations, the newcomers could scarcely hear the harpist playing in the corner of the room.

The wine flowed, and smells of fine dining and sounds of levity filled the throne room as all enjoyed the evening's festivities.

For Daniel, this was the most sumptuous meal he'd seen since Levens. He stuffed his mouth, not paying particularly close attention to any of the guests or toasts. Sammy poked her head up at him from between his legs.

"Please, Danny?" the hound whined. "A tasty?"

Looking about to see if anyone noticed, he slid a bone caked with meat under the table. She wagged her tail appreciatively before darting off with some of the other dogs, making Daniel laugh.

When he looked back up, he could see Sir Caspin watching him from across the table. The captain of the guard gave him a single wink in acknowledgment, and Daniel chuckled in a guilty snicker. He watched the captain of the guard dab his mouth with a cloth and whisper something to a lord from Urocia sitting next to him.

When Sir Caspin looked back to Daniel, he motioned discreetly to him with a nod of his head. Puzzled, Daniel watched the captain quietly stand and walk back towards the kitchen entrance, where servers shuffled in and out.

Daniel hesitated—his mom seemed preoccupied with Nate, and Javier and Kevin were helping themselves to a second serving of food. Sliding quietly from his chair, he walked around the end of the table. Creeping through the shadows where hopefully no one would see him, he sauntered over to the service doorway.

"Sir—Sir Caspin," he whispered loudly, opening the door and peeking inside.

"Over here, Danny Boy! Why are you whispering?" Sir Caspin laughed, motioning for him to enter. Cooks and service maids scurried about, and the captain of the guard seemed to be standing in the middle of it all. He motioned for Daniel to sit with him at a small table in the corner of the kitchen. "I've got something for you, but just a little secret between us, okay? Don't tell your mom or anyone else!"

"Well, you waved me over here," Daniel whispered, blushing but still sauntering in smiling. "I thought you didn't want my mom to get mad because of our drinking the other night!"

"I noticed your mom is protective of you, but man to man, I wanted to talk to you about that. I think she may be holding you back from becoming the man I know you can be," Sir Caspin proclaimed as he stepped aside, and behind him on the table were two enormous goblets of ale. He smiled when he saw Daniel's face light up in recognition. "We all love our mothers, but sometimes we need to draw the line with them and become men, especially at your age!"

"Yeah, she can be a bit overbearing," Daniel agreed. "I think she's just not ready for me to take that next step."

"This ale is about that next step, my friend, but I usually only drink it with my men," the captain pressed. "I would be honored to share it with you. Will you drink it with me, man to man?"

Daniel's grin said it all, and Sir Caspin pulled up two stools where they toasted to their shared pints. The captain of the guard continued to pepper Daniel with questions about where he and his mom had come from, to which the lad could only nod and smile through foamy mouthfuls.

When Sir Caspin asked him about his father though, Daniel became more serious, acknowledging that Nate had been his father's best friend. He told him that when his father died, Nate had stayed as a major part of his family. It was a bit embarrassing talking about his mom to this man who had clearly taken an interest in her.

"I understand, young man. It's a little uncomfortable talking about your mother in this way," Sir Caspin stated as he moved to shift the conversation. "So, Daniel, tell me—have you begun noticing anything different about you, your mother, or your friends? Say, anything special that you can do?"

Daniel stopped for a moment. Sir Caspin's question brought him out of the buzzing stupor he had just begun to feel. *That's a weird question!*

"Oh...that," he burped. He also remembered that Princess Serina had instructed him not to talk about it with anyone but Nicholas. "I'm not really supposed to talk about it."

"Awwww, not even with the king's most trusted advisor?" Sir Caspin coaxed with a smile. "I already know that your mom can heal people, and Nate has lightning inside of him—I don't know what all the fuss is; lots of people can do magic here. In my hometown of Latana, many more people can do magic. Urocia does not exert such restrictions on its people!"

"I thought we weren't supposed to talk about that stuff," Daniel stalled, taking another long draught from his mug, cringing as the long swallow of his drink coated his throat. *Disgusting! I hope I don't throw up!* "Damn, this is good!"

"I'm an advisor to the king and your tour guide," admitted Sir Caspin, struggling not to laugh. "Don't worry—whatever Grand Master Nicholas and the king know, I already know, too. What you share with me will help us keep you and your friends safe here!"

"Really?" This bit of news seemed lost on Daniel, so he drank on, downing the rest of the ale that was beginning to make the room spin. "No one told me about that!"

"Basically, I get to know everything, and that helps me to help you." Sir Caspin smiled, handing Daniel a pinch of mint from a jar with a wink, briefly reducing his voice to a discreet whisper. "This will help cover the scent, so your mom doesn't find out!"

"Okay, I'll tell you just a little," Daniel sighed, taking a deep breath and leaning forward with a grin. "Nate can make lightning, and I can fly. Kevin can glow before he zips off somewhere far away, and Javier can use his voice to punch through things."

The moment he shared it, a wash of guilt and doubt spilled over him, surfacing an uneasy bit of apprehensive. *Have I just betrayed someone—maybe Nicholas?*

"That's very unique," Sir Caspin commented, suddenly interested as the background noise seemed to fade into silence. He seemed to fixate his attention solely on Daniel when, seeing Daniel's face fall, he placed a hand on his shoulder to reassure him. "Your secrets are safe with me! This is going to help you all, trust me! Both Nicholas and King Faund have charged us with your safety: the more I know, the better able I am to keep you all safe!"

"I thought you said whatever Nicholas and the king know, you already knew," Daniel grumbled. "Why bother asking me again if you already knew?"

"This conversation is just between us friends!" Sir Caspin assured him, taking the empty goblets to a nearby sink. He turned and reminded the lad, "We should get back to the others before we are missed. I just wanted to share a brew between us men and our mutual friendship!"

"Yeah, sure," Daniel replied, still awash with doubt. He felt bad enough about talking about something he wasn't supposed to be talking about. The ale had been wonderful, and he felt a sense of fellowship and respect among men he hadn't felt in a long time. *Finally respected as a man, instead of a boy!*

This time, though, he felt different about it. Something about the captain wanting him to keep a secret that supposedly Nicholas and King Faund already knew. He suddenly felt dirty for talking to Sir Caspin; it just didn't make sense. *The captain has been so nice since we met him; why does this feel different?*

≈≈≈≈

Johanna felt quite refreshed but continued receiving a cold shoulder from Nate. She tried small talk with him during dinner but noticed his distraction as he eyed a maiden serving wine. They had exchanged several glances, and the maiden had a beautiful smile that she flashed once his way. Her blue eyes sparkled, and blonde curls spilled over her very full breasts. The maid moved on, continuing to tend to the other guests but looked back occasionally to see if he was still watching.

Johanna fumed but only for a moment. *Do I really mind after all?* She had been flirting with Sir Caspin, so why not Nate? Sighing, she continued to eat her meal—it was delicious, and she'd rather not dwell on something that had to play out on its own.

The long table was filled with the daughters of the visiting lords and ladies, ornately dressed and strutting like peacocks to get the king's attention. *No doubt they all have a daughter that they want to see the king of Tyrna take notice of.*

That was when she glanced back to Daniel's empty chair, noticing his absence. Looking about nervously, she saw her son making his way back to his seat. She waited patiently as he plopped down beside her in a huff.

"Where have you been?" she whispered as he sat.

"Bathroom," Daniel quipped before glancing back over to Sir Caspin. The captain of the guard smiled knowingly and nodded back to him as he turned back to his mother in annoyance. "I'm back now."

"I can see that!" she admonished. "No need to be cranky with me!"

While Johanna missed the gesture between her son and Sir Caspin, Grand Master Nicholas saw the entire interaction from beginning to end, sitting at the king's side near the head of the table. The wizard crinkled his brow as he observed the uncharacteristic cues between the outworlder boy and the captain of the guard.

He was about to stand and motion to Sir Caspin when one of the servers approached with a parchment bearing the seal of the Wizard's Council in his hand. When Nicholas broke the seal and unfurled it, he could clearly see it was a note from Princess Serina.

Hoping my second dove finds its way to you. All is well—I'm studying for my tests at Mondlichtberg now. Council has lots of questions about your new duties in Tyrna, but they're relieved at your coming out of retirement! Confirmed council brought the outsiders here in a recruitment effort. I will remain until Encara's arrival next week, at which time I'll escort your replacement to you unless you decide to stay on.

The letter was brief but to the point. He knew she couldn't write openly of her concerns lest unfriendly eyes read the message, and he didn't know who those unfriendly eyes yet might belong to.

Nicholas folded the paper and pocketed it deep within his robes. The message between the lines for him was that the council was "relieved" of his replacement of Aros. *No wonder Aros was isolated—he had to be careful lest the same happen to him. Interesting that the message contains no mention of Sottis.*

One issue lingered: the fact that no one had notified him that recruitment practices were now extending to people off-world through artificial Shimmerings. It didn't make sense and seemed reckless and frankly uncharacteristic of the council to agree to such a measure. This was not the grand masters' style, neither Yamaro's nor Oaxro's.

He had no doubt that someone was bent on weakening the Wizard's Council and Tyrna simultaneously. He intended to find out who, and his own suspicions were beginning to form as he looked about the room. His eyes rested on Sir Caspin, still eyeing Daniel, quietly eating at the table next to his mother.

Chapter 19

A Day on Our Own

The next day's breakfast proved to be a quiet affair as Daniel and his mother arose soundlessly before the others, going down to the dining nook alone. Tanny and her mother received them with a subdued yet friendly gesture as the servants bustled about, bringing steaming bowls of porridge with a mix of fresh berries, herbs and nuts.

The refreshing concoction's delicious aroma awakened Johanna quickly, the hunger-arousing scents mingling with the cool morning breezes wafting in through the open windows as they dined. She watched Daniel closely, becoming keenly aware that something preoccupied his thoughts beyond a simple desire to return to bed.

"Why have you been so quiet lately?" she coaxed as she stood to ask the question, walking over to her son, and gently brushing his hair back. "You seem more withdrawn than ever—Danny, tell me!"

"When?" he grumbled as he grasped her hand and pushed back the bowl, clearly uninterested in finishing the contents. Her son could scarcely make eye contact with her as he pulled away. "I talked with lots of people during dinner, and..."

"C'mon, Danny; you know that's not what I'm talking about,"

Johanna gently interrupted. "I mean with me; we haven't really talked in days. You even used to talk to Nate more than me, and while I've always been a little annoyed with that, I see you're drifting from him too. I'm your mother, and I can tell when something is bothering you; what is it?"

"Nothing! No reason," he muttered glumly, still reflecting on his last night's secret drink with Sir Caspin. "I just don't like that you and Nate are fighting."

"Well, honey, you don't need to worry about that," she sighed. "Nate's a grown man and can take care of himself. I know you look up to him, and while he is a good man, he's not your father. He's a wonderful role model for you, but being here in this place does accentuate some of the issues we've had with each other all along. My point is, it doesn't have anything to do with you, and I want you to know that."

"Maybe it's because you like Sir Caspin more than him now," Daniel stated more than asked as he glanced at her quickly to gauge her reaction. "He seems to like you; don't tell me you haven't noticed."

"No, no, not really," she lied after a long pause, returning his glance with a sour look. "Sir Caspin is an attractive man, but someone like that is not good for me, or you, for that matter—not here and not now. Nate looks after us both, and I know that. Besides, I still hold out hope we will find a way home soon."

"Yeah, but you said it yourself, he's not Dad," Daniel agreed, although Johanna detected a hint of relief in his response. "Even if we get home, Nate's great with me and all, but you both seem to just piss each other off anymore. Here though, if we get stuck...I just don't know."

She laughed in surprise at his candor and his observance. As her laughter subsided, she started to say something more but thought better of it and changed the topic.

"Would you like to go exploring with me today?" she offered. "I feel like the two of us need some alone time together. Maybe we could go into New Tyrna and look for some new clothes or something. Let's do something fun, just the two of us!"

"You know what—that sounds nice," he decided, brightening further as he chuckled. "Just us! No Sir Caspin."

"I noticed you've met a little friend yourself: our maid, Tanny?" Johanna gently teased.

"Tanny's nice; we've been hanging out a little when she helps with Sammy," he agreed, attempting to downplay their brief interaction yet blushing slightly at the insinuation. "But yeah, let's just the two of us go."

"Of course, but the two of you are about the same age," Johanna sighed with a smile. She stood and glanced out the window, the vista blurred by imperfections in the casement glass. She could hear distant barking outside along with other dogs.

"Sounds like Sammy is having fun with Tanny. She's outside playing with her and the other dogs now. Are you sure you don't want to join her?"

"No, I'm sure," Daniel affirmed. "Let's just us go for once."

"Okay, it's a date then!" Johanna eagerly replied, standing tall. "I'll tell you what; I'm going back up to the room for just a minute. In the meantime, if Sir Caspin comes by, let him know that I'll be right back but today it is just the two of us!"

"Sounds good; I'll be here!" Daniel smiled as he finished his fare as she left the room. He stepped out briefly to watch his mom glide up the stairs to the guest quarters before he turned to sneak over to the servants' entrance for the kitchen. He could hear Sir Caspin's muddled voice through the doorway.

"Hey, Sir Caspin! You in here?" he called inside. Pushing open the door, he looked inside and caught sight of the captain of the guard standing with Sottis and one other man he didn't recognize. Sir Caspin gestured for Daniel to sit as the low conversation between the three men around the table suddenly ceased.

An array of freshly baked muffins and steaming tea lined the table in front of them, and their gently spiced scents filled the room.

Both Sir Caspin and Sottis donned their grey cloaks, shimmering in the light streaming through the window. Sottis's cloak seemed to have fewer dark threads than before, yet the midnight-black threads slowly emerged, creating new leaves and vines with each passing moment.

The stranger had not yet donned his cloak as he held the shiny fine article of clothing draped loosely around his arm. With piercing blue eyes and a handsome muscular build, he surveyed Daniel with mild curiosity, seated relaxed and barely sitting upright, as the lad entered the room.

"Hey, Daniel!" Sottis beckoned with encouragement. "Don't be shy, come on in here and sit with us. We were just talking about you!"

"You were?" Daniel paused. "What about?"

"Only about how glad we are that we have become acquainted of late!" Sir Caspin laughed off the question before turning serious to the matter at hand. "What's going on with you today? How's your mother doing?"

"Nate and Javier are probably going back to Pratenvike today, and Kevin said he wanted to go see Father Jaramillo," Daniel began. "My mom and I are just going to go ahead and do some exploring on our own."

"So, the explorers set out by themselves now, eh?" Sir Caspin joked with a wink. "You don't need my permission, so long as you are all going to stay out of trouble."

"That's the idea; hopefully trouble won't find us." Daniel grinned. "Well, I won't keep you guys; sorry about interrupting!"

"No need to worry—these are my friends," the captain explained. "You already know Sottis. May I introduce you to this handsome guy here: Lord Emelien Legouin of Urocia. He's just passing through and graced us with his presence this day, a most unexpected fortune for us!"

"Nice to meet you!" Daniel greeted cheerfully. "Good to see you again, Sottis. I haven't seen you lately; what have you been up to?"

"Your dear friend Grand Master Nicholas had me 'locked away' with other activities," the valet replied icily. His eyes flickered with a red glimmer as he turned to the Urocian lord. "He's the newcomer boy who can fly I was telling you about."

"So, you were talking about me after all, eh?" Daniel blushed as he turned to Caspin, a sudden wave of unease settling in his stomach. "You know I don't like that."

"Nothing to be ashamed of; that's quite a talent, young man!" Lord Emelien interjected, his voice as smooth as his chiseled features as he presented himself as calmly meticulous and groomed. "There's no need for secrets here; you are among friends! Sir Caspin also tells me your mother retains a unique talent as well, along with your other companions."

"Uh, yeah...she's a healer of sorts, as I guess you'd say around here," Daniel grumbled, caught off guard and suddenly uncomfortable with the openness in this topic of conversation. *Nicholas had sworn them to secrecy!* "I just stopped by to let you know that we'll be out and about today. Feel free to continue talking about something other than us, if you don't mind!"

The other men began laughing, lifting their drinks to the lad and smiling. Daniel shrugged as he returned a forced smile. That same familiar anxiety over the topic began to swell in his chest, making him queasy.

"Daniel, why don't you stay and have a drink with us?" Sir Caspin lowered his voice as he caught sight of the lad's grimace. "You're among friends here, I assure you!"

"Yes, Danny Boy!" Sottis offered, gesturing to the steaming plate of fresh breads on the table. "Why don't you sit and have a delicious fresh muffin?"

"No, I've got to get going before my mom gets back," Daniel politely declined as he backed toward the door. "We'll catch up later and let you know how it all went!"

"That's fine; give her our kindest regards!" Lord Emelien reclined at the table, clasping his hands behind his head and maintaining his ease. "Perhaps I shall have the pleasure of meeting her before I depart back to Urocia!"

"I'm sure you will," Daniel grumbled as he blushed, anxious to be on his way.

The three men seemed eager to engage him further, but this all somehow felt wrong, like being interrogated in the principal's office at school.

"Wait! Before you leave, I want to offer something to you," Sir Caspin called, snapping his fingers to stop him. "You know, whenever you want to practice your newfound abilities, come find me—I would be happy to practice with you. Please forgive us; where we're from, we practice these gifts in the open with each other. We don't hide our light under bushels; we are all friends in that regard!"

"Really?!" Daniel started with surprise. "Do any of you have... certain abilities also?"

"All three of us are from Urocia, Daniel," Sottis assured him. "Those who have powers don't hide it there. We're proud of everything we have to offer to our communities. Our abilities are different than yours, and some are more pronounced than others, but the Emerald Fire resides within us all."

"The Emerald Fire?" Daniel puzzled aloud.

"Daniel, none of us have the same special abilities as you do," Sir Caspin admitted. "Yours is a rare innate power, but we utilize a spiritual power of sorts we call the Emerald Fire. The Order of Etoilenoir retains resources for tapping into that power. If you were to announce yourself openly to the order, I guarantee you would be most welcome! Combined with the innate power you already possess, I am sure you would be a force to be reckoned with, never to be underestimated or discounted by anyone ever again!"

"My friend's point is that newcomers such as yourself are welcomed in our kingdom," Lord Emelien carefully elaborated. "We call all of our gifts an extension of the 'Emerald Fire.' It's unfortunate that your arrival didn't take you through Urocia first. We hope to reconcile that and offer you and your companions the opportunity to live among us there very soon."

"We were kind of hoping to get back to where we came from," Daniel carefully stated. "We aren't looking to stay!"

"What a shame! You would most certainly lose the abilities you are only just developing now," Sottis surmised. "Have you considered what Lord Emelien is offering? Imagine a new life here with us! Just consider the offer, especially if it is determined you are unable to return home!"

"I can't say I miss my old life," Daniel admitted, a slow smile spreading across his face. This seemed to please the other three men, who nodded in approval. "My peeps are here in Tyrna with me, though; I can't just get up and leave them!"

"Of course," Sir Caspin acknowledged. Sir Caspin's eyes stayed locked on Daniel, a hidden seriousness to what he suggested simmering beneath it all. "I would be honored to share with you what I know here in Tyrna, but as a Urocian citizen, you would enjoy greater privilege, access to such knowledge, and not to mention an easier and better life than out here on the frontier. Know that regardless of wherever you and your mother decide to make your home, I will do everything in my power to help you both."

"You really ought to be talking to my mom and Nate about this," Daniel backtracked as his smile faded. "They're the ones making the decisions, and..."

"Daaaanny, are you down here?" Johanna's voice floated through the air, echoing down the hall as she called to Daniel from the other room.

"My mom's calling me," the lad stated. "I gotta go, but we can talk more later."

"We certainly wouldn't want to keep you from your mother," Sir Caspin gently challenged. "We understand that it takes more than just sharing a pint of ale to make a man."

Taken aback by the subtle admonishment, Daniel stood tall, searching for a proper response to the sting, yet the men remained silently fixated on him, awaiting his response.

Suddenly, the kitchen door opened, and a surprised Johanna stood in the doorway.

"Oh, hello, Sir Caspin; I didn't realize Daniel…" She drifted off as her eyes transfixed Lord Emelien as he stood in greeting. Her heart began pounding in her ears and all other sounds seemed to fade from the room as she beheld the stately nature of this new man standing in front of her. Even the previous curiosities of Sir Caspin seemed to evaporate as if they had never been. "H-h-hello, Sottis. Good to s-s-see you again."

"May I introduce myself, my lady?" The regal blond man strode up and took her hand, kissing it. "Lord Emelien Legouin of Latana, capital of Urocia. Let me reassure you, the pleasure is all mine!"

"Oh, yes, nice to meet you; Johanna Langley," Johanna acknowledged in an awkward curtsy and giggle. Quickly composing herself, she turned to her son. "Are you ready to go?"

"Yeah, come on, Mom, we should get going," Daniel insisted, embarrassed with his mother's abrupt interest in the Urocian lord and still stinging from Sir Caspin's earlier rebuke. Grabbing her by the hand, Daniel escorted his mother out of the room. He waited until they were safely out of earshot and back out into the hall, with the kitchen door having shut behind them. "What the hell was that, Mom?!"

"Nothing! Absolutely nothing!" she stated aloud, although her face flushed as they passed through the great hall and double doors to the bright daylight that greeted them outside. They descended the marble stairs into the courtyard, picking up the pace as they went. "Today is about us! Let's go take on the day!"

≈≈≈≈

"His trust is remarkable, still untainted from the wizard's meddling," Sottis murmured after Daniel and Johanna had departed. "The work you've done on gaining his admiration will prove most useful, especially for winning over the others."

"Assuming you don't ruin it with another one of your outbursts," Lord Emelien irritably remarked. "That stunt you pulled on Nicholas nearly exposed us all! You're lucky Sir Caspin and I still hold some influence, even out here in the uncivilized frontier. Rest assured, Sottis, do it again and you will be on your own!"

"We have it under control for the moment," Sir Caspin groaned, no longer smiling. "Now that Aros is out of the picture, we best be on our way before Grand Master Nicholas finds out we've sprung Sottis from his cell. Hopefully by that time, the council members will be in alignment with us, and Nicholas's misgivings will no longer be an issue. His replacement of Aros has proven to be less desirable than initially anticipated!"

"In the meantime, I must find a way to become better acquainted with this Johanna!" Lord Emelien nodded in agreement even as he changed the topic, clearly having been distracted by her visit. "Since you've informed me that she's unmarried to her other companion, I would like to get to know her more!"

"Why you?" Sir Caspin turned on his friend in annoyance. "I found her first and already have built a rapport with all of them, including her!"

"You'll have other rewards coming to you, Sir Caspin," the Urocian lord whispered, still staring at the closed door, deep in thought. "This one is mine; I find her quite intriguing! That is my command, and I expect you to stand behind it!"

≈≈≈≈

Hours later, long after Johanna and Daniel had left the palace grounds, Kevin arrived alone at the doorstep of the Lady of Tyrna Parish. Having just grabbed a muffin for the walk, he donned his cloak, boots and travel garb for his brisk morning walk. Standing in front of the silent white marble guardians, he contemplated his next steps before opening the doors beneath the hovering stone swords held aloft by the giant angel statues to either side. He took a deep breath before swinging open the heavy doors and entering.

"Father Jaramillo?" Kevin called into the darkened recesses of the Lady of Tyrna church. The stained-glass panes shone as brightly and beautifully as they did the day before. However the church was now empty, the daily mass having already been celebrated. The cathedral had a hollow and cavernous feel to it, especially with most of the candles no longer lit. Multicolored morning light streamed through the stained-glass windows as before, illuminating them as jewels gleaming in a darkened background. The streams of light pierced the darkness, warming the otherwise cool air and stirring the tranquil interior to smell much like a leather-bound book.

"Kevin!" a voice called from the choir loft high above him, followed by a pad of footsteps. From the winding staircase to the side of the sanctuary, Father Jaramillo emerged, walking over and shaking his hand warmly. "It's good to see you again, my son! I was just completing the choir folders for Sunday and am now headed out to the gardens; care to join me?"

"Thank you, Father; I'd love to!" Kevin stated as they turned to exit back into the brightness of the day. "I was hoping you could tell me a bit of history about yourself and the church. I hope I came at a good time and am not disturbing you."

"Not at all!" The priest smiled, grabbing two pairs of leather gardening gloves off the garden fencepost and handing one set to him. "The garden may be small but needs tending nonetheless! You would be surprised that even a small patch such as this one can still feed the hungry and those in need! The day is beautiful, and the Lord has granted us that gift—let us not waste it indoors, shall we?"

The scent of freshly tilled earth permeated the warming air around them both as they worked among the variety of vegetables in the quaint garden. The friar spoke mostly about how he had arrived at Tyrna, brown sleeves of his long robe rolled up even as he covered his hands with the labors of the earth. They labored from harvesting cucumbers, melons and beans and uprooting weeds to replanting a handful of tomato plants into a corner of the garden with some wooden trellises.

"I first came to this city back when the outer wall was new and some sections were still under construction," Father Jaramillo recalled as they cultivated the rows. "Tyrna was a much newer city back then;

the people were so eager, and the frontier considered to be exciting and so full of opportunity. We worked with a few early converts to build the church by hand, stone by stone, with mainly tailings from both the inner wall and outer wall. Since before my arrival, most of the population either had no religion or believed in a multitude of gods based on the cultures they had emerged from."

"It must have been quite a challenge," Kevin commented, his own hands dripping with earth. "To start completely from scratch."

"Oh, indeed it was," the priest laughed as he wiped his brow, recollecting and remembering with a sigh. "We had patiently ministered primarily to Tyrna's citizens first and then secondly to anyone who would listen; on the top of this very hill!"

"Here?!" Kevin balked turning to stare at the ancient structure in disbelief.

"On this very location," the priest stated as he pointed at the church's base. "These are among the first stones assembled by the hands of the very parishioners themselves."

"All this was built by hand?" Kevin asked, gesturing to the church with his hand trowel.

"Not all of it," the friar admitted with a smile. "You see, the technological pride of Tyrna was in its ingenious engineering. In the construction of the outer walls and the palace itself, many inventors came together to assemble the great cranes. Built from a latticework of stone, iron and a complex set of chains and pulleys, these massive cranes were able to lift much larger and heavier stones than teams of donkeys and people. The walls had to be built with defenses in place. All of this was to make Tyrna what it later became—a safe and sturdy place to call home on the frontier."

"The cranes had to be able to not only be strong but handle meticulous tasks," Kevin mused. "Much like cranes from my world to build large modern buildings."

"Oh, yes, the same held true here," the priest acknowledged. "Tyrna has always been a city of commerce and ingenuity for all the peoples in the west. With all the cranes and the expertise to build and use them in the possession of the king at the time, I had requested use of but one to build a church for the people and our parish."

"If he was anything like the current king, I don't imagine that he was quick to volunteer that," Kevin commented.

"No indeed," Father Jaramillo agreed, using a hand trowel to shovel more dirt around some cabbages as Kevin assisted. "King Randal was the head of the House of Austrik at the time and the king of Tyrna. He insisted that all the cranes were needed to perform the heavy lifting of boulders onto the wall, and none could be spared."

"What did you do?" Kevin grunted as he muscled another trellis into place.

"I was persistent," the priest admitted as he shrugged. "I had requested an audience with the king every single day to reconsider the assignment of just one of the cranes on the construction project. I saw no issue with it since both projects were occurring simultaneously. After tolerating my persistence for nearly a full year, one day he finally threw his hands up in frustration and allowed my use of the crane."

"So, you got it built," Kevin finished for the priest. "Sounds like a job well done!"

"Not so fast," Father Jaramillo interjected. "My prayers for the crane had been answered, but in my haste, it created another problem that I had not considered. The crane and its operators came condition-ally and with a timeline of only one month. His Majesty would decide to oversee the project himself or end it altogether."

"What?!" Kevin exclaimed. "How did he expect you to do that all on your own?!"

"That, my son, was the exact same question I asked King Randal," the priest sighed. "He told me, 'If your God can perform miracles and move mountains, then let Him help you build a church.' King Randal loaned me the crane and the resources with only a one-month time frame to accomplish the deed. Indeed, it was my single most moment of despair, yet followed my greatest triumph."

"Yet there the church stands." Kevin indicated again with his muddy trowel. "You found a way..."

"Well, in the beginning, a few of the early converts joined in assisting me with the construction," the friar continued, smiling as he stood. "It was just a few spirited souls who were able to assist in moving the first mountain of rocks. As days turned into weeks, people came from as far away as Urocia and the Southern Kingdoms to assist. I have no explanation as to how they heard about the project or even who they were, yet come they did. I continued to perform daily mass and church duties, but I assisted in the construction as well. It was during my daily sermons that I began to recognize many of the faces from the construction site and vice versa. I continued to preach, and they continued to come."

"You were building your parish community at the same time as the church," Kevin mused.

"I was so humbled that I thanked God in my daily sermons for delivering the miracle of manpower added to our original group of volunteers," Father Jaramillo acknowledged. "It truly was a time of unity I have not seen since. The people worked hand in hand, stone by stone, and all who came found God and the spiritual guidance he provides. Our parishioners completed God's house within the timeline King Randal had provided."

"That's amazing," Kevin stated, placing the trowel on the ground and standing up to stretch.

"God's grace extends to places we never thought possible," the priest agreed. "We still represent a very small percentage of this world's people, but we bring God's word to everyone, without reservation. It all started here on this hillside, on this very spot. Now this church serves as a beacon of light to those in this world, illuminating the word of God for them. The fruits of our labor those many hundreds of years ago continue to this day. I am especially grateful for the Austrik's line—this family of kings has been quite gracious to the church ever since dear Randal, who became a convert himself in the end."

"Maybe that was the reason you were brought here," Kevin contemplated aloud. "To have an impact and spread his word in this world.

Don't you ever miss being back in our own world? Don't you want to ever try to go back?"

"I've thought about it many times in the past; however, remember, our lives are not our own," Father Jaramillo said thoughtfully. "I was sent to save native peoples of the new world and instead am working to save a multitude of peoples in another world altogether. Anyone I once knew back in our world is now gone. I think about returning far less than I used to, especially since my work here has far surpassed anything I could have done back there."

"Yeah, I suppose you're right," Kevin contemplated. "Your calling certainly seems to have filled a void in a world that didn't have God in it."

"It certainly would seem that way; our ranks continue to swell even to this day. We now sponsor missionaries to all the surrounding kingdoms!" The friar's grin faded slightly as he winced at the memory. "It's certainly more challenging in resistant kingdoms, such as in Urocia, where they hold no worship of a higher power. The Southern Kingdoms are also difficult in that our beliefs tend to clash with a multitude of other polytheistic and more established religions."

"Much like old Rome, I suppose," Kevin reflected. "It's definitely like a step back in time!"

"In some ways; however, with mystic powers and non-human creatures, it certainly presents some differences too," the priest countered. "The task I've performed over centuries and perform here now is a task I had thought the elves could have assisted with. Alas, though, they are absent, and as I stated, our lives are not our own; I can but do the Lord's work as best I can until the blessed day comes when He finally sees fit to call me home."

"You mentioned the elves?" Kevin squinted. "I understand they are gone and not coming back; is that true? I haven't seen any of them yet."

"Nor will you," Father Jaramillo lamented. "They disappeared when the kingdoms of men began to unify. They retreated to their forests and mountains and other far-off wild places of the world. When the trade routes gained in population and the kingdoms and cities began to sprawl, they disappeared altogether. I must admit to my own prejudices when I first met them, but over time, I grew to appreciate their unique place in this world. It has since been hundreds of years since they were last seen—a beautiful people! A holy people! A blessed people with great wisdom and long lives, even as long as mine; and they are missed!"

"When we arrived here, we began to show certain abilities we hadn't had before." Kevin had been holding a question on his mind but had resisted asking it until now. "Did you receive any special abilities when you came here?"

"It is sometimes difficult to ascertain what is a gift from God and what is not." The priest looked up and smiled. "In the church, we do not believe in what is not specifically given by God. Sorcery is forbidden, therefore I refrained from pursuing any such gift, and no such gift was ever revealed to me."

"Despite the fact you are over 400 years old." Kevin blinked, offering the comment in jest.

Father Jaramillo smiled knowingly as he took a pause from his labors. Wordlessly, he stood to collect his thoughts on the matter, taking a long draught of water from a clay jug sitting beside him before continuing. The fall breeze tussled through his salt-and-pepper hair as the warm rays of the harvest sun gave way to the cooler breezes of autumn.

"The dear Grand Master Nicholas loves debating me and insists that my long life is such a gift, but I continue to believe this is a miracle from God," the priest finally stated as he wiped a bead of sweat from his forehead. "I am very much at peace with doing God's work, and it is my pleasure and my passion to continue to do so. The gift of time *is* God's gift, and He has graced me with much of it, far more than I ever imagined or wanted. It is more of a burden than you can imagine, my young friend. However, I bear this burden with as much grace as I can."

"How so?" Kevin marveled. "To live so long and stay so healthy, you can experience many things! You're very lucky, or blessed, I might say!"

"I suppose that could be true, from a certain perspective," the priest admitted yet shook his head to dismiss the reflection. "What is never taken into account from that point of view is the many generations of people that come and go before me. Additionally, I often lose track of time. Only in moments of reflection, such as now, am I able to even discern the passage of time with any sense of accuracy or measure! For example, I've sometimes mistaken young children in the pews for relatives of theirs, long deceased and gone; it can be rather shocking at times!"

"Geeze, I hadn't thought of it that way; it could be maddening!" Kevin stated as he shook his head. "My friends are really missing out on this! I wish they had come with me here!"

"Each in their own time," the friar assured him gently. "Matters of spirit must arrive in one's heart and cannot be forced by another; you must be called to it."

"Speaking of time, they chose the Pratenvike today, and I think THAT is a waste of time," Kevin reflected. "There are so many things to see here and experience, but shopping and entertainment seems to be what captivated their interest. That obelisk gave me the creeps, too."

"On the surface, the Pratenvike is only a gathering place for fun. Yet, this could easily become a place of vice for others," Father Jaramillo stated unequivocally. "There's nothing wrong with commerce and celebration. However, the newly built structure did displace many people from their homes. Not to mention a large sum of royal treasure went into building it. I fear it may have thoughtlessly taken an improper place within the hearts of many in our community."

"Have you seen it?" asked Kevin, brushing the dirt off his hands on his pants. "Have you been?"

"I have not," the priest admitted with a smile as he knelt again to pad the earth around their transplant efforts, more closely inspecting the fruits of their labors. "I feel the Lord's work is at hand here and abroad—the Pratenvike is simply not the place for me. I might have thought differently when I was much younger, but the trivialities it presents are simply not in my interests, especially given my actual age."

"I can understand the feeling," Kevin sighed. "It's crowded and noisy, not like here."

They continued to garden in silence as a newfound respect and admiration for the priest culminated in Kevin's mind. Despite their newfound kinship, he inwardly marveled at the fact that Father Jaramillo was nearly 400 years old. *And yet he looks like he is just over forty.*

≈≈≈≈

Johanna and Daniel strode past the massive main gate of Tyrna's outer wall, beginning their exploration of New Tyrna. The quaint village smelled of fresh plaster and thatched roofs, peppered with scents of freshly baked breads.

The newly built tiny shops and homes all bustled with peasants and farmers, all mingling with construction workers and their beasts of burden. The unique crowd blended, creating a sense of transition all in the shadow of the great gate of Tyrna, a giant rusting hulk of old in the background of it all.

Daniel noticed that many of the new residences were already occupied by peasants and merchants alike. Many within the morning throng headed to work, yet some continued the ongoing construction efforts at sites close by where they lived. The scent of working animals lingered in the air where construction activity was at its heaviest. Many horses and donkeys trotted by, towing carts of supplies: lumber, thatch and plaster.

"So, who were Sir Caspin's friends?" Johanna casually asked her son as she looked away through storefront windows, pretending to examine a variety of peasant dresses on display.

"Well, you remembered Sottis," Daniel explained. "The other guy was Lord Emelien. I guess they all came from a neighboring kingdom called Urocia."

"A lord from Urocia, that's interesting," she commented as if only half listening.

"Oh, come on Mom, you didn't see the way he was looking at you?" Daniel rolled his eyes. "Between him and Sir Caspin, they're both going to have to go through Nate. Mom, I won't lie; Nate's still got my vote!"

"Danny!" she exclaimed. "That's not very nice! Just because Nate and I are having some issues right now doesn't mean I'm running off with strange men!"

"Sorry, Mom." Daniel blushed, looking away. "I just noticed they took an interest in you."

"That's alright," she sighed, not wanting to address her own wandering thoughts on the matter. "What were you guys talking about anyway when I came in the kitchen this morning?"

Daniel bit his lip, unsure as to how much to say but Sir Caspin's prying into their affairs weighed heavily on him, especially since the captain had clearly shared their private information with his other friends. Still, he had promised to keep their interaction a secret, although the promise he had made seemed to have strings attached to it that he had never realized were there. After a long pause, he turned to his mother.

"There's something I've been meaning to tell you about Sir Caspin," he began. "I'm not sure we should be..."

Screams suddenly arose from a street nearby, distracting them both. A cluster of peasants ran past them as they turned to each other in dismay.

"What was that?" Johanna perked up, distracted by the commotion.

"My son! My son!" A woman's voice cried out. They ran around the corner to see an elderly woman standing over a young farmhand. "Somebody, help us please!"

A cart loaded with wooden barrels had rolled over his legs, knocking and pinning him down to the ground, leaving his mother tugging frantically on his arm to no avail. Several other men were pulling on the two donkeys towing the cart, but the confused animals seemed unable to move forward, due to the cart's other wheel stuck in a rut.

With a loud shout, the men assisted in pushing the cart clear. The injured farmhand gave an audible moan in pain, revealing that his leg had been broken above the ankle. Bystanders were tending to the animals, but the older woman kneeled next to her son, holding her face in her hands as she wept.

"Mom, should we help them?" Daniel whispered.

"We're not supposed to," Johanna stated as she clasped her hands anxiously. They stood there and watched, undecided, when one of the donkeys brayed loudly before breaking free from its harness and began galloping down the street.

The opportunity presented itself to discreetly intervene when the bystanders present began wrestling with the other equine while the woman ran after the fleeing animal with a group of men to retrieve it. For the moment, the young man with the broken leg lay alone in the street, whimpering in pain.

"Okay, let's do this," Johanna whispered, snapping at the opportunity. "Keep everyone's attention away from me up at the front!"

"Hey, sir, can I help?" Daniel waved and shouted to gain everyone's attention. He ran to the man struggling with the lead donkey, still tied to the cart. He glanced back once to see his mother kneeling next to the wounded man's leg.

"The other donkey!" the man shouted. "See if you can help retrieve..."

"Here: I'll hold the reins," Daniel insisted as he reached. "You go after the other donkey!"

"No, I got it!" the man insisted, pulling away. "Why don't you—"

"Aw, come on—I just want to help!" Daniel kept pointing in the direction the others had gone to retrieve the other animal. They had already caught up to the braying beast and were struggling to keep it calm as they led it back to them. Daniel pointed to keep the man's attention away from his mother and the injured farmhand. "You should go help them with the other donkey!"

The wounded man noticed Johanna kneeling near his knee, but when she asked him where his pack animals had run off to, his attention followed to where Daniel had pointed. He didn't notice Johanna cradle his wound in her cupped hands.

"I figure ol' Betsy ran off to..." A searing heat radiated into his leg, and a flash of light coursed from Johanna's hands, and he cried aloud in shock. "What was that?!"

"I don't know," Johanna lied, suddenly pointing at a rat running down the street toward a gutter. "I was looking at your leg when... THERE!"

"A rat?" someone else shouted "Did it bite him?"

"Yes! The rat bit him!" she exclaimed as she feigned fear, backing away while grabbing Daniel's hand. "We can't be here—there are rats! Quick, let's go home!"

They could not continue the charade any longer, bursting out in laughter while turning to flee together down a side alley. Hauling each other by the arm, they both retreated down the street, away from the crowd of people that had clustered around the newly healed man.

"Mom, you pointed at a rat—he's going to think the rat healed him!" Daniel finally managed to articulate through their laughing fits. "You probably started a new health trend of treatments through biting rats!"

"I hope not!" Johanna giggled as she ushered him along, wiping away her tears of mirth. "A rat that heals people when it bites them would be most unhealthy! That debate may call more attention than anything I just did back there; hopefully anyway!"

≈≈≈≈

Nate and Javier had paired up that morning in the hall, finding that the others had already left. After a quick morning bite, the two headed down to the Pratenvike together to see what the center of commerce might provide this day.

The buzz of activity had already begun as they arrived, resuming the action-packed feel of the marketplace. Actors and acrobats maneuvered around the crowd, juggling, blowing torches and creating quite a spectacle.

Nate had never seen Javier so at ease as the younger man flitted from table to table, flirting with nearly half the women he came across. A ginger maiden took a particular interest in him and flirted back, smiling and batting her hazel eyes.

Nate followed him through the sea of people but grew a bit uncomfortable when a group of partying lasses surrounded them. Each smelled suspiciously of overwhelming perfumes and spices.

"Come to our parlor, great sir!" said one, running her fingers down his face.

"Ooooh, aren't you something cute!" exclaimed another, patting him on the rear.

"Rawl," exclaimed a cat-lady. "Ever want to try kitties?"

"Um, Javier." Nate tapped his wayward companion on the shoulder nervously.

"Isn't this great?!" Javier turned back to him, face beet-red but with a big grin on his face. "I don't think I'm ever going to leave here!"

"Yeahhhhhhh," Nate exclaimed weakly. "I don't think they're interested in you as much as they are what you can pay them."

"Hey, boys, what are you into?" a cool voice from the shadows, off to the side inquired.

They turned as a portly, richly dressed man sporting an unshaven face and sandy brown hair proudly presented himself. Sweat beaded his balding head, dripping into uneven tuffs of hair over and around his ears, before dripping into his sideburns connecting to a blotchy beard. Two uncharacteristically young and fair maidens cuddled up with him under each of his swollen arms, stroking his swollen belly affectionately.

"Take your pick; we have many pleasures to offer," he muttered gruffly, flashing a brief grin. He took a sip from a wine goblet before standing, keeping his dark eyes locked on them the entire time.

"I'm Javier, and this here is Nate," Javier began slyly, nudging Nate with his elbow. "What are you offering?"

"Pull your head out of your ass!" Nate whispered. "We don't need to be involved with this crap! We don't even know if *that* is legal here or not!"

"I'm just testing the waters; relax!" Javier hushed back. "Shut up! I know what I'm doing!"

"You can call me Garth," the man proclaimed as he strode forth, a voluminous grey cloak trailed luxuriantly after him, dark threads weaving slowly throughout with delicate interlocking patterns. His voice was as warm as his handshake, although his grip felt a bit moist and clammy. As he shook their hands, his smile dropped, and he hesitated. "Say, you're the outsiders, aren't you?"

"What do you mean?" Nate asked in annoyance.

"No need to play coy; I make it my business to know who everyone is. So, what do you say, young master?" He burped as he gestured to each of the women as they bowed eagerly in turn, eyeing the strangers with anticipation. "Chandra here has a fire needing to be quenched—perhaps the coolness of Methanae to soothe your tired spirit—maybe something exotic, like Kitty?"

"Eh, we'll be back," Nate spontaneously proclaimed before grabbing Javier's arm and hauling him off to the food court. "We have something else to attend to!"

"You know where to find us," Garth growled, watching the outsiders with a red glimmer in his eyes. He settled back into the shadows to reciprocate the caressing of his women.

"Where's your common sense?" Nate chastised Javier, once they were out of earshot of Garth and his entourage. "What the hell are you doing?!"

"Where's your sense of adventure?" Javier retorted, pulling away from him in annoyance. "It's not like Johanna gives a shit anyway! I don't know how you put up with all that, especially with that Caspin guy trolling her, but don't you need a break? It's not like I was actually going to DO something, I just want to see how far they'll go!"

"That's not the point!" Nate spat, even if Javier was right. "How'd that guy even know who we were?"

"C'mon, Nate! It's not like we exactly blend in here! I'm sure word gets around!" Javier exclaimed throwing his hands up in the air before letting out a loud exhale and finally settling down. "Look, I'm sorry for what I just said about Johanna, but the way she's been lately with you, I think you could use a break; I know I can! I'd like to have a little bit of fun while we're here, given what we've all been through!"

"You're unbelievable!" Nate scoffed, unable to say more but could only shake his head. "I'm going back to the palace; do whatever the hell you want!"

For Nate, despite Javier's unrealistic and cavalier attitude toward their situation, the comment about Johanna really stung. As he trudged his way out of the Pratenvike, he couldn't help but reflect on her demeanor since they had come through the Shimmering. Being stranded in another world was one thing, but the situation should have brought them closer together, not pushed them further apart. The fact that even a younger dumb outsider like Javier could spot this made it even more real to him, and worse.

The sound of running feet coming up behind him gave him pause, and he turned to see Javier jogging behind him to catch up. The younger man slowed as he approached and resumed walking beside him back up the road. Red-faced and silent, the pair passed wordlessly through the inner gate as they resumed their trek back up to the palace.

Nate mused with a grin to himself as the two men continued towards the castle's entrance and the fountain's cul-de-sac, leaving the quiet moss-covered gate behind. *At least Javier has come to his senses, even if he doesn't want to admit it!*

≈≈≈≈

When Daniel and his mother returned to the royal palace, they climbed the steps to the main entrance, where Nicholas was waiting for them at the top. He glowered at them with a sense of reprisal as they slowed their climb on their approach.

"What did I tell you about using your powers?" the wizard chastised Johanna, his voice stern over the happily bubbling fountain in the background.

"A man needed my help," was all she could say. "You knew about that?"

"He should have gone to a healer!" Nicholas exclaimed. "I'm trying to protect you; by drawing attention to yourself, others of a more unsavory nature may try to take advantage of you. I can sense your powers and others may be able to do the same, particularly when you use them!"

"I will be more mindful in the future," she admitted sullenly. "I just hated seeing him suffer!"

"You should have seen it though, Nicholas! Trust me, no one noticed!" Daniel blurted out, trying to disarm the confrontation. "We blamed it on the rats! Trust me! No one knew!"

"The rats!" Nicholas scoffed as he escorted them to their rooms. "There are many novel explanations we could offer to cover this incident; however, that's not one I would have thought of."

"We promise to be more careful," Daniel interjected, nervously glancing at his mother. "I promise, though, no one saw!"

"What you don't understand is that I use magic myself so was immediately aware of what you had done," the grand master explained more gently. "Others may not be able to tell *what* exactly or *who* exactly has utilized magic, but they can sense *where* it is being used. More magical beings can discern intent. My point is, your rouse may have fooled the peasantry in the market, but it won't fool everyone, and you never know who else may be watching!"

"So, they may be drawn to us when we use those powers?" Johanna acknowledged.

"Quite possibly," the wizard admitted, satisfied he had their full attention now. "Your innate magic, while not the most refined, is quite strong and naturally potent, particularly when it affects others. Of all the types of powers, it is the most easily discernible by those who can read it. Understand?"

"Yes," Johanna whispered. "It makes sense now."

"What about mine?" asked Daniel.

"Well, you're rather fortunate, young man," Nicholas intoned. "While your magic does not affect others, we can't have you flying about in broad daylight where everyone can see you bumping into things. You're young, but...let's just say I'd prefer if you consult with me first!"

"All right, I promise not to fly when others can see me," Daniel replied glumly. "Where are Nate and the others?"

"They arrived just before you did, and apparently word of you all is beginning to spread," Nicholas sighed, unsure of the validity behind Daniel's promise. "Others are beginning to take an interest in your party, and not all of them may have your well-being in mind!"

"What? Who?" Johanna started with new attention, alerted to this new revelation.

"Merchants around the Pratenvike," the grand master sighed. "I don't mean to be so hard on you; keeping you all a secret for very long was never going to be easy or indeed even possible. If I'm to manage being your Advocate effectively, we need to stay close by and in good communication!"

≈≈≈≈

After dinner that night, Daniel sauntered alone out into the moonlit courtyard to give Sammy a bone the cooks had given to him. She lay with several other of the royal hounds, curled about the fountain. He called her over, and although the other hounds perked up, they didn't move as she eagerly approached the lad.

"Here, Sammy, those cooks are taking good care of you, spoiled doggie!" he whispered as he scratched her behind the ears. The courtyard remained quiet, except for the sound of the fountain babbling softly at the center.

Sammy wagged her tail in acknowledgment, settling at his feet but saying nothing as she gnawed on her bone.

He could see the striations in the grass beside the cobblestone roadway, reminding him briefly of a runway at an airport. He wanted so much to be free of Tyrna's palace and all the restrictions Nicholas and his mother had placed on him. He wanted to see the reservoir at the top of the mountain Sir Caspin had mentioned during their tour.

He stood and trudged over to the corner of the courtyard, deep in thought. Nicholas had told them not to use their powers without his supervision, but he had *also* said that he was young and not as "detectable." *It's dark; no one can see anything!*

Daniel continued to march in a circle to the other side of the courtyard, testing the tempting breeze. Sammy continued gnawing contentedly at her bone, not even stirring at his absence. He looked up and could see the tip of Tyrna Peak high above the uppermost turret of the castle under the full moon. *Somewhere up there is that lake that everyone has heard about, but no one has seen.*

Remembering how planes take off in a life a world away, Daniel throttled his imaginary engines to full power and raced down his imaginary runway. Sammy eyed him warily and began to growl.

"Wherrrrrre you going?" she huffed.

"Stay here, Sammy, wait for me," he snapped. "I've had enough of just walking around! I haven't done this since Levens, and I want to see what I can do!"

Daniel ran through the courtyard past the fountain. About halfway through the courtyard, his speed suddenly increased, and his eyes grew wide as he lifted into the air. His stomach churned as adrenaline surged through him with nothing but air beneath his feet.

"Yeaaahhhhh!" he screamed. With the sensation of a pit opening in his stomach, Daniel heaved up and over the inner wall. He kept climbing as the air blasted him, the sounds of Sammy's frantic barks fading quickly behind him.

Up, up, up he went, aiming not for the outer wall but circling back to the cliffs above and to the rear of the castle. Daniel continued to circle until he could see the path zigzagging like a great white snake on the dark cliffside.

Daniel climbed higher and higher, and the air grew crisp as he climbed. He hadn't anticipated how cold the air could get, but he was having too much fun to stop now. The castle continued to fall away as the lights of the city clustered at its base, peppered below him like fireflies in the night.

His eyes watered as he flew faster and higher, gaining altitude and following Tyrna Peak's southern ridgeline higher and higher. Above him in the full moonlight, Tyrna's Peak came into full view as he began to shiver. Just below the peak, a broad bowl containing a shimmering body of water opened before him.

A few remaining snowbanks lined the sides of the basin, bordering the silent reservoir. The lake was much bigger than he had expected, maybe a mile or two around, and the dam was quite high and built of thick stone, rimmed with bits of ice still floating on the surface. It had several massive floodgates that appeared to be permanently sealed through a combination of great iron bars and stacks of boulders to buttress them.

He descended into the bowl, flying high over the dam and arching around the lake, mesmerized by the stars and moon reflected in them. The air bit mercilessly, cold and unrelenting, yet he pressed on, mesmerized by his flight and intoxicated with excitement.

Going in for a closer look, he skimmed the surface of the lake, daring just to reach out with his fingers to graze the surface of the icy waters. The drag from his fingers and dip of his "wings" changed his flight pattern, and he began to spin, causing drag and threatening to dunk him.

"Argh!" Daniel grimaced. *I'm going to crash into the lake completely if I don't focus!* "Full power!"

His hands emanated a brief pulse, displacing ripples upon the water. The maneuver corrected his trajectory, sending him paralleling flatly above the surface of the lake. He careened toward the dam and could see the froth of the water spilling just over the top ahead of him.

"Terrain! Terrain!" Daniel shouted to himself. "Pull up!"

Up he went—up and over the dam and back out over the valley and the city of Tyrna, far below. He glided so high that the view gave his stomach the butterflies. He circled back over the lake again, but this time climbing even higher, numb to the cold as his shivering wracked his body, his nose running and his eyes watering.

This time, he aimed toward the tip-top of Tyrna Peak itself, steep and rocky. Hard-packed with snow and ice, it glinted cold white in the moonlight. He circled around to the back of the peak where he could see vast plains, stretching further to the east. In the far distance to the northeast, he could see the shimmering glow of a distant city, seeming to produce a light of its own. From this distance, he could only glimpse the glow on the horizon, indicating its presence and the light it produced.

"Urocia," Daniel mouthed through chattering lips. "That's gotta be that Latana place."

Gliding more slowly, he completed his circle back around Tyrna Peak when the Grenze Mountains again came into view. This time, he could actually see over the tops of the massive peaks, revealing even higher peaks behind them. Levens came into view, far off to the north-west, looking tiny, quaint and sleepy. The tiny kingdom's town seemed a mere pinprick upon the telltale turtle-shell hill, alone in a sea of darkness on the northern frontier.

Across from Tyrna, he could clearly see the northern settlement on Long Lake and even the lights from the southern settlement at the other end. *So high, and I can see so much!*

He climbed higher still when his goal finally came into full view: the top of Tyrna Peak. He had gained some confidence from his last tries and realized his hands behaved like engines.

Daniel slowed himself as he approached the rocky top. Tyrna Peak truly retained little in the way of flat surfaces at the summit. One great boulder jutted out on the north end, almost welcoming him like a landing pad. It wasn't much, but it would have to do.

He dropped his legs like landing gear, wobbling a bit in flight as he did so. Making a running motion with his feet, he encountered the flat surface of the great rock. He then brought his hands forward, reversing his imaginary "engines"... and then, all was silent as he landed gingerly atop the pinnacle summit.

The wind whispered silently around him. He could hear his heart beating, pounding at the exertion but also at the excitement. Daniel held his breath, listening to his own heartbeat, clenching his teeth to prevent them from chattering.

Turning briefly, he took in the view with a complete and breathtaking circle. It was beautiful to behold, but frigidly cold. The air up here stung like needles, reminding him briefly of their plunge into Echo Lake, so long ago in that far-off forgotten land of Colorado. As he began to shiver, his teeth chattered.

It is quiet up here, absolute silence! Next time, I'll bring a coat!

Daniel took a swan dive off the flat rock, back toward the lake, then angled to follow the southern ridgeline down instead this time. The exhilarating descent took his breath away. Incredibly fast, he used his "reversers" to maintain control, dodging boulders and rocks and then trees and bushes as he went.

His ears popped and he swallowed hard to clear them but kept going as the air warmed around him. Over the dam and plunging through the narrow valley he charged. Soon he could see the castle returning, rushing up at him. He angled to his left to avoid the Wizard's Tower and the palace's superstructure, zipping past the servant's quarters as he descended in a rush. A quick flare shot him up and over the inner wall, slowing himself over the courtyard, where Sammy faithfully awaited his return and...*uh-oh*—his mom and Nicholas as well.

He was about to pull away when Nicholas pointed him out. *Dang! He could sense me after all.*

He looked about to see if anyone else was watching, but from what he could tell, no one else was present in the courtyard. Aiming for the striations in the grass, he thought he might as well make a good landing out of it. *If I'm already caught, I may as well show them that I can do it!*

Daniel made the best landing yet, running and passing the fountain before stopping and turning sheepishly to his mother and the older wizard.

"Well?" He smiled at the glowering wizard and his mother standing in shock, mouth agape. "What do you think?"

Nicholas's disapproving scowl and his mother's exasperation said everything; Daniel couldn't control the outburst that came next.

"How could you NOT be impressed!" he shouted. "I've got control of this! If I can do these amazing things, then why shouldn't I? No one else saw me in the dark; I swear it!"

"Good, but as I mentioned before, there may be some about who can sense you!" Nicholas huffed, incensed. "We just spoke about this earlier! Now let's get inside before someone else does see you. You must promise me never to pull that stunt again without my permission!"

"Fine, I promise," Daniel sighed, looking at his mother, who just shook her head. "I just want to be on the record that I've contained myself better than anyone else!"

"Onto other topics for now," the wizard sighed, glowering as he reflected on how to continue to best keep these newcomers' presence discreet, or at least with minimum exposure. "I may have some news for you all early tomorrow, anyway. Confound all my efforts to keep you all a secret! Thankfully, despite all the distractions of my daily demands posed by being here, I have not forgotten your plight. I still have more research tonight to do before I share my findings with you."

Chapter 20

The Solution

In the wee hours of the next morning, Johanna stirred in her bed even as it remained dark outside and Tyrna slumbered on. Still haunted by the reflections racing through her mind from the previous day, sleep had not settled easily on her that night.

When the hints of dawn began to illuminate the window in her room, she sat up in frustration, having barely slept. Sammy stood and stretched, turning to her and wagging her tail in anticipation of the morning.

"Tinkle, tinkle?" the hound yawned. "Let's go! Let's go!"

"Yeah, sure, baby, come on; I'll let you out to go potty," Johanna whispered as she stood. Conscientious of Daniel still fast asleep on her room's sofa by the window, she stopped to adjust the single wool blanket draped over him.

As she finished dressing, Johanna glanced back at her sleeping son and exhaled, shaking her head. She had enjoyed her day with him prior to that incident, but even that felt different than it had before.

She had made her own mistake, exposing her power publicly when she tried to help an injured man. She had realized her error after Nicholas's chastisement, yet Daniel continued to reject the wizard's stern advice. Her son's reckless escapade flying up the mountain had shown her that he just wasn't an obedient little boy anymore; he had a mind of his own. He felt more like an adult, and whatever was left of her little boy evaporated even faster since their accident leading through the Shimmering. Every day, all she saw left behind was this angry young adult; even Nate seemed to relate to him less and less each day.

As she closed the door to their room and tiptoed past Nate's closed door, she couldn't help but sigh. She had always thought he was the link that strengthened her bond with her son; now, it was clearer than ever that wasn't the case, leaving her with one less reason to continue the charade of their relationship. There was a time when the two of them couldn't be parted and the attraction had been strong; that time, though, seemed to have long since passed.

As she descended the winding stone stairs with Sammy by her side, her mind began to wander. Caspin's continuous flirtations with her were fun at first but had become annoying as they added to her widening emotional rift with Nate. Keeping a tantalizing diversion at bay seemed the logical choice, given their circumstances as strangers to this world, providing a sense of stability, and setting a good example to her adolescent son.

Everything seemed to turn upside down when she encountered Lord Emelien; the attraction between them could be felt immediately. An awakened electricity, a white heat she hadn't felt since her late husband had surged through her; not even Sir Caspin had tempted her in such a way. *Is it the Urocian lord's regal nature? Is it any different than Caspin's attempts or something more? He's clearly younger than anyone I've ever considered; not much older than Kevin or Javier! Why entertain any of this while Daniel's recent rebellious actions clearly scream silently for attention? Hopefully that was just one moment in time; perhaps I won't see him again and this craziness will fade...*

Leading the hound outside in the courtyard, the moon reflected peaceably in the softly babbling waters. Mourning doves cooed musically as the crisp scents of autumn blew gently around her. She closed her eyes as she took in the peace, trying to adhere it to the chaos and turmoil she silently struggled with deep in her heart.

The moment seemed frozen in time yet passed all too quickly. Once Sammy finished her business, Johanna led her back through the silent throne room and back up the stairs to their quarters. Shuffling back to their room, she was about to return to bed when a soft knock resounded on the door.

"Who is it?" she whispered through the frame.

"Nicholas has asked for us to meet him in his chambers," Nate's voice grumbled back to her. Johanna opened the door and returned the glare he bore her. Daniel sensed the activity and sat up, rubbing his eyes. "I realize it's early but saw you were already up. Besides, we need to talk!"

"Daniel, why don't you go back to sleep and..." Johanna began to turn back to her waking son.

"No, he wants to see all of us—including him," Nate instructed, pushing past her. "What's wrong with you, anyway?! Last night, you didn't even say goodnight to me or anything! We haven't spoken in days!"

"It's nothing, Nate," Johanna sniffed, still ruminating. "Nothing. Now is hardly the time or place."

"Nothing?!" he pressed. "Johanna, we haven't spent any time alone together since we got here. I understand that we may become permanent residents, and while that's a lot for all of us to take in, shouldn't that bring us closer together, not push us apart?"

"You're right," she mumbled, indifferent and laden with exhaustion. "As usual, you are right. I'm just tired, and I'm not sleeping well here. I think this whole ordeal is just getting to me now."

"Yeah, well, that isn't all my fault!" he spat, pushing past her again back into the hallway. Daniel stirred and hastily assembled his clothes, glancing uncomfortably at the arguing pair. Nate clearly had prepared for this confrontation; "Stop taking it all out on me, will you? We're supposed to be a team here!"

"Fine! Let's just drop it for now!" Johanna quipped as she and Nate exchanged heated glares until she dismissed him with a wave of her hand. "I'll get Daniel up and we'll head up together as soon as he's ready!"

"Whatever!" he muttered as he sauntered off, shaking his head before turning back to face her halfway down the hall. "Don't ever say I didn't try! You can't ignore me forever; this passive-aggressive crap you pull has got to stop! You need to decide one way or the other! I can't be the only one to keep trying here!"

"Danny, get dressed," she sighed, tamping down the anger welling up within her even as Nate ascended the tower steps, vanishing up the corridor. "We're needed upstairs."

Daniel dressed quickly, and they joined Kevin and Javier, already ascending the winding staircase of the Wizard's Tower. As they filed into the tower room together, Nicholas stood at the center, overshadowing the large table below a flickering lamp. Maps spilled aimlessly off the table, and a warming fire in the corner of the room took the damp chill out of the air. Fresh muffins and fruit along with a pot of steaming scented tea added a spicy aroma to the room, heavily ladened with a background smell of old leather tomes and book bindings.

"Good morning to you all!" The grand master welcomed them as they entered, standing beside a tall, dark brooding shape. "I'm sorry for waking you so early but it was important. I believe you all remember my protégé; he joins us today!"

"Aros!" the group exclaimed in a simultaneous warm greeting. The dark-bearded wizard stepped into the light, grinning at their surprise.

"Good to see you all again; glad you remember me!" the younger wizard chuckled as he gestured to the table. "Help yourselves to some breakfast and Myrenth tea; it should help wake you. Trust me, with what we'll be talking about, you're going to need it!"

"Again, I apologize for such an early rising, but there's no easy way to go about this," the grand master gently interrupted. "As I mentioned to Johanna last night, I fear all of you have been plunged into something much bigger than yourselves. My efforts to conceal you here have become more difficult; partially from others observing you in public, yet also through no fault of your own. Circumstances now have dictated we must take a new direction!"

"We've at least discovered *why* you are here," Aros clarified with a grimace in agreement. "You seem to have fallen prey to a test at a recruitment effort of sorts. Our order has become a dying breed these days and is not the thriving wizard's order of old."

"Most of what's left of the order stays in the Mondlichtberg, still training in the old ways," Nicholas added. "The senior council members are the only ones capable of opening an artificial Shimmering between your world and ours. The idea was proposed once while I was still on the council; to pull individuals in from other worlds to assist in replenishing our numbers. The idea was dismissed long ago, but I'm almost certain it's been revived, and I'm sure that's what has happened with you here and now."

"That's not particularly ethical by your standards, is it?" Johanna reflected.

"No, it is not," Aros agreed with chagrin. "However, in uncovering *how* you got here, we may have uncovered a possible method to return you to your home."

"Okay!" Nate breathed, rubbing his hands together in anticipation. "Now we're talking!"

"There are two different magical categories employed by our order," Grand Master Nicholas explained. "Spiritual, which takes great practice and discipline. We channel and focus this through talismans, but ultimately, this is assembled outside of ourselves and we internalize it from there. Another is innate ability, such as the abilities you have inherited and are examples of what you are experiencing. When you passed through the Shimmering, innate power is what infused itself within you. Others who exhibit innate power inherit it through their genealogy, such as the case with Princess Serina."

"What about an 'Emerald Fire'?" Daniel mumbled more to himself than to anyone else. He yawned and shook his head, sleep stupor still gripping his mind.

"That is a very new and specific power that falls under the category of spiritual magic," Grand Master Nicholas stated, arching a suspicious eyebrow. "It's mostly utilized in Urocia but not one that our order readily embraces, since its origins are rather unexplored and not fully vetted."

"So, which one of these is what brought us here?" Javier impatiently interjected.

"We believe that neither of these are powerful enough to open such a Shimmering by themselves," Aros concluded. "To *open* a Shimmering, you need something more raw and basic in nature; something not immediately apparent unless it flares the way it did when you arrived."

"I'm not following," Nate muttered, digging into the muffins and fruit, handing several around the table to the others.

"Before we left Levens, Aros directed me to consider a third magic that has long been forgotten," Nicholas elaborated. "Elemental magic infuses all of nature and therefore blends itself into all energy around it. We don't always perceive it because it's around us all the time, operating in a background hum of sorts unless it spikes abnormally into view and perception, such as during a Shimmering event."

"I suggested Nicholas investigate *elemental* magic because I too sensed that strange surge of natural elemental power around the time of your arrival!" Aros reminded them. "I had already begun deeper research on elemental powers when I was called to Mondlichtberg. While I was there, I sensed a great deal of residual elemental traces around the Wizard's Tower. When I asked about it, I was told to inquire no further."

"The elves and other ancient beings were masters of elemental magic, but frankly, most of the derivatives were lost with their disappearance," Nicholas confirmed. "Without the elves for guidance, our order simply omitted it from our repertoires. It's older and less refined, thereby more volatile if not handled properly. We hardly utilize it anymore other than for the simplest purposes; it never occurred to anyone to use it for something as complex as the Shimmering."

"So how would that be utilized for transportation through this 'Shimmering'?" Kevin queried.

"Long ago, the ancient ones worked with the elves to develop talismans to harness the unpredictable nature of elemental power," Aros explained. "They needed to be infused with the power of seeds from the Moleifera tree."

"Pardon, a what tree?" Nate squinted. "I've heard this name before but have yet to have a Moleifera tree pointed out to me."

"Nor will you ever; they are extinct," Aros confirmed. "The seeds from this tree were heavily saturated with elemental magic but could contain the erratic nature of this power. The last of the Moleifera died out long ago within the capital city of Kallah, deep inside the lost empire of Charzera. However, the handiwork done by the ancient beings that lived in the time of the Moleifera trees remains. They utilized specific elements from the trees to create talismans, disguised and forged as swords. They were dispersed and forgotten long ago when the need for them vanished, along with their creators."

"Earth, much like the soil itself, brown in color yet rich with life, hidden somewhere in the southwest wilds or Carthen region; somewhere people don't go," Grand Master Nicholas began methodically pointing to locations on the map with each mention. "Water, a sapphire-blue sword hidden near the shores of the ocean. Air, blowing through the ancient sea of golden grass and fields of flax and corn. Since Charzera's destruction long ago, that extinct kingdom's land is now desert, but that sword's appearance would still likely be. Fire, a crimson sword in the volcanic wastelands of the northeast, nearest to the cursed lands, where the earth's blood flows red in liquid fire. This is also nearest the cursed lands, where the practitioners of the Ghostly Death Fire once cast their spells of darkness!"

"You don't think any would be *inside* the cursed lands, do you?" Johanna whispered, dreading the potential, remembering the shade she had seen in the grand master's vision.

"No, these items were lost and then scattered long before Naehfalar's rise to power, and only the fire sword is even near their borders, but not within," he assured her. "They were displaced to prevent anyone from obtaining them and forgotten even before the great war. Much of their history was lost to those wars and the talismans forgotten."

"That's still a lot of land you're pointing to," Nate scoffed grimly. "I'm not sure I like where this is going."

"It is indeed!" Nicholas stopped, turning to them and clapping his hands together. "Nevertheless, these are the items that would possess the energy and the means necessary to open a Shimmering into your world!"

"Do you think that's how we got here?" Johanna asked. "Maybe someone on your Wizard's Council has already retrieved them?"

"The Grand Master Council's recent behavior leads me to believe that is not the case," the elder wizard answered. "Such a discovery would have been impossible to keep a secret as these were items of tremendous power concentration. I can assure you, the Order of the Moon has something else at their disposal. I'm certain it is elemental in nature, but the timing and chaotic aspect of this whole affair lead me to believe it's something from Urocia. They have often expressed their covetous desire for such power. However, we know their mishandling of something with this magnitude would likely result in anything ranging from unpredictable to even disastrous consequences."

"Yes, that makes sense," Aros agreed. "Grand Master Encara's close dealings with the Order of Etoilenoir, alongside his taking most of the advisory with him, would seem to indicate that they have something beyond their understanding or ability to properly manage. Perhaps they've retained some remnant of Moleifera seeds or something to that effect; it's impossible to know without their admission."

"In either case, that makes our mission to find these relics all the more important." Nicholas glowered. "Our order's desperation for recruits may have put them at a disadvantage with this new Order of Etoilenoir and ultimately compromised their integrity."

"So, neither would agree to help send us back," Johanna sighed unhappily.

"No, I'm afraid not, my dear; especially since they brought you here intentionally," Nicholas exhaled. "That is why I haven't brought you before them. I was naïve to ever believe their silence was simply tabling our disagreements over more aggressive recruitment efforts; they simply moved ahead without me, circumventing my approval in methodologies I would have never condoned. In fact, based on what I remember from our old arguments, they may even try to bring more of your people here, and soon."

"So how are you going to get these swords?" Kevin asked.

"We cannot," Nicholas sighed as he closed his eyes, reducing his voice to a whisper that could scarcely be heard above the crackling fire. "It has to be you."

"What?!" Javier exploded angrily. "Why us? How are we supposed to find these swords when we are complete strangers here to begin with? Hell, we don't even know where we are now! We only found you by blind luck!"

"Their dormant elemental magic makes them impossible for us to sense," Aros gently explained. "Only those who have never sensed elemental magic before will be able to detect them at all. Our lands are saturated with it and have been for all times. We are simply unable to discern them while they sleep until they flare or are brought to life by a user."

"Not only are we unable to sense them, but they also cannot be wielded by anyone tainted with spiritual magic." Nicholas lowered his voice at this point. "They can only be used or even detected by someone such as yourselves who will be sensitive to their proximities and their nuances. Simply put, we wizards and other magic users will be blind to them and unable to see or utilize them."

"That's why it has to be us," Johanna acknowledged in bitter understanding. "Only we can sense these items, in theory."

"Yes, in theory," Aros sighed. "We thought of pressuring the council openly to return you using the means they have, but frankly, even if they agreed to it, there's no confidence in their ability to return you properly. While the Shimmering event was intentional, your arrival through it may have still been accidental."

"So, these swords are still the best shot we have at getting back,"

Kevin confirmed, nodding thoughtfully. "They are more powerful and more accurate than what the council has?"

"While correct, always remember that they are not truly swords, but rather *talismans* that *appear as* swords," Nicholas confirmed. "They've been overlooked over all these centuries because people with innate power are not common to begin with. The few that have it are quickly recruited into the wizard's order and exposed to other powers, swiftly diluting their ability to sense these talismans. That is why they have remained hidden and forgotten all this time."

"Well, wait a minute," Javier began. "You haven't answered my question! How are we supposed to find these items if they are lost?"

"You will sense their presence even in a dormant state," Nicholas assured them. "My understanding is that *you* will *know* when they are close, much the same way I can sense each of you when you utilize your innate abilities."

"Just like that, huh?" Javier scoffed. "We're supposed to wander around looking for these swords until our gut tells us they're close?! What guarantee do we have that will even work!"

"None. I've offered no guarantees, my friend," Nicholas stated bitterly. "What you are suggesting is not far off the mark, and I cannot blame you for your skepticism. We know their general vicinity from the ancient archives but cannot fully locate them without someone untainted by other magic and time. Now that you're here, I do believe they can be found!"

"Well, isn't that convenient!" Nate muttered angrily. "I can't believe that sending us into the unknown on a wild goose chase is your answer! Surely there's another way? We are completely unprepared and know nothing of what is out there!"

"Indeed, that is true," Nicholas sighed. "The alternative is that you accept permanent residency here, as I have done. The secret of where you are from and who you are spreads even now. The council will demand your delivery, and I fear other players from nearby kingdoms will also come for you. Simply put, I will be unable to protect you in the long term. A choice must be made, or one will be made for you; most likely outside of my realm of influence."

"I thought you were our Advocate!" Johanna exclaimed. "How does sending us away help us? Where would we even start?"

"I can no longer simply remain your Advocate here, in this geographic location," Nicholas whispered. "I'm now tied to Tyrna, as with you and your innate abilities becoming common knowledge, I can no longer effectively protect you in this city. I have, in essence, secured the best means to continue my Advocacy for you, and I trust those I shall send to accompany you with my very life!"

"Nate, you and Johanna will come with me to Urocia and make a team of six," Aros gently interrupted to explain the matter further. "I will personally see to your protection and resume the duty of Nicholas's Advocacy. We will search Urocia under the guise of finding a new home for you. Since your secret is out already with many of the Urocians, we should be welcomed there under those conditions. I'm certain they'd relish the idea of receiving outsiders with potential new talents and technology to add to their ranks. The Wizard's Council won't be happy about this, but there already exists a connection between the council and Urocian interests; I may not fully understand it, but I believe a Urocian welcome will keep the council silent and at bay for a time."

"Isn't that a war zone?" Nate laughed in exasperation. "Why would we look for a home there? Who would believe it?"

"The Urocians have the upper hand in that war," Nicholas interjected. "They are technically our allies, and we will be cautious to avoid the front. I've secured a guide who won't know of our quest but will be most familiar with the lands and invested in your safety. He will steer you clear of the heaviest fighting in the far northeast."

"You're not referring to Sir Caspin, are you?" Nate winced.

"No, Lord Emelien of Urocia is passing through Tyrna on business," Nicholas confirmed. "He's of a charitable nature and has already expressed a desire to help. I took the liberty last night of confiding to him that you all may be looking for new homesteads. Allow me to emphasize, though, that he does not know, nor should he know, of your search for the swords."

Johanna's eyes widened, and her heart skipped a beat at the mention of Lord Emelien's name, but she quickly swallowed the notion for flights of fancy. Stakes were simply too high to entertain fantasy interludes or even worry about personal relationships when their circumstances seemed on the brink of drastically changing.

"So, if Lord Emelien is helping Mom and Nate, will Sir Caspin and Sottis be involved with this too?" Daniel swallowed hard as doubt flooded through him. Images of Sottis, Caspin and Lord Emelien talking in private resounded in his mind. "I think they're friends with each other, all from that same kingdom."

"Is something wrong with them?" Nate pressed. "Maybe we shouldn't keep company with this Lord Emelien?"

"I don't have a reason to distrust him to at least escort you safely to Urocia," Nicholas assured. "His loyalties and agendas are centered around his house's standings in their capital of Latana. You will be a unique distraction and opportunity to further his standing there, away from Tyrna and the Wizard's Council."

"What about the other two?" Aros muttered.

"I think it best we do not involve either of them," Nicholas stated. "I have plans to speak with Sir Caspin to further determine where he stands in all of this. However, if you should happen upon Sottis, please notify me immediately."

"Nicholas was assaulted by Sottis recently," Aros revealed the grim news in a whisper, eliciting an audible gasp from around the room. "We are trying to determine if it was an official directive from Order of the Moon or if he was acting on behalf of another power broker. The point is, in either case, he was set free and clearly not acting on his own. For now, I can surmise that the council can no longer be trusted, and Nicholas won't be able to protect you here so close to their influence."

"Assaulted?!" Johanna gasped. "How?!"

"I handled the situation and was uninjured from it, other than my pride," Nicholas grumbled, unwilling to say more. "Let's just leave it at that; we had a disagreement over your futures, but we resolved it. Others like him may already be aware of you and may not have your best interests at heart!"

Daniel perked up at that revelation, almost as if to ask a question, when Nate interjected into the conversation, leaving the lad unsure whether or not to speak.

"So, by spreading out, we will actually be better off," Nate acknowledged with a sigh. The news hung like a shroud over the group as they contemplated their next steps. "I'm happy that at least Aros will watch over us, but what about the others?"

"Javier and Kevin will travel south on Long Lake with another six of my handpicked associates," Nicholas announced. "They are wilderness rangers, and I trust them equally as I would Aros and have known them all for many years. I will introduce you all shortly after breakfast."

"Hardly equal to a wizard," Javier miffed.

"My young friend, the choices I've made for each of your parties are most uniquely suited for where you are going," the grand master assured, placing a comforting hand on his shoulder. "Your company is quite capable and particularly gifted, suited for where you are going."

"What about me?" chimed in Daniel. "You didn't say anything about my involvement!"

"No need," Johanna shushed. "You can ride with us to—"

"I have other plans for you, my fine young friend," Nicholas interrupted gently as he turned to Daniel. "The search for the swords is in pairs to increase the chances of success; no more, no less. I have need of your special talents here."

"Now wait a damned minute," Johanna growled, the color draining from her face as her hands began to shake. "I'm not leaving my son here alone! You just said it was more dangerous to stay here!"

"I can effectively guard one person better than I can five," Nicholas explained, sensing Johanna's apprehension. "Your son will be kept safe, I promise you. King Faund, Father Jaramillo and I will advocate together and look closely after him. In the meantime, he will be my eyes and ears; I have need of his specialized abilities."

"Now hang on, Johanna's got a point," Nate stated, tamping down a sudden flare of his own rage as his protective nature took hold. "I know Daniel's emerging into a capable young man, but he's never been separated from me or his mother!"

"Why can't I stay then?" Johanna interjected heatedly. "Or send him with us and let Aros train him! I am his mother, for goodness' sake! I will not have this!"

"I cannot emphasize enough how important it is that you accompany this quest," Nicholas sighed with a gesture of helplessness on the matter. "I thought about this very deliberately, especially after his flight last night. You need to trust me on this, Johanna; your son is best served here in both safety and discretion. Your own safety and success will also be best served by this arrangement. I am sorry, but some of this you are going to have to accept on faith; your best interests are all served in this way!"

Johanna was at a loss for words and hugged Daniel close. Her mind raced, looking for an alternative that the wizard may have overlooked, yet she could think of none.

"Rememberm your actual purpose is still a secret, even as you set out," Nicholas reminded them. "No one other than your guardians must know of your search. We will make it very clear and public that you all are looking to start new lives with new homes; that will be your cover. Even if your abilities and identities become known, your search for the swords must remain a closely guarded secret!"

"You're sure your wizard's order won't help us?" Johanna whispered. "You said to take this on faith, but is there no one there you can trust?"

"I'm sorry, but I agree with Nicholas on this," Aros interposed. "Sottis's attack has proven that the council cannot be trusted in this matter; they are either behind it or incapable of preventing what's behind it. We dare not share more with you because others, including the council, may have a way of extracting information from you without even speaking to you about it."

"What do we do when we find the swords?" asked Nate slowly, still unconvinced.

"Retrieve them and nothing else!" Nicholas emphasized resolutely, his eyes widening to drive the point home. "You and your innate magic can detect the swords, but you have no training or knowledge about them; in fact, there are few that do. Although you will have the ability to detect them, I cannot foresee what the consequences of awakening them would be. We should meet here again with all present and accounted for, then we can proceed carefully once we have all the talismans in hand."

"Nothing like a bit of field testing, eh?" Javier elbowed Nate with a wink.

"That's exactly what I am trying to avoid!" Nicholas exhaled. "They could be volatile, even dangerous if mishandled. Our histories only record their existence; all knowledge around their abilities has been lost over time."

"Is there no one else who can do this?" Johanna choked in exasperation. "I've never left my son; never! Now you're sending us after dangerous items in dangerous places, leaving my son here alone?!"

"He's not going to be alone; Grand Master Nicholas and his people will be looking after him," Nate whispered in realization, even as he glared at the wizard in doubt. Grasping her closely, he pressed the matter further. "We must trust our Advocate!"

"Nate is quite right on this, Johanna. If there were another way, my dear, believe me that I would employ it immediately," Nicholas assured her grimly. "I swear to you, I will continue to advocate for Daniel as if he were my very own. I continue to advocate for you all, even from afar and through those I trust most closely. You had best prepare for your departure and say your goodbyes. Say nothing to anyone else of our plans; for now, this is just between us!"

As the group ambled down the stairway to their quarters, the grand master grasped his protégé by the arm, holding him back.

"Something else?" Aros eyed his former master warily.

"We must not even acknowledge that you are here; I need everyone outside of our circle to believe you are still in Levens," Grand Master Nicholas whispered. "I suspect your whereabouts will be quickly discovered upon your arrival in Latana. Once that happens, I fear it will set things in motion we have not yet anticipated."

"Understood," Aros acknowledged with a scowl. "Was there something else?"

"Sottis is still loose," the former grand master stated simply. "I don't know how or when he was freed, but none of the guards I tasked with his incarceration seem to know anything about it. I suspect more than one accomplice may be involved, which leads me to believe Sottis may only be a small part in this bigger scheme."

"Are you in any danger?" Aros whispered.

"Hardly, for the moment," Nicholas scoffed. "He'll likely avoid me if he hasn't left the city already, which would be his wiser course of action at this juncture. However, until I verify exactly who I can trust and how far that trust extends, your quest will take Nate and Johanna into the unknown. You must be vigilant to their well-being since you will be the extension of my Advocacy. This will be unanticipated by the council, Sottis or any of their cohorts. If there are nefarious plans afoot, that at least will put us on even ground with our opponents!"

"If that is indeed the case, we may yet gain the upper hand," Aros sighed in agreement. "Well then, may our fortunes follow our bold action!"

"I'll send food and drink up here to you, but please remain out of sight for the time being," Nicholas ordered, patting his protégé on the shoulder. "The longer you stay hidden and out of the picture, the further ahead in this game we will be. I'll head downstairs to complete our arrangements."

As Nicholas departed, he closed the door softly behind him and descended the winding stairwell. Tapping his staff softly with each stride, he passed the residential quarters and emerged into the throne room.

The grand master paused when he saw Sir Caspin leaning up casually against one of the stone columns in the shadows, waiting for him.

"Greetings, Grand Master!" Sir Caspin hailed as he stood erect, bowing as Nicholas approached. "I understand you were looking for me earlier?"

"Indeed, I was! Greetings, Sir Caspin!" Nicholas shook his hand warmly. "I'd like to thank you for your time showing the outsiders around the capital while I was otherwise indisposed."

"It was my pleasure to do so, Grand Master!" The captain smiled agreeably. "I found them intriguing and attentive! They make me appreciate what I've previously taken for granted in my role here as I showed them around Tyrna."

"Indeed, they are intriguing, which is what I wanted to talk to you about." Nicholas's smile faded. "I would like to know more about your interest in the boy, Daniel. I noticed you speaking with him on occasion in private and away from the others."

"Ah, yes, Daniel reminds me of me when I was young," the captain of the guard reflected, a sudden look of sadness overcoming his face. "He's alone in a new world, with an overbearing mother and without someone to help point out the traps and pitfalls."

"I thank you for your personal concern in that matter," Nicholas stated tactfully. "However, I would caution you against becoming too attached; it may not be in the best interests for you or the boy."

"Oh, come now, Grand Master," Sir Caspin chided. "Surely the occasional ale and treating the young man to a glimpse of an independent future as a man is just as much in his interest as showing him how to navigate the city!"

"I've been discussing their situation with the Wizard's Council," the wizard explained. "You see, we've come to an agreement that they don't belong here, and we will be returning them to Mondlichtberg and subsequently, their home."

"Really? When?" The captain's face darkened, and his voice betrayed a slight strain of surprise. "You've spoken directly to the council about this?"

"Oh, yes, and in great length, just last evening!" Nicholas watched the captain's face closely as he spun the lie. "Grand Master Yamaro has found a way to reverse their coming; no easy feat, I can tell you that! Since my position as Advocate for them will be coming to an end, your participation in assisting me with that role is also ending. You may resume full attention to the captain of the guard at this time!"

"The council agreed to this?" Sir Caspin's eyes narrowed as a momentary flash of anger passed through him. "I had understood that return was not possible for them after the council made such an effort to bring them in the first place..." He drifted off, muttering to himself and turning away as if having said more than he had intended.

"Go on—you were saying?" Nicholas probed gently before waving his hand dismissively to the issue. "You seemed surprised, especially in the matters of wizards. First the king's financial meetings and now the Wizard's Council? I do hope you aren't spreading yourself too thin; I would have imagined the news would come as a relief for you!"

"King Faund demands my presence in the financial matters of Tyrna!" Sir Caspin balked. "Are you questioning his judgment on that matter?"

"Not at all!" Nicholas sighed with a pleasant smile. "I respect the king's authority in this matter, just as I respect the Wizard's Council's authority in the matter of the newcomers! Since you have been involved with both lately, much to my appreciation and admiration, I'm merely serving to inform you. I do this to conclude our cooperation, open respect and communication around these newcomers!"

"Indeed." Sir Caspin grimaced, unwilling to say more on the topic. "If there's nothing further, then I shall take my leave."

The captain spun and departed abruptly down the hallway.

"Now, where could you be off to in such a hurry, I wonder?" Nicholas mumbled smugly to himself, watching him go.

The captain's knowledge of both matters of the kingdom and the wizard's order had revealed the captain of the guard had far more involvement in affairs well beyond that of his simple title. Their discussion indicated Sir Caspin's involvement not only involved the king of Tyrna but even the Wizard's Council itself, although to what extent, Nicholas could not be sure.

At least Lord Emelien's dealings with Sir Caspin appeared superficial at best. The Urocian lord's volunteering to take the group to a potential new homestead in Latana seemed aptly timed to separate him and his influence from Tyrna's captain of the guard. Lord Emelien would be less familiar with the newcomers' situation and likely more focused on Urocian agendas.

Nicholas knew he had to move quickly, though; the lie he had just spun to Sir Caspin would be discovered before too long. Once the council discovered he wasn't sending the newcomers to them after all, more would certainly be revealed.

Chapter 21

Departure

By late morning, everyone had discreetly packed their bags and met the grand master at the castle's main entrance. Hints of dawn had scarcely crested the ridgelines of Mount Tyrna when Nicholas led them out behind the courtyard fountain to a secret entrance, beneath the stone steps for the parapets of the inner wall. Instead of following the steps up, he produced a small key from his white robes, inserting it into a hidden crevice.

With an audible creak and groan, a narrow doorway opened in the stone. Muttering a few words aloud, his staff glowed with power, lighting the way as they followed him into a long and dark corridor, set deep within the cold grey wall. Light from the outside rapidly faded behind them as the heavy stone door slid back into place, leaving only the glow from the wizard's staff to light the way. Once the door closed behind them, he cleared his throat in the dusty passageway to speak.

"Follow closely now, you mustn't get lost in here or you'll never be found again!" the wizard explained ominously. "We go through a series of underground passageways that connect the royal palace to the outside of the city. I've secured a quiet location, just outside of the city's wall along the south end. From here, we go through the city's conjunction of the inner and outer walls."

Other than the dull scuffling of their feet, no sound could be heard in the empty cavern-like passageways. They brushed aside the occasional cobwebs; however, nothing ever seemed to frequent these tunnels. Cold yet dry, the endless expanse of the intricate stone maze stretched in every direction, some passageways massive while others narrow.

"These corridors were created for maintenance and emergencies. They were ways to enter and leave the city without the use of the main gate," Grand Master Nicholas stated, his voice muffled in the tomblike atmosphere. "Stay close; we're nearly there!"

Stymied by the immensity of it all, the newcomers clustered behind the wizard, who appeared nonchalant as he confidently strode ahead, seemingly completely assured as to where they were headed. Eventually, the characteristics of the stone changed from round grey to red brick, yet the passageway seemed to dead end after a turn into a long, nondescript corridor.

Just when the newcomers began to sense a mutual apprehension, Nicholas pressed on the stone wall, his hands aligned in a strange pattern. The massive wall seemed to swing effortlessly away, and they emerged into blinding daylight through the southern base of the outer wall. A friendly local farmer stood outside, and he greeted the grand master, beckoning them forth.

As they emerged, the doorway slid silently shut again behind them, sealing off as if it had never been. The retired wizard led the newcomers closer to a quaint barn, where mules grazed peacefully on hay. The lean farmer's wispy white hair danced sparsely on his head as he resumed his mundane duties, loading bales of hay atop a modest cart for his goats and mules.

As their eyesight adjusted, they could see other farmers and carts mulling through the fields in the distance as gentle warm breezes caressed the fall harvest, spreading the smells of tilled earth and dry-cut grain throughout the wide valley.

Aros emerged quietly from the rickety wooden barn, tapping the elderly farmer on his shoulder and then handing him a bag of coins. The man grinned to Aros's satisfaction before returning to his hay bales.

"There! That's settled," Aros exhaled as he approached. "As we discussed, I will be accompanying Nate and Johanna to Urocia. However, before we begin, I have a gift to share with you."

Motioning to the barn at the edge of the fenced enclosure, four horses emerged, towing a rather large, covered wagon. Driving the wagon, a gruff-looking middle-aged man in rider's garb coaxed the horses forth from the barn's shadow. The man's dark hair and weathered skin indicated he was someone who was accustomed to spending most of his time outdoors.

As the driver brought the wagon to a stop in front of the group, Aros took hold of the canvas, and with a dramatic tug, he flung aside the loosed cloth to behold their long-lost Jeep. The glass glistened as a new vehicle would, as did the speckled brown paint and body. All signs of wear had vanished as if nothing had happened to it.

"How..." Nate gasped alongside the other members of the company, all equally shocked. He stood and ran a shaky hand alongside the vehicle as if for the first time.

"One of my special innate talents," Aros announced with pride as he caressed the automobile like a newfound love. "You see, I am obsessed with the sciences and items from your world; they are indeed fascinating to me. I had your beastless carriage brought back to Tyrna with me after I studied it."

"Studied it?!" Javier laughed. "You fixed it!"

"Well, specifically, I probed it," the wizard clarified. "I must confess, although I can identify how it is assembled, I do not know how to operate it. What I found is that it is composed of a multitude of polymers, metals and glass. I discovered channels within the structure made of conduits through which puzzling liquids flow, for which purpose I know not. I simply reproduced it all and repaired what was broken."

"The windows, too?" Johanna shook her head, unbelieving. "It's incredible!"

"Unbelievable!" Nate gasped as he opened the door. The Jeep looked to him like the day he had bought it from the dealer back home. "Okay, but how did you clean it?"

"That took simple elbow grease and the hands of our squires," Aros admitted haughtily. "It should run; can you make it do so?"

Nate climbed into the driver's seat, and the keys were still in the ignition where he had left them. He glanced back at Aros, still beaming with pride, waiting for the fruits of his labors in excited anticipation.

"Not yet." Nate smiled, setting the parking brake and stepping back out of the vehicle.

"What's wrong?" Aros asked.

"Go ahead and do the honors!" Nate beamed as he stretched out and dropped the keys into Aros's hand. "You fixed it; make it start!"

"Well, I examined the functionality back in Levens, but I didn't want to try the whole process without you being there," Aros mumbled. The proud wizard nearly dropped the keys as if they were on fire and too hot to hold, fumbling with them in excitement. Nate patiently directed him to sit in the driver's seat, guiding him into the vehicle. When the wizard inserted the key into the ignition and nothing happened, he glanced briefly at Nate.

"Reach out with your power and watch the mechanism work," Nate encouraged. "I think that will reveal to you the aspects of the vehicle you didn't see before."

"I can't believe I'm taking magic advice from someone who's not even familiar with the practice," Aros mused, yet he eagerly rolled his eyes back as his hands glowed.

"Just turn the key, Aros," Nate laughed. The wizard took a deep breath, and after concentrating, he turned the key.

The Jeep backfired with a loud pop, sending fowl and bystanders scattering. Even a startled Aros jumped, hitting his head on the roof. Nate laughed so hard he could barely speak as he directed Aros to pump the accelerator twice before trying it again.

A red-faced Aros did so, and this time, it worked! As the Jeep rumbled to life, the engine purred as if new, yet Nate's face quickly fell.

"Looks like we're still low on fuel," Nate stated, reaching in front of the brawny wizard and tapping the fuel gauge. "That 'E' on the gauge indicates we won't be going very far. We need that gauge to read 'F,' and I don't know where we are going to get gasoline."

"I surmised as much," Aros stated smoothly, regaining his composure. He smiled knowingly and pointed at the hatchback behind them. "Those empty cans in the back—is that what those are for? They contain the same liquid that this 'gauge' seems to measure in a tank under the carriage."

"Yes," Nate acknowledged. "But as you said, they are mostly empty."

"This time, allow me to surprise you!" Aros quipped as he stepped out around to the back of the Jeep and opened the hatchback. He pulled a gas can from the back and poured a cup full of gasoline into his hands. Closing his eyes in concentration, his hands again glowed briefly as he examined the contents.

Shaking his hands off, he walked over to the watering trough next to the feeding livestock. He plucked some grass and threw it in, added horse manure and dirt before mixing it all. He reached into the horses' water trough, scraping off bits of algae and stirring it in the mix with his staff.

Satisfied that the mix was sufficient, he dipped his hands into the water. Aros could see the molecules of gasoline, their structure and their substance. For a moment, nothing happened. Then, the water around Aros's hands began to softly glow. He could feel the interaction occurring as he willed it forth, spreading from his hands until it filled the entire trough, molecular bonds shifting, breaking and reassembling.

Steam rose from the bubbling surface, and the light filling the trough pulsed several times before finally fading. The pungent smell of gasoline wafted in strong vapors as everyone stood back.

"There," the younger wizard proudly proclaimed in satisfaction. "Fill your metal beast and your cans and let's be on our way!"

"Our own portable gas station!" Nate exclaimed, bursting into laughter. "That's fantastic!"

"Aw, man!" Javier exclaimed. "They get the Jeep, and we're on foot?"

"Where we're going, even your metal beast would have difficulty," declared the gruff driver, stepping down from the wagon. "Allow me to introduce myself. My name is Dex. This metal beast of yours will best serve you in the long, rolling plains of Urocia. We will be deep in the forests and wilds around Long Lake, where wide roads are few and obstacles are many."

Dex walked up from behind the covered wagon and began removing the towing harnesses from the horses. His rich brown beard gave him the tough appearance of a mountain man, but his eyes glinted with friendly knowledge he was happy to share.

"Dex, huh?" Javier viewed the man skeptically. "Are you a wizard too?"

"Hardly," Dex laughed dryly, cutting right to the chase. "Tracker, huntsman and special guard for Tyrna's interests in the wilds. However, for your quest in the west, I will be your leader."

"Just you?" Javier countered skeptically. "No offense, but I hardly think Micker and I will do very well with only one guy leading us into the unknown!"

"Allow me to introduce you to the rest of our troupe," Dex announced. He turned and whistled back to the barn, and nine other men emerged. Five joined him in adding riding saddles to the steeds. They waved in turn while Dex introduced each of them.

"I'm Warley," the dark-haired guy introduced himself. He seemed a younger and thinner version of Dex, striding forth with purpose, sporting a moustache instead of a beard. He extended his hand, and his grip was iron, even as he gestured to his companion. He was accompanied by an even younger man, clean-shaven with blond hair cascading down his shoulders. "This one's Fliegel!"

"Hey-ho, Warley!" Fliegel exclaimed. Both young and enthusiastic, they greeted Javier and Kevin as fellow youths as if on a sports team.

Clapping each other on the back and grinning, they exchanged hand-shakes. "Give a guy a chance to speak!"

Javier laughed at the exchange as another two approached more cautiously, their gaits swaying more than the others. His smile formed a quick "O" of astonishment on his lips. *Cat-people!*

"Rwawl, pleased to meet you! I'm Crisken," the orange-and-white-furred feline exclaimed, green eyes agleam with curiosity as he approached Kevin first. "Brythen won't mind if I speak for him; he just finished eating!"

Brythen clearly had just taken a bite of jerky and was mid-chewing with a mouthful, still swallowing as they approached. His jet-black fur shone in the sun, and his coat sparkled and rippled as he moved.

Kevin shook their hands, amazed at how paw-like they seemed to be yet how they still retained actual fingers, albeit stubby and short. Their fur felt soft and well preened, yet they hid what clearly were sharpened claws, retracted, stowed and out of sight for their civil discourse now underway.

Both Carthenians observed the newcomers with typical slitted green eyes, sparkling with inquisitiveness. Both remained friendly yet approached them cautiously as outsiders. Spotlessly well-groomed, clean, yet still feral, they retained a pleasant yet faint aroma of spice-like cinnamon on their fur.

"This one is Davyn," Dex introduced with a grin, pointing at a stocky albino man emerging from inside the barn. The muscular man muttered a gruff greeting when introduced, waving briefly with a thick, muscular hand. "He doesn't say much, but he knows the land well for our journey west!"

Built like an ox and balding, Davyn motioned Dex over, conversing quietly with him in earnest. Seemingly apprehensive, the albino seemed focused on some unspoken detail while Dex exuded a reas-suring confidence. Javier noted a massive broad sword strapped to the side of the albino's horse, allaying any doubts that this man would be just as physically formidable as their leader if ever needed.

Javier followed Kevin's lead and began helping Warley load the saddlebags with the supplies Fliegel handed to him. The other four men sauntered over to Aros and introduced themselves in turn to Johanna and Nate.

"Allow me to present myself; my name is Crand," a tall, dark stranger stated with a warm voice as he strode to the forefront from behind the Jeep. He bowed low with a smile, his almond skin and warm eyes showing that he too was no stranger to the sun. "I'll be most familiar with the lands east of here to help navigate the lands and customs between the civilized and uncivilized."

"I suppose that means you'll be in our group," Johanna surmised. Although he looked similar in age to Nate, he had a youthful voice and a sweet smile that gave Johanna the impression he was closer to Javier or Kevin in age despite his weathered appearance. "You all seem so young!"

"Do not let our youthful appearance deceive you, my lady," Fliegel admonished her playfully. "We may look young, but we are far from inexperienced!"

"My bright and brash companion is quite correct!" Crand laughed with gentle mirth. "He is from Tyrna but knows the wild lands west of here quite extensively. Myself, I was born and raised in a semi-arid region east of here, where my family farmed before the historic blight hit our lands. We were forced west, where I met up with my fellow trackers. All of us retain knowledge of our homelands, lands we will all be traveling to soon!"

"Yeah, we all spent a lot of time together at the Tracker's Guild," Davyn grumbled in agreement as Lord Emelien approached from another side of the stable out of the shadows. "All except him; but he's going to be your key once you arrive at Urocia's capital!"

"I apologize for my tardiness!" the Urocian lord called, announcing his approach with a rich, jovial tone, his bright blond hair shimmering in the sun. He sauntered up before them, huffing out a sigh of relief. "I'm afraid the trek from the front gate to here is rather lengthy, and I didn't realize our meeting spot would be so far!"

"Glad you could join us," Dex commented coolly. "We are fortunate to have your lordship to guide our newcomers on the eastern portion of their quest."

"I was only told that I was showing some outsiders my home city," Lord Emelien confirmed, raising an eyebrow. "What's this about a quest?"

"Hardly a quest," Grand Master Nicholas quickly interjected. "More of a search for future potential residence."

"Well then, Grand Master, I'm glad you came to me!" Lord Emelien grinned, eyeing Johanna. "Sir Caspin seemed to have some confusion about their destination, something about being delivered to Mondlichtberg. However, I am only all too happy to show the outsiders proper Urocian hospitality! Although I am unsure what the point would be to show them anything west of here."

"Oh, come now, your lordship," Dex chided. "You know not everyone is drawn to the city and civilization. Some among us are 'self-made' men! We may have a few farmers or trappers in the making among them!"

As the men laughed, Johanna's heart skipped a beat as her eyes briefly met Lord Emelien's. She glanced briefly at Nate, but he was still busy with Aros at the Jeep. The Urocian lord's short blond hair and manicured facial features were beautiful to behold, but he remained rather aloof, only cordially introducing himself before mounting his black horse, even as his piercing blue eyes lingered on her.

Grand Master Nicholas next introduced Owl and Rabbit, members of the Clay Tribes to the south. They emerged from the barn and their garb stood out differently than the others, made from deer leather and rabbit furs. Rabbit's exuberance clearly indicated him being the younger of the two hunters, although both sported long, flowing jet-black hair. Although shorter and stockier in appearance, Owl clearly retained the appearance of wisdom and age over Rabbit. His hair was specked with bits of silver while his facial features had a weathered and wise look to them.

"Our people live south of here, mid-way between the Southern Kingdoms and Tyrna," Owl stated, taking a slow but deep and deliberate tone, speaking quietly yet with authority. "We have the land of high mesas and valleys of springs and wild game, similar to where our ancestors came from."

"I can't help but notice some similarities with Native American tribes of the Southwest in our country," Johanna commented. "Were some of your people ever in our world?"

Rabbit pushed in front of Owl, more in excitement than rudeness. He almost reminded Johanna of a native version of Daniel, maybe only slightly older. He grinned with the same enduring enthusiasm she hadn't seen in her son for some time.

"Our tales tell of a great spirit guide who led our people out of a terrible drought," he stated with adolescent enthusiasm. "We had many cities but were losing crops when she came to save us. When we came to our new lands, many people developed new abilities to hunt, fish, farm and some even shape-shift!"

"Come, Rabbit," Owl gently chastised him. "She doesn't need to know everything before we leave. I doubt she's familiar with our ancestry!"

"If she came from our ancestral homes, then why shouldn't she be?" Rabbit protested in annoyance.

"No, it's fine," Johanna gently interrupted. "There was once a vast tribe of people who vanished from the American Southwest long ago. Many of them were cliff dwellers and built great multi-layered structures and dwellings. Where they went is a mystery in my world to this day. We called them the Anasazi, and they built cities of stone in places we called Chaco Canyon and Mesa Verde."

"It could be the cities of our ancestors, who's to know?" Owl shrugged, clearly intrigued yet unsure as to the unexpected correlation this newcomer had suggested. "It certainly describes the way our people live to this very day. Some in our families still pass the stories of previous generations to remind us that we came from another home and that our ancestral spirits delivered us here."

"I wish I was going with you both," Daniel whispered sullenly, pulling on his mother's sleeve. "I don't know why I'm being kept back!"

"I wish you were too," Johanna replied before smoothing back his sandy hair. "Nicholas is right, though. You will be safer here and there will still be lots of things for you to do. You need to keep Sammy safe and stay out of trouble. I'm a bit jealous that Nicholas will be showing you some more about your power while we're gone!"

"Jeep?" Sammy wagged her tail furiously. "Going? Going? Going?"

"No, Sammy, you stay here with Daniel and guard him too," Nate directed. "You both look out for each other! I expect to come back and find you both in good shape so we can share our stories! Stay out of trouble and listen to what Nicholas tells you to do!"

"We will," Daniel sniffed. "I promise...but I'll still miss you guys!"

"Danny!" Sammy pushed herself into Daniel's leg and sat at attention. "Keep safe! Stay with me!"

"That's right!" Nate winked, holding back the lump in his own throat. "Sammy has always been more attentive to you anyway, Daniel. You both were made for each other; see to it that you keep safe until we get back!"

"As soon as you have found what you are seeking, return quickly and return to share your knowledge with the others!" Grand Master Nicholas announced. "We look forward to your success and eagerly anticipate your safe return!"

≈≈≈≈

It seemed like moments later, but hours had passed when the two teams finally departed. Nate drove the Jeep, and Johanna sat beside him in the front, not wanting to look back, lest she regret her decision and turn back to her son. Owl and Rabbit chattered in the back of the Jeep while Aros led with Lord Emelien just in front, both imposing figures atop their dark steeds.

Behind the Jeep, Javier and Kevin followed, conversing with Dex and Davyn astride their horses. The rest seemed content to follow on foot as they began their journeys.

The main road split in two at an intersection less than a half-mile to the south amid the waves of golden fields of grain. A simple wooden sign marked with arrows pointed the way. The eastern fork led to Urocia, and the western fork curved slightly south and downhill to the distant glittering shores of Long Lake.

They turned to each other as the two companies parted ways. Johanna became tearful again as she and Nate hugged Javier and Kevin, glancing anxiously back toward Tyrna's still-looming walls and their crimson heights. The four newcomers finally turned their backs to each other and Tyrna as they began separate journeys.

The Jeep's rumble diminished as the vehicle disappeared over a rise, the billowing dust vanishing with it. From there, they continued onward over the edge of the steeper ridgeline, the sound of the vehicle fading as it lumbered onward, tracking further off the shoulder of Tyrna's Peak and the next subsequent ridgeline. A cluster of boulders at the top hailed the entrance markings of Tyrna Pass.

Dex's group descended in the opposite direction, gliding down the trail and fading down the broad valley, toward the glittering Long Lake in the distant west. Only the lone crossroads sign remained in the settling dust, surrounded by long blades of grass and grain, blowing quietly in billowing waves, driven by the intermittent wind.

Chapter 22

The Gift

The morning of the caravans' departures, Daniel stood with Sammy, deep in thought and waving goodbye. He stared longingly after them as the Jeep's engine revved and then idled, bobbing slowly in the distance down the winding dirt road. Escorted by the group of horses and men, the vehicle kicked up a brief but billowing dust cloud as it ambled through the wind-swept long grass. Soon, even that too dispersed and vanished.

"Well, it looks like it's just you and me now, Sammy," Daniel sighed as he hugged the hound to his side. The dog whined sadly but said nothing as he stroked her fur.

Nicholas looked on with sympathy; clearly, the lad felt left behind and out of place. He waited patiently for the moment to recede before sauntering quietly over to Daniel's side and clearing his throat to gain his attention.

"Trust me, they are in good hands, as are you," the wizard assured him quietly. "What do you say we begin the afternoon exploring what you can do with your newfound abilities?"

The offer brightened Daniel's perspective as he followed Nicholas back into Tyrna through the secret side wall entrance to the city. The tunnels seemed as empty and somber as ever, and he simply blocked it from his mind as he followed the wizard back through the empty stone maze. When they reached the palace courtyard fountain, the grand master stopped as the secret door closed behind him.

"Daniel, I need to see the king briefly about something important," Nicholas recalled suddenly. "I may be a little while; would you mind staying here in the courtyard with Sammy until I return?"

"And then we'll practice my magic?" Daniel grumbled.

"Absolutely; just give me some time to attend to some neglected duties first," Nicholas promised before striding back up the stairs into the throne room's entrance.

Sighing aloud, Daniel took a seat on the edge of the fountain, petting Sammy, who laid her head in his lap as they watched the fish inside swim in lazy circles. Glints of light reflected off the dew-covered leaves of ivy, giving the enclosure a glistening sparkle of promise to the beginning of a new day. The serenity of the scene remained lost on him; he just couldn't bring himself to feel happy about being left behind, alone and bored.

Lethargy began to settle over Daniel as his eyes drooped, the rising sun warming the courtyard around him. Moments passed by when he noticed a shadow detaching itself from the wall on the far side of the courtyard. Sammy growled as he stood, squinting to see who it was. In the bright sunlight, it was hard for him to tell who was approaching, but he soon recognized the man as Sir Caspin as he approached. The captain's grey cloak billowed behind him as he came, glinting in the sunlight with hints of scarlet between the intricate thin dark threads. The threads seemed to pulse, weaving intricate patterns of vines and leaves as he strode.

"Hey, Caspin," Daniel greeted, doing his best to appear cheerful. "I didn't recognize you without your captain of the guard uniform! You look all dressed up!"

"This is my formal attire when I'm at court, especially when presenting matters of finance," Sir Caspin replied with a grin, his hands clasped behind him beneath the cloak. "Where is everyone?"

"They're out and about," Daniel dodged. "I didn't feel like going around town today."

"I could certainly understand that! Not after exploring your other method of getting around," the captain laughed. "I've been meaning to ask you; did you enjoy your escapades last night?"

"What do you mean?" The boy blushed slightly.

"Oh, yes, I make it my business to be quite aware of what happens behind the Inner Wall!" Sir Caspin smiled, enacting the boy's flight with his hand in the air, his hands completely gloved in grey leather, matching the cloak. "I don't have to see it to know that it happened."

"How did you know about...?" Daniel whispered, eyes wide and face flushed.

"Don't worry about it, little man," the captain winked. He reached back into his cloak and pulled out a large red apple. "You've done nothing wrong."

Sammy sat up and growled a low, deep, rumbled warning as the captain moved to hand the apple to the lad. The dog's eyes locked onto Sir Caspin, and she bared her teeth, her hair standing on end.

"Sammy! What are you doing?!" Daniel exclaimed as he accepted the morsel. "I think your gloves or your cloak is freaking her out."

"Indeed." The captain stepped back in surprise. He reached out again to pat the hound's head. "It's okay, Sammy, it's just a cloak."

"NO!" Sammy snapped, baring her teeth, fur bristling.

"Sammy!" Daniel shouted, holding her back. "I'm so sorry, I don't know what's gotten into her! Thanks for the apple; it looks delicious!"

"Harvested from local farmers; they are the best!" Sir Caspin laughed it off, withdrawing his hand. "I have other matters of the court to attend to, but what do you say I stop by and visit this evening? Maybe after dinner?"

"Yeah! That would be great!" Daniel said but then paused. "I could use the company, but..."

"You have other plans?" Sir Caspin saw the hesitation and took the opportunity to query further. "I was told you all would be leaving for Mondlichtberg soon, or is it later? I was told there may have been a detour to Latana, which hardly seems to be on the way. I seem to have conflicting reports on the matter; do you think you could clear some of that up for me?"

"Well, Grand Master Nicholas and I are going to work on my magic today," Daniel began. *No sense in hiding something Caspin already knew about.* "I know that the others had some things to check out elsewhere, but they all thought it best if I stayed here."

"Funny, I take you all on a tour and now they depart without notice, leaving you here alone?" Sir Caspin seemed wary but still smiled, nonetheless. "Did they mention where they were headed? It just seems so out of character to just leave you here like that."

"I don't mind; plus, they said they won't be gone long," Daniel insisted, still struggling to hold back Sammy, tugging against his restraint, snarling and hair bristling. "This gives me a chance to do some things on my own. I'm kind of the only 'kid' in the group, anyway."

"You're far from a child, nearly a man yourself!" Sir Caspin reminded him. "Very well then, it's settled: I'll check in on you later to be sure you're getting along okay, my fine young friend! I won't allow you to be sidelined; I don't allow men I look out for to be treated like that!"

The captain of the guard threw him a wink as he turned and walked back around the corner of the palace, his cloud-grey cape billowing behind him. Sammy finally settled, glancing back at Daniel worriedly.

"What's wrong with you, anyway?" Daniel snapped, admonishing the hound. "It's not like you've never met him before!"

"He smells different!" Sammy whined, finally calming. "He changed!"

"Of course he did!" Daniel scolded the hound. "Now he's having to work with advisors, important leaders from other kingdoms, and stuff like that!"

Nicholas watched the entire interaction from behind the doorway above the stairs as the hound finally sighed, settling down to a resting position at the lad's feet with a huff. The wizard purposefully waited another few moments before descending the stairs and greeting Daniel with a smile.

"How is the captain of the guard these days?" Grand Master Nicholas asked mildly.

"I guess he's busy," Daniel groaned a with shrug, refusing to meet his gaze. He glanced up at the high walls of the royal palace and the Wizard's Tower, looming high above them to unseen heights. The tell-tale Tyrnaese red brick walls became more apparent higher up, their bases covered with ivy vines between the intermittent casement windows "I wasn't talking to him long before he said he'd check in on me later. Don't you see him more than I do?"

"One would think so," Nicholas scoffed, motioning the lad to follow him around the back of the castle. The two walked together around the south side of the palace, under the shade of the fruit trees. "Would you be surprised to learn that I actually do not?"

"He said he thought we were going to Mondlichtberg but seemed confused that I'm still here while my mom and the others left," Daniel confessed, finally turning to the wizard with a confused exasperation. "I'm so confused! I thought he was part of our guard, taking care of us, but now he's not? I lied and said they didn't go far, but I don't know what else to say!"

"The captain has other duties now, and you are my charge, just as Aros now has charge of your mother and Nate," the grand master clarified. "I've found it necessary to restrict information to only certain individuals on your movements and well-being. I hope you understand that this does not yet include Sir Caspin, but I'll let you know when it does, do you understand?"

"Sure, why not," Daniel groaned. "It's just all so confusing now!"

Nicholas escorted Daniel through another vine-strewn gate to the back gardens, placing a reassuring hand on his shoulder. With subtle ease, he let his fingers brush the lad's neck, gently probing his thoughts. Within Daniel's mind, he found a fiercely protective image of Sir Caspin, despite feeling somewhat conflicted about it.

"This area of the palace grounds is mostly vacant, only ever visited by the city's aquatic engineers," Nicholas began with a disarming smile, content to change the topic for the time being. The wizard took a seat upon a stone bench quietly in the shade, directing Daniel's attention to the base of Tyrna's Peak rising before them. With the castle to their back, the grand master grinned as he gestured to the grounds around them. "We will begin our training here!"

"I already flew that yesterday," Daniel complained. "I did it fast too; you want me to do it again?"

"No, I know you can fly far and fast, but can you hover like a bee?" the wizard began, his eyes narrowed even as he explained gently. "Can you maneuver like a hawk? How high can you go? How much can you carry? These are the questions I want you to start pondering during training."

"Why are we starting so small? I can do so much more!" Daniel insisted. "Are you sure you don't want me to fly after my mom and..."

"No, we cannot expose you or them like that," Nicholas gently replied. "You'll see them again, but for now, I need you to focus on the matters at hand. I have great need for your abilities, and much will be asked of you in the coming days. You've also already proven your speed and altitude; I want to expand your abilities at this point."

The grand master took his staff and threw it like a javelin into a nearby pine tree. The lad watched with mouth agape at not only how deceptively strong the old man appeared to be but how accurate he was as well. The staff flew high up into the tree with a whoosh and lodged itself, sticking out between the branches near the top of the tree, more than forty feet off the ground.

"Retrieve that for me, but I have an additional condition," Nicholas emphasized with a single finger. "Carry this out for me without getting any sap on you or touching a single branch."

Daniel nodded and spread his arms, levitating into the air. He was halfway to the tree and more than twenty feet off the ground when Nicholas called to him with a grin, producing an hourglass from his robes.

"Oh, and by the way, retrieve the staff before time runs out," the grand master called, displaying darkened sands draining slowly away. "Time is of the essence!"

"Awww, great!" Daniel continued, having only looked back briefly to avoid losing concentration. It seemed impossible to get to the staff without touching the branches of the tree, all laden with sap. The boy tried lying flat, standing, hovering above, and reaching down, but each time, the tree branches lacquered him in sweet-smelling sap.

Sweating from the effort, he reached in vain for the staff when Nicholas called, "Time!" just below him.

"Crap!" Daniel exclaimed. Letting himself down to the ground, shoulders hunched in rejection. "I just can't reach it!"

Nicholas was ready for this—he produced a parchment from his robes a charcoal piece and drew the tree. He sketched the staff at the top, then turned to show the boy.

"You're thinking two-dimensionally," the wizard said. "You *think* propulsion comes from your hands, and you are currently using this method—I see this. That will be to your advantage when speed or power is of the essence. However, this task requires precision!"

He continued to draw the diagram of Daniel hanging from the sky at a very awkward angle and then using his hands to retrieve the staff. Turning back to the lad, he faced the tree.

"Focus on the propulsion coming from somewhere else," the wizard proposed, waving his hand haphazardly around the boy. "Use all aspects of your body in concert with your power, working together to achieve your objective!"

Daniel acknowledged this, launching himself straight up beside the tree. *More like a hovercraft or a helicopter.* This time, he pictured propellers in his belly with smaller ones on his legs. Tilting his body, the blood rushed to his head, but he was able to maneuver himself between the branches. It took a few adjustments mid-hover, but he was able to grab the wizard's staff before returning to earth triumphantly.

"I did it!" Daniel exclaimed proudly as he handed the staff back to the wizard. "I figured it out!"

"Very good!" Nicholas proclaimed in applause to Daniel's delight. "I've got a few more for you to try!"

The lad sweated freely as the exertion mounted throughout the afternoon. Training continued with retrieving a variety of objects from the cliffside to the castle wall, the trees and around the garden. Sometimes the challenge had nothing to do with his power, but more on learning to use keen eyesight and spot his target from the air.

Nicholas taught him to hover only inches off the ground and to switch into full motion immediately, hurtling up into the sky like a rocket. It was nearing sundown when he noticed the fatigue in Daniel's eyes. A small dribble of blood began to drip from his nostrils.

"One thing I must point out to you, my young friend, is that the use of magic requires much energy followed by a good solid rest," Nicholas insisted. "You have incredible stamina, more than I've seen from anyone in a long time, but you need a reprieve."

Daniel reluctantly agreed, bags under his eyes, wiping his nose with his sleeve. They started back to the fountain courtyard when the wizard stopped him.

"Daniel, do you trust me?" Nicholas asked, a sad seriousness overcoming the conversation like a dark cloud. A cold evening breeze brushed through the grand master's white hair, accentuating the soft sadness that had taken his face.

"Of course!" the newcomer pupil stated in surprise, nodding vigorously in affirmation.

"I'm worried for your mother and the others," Grand Master Nicholas started. He had not originally intended to discuss this matter, but Sir Caspin's interaction with the lad still weighed on his mind. "I know this whole circumstance is difficult for you and is requiring you to grow sooner than your mother would like, and likely even sooner than you're ready. I hate to burden you with matters beyond your years and out of your control, but I must,"

"Why?" Daniel asked, the statement catching his attention. "What's wrong?"

"Someone has been lying to me: King Faund, the other wizards, perhaps just the people who serve them," the wizard began, his voice descending to a whisper. "Recently, many have taken an interest in you, your mother and your friends. I had intended not to involve you in our internal affairs, but I sense that certain interests are deliberately moving against me. They may try to harm you and the others in your group while posing as friends. It's actually partly behind the reason why I had to send them away."

"For their own protection?" Daniel seemed to be working out something in his mind but had not yet arrived at a decision. "You said that earlier."

"Indeed, I did," Nicholas confirmed as they resumed their stroll at a deliberately slower pace. "The central source of this problem may be someone you don't know, but it could also be possibly someone you know very well."

"I-I-I don't know what you're talking about," the lad spluttered.

"Daniel, I cannot stress the seriousness of the situation enough," the wizard warned, letting the thought hang in the cool evening air. Their stroll slowed, the water fountain still ahead, and they lingered on the narrow side pathway of the palace. "I wasn't going to tell any of you before, but I feel now that you should know: Sottis tried to kill me earlier, and I had him thrown in the dungeons for it."

"He tried to kill you?" Daniel gasped. I thought you said he just assaulted you, and then you and Aros downplayed it. What exactly happened?! You had me thinking he bitch-slapped you!"

"Bitch-slapped," the wizard repeated softly, gently laughing. "No, I can assure you, his attack was far more than that. The intention certainly was."

"How?! Why?! I had no idea—why didn't you say something?!" Daniel pressed, still in shock, jolted out of his stupor. "He's friends with Caspin and that other guy, Emelien, who left with my mom! He was with us since Levens!"

"I'm aware my secrecy may have resulted in a lack of knowledge in some cases, but trust me in that it's for your own good," Nicholas intoned, grasping Daniel by the shoulders, locking him with his gaze. "I am including you in this information now; this is why I need to know if anyone has been asking you questions or offering you favors in exchange for information. I went to interrogate Sottis over the matter and discovered someone had released him against my orders. I want to be clear in this matter: I can handle myself, but I'm worried for your safety and the safety of those you came here with."

"Just Sir Caspin," Daniel whispered, still in shock over the revelation. "But he's with the king all the time, and he's with you, isn't he? What about that Lord Emelien guy?"

"Lord Emelien appears not to be involved, for the moment anyway," Nicholas reassured him. "I know you are close with the captain of the guard, so let's make *sure* he's okay. Let's prove to ourselves that he's not tied in with whatever Sottis's dealings are. What specifically has Sir Caspin been asking you?"

"He wanted to know more about our powers," Daniel whispered even as a sudden sense of shame seized him. "He even offered to work with me on mine."

"Why would he do that?" Nicholas initially scoffed, although a chilling realization began to settle in as the smile faded from his face. He wasn't completely sure, but what he heard from Daniel was not only unexpected, but it also made his blood run cold. *The captain of the guard's involvement in the king's finances is strange enough, but the Wizard's Council, and now also the newcomers' magical abilities?!*

"He was just curious," Daniel said, flushed and feeling guilty for betraying his friend's trust. "It was supposed to be our secret. He said it's not a big deal and everyone in Urocia is open about that sort of thing."

"Daniel, do not assume guilt over this," Nicholas directed as he stood tall. "I promise you, I will do nothing to hurt your friend. Let me remind you—I only need to know *why* he wants to know this. Have you noticed anything strange about him lately? Anything at all?"

"No!" Daniel protested in a fluster. "He's nice to us, that's all; especially when everyone else treats me like a child! He treats me with respect!"

"I'm sure he does," Nicholas sighed as he calmly called Sammy over.

"Sir Caspin," the wizard whispered in the captain of the guard's own voice. Stroking the hound on the neck, he probed the dog's thoughts as she met his eyes with her own concerned gaze of innocence. He spoke aloud to the hound as his eyes rolled back in concentration. "Hear me, oh, Sammy. Sir Caspin!"

The hound became downcast, her tail dropped, and a low growl reverberated through her throat. Nicholas was sure he was going to sense anger or protection, but he sensed something else: *fear*!

"Sammy only barked at him this once!" Daniel spluttered. "Just this once!"

"Why, Daniel?" Nicholas persisted, his eyes normalizing as he quietly squinted back at the lad, challenging him to think about it. "Why would she do that after all this time? What was different this time?"

"I don't know!" Daniel threw up his hands in exasperation. "Sammy said he smelled different, but I didn't think anything about it! He just was wearing that stupid grey cloak and those gloves, but other than that, he was the same!"

"I see," Nicholas acknowledged softly. He cleared his throat when he contemplated the matter more. "Daniel, why don't you just stay close to Sammy while you're under my protection, especially when I'm not around?"

"What about Sir Caspin, though?" Daniel sighed. "I was supposed to meet with him after dinner tonight!"

"You may still see your friend, but say nothing of our conversation here," the wizard warned. "I just need to know when anyone asks you questions such as these. Sir Caspin truly may not be the source of the problem, but he may be connected to those who are. Even Sottis, with all his foul intentions, may not be at the heart of it all. Whoever is behind this may be using innocent people to obtain their objectives. My job as both chief advisor to King Faund and Advocate for you is to be able to sort that all out!"

"I promise I'll be careful," Daniel grumbled as they climbed the stairs to the front entrance. "What should I tell him if he asks about my mom and the others?"

"Tell him I sent them on a brief scouting tour to look for a place to settle, should the efforts at Mondlichtberg to send them home fail," the grand master instructed. "Tell him you stayed behind as my ward to assist me in matters here; it's not far off from the truth."

"These lies are getting more difficult to hide by the day," Daniel muttered.

"They are, indeed, my young friend!" Nicholas agreed, patting him on the back. "They are indeed."

≈≈≈≈

Later that night, the king's hall in Tyrna never felt so large and empty as Daniel ate dinner alone in the dark. The chandeliers tinkled softly high above, casting a gentle flickering light throughout the chamber as Sammy sat at his feet, gnawing a bone. The lad picked sullenly at his steaming plate of pasta and meatballs; it was delicious, but without the king or anyone else around, it felt quite lonely. He was tempted to pick his meal up and move to the breakfast grotto nearer to the kitchen when Sir Caspin strode up from out of the shadows.

"Where is everyone?" the captain of the guard announced himself, exclaiming the joke with a broad grin. "You are still here by yourself!?"

"Yep, you know me; always on my own," Daniel muttered, letting food dribble from his fork while refusing to look the captain of the guard in the eye. Sammy looked up, and as a brief growl emitted from her throat, Daniel swatted her head in annoyance to get her to stop. "I guess they get to tour the countryside while I hold down the fort."

"I understood you all were leaving soon," Sir Caspin prodded. "Have they not found a way to return you back to your world?"

"Well, supposedly, they're fine-tuning that, but once we head back to Mondlichtberg, that'll be the plan. In the meantime, the others are scoping out a plan B." Daniel shook his head as he tossed his fork onto his half-eaten plate, finally turning to face the captain, his eyes locking his gaze in accusation. "What is your interest in me, Sir Caspin? I appreciate you checking in on me and all, but I just don't get it!"

"What's going on, Daniel?" Sir Caspin seemed taken aback. "Why have you taken this attitude? Has something happened?"

Daniel immediately remembered Nicholas's warning. *Sir Caspin's not in trouble, but it will do no one any good if the captain finds out he's a topic of conversation with the wizard.*

"Sorry," Daniel muttered, looking away again. "I'm just sick of being left behind on everything—sick of being 'the boy' when I'm practically the same age as Javier and Kevin. I just don't want you to start treating me the same way my mom and Nate do."

"I understand," Caspin acknowledged with a coaxing smile. "Surely, though, you understand that I hold you in great respect! I'm sure they love you, but they don't see you as I do. I respect you as the man you are becoming, and I see your potential! I have many young men in my service close to your age and recognizing that potential in them is part of my job. When I say, I understand, trust me, I do."

"Thanks." Daniel managed to keep the sarcasm from his voice, gesturing to an empty seat beside him. "Why don't you sit down and join me for dinner?"

"Daniel, I'd love to, but I confess that I have a brief mission assigned to me this very night and cannot stay," the captain sighed. "Before I depart Tyrna, I have something for you in the kitchen, a going away gift; please, come with me."

Sir Caspin motioned for him to follow as he turned, voluminous grey cloak ruffling past his shoulders. Daniel dropped the fork on the plate and followed, his interest suddenly piqued.

The captain's cloak billowed like waters on the ocean as he walked, floating in the air in ripples, giving him an air of authority and grace that Daniel couldn't help but admire. Sammy padded protectively close behind them, panting nervously as they entered the servants' entrance to the main kitchen.

Sir Caspin opened the kitchen door and pointed to the cook's table. There atop the table sat a small wooden box.

"That, my young friend, that is for you," Sir Caspin stated. "Go ahead, open it."

Daniel walked over to the table and opened the chest as the aroma of fresh oak wafted to him. Folded neatly inside lay another luxuriant grey cloak with stitching threads as dark as night. It rippled in the torchlight the same way Sir Caspin's did when the boy retrieved it, holding it high. He gasped at the touch, silky and light yet warm and comforting. A barely perceptible amber glow coursed through as the lad pulled it forth and examined it. Sammy growled once but settled at his feet, her eyes fixed on the strange garment.

"I don't know what to say," Daniel shook his head as he ran his hands through it again. "This is awesome! It's gorgeous; so soft!"

"I cannot tell you more about my mission yet, but you will know in good time," Sir Caspin stated, handing the box to Daniel. "When that time comes, you may wear this with my blessing, but not until then. You once asked me what this special grey cloak is for; I'll tell you this— we must earn it!"

"So Sottis earned his, too?" Daniel mentioned and casually caressed the dark cloth, careful not to look Caspin in the eye. Dark gossamer threads formed on the grey background, twisting and turning hypnotically into a pattern of vines before dispersing back into nothingness.

"Yes, Sottis did great deeds for king and country back in Urocia." The captain of the guard glanced at him quizzically before the look quickly faded from his face. "However, I've recently discovered that he's in a bit of trouble lately. If you should see him, please let me or Grand Master Nicholas know as soon as possible. You haven't seen him, have you?"

"No, but I'm glad you told me." Daniel did his best to appear surprised. "I'm sorry to hear that, I had no idea—what did he do?"

"Nothing that cannot be reconciled; it's a trivial matter," Sir Caspin assured him. "For now, just stow the cloak, safe and secret in your quarters until I return. I should be back before your journey to Mondlicht-berg, should that still be your destination."

"Really, Sir Caspin, thank you," Daniel thanked him softly as he folded the garment and placed it gingerly back in the trunk before closing the lid. "I shall wear it proudly!"

"Not yet, but you will," Sir Caspin stated. "I will tell you when the time is right, and then wherever you go, the cloak will follow as a reminder of our time together here. Just as Grand Master Nicholas was Advocate for you and your friends, my gift to you with this cloak is my personal advocacy for you."

The pain and guilt washed through Daniel even as he accepted the grand gift. *Why are Nicholas and Caspin at odds?! Yet still, something feels off regarding his response to Sottis and the "trivial" matter of attacking Grand Master Nicholas.*

With that, Sir Caspin strode out, the grey cloak billowing behind him as Daniel watched him go. With his mother and his other friends gone, the captain leaving too made him feel more alone than ever. Reaching down and patting Sammy, panting again and eager to be on their way. He grabbed the case, carrying his new gift, and set off to his room, leaving the rest of his dinner back on the table, the loyal hound following close to his heels. *I'm just not hungry anymore.*

Chapter 23

Promotions and Rewards

Princess Serina slept well in her new quarters at Mondlichtberg, better even than in her own palace bedroom in Levens. The bed and pillows were goose down, and the sheets bleached white and soft; she likened it to sleeping in a cloud. As a royal guest of the wizard's keep, her accommodations were among the best Mondlichtberg offered, near the back of the southwest wing and closer to the ridgeline. She had left her window open a tiny crack to let the cold mountain breezes waft into her room throughout the night.

Upon awakening with the coming of the dawn, she could just make out the frost beginning to melt on the sill. The music of mountain birds singing carried on the breeze as she lay back to contemplate the new day that would lead into the rest of the week.

She recalled her deception to Grand Master Yamaro with distaste about her reasons for coming to the wizard's keep. The purpose was true, even if the timing had been rushed to provide cover for her secret assignment from Nicholas. At least for now, the clandestine portion of her mission to search out and expose the undermining forces of the council's decisions could wait. Until she could figure out how to make contact with this mysterious Mistress Amina, her mission for Nicholas was at a standstill.

For now, her real passion and primary focus were set on her studies and her promotion to a full-scale magician. Now, she could fully devote time to explore her talents and throw herself into her progression within the Order of the Moon!

A soft knock on the door interrupted her thoughts. She smiled at the thought of an apprentice boy most likely, standing and meekly calling to her through the door.

"My lady, breakfast will be served in thirty minutes," the cringe-worthy and squeaky voice of the courier called to her through the door. She smiled as a slight rustle caught her attention from beneath the door frame. Resembling a small mouse, a flattened scroll pushed through the crevice and into her room. "The avian scroll master asked me to deliver word to you; arrived from Tyrna this morning!"

"Thank you," she replied as she tussled her hair and tiptoed out of bed to retrieve the parcel. When her feet touched the cold stone floor, she gasped but ignored the shock as she recovered the parchment bearing the crimson seal of Grand Master Nicholas.

"There's one more point of order, Your Highness," the courier replied before shoving another parcel through, a flattened sheet of parchment with a handwritten list. "Grand Master Yamaro also listed assignments for you today and requests your presence for training before dinner tonight."

"Most kind!" she called over her shoulder as she retreated gingerly to her bed-stand to dress. "Please let the grand master know that I'm up and about; I'll be sure to check in with him before dinner!"

The footfalls of the courier faded down the hall as she turned her attention back to the rolled scroll. Breaking the ornate wax seal, she opened the scroll from Tyrna and read to herself:

Apprentice Sottis taken into custody; will explain later, but consider him dangerous. Proceed with caution as he claims to follow council orders. I'm not convinced of council involvement. Until certain, stay alert...find Amina!

"Well, that sounds ominous," Princess Serina exhaled aloud as she dressed herself, tossing the parchment into the dying embers of her stone fireplace. The message had been an unwelcomed reminder that her visit to Mondlichtberg was clearly intended to go beyond simply studying and enjoying the fresh mountain air. *At least Aros's bane has been identified and dealt with; justice, in this case, seems to have prevailed.*

Her day began with supervising the squire's chores, much below her standards of a princess. She shouldered them without complaint since it gave her access to all the other occupants in the castle and their rooms. It also allowed her to familiarize herself with the layout of the castle and its inhabitants.

Going from room to room, she assisted the squires in changing bed sheets and gathering laundry while she checked for closed tomes on the desks and tables. When she happened across any material taken for night reading, she would collect and return it to the main hall library.

With each room she visited, she'd throw open the curtains and the windows, letting the fresh mountain breezes blow through the mustiness of each room and the corridors. It was as if the wizard's keep had been holding its breath all night, and she was determined to bring new air to the stale confines of the stone walls.

Each time she met one of the apprentices, she would try to make physical contact with her hand and probe their minds the way Grand Master Nicholas had taught her. *Any contact must be light as a feather and focused upon a specific thought so as not to be detected. Do not linger...*

She could cover the quick probe with a flashing smile, a gleam in her eyes, or a blush of the cheek—all feminine wiles she brought to bear and practiced to an art yet never used for the purposes for which they were designed. She had no intention of finding a suitor here, but her flirtation came as a useful tool indeed.

She had to be more careful when researching the few and far between female students. In such situations, she would approach them with a sympathetic touch or a comradely pat instead of her standard male-appealed flirtations.

As she went room to room, no one suspected she was up to anything other than her chores. Each time she touched someone, her carefully targeted probe would flash a vision in her mind.

A younger, lightly yet sparsely bearded albino dwarf: *How much he wanted to explore a local cave for jewels. The quartermaster had provided a wand recently to detect such jewels, and he was anxious to use it.*

A grey cat-lady with green eyes named Vivera: *How pleasant it was to see THE Princess Serina of Levens in her quarters; she couldn't wait to tell her twin, Minx.* Princess Serina smiled and curtsied.

The young apprentice boy, Ollen: *How he missed his mother and father in the Southern Kingdoms. How glad he was that the arrangements for Barley's return to Levens had been secured and were underway now. Since the princess of Levens herself now stood before him, it was a good reminder to follow up on the success of the horse's delivery later today.*

"I meant to thank you for taking care of my steed," Princess Serina began. "He's such a good horse and a loyal companion; I shall miss him terribly."

"I should receive word on his safe arrival by pigeon carrier this afternoon," he assured her. "I promise to check on the matter myself!"

She thanked him and continued to make her rounds. At one point in the afternoon, she even stopped by the stables where the avian and quartermaster were both busy coordinating their inventories for communication and supplies. The Urocian lads nodded in recognition as she approached but said nothing as they continued their work.

"Pardon me while I squeeze by," she muttered in friendly greeting, moving behind them within the cramped quarters of crates, parchments and bird cages with their squawking contents. "I just need some pen ink."

Though her cursory hand brushed by each of them, their thoughts revealed little beyond the demands of their positions with the grand masters: *supplies...trade...inventory...cloaks...blankets...boots...store-house...preparations for the coming winter...*

As she moved her rounds back into the castle and the dining hall, the few Levenese present recognized her immediately, downright ecstatic to see her. They bowed excitedly, eager to make her acquaintance.

Her subsequent probes with each individual introduction revealed nothing. No one had Sottis or any plot on their mind regarding the order or Grand Master Nicholas. Any preoccupation of their thoughts seemed far from undermining anyone at the order; they were completely, loyally focused on their duties. Of all the representatives' kingdoms across the known world, no one seemed intent on a foul deed.

One common thread surfaced from everyone she met: all seemed focused on their studies yet slightly on edge. Nearly all felt a general lonely longing, isolated and depressed. While all remained loyal, morale among the Order of the Moon clearly had never been lower.

Nearer to lunchtime, she sauntered out into the courtyard, slightly depressed at the situation at her long-awaited trip to Mondlichtberg. She set her sights back at the main entrance and on the well in the courtyard, intent on retrieving a bucket of water to wash the morning duties' grime from her hands. As she rounded a corner, she nearly bumped into a tall-cloaked figure and squeaked in surprise at the near collision.

"Watch where you're going, apprentice," the gruff woman's voice chided her from the long folds of the grey cloak. Dark hands reached up, pulling the hood back and revealing a glowering yet chiseled ebony face. Her icy blue eyes glared back at the princess as if daring her to speak.

"My apologies, Mistress Magician." Princess Serina smiled courteously. *I owe no such courtesy but want to minimize any impact I would have on my identity here at the keep.*

"Sorceress," the woman reminded her coldly. "I am a master-level sorceress!"

"I'm sorry, come again?" Princess Serina asked, her eyes narrowed.

Could this be someone behind the scheming here at Mondlichtberg? She seems to deliver a colder reception than anyone else I've met thus far.

"I'm no magician, nor am I the local help," the woman growled. "I am Sorceress Amina, master-wizard level to the rest of you!"

Princess Serina's heart leapt; *this is who I'm looking for!* The princess glanced to either side to ensure no one else was present.

"I'm Princess Serina of Levens," she whispered. "I was sent by Grand Master Nicholas to finish my training here. More importantly, I was to seek you out while I was here and pass along word to you as soon as I could."

"So, you're what all the fuss is about among the new recruits!" Mistress Amina nodded, her features softened, although the frown never left her face. She accepted the princess's offered hand and stared deep into her eyes. "My apologies, Your Highness. I hadn't realized I was getting assistance so soon."

"Assistance?" Princess Serina asked quizzically. She gently shook the other's hand, simultaneously readying her mental probe. As their hands grasped, she sensed Sorceress Amina evoking the same probe!

Both of their eyes rolled to white as their consciousness met. Wrestling briefly, the mistress's clearly stronger force pushed through, and Princess Serina found herself standing in a grey fog facing the sorceress.

"What?! Where are we?" the princess demanded. "What have you done?!"

"My apologies, Your Highness," Amina laughed, a musically sweet sound like mahogany. She flashed a dazzling smile, putting the princess somewhat at ease. "I know this is terribly intrusive, but it's obviously no different than what you are doing here at the keep to me, or indeed everyone else you've apparently come in contact with!"

"Now wait just a second?!" Princess Serina started to object, but Amina held up her hand. "Who told you that I was—"

"No need to deny it," the sorceress interrupted playfully. "I recognize the type of probe you're using because it's the same one Grand

Master Nicholas taught me many years ago. I suspect you've been using it all over Mondlichtberg, although I would advise caution in attempting it with the upper echelons of our order. We were taught by the same master, and they will recognize it. Trust me, don't try it. Just be assured that your mission for Nicholas is safe with me; he was wise to have you seek me out!"

"You found all that out just now?" the princess retorted, eyeing her with skepticism.

"Indeed, I did, Your Highness," the sorceress confirmed. "Don't be too hard on yourself about it, though; I have eons of practice! In any case, you're fortunate I found you first."

"Well, now that I've found you, what can we do?" Princess Serina shrugged. "You know my mission—who's lying to Nicholas, and why is Aros being targeted?"

"For the moment, we can do nothing because I don't know either," Amina stated, her ice-cold eyes driving home the warning even more than her stating it. "Everyone is on edge for a reason—the Grand Master Council has recently come down hard on the apprenticeship and the Master Advisory. There is no tolerance for detractors, and many have already been demoted or even summarily dismissed!"

"I've been sensing that in my probes," Princess Serina confirmed, shaking her head sadly. "I cannot believe Grand Master Yamaro could be so..."

"You don't know your old friend as well as you used to, I can promise you that," the sorceress sighed bitterly. "Times change, Your Highness. Even the closest ties can be challenged when they do. Desperation can alter even the most loyal and wisest of our order."

"It's not all Grand Master Yamaro, is it?" the princess exclaimed, balking at the insinuation. "I mean, surely there's other forces at work here!"

"In all fairness, the fault is not solely his," the sorceress grudgingly admitted. "It's a culmination of their plight combined with the pride of eons. Grand Master Encara has taken advantage of the situation to promote himself, even as he's stepped on everyone else to do it. He's ambitious, yes, but he's also inexperienced, an opportunist and reckless. The council's fault was to welcome him in along with the risks he's taking. I'm afraid their desperation will lead to the detriment of us all."

"So Grand Master Encara's ascension allowed someone to infiltrate the order and set into motion their own agendas?" Princess Serina asked.

"Maybe more than just one person, or maybe just him." Mistress Amina shrugged in disgust. "In either case, I've been effectively side-lined as the order's core values collapse around us. I'm powerless to stop any of this, and they've kept a close watch on me since I first tipped them on my position, opposing their direction even before Encara's initial ascension into the Master Advisory Council."

"Surely you don't believe Grand Master Encara is behind this, do you?" the princess exclaimed, squinting in disbelief. "I'm aware there's some bad blood between you, but being a revolutionary is hardly traitorous!"

"Perhaps you're right, but the differences between him and me go far beyond simply not sharing the same opinions," Sorceress Amina scoffed. "I would think some level of respect and attention would be offered, particularly at Aros's level and certainly at mine. We've been shown neither! Not by him, nor by the Grand Master Council! Their demands for blind loyalty and support without discussion and under threat is like nothing I've ever seen in the Order of the Moon!"

"What are we going to do about it, Mistress Amina?" Princess Serina whispered as the shock roiled through her. "We can't stop the chaos and dissent amongst our superiors, but that's not my mission. My mission is to find the saboteur behind it all, likely fomenting all of this to begin with!"

"Yes, I understand," the sorceress assured her darkly. "It's going to be a much harder task than you realize though; particularly with the way things are now. In fact, it's likely best that you and I aren't seen together while you're here."

"You mean like we are right now?" Princess Serina became nervous, glancing around at nothing in their surroundings of darkened swirling mist. "I was just heading to clean up for lunch when we met. How long have we been standing here?"

"Not to worry," Amina assured her with a smile. "We are still standing by the well, and our conversation here in this fog is simply in our minds; it is truthfully taking less than a flicker of an eye. We are communicating with the speed of thought!"

"How did it ever get this far?" Princess Serina sighed, turning her attention back to the conversation at hand. "Why all the secrecy and subterfuge?"

"I'm not sure yet, and I suspect that's why Nicholas sent you," the sorceress's features hardened again as she stared off into the swirling fog. "The grand masters have kept to themselves since Encara pilfered the advisory away with him back to Urocia for his own private pleasure. You're likely the only outsider that would be welcomed in with a certain leniency most of us would not be afforded."

"It certainly seems appallingly out of character." The princess shook her head. "We're going to work together to uncover this!"

"Yes, and your fresh perspective may be just the spark we need!" Sorceress Amina nodded in satisfaction. It was short-lived as a sadness stole her eyes. "However, we must tread carefully. Most recently, the Grand Master Council has isolated two other wizards, formerly up for promotion to master-wizard level and demoted at least ten to magicians. Leadership has become a dictatorship, by intentional design."

"How? Why?" Princess Serina asked in exasperation, waving at the fog to clear it from the sorceress's face becoming obscured by the encroaching mists. "You would think with all this talk of recruitment, they would want to increase their numbers, not decrease them!"

"I don't know, and they won't tell us," Mistress Amina fumed. "It all started when Encara was promoted to Grand Master of Urocia after Nicholas retired. It was a post I was assured would come to me, and I coveted it. Apparently, Encara the Golden's connections with Latana and the Order of Etoilenoir ultimately weighed greater with the council than my experience, so they changed their minds."

"Nicholas never mentioned this before," Princess Serina reflected. "About you, the council and Encara. Not in such detail!"

"Nor would he," the sorceress assured her as her form began to fade into the swirling fog, losing its color and form. "It was considered a council matter, and frankly, most of those decisions were made after his departure."

"Mistress Amina, our connection is fading!" Princess Serina called as the mists thickened, obscuring her view of the sorceress.

"Yes, my dear, our time here at the well now draws to a close!" The sorceress's voice floated ethereally back to her. "Harken to me on this before we depart—although the Grand Master Council has no suspicions of you for the moment, the system of checks and balances from the master wizards is now viewed skeptically as outsider intrusion. The timing of your arrival couldn't have been better! You are the last vestige of goodwill between Nicholas and Yamaro. I only hope it's enough to bring unity back to the order again!"

"I do too," Princess Serina sighed as the mist closed in around them, fully obscuring one from the other. "I had no idea that it was this bad or had gone this far."

"Nor would you." Mistress Amina's voice echoed distantly. "That is why your contact with me must remain limited and unknown. Say nothing to anyone of it. Remember, I'm being watched all the time and already viewed with high suspicion. They look for any excuse to demote me or anyone who associates with me."

"But I have so many questions!" Princess Serina protested. "There's so much I want to ask you..."

The grey fog suddenly vanished, and Princess Serina found herself staring back at Mistress Amina in front of the well, outside the castle within the courtyard. The sorceress nodded curtly at her, donned her hood and strolled briskly past her to the entrance of the great hall.

≈≈≈≈

Princess Serina reflected on her situation at the keep throughout the remainder of the day. Her run-in with Sorceress Amina had been unexpected and fleeting, but she abided by the sorceress's warning to not reveal their connection.

Continuing with her afternoon the same way she had started the day, she remained unable to uncover any other presence of foul intent. Perhaps tomorrow she would try the personnel in the stables and gardens, but she would be more cautious with her mind probes as Amina advised.

By the time evening dinner was served, she was exhausted and ready for bed. Entering the great hall, the massive stone fireplace crackled with new life, and the aroma from the evening meal caressed her senses alongside the muffled low conversations of those at the long tables. Quietly obtaining a heaping plate of fried fish and greens from the kitchen, she easily found an unoccupied corner among the sparsely spaced inhabitants of the keep.

Grand Master Yamaro approached her midway through her meal, placing a gently wavering hand on her shoulder to gain her attention. She looked up expectantly, dabbing her mouth with a cloth napkin.

"How was your day, my dear?" the grand master asked inquisitively.

"Wonderful!" she exclaimed, smiling gratefully and patting a seat next to her on the bench. "It was a bit exhausting, but I don't mind hard work. Care to sit with me for a moment? I know you wanted to speak to me this evening."

"Unfortunately, I cannot sit at this time," Grand Master Yamaro intoned gently. "There are some matters that demand my attention, but I would like you to come by my office in the tower after you're done with your meal."

"Very well, Grand Master." Princess Serina's smile remained, yet she utilized his title, noting his official tone of the interchange. As he shuffled off to speak with other students, she couldn't help but notice his request invoked a slight sense of apprehension as she finished her dinner alone. *I wonder if he noticed me by the well earlier with Mistress Amina?*

As the other students and staff finished departing the dining hall, Princess Serina cleared her dishes and turned to the steep and winding stone staircase of the central tower. The narrow entrance to the tower stairwell seemed as little more than a closet next to the massive central fireplace in the dining hall. Cold wisps of air gusted down the stairwell, past vents in the fireplace, stirring the remaining coals aglow with an orange flare.

She nervously entered and began the ascent, her mind racing with the possibilities as to what this summoning could mean. The evening breezes moaned through the passageway as if to warn her, sending chills down her spine and adding to the sense of foreboding as she climbed.

The princess climbed the steps two at a time, marveling at the engineering of the staircase around the chimney. The stone radiated warmth and intermittent vents emitted additional heat into the corridor somehow without allowing smoke. She swallowed hard as her throat dried, gulping the nervousness she struggled to hide.

After four turns around the central column, she neared the top. As she approached the grand master's entryway, she found the thick oaken door closed. *Is he here?* Not knowing his whereabouts, she knocked softly.

"Come in," Grand Master Yamaro's voice wheezed from the other side.

The latch clicked, and the door groaned as she pushed it open. The darkened interior flickered with intermittent candles as the sweet and spicy aroma of Myrenth tea mingled with old leather-bound books wafted forth.

A sudden bright flash of white light dazzled her eyes, and she threw up her arms reflexively. Gasping in surprise, she shielded her face with her hands, projecting her innate shield with a solid, vibrating hum of tendrils of rose-colored strands. The light scattered around her, the crimson shield illuminating the protective bubble with which she surrounded herself.

"Excellent, my dear!" exclaimed the grand master as the intrusive light ceased. "You have wonderful reflexes!"

"What's the meaning of this?" Princess Serina inquired, lowering her hands along with her protective shield, and retracting the rosy tendrils within her wrists. She blinked to dismiss the stars dancing feverishly around her field of vision.

"You're in a wizard's castle, are you not?" the elder Silver Wizard exclaimed, grinning smugly. "I wanted to see how your reflexes held up despite your exhaustion from your daily duties. That ray would not have harmed you, but you blocked it nevertheless! I would say you passed your first test of many more to come!"

"I've practiced my shield deployment with Grand Master Nicholas on many occasions," she exhaled in relief, softly laughing herself. "I've focused on both strength and speed. I just had not anticipated using it this night!"

"Expect the unexpected!" Grand Master Yamaro cooed approvingly. "That is good—now let's see what *else* you can do with it!"

"What else *is* there?" Princess Serina asked, her curiosity now piqued along with the relief that clearly, this was to be a training session, not an interrogation.

"I shall show you," he eagerly intoned as his face erupted into a mirthful exuberance that she had never seen before. "My dear, I am ever most eager to complete your training. Nicholas sending you to me is a greater gift than even you realize, and one that I will not forget! I won't go into all the personal details between him and me, but time and circumstance have driven a wedge between us that I hope your being here will help remedy. The time to heal this rift is long overdue, and I believe the opportunity is finally upon us!"

"I certainly will do anything I can to help!" Princess Serina balked, unsure of what more to say at the revelation, knowing she must balance what she already knew with anything coming from Grand Master Yamaro.

"I recognized promise in you at a very early age, long before you ever showed signs of innate power," the grand master elaborated. "I had hoped to retire before Nicholas and assume the very position he retained in Levens alongside your father with your family. I will always envy him for beating me to it. For him to send you to me after all these years; it's the olive branch I've been waiting for!"

"An olive branch? You both may be stubborn, but you don't need that," Princess Serina scoffed. "You and Nicholas have eons of history together that should mend whatever rift you've suffered!"

"Quite right, my dear! Quite right! No need to linger on such unpleasantries that have already taken up more time than their allotted worth!" The grand master's enthusiasm beamed unrestrained as he sauntered over to his desk, where a steaming pot of tea sat brewing atop a candle burner. With a slight tremor, he poured the tea into a small, delicate porcelain cup and offered it to her. "You and I have some late-night work ahead of us! I took the liberty of brewing some Myrenth tea for just the occasion!"

"Grand Master, have you ever heard of anyone named Sottis Bisset?" she asked as she gratefully accepted the offering, carefully sipping at the ornate teacup.

"No, I can't say that I have; should I have?" he wondered aloud. "Is that perhaps a friend of yours from Levens? An acquaintance of Nicholas's?"

"No." The princess smiled dismissively. "He was Master Aros's apprentice and valet."

"Apprentice?!" Grand Master Yamaro laughed. "No guest apprentice would ever be assigned as a valet; our council would never allow that! We may be short-staffed, but surely you are mistaken! I do remember the valet driving Aros's carriage on his recent visit. A guest from that Order of Etoilenoir happened to be available for the assignment. If I recall correctly, he swapped out for his protégé, Durant, when he was needed in Latana. Indeed, this was solely for the purposes of transportation, nothing more, or so as I recall it."

"Indeed, perhaps I am mistaken." Princess Serina drifted off in thought as she took another swig from her teacup, a pit opened in her stomach. *How could the Grand Master Council be unaware of a guest apprentice in the order?*

"Grand Master Encara has laid developing plans with the Order of Etoilenoir, but that is not a discussion for us here and now," Grand Master Yamaro chided. "Come, let us begin!"

Chapter 24

Eastward

Johanna had a lot to think about, lying under the stars on the ground near the front of the Jeep. It had been a long day since their departure from Tyrna, but the cool evening breeze caressed her hair, and she was surprisingly comfortable despite sleeping outside.

Earlier that day, they had paused atop Tyrna Pass for lunch and to overlook the plains below, an effective distraction from Lord Emelien's intoxicating stare. It had been such a beautiful spot that she wished they could have lingered longer to absorb the view.

Alongside her companions, Aros had explained that Tyrna Peak, to their immediate north, retained the title of the highest in the mountains referred to as the Torweg Range. They were rockier and drier than the Grenze and typically hosted occasional scrub, juniper and pinion pines. Only Tyrna's Peak retained the alpine aspects of the Grenze due to its uncharacteristically high elevations, broad shoulders and ability to catch moisture from the storm clouds.

"So, what lies ahead?" Nate had eagerly asked, gesturing out over the expanse.

"All the lands north of the desert and east of those mountains are the great plains of Urocia," the wizard had indicated. "Our travels are taking us there, to the town of Cierna and then beyond to the great city of Latana."

After their brief respite atop the crest, they descended a series of forested switchbacks into a narrow pinion- and juniper-choked valley before emerging Tyrna Pass out onto the plains below. From there, they emerged from the cover of the forest, continuing into the better part of the day, out onto the grassy plains along the broad southeastern base of Tyrna Peak.

When the sun receded behind the ridgeline, they had found an ideal spot to camp near a fresh spring along the roadside. Like a great lidless eye, the blue depths of the pool stared skyward in a great blue oval nearly a hundred feet across. Three lonely cottonwood trees grew over the pool alongside an enormous worn boulder and provided some shelter in the fading sunlight.

Nate had discreetly bent down and snapped his fingers, letting off a little spark, promptly lighting their evening fire to cook. He winked at Johanna as Aros looked on, frowning in disapproval, but he said nothing since everyone else had been busy elsewhere and the wizard was also hungry for dinner.

The group refilled their water and rested, although Johanna had gladly busied herself from her worries to make a meal for them. She started with diced meats and potatoes when Crand surprised them all by bringing a couple of fish caught from the spring. She added these as a delicious side dish and diced them up with some spinach as Lord Emelien looked on expectantly. Soon, the glade around them mingled scents from the coming meal alongside the reeds and the mossy embankments of the watering hole.

Once the meal was over and the dishes were done, everyone else fell asleep, leaving Johanna to sprawl out and again observe the night sky. It was a wonderful distraction from the Urocian lord, whose image kept infiltrating her mind's eye, even if he was out of sight.

Nate gently snored beside her at the front of the Jeep, facing away, mind occupied by their new mission. Aros slept near the spring with

Owl and Rabbit. She had put the seats down and invited Crand and Lord Emelien to try the Jeep out, but only Crand had accepted the invitation. The Urocian lord insisted he take the first night's watch and that everyone else get some rest.

Thankfully, no one had yet taken notice of Lord Emelien's interest in her. This night, he sat alone atop the large boulder overlooking the spring and the entire vicinity, a distant and vague silhouette in the dark just beyond the light of the dying campfire. *Perhaps his persistent stare will die off before Nate notices. Perhaps my own curiosity will die with it. Has he caught me returning his glances?*

As she drifted off to sleep, her pondering of the day behind her faded, leaving her only to wonder how Daniel was doing, the smell of the curing long grass lulling her into a relaxed state. Was he going to be well-fed, watched over and taken care of? She finally admitted to herself that she preferred him staying where he was now, safe with Grand Master Nicholas, but she missed him all the same. *He would have loved to see all these stars.*

Unsure as to how much time had elapsed, a rustle of whispers jolted her suddenly awake. She sat up briefly but saw nothing; everyone still slept. The campfire had died down to mere coals, and the breeze had ceased as the chill from the wee hours of the night settled over the grass.

She calmed her nerves and lay back down again to admire the night sky. She tried to find familiar constellations, yet none seemed to shine here. The moon was just a sliver, and the stars shimmered in nondescript patterns above like a vast carpet. Beginning to drift off again, she heard the same whispers, but louder this time, a blur of hissing through the air.

Sitting up again with a start and looking around, for the first time, she noticed something was different. Although the whispers silenced, there were no other sounds: no crickets, no breeze, no crackling from the dying fire, nothing. *Simply dead silence.*

She peered under the Jeep, looking for anything, but the evening's fire had gone cold, and only a few coals winked back at her.

Just past one of the cottonwood trees on the road ahead, she saw movement. A dark shadow she recognized as Lord Emelien strode slowly over to the spring along the base of the large boulder. She followed his movements until he got to the water's edge and began to undress. His chiseled form glistened in the moonlight, and his lean muscles rippled with every movement he made.

Feeling a bit ashamed of herself for allowing her gaze to linger, she began to lie back down. He obviously wanted to bathe, and this might be the last chance; no wonder he wanted the "night watch." *He can't be that much older than Kevin or Javier; stop it, Johanna!*

Unable to resist the temptation, she glanced back at the cottonwood tree where he had been. The shadow beneath the tree remained even after the Urocian lord dove into the placid waters with a loud splash. Perplexed, she rubbed her eyes and squinted, and the shadow appeared to shrink and diminish, yet it remained.

Listening intently, only the sound of her heartbeat boomed above the gentle splashing of Lord Emelien's bathing in the spring. *Yet the shadow stayed aside the rock? Was that from one of the trees? No, the shadows from the trees are clearly splayed across the spring's surface.*

With another loud slosh, Lord Emelien emerged from the spring, water dripping from his every appendage as he reached for his cloak to dry off. She jolted back into a sleeping position, hoping no one had seen her staring. Indeed, no one had. Everyone remained asleep, and their Urocian guide resumed dressing.

She could hear the call of crickets returning over the sound of her pounding heart and thought nothing more of it, receding back into her night's sleep. It had been a long day, after all, and her exhaustion had clearly affected her vision. The soothing scents of moss and cottonwood trees among the reeds caught her attention as sleep regained its hold on her. *Strange how the whole landscape seemed to hold its breath yet now seems to breathe freely again...*

≈≈≈≈

The next morning, Johanna decided to ride one of the horses while letting Owl and Rabbit ride in the Jeep with Nate driving. She thought to ask Lord Emelien more about what she had seen last night, pulling her steed alongside his in front of the Jeep.

"Good morning, my lord," she started the conversation, gently guiding the reins of her steed alongside his. "Please don't be offended, but I'm surprised you aren't, well..."

"Good morning, my lady," Lord Emelien greeted, smiling with his flirtatious grin. "What curious offense could possibly trouble you on such a lovely morning, the beauty of which is dwarfed only by your own?"

"...engaging much with the others," finished Johanna, not at all happy about her own choice of words. She tried her best not to sound as if she was levying an accusation, but clearly, he intended on flirting, causing her to blush. "I mean, you're from our destination, Urocia—but Crand is too; Owl and Rabbit aren't though. My point is, I just don't see you interacting with any of them very much."

"We actually didn't know each other prior to this mission," he replied, not sounding the least bit perturbed. "I only met Crand in Tyrna a few days ago. I was headed home anyway, Grand Master Nicholas said you newcomers needed a guide when you reached Latana, and so I volunteered. It was the least I could do for him, for Tyrna's royal court and the Grand Master Council."

"Our mission?" Johanna wondered. *How much does he know?*

"To help you find a new home—I wanted to personally make the case for Latana as we welcome you all, especially those with special abilities," the Urocian lord stated confidently. "You see, I know the other kingdoms are not quite as welcoming to outsiders, especially those with the ability to use magic. I believe you will find our humble utopia quite agreeable and a good choice for resettlement. You may even prefer it over any potential offering Mondlichtberg may extend for you to return to your world."

"Yes, well, I certainly appreciate the welcome," she replied, smiling with relief. Shifting the conversation back to the original subject seemed like a better idea given Grand Master Nicholas's warning not to talk about their primary mission for the swords. "The others really seem to be nice guys. I just don't see why you don't join in with them more. I make no judgments about you personally, but you seem rather aloof."

"I don't suppose there's much division in society where you're from?" He laughed before turning to Johanna quietly. "We have a clear hierarchy in Urocia."

"Well, yes," she began, her horse nickering as she adjusted her reins. "Some have more wealth or opportunity, but generally, where I'm from, we all have the same shot at whatever we want to be and follow our dreams and aspirations to their conclusions. Some succeed, some fail, but ultimately, we are the product of our choices."

"Sounds rather nice for the peasant folks; no offense," Lord Emelien chuckled disarmingly. "That would not work here; how would you maintain order?"

"I don't know what you mean by that," she replied, squinting and feigning annoyance. "That sounds rather judgmental."

"Urocia is more class-driven," he sighed. "It always has been, and I suppose it always will be."

"Sounds like a typical monarchy," Johanna quipped. "We did fine when we ditched ours."

"Our caste is made of several families, but we're all pretty much interrelated now; we could use a fresh infusion of new blood," he suggested, looking off into the distance. "Perhaps your people might be just the infusion it needs. I would personally guarantee your people would never be on the lower rung!"

"I don't know how well we'd mix into your caste system," Johanna admitted. "I'm sure we'll consider it, though."

"It's not bad; even the peasants are happy with it and benefit greatly," he admonished proudly, turning back to her with a gleam in his eye. "Farmers are farmers, and they will always be such. Blacksmiths are blacksmiths, and that won't change either—my point is, our caste system is older than Tyrna itself. Tyrna was originally an outpost for

Urocia—just as now Levens is an outpost for Tyrna. I bet no one mentioned that before!"

"I'm sure there may be some disagreement on that matter had we brought it up there," she teased.

"Tyrna exists at our pleasure. What we require, we receive," he stated, leaning in closer to her until she thought he might fall off his horse. Just then, his face took a sterner tone, and Johanna detected a notable indignance welling to the surface. "Make no mistake about our standing; we are superior in every way."

"Oh." Johanna blinked. That answer had not been something she had expected. "That seems rather, oh, how shall I put it—arrogant?"

"Arrogant?" he questioned, looking uneasy for just a moment before he flashed his dazzling grin again. "Just something my father told me long ago, a saying we have."

"Superior," she scoffed. "Sounds very unevolved."

"Please don't misunderstand my pride for arrogance," he back-tracked. "We have a very proud history, and I really do hope you enjoy your stay in Latana. I will be very honored to show you around when we arrive. Johanna, you are from another world, but trust me on this—if you liked Tyrna, you will love Urocia. You'll see; the people of our kingdom are happy regardless of what part they play in our society."

"I'm sure," she stated dryly, letting the awkward moment fade as the sun shone on his face. They continued riding on through the after-noon, forgetting the awkward political disagreement and just enjoying small talk.

He turned the tables, asking her simple questions about where she was from and what her interests and hobbies were. She spoke about her passions for helping others, cooking, and even gardening. She even laughed that she was enjoying herself this day because she had often excelled at horseback riding as a young girl and hadn't had the opportu-nity to enjoy that again until now.

The more she opened up, the more intently he listened, saying very little other than to offer a comment of surprise at "how industrious" she was and amazement at how "versatile" her interests were.

"You truly are an amazing woman, Johanna," he stated at one point, a glimmer in his eye as he locked her in the grip of his gaze. "I really know no one else like you; the women of my world tend to follow a single path. You seem to excel at many things!"

Nate watched from the Jeep, taking in the scene playing out before him in a cold and quiet contemplation. He had expected the turn of events leading them here would bring them closer together, yet ever since they had come through the Shimmering, he couldn't help feeling they were moving further apart. The whole Sir Caspin ordeal led him to believe they were not drifting but accelerating apart.

He might find it distasteful, but Johanna had every right and was free to explore other relationships if she really wanted to; he just couldn't imagine her exploring one here, in this world. Certainly not with a captain of the guard from Tyrna! Still, he shook his head when he thought about it. Sir Caspin's advances had annoyed him in Tyrna, but now that they were on the road, he had thought it a fluke and that it all was well behind them. Seeing her now with Lord Emelien, had he been wrong?

Aros rode up beside the Jeep and knocked, interrupting his thoughts. "We'll be coming into Cierna at nightfall, and I'd like to ensure that we will have lodging," Aros announced when Nate rolled the window down. "It may be late, so I'd like to ride ahead with you in your 'metal beast' to make arrangements."

"Sure, hop in!" Nate invited before pausing to whistle to Johanna. When she looked back, he shouted, "Hey, Aros and I are going to push on to Cierna; do you wanna come with us?"

"Um, I may be able to help more here," she stated, glancing briefly at Lord Emelien, then back to Nate, considering the option before offering a polite smile. "Yeah, I'll stay with the others for now and just catch up to you there."

"Suit yourself," he replied. The interchange, albeit brief, left Nate annoyed. She had said little to him the previous night and even less to him this morning. With Sir Caspin no longer in the picture, he had hoped she would resume time with him; however, their rift only seemed to widen. *Now this Lord Emelien seems to catch her interest; he's too young, and that flight of fancy should pass quickly. Better him than that Sir Caspin jerk!*

Owl and Rabbit were happy to retake their horses, and Nate stopped briefly to allow the native trackers to unload while Aros jumped into the front with him. After a brief goodbye, Nate and Aros drove ahead, pushing on to Cierna.

Within the hour, thunderheads began to stack and build across the plains, casting shadows over the billowing grass. As the winds began to pick up, a smattering of rain began to dot the windshield. The scent of rain on the horizon brought with it the promise of cooler air and moisture.

As the coming storm stirred up the dust on the trail, Nate pressed the Jeep faster when the clouds above released rain in sheets. He turned on the windshield wipers and chuckled when the movement caught Aros by surprise.

The moment encouraged Nate to explain more about the electrical systems in the Jeep, which Aros could explore by reaching out with his power as Nate turned on one system at a time. It was difficult to explain the radio since no radio signals were present, but Nate popped a CD into the player.

The wizard seemed startled at first by the sounds coming from the speakers around him. When he placed his hand on the CD player, it flickered briefly as Aros explored the wiring to the speakers within the system and seemed to understand.

Time suddenly seemed to fly by as the duo exchanged ideas and theories behind the elements utilized for electrical flow and how they may be utilized and altered. Conjecture and theory arose out of the conversations on how magic could be augmented with science to further the practice.

For Nate, the diversion from Johanna's deteriorating affections was a welcomed one. The wizard's never-ending curiosity about the technology afforded Nate the rare opportunity to express his own expertise around electronics and the way the systems functioned.

It was well after dark when the Jeep reached the first signs of civilization. By then, the thunder had ceased but the clouds blotted out the final rays of sunset. Rain descended on them in sheets of a relentless downpour. The once dust-covered roadway transformed into a thick, muddy and soupy mess. The SUV carved deep swaths into the passage as Nate was forced to engage the vehicle's four-wheel drive, struggling to guide the vehicle closer to town.

"At least it doesn't seem as cold down here," Nate grunted at one point as he drove. Slipping and sliding on the muddy road, he struggled to keep the vehicle centered as they ascended a hill.

"We're much closer to the sea and the Bay of Uorcia the further north we go from here," the wizard gasped, holding onto the grab handles and dashboard with white knuckles. "It will be much warmer from here to the capital. Although I must admit, this storm is unseasonably warm!"

In the failing light, they could make out the lights from the town ahead, a collection of wooden structures haphazardly strewn to each side of the road. Faint candlelight shone through the myriads of windows and shadows bustling about between the buildings, passersby struggling to stay dry in the deluge.

"Hold on!" Nate turned to the wizard and winked, bringing the vehicle to a stop. They had neared the top of the rise, and the Jeep's headlights blazed upon a crooked wooden sign reading, "Welcome to Cierna." The lettering was displayed clearly despite the worn sign swinging in the breeze. A wide grin spread on his face as he read it aloud. "I have an idea."

"Now, Nate, we attract enough attention to ourselves already, there's no need to—" Aros never finished his sentence.

Nate gunned the engine, running the Jeep down the road and straight into town, horn blaring and lights ablaze. As they reached the center of town, Nate slammed on the brakes, bringing the Jeep to a sudden stop just short of gathering crowds of people awash with terror and agitation. Stricken in fear by the sounds of the "strange beast" running up the road toward the town, they had all come out into the streets to see what was coming.

The headlights illuminated a line of pale, stricken faces as a phalanx of soldiers rushed to greet them, spears drawn. Aros glared briefly at Nate as they came to a stop, blocked by the commotion and cluster of people gathering and shouting.

"I'm sorry, I'm sorry," Nate roared with laughter. "I just couldn't help myself!"

"I suppose maintaining a 'low profile' has been all but forgotten?" Aros muttered, shaking his head. He opened the door with an audible sigh and stepped out to calm the crowds. "Nothing to see here; everything is okay, just something new we are trying out with the order."

Quickly recognized as a member of the Order of the Moon, calm was restored among the throng. A somewhat unkempt, portly man, balding with a scraggly beard stepped forth and removed his helmet. The captain of a phalanx from Tyrna beheld them with wide eyes before bursting into laughter. A second contingent of trembling soldiers had hastily assembled a smattering of spears and swords nearest a saloon. Their ranks swelled as a motley group of partially armed and half-drunken men also stumbled out to see what the cause of the commotion had been.

"You had us all going there for a minute, wizard!" the commander hooted. "This past quarter hour, the whole town was up in arms, wondering what roaring beast breathing fire was headed up the road to devour them!"

"We apologize for any disturbance our arrival has cost the town," Aros muttered, shooting Nate an annoyed glare.

"Not at all!" The captain was laughing so hard; tears were streaming down his face. "You should have seen the look on my first officer's face! When I ordered the men to line up, he thought they were about to meet their doom! Only halfway to Latana and the snake-men already had a surprise waiting for us!"

Indeed, many of the town folk had gathered around the idling Jeep, purring like a great cat. Murmuring, they ran their hands over the head-lights and the engine hood.

"What sort of metal beast is this anyway?" the captain asked. "I've never seen anything like it!"

"Everyone asks me that!" Nate proclaimed, priding himself on the coming explanation. "It's just a fancy chariot made from metal and bits of scientific ingenuity. Got over 400 horsepower in here!"

"But where are the horses?" another soldier asked, unbelieving as he tapped the hood. "In here?!"

"They're under the hood, all packed in nice and neat!" Nate explained. "We measure the output of an engine in horsepower, not actual physical horses. It's run by an engine; all just science, not magic, and nothing dangerous. Feel free to check it out, but I'm going to lock it up after we park!"

Along the street, squat buildings were interspaced with pens for beasts of burden. The buildings were barely held together by wooden pegs, and they leaned slightly over muddy streets with livestock mean-dering between.

People scattered ahead of them as Aros pointed out the Cierna Inn midway through the town. When Nate parked the Jeep in front of the covered wooden porch, the wizard went inside with his coin pouch in hand, reluctantly glancing back to make sure his ward stayed out of trouble.

"Don't worry, Aros, I'll wait here on the porch for Johanna and the others!" Nate called out with a grin. "I promise, no more outbursts or tricks for the locals!"

The wizard seemed satisfied with his word and went inside. Nate's mirth faded as he took a moment to look around, even as the rain pattered down. The onlooker's curiosity was quickly dispelled by the coming rain, and they began to seek shelter even as steam wafted from the resting vehicle.

The Cierna Inn stood as a plain and rickety wooden building, much like The Wanderer Inn they had stayed at in the deep forests between Levens and Tyrna before. The other buildings were smaller and no more grandly constructed. This town was obviously a wayside stop between places and resembled a ranching and farming community on the plains. Nate likened it to an old Western movie set.

Inside, the Cierna Inn had small windows and not many decorations other than candleholders dotting the walls. For such a plain accommodation, though, the inn seemed to be the center of activity for the town as both locals and outsiders mixed in the main lobby for evening socialization and entertainment. The smells of the evening meal mingled with the scents of leather chaps and damp riding boots among the patrons crowding inside.

Given the crowds jammed inside, Nate opted to stand in the entryway, peeking in now and then to see Aros's progress in securing accommodation for them with the dual-duty bartender and innkeeper. He continued to stare down the south road leading into town, waiting for signs of his entourage from the shelter of the porch.

Watching the occasional passerby brave the rain pause to examine the Jeep, he laughed to himself as they muttered suspiciously to each other. Interest in the vehicle seemed to be waning though, tamped down by the weather. As he waited for Johanna, he noticed that nearly half of the people in the tiny town were soldiers dressed in peasant garb, crowded in among the likely few permanent inhabitants.

With the passage of time lengthening, Nate became worried and began to pace. Just then, Johanna finally came riding into town, soaked and covered with sludge. Riding tandem with Lord Emelien, she had somehow lost her horse, and he had his arms wrapped around her from behind, trailing the remainder of their entourage behind them.

Holding her firmly in front of him, her breasts and nipples stood out as faintly visible through her wet clothing; she seemed to relish his grip. She laughed and carried on the way she had with him many months earlier—and hadn't since.

The Urocian lord seemed to hang on her every move while helping her down off his horse, like a "true gentleman," and even kissed her hand. His icy blue eyes fixed on her every move as she blithely skipped atop the mud over to the inn's porch, floating on a high of elation.

"Oh, Nate, it was terrible! You should have seen it!" Johanna laughed when she saw him glowering back at them from the entryway. "I fell off my horse when the downpour started, and it ran off without me! I was covered in mud, and Lord Emelien had to pick me up—"

"Yeah, I can see that!" Nate shouted, cutting her explanation off, uninterested in hearing more. The rage in his tone caught the attention of the others in their group as they arrived. Embarrassed, Johanna brushed herself off and cleared her throat but said nothing. "Why don't you come inside and quit making a spectacle of yourself!"

"Oh, Nate, it's nothing," she stammered. "I'm just a mess and wet..."

"I can see that, and it's not just from the mud and rain!" Nate spat.

"Allow me to explain, if I may," Lord Emelien offered.

"No, you may not!" Nate snapped, throwing him a glare before ushering Johanna inside. Nate flushed briefly, fists clenched and trembling with rage before realizing how loud his retort had been. He didn't bother to look at anyone else, particularly at the Urocian lord, who stood smirking in the rain.

Once the group entered the inn, Aros handed out keys in awkward silence as Nate took an extra for Johanna.

"I made sure I got you one next door to me," Nate fumed as he handed her the key. "We may not be able to sleep together, but we wouldn't want you doing something you might regret, would we?"

"We're *not* doing this here!" she whispered in a brisk retort. The spat in the lobby clearly drew attention of those inside, and a brief silence ensued. Snatching the key out of his hand, she stomped up the stairs to her room as he followed. Blushing and holding her bags close to her soaked blouse, she ascended the stairs quickly, refusing to turn even as he followed.

"Why not?" Nate shouted as he turned to follow in pursuit up the stairs. "You didn't seem to mind the whole town see you wallow in the mud?"

She ignored him until they were well down the long hall and stood in front of the door. Turning to him in the hallway, she clearly indicated that he would not be welcomed into the room. He pushed inside anyway and forcibly shut the door behind him.

"Who the hell do you think you are, talking to me like that?" she snarled, following him inside. "I would never do that to you in front of others!"

"In front of others?! What the hell were you thinking, parading yourself around out there like that?" he lit into her. "It's one thing that you insult me in one world, but you've taken it well beyond the pale in this one! You're unbelievable!"

"It was nothing, Nate!" Johanna fumed as Nate ranted and raved before her. "I don't know what to tell you!"

"Don't know what to tell me?!" he shouted, throwing his hands up in the air. "Normally, you're a practical woman! Now, you have nothing to say about it?! It sure as hell didn't look like nothing to me!"

"Nate, I'm so sorry," she said suddenly when she saw through the anger and recognized the pain behind it all. The rage within her receded, leaving only an invisible chalky foam of guilt in her core. When his incoherent rant faded, the empty sadness she felt choked her response down to a barely audible whisper. "Really, though, don't you think things are different now?"

"Different how?" he demanded, still venting the unseen pressure below the surface of his furrowed brow. "First Sir Caspin and now Lord Emelien?! What the hell are you trying to prove? Working on seducing your way up a corporate ladder?"

"That's not what this is, and you know it!" she whispered, swallowing the painful ache in her throat as she searched his eyes, her lower lip beginning to tremble. "Being here in this new land changes everything; I fell off my horse, he helped me, and that's it! You need to just get over it!"

"I don't know what the hell you're talking about!" he shouted. "This wasn't just falling off a horse. You were literally parading yourself around with the next man who looked your way since Sir Caspin back in Tyrna! I know you all too well, Johanna; I could see it written all over your face!”

“Fine, I enjoyed it!” she snapped. “You satisfied? Everything's changed since we got here, but we've had these issues all along, even back in Denver! Things are different now, and I just don't see you and I staying the same, given how things are going!”

“What? Are you insane? After all we've gone through, you want to drop me like a hot potato and find a new love with someone from *here*?” he emphasized, gesturing in frustration with his hands. “We're trying to LEAVE, are we NOT?”

“Keep your voice down,” she whispered in a harsh hiss. “I went with you on that drive from Denver for a vacation, a break and to get away! You've known all along that I was married before and that I wasn't ready to settle! I'm sorry, but honestly, even there, we were not doing well! Now we are here and well, I need more time for myself!”

“Time for what?” he yelled, throwing his hands up again. “Time to go shack up with some other guy and then say, ‘Oh, poor Nate, thanks for hanging in there, but second place isn't good enough for you; now you go to third!’ That's bullshit, Johanna—I've stuck with you every step of the way since Bill died, and he was my best friend!”

“I was his wife!” she cried out before she could stop herself.

“Yeah, and I was there for all of you!” Nate finished coldly after a long pause. “I'd ask Bill for his opinion on this, but he's not here. I think he would agree with me, though; I deserve better from you, and you know it!”

He let that last statement stick in silence, glaring at her from across the room. He hated that his voice had quavered when he said it, but he had needed to say it for quite some time, and now it was out there.

“Nate, please,” was all she could manage, the guilt of the unspoken truth between them resurfacing. Her own voice cracked as the truth threatened to flood forth. She still cared, but this argument was a long time coming. “I'm sorry for letting this linger for so long, but things are only recently clearer to me.”

"No, I've had it! I've had it with you and your unstable personality! I deserve better!" he stated hoarsely before leaving the room, slamming the door behind him and storming back down the hall.

Walking downstairs, Nate caught sight of Aros standing alone near a window, watching the rain fall. Strangers clogged the walkway between the bar and the dining room, milling about and feasting on malt beer, meats and potatoes. Scullery maids bustled busily, hustling to take care of all the guests. Nearly half the room was filled with the soldiers from Tyrna.

At least no one down here would have heard us upstairs, not with all the racket going on down here; where'd they all come from anyway?!

"Nate," Aros greeted him sympathetically as he approached. "I'm not sure what happened earlier, but I hope you and Johanna..."

"Never mind her, I'm done with that," he miffed irritably. "Where are the others?"

Aros gestured at the bar where Lord Emelien was laughing it up with some men in guard uniforms, obviously leaders of their houses since their tunics contained emblems of the family crests on them. One had an elm tree, another a fox and many more with the telltale Tower of Tyrna. The Urocian lord turned and lifted his mug of ale in a toast, a knowing twinkle in his eye.

"How long do we have to rely on that guy?" Nate fumed in disgust even as he clenched his teeth to return a forced smile. "No, never mind! Don't answer that; I'm going out before I walk up to him and knock his teeth out!"

Aros sighed to himself as he watched Nate go, then glanced back at the gloating Lord Emelien in contemplation. Nate's question weighed heavily, and he was glad he didn't have to answer it for the time being.

The wizard knew little of the Urocian lord's history. When Grand Master Nicholas had called for assistance on their mission, Lord Emelien had stepped up immediately. His father's connections, wealth, influence and knowledge of the region would be critical to their success once they reached Latana.

Lord Emelien's manners, however, were proving less than desirable, particularly since he had unexpectedly inserted himself between Nate and Johanna. The lord's flirtations came across in bad form, especially for a highborn of his caliber. Given all the eligible pairings both within Urocia and beyond, it had come as a bit of a surprise that Johanna appeared to have caught the lord's eye. Older, a complete outsider and clearly with another man, the lord's choice seemed quite out of character for a highborn of his station.

"This may turn out to be a problem we do not need!" the wizard muttered aloud to himself.

≈≈≈≈

Nate stepped out into the cool evening air, and the relief was immediately palpable. The rain had stopped, and the air cooled as clouds raced in retreat across the evening sky, clearing as stars began to pepper the evening twilight. Soldiers still bustled about, and Nate found one to converse with, standing alone and guarding their horses. The pungent smell of mud permeated the air, but the fresh winds had already begun drying the roads and kept the air clean and cool.

"So, what's the deal with all the infantries?" Nate asked in casual conversation. "Staying out of the mud, hopefully?"

"Training, sir!" the young man answered. His eyes shone with pride, even if he was a bit scrawny. Obviously, this meager detail was aptly assigned to a recruit. "The fighting is in the east, near Farsperk. The snake-men are poisoning crops and demanding land from us all, but we'll crush them despite the mud! It should all dry by tomorrow; so we're told anyway!"

"Is that so?" Nate mused, the conversation proved uninteresting so far, but it was far better than going back to the inn.

"Tis!" exclaimed the young soldier. "The mud hindered us this evening, but with the storm clearing out and a good day of sunshine, we should be alright! Whatever's left over the grass will soak it up and we'll be underway on the morrow!"

"So, where are you from?" Nate asked, not expecting to really know even when he was told.

"Just north of Levens, sir," the young man replied. Nate perked up at this. "Northern Guardian burnt my home, and me mum and dad moved into town. I had nothing better to do since we sold half the harvest before the rest was destroyed, so I joined up with this lot!"

"Ah, yes; I know the area," Nate said, "We came in from there not long ago."

"Really?" the young soldier replied, his attention perked. "There's not many settlements out that way—I don't ever remember seeing you before. My family and I know everyone within twenty miles of our home!"

"Sorry, no, we came *by* that way," Nate clarified, realizing that he probably shouldn't have said anything.

"Strange way to come here," the young man noted skeptically. "Where are you from exactly? Just wilderness, out beyond where I'm from. I never believed anyone else was out there—just wizards, hermits and wolves!"

"Yes, but it's so beautiful," Nate interjected, anxious to leave the conversation now. "Especially this time of the year. We're explorers... and fur traders."

"So why are you headed to Urocia?" the young man probed. "You and your fancy beastless carriage? This all part of the Order of the Moon's new experiments?"

"It's all for the war effort." Nate winked, inwardly exasperated now with the interchange and anxious to leave. He feigned a quick salute before turning to depart. He slogged his way through the mud toward the barn at the back of the inn, muttering to himself, "I'm not going back into the inn, but I'm going to get myself into trouble talking with the locals!"

Inside the small, rickety barn, he found Owl and Rabbit playing a game of chance with a set of bones, stones and twigs. They looked up and smiled when he walked in and invited him to sit atop the mounds of hay piled around the floor, scooped away from the center, where a single candle burned. The barn with the candlelight provided a surprising sense of warmth out of the cold and damp.

"Don't get up for me, fellas," Nate sighed, plopping down on the ground next to them, "Show me what you got going here; maybe I can just jump in!"

They explained that the bones and twigs had one set of values and were dependent upon the array of stones that fell at their sides. Each player added up the points and could retain that value to cash for trades on additional tokens. Nate took right to it and relished in the simplicity as well as the diversion from the previous confrontations of the evening.

"So, where's the lady of the group?" Rabbit asked with a smile. "She coming down to join us too?"

"Nah, I'm really enjoying this, sitting around with just us guys tonight!" Nate stated before changing the subject. He looked up inquisitively as an impulse seized his thoughts. "Why do they call you members of the Clay Tribes?"

"It's what our people do," Owl explained, beaming with pride as he reflected on the name. "We've always utilized the land and bounty around us for our day-to-day needs. Our lands are rich in many types of clay, which we use for our homes and our pottery. If indeed we are the descendants from the 'Anasazi,' as your woman referred to them, we've continued their traditions."

"My woman," Nate scoffed, shaking his head. Owl and Rabbit glanced at each other but said nothing as they began to play. "Sorry, guys, I don't mean to involve you. If you couldn't tell, we aren't exactly getting along right now."

≈≈≈≈

Johanna had mulled at her situation long after Nate left. Relieved to have him gone, she wondered to herself if he could be right. He had slammed the door in her face, but it seemed odd that the fiery exchange had bothered her less than she anticipated. She knew he was right as she stared at the closed door long after his departure but couldn't help that she felt differently now.

She still cared for Nate, but her day with Lord Emelien had left her feeling elated, and she couldn't deny it. For the first time since they had come to this world, she hadn't felt afraid. She had enjoyed herself this day and refused to regret it. She sat on the bed, still staring at the shut door, unmoving and deep in thought. *Am I being selfish? Is this just a flight of fancy, and should I just pull my head out of the clouds? Nate was a good man—Nate IS a good man...I just don't feel anything anymore!*

Johanna was just starting to lie down on the bed when she heard a soft knock. She walked over to the door, figuring out what she was going to say to Nate, assuming it was him, before opening it. *Perhaps he has returned to apologize?*

It wasn't Nate—Lord Emelien stood there, smelling slightly of ale but as gentlemanly as ever.

"I stopped by to make sure you were comfortable," he soothed, flashing his intoxicating smile. "I do not wish to intrude, but I noticed you and Nate arguing earlier, and I wanted to stop by and make sure you were faring alright. I wanted to apologize if I did anything to cause you distress."

"Oh, yes, I'm fine, thank you," she stammered. "Nate went out to get some fresh air. I'm just going to call it a night early."

"You needn't lie to me about him, Johanna," Lord Emelien stated softly. They stood staring at each other in an awkward moment of silence before the Urocian lord spoke again. "I have many men just like him under my command, just like him, and they are all good men. I hope I am not overstepping my bounds here?"

"You're not overstepping, but I'm not lying either," she protested yet looked away. "He's just a little jealous, and I can't blame him—"

"Nor can I blame him," he interrupted, placing a firm yet gentle hand on her shoulder, giving it a barely perceptible squeeze and caress. "He's a leader and provider, now far out of his element. However, I'm not here to talk about him. I wanted to check on you, especially since I just couldn't imagine you here awake, upset and alone."

"Well, I actually asked to be left alone," she stated, quickly becoming self-conscious with the building tension at the doorway, desperately wanting to pull away from his hand sending heat into her being yet unwilling to offend the extension of his gesture. "I'm fine, thank you, Lord Emelien—in fact, I was just headed to bed."

"Tsk, tsk, tsk," the Urocian lord playfully scolded, releasing her shoulder to her relief (*or was it disappointment?*). "You mustn't go to bed alone, especially after such a terrible argument with your, I don't know what to call him: Spouse? Love interest? Caretaker?"

"Nate is just upset," Johanna scoffed. "He's a fine man and is just under a lot of stress! He was a dear friend of my late husband, who has since passed away. He's a great friend, and you are right—he's a good guy! But to answer your question, we aren't married, but..."

"You don't say!" the Urocian exclaimed. His smile filled her with delicious guilt, making her heart jump as he leaned in closer to her. "Well, while I'm sorry to hear about the loss of your husband, I daresay that leaves you open to other suitors, does it not?"

"I thank you for your sentiments," she muttered, looking to the floor, not wanting to pursue the interaction further even as she blushed. "After everything we've been through, this is hardly the time for that conversation, with me or anyone." *If Nate comes back while he is here...*

"Nate's done a fine job keeping you safe despite your ordeal; he obviously cares for you and your son," Lord Emelien complimented. "I just want you to know that in your search for a new home, if you were to choose Latana, I would personally ensure that your choice was well-founded. I would not only look after you, but in my utmost respect for you, after your son and even Nate as well."

"Why would you do that?" She cringed, meeting his gaze again to ascertain his meaning. "We're strangers to you and your family!"

"Perhaps the ale is getting the best of me, but hear me out," the Urocian lord laughed, his eyes twinkling with eagerness and anticipation. "You and your people are quite unique, even amongst ours. At face value, you have much to offer any community you choose to settle. That aside, I am most intrigued by you, Johanna from the lands beyond the Shimmering! I find you...simply refreshing!"

"That is most generous," Johanna stated, picking her words carefully as she said them. "I'll have to think about it and talk to the others about it as well. Grand Master Nicholas is our Advocate, and by proxy, Aros."

"My courtship of you would come with additional benefits," he promised. "You would have no need for a continuation of Nicholas's Advocacy; my family name would assume full responsibility for your well-being. I would be your Advocate!"

"Courtship?! We've only just met! Good night, Lord Emelien!" she managed to say, flashing her own shaky smile before quietly shutting the door. She rolled her eyes even as the latch caught. "I'm sure we'll talk more about it another time!"

"I know we will! Goodnight, sweet lady!" he sighed, pausing as he maneuvered his mouth to the gap in the door frame. Placing her back against the door, she could hear him lean into the door to whisper. "I know you saw me bathing back at the spring last night! I only wanted you to know that your secret is safe with me! That, and that I didn't mind; you can watch me bathe anytime! In fact, if you decided to do more than just watch, I would welcome it!"

With that, he walked away, leaving her heart pounding. *Did he just say that?*

Her heart swooned, although she dared not respond to his words setting her very flesh afire. His soft whisper had pierced through the door like a hot sword into her chest. *That was unlike anything I've ever heard before—so direct and so open! Just because we are in a fantastic land doesn't mean I have to live in fantasyland!*

The moment passed, and she breathed a sigh of relief when his boot steps faded down the hallway. Putting on her nightgown, she climbed into bed. She lay there for nearly two hours, dozing on and off before hearing Nate's footsteps at the door.

There was a long pause at her own door as Nate seemed to be

making up his mind about whether or not to knock. She listened quietly, pretending to sleep as she heard him sigh, before turning and entering the room next door. From there, she could hear him undress before struggling to find comfort alone in the other bed. When the noises in the other room fell silent, Johanna's shame flooded through her as she choked back tears of confusion before finally falling asleep.

Chapter 25

Westward

Javier rode his steed alongside Dex as they started down the trail, surveying the landscape ahead to get the lay of the land and take in the expanding view of Long Lake as they marched closer to its distant shores. The heat of this day would have been summer-like had it not been for the cool fall breezes descending from the Grenze Mountains' high country, billowing through the waving grasses.

"Once you are on the north end, you cannot see the shoreline of the south and vice versa," Dex explained with gruff pride. "Even on the eastern side, the shoreline in the west is not visible, although the Grenze Mountains are so high that, on a clear day, you can see their faint outline in the distance."

"Like today," Javier observed aloud, pointing at the expanse of the lake at the foot of the mountains. "I can't believe how big that lake is! Reminds me of one of the Great Lakes in the Midwest, except with huge mountains right behind it!"

"Like today," Dex agreed. "Grand Master Nicholas selected our group of men from the Tracker's Guild because of our knowledge of the wilds and the least-traveled routes. The western shore has one seldom-used trail but is mostly a wilderness frontier, save only the occasional fur trapper. It's quite wild and can be dangerous, but we are suited for it should we need to forage along the way."

Javier glanced back over his shoulder at the others. Davyn plodded close behind them, the silent albino saying nothing yet following closely. His white hair was almost blinding in the sun, and he turned his head from side to side as he surveyed the way ahead with eagle-like eyes. Kevin followed, chatting eagerly with the two cat-men, Crisken and Brythen. Warley and Fliegel brought up the rear of the column, speaking in low tones to each other, keeping pace with the group ahead of them as they descended through the fields of Tyrna, towards the vast expanse of Long Lake.

"What of the eastern shore?" Davyn interjected, noting attention had shifted his way. "I still don't know why we don't travel along better roads!"

"Worry not, my pale friend, we won't be traveling upon either," Dex acknowledged. "The grand master indicated we were to keep a lower profile for this trip. In order to keep the lowest profile possible, we will charter a sail barge to sail south upon the lake. Many merchants utilize Long Lake for trade and transportation of large volumes of cargo; we'll stow alongside one of them."

"What's past the mountains?" Javier asked.

"Only a few explorers have ever returned from beyond the mountains to the west," Dex surmised. "Great beasts guard those passes and tales are that the Grenze Mountains fall right into the sea. There's one known pass to the southeast, where the mountains descend and become passable in a narrow canyon. Some say a lost sect of wizards fled civilization through there, but none have returned to verify that. Most travelers curve alongside the diminishing foothills of Carthen to the southeast until they reach the Southern Kingdoms, where one may access friendlier pathways to the ocean. Otherwise, the Grenze Mountains are known to be impassable and wild, stretching all the way from Levens to the Southern Kingdoms."

"Ah, well, I don't suppose we'll be going that way then," Javier muttered, drifting off in thought. "I would love a beach day!"

"Well, the best beaches are near the Southern Kingdoms, if that be your wish," Dex intoned with a grin, yet turning serious as he lowered his voice so no one else would hear. "Nicholas told me about the swords you seek. The brown sword is likely somewhere south of Carthen, in a very heavily forested region. However, the blue sword is going to be somewhere in or near the ocean beyond. If the swords had been closer, they surely would have been uncovered by now. We are going to have to go beyond known civilization before we can even expect to begin looking for these ancient lost talismans!"

"So, we're in for a difficult journey after all," Davyn laughed aloud. "No leisurely beach days!"

"I'm just saying it would be nice," Javier grumbled, wiping the sweat from his brow as they rode. "When you put it that way, it makes me wonder what chance of success we have at all."

"'Tis a challenge, to be sure," Dex agreed. "Grand Master Nicholas has a hidden asset that lives in the wilds not far from South Long Lake. We may solicit his help if the need is dire, but otherwise, we are not to engage with him. Grand Master Nicholas wanted our company to ride in secrecy, and I promised that we would. Once we reach the shores of Long Lake, we will charter a boat to take us to the southern settlement. Once aboard and safely out on the lake, we will brief the rest of the men en route."

"Well, if you can't trust your own men, who can you trust?" Javier smiled. The comment seemed to put Dex at ease, and the trapper sat up straight on his horse with a look of satisfaction.

"I like your attitude, young man," Dex laughed, slapping Javier on the back. "We seem to understand one another, but I gave my word to the grand master! Not until we are underway without risk of eavesdropping from anyone other than Davyn here, who was party to my original briefing!"

Kevin glanced ahead at Javier conversing with Dex and Davyn but kept his attention on the cat-men. Brythen and Crisken welcomed him among them and made a space for him to ride between them. Although fascinated by their mewling accents in their own language, they readily shifted into the common tongue as he rode beside them. Conversation flowed easily as they were as curious about his world as he was about theirs.

"Mrawl, so tell us more about cats in your world, Kevin," Crisken coaxed with a yawn. "Are you friends with any there? I heard you were a student there; do they go to school with you?"

"Um," Kevin began, unsure how to answer, "cats in my world are revered and loved, but not like you and Brythen here."

"We're different?! How so?" Brythen seemed taken aback. "You and Javier look like Fliegel and Warley. Your kind blend together most readily. I can't imagine it being that different."

"Well, most cats are not as intelligent there as they are in this world," he fumbled. "They're more like Sammy, the hound you saw with Daniel before we left. You're also much larger and, um...more active!" *How am I going to explain this?*

"Like a dog?!?" they exclaimed together. That elicited a laugh out of the feline pair as they continued chatting happily. "I cannot imagine our kind would be anything like a hound!"

The group continued through the day, snacking on apples, jerky and nuts as the sun bypassed the travelers overhead on its march down to the shores of the vast Long Lake. When the sun began to kiss the distant peaks, a gentle pink hue settled across the sky.

The scent and humidity from the great lake began to permeate the air as they descended from the higher fields. As they drew closer to the shoreline, thicker grasses grew green and tall, having not yet turned with the season. Large shrubs began to cluster in thick groves around them as the scent of water and cool, moist air hung about them.

Twilight descended, and a few lights dotted the vast lake as barges traversed the watery expanse ahead of them and lit their evening lanterns. In the distance, Dex pointed out the lights of the northern settlement winking at them through a cluster of buildings and docks on the northern shore of the massive lake.

As the trail met a roadway, foot traffic became heavier. Beasts of burden towed carts of supplies to and from town along the thoroughfare. They joined the throng, passing by a multitude of docks lakeside. Parked by each of the docks, a great number of wooden vessels, barges and fishing boats in a variety of sizes bustled with activity. The scent of fish and fresh mud filled the air.

Men hoisted fishing nets and other cargo off the vessels while seagulls cawed, fighting over the scraps littering the mud flats. Errant boxes lay half submerged in the muck, having dropped from nets as crews struggled to hoist most of the cargo dockside.

"The lake level looks a bit low," Kevin commented, noting that most of the smaller docks appeared empty and exposed in the mud. "Seems like only the longest docks are accessible."

"Yes, the fall harvest is upon us, and the lake level falls this time of year," Brythen mewled. "Especially when the north winds blow."

As they drew nearer to town, the larger docks crammed with activity, jutting out into the water where hulking barges and smaller fishing vessels jammed together. The bustle concentrated on the few deepwater docks where men worked in a frenzy to unload their cargo.

The lake had receded beneath smaller and shallower docks, exposing glistening mud flats beneath them and stranding any smaller vessel that had docked earlier. The overnight shift in the harbor's depth relegated the shallower docks to mere temporary storage and the stacking of crates to make room for the fervent use of the larger docks.

"This could become an issue for us tomorrow," Crisken pointed out, calling to Dex riding at the front. "Mrawl! Dex, we had better secure transport quickly; if the north winds pick up, this could be a problem!"

"Agreed!" their leader called back, waving them on impatiently. "For now, we must find a place to spend the night. My contact will let us know what we need to do once we're settled."

As the dirt road faded behind them, they plodded onto the cobblestone streets leading to the center of town, the waterfront near the docks still a flurry of activity. Fishermen folded their sails and stowed their nets as shopkeepers closed for the evening. Here, in the oldest and most condensed part of North Long Lake, the roadway joined and followed the south end of the Rhane River, flowing to the lake's northern edge. The river emerged from the northern forests, cutting through the center of town before spilling out onto the lake.

Upon reaching the convergence of the river and the lake, the group dismounted from their horses and walked them along the busier thoroughfare.

"We'll lodge here tonight," announced Dex as they gathered around him. "The local lodges should be full of lake captains for hire, and we should be able to secure a boat for tomorrow. My contact has several he works with, and we should have no trouble securing one."

Across the slowly flowing river, Kevin could make out the other half of town, not more than a hundred yards away. Brythen sauntered up to his side, standing by the roped railing, staring across the river.

"We could just walk across, couldn't we?" Kevin commented.

"If it's all the same, I'd rather not cross on foot," Brythen commented through a needle-sharp grin. "I hate getting wet."

"It seems that's another thing cats here have in common with those from my world," Kevin chuckled. "You appear to share the same aversion to water!"

"Mrawl, don't let appearances fool you!" Crisken warned. "The river can be treacherous, even outside the wilds. This one flooded the town recently, and although it appears shallow, there are many hidden pockets that are well over even the heads of our steeds!"

"Well, it looks like tomorrow's problem," Kevin sighed, pointing to their leader already gathering the group together in the fading light off to the side. "Looks like we've got lodging tonight settled!"

Dex guided them to the Bog King's Inn, ironically represented by a banner of a large frog wearing a crown, not far from the riverfront. The rickety wooden building had a soft layer of green moss lining the stones and wood of the outside. When they entered, they passed a roaring fireplace as they walked to a dining room with less than ten tables, serviced by a scullery maid with scraggly blonde hair and missing teeth.

"Make yourselves at home, boys, I'll be right with ya," the maiden hollered as she bussed tables and welcomed the new patrons as they entered. She had a slightly burly build to her, but she smiled shamelessly in a warm greeting regardless.

"Take your time!" Dex called back, smiling appreciatively. The scent of roasted vegetables and mutton filled the tavern as they clustered inside. "That smells delicious!"

"Pa!" she screamed, turning to shout into the kitchen. "Guests!"

An elderly gentleman appeared, lean and balding with grand spectacles perched on his beak of a nose. He had an odd hunch to him as he shuffled across the wooden floor to the podium at the entrance.

"Eight for dinner, is it?" the caretaker asked. "Or ye wanting lodging too?"

"For dinner and for lodging, if you've got it!" Dex stated as he pulled a bag of silver from his cloak, jangling lightly to accentuate their readiness to pay.

"We do indeed, although you'll need to double up." The older man smiled as he handed out keys for two rooms. "I advise dinner first; we are at capacity these days, what with the north winds a-blowin'!"

"Point taken." Dex nodded back to the group, gesturing at the larger table with benches near a small window. "Best take that spot soon before they fill up!"

They quickly sat and the scullery maid promptly brought a hearty meal of mutton, offering an option of fried fish for those who didn't want meat. Potatoes and a variety of greens accompanied the fare, and the group ate in silence, observing the influx of noisy patrons at the bar and the surrounding tables.

After dining, Javier and Kevin accompanied Dex and Davyn to their room. The stairwell they took led to the second floor and had a musty smell to it; clearly showing the inn's older age. Dimly lit by wall-sconced candles, the light gave a soft glow down the narrow hall to the otherwise meager choices of rooms, giving the establishment more of a cottage feel than a hotel.

Kevin burst into laughter when Davyn opened the door and he saw their accommodations. He pointed at the thatched roof and tiny beds parked side by side near the window.

"Something wrong?" the pale Davyn asked.

"No, it's fine," Kevin snickered. "It looks like a room from the tale of *Snow White and the Seven Dwarfs!*"

"Which dwarves? I see none in this entourage," the albino muttered, shaking his head. No one else seemed to understand what he was talking about, so he let the comparison go. "We're all gathered in one great room; at least we can keep track of each other that way!"

"Eh, no worse than a college dorm," Javier intervened before turning quietly to him, prodding him gently back out into the hall. "C'mon, Micker, let's go back out and explore the town!"

"Don't be gone long!" Dex called after them, catching sight of the two newcomers making their discreet exit as the rest of their party filed in. "We have an early start tomorrow morning just as soon as we locate and pay for our charter!"

"Got it!" Javier shouted back over his shoulder as he and Kevin departed. They raced back down the narrow stairwell, laughing, pausing only briefly in the dining room to scan over the crowds filling the tavern, just as the innkeeper had warned. Pushing through quickly while they still could, they exited into the cool evening air. "Aye! That place got busy!"

As they exited the Bog King's Inn, they quickly noted that the north winds had stalled and quiet had settled in along with the crisp coolness of night. Lanterns flickered gently, and crickets chirped as the Rhane River bubbled black under the night sky alive with stars. The duo strolled disappointedly past a multitude of stores, closed and dark within for the evening, leaving them to window-shop. As they meandered from window to window, a thin fog rolled in off the lake, bringing a slight chill to the air, and they hugged their tunics around them.

Conversing in low tones, they said very little as they explored the empty side streets of the medieval village. They had not gone far when a young boy stepped out from behind a cart in an alley. The boy had mussed curly brown hair, and his face was smudged with dirt. His hands appeared worn, obviously from a day's labor.

"Hey, what are you looking for?" the lad asked. "I got a few apples left in me cart if you wanna buy 'em?"

"No, we had dinner already," Javier volunteered casually. "We wanted to shop, but everything's closed around here."

"Of course, everything's closed—no use in opening when no one can get here at night," the boy replied as if nothing could be more apparent. "Supplies held up at the docks when that northern wind's a-blowin'. Eastern roads are full of traffic. Other than trappers, rumors of the Beast of the Forest keep people from usin' the western trail, so there's no sense in being open!"

"Beast of the Forest?" Kevin began. "What's that...?"

"Surely there's a pub or fun place to go," Javier quickly interrupted him. "What do you people do around here for fun?"

"Fun?" The lad squinted, perplexed. "Don't you work? When we have time, we play along the lake or maybe visit the Pratenvike in Tyrna."

"Well, we just came from there," Javier groaned in disappointment. "The guys we are traveling with are looking to leave in the morning and head south, so we're looking for something now."

"Oh, well this area of town is mostly for trading. My dad and I fish here, and that's our shop," the lad proclaimed, pointing over his back with his thumb to a shuttered store. "We'll be open in the morning with fresh catch, more produce and maybe even some textiles from the south if you wanna browse what we have then."

"Good enough!" Javier stated, giving him a thumbs-up, but this time, it was Kevin who interjected.

"What about this Beast of the Forest?" Kevin persisted. "What's that about?"

"Everyone knows about the Beast of the Forest, even in Tyrna!" the boy scoffed before explaining the situation. "It started coming down from the Grenze Mountains last summer to hunt. Won't bother you if you're indoors or in town, but best not be on any road west of here at night! Trappers at the outpost west of here swear it takes their animals, but even people have been known to disappear from time to time."

"It doesn't come near here, does it?" Kevin asked.

"Nah, it hates being seen by people, especially near town," the boy dismissed, wrinkling his nose at the notion. "Some say they've seen it prowl near the river on the other side every once in a while, but mostly, it stays far west of here...well, mostly." He drifted off as if suddenly doubting his own statement.

"Enough of the fairytales," Javier interjected, eager to change the subject. "Why isn't there a bridge to the other side of town?"

"Wow, you really aren't from around here!" the lad exclaimed, shaking his head. "Several seasons ago, we had a big flood after spring rains hit the snow up in the mountains. All the water came down and washed out our bridge. Wiped out a bunch of houses in town, too. They haven't rebuilt it yet, and the river stays deep enough that we have had to ferry across ever since!"

"Must have been quite a flood," Kevin murmured.

"It was," the young lad agreed with a yawn. Beginning to tire, he looked away. "Well, I'm happy to sell you an apple or fish, but you said you already had dinner. I'm settling in for the night, and my dad's expecting me home."

They bade the lad a good night, and the boy wandered off down a torch-lit alleyway. Disappointed by not finding any other open establishments, they turned to go back to the Bog King's Inn. Passing briefly by an empty wagon with furs hanging from an open line, Kevin caught sight of movement behind the cart.

"Whatcha lookin' at?" Javier elbowed him.

"Nothing, it just reminds me of something I saw earlier," Kevin sighed. "I ran into a guy who described a wagon like that back in Tyrna; maybe it was in Levens. I don't see the guy though."

"Probably indoors like the rest of these people in this place." Javier shrugged. "Would be pretty weird to run into the same guy here though, wouldn't it? Besides, no one has really bothered us yet, and we've been careful not to expose ourselves too much."

"Probably; he'd have to be following us the whole time! He did say they hunt in this area though," Kevin recalled as he sighed. "Looks like our evening exploits are a bust! Seems to be no one else around. Not exactly party central!"

"Well, I guess so, Micker," Javier scoffed. "Just you and me, and other than a toothless beauty back at the inn, looks like no women for us tonight!"

Kevin rolled his eyes but acquiesced. North Long Lake clearly had shut down for the evening, and the Bog King Inn had the only action they were likely to find.

When they arrived, Dex was outside talking to a short, squat man with only one eye and a red beard. They stood beneath the swinging sign of the frog with the crown. Seeming to have concluded their business, the man turned and waddled off into the night.

"Kevin! Javier!" Dex called out when sighting the pair, motioning them over. "We've secured transportation in the morning. The man I spoke to is a trader from the south end of the lake. He goes by the name Lefty Jeck, and his barge is west of here, anchored just offshore."

"I guess that means we found our ride." Javier winked. "Don't worry, Kevin, it's still in town and free from the clutches of the Creature of the Trees!"

"The what?" Dex coughed, stifling a laugh.

"Just something some kid was telling us about," Javier laughed. "Had Micker in an uproar."

"Beast of the Forest," Kevin corrected him, blushing slightly. "I wasn't in an uproar, I just wanted to know what it was. After hearing about Grimmigwulfs and God only knows what else, I figure we'd better realize what we are dealing with."

"Ah, yes," Dex sighed, his face a sudden sober reflection of understanding. "It's very real, Javier—at least to these villagers. I can't say I've ever seen it since it sticks to the deep wilds of the Grenze Mountains, but there are rumors of it hunting along the western edge of the lake on rare occasions. It's a solitary creature, even more so than the Grimmigwulf, and they avoid civilization and each other. I don't plan on encountering either!"

"See, Javier." Kevin pointed. "I told you that—"

"Kevin, Javier's right about one thing, though. I wouldn't worry about it since I've secured passage across the lake," Dex gently interrupted. "We will be traveling by barge; the important thing is that you both have a big day ahead of you and an even bigger journey until we reach the southern shore. Go inside and get some rest now while you can!"

Chapter 26

Friends

Princess Serina had been working hard all day at Mondlichtberg, and upon careful self-reflection, she was content with her progress in preparation for her final trials. She had always known how to project a bubble around herself to deflect rain, rocks, hailstones and bugs. Now, she knew how to create movement on the shield's surface, not just for deflection but even calculated redirection.

She spent most of the day strolling the gardens with Grand Master Yamaro to practice for her tests. The more she learned, the more she realized how little she had known before. She had always assumed her force field was merely a sphere of energy she could conjure. Far more intricate than she had realized, the grand master taught her untried strategies and methodologies to alter her fields' shape and intensity.

During one session, she kept the force field as a sphere but double-layered it into a disc. She lengthened it into a rod and used it like a hammer, testing it on several large stones in the courtyard.

Additional manipulation of the fields into sickle shapes illustrated an ability to throw an opponent if ever needed. She cringed at the idea initially, but when Grand Master Yamaro added, "or an improper suitor," they both broke out into laughter at the prospect.

Throughout the day, she and the grand master worked together as they toured the compound. As they moved throughout the castle grounds, a nagging surprise gnawed on her at how few students resided at the keep. As the day ended, they moved their activities back into his office, high above in the central tower.

She secretly relished her time in the grand master's tower since the ambiance reminded her much of the Wizard's Tower in Levens, only slightly larger and more richly appointed. High in the tower, the wizard used his silvery staff to gently highlight and identify the exact outline of Princess Serina's field even as she extended it.

The princess observed the glowing blue line he highlighted around her field with great interest. He carefully traced the boundary of her personal shield on the stone floor in front of her. She smiled as a sudden thought occurred to her. *I can sweep dust; this will come in handy for Charla, my housekeeper.*

"Now, carefully shift it away from you," Grand Master Yamaro said, interrupting her thoughts as he withdrew his staff to his side. "You can do it; instead of wielding it like a hammer, operate it as you would a fine instrument!"

"There!" she said. The dust on the floor moved faintly away from the field as her barrier seemed to blur and turn blue. *It isn't blurring—it's moving!* Now, she rotated the field the other way, and the dust seemed to move with it as her field shifted from blue to red.

"You should take stock of what you've learned and focus on practicing just this for the remainder of the week," Grand Master Yamaro advised, a smile of satisfaction on his face. "After this, there's one more thing I'd like to show you."

"What is it, Grand Master?" Princess Serina nodded in agreement, breathing heavily from her exertion.

"Turn your field inside out," he said, clasping his hands together and then wringing his palms out for emphasis.

"Why would I do that?" she asked.

"Two reasons," Yamaro stated. "One is to penetrate another field, and the other is to bring something *to* you."

"Okay, I'll give it a try," she sighed as he pointed to a vase on the bookshelf near his desk.

"Gently, now, use the 'rod' to push the vase slightly," he encouraged. "Just slightly!"

She reached out with her mind, pointing with her hand, and created a narrow beam in her mind's eye. Nevertheless, a faint blue hue, narrow like a tube extended from her hand to the vase, just touching it. The vase shuddered and then shuffled an inch, dangerously close to falling to the floor.

"Now, turn it inside out," Yamaro whispered. "Gently, now; slowly!"

The field brightened for a moment, and suddenly the vase whisked across the room and straight into Princess Serina's outstretched hand.

"Whew!" exclaimed Yamaro with a laugh. "I was afraid we would have to replace that!"

"The time we've spent honing my field prevented that necessity!" Princess Serina smiled. *This could be useful, indeed.*

"I'm afraid we've well missed lunch entirely and must ready ourselves for dinner!" the grand master mused, glancing out the darkening window into the sunset. "We can work on perfecting that more at another time!"

"What?!" Princess Serina exclaimed, suddenly realizing her stomach was making noises. "I hadn't realized so much time had gone by!"

"Time has indeed gotten the better of us this day, I'm afraid," the old wizard chuckled. "Let us join the others for dinner. We've done enough for today!"

The pair descended the stairs into the main dining hall and Princess Serina caught a glance of Sorceress Amina, glowering in the corner of the room alone. Grand Master Oaxro beckoned for Yamaro to join him from a table near the roaring fire.

Although the princess had never met Oaxro personally, his reputation as an oversized, dark-yet-brooding man preceded him. He had just returned from another recruitment trip in the south, and his ominous features and black beard gave him the appearance of perpetually scowling, even when he was happy.

"Why don't you mingle with the other apprentices and make some new acquaintances?" Grand Master Yamaro suggested when he caught sight of the Copper Wizard. "I'm afraid I have some business to attend to."

The two grand masters strolled off together, seeming to launch into discussing something unpleasantly intense. As Princess Serina watched, she turned and made her way to join the younger apprentices. Glancing back, she noticed the sorceress observing her as if anticipating her attention.

"I cannot expose you. The time is not right to reveal our hand yet," Amina projected her voice into Princess Serina's thoughts. *"We will meet later, I promise."*

The princess casually nodded, as if to herself, and turned to find an empty seat among the bulk of the students, risking a quick glance back at the sorceress to let her know she understood.

After eating a few bites of the pot roast and asparagus, the princess decided to engage with the others around her in the rare moment they had together away from their studies. *Pondering what impossible puzzle the two leaders of our order are shouldering seems far less an appealing prospect than meeting fellow magicians!*

Although most of the other apprentices kept to themselves, she still could detect no animosities or subterfuge in any of her contacts. As far as the other upper-level master wizards went, Amina and Aros were the only ones she had seen since Grand Master Encara had taken the others with him to Latana.

A tap on her shoulder caught her attention, and a dwarf introduced himself to her as Merek. He gestured to a pale and skinny young man he introduced as Peith. The pair took an immediate interest in her and insisted on keeping her company for dinner.

"We've been watching you," Merek grumbled in a sudden shift of topic, even as Princess Serina had just begun to introduce herself.

"Oh, is that so?" Princess Serina arched a sly eyebrow, struggling to hold back a burst of laughter at the surprise that comment garnered.

"What he meant to say is that we noticed you've been sitting alone and are glad you joined us." Peith broke in, blushing in embarrassment.

"Oh! Well, in that case, I'm glad I did," Princess Serina laughed. "I've seen you two skulking around but didn't realize I had become the object of your fascination!"

Merek's demeanor seemed initially gruff, yet his words stayed kind. His kinship with Peith initially seemed like a misplaced pairing yet soon became quickly apparent. Peith's pale complexion combined with his tall and lanky form seemed to contrast notably with Merek's short and stocky form, darkened gruff skin indicative of desert dwellers.

Both seemed so opposite in nature, yet they shared an unspoken bond that the princess could only sense and an insatiable curiosity for the royal visitor. They scooted along the bench in tandem, closer to her to engage in deeper conversation more closely.

Conversation continued to flow more naturally as the awkward introduction was quickly forgotten. Soon, a sandy-haired and freckled younger lad joined them. He reminded her of a much younger version of Daniel, the newcomer she had met days ago.

"I've seen you before; what's your name?" she asked, mild curiosity beaming through her sparkling azure eyes. The young lad blushed briefly before gathering his wits and responding.

"I'm Brice," the boy stated proudly, bowing awkwardly to the princess. Short and somewhat scrawny, he seemed yet another awkward addition to the pair before her. Yet nevertheless, he sat with them as comfortably as ever. He seemed to chitter like a squirrel, his wide, bright brown eyes surveying everything with a nervous energy.

"Well, hello, Brice, it's nice to meet you," she replied with a smile. He blushed as he sat directly across from her, unsure as to what to say next. "You really are an interesting trio, aren't you!"

Peith reddened at the comment but quickly broke the awkward silence with a peppering of questions about her time as a royal in the court of Levens. She was all too happy to oblige, and from there, the conversation continued its natural flow, unabated without further interruption or distraction.

As the meal concluded and the dining hall patrons thinned, the sun set behind the ridge at Mondlichtberg. Princess Serina excused herself and climbed the stairs back to Grand Master Yamaro's office. The past few days had been marvelous, and she wanted to wish her new master a good evening. He had somehow departed the dining hall without her noticing.

Her nagging worry about finding no collusion or ill will among the apprenticeship lessened as her time spent at the keep went by. She had heard very little from Grand Master Nicholas lately other than the enigmatic Sottis escaping captivity in Tyrna. No one at Mondlichtberg seemed to know anything about him, but that didn't mean that there wasn't a connection. *After all, wizards are always secretive, even amongst each other—are they not?*

As she approached the top of the stairs, she could hear voices inside even though the doors were closed. Not wanting to disturb them, she peeked through the keyhole.

Grand Masters Yamaro and Oaxro stood before the tall magic mirror, and from within the reflection, the third grand master, Encara. Their counterpart stood within the mirror, tall and glowering in his telltale golden robes. Deep in a heated conference, Yamaro's elderly figure seemed dwarfed by the abnormally tall Oaxro, while Encara's faded image in the mirror still clearly depicted the man's displeasure. The younger grand master's bald face pulsed crimson with anger, and his eyebrows arched as he argued with the other two. His rageful demeanor contrasted with the regal nature of his long yellow robes, interwoven with fine gems and golden thread, relegating his unofficially given nickname of "the Golden Wizard" to a verifiable truth.

"This is not what we agreed to, gentlemen!" Grand Master Encara roared through the mirror. "You've kept the lesser wizards out of the mix for this ordeal, and I commend you for that, but now you're slipping!! We simply cannot have this level of failure!"

"Grand Master Encara, calm yourself!" Grand Master Yamaro scolded in exasperation. "This exchange is hardly becoming of our circle!"

"Nicholas must have had his reasons!" Grand Master Oaxro rumbled from behind the folds of his long coppery cloak. "He always does!"

"Indeed, we have all known him for years; there is no reason for him to lie about Aros. Surely, he was misled as well," Grand Master Yamaro echoed his agreement. Only the wizened lines that danced on his face betrayed any sense of angst. "We must investigate further to—"

"That's not the point!" raged the Golden Wizard. "Aros was supposed to be contained, NOT roaming the countryside with the outsiders!"

"Our informants have been telling us Aros is in Levens," the glowering Oaxro insisted. "He is seen nightly at his quarters there, contained and comfortable in Levens. It's common knowledge to see his reading lamp lit, high above the town in the tower each and every night!"

"And my sources say otherwise," seethed the grand master of Urocia. "Did your informants actually *see* him or just someone lighting a candle in the Wizard's Tower of Levens?"

"We are a council of equals!" exploded Oaxro, losing his temper as his voice boomed. He gripped his copper staff angrily in frustration as he spoke. "We do not answer to you—we are your peers, not your subordinates! Regardless of where Aros is, it should have nothing to do with opening another Shimmering!"

"Gentlemen, gentlemen," chimed in Grand Master Yamaro, attempting to keep the peace as he gently rolled his silver staff back and forth in his hands. "We *are* a grand master council with much to celebrate in our accomplishments! Oaxro, you've done a splendid job with recruits of late, and we thank you. Encara, your bold idea of bringing in the outsiders *does* appear to work, and we are also immensely grateful for that feat. The mishap with the dragon and the wolves was only a mere setback that we've since corrected for future attempts. The hermit has also assured us that superior sources of wood for staff and wands have been located, and more are coming!"

"Grand Master Yamaro!" Oaxro exclaimed, turning to his counterpart and beginning to shake until Yamaro calmed him with a steady hand. "The hermit has proven most resourceful, but that is hardly the point at hand here!"

"It IS the point, gentlemen; better days are ahead for us!" Grand Master Yamaro interrupted, squeezing the Copper Wizard's arm gently as he turned to face his golden counterpart. "However, Oaxro's question does have merit; what difference does it make if Aros is indeed accompanying the newcomers to Urocia? If that's the case, then they are coming right to you! Take matters into your own hands then. You can confine him, reprimand him, congratulate him...whatever you want to do! You're his superior, and if indeed he arrives in your jurisdiction, we would support you! Let's just discuss that if and when that happens. Enough with the conjecture! This is a non-issue!"

Princess Serina could feel Grand Master Encara's animosity seeping from the mirror even through the very keyhole in the door.

"I will not accept being lied to," the Golden Wizard hissed. "Not by that retired purist fool Nicholas, not by his protégé Aros, and certainly..." He paused, considering his next words carefully as his gaze shifted from the mirror. "Not by anyone else."

"None of us are lying to you, my friend; we are—all three of us, after all—equal members of the sacred Council of Three!" Grand Master Yamaro cautioned, the implied meaning by Encara clearly received. "Nicholas is still a true and trusted ally, but he is no longer on the council. *We* are the core leadership! I have Sorceress Amina under my close supervision, restricted here to the keep, just as you requested. Although Nicholas's actions are unclear at this time, we cannot doubt his intentions. I move that we enlist his assistance the next time we create the Shimmering."

"I object!" Grand Master Encara exploded. "He's proven untrustworthy, and this obsession you have with bringing that prune out of retirement to satisfy an old reconciliation matter is jeopardizing our efforts with the Order of Etoilenoir! Besides, the spell only calls for three, not four!"

"I have all fourteen crystals right here!" trumpeted the crimson-faced Oaxro, snatching a sack next to them and unceremoniously dumping them on the floor. Green, purple, red, yellow, green, blue, white—all different colors of the spectrum like rare gems spilled out in a pile, clattering onto the stone floor. "Why not bring Nicholas in? He's certainly a lot more readily available than you are; only a day's ride, two at most! If we temporarily reinstate him for this one spell, your precious timeline is not threatened. The first winter snow is just weeks away!"

"We have a war here in the east, or have you forgotten?" blasted Encara. "I don't need that old fool taking MY place at—"

"Isn't that the whole point?!" Oaxro shouted, throwing his hands up in the air. "We need recruits now! Your obsession with having your fingers in everything is what's slowing us down! Stick to the plan and let us handle Aros and the others as we originally agreed!"

Oaxro said nothing further as Yamaro placed a gently reassuring hand on his arm again. Brooding silence passed between the three until finally Grand Master Encara closed his eyes and took a deep, shaky breath before speaking again as he collected himself.

"As I said earlier, if Aros shows himself in Urocia, I will move up our timeline," Grand Master Encara began, voice low and determined as he opened his eyes. "We don't have time to consult with Nicholas; convince him, and bring him up to speed if you must. I will remind you, though—he clearly voiced his opposition to our plans long ago. If he wants to support us when we bring in more recruits, I suppose he could aid in their training, much the same way he has for the princess of Levens. However, I would consider his addition as nothing more than as a consultant in the Advisory Council, holding a ranking no higher than an honorary returning master wizard."

Before the two grand masters could respond, the Golden Wizard waved his hand, severing the image's connection. The two remaining

Grand Masters began to shout immediately, whether in agreement or against each other, Princess Serina could not tell. Unwilling to be caught eavesdropping, she retreated back down the winding staircase. The muffled voices of the other two head wizards' heated argument faded behind her in the silent stairwell as she left.

Padding down the stairs silently, she gasped for breath as she nearly collided again with a patiently brooding Amina. The sorceress had been waiting for her in the great hall at the base of the stairs.

"Eavesdropping, Your Highness?" Mistress Amina growled from the shadows of her cowl, arching an eyebrow. "Hardly becoming of a royal!"

"Mistress Amina," Princess Serina said, finally finding her words. "I was wishing Grand Master Yamaro a good night, but he was in council with..."

"No need for pretense; I could hear them from here!" the sorceress scoffed, her eyes narrowing like a cat's. With a forceful hand, she directed the princess behind the stairwell, sheltering them both from any prying eyes in the dining hall. "I may not have the full details, but it did sound tense. You're not the only one highly interested in that conversation!"

"The three of them brought the newcomers here as part of their recruitment efforts!" Princess Serina confessed. "I cannot believe it; against Grand Master Nicholas's advice and pressured by Grand Master Encara, but they did it! They also seem to know Aros..."

"Grand Master Encara is still in Urocia," Mistress Amina said. "With the three of them still separated, then whatever they were up to before has not yet happened. No wonder they've kept the rest of us out of their secret meetings again! This goes beyond simple pragmatism and is against our very teachings of involving outsiders in our affairs. This is downright abduction of outsiders to our world altogether!"

"What are we to do?" Princess Serina asked. "Grand Master Encara mentioned moving up the timeline if Aros arrives at Urocia."

"For now, nothing," Mistress Amina resolved. "Aros is in Levens, so that shouldn't be an issue."

"That's my point; he's not in Levens," Princess Serina admitted in a whisper. "He's with the outsiders on his way to Urocia; I dare not say more!"

"Agreed, let's refrain from discussing this further!" the sorceress gently shushed the princess gently with a gesturing pointer finger. "However, if Encara moves up his timeline, that could change everything, and more drastic measures may be needed!"

"I will let you know if anything changes," Princess Serina promised, turning to leave before saying, "I've been meaning to ask why you were sequestered away from the advisory."

"I suspect it's because they don't like my input and haven't for some time," the sorceress sneered, suddenly conscious of her harsh demeanor. She looked away briefly as her features softened. "A common perception I imagine among others."

"You don't like me very much, do you?" Princess Serina dared to lock eyes with the other woman as she whispered her suspicions aloud. "I just want you to know, I'm not trying to supplant you or your work here."

"Dear princess, it's not that I don't like you," Amina sighed, her rigidity deflating somewhat as she spoke further. She sat down heavily on one of the hallway benches, a sad look washing her cold stare away as she looked out a darkened, narrow window to the outside. "You are royalty and a subordinate, so it makes this all very awkward. Grand Master Nicholas was my mentor, and I felt like our time was cut short for his retirement...before he started mentoring you."

"Grand Master Nicholas moves in mysterious ways and to his own rhythms," the princess agreed, nodding solemnly. "I may have a royal title, but I can assure you that this was not the cause of his moving to something else."

"My dear, you mistake what I said for jealousy of your regal status," Mistress Amina stated, smiling knowingly. The sorceress spoke with a warmth and sadness that Princess Serina had not before heard from her before. "You and I are frankly *very* similar. I too come from the regal house of Bokumba. I'm the daughter of a great countess there, yet my family was not as understanding as yours."

"I had no idea," Princess Serina sighed in understanding, taking the sorceress's hands within her own. *They are ice-cold and tremble with nervousness; this is clearly a very private matter for her.*

"'The dark terror' they used to call me," the sorceress scoffed in confessional relief. "I learned of my ability early on and my fascination with fire. They didn't know what to do with me since, as a child, I loved lighting the torches leading to the great pentagonal temple. I was always scolded and told to keep my innate ability a secret. When I rebelled, they forced me to bathe in ponds and drink large volumes of water until I choked. They said it was to quench the untamable fire within me!"

"What did you do?" Princess Serina balked, reflecting on her own upbringing.

"I rebelled," the sorceress stated simply with a laugh. "I set fire to my bed, my furniture, everything I could come across. Not long thereafter, they stripped me of my title and were about to send me into exile near the cursed lands—my own family!"

"I-I can't imagine!" the princess stammered. "That's unbelievable!"

"It was for me too; even in the South," Mistress Amina recalled as her tone grew bitter, and her face set like stone. "That's when Grand Master Nicholas came to my aid. He stole me away in the night before the caravan of my exile was to leave and brought me here to Mondlichtberg instead."

"All those years, long ago!" Princess Serina sat back thoughtfully. "Did your family ever know what happened?"

"Grand Master Nicholas sent notice three times, twice by carrier pigeon and once by personal courier. They never responded but trust me—they knew." The sorceress stood and gently pulled her hands away from the princess. "My dear, my greatest pain was not from my family; it was when the opportunity came to achieve the grand master title in Latana, capital city of Urocia, and that was taken from me. I would have emerged at the top of this order, and my name and accomplishments would be proclaimed for all to see, whether or not they approved."

"You thought Nicholas betrayed you by leaving early for his retirement only to work with me," Princess Serina sighed as clarity seeped in.

"While I do not deny I had those feelings initially, I came to recognize the truth of the matter," Mistress Amina exhaled. "I really had progressed far enough in my studies to continue on my own. When Encara the Golden emerged as Urocia's grand master wizard to replace Nicholas, I realized the Wizard's Council was no longer the center of the magical world. They had become weak and desperate, grasping for life at outsiders in a slow, withering, decaying decline of their own making."

"You were a better fit for that role," Princess Serina acknowledged.

"I still am!" the sorceress spat, shaking her head bitterly with a smile. "That post should have been mine! Urocia would have eventually accepted me; I know it! However, I've come to accept that regardless of rank, we cannot be in control of everything in this world that affects us. That's life; it's just the way it is."

"While true, I don't know why Grand Master Yamaro didn't see it and act on it," Princess Serina sighed.

"You're close, the two of you," Mistress Amina observed soberly.

"He's been a loyal friend to the Levenese crown for centuries, particularly to my father," Princess Serina admitted. "I knew him as a small child, but it's been ages since I last saw him; that is, until I came here."

"That explains your frequent meetings with him then," the sorceress contemplated. "I don't hold that against you or him. Although, if he showed half that concern for his other students, this order would be in a far different state!"

"Something else has seized his passion for this order," Princess Serina stated. "I know it; I sense it! I just don't know what it is. If only he and Nicholas had stayed close, this would never have happened!"

"Oh, yes, the two of them had a significant falling out, spread out over time," Amina recalled somberly. "They were both great men in their own ways, but Yamaro preferred and offered a kinder, gentler, more subtle hand in leadership. Nicholas was always more of a realist and preferred a direct approach. We were all at a crossroads when Nicholas left as interest in the order waned. It wasn't any one argument that did in their friendship; it was a series of bitter disagreements over the years."

"Why didn't the advisory step in on any of this?" Princess Serina asked.

"The advisory! You overestimate their influence!" Amina scoffed. "They are an overrated bunch of sniveling cowards, blindly following Encara's golden façade, all in the name of pragmatism! Master Aros and I refused to worship his special brand of idiocy! They lap it up like dogs! I tell you, it is no accident Aros and I were excluded from that little maneuver!"

"That explains it then; Nicholas gave up, and Grand Master Yamaro blindly embraced a new direction in hopes it would lead to something better," Princess Serina exhaled as the two women surveyed each other anew in the dying light of the dining hall fireplace. "Thank you again for your candor, Mistress Amina. It really has cleared up a lot for me, and I hope we can be friends through this all."

"Friends," Mistress Amina chuckled appreciatively. "My dear, I would love to be your friend and even your guide through some of the pitfalls I have discovered along the way, Your Highness!"

With that last comment, she ended with a wide grin and a bow, to which Princess Serina responded in kind. With their new understanding, both women bade each other a good night. The sorceress watched the princess go as she ducked back under the stairs to rejoin the others in the dining room. The firelight reflected in her eyes, gleaming with newfound hope as she reflected on what they had shared.

≈≈≈≈

The next morning at breakfast, Princess Serina mingled again with the other recruits she had met the previous night. Grand Master

Yamaro had a messenger deliver the news to her that he and Grand Master Oaxro were going to be busy over the next few days and that she was to practice on her own what she had already learned.

They had been assigned duties outside to conduct touch-up repairs along the keep's outer wall. The day warmed quickly despite the early morning frost still clinging to surfaces.

Merek grunted, shoving some bread her way in his typical dwarfish temperament even as the tall, lanky Peith commented on how warm the weather had become again. Indeed, over the past few days, the grass outside had turned and was going to seed, but flies and bees still buzzed about the castle grounds throughout the day.

On both sides of the entrance, Mondlichtberg maintained a grassy garden between the twenty-foot stone barrier and the main castle for a protected outdoor area of reflection and contemplation. Dotted with stone benches and small trees, it also provided a small sanctuary for relief from the indoor oppressiveness of the keep.

While they worked throughout the day, she learned that Merek had a talent for mixing potions. Apparently, he was more of an alchemist, and Oaxro had discovered him on a trip to the southern dwarf kingdoms. He had refused to be drafted without his friend, Peith, from the outskirts of the southern unified kingdoms. When it was found that Peith had the ability to find things, Oaxro seized the opportunity for their recruitment.

Peith had come in especially handy since the young Brice had been getting out of hand at Mondlichtberg lately. A ward of Encara from Urocia, Brice had been an orphan deposited at the sanctuary because he had demonstrated the opposite ability—to hide things. Sadly, the boy seemed starved of affection and knew little of his own background. He also seemed singularly bent on mischief. After a short period of time, Grand Master Encara insisted Brice would be a better fit at Mondlichtberg rather than becoming a member of the Order of Etoilenoir or taking up his time under personal tutelage.

Upon Brice's arrival at Mondlichtberg, Peith and Merek took him under their wings. Peith had been able to thwart Brice's mischief, and

Merek had taken a stern approach with the lad, enforcing a new sense of discipline for the boy he had never followed. While outwardly Brice had resisted the approach, it was the first time anyone had shown personal interest in him, and he adopted himself out to the pair.

Princess Serina listened with great interest as they worked. As she got to know them better, she began to feel more confident in her interactions with them. Their skills with masonry seemed uncanny as she quickly learned not only by working with them, but also by watching how they handled the clay, bricks, and plaster. Their personal stories and their diverse backgrounds intrigued her as the rest of the day and evening seemed to fly by along with the repairs to the wall they had been assigned.

When the bells tolled and the sun began to set, signifying the end of the day, they strolled back to the main entrance together. The evening air had a crisp feel to it again, and they let the coolness wash over them as they strode along.

Princess Serina laughed when Brice loosened Peith's change purse dangling from his grey magician's cloak. She watched the change purse drop to the ground and seem to vanish, realizing that Brice was using his power to hide it. Peith immediately closed his eyes in concentration to locate it, which Brice anticipated would happen almost immediately.

To Brice's great glee, she even contributed to the mischief by moving the tiny bag about with her own fields, sliding it along with her innate power through the grass to a nearby shrub. She winked at Brice, who giggled as Peith's concentration seemed interrupted and a look of confusion overcame his narrow face.

Once he located the lost item, Peith took it all in stride, turning to the princess and pointing a knowing finger at her. Even Merek had cracked a rare smirk at the spectacle.

It was nice to have friends to dine with that evening. They quickly cleaned themselves up for the evening meal, barely skipping a beat to pick a table not too far from the fireplace as evening temperatures dropped and a cold draft percolated near the main entrance.

To have peers whom she could enjoy was something beyond her

experience as a royal, and this was the camaraderie she had been searching for. They compared notes that evening on their teamwork, their strengths and their challenges. At least for now, all sense of rank and etiquette had vanished, leaving only a group of four comrades happy for each other's company.

The mission she had been sent here to accomplish haunted her, but making some new friends along the way didn't have to hinder it. As much as she wanted to get to know Amina more, this new group of friends didn't have the hierarchal limitations she currently had with the sorceress. For the first time since her arrival at Mondlichtberg, she allowed herself to briefly forget the mission for Nicholas and enjoyed what she always wanted—be an apprentice for the Wizard's Order of the Moon and experience the camaraderie with the other apprentices as an equal.

When the dishes for the evening had cleared and the hearth's fire had died to a low glow, Princess Serina almost regretted having to retire for the evening. Returning to her room, sleep initially eluded her as she anxiously awaited the next day, excited as to what new experience with her newfound friends it may bring.

≈≈≈≈

The princess of Levens awoke the next morning, her jet-black hair spilling about her feather pillows, blue eyes red and irritated from the lack of sleep from staring at the ceiling as she had awaited the coming day.

Plagued with new doubts about the Grand Master Council, her mission for Nicholas, and her newfound friends, her night of sleep had been fitful at best. It had been a long night and hardly restful, yet she felt compelled to push on. The distant howling of wolves through the night had echoed through her partly opened window, accentuating the sense of foreboding.

Keenly aware she was overdue to report back to Nicholas, she vowed to start with that task, forcing herself to get out of bed and get dressed. Since her arrival at the wizard's fortress, her efforts to find a source of conspiracy against Aros or Nicholas had been frustratingly futile. This whole charade of sleuthing around the Order of the Moon seemed pointless, and the only conspiracy she could find was that of a dilapidated bureaucracy. The problems here seemed to point more to a matter of overcoming a decrepit establishment than that of an outright plot to overthrow leadership.

As she opened her bedroom door to go to breakfast, her worries melted away as Peith, Merek and Brice greeted her at the doorway, waiting patiently for her to emerge. Her new friends jumped at the suddenness of her emergence, vaguely hiding a small wooden cart behind them.

"Gentlemen," she muttered in surprise, raising an eyebrow. "Rather early, isn't it? As happy as I am to see you, I must ask—what are you doing skulking outside my bedroom?"

"Your Highness! We didn't want to disturb your rest," Peith stated as he bowed low. His thin form bent playfully as he blew a long lock of sandy hair away from his eyes. "We wanted to get an early start on the wall again today with you!"

"The wall's not here, my friends," Princess Serina laughed. "It's outside, and I need breakfast first."

"That's why we brought you this!" Brice jostled the cart forth from behind the trio, the younger boy clearly eager to please. Lifting the cover atop a plate, he revealed a steaming plate full of scrambled eggs, sausage and toast. The scent of freshly cooked food hit her immediately, and her stomach growled in protest. "We've already eaten so now it's just about waiting for you!"

"For me?!" Princess Serina smiled at her new friends appreciatively. "I don't know what to say!"

"Say you'll hurry and eat it so we can get going," Merek grumbled through his scraggly, dark beard. "We have a lot of work ahead of us!"

The stocky dwarf clearly wanted to get going, but through his gruffness, the princess could see he was equally vested in her joining them.

She invited the trio into her room as she quickly downed the morning fare.

"You shouldn't rush her like that," Peith whispered to Merek.

"It's okay, really," Princess Serina intoned through a mouthful of food, dabbing her lips with a napkin. "I was looking forward to helping you guys out, anyway. Frankly, I had something else on my mind, and you've made my morning much better!"

"You have somewhere else you need to be?" Brice raised an eyebrow. His freckles seemed to sparkle with the same curiosity in his hazel eyes. "Grand Master Oaxro told me wall repair must be completed before the first snows. Mondlichtberg is so isolated and high up in the mountains and we're the only ones around to keep up with this sort of thing, and..."

"There's nowhere that's more important than with you three!" she stated absolutely and without hesitation. Princess Serina winked as she set the matter aside, taking in a deep breath. "Okay, let's get to it, shall we?"

Within no time, they were out at the castle's wall again, teaming up to patch loose portions of the wall as regular maintenance. This time, they worked near the main gate, where a set of wooden scaffolding lay propped up against the wall.

Merek produced several vials and mixed them into a set of waiting clay pots beneath the scaffolding. After muttering a few words and a brief flash of light, he produced several steaming buckets of foul-smelling, bubbling muck, almost like algae heated with tar.

"Slather the bricks with this and it will strengthen the replacements to adhere bricks to the walls," the dwarf instructed and pointed. "I've already stacked replacement bricks along the base of the wall."

"Okay, well, with me here, you won't need the scaffolding," Princess Serina announced. Without another word on the matter, she lifted her arms, spinning the familiar glowing rose threads from her fingertips. Enveloping a waiting Brice in the warm glow, she raised him up to the top of the wall. High atop the ledge he perched, followed by several of the steaming pots of Merek's concoction, which she levitated after Brice. The lad began the work on the upper sections, leaving Peith and Merek to fixate on the lower portions.

As the sun continued its trek across the sky, Princess Serina looked on with admiration at her newfound friends. While their labors continued throughout the day, smiles and laughter abounded despite the pungent smells of plaster and grout dripping from bricks and onto their robes. *This is living!*

Chapter 27

Latana

When the caravan led by Aros left Cierna bright and early the next day, they were pleased to see they would be the first on the drying roads. Johanna opted to ride with Nate in the Jeep to try to reconcile their differences from the previous night. Nate drove and Aros rode horseback alongside the Jeep with Lord Emelien and Crand taking point. Owl and Rabbit delighted themselves with riding on the roof rack of the vehicle as if they had broken in the metal beast and now utilized it as a traveling lookout post.

Peasants and soldiers alike gathered to stare at the odd group departing from town, milling about to gaze a final time at the metal beastless carriage. Many stood, shaking their heads in disbelief until the bizarre caravan disappeared completely down the road, vanishing along with the blowing prairie wind as the rising sun brightened the landscape.

Johanna initially tried to make small talk with Nate for the first few hours as they bounced and jostled down the dirt road but found that he simply wouldn't engage. Seeing that chitchat about the weather and their other companions was going nowhere, she finally lay a comforting hand atop Nate's, resting on the armrest console between them.

"Nate, I get it," she began anew with a deep breath. "We touched on a sore subject last night. It's been there before, and we've both felt it even though we haven't spoken about it. Our relationship: we've drifted apart and it's not the same, but it hasn't been for some time now."

"How can you say that?" he chastised her sullenly, withdrawing his hand. "After everything we've been through. What about all this time we've spent together, even before we got here?"

"C'mon, Nate, it's obvious we still care for each other," she pressed. "I would feel better knowing that at least this wasn't a one-sided issue. It began before we even came through the Shimmering, but now we're stranded and the strain we've been under only makes it more obvious. Tell me you don't agree!?"

"I don't agree!" he bellowed suddenly. "For God's sake, Johanna; we even talked about getting married and having kids together at one point!"

"But we didn't," Johanna whispered, driving the point home like a knife. "You brought it up once long ago, and I told you I wasn't ready for that. We never spoke about it again, and with good reason. Bill's death hit us all hard and in different ways. Having a conversation like that would not only be improper, it would be nothing but a fantasy considering we were all still going through so much pain!"

Nate said nothing. He looked over at her briefly, but when he looked away, no words were needed. Both he and Johanna seemed unable or unwilling to push the matter further since neither could deny the decline in their relationship.

To Johanna's relief, they switched back to talking about other members of their caravan. Nate changed the subject, conveying what he had learned about Owl and Rabbit during the strange game they had played in the barn the previous night. He had asked them about their descendants from a long line of tribes that sounded to him much like the Anasazi cliff dwellers that had vanished from North America.

He had asked them about how they felt standing out among other cultures, such as in Tyrna and Latana. Owl had admitted that there was some discomfort, but truly the diversity in the world was so wide, they felt like just another part of it. Rabbit pretty much agreed with whatever Owl said, so it was difficult to ascertain whether the two were always of like mind or if Rabbit was ever really listening to the conversation. His enthusiasm always prevented anyone from questioning his engagement.

"From what they've told me, I think you're onto something," Johanna added. "They remind me a lot of what those rangers told us about Chaco Canyon and Mesa Verde during our last trip there. Their tribal history just has too much in common with the Anasazi to be ignored."

"Who's to say their ancestors didn't end up here the same way we did?" Nate remarked with a smile.

"What is it?" Johanna smiled back, glad to see Nate's mood lightening.

"Those two." Nate shook his head, pointing at the roof with his thumb. "They really complement each other. Owl is the brains of that operation, but I think Rabbit keeps him going—all that nervous, youthful energy."

On impulse, he pounded on the roof of the Jeep with an open palm and surprised them both.

"Hey!" their muffled voices yelled back to him from outside, eliciting another chuckle from the driver.

The moment of levity was short-lived, and soon, they sat again in silence. The unspoken looming admission of earlier seemed to catch up and take a back seat, only to inflate until it permeated the entire vehicle.

Johanna sat across from him wordlessly, staring out the window, her smile fading as Nate glanced warily over at her. The history with her passed briefly before his mind's eye. *Surely, she is worried about our relationship too! Now, it all seems more like a fantasy! Even if I adore Daniel, maybe I should just let her go...maybe I should quit trying.*

"So, what if we don't get back?" he asked suddenly. "I mean, what kind of plans, if any, should we be making?"

"What was that?" Johanna asked, turning back to him with practiced politeness as if she hadn't heard. *I'm not sure how to answer.*

"I mean from this world back into ours," he repeated, refusing to believe she hadn't heard him. *She is clearly stalling to think about her answer.* "I don't mean to focus on a negative, but it's a distinct possibility that we might not be able to return."

"Then we'll all make do, I suppose," she considered, her face dropping slightly. "I have a lot to offer with my healing skills. You do, too, mister electricity."

She winked with a brief flicker of humor before looking down and away again. *He's not having any of that. Best not to joke about this.*

"Yeah, we both have skills to offer..." he trailed off into bitter silence, contemplating his next words. He began slowly but purposefully. "Things really have changed between us though, haven't they?"

"They have," she whispered, turning to him and grasping his hand again. Despite taking a deep breath, she said nothing further to deny it but held his hand loosely, not wanting to interrupt.

"I feel it, too," Nate admitted before summoning the passion within him for a final attempt. "Sometimes, real relationships take work. But Johanna...we have history. Are we really ready to throw that all away?"

"We do have history," she acknowledged. "Ask yourself, though, Nate: do you want to keep reliving history?"

"Probably not," Nate agreed with a sigh, turning his attention back to the road. Releasing her hand gently, he did his best to do so without the bitterness in his voice. "Depending on how this Latana and Urocia turn out, maybe we'll want to make a new home there. Maybe we'll just go back to Tyrna, or even Levens. Maybe you'll go to one place, and I'll go to another; part company and be on our merry ways!"

"It's not something we have to decide right now," Johanna assured him with a smile of sympathy. "Are you going to be okay? I mean, with Lord Emelien or anyone else who may come along? At some point, you might be the one to find someone new, and I'll have to get used to that. You are still a very attractive man, you know."

"Thanks," Nate managed to say through a clenched-teeth grimace.

"I'll be fine. I just wish these jackasses weren't so obvious about pursuing you; it's downright disrespectful! I mean, no offense, Johanna, you're also a very attractive woman, but this Lord Emelien's gotta be half your age!"

"Half! I don't think so," she admonished lightly before becoming serious again. "I'm sorry, Nate. I wasn't being very sensitive either; you have been truly a gift for both Daniel and me. Just know that I wasn't pursuing anything with him or Sir Caspin. I'm just trying to be polite to those who are helping us."

"Yeah, well, I don't have to like it," he sighed, not quite believing her explanation. "Just give it time, I suppose."

"Yeah, I think that's best," she agreed. "Speaking of time, we're well past lunch; why don't we give our friends a break from the sun?" she suggested, changing the subject.

"Go for it," Nate chuckled, absent of bitterness but with a certain degree of reluctant acceptance. *This conversation has been way overdue, but it still feels unfinished and unresolved.*

"They'll appreciate it," Johanna assured him as she rolled down the window and tapped the roof. "Hey, guys, anyone want to ride inside?"

"Sure!" the exuberant responses from the native men came back. Nate rolled down the back windows, and without even stopping, the two Clay Tribesmen slid through with little effort, limber and agile.

"Thanks," they echoed each other enthusiastically, smelling of sun as they settled themselves in the back seat for the ride.

The landscape continued to roll on by with gentle hills and very sparse trees—mainly elms, shrub oak and the occasional cottonwood. The grass grew long and flowing, rippling with the wind as far as the eye could see. Whenever the breeze shifted, the patterns would flow through, extending for miles, like waves of water on the ocean.

Later that afternoon, Nate could see Aros and Crand in front of them stop and discuss something atop their horses. A little further ahead, Lord Emelien had intercepted a wagon being drawn by two oxen and was conversing with the drivers.

"What's this?" Johanna pointed as Nate brought the Jeep to a halt.

"Looks like someone they know. I'm going to go have a look," she stated as she exited the Jeep, gently shutting the door behind her.

A balding man with white hair and plain traveler's garb sat atop the wagon between two pale dwarves with full dark beards. Both dwarves held the appearance of wealthy merchants and looked like twins, donning long brown beards and over-embellished clothing with purple and red stripes. Their eyes shifted nervously about, but their wizened faces had a playful look to them. The canvas from the wagon overshadowing them comically matched their attire, keeping the riders cool from the lowland sun.

"Everything okay?" Nate inquired when Aros trotted his horse back to Nate's window.

"Oh, yes, I believe so," Aros replied, a bit distracted by the scene ahead. "This is apparently a merchant Lord Emelien's father has dealings with often. I overheard them say that they're returning to Long Lake's southern settlement. We'll be on our way again shortly."

Nate drummed his fingers impatiently on the steering wheel as Lord Emelien pointed to the west and then to the south. The dwarves nodded vigorously, seeming to confirm something he was telling them. *What's taking them so long?*

As if reading his mind, Aros rode up and announced himself to the wagon. Nate could see that they had stopped their conversation and warmly acknowledged the wizard as he introduced himself.

"How rude of me! Please allow me to introduce my companions," Lord Emelien exclaimed, cued by Aros's appearance. He pointed to each of them, from the Jeep to the horses, who in turn waved.

"Nice to meet you," Nate called from the Jeep, declining to step out.

"This is Beloun and Dorieon; they own the Inn at the Oak, a lovely lodge in South Long Lake, friends of my father," Lord Emelien indicated. "Their driver, Hannok, is returning them from a rather lucrative expedition to Latana."

After niceties were exchanged, the wagon master assured them that they were nearly to Latana and should see it over the next rise come sundown. The dwarves and the wagon master eyed the Jeep suspiciously but said nothing openly about it.

Soon, Lord Emelien bade them farewell, and in return, Dorieon reached back into the covered wagon for a sack of fruit. When Aros opened the bag, the contents resembled peaches, and he handed individual ones to the men on horseback while handing the remainder to Nate in the Jeep.

"With my compliments!" Dorien proclaimed with a wooden voice. He smiled, nudging the man they rode with to drive on. "Nice wagon—if you ever want to sell it, come see me at the Inn at the Oak in South Long Lake. I could use a beastless carriage such as this! Remember—Dorieon or Beloun!"

"You bet I will!" Nate laughed, patting the side of his prized vehicle. *We may just do that if we end up living here.*

"I'm going to take a break and ride for a while," Johanna stated, tapping Nate's arm as she opened the passenger door to exit, pausing briefly as her eyes met his. Flashing a brief smile, she looked away as she shut the door behind her, calling out to Crand to offer her seat in the Jeep.

The dwarves continued onward, diminishing from sight down the road behind them.

Nate silently watched her go, holding himself back from interfering. Crand offered her his steed before dismounting and returning to the Jeep and taking the passenger seat, closing the door behind him as Aros motioned for their expedition to move onward to Latana, presumably just over the next few grassy hills.

As the group resumed their journey, Johanna examined the bright, fleshy fruit in her hand. Taking a bite, she took in the sweet, succulent flavors as the juice permeated her mouth.

"Oh, Nate, these are wonderful!" Johanna called out to him as she bit into the strange fruit. She flashed a final smile before riding to catch up to the other riders in their group.

"Would you like to try one?" Crand offered to Nate. "We call them Nacovine; they are native to the lands around the Bay of Urocia and are said to hold great healing properties as well as sustain one's thirst."

"Sure, when in Rome," he muttered as he put the Jeep into gear, resuming their trek down the road. When he bit into it, the fruit tasted more like strawberries yet was infinitely juicier. They had to keep peeling spines off the skin, but it was well worth the effort. He felt more energetic, and his hunger seemed to dissipate as they followed the road onward.

Distant thunderclouds appeared on the western horizon, the rumble pealing across the vast plain. Despite the oppressive heat, cool breezes began to gather and blow, descending out of the highlands, unseen from this vast distance and drying the remnants of the mud puddles still dotting low areas on the dual trackway ahead. Nate was about to ask how much further when they cleared a rise with a single windblown tree on its crest. To the northeast, the great capital city of Latana lay splayed out before them.

No introduction was necessary. The city sprawled out before them like a spectacular glistening gem, giving the appearance of having been sculpted out of ice formed naturally rather than having ever been built. Thick crystalline columns rose around the city, forming its towering wall. Like two massive arms, the walls stopped just short of meeting, allowing traffic to flow in and out through the yawning gap between.

Behind the city was an expansive glittering bay dotted with wooden vessels donning white sails, the body of water stretching out for as far as the eye could see. From fishing boats and other ships of trade that moved in and out of the harbor, the massive bay spread out well beyond the visible horizon, resembling more an ocean than any inland body of water.

"I never get tired of this view," Lord Emelien murmured softly as he pulled his horse up beside Johanna and dismounted, beaming with pride. "A great iron gate once protected that archway entrance, much like Tyrna's entrance. Long ago, Latana was built from brick and mortar, like Tyrna's walls. My ancestors tore those down and embraced a different path."

"Urocia's mines, somewhere further along the coastline to the northeast, yielded a great crystalline bounty," Crand stated as he jumped out of the Jeep and sauntered to Johanna's other side. "It was further discovered that the crystals could be grown with the proper invocations of magic, heat and salt water."

"This is all something Latana has in abundance," Lord Emelien reminded him. "We also don't retain a stigma other cultures have for using magic when the need suits us."

"Perhaps I'll get to know more about it soon," Johanna murmured, suddenly conscientious of the Urocian lord's proximity to her own and Nate's gaze boring into her back. With a click of her heels, she spurred her steed onward at a gentle trot. "We are, after all, newcomers here."

"Indeed, you will," Lord Emelien muttered, grinning as he spurred his own steed on, following Johanna as they descended the hillside toward Latana. Aros steered his own horse closer to where the two had left Crand standing alone where he was.

"His affection for her may become an issue in the coming days," the wizard said.

"Oh, trust me, it already has," Crand assured him, shaking his head as he strode back to the Jeep. "At his societal station, I personally take no offense. His pursuit of her though is most perplexing, and I have no doubt will annoy many ladies in waiting!"

"What was that all about?" Nate asked Crand with a wary glance as the tracker climbed into the vehicle. "Our host is going above and beyond, wouldn't you say?"

"Just our Urocian host blustering on again about his city," Crand sighed, trying to minimize the situation. "It seems she heard enough and just wants to get there, like the rest of us."

"His city," Nate scoffed to himself. "If permanent settlement becomes the goal, remind me to scratch this place off the list!"

The caravan continued along the grassy roadway, leading down the hillside toward a slow-moving clear yet shallow river. The tributary flowed in from the western horizon and around the front of the gate, forming half of a natural moat. From there, the waterway widened, flowing around the eastern portion of the city and dispersing into a delta clustered in willows and reeds. A notable amount of steam rose from the eastern end with steady plumes like cotton, puffing in voluminous columns before the water below emptied out into the bay.

Quaint small farms with cream-colored stone houses and barns dotted the pleasant lowlands between them and the city. As they approached the city, several roadways converged onto the one they traveled.

They soon merged into peasant foot traffic, destined for the main thoroughfare, all streaming toward the city's entrance. Unlike their previous stops, the Jeep generated little more than curious acknowledgment from the local population.

Even elderly couples smiled and waved as the group ambled by, careful to maneuver the vehicle safely in with the pedestrians, who parted in kind to allow entry into the traffic flow. Regardless of age, nearly everyone they encountered retained smooth features—tall, lean and toned.

"Everyone seems so friendly, so healthy," Johanna muttered to Lord Emelien as he pulled again alongside her protectively. "No one seems bothered by the Jeep or us!"

"Strangers are welcome here; I told you this before. This could be your home!" Lord Emelien reminded her. "You and your son both could live here in this utopia, with me. My family name goes far here, and you would be well cared for!"

"Lord Emelien, I mean no offense, but as I also told you before, I'll need to think about it," she blustered in annoyance before pushing her horse ahead of his. While appealing, she wasn't sure she was ready to accept such a drastic change to her life. "I'm not just going to abandon Nate and the others!"

"You wouldn't be abandoning anyone," he called after her. Pushing his horse alongside hers again, he lowered his voice intentionally so only she would hear. "Your loyalty is most admirable, my dear. I am not a jealous man and would see to Nate's comfort as well, but you and your son would be my top priority! I know you are going through a difficult time right now but please know this: All of you would ultimately be welcomed, even if you choose to rebuff my advances. However, I believe our match would go far beyond simply a good arrangement. Give me a chance, Johanna! Allow me to prove this to you!"

"Stop it!" she hissed. "We hardly know each other! Your incessant flirting is—"

"I know you feel it too," he pressed softly. "You know this is well beyond just flirting, my dear. I will let you be, but please don't turn me away!"

Johanna's heart felt like it was about to burst, conflicted yet almost conceding the notion the Urocian lord expressed. *It's as if he knows!*

Deciding not to answer at all, she turned her thoughts and her gaze to the city as they arrived. As the group drew closer to the city, the walls loomed ahead of them, and the traffic flow began to thicken. Progress slowed yet the city's immensity seized the attention of everyone in their caravan.

Johanna stayed behind Lord Emelien at this point, evading his invitation for her to ride beside him. She certainly did not want to hurt Nate with him driving just behind her, witnessing the Urocian lord's pursuit of her attention.

Soon, the roadway ceased meandering and joined the main cobblestone thoroughfare, paving a direct line to Latana's front gateway. Massive spires rose within the walls, each consecutively taller than the next the closer one got to the city center. If the buildings at the front of the gate looked like clusters of short knives pointing up from the open plain, the buildings in Latana's interior appeared as great swords, fewer in number but each well taller than the massive crystalline wall they approached. Massive banners hung to each side of the city's entrance, the banner of Urocia: a white crystalline "X" in a field of gold with a dark line of blue at its base.

The common structure appeared as glass from a distance, yet as they drew nearer, closer observation revealed the material maintained an opaque milky ivory color.

Windows and doors dotted the structures and appeared as long vertical slits—some covered in thin glass and others opened altogether.

The crowds moved in and out of the entrance to the city in a surprisingly organized manner, all under the single gaping archway entrance. As the group moved through, they crossed the river atop a squat wooden bridge, interlaced with that same crystalline material utilized in the city's construction. Only brief whiffs of sulfur were carried on gentle breezes throughout the city, barely perceptible and faint so as not to be unpleasant.

Johanna blushed to herself in a brief flash of shame as they entered the city's main gateway and people began to recognize Lord Emelien in their midst. Calls of his name and waving elicited a practiced yet friendly response from the lord. She hated to hurt his feelings, even if this new courtship from the Urocian lord had awakened an excitement within her that she hadn't had since she could remember.

Glancing back to Nate, she realized that this time, he appeared not to be fixated on her or Lord Emelien. The glittering heights of the crystalline towers above seemed to have him captivated for the moment, even as he glanced occasionally at the road ahead to ensure he wasn't bumping into anyone.

The bottleneck in the crowds forced the caravan more tightly together, and Nate rolled his window the rest of the way down as Aros took station beside him. All on horseback dismounted and led their steeds going forward, clustered more tightly together so they could converse.

"Latana discovered long ago that the crystals they employ are able to absorb and harness the energy of geysers that vent near the city's eastern flank." Aros pointed to great columns of steam that arose above the eastern wall. "There are a series of springs here that provide much of the heat and water for the entire population."

"It is rumored that Latana is one of the cleanest cities in all of the kingdoms," Crand offered from the passenger seat.

"It's no rumor," Lord Emelien assured, pushing back up alongside

Johanna. While she had hoped their striding side by side would be too wide for the road, the peasants dutifully made room for him. "Waste is funneled into one particularly hot vent near the wall and has been for centuries. It is boiled, churned and never seen again. Whatever is left over spills into a series of ducts that empties into the bay, but at that point, everything in the water has been cleansed and is as pure as when it had arrived."

"Is that why everyone is so healthy?" Johanna marveled.

"Indeed, it is. Longevity and vitality are notable traits among many of our citizens," Lord Emelien stated proudly. He glanced briefly over the wizard at Nate driving the Jeep before whispering with an inviting smile. "We also have an interesting mineral water bath bubbling up from the base of the south wall—a hot spring with waters that you can get nowhere else in our world. I'm anxious for you to sample it with me later."

Johanna gulped at the invitation, feeling a surge of heat flow through her. All she could do was look away and hope no one heard or noticed. Aros squinted in the sun glinting from the buildings. *Or is it disapproval?*

"Most of Latana's trade and travel occur by sea," Aros began after clearing his throat, shifting the conversation back to the capital. "It's a far less dangerous route via ship than the desert caravans to the southeast, but also much longer. The route takes merchants out of the bay and around the eastern coastline to the Southern Kingdoms."

"Nearly a month of seamanship," Crand mused. "All that to avoid the cursed lands."

"That is why my father invested in several merchants with camels," Lord Emelien bragged, pointing to a long line of camels approaching, tied together in a line of colorful rope. "Look, there's one of them departing the city now!"

"The desert caravans brave the fringes of the cursed lands and make runs directly between Urocia and the Southern Kingdoms," Aros stated somberly. "It's frankly somewhat of a controversy because the route runs adjacent to the cursed lands. Although the compensation is high, the route is dangerous. Many are lost and are never heard from again."

"Controversy—meh!" Again, Lord Emelien rolled his eyes. "The wizards from the Order of the Moon always were overprotective. Anyone can get through with the proper guidance and a little determination. My father's merchants make the route regularly. Oh, sure, they claim to run into a wayward phantom here or there, but they make it every time. The cursed boundary remains intact, and although adjacent to the route, unmolested!"

"Didn't your father lose a few men on a run last year?" Aros probed gently to avoid mocking Lord Emelien.

"Indeed, they did. They were new and untrained; fresh from Tyrna, I believe," the Urocian lord parried. "Cursed lands aside, the desert comes with its own natural perils!"

"What's east of the cursed lands?" Johanna asked in idle curiosity as the caravan passed them by. "Between the eastern shores and there?"

"The lands have been cursed for so long that no one really has explored beyond that," Aros divulged as everyone looked to him for the answer. "Nobody really knows the boundaries of the curse to the east, but ship captains report those lands being wild and untamed, under a blanket of a vast forest. The beaches are long and untouched, but no one that we know of lives east of the cursed lands except for the snake-people and a smattering of seaside villages they inhabit. Downwind and east of the cursed mountains, it's difficult to ascertain where the curse ends and where wilderness begins."

Conscious of Nate's eyes moving from the spectacle around them having returned to her, Johanna moved her horse back to the side of the Jeep. Positioning Aros between her and Lord Emelien, she resumed her ride, attempting to strike up another conversation with Nate.

"Can you believe this city?" she exclaimed, hoping the effort didn't come across as appearing forced. "I've never seen anything like it!"

"Neither have I; it is incredible," he agreed, stealing a quick satisfying glance over at an annoyed Lord Emelien, miffed at her return to the Jeep and him. "You know, I must admit, though, it seems a bit off-putting."

"What do you mean?" she asked.

"The shape of the buildings: sharp edges, pointy spires and harsh light reflections," he stated as he gestured with a sense of irony. "If they were any other color, it might actually look vicious and not look as nice."

The pair continued to converse, awestruck as they passed down the main thoroughfare. The whole capital reminded Johanna of a futuristic city, cylindrical buildings joined by an intricate latticework of walkways and bridges, all glinting in the sunset light from the same ivory crystalline material. The walls surrounding the city were easily over 100 feet high, but these massive towers dwarfed the walls altogether.

As the group approached the city center, Latana's royal palace lay directly ahead. Three gargantuan columns formed the base, with the thickest and tallest of the three in the center. The tallest structure, the Wizard's Tower of Latana, thrust high into the air, nearly three and a half times as tall as the wall, peering over all the other structures in the city.

Johanna could see a balcony at the top, like a great ivory seashell jutting out from the top of the spire. Someone in long, flowing yellow robes stood next to a shorter, squat man in royal red. The setting sun cast a myriad of colors across the crystalline walls, highlighting the colors of their robes.

"That's Grand Master Encara and His Royal Highness of Urocia, Emperor Vandroff the second," Aros stated quietly as he pointed them out to her and Nate. Glancing quickly at Lord Emelien, he ensured the Urocian lord had become occupied with the crowds around them before speaking further. "Now we test just how welcomed we are here—some of our answers for this enigmatic mystery may play out very soon. Keep your eyes open, and stay wary!"

As the company approached the royal palace, trumpets hailed their arrival. Nate parked the Jeep next to the broad set of marble stairs and locked it while the rest of their company handed over their steeds to the palace's attendants. Dressed in fine grey cloaks, the young equestrian men took the reins without a word as the group assembled and strode up the white marble stairs together.

Colossal crystalline doors swung soundlessly open at the top of the stairway as they entered the great hall. Transparent support columns curved to the top, disappearing into unseen recesses of light seen as a blurry mist in the throne room high above.

Towering statues built from white marble lined each side of the hallway between elongated draped banners representing the thirteen original kingdoms of Urocia, each flying beneath the unified banner, signified by the white crystalline "X" in a field of gold with a dark line of blue at its base.

The first statues were apparently of ancient heroes or soldiers, but as they approached the throne, each statue grew more regal, celebrating prior to more current kings and emperors, clearly depicted by the intricate and monumental crowns they wore.

Natural sunlight highlighted each statue from far above through crystalline skylights of massive proportions, yet they were wafer-thin. The slats were tilted open and held in place as if by some unseen force. The largest skylight above shone directly onto the throne itself, residing atop a wide marble podium, an oversized marble chair with a single plush cherry cushion with golden tassels.

Everywhere they looked, a soft white light seemed to radiate from the very walls, illuminating the cavernous room as if in a sunlit cloud. Guards lined the hall in front of each statue, donning intricate grey capes that, when rustled, glinted with a hint of crimson. As they neared the royal throne, a crowd of lords and ladies filed into the room and around the thrones, whispering among them, all wearing the same plush grey cloaks with the ever-swimming intricate black stitching.

The golden-robed figure Aros had pointed out strode forth from behind the throne with a purpose, eyes focused on the newcomers as a golden cape billowed behind him. He wore his long yellow robes with an exaggerated high collar glimmering with golden threads that framed his head well above his neck. His bald scalp reflected the light from the walls as he approached.

"Grand Master Encara," Aros greeted his superior in a reverent voice of deference, bowing low.

As the grand master stood before them, his face betrayed no emotion. His thin, dark eyebrows almost appeared stenciled, making his age impossible to guess since his face had neither a wrinkle nor a blemish. His sharp eyes shifted with curiosity as he surveyed the group, allowing the awkward moment of silence to ensue for a time.

"Master Aros, you may rise," Grand Master Encara suddenly greeted in return, as if rushed into an afterthought. His voice pierced the silence with an air of authority, high yet purposeful. "May I present the Grand Emperor of Latana, Laurent Vandroff the second!"

The shorter squat man Johanna had seen on the balcony ascended the podium from behind the throne to stand at its right side, flanked on either side by veiled and silent guards wearing telltale grey cloaks aflutter with the same strange black threads. Armed only with ceremonial spears, the banner of Urocia hung from each.

The emperor approached them, grinning through a clean-shaven smile and sporting a full head of white hair, yet his face bore no wrinkles. He surveyed the group with piercing grey eyes, like grand diamonds. His crimson robes dragged behind him yet collected no dirt or dust.

"You've traveled far and are surely wearied," the emperor stated with a voice as sweet as honey. Flanked by his guards, he turned and motioned for them to follow back outside. "Come, take sustenance, and find solace in our kingdom of Urocia! Let us first gather your belongings; I am most curious to see your beastless carriage!"

"We thank you on behalf of Grand Master Nicholas and His Majesty, King Faund, in Tyrna," Aros stated, turning to acknowledge the monarch, bowing his head briefly in greeting. "We hope not to impose on your hospitality for too long but are most grateful for your offer!"

"No imposition at all! Lord Emelien is a most efficient guide and sent word of your arrival prior to your departure," Emperor Vandroff stated. His trancelike voice had a sleepy sound to it, flowing like background music with a kind yet lighthearted disinterest. "I know of your search on behalf of the newcomers for a place they may call home. Aside from our little skirmish in the east, I hope you will place serious consideration on Urocia!"

The entourage exited again, and the monarch's pace quickened when he caught sight of the Jeep glistening in the sun. Nearly leaping down the stairs in sudden exuberance, the move startled even his guards, who raced after their emperor in haste to keep up.

"My oh my, what a glorious chariot," the emperor exclaimed. "I would love to hear more about it!"

"Of course, Your Majesty," Nate volunteered as he bowed. Everyone followed as he took the lead. "I'd be happy to demonstrate it to all of you if it pleases you!"

He took it upon himself to walk closest to the emperor, pointing out the various features of the parked Jeep. The emperor nodded in wonder as Nate described the headlamps, the engine, the wheels and various other features. He began to feel an emerging sense of agitation, however, when Lord Emelien pushed to the front and pressed himself closely to the monarch as they circled the vehicle.

To Aros's clear annoyance, the Urocian lord cleared his throat and began adding in his own bits of information about the vehicle from another world.

"It's really a fascinating machine, sire. It has the ability not just to move on its own but haul as well," Lord Emelien stated, informingly pointing out the hitch at the back. "I've become quite acquainted with it on my way here!"

"That is most fascinating. I would love to see more!" the emperor complimented, suddenly turning to Lord Emelien. "You've done well, nephew!"

"Thank you, dear uncle," the Urocian lord remarked. Nate and the others stared, jaws agape, as Lord Emelien smiled anew with pride. "The outsiders have proven themselves to not only have capable technology but also seem to bear many talents of their own. They would make fine additions to the citizenry of Urocia!"

"Your investment of time you've spent in Tyrna has indeed paid off well!" the emperor muttered aloud, still transfixed by the Jeep. "When can we expect more of these?"

"Sire, this is but the test vehicle and the few people that came with it," Grand Master Encara huffed as he pushed his way back up to the front. "As promised, we at the council will deliver! However, we must first ensure that we are fully stocked and ready to care for and properly maintain such tools as these. They are very complex—are they not, Master *Aros*?"

The grand master's tone had a sudden and very deliberate thrust when he spoke the subordinate wizard's name.

"Wait a minute; a test vehicle? More?" Nate's brow crinkled, taken aback. "This is mine..."

Nate drifted off as the grand master interposed himself between the group and Aros. Up until that point, Encara had been nothing but pleasant, yet now he motioned Aros forward almost impatiently.

"Um, yes, Grand Master—these technological devices are quite complex; very demanding to operate and maintain!" Aros reluctantly agreed, locking eyes briefly with Encara's, his superior glowering over him. Aros shook his head as he turned back to the emperor, refocusing on a more obvious question. "Sire, what need have you for an outworlder vehicle such as this?"

"That was my question," Nate muttered from behind, yet suddenly no one seemed to pay him heed.

"The emperor's needs are not for you to question! They are mine to supply and...aren't you supposed to be in Levens?" Grand Master Encara became incredulous, a shrill tone pervading his voice. The two wizards locked eyes again, but this time, Aros did not back down; his eyes smoldered in rage as he viewed his mentor.

"I have need for larger such vehicles, my new outworlder friend, and a great deal more of them," the emperor intoned, breaking the awkward silence. He surprisingly turned to Nate to ask the question. "Do such others exist?"

"Uh, well, they exist, Your Majesty; just not here," Nate managed while maintaining his composure, unsure as to what exactly was transpiring. "They are called buses and vans and such. There are many where I come from, but as far as this vehicle goes, I must insist this Jeep stay with me."

"Very well then, you may keep yours!" the emperor proclaimed as he turned to Grand Master Encara. "If you wish to serve me well, I have an immediate need for at least thirty. The Jeep is fascinating; I shall have one like it for my coach. I need not remind you, Grand Master: our need is pressing! We have a war to win, after all!"

"Of course, sire!" The Golden Wizard grinned through clenched teeth even as he bowed in deference.

"Come, everyone! Let us see to your accommodations here in the capital!" the emperor motioned, and the group followed the monarch back into the main hall. As the sovereign turned to leave, Lord Emelien stopped him.

"Sire, may I take our guests around Latana?" the Urocian lord eagerly requested. "I wish to personally show them our home. I feel we have mutual interests that could be served by my continuing to advocate our capital as a top choice for relocation."

"Of course, dear nephew!" The emperor perked at this proclamation and smiled, turning a wary eye to the group. "Additionally, I hope you all will consider attending the festivities in just a few nights' time! We have an annual ball, and we would love to honor your visit at the occasion!"

"I know I speak for everyone here when I gladly accept the invitation!" Lord Emelien turned for confirmation. "I hope I am not overstepping my role here, Master Aros?"

"We had only anticipated staying one evening and perhaps the next day," the wizard sighed, nodding in appreciation and bowing again to emphasize the point. "However, if you would like us to extend that, we could..."

"Splendid, then it's decided," Emperor Vandroff exclaimed happily before turning to leave with his vanguard. "It shall be a most joyous occasion!"

"I was about to say consult with—" Aros began before his superior interrupted him.

"I have business elsewhere, so I'm afraid I will not be able to attend the ball, but please enjoy," Grand Master Encara announced, letting his glare linger on Aros for a moment longer as if deep in thought. Suddenly, the animosity seemed to vanish, and a weary smile took his face. "Speaking of which, I have some matters to attend to at present as well. Master Aros, you may attend in my stead. Will you join me in the Wizard's Tower so we may conclude any remaining business of the order?"

"Yes, of course, Grand Master," Aros replied, stealing a nervous glance at the rest of the group before sauntering off after the head wizard. Nate and Crand exchanged a worried look, but Johanna and the others seemed oblivious to the exchange.

"Well, what say we get acquainted with our new quarters, shall we?" Lord Emelien broke the silence with a wide grin. They followed their guide behind the throne room to a narrow corridor, extending to the emperor's personal guest quarters.

The Urocian lord led them up three floors to an identical hallway, making up the northern wing of the palace. The stairway emptied into the crystalline corridor, punctuated by a simple window where the staircase ended. From this vantage point, one could look out the window and back into the vaulted throne room below.

Each of them fanned out to their own assigned rooms, even the inseparable Owl and Rabbit. Nate noticed immediately that both the Clay Tribesmen were assigned rooms between his and Johanna's. While initially ecstatic at the extended stay in the Urocian capital, the exultation seemed to already be wearing off as they viewed their minimalist quarters. They quickly found all the rooms identical, remarkably sparse in furnishings and decor. Only the oversized windows of the rooms on the north side looked over a great dark obelisk at a parkway in the city center.

The monument stood out tall and in dark contrast with the buildings around it, identical to the one he had seen in the Pratenvike of Tyrna except in size. This one was nearly 100 feet tall. All around the plaza with the obelisk at the center, activity from the main road continued unabated, buzzing with vendors, shoppers and pleasure-strollers alike. Behind that in the distance, the roadway led to the bayside docks.

Inside each room, the curvature of the walls peaked out into the ceiling and a single crystalline chandelier, both glowing with a light of their own yet, without a single incendiary source. Despite the absence of candles or torches, the room was clearly illuminated by the soft glow coming from within the translucent walls.

A single polished wooden bed, dresser and wardrobe appeared to be the only furnishings, along with a corner chair—all made from a material Johanna could only guess to be blue marble.

The group politely declined Lord Emelien's insistence on trying the hot springs and opted for the local bathhouse where they could wash in private. Only a short time later, dinner was served in a guest dining hall. After a short but filling meal of roasted chicken and locally grown fare, the group retired to their own separate rooms for the evening. The day had been long and tiring, and most were eager to rest.

Johanna returned to her room first and flopped down on the bed, the silken sheets and down comforter caressing her newly cleaned body. Exhausted from the travel and days away from civilization, she fell asleep immediately.

Within a matter of a half hour, Nate stopped by Johanna's room to check on her. Raising his knuckles to knock, he paused nervously. Taking a deep breath, he gently rapped on the crystalline door, resulting in an odd metallic sound. Standing in silence, he waited outside patiently. After two times knocking, he gave up and returned to his own room.

For now, other more pressing thoughts had entered his mind. *Lord*

Emelien is the emperor's nephew? What was all that discomfort between Aros and Grand Master Encara about? How much does this grand master know of our quest or indeed of us, and how much SHOULD he know? I really needed to talk to Aros about this...

Nate never saw the room across from Johanna's open a crack while he had been standing in front of her door—nor did he see it close after he left. Lord Emelien, who had been staring through the crack, smiled in satisfaction. He waited patiently as Nate's door closed, his own gaze lingering on Johanna's door.

Johanna had awakened when she heard the knocks on her door but was not coherent enough to realize whether something tangible had disturbed her slumber. She stirred, moaning in an effort to wake, before forcing herself to sit lethargically upright in bed.

"Nate, is that you?" she finally called at the door.

When no one answered, she struggled out of her bed and threw on her plush robe before opening the door.

"Nate?" she called out into the empty hall.

She was about to close her door and return to bed when a shirtless Lord Emelien standing at his own doorway across from her caught her eye. Her gaze drifted from his piercing blue eyes and spiked blonde hair down past his massive chest. The lack of body hair accentuated the curves of his muscles, and his abs gave the appearance of being carved granite, as did his legs. He wore an undergarment over his loins made from the finest silk, but it seemed to hug his lower frame suggestively, bulging with...

"My lady," the Urocian lord greeted with a smile, redirecting her gaze to his face. "My apologies for my current lack of clothing, but I heard a sound and wanted to ensure everyone was well-accommodated."

"Oh, I'm sorry—yes, of course," Johanna stammered, her face pulsating from the blood rushing to her cheeks in a blush as she spoke. "We're all very comfortable. I also heard...I mean, I was looking to ask if..." She could say no more and began to turn to leave.

"No need to leave, dear Johanna!" Lord Emelien let out a laugh that sounded like wind chimes to put her at ease. "I'll dress now; I was actually really looking forward to catching up with you! Please, come and give me your honest appraisal of your quarters!"

"They are very comfortable but a bit sparse," she sputtered, turning about to face him again.

"Sparse?" he replied with a smirk, raising an eyebrow and shifting to face her as he slowly donned his shirt, neglecting the buttons and allowing it to fall open. "They are meant to be clean and focused solely on the inhabitant's comfort."

"Oh, forgive me!" Closing her own door behind her, she could feel her heart pounding in her chest. On impulse, her feet began moving by themselves against her wishes, carrying her across the hall to his entryway. "They ARE most comfortable!"

"Something the matter?" He grinned, stretching his arms in a suggestive embrace even as he flexed.

"Oh, I'm sorry," Johanna gasped, rushing to him even though he was only halfway through buttoning his shirt. She hesitated for only a moment before the heat of the unspoken exchange took her. "You've been nothing but kind and generous, and I think that maybe if we just tried to..."

He caught her suddenly, drawing her in. She gulped, losing herself in his sky-blue eyes—she only meant to approach, not be embraced. She relaxed as she felt him pull her closer, relishing his body heat enveloping her as he gently whispered in her ear.

"You do not need to say anything further," he whispered gently in her ear. "I know, and it's okay, really. Just relax..."

"It is?" she gulped.

"Oh, yes! I will take care of everything!" he stated, smiling as he pulled her into the room, shutting the door gently behind her. He placed her hand on his barren chest. She could feel his heart thumping beneath. "Latana is my birthplace, and I want to share it with you. Latana is also my home and the home of my ancestors. It is very special to me, here in my heart, as it could also be for you."

"We shouldn't do this, not yet!" she whispered, almost choking on the words. "You're so young! I'm sure you have plenty of better-suited choices for your house! You've got..." She stopped talking when he placed his finger on her lips.

"I can feel it in your heart too," he persisted. He gently slipped his muscular hand beneath her silken gown, locking her gaze with his eyes as she drowned in his piercing stare. "It's special in a way that few people know. You get it, Johanna. You understand. That's why I'm drawn to you. The others know it, too—I can't blame them for being jealous, but we shouldn't resist who we are...or where we belong."

Johanna went completely limp, her heart pounding as Lord Emelien drew her into the room, kissing her long and deep. His mouth tasted like tangerines, and she could feel her will to resist him fly from her. As her eyes closed, she kissed him back, hard and unrelenting, pulling him into her.

She groaned in sweet agony as he lifted her, and she wrapped her legs around him. Carrying her over to the bed, their kisses intensified as they fell together upon the plush mattress, rife with pillows and his wadded comforter. When she felt the summary of his desire press against her abdomen, she realized she was unable to stop, and she moaned his name aloud in deep surrender.

Chapter 28

Summoned

Aros climbed the crystalline stairs, wearily leaning on his staff with each step, watching Grand Master Encara's back ahead of him with trepidation. Keenly aware of the quick pace the grand master took, he pushed himself to keep up and prove his physical stamina on the circular staircase.

The very steps beneath his feet lit as he climbed, aglow as if to guide him toward the inevitable end of his journey, where he dreaded the coming conversation. Breathing steadily, he vowed to prove at least his physical equality with his former rival, now superior.

Latana slept below as they wordlessly ascended the glassy staircases up to the top of the tower, overlooking the city. As Aros peered through the slotted windows, he could see the soft radiance of the buildings and walls below. As they climbed higher, he could look down on even the tallest pinnacle and column structures through the narrow viewpoints.

They finally arrived at the large doorway at the top, where a great crystalline doorway greeted them, nearly blending in completely with the walls around. The grand master produced an iron key and slid it into a nearly imperceptible slot in the entryway. The massive door opened soundlessly, and he turned to Aros, ushering him inside before closing the door in effortless silence behind them.

"Dear Master Aros!" Grand Master Encara exclaimed with a broad smile, startling him with loud exuberance. In a surprisingly warm embrace, he took Aros's hands in his own as if greeting an old comrade. "I must apologize for earlier, but His Majesty insists on strict formalities! Please, make yourself at home in my humble abode! I must say, though, I was rather surprised at your sudden arrival!"

"I apologize for my unannounced visit," Aros stated as he peered about the room that was anything but humble, dwarfing what he had once considered the elaborate Wizard's Tower of Tyrna. "The arrival of the newcomers seems to have the order shuffling their duty assignments lately, and these newcomers ended up being my charge..."

Aros's voice caught in his throat at the magnificence of the Wizard's Tower of Latana, a round rotunda built from the same crystalline structure as the rest of the city, smooth and implacable. Four large seashell-shaped balconies protruded on all sides, facing each principal direction of the compass.

There were no stray parchment or maps lying about. Neatly stacked bookshelves squared off each of the rounded walls, interrupted only by a map indicating what landscape lay behind the wall. Large and spacious, Latana's Wizard's Tower held the grand appearance of being inside a glass oyster with support beams curving gracefully throughout the superstructure. The whole place glowed with ambiance and power. Notably, the absence of any scent at all caught his attention —only a sterile, clean and ambient background.

Warm and cozy, a low blue flame flickered within a narrow single hearth in the southwest corner, casting a light glow but giving Aros doubts that it heated the entire room on its own. Absent smoke, any fumes produced seemed to be channeled up a lean glass funnel, blending in with the crystalline ceiling. Nearby, the grand master's bed awaited, surprisingly small yet extremely plush with white pillows and comforters. Only a single standing mirror stood near the foot of the bed, next to a large chest and wardrobe. The grand master's quarters seemed otherwise sparsely furnished, for such a large room.

"I, in turn, must apologize for the condition of my modest accommodation," Grand Master Encara joked, raising an eyebrow as if reading his counterpart's mind at the clear lavishness of the room. "The disarray reflects our sad current state of affairs these days!"

"Yes, well, I suppose we all make do," Aros replied with a forced grin, still wondering why he was summoned. *Everything about this place is anything but modest or in disarray. Does he say that knowing the towers of Levens and Tyrna are nowhere near this tidy?*

"I must say, whoever designed this office had a very literal sense of humor," Encara mused as he beckoned Aros to his side. "Come, join me on the north balcony, and let us take in the view of the harbor!"

Aros obliged, and the two stood at the threshold as moonlight glistened off the bay in silence. The ornate balconies splayed out before them, hundreds of feet above the bustling streets below. Up this high, the city's sounds wafted up only as a dull and muffled background, eclipsed only by the gentle whistle of the cool evening breeze, blowing in from the bay.

"It's beautiful, even serene, isn't it?" the grand master began with a sigh. "A most unfortunate circumstance, your reassignment from Tyrna; I must admit, I was most distressed to hear of it. I had aimed for you to join the rest of the Master Council of the Advisory here in Latana. But alas, the council's aims overrode mine."

"It's enough to keep you up at night, that is certain," Aros lamented. "You just never know what new assignment may come your way next. I suppose at master level, that is my bane, to be prepared and stay adaptable to the needs of the Grand Master Council."

"Indeed, but you are no longer a master-level wizard, are you? New assignments, changing directives and glorious views are no longer what keeps us up late at night, are they?" Grand Master Encara's mood sobered as he turned an icy stare onto his subordinate, lowering his voice to a harsh whisper. "Tell me, Wizard Aros, since I may no longer address you as 'Master'—what is it that *truly* keeps you up at night?"

"It's been a long road." Aros dodged the question through a strained smile despite the grand master's stinging dig at his demotion. "I advocate for our newcomers and their well-being." *We were once at the same level, and after he gets promoted, I get thrown down a level; oh, the irony!*

"Ah, yes! The duties of an Advocate, or rather, a surrogate Advocate, in your case; most trying indeed!" the grand master opined as he drifted off thoughtfully before snapping his fingers. "I'll tell you what keeps me up at night, dear friend! I get such few visitors here from the wizard's keep! 'Friend,' I hope you don't mind me calling you that?"

"Not at all," Aros lied. "I'm pleased to see the feeling is mutual!"

"What keeps me up at night are surprises," the grand master prattled, a gesture of acknowledgment. "You see, I pride myself in my planning, my organization and my ability to create order. Look around you; notice how everything has its proper place and is organized neatly by category?"

"Yes, Encara, it was difficult to miss," Aros acknowledged.

"Grand Master Encara—I am your grand master now," the Golden Wizard emphasized with his eyebrows, not bothering to hide his annoyance. "Your other friend, retired Grand Master Nicholas, had his time and his place; now I have mine. You and I, we once shared the same title level of master; we had that in common. I believe that hopeless Sorceress Namina, or whatever her name was also…"

"Oh. Did you mean Mistress Amina, Sorceress of the Southern Kingdoms and High Countess of Bokumba?" Aros feigned ignorance while still driving the point home.

"Perhaps," Encara replied, smiling dryly while waving his hand at the irrelevance it held for him. "At any rate, my friend, I hope you don't mind that I offer you a helping hand. Consider it a bit of advice from someone who led the way to higher stratum, breaking the ground for the younger members of our order. I offer you a window into something that led to my success, especially considering your difficulties of late with the Grand Master Council. Whether you choose to take that advice is ultimately up to you, but I must insist on your use of my proper title since I've earned it, even if you have yet not."

"Yes, of course, Grand Master Encara," Aros muttered as he nodded in deference. *This conversation is becoming more annoying by the second, yet I hold my tongue!*

"I say this not to insult you, my dear friend," the grand master encouraged. "You are a perfectly capable wizard, and I daresay in my own eyes, a worthy master wizard. Why, if I had my way, you would have retained your master title! However, our status in the order is not why I called you here."

"Then why am I here, Grand Master?" Aros tried not to spit the words.

"That *is* the question of the evening, isn't it?" Grand Master Encara took a step uncomfortably close to Aros and stopped, leaning in, his eyes narrowing like a cat's, his voice a whisper. "Why indeed ARE you here?"

"I told you; I'm Advocate for—" Aros began.

"No, no, no!" Encara interrupted, waving his hands about as he would if shooing an insect away. "I know why you *said* you were here, but I'm not interested in your cover story. Again, I ask, WHY are YOU REALLY here, in the Urocian capital of Latana this...very...night!?"

"Ah, yes, I see now," Aros murmured, pausing as understanding settled on him. *Grand Master Encara is comparing what I tell him with what his other sources say.*

"I was initially told by the Grand Master Council that you were in that peasant kingdom of Levens!" the grand master pressed when Aros failed to respond further. "Another source stated they witnessed you in Tyrna. Then, I suddenly hear from yet another source that you were on your way here with the newcomers! It's just all so confusing!"

"Emelien told you that," Aros stated rather than asked.

"Lord Emelien to you, but actually, no." Encara turned away from him and began to pace, his brow furrowed in concentration. "He's not the only Urocian in the Tyrnaese court in dual service to Urocia. We are, after all, allies, are we not?"

"Forgive me, Grand Master," Aros interrupted gently while attempting to retain the cordial interchange. "I cannot speak to the well-being of Urocia, but it seems things are going rather well here in Latana compared to Tyrna. I was under the impression vast resources were needed here for the war effort."

"Security, Aros!" Encara hissed, stopping to throw a glare of importance to him on the topic. "This isn't just about us; we are providing security and well-being for *all* the kingdoms of the west! I assure you, those resources are very much needed and well-invested!"

"Does that include the Order of Etoilenoir's push for 'free magic for everyone'?!" Aros balked. "Seems a bit reckless, does it not?"

"Of course it does!" Grand Master Encara snapped as he stepped back in front of Aros to reassert his dominance. "Desperate times call for desperate measures! We must reciprocate some of the Order of Etoilenoir's ideals to thereby in turn recruit members to our cause at the Order of the Moon! Compromise is needed on our old, rigid ideals; surely you can see that?! Your fellow master-level wizards do!"

"I see it as well," Aros threw in, not certain whether the grand master's stance on the subject was valid. "What does the Master Advisory say about this? Is that not why they are here, to advise you directly in exchange for your tutelage?"

"Their input has been most helpful," Grand Master Encara sighed, shivering slightly as the outdoor breeze grew colder. He turned and escorted his subordinate back inside, closing the balcony doors without a sound behind them. "I am now their sole benefactor, and their relevance is evermore stronger here than wasting away at Mondlichtberg. They interface directly with me on the front line of societal evolution, and we keep the leash on the Order of Etoilenoir, as promised to the Grand Master Council."

"I would very much like to commune with them, if you don't mind," Aros gently requested as he turned away from the grand master, staring into nothing as if deep in thought. "It's been some time since I had the opportunity to consult with my peers."

"I'm sure that can be arranged," the Golden Wizard promised before leaning in from behind to whisper slowly in his ear. "Before you commune with your peers, though, you must answer my remaining question: Why are you here when my associates at the Wizard's Council and in Tyrna told me you were elsewhere? Answer truthfully! Stop conflating the many issues to avoid answering!"

"I...came on my own accord." Aros paused before blurting out suddenly, as if revealing an unwanted confession, "I won't lie, my dismissal from Tyrna stings greater than I would admit to anyone, and I'll admit to you that I don't relish discussing it further! Although I retain great personal loyalty and respect for Grand Master Nicholas, he is the one who dismissed me to his former post in Levens, taking Tyrna for his own!"

"Ah, yes, honesty at last; we may yet be allies in our causes!" Encara sighed. "I hated to think we had a breach in trust. I can imagine that reassignment must have stung, especially coming directly from your former master."

"It did," Aros exhaled in a shaky breath, allowing the tension to leave him as he closed his eyes, his face flushed with regret. "If you don't mind, I'd prefer not to speak of it further!"

"Forgive me, my friend, I did not mean to pressure you. Latana is an elegant capital of trade and commerce, but in the circle of the Order of the Moon, I am out here on the eastern fringes," the grand master explained. "In order to remain informed, I must work harder than my peers. I too share an unspoken isolation within our order, albeit a different one at my level. I sympathize with your plight and even share it to a certain degree!"

"Really? I had thought your assignment here to be a great honor, indeed a privilege!" Aros blinked, feigning surprise. *Despite the grand master's perceived arrogance in his own title, that makes sense; a grand master unaware of significant movements would be quite troubling. The weight to lead the entire Master Wizard Advisory, convert the Order of Etoilenoir and lend support to the Urocian crown during a time of war is indeed a heavy burden.*

"It may seem so initially," the grand master acknowledged somberly. "However, I daresay I did the Sorceress Manima a favor by denying her this role in a particularly patriarchal society!"

"When given the opportunity to accompany the newcomers and begin fresh again, I took it," Aros recollected, ignoring the golden wizard's comment about the Sorceress Amina. Noting the grand master's interest spark as he spoke, he channeled his next statement louder and with more deliberation in an effort to portray newfound trust while also changing the subject. "It was a last-minute decision, to be sure, since I felt guilty about abandoning my prior assignments. I knew the newcomers wanted to explore the land, and word had reached me in Levens that they were doing so. They wished to hunt out possible places to take up residence, and Nicholas allowed this dalliance since Levens is but a minor kingdom and so close to Mondlichtberg. This is one of many stops for us, but I couldn't pass up the opportunity to meet with the advisory, and you."

"I'm honored by that, but what of the other two newcomers; why are they not here with you?" Grand Master Encara asked, turning to close the doors of the other terraces, stopping with the west-facing balcony. "What are their names again: Kevin and Javier, or so I'm told?"

"Yes, those are their names," Aros confirmed, unsure of the grand master's belief in his explanation. "They carry a strong affinity for the western wilds and the lands there. My given charter did not encompass them, so I know very little of them beyond our brief introduction."

"Interesting," Encara scoffed. "Yet another report of mine is proving inaccurate! I had been informed that at least one of them rather enjoyed the Pratenvike and all its activity. Hard to believe that he would suddenly prefer to be in the wilds, wouldn't you say?"

"These newcomers are always such an unpredictable surprise," Aros sighed, straining to carefully balance his own lies against the truth. "I must admit, even being the appointed Advocate for only two is a challenge. They are all quite erratic, a contradiction for themselves. Perhaps Nate and Johanna will return to Tyrna and convince them to come this way when all is said and done!"

"Perhaps there will be no need to return to Tyrna. I certainly hope you give your quaint entourage a fair appraisal of Latana and the many advantages to living here..." The grand master trailed off thoughtfully before turning back to Aros. "If you truly are looking out for their better interest, Latana would make a most logical choice, wouldn't you agree?"

"Well, we shall have to see, won't we?" Aros countered. "I'll be sure to bring it up with them. I promise you that I will bring to their attention every positive aspect of each of our visits, but ultimately the decision is theirs to make."

"It is your duty as Advocate to ensure they make the right one," the grand master surmised, almost to himself. His tight lips creased against his teeth in anticipation even as he stated his proposal. "Although you are not here under my wing with the advisory, understand that I would be happy to assist you there, when or if needed or desired! I see you as one of us, the younger generation of the Order of the Moon whom I represent!"

"Indeed, a most generous offer, Grand Master. Kindly appreciated!" Aros managed as he inwardly bristled at the idea of abandoning the newcomers to Grand Master Encara, the Order of Etoilenoir and the royal house in Latana. "Perhaps I could impose only a little further and ask you to obtain an invitation for me to join the Advisory Council in conference? Perhaps tomorrow?"

"Ah, yes, you would like that," Encara murmured through a smile. He moved in to embrace Aros again, more as a move of dismissal than affection. "All in good time, my friend; all in good time. I'm afraid that decision must be made in the Master Advisory, since I do not control their schedule. They are most busy as of late, providing training and guidance to the leadership within the Order of Etoilenoir. I promise you this, though—I will advocate most strenuously on your behalf!"

"I thank you for that, Grand Master," Aros replied, bowing his head again in deference, gathering his robes about him to signify his intention to depart. "I had one other question, if I may be so bold, regarding the Emerald Fire—it's a term I've heard among the Order of Etoilenoir. Are you familiar with it?"

"The most basic fire spell, conjured up among simpletons, perfected by our order and then shared with the Order of Etoilenoir!"

the grand master assured him without hesitation. "We collaborated on it in a gesture of good faith of trust between our mutual orders."

"Very well." Aros nodded, unsure whether the information was sound or not or whether it even mattered. Observing the grand master carefully, he scrutinized the otherwise unreadable, placid face of his superior for a response. "I was just wondering if there was any further significance to it, perhaps an altering of that spell during our exchange of goodwill?"

"Hardly!" The grand master's countenance darkened even as he said it. "As I said, it was just an entry-level spell I recommended to impart on the Order of Etoilenoir early on in negotiations."

"Very well!" Aros grinned. "I shall await your word on when I may meet with the advisory. Perhaps in the morning, we may speak of it further."

"I understand you are quite close with Master Durant in particular," Grand Master Encara reminded Aros. "I'll extend my goodwill and send for him specifically, if the others can spare him. You've had a long journey and must get some rest in the meantime! I may not be able to summon the entire Advisory Council for you, but summoning Master Durant is the least I can do!"

"I am most grateful and look forward to seeing him," Aros stated with renewed hope. *Speaking with Durant will go a long way in earning my trust!* "Thank you for summoning me, Grand Master, and for letting Master Durant know that I am here. May I add how much I appreciate our newfound friendship and understanding!"

"And I yours," Grand Master Encara stated coolly as he nodded in his direction yet more towards the stairwell door.

"Very well, a good evening to us both," Aros stated as he turned to leave. He stopped in the doorway and snapped his fingers, turning back to the grand master, again feigning an errant thought. "I had one more question, if you don't mind, Grand Master."

"Go on," Encara sighed, arching an eyebrow.

"With all the talk of the great war in the east, I see no evidence beyond the large numbers of military buildup here in the city," Aros mused dryly, allowing a long pause before continuing. "So...where's the war? I had assumed Latana itself lay under siege by the way the rumors had flowed."

"Latana would never be under siege; our emperor has seen to that!" The grand master scoffed in indignance at the insinuation. "The war remains at our eastern flank, near the cursed lands. Urocia remains the bastion of civility and strength for the rest of the west. I assure you, Aros, your efforts in Tyrna to secure resources for our fight were carefully and judiciously regulated and never wasted!"

"Naturally," Aros acknowledged with a smile. "Since we are both confirming our sources this evening, I felt the need to ask. The peace and tranquility of Latana seem to conflict with what the Urocian advisors have conveyed to King Faund, since I too understood the need to be so dire."

"King Faund's generosity is valued, but he is also well compensated!" Grand Master Encara suggested as his tone soured. "Concern yourself no further from your previous post and focus on your advocacy for these newcomers! You may convey that bit of information to Grand Master Nicholas upon your return, if you wish, but I recommend you leave Tyrna to him now!"

"Of course, Grand Master," Aros stated in finality as he bowed low. "I meant no offense."

"None taken," the grand master corrected through a thin smile even as Aros turned and left. "We shall see you and your wards tomorrow at dinner, perhaps!"

Grand Master Encara stayed seated even after the visiting Aros departed, as if anticipating something else to happen. A few moments passed before two grey-cloaked guards entered, dark leaves descending to either side of their mantles.

"Have my carriage readied and call up the legion," the grand master growled. "There's a change in plans I need to discuss with the captains; have them brought to the stables where I will confer with them immediately!"

"Which ones, Grand Master?" the lead guard inquired.

"All of them," Grand Master Encara directed in a whisper. "We leave tonight, as soon as they're ready!"

≈≈≈≈

Never seeing the two grey-cloaked guards hidden in an alcove of the stairway just outside the door, Aros descended the tower stairs. A newfound sense of peace came over him. He would proceed with his plans to leave with the others as soon as possible.

Whatever Grand Master Encara was involved with, the Golden Wizard had not yet contacted the wizard's order or Nicholas about it. The grand master seemed preoccupied with something; his calling Aros to account had been a result of his surprise visit. Additionally, Encara's overtures of friendship at least gave the indication that his mission's real purpose remained undiscovered at this time.

If he could keep out of disrupting the grand master's plans, whatever they were, then he would be allowed to continue to lead his expedition, at least for the time being. Perhaps once he could meet with Durant, more light would be shed on the subject.

Chapter 29

Into the Wilds

When the sun rose over North Long Lake the next day, Dex and Davyn were already sipping their steaming morning tea outside the doorway of the Bog King's Inn. Javier and Kevin had slept so soundly that Fliegel had to return to the room and rouse them from their beds.

Upon Fliegel's hasty entry, followed by his incredulous laughter at their slumber, they leapt out of bed in a shambled disarray. Embarrassed and flustered, they quickly gathered their belongings and made their way down the creaky stairs to the dining room where the others had already gathered to eat their breakfast of oats, barley and fruit. The happy maiden seated them again and bustled about to work them into the morning's rush.

After scarfing down their breakfast, Dex paid the innkeeper, and they ambled outside. The morning air felt crisp and cold, yet as the sun rose, the landscape warmed. Even as the first rays of the sun touched the land, fresh scents of mud and fish permeated the air as the morning mists evaporated above the lake's waters, lapping on the muddy shoreline.

Dex gathered the group with their horses near the river docks to introduce them to the short, squat man they had seen the previous night. From his stocky appearance, it seemed the one-eyed captain's name was well-earned. He retained a nasty scar over where his right eye would have been, more clearly visible in broad daylight.

"I want to acquaint you all with the captain of the barge we will take to the southern shore; he goes by the name of Lefty Jeck," Dex proclaimed, stepping aside and gesturing to the portly man with dingy hair and unkempt rusty beard.

"Pleased to meet you," Lefty Jeck spat, eyeing each one of their company with a skeptical rolling eye, quietly contemplating his next words. "We won't be able to catch the barge here, not at this time, unfortunately."

"That's most disappointing to hear," Dex replied, clearly annoyed at the proclamation. "How long of a delay can we expect?"

The announcement elicited groans from the company, but they gathered around to hear the rest. The barge captain pointed out the ferry terminal, where the raft ferries ran regularly to transport passengers across the Rhane River to the western side.

"You'll need to cross there; I cannot return my barge to the main street docks," Lefty Jeck announced in a gruff voice, grating like sandpaper. "There are three ports on the other side of the river, and all three have other barges already backlogged and waiting for cargo transfer. I would have to get to the back of the line and as of now, that's looking to take until well into the evening or even later, depending on the weather. There's a storm blowin' in from the north, and it's exposing the alternative shallower docks around town, further limiting our options. With all your horses and supplies, I need the deepest water which, as you can see, is in short supply!"

"Well, so you think this will clear in the next few days?" Dex asked, scratching his head.

"That's what I'm sayin'," the barge captain stated, shaking his head in visible frustration. "The next couple of days at the earliest! There's potential that this storm's gonna expose even the deeper docks, which means your delay could go well beyond several days, perhaps even into next week and beyond!"

As if on cue, a sturdy wind picked up from the north, scattering the last remnants of the morning mists, revealing the situation even as described. The team peered over Lefty Jeck's shoulder and sure enough, the muddy shoreline extended for miles, revealing a line of completely exposed shorter docks to dry land. Only the dredged main docks bustled with increasingly urgent activity, bottlenecking the backup of commerce and sailing traffic upon the lake near the town of North Long Lake.

Boats that hadn't been so lucky or quick enough were already mired in the muck, making it impossible to unload their cargo, even stranding their crews struggling to make for the shore in hip-deep mud.

"Is there any alternative?" Dex breathed, eyeing the brewing chaos dockside.

"Not since the great flood widened the river here and filled most of the dredged ports with debris," Lefty Jeck pondered bitterly. "We can wait and hope for another two or three days. Of course, that delay adds to your cost—lodging, crew and all."

"That's it?!" Davyn spat, turning to Dex. "We can always push through the main roads to the east!"

"Rawl!" Brythen chimed in. "The cat-people in Carthen would welcome us, but while we are welcoming to strangers, we are also curious people!"

"We would have an entourage in no time, scouring the countryside alongside us!" Crisken laughed at the notion. "Oh, yes, our strange party would create quite a stir in Carthen!"

"Come now, surely it wouldn't be like that!" Davyn snapped at the cat-men before turning back to Dex, the albino unusually flushed and vocal about the matter. "Brythen and Crisken know those routes, and..."

"We cannot travel through Carthen!" Dex stated resolutely. "Grand Master Nicholas expressly directed us to stay clear of those heavily traveled thoroughfares."

"I do have one other option," Lefty Jeck interjected, wringing his hands. "There's a trapper's cabin about a half day's ride west of here that I make occasional deliveries to. The trip to the outpost won't be easy; it's a bit of a slog through the swamps, but the outpost dock extends out far enough onto the lake to accommodate my barge. The waters are deep nearer to the mountains and even with these winds, it would be a guaranteed option."

"Yes!" Dex didn't even have to think about it as he nodded in agreement. "Let's take your option, and we'll meet you there by sunset."

"Very well then, it's been decided!" Lefty Jeck spat. "I'll be anchored at the dock's edge when you arrive!"

Without another word, their monocular host feigned a salute, climbed down a dock-mounted ladder into his dinghy, moored to a pylon. He quickly threw the rope clear of his tiny craft and without a second glance, was gone, cursing and rowing furiously as he went. They watched him go, as he navigated the boat down the river's current and out onto the lake toward his waiting vessel, clearly struggling to beat the rush by the other sailors out onto the lake.

Kevin could see Lefty Jeck's barge anchored offshore, which was more like a large raft with a barn enclosure on top. A small wisp of smoke drifted from a corner chimney. Fore and aft, large masts supported even larger sails, currently stowed while in port.

As Lefty Jeck boarded the vessel, the ferry from across the river arrived. Two tall and muscular men operated the large raft affixed to both docks on each side of the river with pulleys and ropes. The ferry seemed a hasty contraption, turned into a thriving business, thrown together by the townspeople. Dex paid the toll in silver coins and began the process of ferrying their horses over two at a time.

Javier and Kevin were in the last group to cross, standing packed in tightly with their horses alongside the silent Davyn. The two husky ferrymen gripped the rope draped across the river, pulling together for the other side. As the large, burly men grunted and strained, the raft moved across the nearly hundred-yard expanse dotted with the stony remains of houses and shops that had once stood.

"Quite a flood," Javier muttered quietly as they surveyed the scene. "Looks like it took out some of the town."

"Oh, yes," one ferryman grunted, pushing them along with a long pole to stay on course. "The river wasn't even half this wide before!"

"Say, have you heard anything about a Beast of the Forest?" Kevin asked.

"Don't be such a child, Micker," Javier muttered.

"Oh, it's not a child's tale; it's quite real!" the other ferryman insisted, grunting as he continued hauling on the ropes to move the ferry along. "Not usually near here, but some say they've seen it from a distance."

"What exactly is it?" Javier sighed skeptically.

"Some people say it's a large bear, others a rabid beast. Regardless, it stays mostly on the western shore. I shouldn't worry," the first ferryman assured, putting aside the pole and assisting his partner with the pulleys. "Every once in a while, it may wander north near the trapper's cabin but never into town."

"Near the trapper's cabin?" Kevin winced.

"That cabin is a way station for such tales," the other ferryman laughed, his massive arms flexing as they pulled at the ropes. "That outpost is a crossroads for the many trappers who come through there. It's frequented year-round from all over without incident, save for the tall tales the men that visit it spin for each other's amusement!"

"See, told you so," Javier whispered as they rejoined their companions on the other side.

It took less than an hour, but soon, the whole company was safely on the other side of the gently flowing Rhane River. Davyn remained a brooding presence, clearly disappointed in them not choosing the roads he had suggested earlier. The rest of the group set off with high spirits though, eagerly embracing the coming venture.

As the group walked their horses through the western part of town, they joined the lakeshore road, bustling with activity. They passed the three large docks crowded with all sorts of barges of different sizes, loading and unloading cargo. Most had the same peculiar shape as Lefty Jeck's barge, yet some looked like sailing ships meant for the sea.

As they passed the docks, the chaos diminished, and the population became sparser and more spread out. This area of town was more exposed to the elements and not in the lower valley the river had carved. Most homes were farms, and fewer people walked about the roadway turned dirt from the better-maintained cobblestone roadways behind them.

Finally reaching the end of town, the road became little more than a trail, disappearing into high shrubs and bushes mixed with tall grasses and reeds. Dex led the group single file, followed by Fliegel, his blonde hair glistening in the sun, and Warley, who wrinkled his nose at the mud their horses were stepping in as the path descended toward the lakeshore. Javier followed with Kevin and both cat-men while Davyn brought up the rear, grumbling aloud to himself as they hiked.

It only took less than an hour before their path muddied, and their slogging began through the muck that only loosely resembled the trail.

When the wind blew, it laid the tall grasses and the reeds flat, pointing them toward the lake and the receding waters along the muddy shoreline. As unpleasant as the wind was, it grew far worse when the wind subsided, as biting flies and mosquitoes emerged to torment them in a cloud of pestilence.

Kevin surprised everyone when he pulled from his pack an aerosol can that hissed like a snake, spitting out a mist of mosquito repellent. They watched in bewilderment as the newcomer covered his body from head to toe in the foul-smelling mist before Javier tapped him on the shoulder.

"Hey, save some for us, will ya?" Javier exclaimed as he playfully snatched the can from him. "At least we still have a few things from home that can help us out here!"

"It really works," Kevin encouraged the others. "Try it!"

Most reluctantly allowed Javier to douse them with the mysterious spray and were pleasantly surprised by its seemingly magical ability to keep the pests at bay. However, the cat-men declined, swearing it burned their sensitive nostrils.

At one point during their trek, they were able to stop for a brief lunch the innkeeper had packed for them in their saddlebags. Although cold and uninteresting, it was a welcomed break from the mud-slugging and insects.

While eating his lunch, Kevin noticed the buzz of the insects suddenly ceased, yet not from the wind nor from his spray; it seemed as if the entire landscape collectively held its breath. He turned when he heard rustling in the bushes behind them, glancing over to Brythen and Crisken, whose hair stood on end as they fixated their attention on the tall grass and reeds.

Kevin was about to ask them about it, but just as suddenly as the episode began, it was over. The insects swarmed again, and the cat-men went back to eating as if nothing had happened.

Continuing onward through the afternoon, the horses began to struggle with the mud and the narrow trail. The group elected to walk single file and lead the pack animals rather than ride to give the equines a break. The muck smelled strong here, thick with algae and decomposing reeds.

"Something back there?" Kevin asked the cat-men, noting the cat-men's frequent nervous glances over their shoulders.

"Nothing to be concerned with, as long as we push on," Brythen replied, panting and pointing ahead. "Keep moving; we're nearly there."

Unsatisfied with Brythen's response, Kevin pushed anxiously forward in line to Dex just ahead of him on the sweltering trail.

"Dex," he called out, "I was wondering, have you heard of this Beast of the Forest, or do you think it's just wolves the townspeople were talking about?"

"I highly doubt the Beast of the Forest actually ever comes this far north," Dex assured him, although their leader did not turn to face him as he spoke. Sweat glistened on his face and he wiped his brow as his tone grew soft. "We have had a rash of attacks on the frontier recently, from wolves and such, primarily on livestock. They occur at night and mostly stay clear of people. Some say the Grimmigwulf are behind the pack attacks. I suppose out here in the wilds, anything is possible."

"Do you think this 'Beast of the Forest' could be a Grimmigwulf?" Kevin persisted. "Nicholas told us they don't bother civilization, but suppose one went crazy or something?"

"No, they are separate and unique creatures. They likely would avoid each other as natural rivals in the wild," Dex assured him. "The Beast is a solitary hunter and mostly prowls the southwestern shores while the Grimmigwulf and their packs roam the lands to the north; again, not typical in this area."

"Kevin, I know you're freaked out about the wildlife, but I know these types of guys!" Javier broke in. "The woodsmen tell big stories, one-upping each other about who saw it last and how big it was, right, Dex?"

"Your friend is correct, Kevin. I wouldn't fret," Dex sighed, wiping the gnat-stained sweat from his brow again in annoyance. "We're nearly to the trapper's cabin, and as you were told earlier, these natural predators stick to the wilds. We are only going *to* the wilds, not *through* them. We will board our transport from there."

"Yeah, Micker, lighten up!" Javier scoffed "I told you to stop being such a pussy!"

"This 'pussy' can best you, watch it!" Crisken hissed, his orange fur bristling.

Javier laughed before blushing and turning away, saying nothing further.

"Don't worry, I can smell dog a mile away!" Brythen mewled softly behind Kevin, tapping him on the shoulder with a dark paw. He glared at Javier briefly in offense at the name-calling before offering further reassurance. "I'll know if something's close: Beast, Grimmig or otherwise!"

Kevin smiled, noticeably relieved, albeit a bit embarrassed that he had unintentionally exposed his fear to the group. *Although Javier's attitude toward me has improved, he's still being a bit abrasive in front of others!*

"Not all these tales are true, you know," Brythen added quietly over Kevin's shoulder in sympathy. "At any rate, we'll all be on the water soon and sailing past it all!"

"Thanks, and don't worry about Javier; he didn't mean to offend anyone," Kevin feigned a nervous laugh. "As for me, I didn't mean to sound over-concerned; I was only asking!"

"I took no offense," Crisken whispered, flashing his needlelike teeth in a broad grin. "Go catch up to your friend and make sure he knows that!"

Kevin nodded and pushed through the reeds to catch up to Javier even as the two cat-men waited briefly until the others were out of earshot.

"Did you catch the scent?" Crisken quietly asked in a mewling whisper, holding Brythen back with his orange paw. "I don't want to scare the newcomers, but I'm certain Dex is aware of it."

"It was strong during our lunch, but it's faded since," Brythen growled, the sun glistening off his jet-black fur standing up on end briefly. "What I smell now is faint, but they're still not far away. They are holding off for now, but for certain they are following us! From this distance, it's difficult to discern if it's stalking or just curiosity."

"If they close in again, we'll have to tell the others without alerting those that pursue us," Crisken replied with a growl of his own. "If they know that we are aware of them, they may move in to attack!"

"If they come that close again, we won't have a choice," Brythen sighed. "I'm hoping we'll be on the boat by then. We still have daylight for now, and that's keeping them back. Fighting dog in a swamp is the only thing I hate worse than being wet!"

"Best keep this to ourselves for now," Crisken reminded his feline companion. "We don't want to set the newcomers off!"

The two cat-men continued conversing as Kevin pressed past Dex, squeezing by through the tall grass and reeds to catch up with Javier.

"Did you hear all that about these Grimmigwulfs?" Kevin pressed nervously. "Like werewolves?"

"Of course, we talked about them in Levens, remember? What are you worried about? You can just whisk yourself out of any situation if you can focus on it and see it," Javier snorted, brushing it off in annoyance. "Me, I'll yell at it like good ol' Nick showed us. We can handle it!"

"Yeah, but we're not supposed to use our powers because it will attract even more attention!" Kevin persisted. "I overheard Crisken and Brythen talking about a scent they caught on the wind."

"Scent?! Micker, what does it matter?" Javier retorted. "I can't smell anything beyond our mosquito repellent and the swamp we're slogging through. I tell you, we're on our own out here. Look at the group we're in; they know what they're doing! Kevin, just relax, will you?! Dex and the others, they've got this!"

Kevin begrudgingly conceded the point, content to walk on in silence. The day wore on, and once again, the sun began to set atop the high peaks in front of them. A more ominous orange hue took the horizon, and the glare of the setting sun burned their eyes as they walked into it. The trail led them up a brief rise to where the grass wasn't quite as high. From the top of the mound, they could make out the dark line of mountains looming in front of them for as far as the eye could see. Below them to the south stretched the dark waters of Long Lake, reflecting the blazing glory of the sunset.

The trail meandered through the mud ahead, disappearing again into a vast cluster of shrubs and reeds even as the swamps receded behind them. Even though the grasses towered well over their heads on the trail before them, their spirits lifted seeing they had already cleared the thickest parts of the bog.

The odor of decay from the swamps finally receded, replaced with the pleasant aroma of pine. Even the muddy shores of the lake smelled fresher as the welcomed scents filled the evening air. The sun descended behind the mountain peaks even as they took in the view, and the evening breezes began flowing through the forests bordering the wilds.

Not more than a mile ahead and atop a second knoll, they could make out the trapper's cabin on the shores of Long Lake. The path emerged from the mud and reeds on the first knoll but ascended further to the final knoll, marking the end of the swamp and the beginning of the foothills to the great Grenze Mountain range.

The brush and reeds had been cut well around the cabin, and the steep foothills of the mountains inclined immediately behind the property. A single dock extended outward onto the lake, following a set of stairs leading from the cabin's porch. The long boardwalk was positioned between a series of large half-submerged boulders, which gained access to the deeper water, just as the barge captain had told them.

Lefty Jeck's barge awaited them, tied at the end with sleepy wisps of smoke emerging from the smokestack atop the barge's wheelhouse, sails stowed and moorings secure. Other than a single candlelight shining from the barge's wheelhouse window, no light shone from the cabin on land, windows appearing darkened from their hilltop vantage point.

"Looks like ol' Lefty beat us here," Davyn commented, pointing at the end of the dock. "Hope he hasn't had to wait for us too long!"

"He got here in quite a hurry," Brythen mewled. "If we didn't have all these supplies and horses, we could have skipped the swamp and left with him on his dinghy!"

"We'll need those supplies," Dex irritably reminded the group. "We may be traveling much further than South Long Lake. Let's just get there and quit complaining, shall we? We're nearly there!"

The party descended into the mire again, pushing on through the last glade, the gentle sucking sound of mud at their feet. At what Kevin imagined was halfway, the reeds got so thick that they had to dismount again to assist the horses through.

Kevin noticed the cat-men appeared nervous at this point, and they began to growl, their fur standing on end. Suspecting they hated being wet, he turned to ask Dex a question when he noticed a reed just in front of his face glowing in a faint emerald hue.

"Hullo, what is this?" Kevin exclaimed in fascination. He paused to examine the light closer when a pair of delicate wings emerged from behind the reed. Like that of a large insect, they flexed briefly and buzzed at Kevin's approach.

"It's just a dragonfly!" Javier snapped his fingers at Kevin, seeing he had stopped, mesmerized by the glow in the dying evening light. "Come on, Micker, catch up!"

"I don't think so," Kevin murmured as he leaned in for a closer look. He paused when he realized that many more wings had emerged from around them in the forest of reeds. The whole meadow seemed to pulse in a new glow, awash in an ever-increasing number of green lights emitting from the edges of the thick leaves.

Fixated on the one immediately in front of him, Kevin spotted a tiny green girl with wings, only a few inches tall, poking her head from behind the reed. Her skin glowed with an emerald gleam, and her jade eyes blinked curiously back at him. She yawned and stretched, but as Kevin drew closer, she perked up. Looking anxiously about, she began to chitter, much like a nervous squirrel.

"Hey, guys! What is this?!" Kevin shouted excitedly to his companions, "Javier, Crisken, Brythen—check this out! Is this a fairy?"

Javier turned first but saw other tiny emerging faces from behind the reeds near where he stood. Hundreds of fuzzy green lights began to multiply throughout the grasses and reeds. Now, even he stopped as fascination kindled within him.

"Hey, little chickie!" Javier softly teased, reaching out toward the nearest one. "You sure are cute."

"No, wait!" Dex shouted back at him. "Don't touch it; that's no fairy!"

"Wood sprites!" Crisken yowled, seeing what was happening, "Stop! Do not disturb them!"

Crisken tugged on Brythen's tunic, but the other cat-man's attention was focused through the reeds off trail, just to their immediate north.

"We've got bigger problems coming! They're back!" Brythen hissed, quickly ascertaining the situation. His breathing quickening, he shouted, "They waited for this spot intentionally; we're walking into a trap!"

Javier, still unaware of the commotion building behind him with the cat-men, focused on the tiny green wood nymph. He couldn't help himself, drawn to the unusual spectacle unfolding before him. He touched the tiny girl on the head, who squeaked and buzzed like an indignant angry bee in response. Her eyes flared a glowing red as she glared back at him before taking to the air, dive-bombing him as he ducked reflexively.

"Crazy bitch!" Javier laughed, swinging his arms in the air. "What are you guys talking about over there? Who's back?"

Suddenly the entire meadow erupted in a blaze of glowing red eyes. The green glow from the hundreds of wood sprites intensified into a sharp, almost blinding haze as the swarm took to the sky. The flurry of wings that followed released a pale dust that quickly caked everything around them.

A sharp, overwhelming odor like ammonia permeated the air around them. Crisken and Brythen caught up to Javier and Kevin, grabbing each of the confused newcomers by the arm and propelling them forward. Buzzing filled the air as the cat-men began uncontrollably sneezing.

"It smells like a cleaning solvent!" Kevin shouted as a murky sleepiness began to overtake him. He turned to Javier, who began to stagger as they ran, dropping the reins of his steed.

The horses whinnied and neighed, bolting up the trail ahead of them to the first knoll. As the group consolidated, Dex and Fliegel covered their noses with their tunics and motioned the others to do the same.

"We've got to keep moving! We've got to get out of here!" Brythen shouted to Warley and Davyn, who had stopped to gather a fallen bag that had dropped off one of the fleeing horses. "They're coming at us from behind!"

"Who is?" Davyn coughed, grabbed his axe and turned, eyes watering. "The sprites are all around us!"

"We've got to run!" Crisken grabbed Davyn's tunic and shook him. "Axes aren't going to help! There's too many of them, and the horses are getting away!"

The men agreed in unison and turned to flee; however, running through the swamp proved nearly impossible. The hazy dust from the wood nymph's wings continued to layer over all of them as their swarm's dive-bombing intensified. Between their wings, scorpion-like stingers emerged, and the attacks became a crazed frenzy, buzzing them in an intensified cloud like an angry horde of wasps.

Kevin screamed as the first wood nymph stingers found their mark. He could see through the green mist and pain that Javier was no better off, collapsing into the mud, swinging wildly with his hands. He seemed to be fighting off the brunt of the wood nymph attack but had already sustained several stings. Kevin ran to him, grabbing him by the arm and jerking him to his feet, several of the miniature female shapes clinging angrily to his tunic, jabbing him repeatedly with their tail stingers.

"Come on—move!" Dex shouted from behind them. Together, they charged blindly through the grass and up the trail to the crest of the knoll where thankfully, the ground was hard and dry. From there, they stumbled up to the trail toward the lengthening shadows of the trapper's cabin, pursued by the angry swarm.

"Dex, help!" Kevin croaked as his body began to tingle with the venom from the stings taking hold. He had difficulty holding Javier up, his companion's eyes already rolling as he foamed at the mouth.

Dex lumbered back and grabbed each one of them by the arm. Continuing to push Kevin along, he dragged Javier behind him as they continued their struggle up the hill.

Meanwhile, Davyn broke through the rear and charged past them in a blind pursuit of the horses, shouting and whistling for the equines as he ran. Brythen and Crisken could scarcely help themselves, nearly convulsing with sneezing as the group topped the final knoll, swinging wildly at the air to rid themselves of the pests.

Kevin was only vaguely aware of Dex shouting unintelligible

instructions when suddenly another set of hands grabbed his other arm and began helping him along; it was Warley.

Somehow, Kevin had halfway fallen and hadn't even realized it when the taller tracker came up from out of nowhere, scrambling to help him to his feet. He swooned as the tracker steadied him, standing upright only with great difficulty.

"Not far now, my friend, we're almost there," Warley grunted into his ear, his dark moustache brushing his neck. The tracker's wide eyes skimmed the trail ahead for threats. "Just press on! We're nearly there! It's just the wood nymph's stings; they're potent but short-lived. You'll be alright!"

The Grenze Mountains loomed above the tree line, fading into a dark outline with no discernible features against the now blood-red sky. Emerging from the last bramble of the swamp, they staggered toward the front porch of the cabin, constantly harassed by the furious green cloud of wood sprites every step of the way.

Their visions blurred from the wood nymph poison and the lengthening shadows from the neighboring pines, making them oblivious to the mangled body lying to the side on the front porch in a dried pool of blood—arms and legs and torso torn to shreds, yet with no head.

"Fliegel, wait a moment!" Dex called, seeing the body first even as the blonde man reached for the doorknob, brushing out an errant nymph caught up in his hair. He flailed wildly, combing his fingers through to dislodge the angry tangle of wings, arms, legs and stinger buzzing around his ear.

Fliegel either didn't seem to hear or care; he pushed on the closed door, and it popped open with a loud creak. Strangely, no light greeted them from the cabin. The place smelled like dust as if uninhabited for days. He turned to motion them in, his bright blonde hair sticking to his sweat-streaked face even as a new smell, like a wet dog or a dead animal, wafted out to him.

The group pushed onto the porch behind just as a massive grey wolf slammed into him from inside the cabin. Poor Fliegel never knew what hit him. He went down hard in an instant as the wolf savaged his neck, blood spraying all around as the beast ripped half his throat out, leaving him gurgling and writhing on the porch as his attacker gorged itself in a feeding frenzy.

Dex lunged at the beast, sword drawn, swinging like a madman. The wood sprites parted only briefly before renewing their attacks as the predator dodged to the side, bounded off the porch and dove into the brush.

The wolf snapped once at Davyn as it ran, surprising the albino, who managed to dodge the bite, still trying to collect the horses. The bloodstained beast wheeled on the pale tracker, jaws agape when, with a loud yowl, Brythen and Crisken pounced from out of the shadows. Needle teeth snapping and claws ripping, they raked their opponent, who leapt clear to avoid the assault. Without hesitating, the great wolf dove into a cluster of gamble oak, rustling the bushes as the chaos continued.

A long, low howl broke out at the edge of the glade, where the wolf had vanished.

The answering howls erupted into a deafening semi-circle, enveloping the cabin from all sides. With a cold, blood-chilling realization, the group in unison became aware of movement swaying the reeds and bushes from everywhere but the lakeshore.

"Hurry!" Dex seethed, waving a free hand in front of his face, attempting to ward off the stinging wood sprites. "Get inside!"

Kevin crawled on all fours as Warley lifted the nearly unconscious Javier onto the creaking porch. With a final heave, they pushed themselves inside and collapsed onto the dusty floor inside the cabin.

Dex retreated inside last, sword drawn, and guarded their rear flank. Dragging Fliegel's lifeless body behind him, he slammed the door shut and turned to the group, shaking his head. Breathing heavily, he knelt down in a growing pool of blood to examine the lifeless tracker, his blond curls soaked in crimson mire spurting from his neck.

"Oh, no; Fliegel!" Warley screamed when he saw his friend's bleeding corpse. He rushed to Dex's side only to be held back by their leader's firm grip affixed to his arm. "What about the others?"

"I need you here, Warley! There will be time to grieve later," Dex insisted, his voice hard and icy. "Davyn's on his own with the horses. Brythen and Crisken will help him, and they can climb trees if they have to. It's us I'm worried about!"

A quick check outside the window revealed several horses neighing and kicking before bolting out into the woods, Davyn's bulky form chasing after them. Crisken and Brythen stood back-to-back, and more chaos ensued as a ring of five dark shapes launched at the pair. A cacophony erupted as the cat-men let out a unified screech, claws shredding the attackers as the battle ensued.

"What do you mean?" Warley exclaimed. "We're indoors! They're out there!"

"Think about it!" Dex shouted as he began to frantically search the inside of the cabin. "That attack came from INSIDE the cabin!"

"We're not safe in here, are we?" Kevin gasped with a sudden realization. That statement sent a chill coursing through him even as he stated it, his mind beginning to already clear from the wood nymph's poisons. *How did the grey wolf get into the cabin in the first place? Are any others inside?*

"This ought to hold them back for a bit!" Warley offered as he overturned the table, slamming it against the door.

Kevin began to search about also, finding very little sign other than the two broken windows on how the wolf could have gotten inside. A dusty grey rug lay haphazardly beneath the window frames, shards of sharp glass peppering the splintered wooden floor. Faded checkered red and white linen curtains hung to either side of the windows, fluttering lightly in the breeze. A third smaller window near a sink in the kitchen posed no threat.

The room they were in revealed very little as it was completely dark with nothing more than a small, cold stone hearth and a plain wooden table with a bench. Other than an iron stove with a variety of pots and pans and a single oil lantern, the wooden shelves also revealed a sparse supply.

Directly across from the entry door they had come through, Dex found an open door leading to a hallway with two bedrooms, one to either side. The exit at the far end of the hall stood wide open to the outside, facing the dock and Long Lake. The dead animal stench seemed to come from down the hall, and he audibly choked as he caught wind of it.

"Well, that's how they got in," Dex muttered, slamming the kitchen door shut and bolting it closed.

"The door at the end of the hall is still open," Kevin rasped. "Can't they still get in?"

"Undoubtedly!" Dex scoffed. "You want me to open the door so you can walk down there and close it? Give me a moment to think!"

They could still hear the horses whinnying outside. Davyn's shouts seemed to be directed at their steeds, and for the moment, the pack seemed to be ignoring him and the horses. The brawl with the cat-men had also faded as the two had climbed nearby ponderosa pines to get clear of the wolf pack now surrounding the cabin. Snuffing sounds and footfalls outside the windows made his skin crawl.

"They aren't going after the horses or the others!" Dex realized aloud. "They're coming after us!"

"That makes no sense! This does not follow normal pack behavior!" Warley muttered as he carefully glanced out the broken window between dusty and tattered curtains. "The wolves waited in the swamps to corral us in here! They got here first, before we did, broke in, and killed whoever was here first!"

"Now don't get jittery!" Dex hissed. "If that's true, then this is no shelter; this is indeed a trap, just as Brythen and Crisken said earlier!"

Just then, the howling outside turned to growls and sniffing and scratching on the front porch. Kevin's heart pounded as his attention focused on the broken window. The glass had provided little protection as it was; now, only the half-open curtains remained as the only barrier between them and what was coming for them.

"Shhhh!" hissed Dex as he and Warley drew their swords and moved to the windows. "They're right outside; a whole bunch of them!"

Kevin took one of the ragged curtains from the smaller, unbroken window and wet it in the sink. A pump faucet provided water to the cabin, and after several quick strokes, it provided enough output to wet the rag. He tended to his own stings first before turning his attention to Javier, dabbing his companion's swollen face. Javier's breath came in long, slow and ragged draughts until suddenly he gasped, sitting upright, eyes wide with fright.

"Hold still, we're alright for the moment," Kevin whispered. "But they're right outside!"

Still breathless, Javier shook his head and then vomited all over the floor. He gasped for breath but shuddered with each heave as he struggled to stand. As his nausea calmed, Kevin gave him a swig from his canteen, holding it to his friend's mouth.

"Warley said the poison should pass quickly," Kevin assured him, shaking him gently and trying to get him to focus. "Javier, do we have matches or something? We need some light."

"Here," Javier croaked. With a shaking hand, he pulled a cigarette lighter from his pocket. With a flick of his thumb, he displayed how it functioned before handing it over to Kevin.

Dex and Warley paused in amazement at the off-world invention before grabbing torches from the walls and lighting them one at a time.

"A stick with fire and a hissing can that creates a magic shield against insects," Dex murmured. "What else do you have in that pack that might help us out of this quandary?"

Before Kevin could answer, a mad buzz flooded the room as hundreds of angry wood sprites spilled into the cabin through the window near Dex, forcing him back, clawing at his face. Like an angry glowing green cloud, they spread over everything, swarming and stinging the company as the emerald light filled the cabin along with the overwhelming stench of ammonia.

Kevin snatched the can of mosquito repellent and held it up to the flame of the cigarette lighter, depressing the trigger even as the pale dust permeated the air around him. Raw fire belched from his homemade flame-thrower, and little green bodies fell from the air around them, squealing and twitching with rage.

Revulsion and anger overcame Kevin as he went on the offensive, spraying down the flying horde, assaulting the cloud in a fiery frenzy. He sprayed the torches his companions held, sending billowing clouds of flame into the buzzing hoard.

What remained of the attacking cloud flew back out the window through which they had come. He chased them right up to the window, accidentally lighting the sparse drapes. He watched as the glowing green cloud faded into the swamps, the buzz subsiding into the night along with the glowing swarm.

"That showed 'em!" Javier gasped, his bitter laughter subsiding into a coughing fit. His mirth faded as he caught sight of the blood on the floor. "Oh, man, what happened to Fliegel?!"

Kevin scarcely had a chance to catch his breath when a great black wolf head burst through the window frame, jamming through the broken glass, snarling and snapping. He screamed in surprise, falling back yet aiming the flaming nozzle only inches from the snapping maw. The wolf retracted, yelping as it ducked back outside, bathed in Kevin's fiery blast.

The blazing drapery had the outside threats at bay for the moment, but the flames began to spread. The curtains quickly burned away, but as the flaming shreds dropped to the floor, they landed on the dusty grey rug, setting it ablaze. Traces of fire licked at the dry wooden window frame, the edges of the splinters beginning to smolder.

"I guess we had better put that out?" Kevin wondered aloud.

"There's no time, and that's the only thing keeping them back!" Dex shouted out the broken window as the flames roared to life around the frame. "Davyn! Brythen! Crisken! We're going to make a try for the barge!"

"We're going back out THERE?" Javier gasped. "Can't we stay here for a bit and..."

"We can't stay here," Dex warned. "They've overrun this place before, and they're about to do it again!"

"What about him?" Javier gestured at Fliegel's motionless body curled up in a pool of blood beside the front door and upended table.

"I'm afraid there's nothing more we can do for Fliegel at this point," Dex coughed as billowing smoke began to fill the room. "Come on now, before we all catch fire!"

"Poor guy! I guess we run for it then!" Javier muttered. Snapping his fingers at Kevin, he locked eyes with his companion. "Better give me the canteen; we may need my voice soon!"

Kevin nodded dumbly and handed his canteen to Javier, who quickly guzzled the contents, clearing his throat with each swallow, even as the flames began to spread.

Suddenly, a loud thump impacted the front door, nearly startling him out of his skin as it shook the entire cabin.

Then another. A third made a sickening cracking sound as the wood began to splinter. The snarls and growls outside began to turn to barking and scratching. Yellow eyes and lolling tongues appeared in both broken windows now as the wolves stood tall, peering through the flaming windows with an eager hunger.

Dex moved decisively to the door leading to the bedrooms. As he unbolted the door, he turned to the others. "Are you ready?"

A loud crash from the front door gave them no choice. The massive black wolf with a now-seared nose dove through, followed by the large grey one with blood-smeared jaws. Quickly on its tail, another three shadows paced just out on the porch. Without thinking, Kevin sprayed his homemade flame-thrower directly in front of them, completely dousing the rug before him in knee-high flames.

The distraction was devastating to the cabin but enough to erect a flaming barrier between the wolves and them. Smoke billowed anew, filling the room they occupied even as they pushed through the door Dex had opened and into the hallway. Standing between two small bedrooms, they slammed the door shut behind them, even as the fresh stench of rotting meat assailed their senses.

It took a moment for their eyes to adjust, but both doorways on either one of the side bedrooms were completely dark. At the end of the hallway, the back door to the cabin still lay wide open. Just past the porch, they could make out the barge, still docked, with its single light at the edge of the pier, silhouetted against a violet night sky.

A slurping sound caught their attention on the floor before them and a dark mound seemed to move on its own. As their eyes adjusted, two large dark shapes feeding on another half-eaten carcass looked up, glowing yellow eyes and slavering jaws dripping. Chunks of meat fell from their lips as they snarled, lips curled back, revealing their gore-covered jaws.

"Oh God," Kevin gasped as the wolf shapes stood, crawling forth to close the gap between them.

Warley shoved Kevin into the bedroom on the left even as Dex pushed Javier into the room on the right. Both slammed the doors shut behind them before the predators could get to them.

≈≈≈≈

"There's no latch!" Warley exclaimed as he held his back to the door. "Quick!"

"The bed!" Kevin pointed for the only solution, gasping for breath as he tugged and pulled on the heavy wooden furniture. Every time Warley moved, however, something heavy slammed into the door from the other side.

"I can't move, or they'll get in; you'll need to move it quickly!" pleaded Warley, struggling to hold back the door.

With a surge of adrenaline, Kevin pushed and struggled with the bed and finally managed to slide it in front of the door. Warley moved aside as they slammed the furniture into place.

Suddenly, the struggle stopped. They held their breath, waiting, when they heard a crash and Dex yelling from the other room. Apparently, their counterparts had not been as lucky and were now fighting for their lives.

≈≈≈≈

Across the hall, Dex also had found there was no way to lock their door. He could hear a commotion outside but could do little else but hold the door shut. Unfortunately, in this room, a large window was also broken with nothing but useless tattered curtains swaying in the breeze to separate them from what waited outside.

Seeing movement approaching the windowsill, Javier grabbed a long knife from his belt and fended off two snarling wolves, each trying to push through the broken glass.

Dex could hear pounding on the other bedroom door and then heavy furniture being moved into the other room. He was about to turn and help Javier when suddenly, their door crashed open, sending him sprawling across the floor as a massive grey wolf pushed through the doorway.

This wolf was different; the head and jaws were more massive, the front paws looked more like claws and the shoulders were broader. Its hair stood on end as it entered the room, easily shouldering through the doorway as it surveyed its prey with a cold intelligence.

"It's a Grimmig!" Dex shouted as he blocked the predator's entry, parrying with his sword.

The creature stood tall on its hind legs, massive front claws stretching to reach for him. The smell of wet dog permeated the room as the legendary Grimmigwulf roared like a bear, closing in on them, towering nearly to the height of the ceiling.

Dex faced off squarely, locking eyes with the creature as he lunged with his sword to drive it back. Javier began to panic as he cleared his throat; he had no choice now. Focusing his energy on the Grimmigwulf, he threw his voice at it as he would a projectile, hammering at its chest as he would wield a bat.

"OUT!!!" Javier screamed, directing the sound in front of him with a fling of his hand.

The impact threw the creature off its feet, blasting it through the wall behind it in a blizzard of splinters. Chunks of bloody fur flew from its hide as it rolled, claws flailing. It screamed an inhuman screech, rolling back to the edge of the room in a protective crouch, bleeding onto the floor. Heat hit them from the inferno blazing in the room they had just come from as the beast rolled clear of the flames.

"How did you—" Dex gasped.

"Not now!" Javier sputtered. "It's coming back! I'll try to hold the other two off!"

The wolves outside behind Javier peered cautiously through the window, curious to see what had just happened. Smoke quickly filled the room, and Javier began hacking and coughing, even as he turned. Preparing to strike again, he took aim with an extended arm, this time at the pair of wolves climbing through the windowsill to get inside.

Dex meanwhile swung his sword at the returning Grimmigwulf, cutting into the flesh beneath the grey chest fur. It roared in pain as blood spurted forth, the creature curling back toward the doorway.

Dex mistook the Grimmigwulf's falter to be more serious than it was, and he lunged at it again, cutting another deep gash into its shoulder.

"Dex, be careful!" Javier shouted as the two wolves outside renewed their attempts to breach the window. He turned in time to see the standoff between their leader and the Grimmigwulf. "I don't think it's as hurt as..."

From its crouched position, the creature snarled once before lunging back into the room at Dex with its claws extended. With a loud zipping sound, it tore a gash in the man's flesh, from neck to stomach. Javier watched in horror as his leader reeled back, gurgling and clutching at his mortal wound, intestines spilling onto the floor in a fountain of blood.

The Grimmigwulf leapt atop Dex, knocking him onto the floor and gorging itself on its victim's midsection. Tearing into Dex's body while he writhed, the predator's maw shredded and snapped, spraying gore in a frenzy around half the room. As their leader's convulsions subsided, the attacker looked up and stood tall again with a malicious, dripping grin.

"Noooo!" Javier gasped, tears flowing down his face. He tried not to vomit as the smells of carnage hit him as quickly as the choking smoke filling the air around him. Pressing his back against the wall, he turned again toward the window, attempting to keep all the attackers in sight.

Smoke and fire spilled into the room, and Javier coughed as he shielded his face from the heat and flames, the wood nymph's poison still clinging to him in a stubborn fog.

The Grimmigwulf seemed unaffected by the calamity blossoming around them as it ducked low, grabbed Dex by the throat and dragged his body back into the hall, keeping its raging eyes fixed on Javier the entire time.

A chill ran through Javier's bones despite the unbearable heat now coursing through the flames. He couldn't break free from the fiery gaze of the predator's eyes, and his knees went weak as the flames began to surround them both in the stare-down. The creature's eyes reflected the fire from the burning cabin as its hungry glare bored straight into his. *Eyes that seem to convey the wordless sentiment—you're next...*

The two snarling wolves outside resumed their advance through the broken windows. The distraction was enough to catch his attention, and he turned, standing tall to greet the two dark shapes in the room and bounding towards him.

"OUT!!!" Javier shouted in a focused blast. The concentration and effort nearly sent him to his knees, but the window and wall exploded in front of him. Blood, fur and wood flew everywhere, and when the dust cleared, nothing remained but a massive, splintered hole in the side of the cabin.

Wasting no further time, he threw himself outside, falling to the ground, smoke pouring out behind him from the orifice he had just carved into the side of the outpost. First crawling, then limping, he made his way free of the burning cabin, not even turning to see if he was being followed. Sounds of the pattering of paws on the deck drove him away from the dock and into the brush.

A flash of light and the sound of breaking glass caught his attention as he scrambled along the lake shore, seeking thicker brush to hide in. He turned briefly to see countless wolves flooding onto the back porch and onto the dock; *I can't go that way.*

Alone, singed and shaking, he looked back at the cabin again, yet still nothing emerged to follow him. For the moment, he remained undiscovered and alone. He stood and stumbled on, diving through reeds and brambles as he went.

Smoke billowed from the cabin as flames consumed the entire cabin, belching forth from the windows and doors, setting the roof ablaze. As he looked on, the adrenaline carrying him through subsided slightly, and a sudden weariness seized him, brought on by a resurgence of the wood nymph's lingering poisons and smoke inhalation.

Javier's eyes fluttered, tearing profusely as he struggled to see, gasping for air as he walked. His knees buckled where he stood, and he lay briefly unmoving, unsure whether to call out to the others. His head swooned, and the sky above seemed to spin.

From behind him, within the bushes, the leaves rustled. Suddenly, a clawed hand reached out, grasping his mouth shut and yanking him off his feet. He struggled in a silent scream before being pulled deeper into the brush. His vision grew dark, and he managed only a brief muffled moan. The leaves in the brush around him shook violently for a few moments, and then, the glade subsided back into silence as he went still.

≈≈≈≈

In the other bedroom, smoke poured in as flames began to seep in through the doorframe and along the walls. Kevin wanted desperately to help but still had trouble standing. A sudden boom echoed through the cabin, shaking the outpost to its very foundation.

"What the hell was that?!" Warley cried.

Kevin didn't answer; he had noticed that the window in this room had not been broken—he could see the barge clearly despite the warped features within the crude glass. Focusing on the single light in the window of the barge, he could make out the dancing features of the lone candle flame as a plan formulated in his mind. A faint humming sound permeated the air...

"Warley, hold tight to me!" Kevin called insistently, motioning him over.

"What are you talking about?" Warley gasped as he hesitated. All had now gone silent. Suddenly, another explosion rocked the cabin as they exchanged terrified glances.

"I don't know what that was, but if my plan works, we won't have to find out," Kevin insisted. "Now get over here!"

"I don't know what you're up to, but you better do it fast!" Warley warned as he moved over to steady his companion.

Soft shuffling and scratching at the door were suddenly followed by a splintering slam. They looked back to see the top half of the door disintegrate and fall to the floor.

The great grey wolf's maw, dripping with blood, pushed into the room near the top of the doorframe. The beast shoved the bed aside, pushing itself further into the room. It roared in triumph as it entered, rearing up high upon its hind legs.

"It's a Grimmig!" Warley gasped. "I never thought..."

"Hold tight to me!" Kevin rasped, moving quickly to grasp his companion forcefully around the shoulders. Cradling Warley's head into his neck as he reached out for the single candlelight of the far-off barge, atop the glistening lake.

"What are we...?" Warley began, but Kevin wasn't listening. He turned his complete focus through the window and onto the candle's flame, floating forlornly on the distant barge, so far away...now closer... *Now I can see the inside of the barge...wooden paneling, a picture frame painting of Lefty Jeck, hanging lopsided on the wall...focusing...focusing...drawing it closer to me.*

Behind him, he heard a distant crash and the scratch of nails on wood and felt the heat from the putrid breath of something large coming for them.

Kevin focused his power as sharply as he could, and a familiar crackling sound filled the air as white sparks filled his field of vision. Thrust forth through a tunnel of breaking glass, across the dock, and toward the barge, his vision warped the boat closer to him.

Suddenly, Warley tumbled over the top of him, and they both rolled together onto Lefty Jeck's desk inside the barge's wheelhouse, snuffing out the candle and smashing it beneath them. Broken glass spilled across the desk as they collected themselves and fell to the barge floor.

"What the hell did you just do?" Warley exclaimed as he swooned, struggling to stand. Jerking upright he retched, grasping the wooden desk to steady himself.

"I saved our asses," Kevin cried out in triumph, trembling as he stood and looked about. "For now, anyway; we have to get the hell out of here!"

Warley dismounted the table and tripped over Lefty Jeck's body lying on the floor, completely disemboweled. A dried pool of blood caked the floor beneath the desk, and a wave of nausea hit him with the fresh scent of decaying meat.

"Crimey," was all Warley could manage to say. He couldn't even finish his sentence when a howl went up from all around the cabin, now roaring in flames. Smoke billowed out over the water to them, filling the night air with the scent of burning wood.

The sound of paws from the porch sprinting onto the dock caught their attention. Shadows of running wolves mingled with the branches of the pine trees, writhing from the heat emanating from the outpost's fire.

"Get the masts!" Warley shouted as they dashed outside the wheelhouse to the two ropes holding the barge in place to the dock. "I'll get the moorings!"

Kevin clambered to the masts, undoing the knots holding the sails up. With a loud *whoosh*, they fell and quickly took in the evening breezes. He glanced at the stern to see Warley untying the mooring.

"One!" Warley yelled, yanking the stern rope free and dropping it in the water.

"I've got both masts!" Kevin yelled back as the bow sail unfurled with a loud flap. With all sails deployed, the boat creaked and groaned as it strained against its bow mooring.

"I can't get the bow mooring!" Warley exclaimed as he struggled to undo the knot holding the vessel in place.

Kevin panicked; the wolves were halfway down the dock to them now, passing the second of three boulders the dock sat upon. *They are almost on us!*

Warley jumped off the barge and onto the dock. He pulled his sword and began hacking desperately at the last rope, holding the barge fast at the bow end. The vessel creaked and groaned as it turned a lazy half circle, the stern end swinging around out onto the lake.

Suddenly, the line snapped, and to Kevin's relief, the barge began to pull away from the dock. As the ship began to pull away from the dock, spinning slowly out into deeper water, it left Warley behind as he ran to catch it even as it pulled away.

"Warley!" Kevin screamed as he ran to the bow. "Hurry! Jump!"

Warley made a lunge for the barge...and missed, dropping into the darkened waters. Wet and flailing, he grasped for anything, but the barge floated further from the dock with no direction except the way the breeze carried it out into the lake.

Three wolves reached the dock and didn't hesitate, launching themselves into the water as they paddled after their prey.

"Warley, here!" Kevin hollered as he reached the bow and tossed the frayed mooring out into the water for his companion. When the line missed, he pulled it around him and prepared to try again. "Keep coming! Don't look back! They're right behind you!"

"I...can't...get to it!" Warley gasped, spitting out mouthfuls of water as he struggled to swim and stay on the surface. Against Kevin's advice, he turned with his head barely above water; one of the wolves paddling after him had closed the gap to less than a few feet. He hacked with his sword and missed but forced the wolf to circle back, paddling just out of reach with a snarl.

With the last of his strength, Warley turned his attention to swimming, pulling awkwardly for the drifting vessel, sword still in hand. Kevin tried again, throwing the severed bow line back in the water; this time, Warley caught the frayed end.

"Hold on tight!" Kevin grunted. "I've got another idea!"

Turning back into the wheelhouse, he grasped Lefty Jeck's corpse and hauled it over to the railing, dumping it unceremoniously over the side. The bloated body floated past Warley and toward the pursuing wolves swimming after them.

As Kevin hauled Warley in, the wolves paused in their pursuit, confused by the splash that had caught their attention and the easy body that came with it. They turned their attention to Lefty Jeck's corpse, dragging it back with them to shore.

Finally, to safety and standing behind the railing, Kevin and Warley stared back to the shoreline as their drift picked up speed. The trapper's cabin blazed, lighting up the night sky and the entire shoreline, reflecting off the waters.

Arriving at the end of the dock, the grey Grimmigwulf stood tall at the edge on its hind legs. It glowered at them with gleaming yellow eyes, covered in blood, watching the fleeing barge as if to ascertain whether to give chase. It huffed once before turning back, dropping on all fours. It looked back once over its shoulder before trotting off back down the dock and into the night.

Silence enveloped the shoreline, interrupted only by the roar of the burning outpost, completely engulfed in flames. With a loud crash, the cabin's roof caved in, sending a column of sparks like fireflies up into the night sky. Even as the scene began to recede further and faster behind them, the glow from the inferno cast an eerie orange glow across the glistening black waters of the lake.

Epilogue

Grand Master Nicholas lay in bed, asleep but agitated. A sense of dread crept through his dreams, intruding on his night's sleep. High above the city of Tyrna in his Wizard's Tower abode, his linen sheets soaked with sweat from his nightmares as he tossed and turned.

"Emerald Fire! Emerald Fire!" a voice whispered in his mind.

I'm missing something; it's new, isn't it? Aspects of it certainly are new; however, mentions of it in much older texts come to mind. While searching for information about the elemental swords, a chance page mentioned "practitioners of a ghostly fire" to the east...

The page seemed to come alive in his mind's eye, yet he couldn't recall where he had read it. *Could it be the same? Is it something different? Where is it from?*

New distractions peppered his thoughts, and the Emerald Fire was quickly forgotten. Worry over the newcomers from his former world surfaced. When the newcomers had first arrived, the grand master had perceived their collective presence in his mind. They appeared to him in a dream state as nothing more than lanterns of different colored lights, ablaze in the darkness of the wilderness. A spectrum of diverse colors, their lights gave off a telltale sign of their presence.

When they had approached Levens, he could even make out their individual magical signatures and see glimpses of their faces, although the distinctly peach and violet ones had gone dark. After bonding with the newcomers to aid in the discovery of their innate abilities, Nicholas could discern their embodiments even more clearly, much as he could sense Princess Serina and Aros.

Now that the quests for the swords had begun and the distances between them grew, the newcomers' individual signatures faded, becoming more difficult to sense as they moved out of range. Only when one of them used their innate powers did their likeness flare anew.

Javier had a blue hue; Kevin had a green one. Nate retained an orange hue while Johanna had a red one, and Daniel had a bright yellow light. These lights always seemed to surround their faces.

Other than when Nate briefly lit a campfire during their trip to Latana, the group heading east moved off unhindered. Nicholas had smiled smugly when he saw his protégé lecturing the newcomer about that stunt before the vision faded. Now that the group had arrived at Latana, a troublesome cloud seemed to obstruct his vision of them. Even his link with Aros appeared clouded in his mind; it was a faint lamp in a misty fog, blending and blurring with the newcomers. *It's as if I'm being blocked...*

As troubling as his inability to see those in the east was, it was the group heading west that bothered Nicholas this night. Visions of wolves in a forest flashed through the grand master's dreams, and he tossed and turned through the night. They ran as a pack, gnashing their teeth and charging at prey—*human prey.*

Both Javier and Kevin used their innate powers freely now and with a sense of urgency. Their green and blue lamps flared clearly in his mind's eye as he'd never seen them do before, their faces reflecting sheer terror as they fled, yet their distinctive powers flowing strong and sure.

A brief flash of Javier struggling in the bushes near the lakeshore came to mind; then, Brythen's catlike face whispering for him to be silent popped into view. Just as quickly as the vision appeared, it was gone. His blue hue remained, shining strong in his mind, even as Kevin's green one seemed to separate over a large body of water.

Something else confronted them—a flicker of the two newcomers who had been killed earlier. *Tim? Becky? Had those been their names? I never met them, but I remember the faint outline of their peach and violet signatures as I had once seen them when the Shimmering had first been opened. Now they appear again, this time paler and almost meshed.*

It made no sense, though; they were dead. Like ghost images in his mind's eye, they had confronted both the newcomer lads alongside the wolves and then were gone as quickly as they had appeared.

Nicholas's eyes snapped open as he gasped for breath. Whatever had happened, it was over, and they were too far away to do anything about it now. He had to trust the members he had assigned to each quest and those who led them.

"Javier and Kevin, it seems you've both had quite a close call," he muttered under his breath. He could still clearly sense them both, even as they moved further away from him. This time, they were apart from each other, but both still very much alive.

Throwing the covers off his bed, he began pacing the room nervously, muttering to himself. Snapping his fingers suddenly, he ceased his rant and sauntered over to his desk, spreading the map of the west lands before him.

"We must find a way to increase the newcomer's chances of survival and ultimately success! I'm afraid your time for seclusion is at an end, my old friend," the wizard sighed, tapping his finger on the map at the southwest corner of Long Lake. "I may yet need to call upon you and your resources at your hidden castle of Montagna Sole. You won't like it, but I need you nonetheless!"

THE ADVENTURE CONTINUES IN *THE CITY OF THE GLASS VEIL,* BOOK TWO IN THE SHIMMERING PASSAGE SERIES.

References

Brawny is a trademark of GPCP IP HOLDINGS LLC.

Etch A Sketch is a trademark of Spin Master LTD.

Grand Cherokee is a trademark of Chrysler LLC.

Jeep is a trademark of FCA US LLC.

Hand, David, David Hand, Larry Morey, Wilfred Jackson, Ben Sharpsteen, William Cottrell, Perce Pearce, directors, *Snow White and the Seven Dwarfs*. 1937: Los Angeles, CA: Walt Disney Productions, Film.

Lincoln and Lincoln Town Car are trademarks of Ford Motor Company.

Thermos is a trademark of Thermos L.L.C.

About the Author

Eric T. Schönfeld was born in the American West and lived in rural settings across several states. All throughout his years in school and earlier careers in corporate communication, he balanced the diverse human pursuits of career growth with the realities of the business world. For him, the key to finding peace within that turmoil was to hold onto the value his ancestors gave to him on embracing his inner silence.

He always had been inspired by the great novelists in fantasy writing, noting the appeal across the spectrum of cultures and diverse yearnings for life beyond the norm. Since childhood, he also retained a love for the outdoors, hiking in the wilds and the peace that comes from experiencing God's gift of nature.

He now resides in Denver, CO, where the balance is challenged in the noise and chaos of everyday living. However, he's managed to rediscover that inner peace even in the city through the quiet contemplations in church and the musical contributions. Through this book series and his other works, he hopes to bring an enjoyable escape and peace amidst the chaos of all our daily lives.

You can find Eric at https://erictschonfeld.com/.

facebook.com/erictschonfeld

instagram.com/erictschonfeld

linkedin.com/company/eric-t-schonfeld